SOMETHING HEAVY FELL ACROSS VALEDAN'S LEGS

and convulsed there, writhing. A man. A dead man.

Valedan threw himself off his sleeping cushions, pulling his legs out from beneath whatever—who-ever—it was that had fallen so heavily.

"Valedan," a voice said in the darkness. "Do not move."

He didn't recognize the speaker, but he did as she commanded. A ring of pale orange light, an inch wider than his feet on all sides, appeared across the ground.

Fire consumed the cushions as the dead man rose, limned in red, red light. The creature's lidless eyes flickered over Valedan a moment as the young man stood frozen. But when he spoke, it was not to the boy. It was to the shadows.

"Do not interfere in what is not your concern, and you may be spared."

"And are the half-named kin to decide what is, and is not, my concern?"

Fire flared, the heat almost scorching. Valedan crossed his forearms in front of his face as the intensity almost forced him back. But he did not move. He did not lift his feet. Because he knew, without knowing how, that to lift his feet was to die here, consumed by flames.

"You know the kin," the creature said. Great wings unfurled; long obsidian arms glittered in the unnatural light of fire. Horns, black as pitch, and pale, long teeth filled out the contours of its face.

"Yes." Bereft of shadows, a small figure in robes the color of midnight nodded her hooded head.

"Then know this. You will not be killed by any half-named kin. Be honored. . . ."

DAW Presents
the finest in Fantasy from
MICHELLE WEST

THE SUN SWORD:
THE BROKEN CROWN (Book One)
THE SHINING COURT (Book Two)
(forthcoming)

THE SACRED HUNT:
HUNTER'S OATH (Book One)
HUNTER'S DEATH (Book Two)

The Broken Crown

The Sun Sword: Book One

Michelle West

DAW BOOKS, INC.
DONALD A. WOLLHEIM, FOUNDER
375 Hudson Street, New York, NY 10014

ELIZABETH R. WOLLHEIM
SHEILA E. GILBERT
PUBLISHERS

For Thomas,
Because Kiriel was always for you.

ACKNOWLEDGMENTS

Ken and Tami Sagara made the writing of this book possible, period. If I start to list everything they do, I'll feel like I'm *a* child, not *their* child, although I admit the distinction in their minds has probably blurred more than it should have by now.

Thomas made the writing possible, because he offers me both encouragement and advice without being either cloying or hurtful—and for this book, I needed a lot of both. And everything else that gets taken for granted when I'm in the middle of obsessive writerly vision.

Kelly Sagara read the page proofs when I was too sick to do so—which takes a special fortitude all its own—and because of her help, I didn't miss what otherwise would have been an impossible deadline.

And Sheila Gilbert made the writing of this book as difficult as possible—because when she's right, she doesn't give up; she cares about the *book*. Which, in my humble opinion, is exactly what an editor should do. I hope I lived up to the challenges she set.

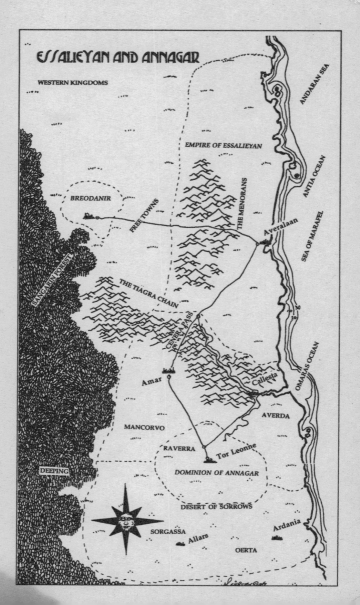

Annagarian Ranks

Tyr'agar	Ruler of the Dominion
Tyr'agnate	Ruler of one of the five Terreans of the Dominion
Tyr	The *Tyr'agar* or one of the four *Tyr'agnate*
Tyran	Personal bodyguard (oathguard) of a *Tyr*
Tor'agar	A noble in service to a *Tyr*
Tor'agnate	A noble in service to a *Tor'agar;* least of noble ranks
Tor	A *Tor'agar* or *Tor'agnate*
Toran	Personal bodyguard (oathguard) of a *Tor*
Ser	A clansman
Serra	The primary wife and legitimate daughters of a clansman
kai	The holder or first in line to the clan title
par	The brother of the first in line; the direct son of the title holder

Dramatis Personae

ESSALIEYAN

AVANTARI (The Palace)
The Royals
> *King Reymalyn:* the Justice-born King
> *King Cormalyn:* the Wisdom-born King
> *Queen Marieyan (an'Cormalyn)*
> *Queen Siodonay The Fair (an'Reymalyn)*
> *Prince Reymar:* son of the Queen Siodonay & Reymaris
> *Prince Cormar:* son of the Queen Mareiyan & Cormaris
> *Princess Mirialyn ACormaris:* daughter of Queen Marieyan & King Cormalyn

The Non-Royals
> *Duvari:* the Lord of the Compact; leader of the Astari
> *Devon ATerafin:* member of the Astari and of House Terafin
> *Commander Sivari:* former King's Champion (at the Summer Games)

The Hostages
> *Ser Valedan kai di'Leonne (Raverra):* the heir to the Sword of The Dominion
> *Serra Marlena en'Leonne:* Valedan's mother; born a slave; granted honorific "Serra" because her son has been recognized and claimed as legitimate

> *Ser Fillipo par di'Callesta (Averda):* brother to the Tyr'agnate of Averda
> *Serra Tara di'Callesta:* his Serra
> *Michaele di'Callesta:* oldest son
> *Frederick di'Callesta:* youngest son
> *Andrea en'Callesta:* his concubine

Ser Kyro di'Lorenza (Sorgassa): the oldest of the hostages

Serra Helena di'Lorenza: the only wife he has; he has taken no others

Ser Gregori di'Lorenza: his son

Ser Mauro di'Garradi (Oerta)

Serra Alina di'Lamberto (Mancorvo)

Imperial Army

The Eagle: **Commander Bruce Allen.** Commands the First Army

The Hawk: **Commander Berrilya.** Commands the Second Army

The Kestrel: **Commander Kalakar.** Commands the Third Army & the Ospreys

THE TEN:

Kalakar

Ellora: The Kalakar.

Verrus Korama: her closest friend and counselor

Verrus Vernon Loris: friend and counselor

The Ospreys:

Primus Duarte: leader

Alexis (Sentrus or Decarus)

Auralis (Sentrus or Decarus)

Fiara (Sentrus)

Cook (Sentrus)

Sanderson (Decarus)

Berriliya

Devran: The Berriliya

Terafin

Amarais: The Terafin

Morretz: her Domicis

Jewel ATerafin: part of her House council; also seer-born

Avandar: Jewel's Domicis

THE ORDER OF KNOWLEDGE
Meralonne APhaniel: Member of the Council of the Magi; first circle mage
Sigurne Mellifas: Member of the Council of the Magi; first circle mage

SENNIEL COLLEGE
Solran Marten: Bardmaster of Senniel College
Kallandras: Master Bard of Senniel

ANNAGAR

The Tor Leonne
General Alesso par di'Marente - par to Corano; General to the former Tyr
General Baredan kai di'Navarre: General to the former Tyr; loyal to Leonne.
Widan Cortano di'Alexes: the Sword's Edge
Lord Isladar of the kin: the link between the Shining Court and the Dominion

THE CLANS

Callesta
Ramiro kai di'Callesta: the Tyr
Karro di Callesta: Tyran; half-brother (concubine's son); the oldest of the Tyran
Mikko di Callesta: Tyran; half-brother (concubine's son)

Garrardi
Eduardo kai di'Garrardi: the Tyr'agnate of the Terrean of Oerta

Lamberto
Mareo kai di'Lamberto: the Tyr'agnate of Mancorvo
Serra Donna en'Lamberto: his Serra
Galen kai di'Lamberto: the kai (former par)

Leonne
Markaso kai di'Leonne: the Tyr'agar
Serra Amanita en'Leonne: the Tyr'agar's Serra
Illara kai di'Leonne: the heir
Serra Diora en'Leonne: also *Serra Diora di'Marano*

Ser Illara's concubines:
> *Faida en'Leonne:* Oathwife to Diora
> *Ruatha en'Leonne:* Oathwife to Diora
> *Dierdre en'Leonne:* Oathwife to Diora

Lorenza
> *Jarrani kai di'Lorenza*: the Tyr'agnate of Sorgassa
> *Hectore kai di'Lorenza*: the kai

Marano
> *Adano kai di'Marano:* Tor'agar to *Mareo kai di'Lamberto*
> *Sendari par di'Marano*: his brother; Widan
> *Serra Fiona en'Marano*: Sendari's wife
> *Ser Artano:* Sendari's oldest son
> *Serra Diora di'Marano*: Sendari's only child by his first wife

Sendari's concubines:
> *Alana en'Marano:* the oldest of Sendari's wives
> *Illana en'Marano*
> *Illia en'Marano*
> *Lissa en'Marano:* given to the healer-born
> *Serra Teresa di'Marano:* sister to Adano and Sendari

Caveras
> *Ser Laonis di'Caveras:* healer-born; his wife is *Lissa en'Caveras.*

THE RADANN
> *Radann Fredero kai el'Sol:* the ruler of the Radann
> *Jevri el'Sol*: his loyal servitor
> *Radann Samiel par el'Sol*: youngest of the Hand of God
> *Radann Peder par el'Sol*
> *Marakas par el'Sol*: contemporary of Fredero
> *Samadar par el'Sol*: the oldest of the par el'Sol

THE VOYANI

Arkosa
> *Evallen of the Arkosa Voyani*: the woman who ruled the Voyani clan
> *Margret of the Arkosa Voyani*: her chosen "heir"

Havalla
> *Yollana of the Havalla Voyani*: ruler of the clan

BIRTH

I: ASKEYIA

20th of Henden, 411 AA
Averalaan, the Common

Children were always the worst.

Five years spent cramping knees at the feet of Levec, the most notorious healer on the isle of *Averalaan Aramarelas*, had drilled into Askeyia a'Narin the fundamental lessons about how to be a healer in the Real World. But although she could now walk past crippled men, injured women, people in pain so great that they hid it behind enough ale to flood a river, she found it hard to bypass the children.

So she did what many of the healer-born did when they went about their errands in the city outside of their walls: she dressed like one of the poorer merchants, and she kept the medallion which proclaimed her birthright—the talent with which she'd been born—hidden. It meant that the needy had to actually know *who* she was before they could approach her with their tales of woe.

It was so hard to say no. It was still hard. She wondered, as she pulled the edges of her woven shawl more tightly around her shoulders, if she would ever find it easy. Levec had perfected such a look of temper that people were afraid to speak to him—and he was the only healer who wore his medallion openly no matter where he traveled.

Of course, Levec also had a single brow that crossed his forehead in a dark unbroken line, and his temper suited the perpetual frown he wore; had she been injured, with nowhere to turn, she'd probably have to be *paid* to approach the taciturn healer.

Askeyia a'Narin had no such brow. She had no height to speak of, although she had so hoped that she would

take after her father's family and grow all tall and willowy by the time she'd reached her name age. It hadn't
happened; she'd slimmed down a little—hard work and a
poor harvest always had that effect—but she'd only
gained an inch on her mother, and her mother was, to put
it politely, short.

She'd tried different hairstyles, something suitably
severe, but they made her chin look chubby, and she had,
although Mother knew it was childish, her vanity. She
also had an uncanny ability to be recognized for what she
was, although how or why she couldn't say.

Heal one of them, Levec would say sternly, *and they'll
follow you around like rats for the rest of your life,
gnawing at your strength when you can least afford to
lose it.*

*You think you can save the world because you're
young. You can't. And if you let the pain of the world drag
you in, you'll find the undertow is too strong; you'll be
swept away by it, and all of the good you could have done
in a long life of healing will be lost.*

*There are always dying men. Dying women. Dying chil-
dren. They need and will always need. But you don't owe
them your life, is that clear? If you were meant to live
their lives, you'd have been born them. You weren't.
Those people with broken ribs or infections or illnesses—
they don't care who you are; they reach for you blindly,
the same way they reach for a drink. They'll drain you as
dry, if you give them half a chance. You can't afford to be
swallowed by those needs. Askeyia, are you listening?*

She had nodded politely, thinking that Dantallon was a
healer without compare, but a gentle man, a quiet one.
Most of the healer's students felt that way, but they'd
long since refrained from pointing him out as a counter-
example. She'd tried it, once.

Of course, he's gentle, had been his reply. *He's the
Queen's own healer. A commoner with a cold comes near
him and the Kings' personal guard will make the matter
of a healing entirely moot. You, on the other hand, are far
too approachable. I tell you, Askeyia, you're the softest
free towner I've ever met.*

Words meant to sting, and they did.

Because he was right, and she hated it.

As proof of this, as proof that his words held both sting

and truth—as if words with no truth could sting at all—
she looked up from her reverie and saw a woman standing
in the cobbled streets of the Common. The bowers of the
Rings—the ancient stands of trees that were famous
throughout the Empire—caught the height of the midday
sun and made of it shadow, short and dark, that pooled
around the woman's feet. Her eyes were wide, her skin
unnaturally pale, and the collar that framed her neck was
worn to threads; Levec's second youngest healer thought
that the shift she wore had once been a deep blue by the
edge of color near seams that were splitting with age; it
was pale now, whatever its color had once been.

Askeyia started to lower her face again—she found it
easier to walk through the Common with her eyes cast
groundward—but she stopped as she saw that the
woman's arms were rigidly curved on either side of a
bundle of cloth. A still bundle.

People were always in a hurry in the Common; they
glared at the woman as they shoved their way past her,
flowing to either side like a sluggish river. The woman
swayed as shoulders and elbows brushed her to either side,
but she stayed her ground as if rooted to it. Raising her
glance from the bundle to the woman's face, Askeyia made
her first mistake: she met the eyes, dark-ringed, horrified.

You couldn't meet eyes like that and turn away. You
couldn't do it; you'd have to leave shreds of soul behind
just to tear yourself free.

Swallowing, she glanced over her shoulder once, but
there were no other healers in sight; Jonas had run ahead,
and Mercy—Aristide, really, but everyone called him
Mercy, for reasons which were clearly lost on Askeyia—
had disappeared into a stall full of people with too many
elbows for Askeyia's less prepossessing size. Neither one
could see her, and what they couldn't see, they couldn't
report.

Besides, it wasn't as if she was going to heal the babe.
She was just—she was just going to see if the babe needed
help. That was all. She was just going to take a small look;
just touch the child. Nothing too dangerous. And children—well, if they were the most compelling, they were
also by far the easiest to heal all across the spectrum; their
bodies helped.

Taking a deep breath, Askeyia a'Narin reached into her shirt and pulled out the medallion of the healer-born. It glittered in the sun as she laid it flat against her breast, a platinum rectangle, simple and severe, with only the golden glow of two hands, palm up, to alleviate the starkness. No one in the city could mistake the medallion itself for anything other than what it was.

The flash of light cut the shadow and drew the woman's attention, and although she made no move toward Askeyia, her dark eyes lit with a hunger, a hope, that the healer had seen so often it shouldn't have been jarring. But it was.

"Healer," the woman said. "Healer, I know—"

Askeyia lifted a hand that was at once gentle and imperious. She held out her hands but the woman's arms, thin and fragile, seemed locked in a position that she herself had forgotten how to break. Shock—or worse. The woman started to speak again, and again Askeyia lifted a hand. Of all the things that she found difficult, the pleading was always the worst; it cut her, to hear a voice so devoid of pride.

"I am Askeyia a'Narin," she told the woman gently. "And I'm—I'm about to start my day at the Mother's temple in the thirteenth holding." It was absolutely true. "If you'd—if you'd like, you can accompany me." She held out her arms again.

This time the woman seemed to break; her feet left the cobbled stones as if she'd yanked them free. "It's my boy—he's hurt my boy—Healer, my boy—"

This close, she could see the blood that trailed out of either corner of the child's mouth. He was young; no newborn, but not yet crawling. And as she touched his face, as she concentrated, calling upon the talent that was bane and boon both, she knew. Ribs, thin and flexible, had been crushed with enough speed and force to pierce lungs; blood filled them, even now. He was dying. Not so close to death as to threaten her should she attempt the healing, but not so far that his mother had the time it would take to walk to the Mother's temple and wait for the healer to arrive.

Not so close to death?

He's only a child, she thought. *He's only a child. And children aren't so costly to call back. Everyone knows that.*

She did not look over her shoulder again. She did not wonder where Jonas and Mercy were. She held the life in her hands, and the life was almost everything. It was why a healer couldn't freely touch the injured or the dying at her level of skill; the call was almost impossible to ignore. Not that she would have ignored it; she was, as Levec had said, the softest free towner that he had ever met.

She brushed a stray strand of limp, dark hair from the curve of her cheek; it was shorn by fire, the candle's kiss—one she'd been too tired to completely avoid. With care, she took the child from the arms of his mother.

He's only a babe, she thought. *It won't cost much.*

Babies were need defined, but their needs were simple; eating, sleeping, physical comfort. Askeyia felt the warmth leave her hands in a rush as the baby's thoughts, inarticulate pictures, smells—the smells were *strong*—images of a face, smiling, joyful, tearful, tired, and sometimes angry filled her vision. She could not recognize this woman in the woman who stood in such desperation, beneath the trees in the Common; *this* woman was safety. Had this child known loneliness? Not yet; not yet.

He was 'Lesso; a diminutive, Askeyia told herself, although it was a struggle to find the word. When he was hungry, he called for his mother, and she came; she was warm when he was cold, she was sound and sight and smell.

'Lesso thought that Askeyia was his mother, and when she called him, when she held out her arms, he came with ease and joy—or rather, he wailed the louder for the sound of her voice bearing his name in the shadows of the foothills that led to Mandaros. She called him again, and again he wailed, louder; one last time, and she was there, he was there; she picked him up and held him tight against her, *within* her, bringing him back to himself.

And all about her, too strong to be memory, too visceral to evoke that naive yearning, the things by which a young babe knows a mother. By which, in turn, a young mother knows her child. And this was her child, this 'Lesso, this babe; this was hers, to protect and heal and comfort. He fell into the cradle of her healer-strong arms and rested there as if those arms were made to do no more than hold him.

Really, as she'd told Levec a hundred times, a *thousand* times, healing babies was no risk at all.

Really.

But she couldn't explain the tears that coursed down her cheeks as the world returned to her eyes—to her adult eyes. Couldn't explain the way her arms tightened around the swaddling cloth, the way she pressed the babe tight, too tight, to her chest.

She spoke phrases, things meant to separate the healer from the healed—but words offered no separation.

The screaming, thin and terrible, did.

Turning, sloping groundward with the sudden disorientation of motion, she saw 'Lesso's mother—his terrified mother, his strong, his happy, his angry mother—chalk white, white as snow on mountain peaks.

"Healer!" she cried, pointing to a place beyond the vulnerable healer's back.

Askeyia spun again, lighter on her feet, surer now that the pounding of heart was without question *her* heart, not his. And as she gazed at a man who was moving from the center of the Ring beneath which she stood, she remembered what 'Lesso's mother had said.

He's *hurt my boy*—

No healer had ever come out of the call with such speed, such terrible urgency. Was it 'Lesso's fear? Her own vulnerability? The weakness of a healing? She turned, handing the child to his mother, to his *other* mother, and then turned again, a single word having passed between them: *Run.*

He was well-dressed, but not so well-dressed that he needed guards or a palanquin; she thought him a Southern noble, some minor clansman, not the valley Voyani whose descendants now crowded many of the hundred holdings in their attempts to make roots—a place for themselves that their Southern compatriots neither wanted nor claimed. His hair was dark, and his skin quite pale; his shoulders were broad and his hands unblemished. His teeth—rare enough in a man his age—were perfect, as was his brow; he had the look of power about him.

He carried no obvious weapon, wore no visible armor.

In the light of day, he should have looked like just another man, another foreigner.

But the light of day shunned him.

She glanced once over her shoulder, just once, to make sure her child had escaped, and then she, too, ran.

Light, as distinct as a bird call, she heard his chuckle cross the Common as if nothing at all separated them.

Askeyia a'Narin was good at running. A life of relative luxury and indolence had not robbed her of the skill—or the instincts that had honed it. Air crested her open lips and slid down her throat in a rush. The cobbled stones beneath her feet were hard and solid; they provided an even ground with no treacherous dips or holes, no unseen roots or branches.

As a healer, she had a value.

It was beyond money, although money was paid for it. Untrained, unknown, and unregistered, she was worth half of the naval fleet's best ships to the right man, if he could catch her and remove her from view before he could be stopped. It was, of course, completely illegal; the punishments for kidnapping and forced indenture were almost as harsh as those for murder. But murder didn't stop, either.

Askeyia knew how to keep her wits about her while she ran. It was a strength, and time and again, it had proved her salvation. And the running itself cleared her mind; the depth of the breathing, the ache of her lungs, kept her firmly in the here and the now. It was harder to panic if she was *doing* something.

And it was hard to do something with the press of bodies grown so thick at the height of day. In the summer months, the height of day was the emptiest time in the Common, but in Henden, what with the cool breeze and rains, it was the most crowded. She had no time to apologize, although she heard the curses at her back and to either side. She hoped that none of the men or women were foreign, and that none of them had tempers, because she couldn't afford to be called to task for the clumsy, horrible run. She had to find—

There. Authority guards. Armor gleaming ostentatiously in a day that was cool enough for it. Their helms were down; the metal bridges that followed the line of the nose usually made her think of sculptured birds.

Not today. Her feet slowed their stride as they responded to the giddy relief she felt at arriving, untouched, before the men who kept the Kings' Order in the Common. Safety, here, although in her youth she'd been raised to distrust Imperial authority. A free towner's daughter, but not a free towner at heart. Beneath her chin, the medallion she wore caught the light, bending it, scattering it, and holding it as she caught her breath.

"Healer?" A guard who Askeyia thought wore the insignia of a Primus said, eyes widening slightly. Her medallion wasn't a common sight in the open streets.

"I—I'm being followed," she said, drawing a harsh breath—a series of harsh, quick breaths. "Foreigner."

The guard—a man she vaguely recognized—frowned as her words and her medallion made clear what the threat was. He turned at once, waving his three companions forward. She huddled behind the mass of their armored bodies, feeling the safety of their height, their obvious weight, and especially of the arms that they were even now unsheathing in a rough scrape of metal against metal.

The stranger walked into view. *Walked.* Yet he followed no more than twenty seconds behind her; less, if she were a capable judge. He was completely unruffled, as finely turned out—in a city sort of way—as he had been when she'd first set eyes on him.

And the shadows that the trees cast still flowed from the edge of his cloak, bleeding into the stones like a thick, rich liquid. He smiled, glancing between the guards as if he could see through them.

The safety she felt vanished then, as if she, too, could see through armor and arms and simple physical strength as the illusions they were. Had her eyes widened? Had she made a noise—any noise other than the simple and unavoidable rhythm of drawn breath? She thought she must have, because he smiled. Winter on the mountain had been just as cold and just as deadly as that smile for a healer-born girl who didn't understand what the word storm meant.

And she was a healer-born girl, with all that that implied. All of it.

"Primus," she said, standing forward, the heart beneath

her rib cage telling the tale of the fear that she forced, with so much difficulty, from the lines of her face.

"I'm a Sentrus, Healer," he said, as the stranger drew closer. There was a smile in his voice, a friendly correction offered to a woman who had seen enough of the effects of a sword, but never seemed to know enough to recognize the rank of the person who wielded it.

"I—I think I've made a mistake."

He looked back over his shoulder, his eyes narrowing.

She swallowed, pale in the fading day, the weariness replaced by the giddiness of too much fear.

"Healer—are you certain?" He didn't believe her, of course. Askeyia a'Narin was a terrible liar. Especially when the lie was forced out of her by an instinct that she only barely controlled: the desire to preserve, at any cost, the lives of those around her.

Because she knew, without knowing why, that in seconds, these men would lie aground, dying just as surely as the babe had been, but with no one to come and rescue them all. No one to come for even one.

All healers learned to hide from the instinct; to deny it. There wasn't enough power in the world to stop death from coming to those who heard the call; not enough power in the world to save every man, woman, and child who was worth saving. But there was guilt enough to destroy a healer, and a healer's life.

And if not guilt, there was the call itself. To guide a man back from death was the most harrowing journey that either the dying man or the living healer could make. Or so she had been taught.

But she didn't believe it, not now. Because she saw the death in the stranger, writ across the living shadow in his face, and she could not imagine that anything could be harder than this: to swallow, to smile, to force a foolish young expression across her face instead of huddling behind swords and armor, or better, fleeing and gaining the moments each guard's death would take.

The stranger had stopped completely; he still looked at her, through the guards, but his expression lost all smile, all edge of expensive pleasure.

"Askeyia a'Narin," he said, and she saw that his eyes had no whites. "I am Isladar."

She wanted to run, but the guards wouldn't—couldn't

it seemed—quite leave her, and she knew that the moment she unleashed her struggling fear, the moment her feet hit the cobbled stones, they would fulfill their duty.

And wasn't that what they'd trained all those years for? Wasn't it what they swore their oath to do? Wasn't it what they—*say it, Askeyia*—risked daily, with full knowledge? Ah, she wanted to listen; the words were the strongest they'd ever been. But she stayed. Because she was healer-born. Because she knew now that 'Lesso's injury had simply been the trap that had closed around her; this man had injured the babe to catch her out, and a man who could do that, could do anything.

Levec would be angry, when he learned how she'd let herself be caught.

"Isladar," she said, turning the word around in a dry, dry mouth. "W—what do you want?"

He offered her his arm; she reached out, hesitated, and then let her hand fall limply to her side. She couldn't touch him. She could not.

He stared at her, his eyes narrowed, his lips a slender line in his pale face. Then he smiled, and this smile, unlike the other, was, if not friendly, benign. "Let us," he said, withdrawing his arm, "walk. I have so little experience of the healer-born."

She swallowed, took a step forward, stood near enough that he might actually catch her in the circle of his arms. But he did not touch her; instead, he smiled more deeply. "Your fear," he whispered, "is so strong. I am almost surprised that you remember how to walk."

So was Askeyia.

He did not wish to injure her, but he could not quite bring himself to say this; there was no gentleness in his nature, nor could there be. He was First-born, he had Chosen, and he resided in a place of power among his kin: Kinlord. Demon. *Kialli.* Isladar.

Months had gone into the careful watching and studying of the houses of healing on the isle. The healing houses were notable for the security of their walls, the profusion of guards that protected the students within them, and the personalities of the people who claimed to own them. He studied them, but always at a distance; he would cause an injury, pay for its correction, and then take the information from the mind of the man or woman so healed. Time-consuming.

Yet in the end, he had settled upon the house of healing owned by a man named Levec. Healer Levec. Taciturn, sharp-tongued, and more possessive by half than the next man who undertook the running of a house of healing, he had caught Isladar's attention. If he had a family name— as most of the mortals did—it was not one that Isladar could find easily, and the various records of the Authorities were open for his inspection. In all of his dealings, he was simply Healer Levec, and he was known to any man of power who made his home on the Holy Isle.

That isle was no home to him, and he did not cross the bridge that separated *Averalaan Aramarelas* from the rest of Averalaan happily, but he knew what he sought when he left his Lord's side, and knew further that it was upon the isle, and nowhere else, that it could be found.

He chose Levec's House, and from there, his intense personal scrutiny began. Levec, of course, was not useful in the grand scheme—but Isladar believed that a man of Levec's temperament was prone to foster those who were. He was not completely certain; the younger healer-born students did not have a *Kialli*'s way of measuring the depth of mortal affection, and they took his words, often, as words that held all of his many meanings.

His smile folded into a line; his face grew remote, as it often did when he contemplated the plans that lay, stone by carefully placed stone, ahead. Always ahead. If he was honest, and in the silence of his own thoughts, he could afford to be little else, he had chosen the House of Levec for one other reason: Levec was a man who would be . . . injured by the loss of one of his students. Even one.

And so we prove ourselves, again and again, true to our nature.

There were many healers who fit the kinlord's needs in a purely emotional way, but they were more often than not young men, and for his particular plan, a young man was out of the question. Yet in the case of a house such as the house Levec ran, the young women were often more guarded—in both senses of the word—and it was not until he found Askeyia a'Narin that he knew, with as much certainty as it could be known, that he had found the one.

Narrowing the scope of his search had been simple, and

following her had proved instructive, although what he said remained true: healers were almost beyond his ken.

"Askeyia a'Narin," he said, as he brought her to one of the standing rings. "I have been waiting many months for this opportunity." He reached up, caught the underside of a leaf, and followed its veins up to the thin stem that fixed it to a branch. With a quiet snap he pulled it free, turning it over in his palm as if that, and nothing else, had been his purpose.

"What do you want?" she said again, the fear thickening her words less. "Why have you—why did you—"

It was hard not to frighten her; she was so close to the brink of hysteria he had only to speak the right words and she would fall over the edge. In truth, he greatly desired it, but that was the visceral, and Isladar was known for the control that he exercised over base impulse. Over any impulse. He handed her the leaf, taking care to cause no contact between her flesh and his.

Shaking, she took it, pressing it unconsciously between the palms of her hands as if it were a flattened glove. The leaves very much resembled wide, oddly colored hands.

"You are about to become a part of history, Askeyia. It falls to you to begin the greatest empire that the world has ever known."

She was mute; she stared at the leaf, as if meeting his eyes was painful. He pondered a moment, wondering if she could see his true eyes. A rare self-annoyance troubled him; of course she could see them. What other reason could he have for her terror? The healers saw much that he had not expected. He reached out to touch her, and pulled away as her nostrils widened. The sun was falling; the shadow was growing.

"Askeyia," he said, his voice soft and neutral, "I do not intend to frighten you."

At that, her eyes flashed. "You're lying," she said evenly.

"Am I?"

"Yes." Pause. "No."

He laughed, although he knew she would find the laughter unpleasant. "You speak truth. And it is thus with my truth: that opposites are in equal measure valid." He frowned, fell silent. He had not intended to say as much.

It annoyed him.

"What do you want from me?"

"Everything," he said gravely, "but not for me." Her fear was as strong as any fear he had tasted in this domain; he had, after all, been cautious and infinitely human in his interaction with other mortals. But this one, this girl—she would see much more than a simple *Kialli* indulgence before her life ended.

"For—for who?" She edged away, hit the bark of a tree that unexpectedly barred passage into the Common that she had traversed freely for years.

He stepped forward, coming upon her quickly, moving with all of his speed, all grace. Her eyes widened, becoming white circles around dilated pupils; the fear made her wild, and it was wildness that he craved. She threw up her hands in denial, seeking to wedge them between her body and his chest. Too late. He was upon her; his shadow ran up the sides of her face, her throat, the back of her neck; he caught her as she flailed, trapping the sound of her scream in her throat; letting enough escape for his ears, for his ears alone.

It had been millennia.

It would be millennia again.

How odd, that the one girl he found suitable was also, in her fashion, the one he found most tempting. The temptation itself was an unexpected sweetness, a small element of risk. For he needed her, and he needed her alive. And sane. He walked the edge, carrying her as she flailed. Knowing that he could not give her the consummation of her fear, of her dread, of her certainty.

He lowered his head; his face, wreathed in the shadow that healers alone could find so corrosive no matter what its intent, rested a moment in the crook of her neck. His lips touched her ears, and into the shadows, into the sounds of her terror, into the crackling sharpness of the fantasies of death that he now let run like the Wild Hunt through her thoughts, he said, "For who? My Lord, dear child; the only Lord that any of the kin have willingly chosen to serve. *Allasakar.*"

And although the word sank and took roots immediately, although her fear gave the name as great a weight as her imagination allowed, the speaking of it freed him.

Impulse.

Control.

"I—apologize," he said, with some effort. "We are both creatures of our nature." His smile was a glimmer in the darkness of his shadow; it started and stopped almost at the same instant. She could not see it.

He did not release her, but only because he could not; the spell was near completion, and this particular casting of it required physical contact. He was not, after all, a lord who chose ostentation in any of his endeavors.

He cast a glamour upon her, something to take away the fear that she radiated; in the Shining City, there was no faster way to be noticed. No better way to call the kin, be they greater or lesser, to feed. She was not ready for that—nor would she ever be.

The kin that had been called to these plains for the first time in millennia found the absence of Those Who Have Chosen a far more bitter thing than any, even Isladar, had suspected.

And Isladar, of the kin, was the wisest.

He came to the stone tower that had been built upon its own foundation. Steps, of a piece, were sheared up the tower's side; they were small enough for human feet, and they would serve until such a time as human feet no longer found it necessary to traverse them. The tower of the Lord had no such steps; his audiences were few indeed, and he chose to hold them in the basin at the foot of this, his Shining City. The kinlords, each and every one, were capable of rising to the height of his doors without the need to touch anything as rough as hewn stone; it was a subtle test, another proof that only the powerful reigned in the Hells.

In the Hells.

But in this rocky, barren place, the skies were clear; the snow, when it fell, fell in a clean, white storm of ice from the heights; the rivers that ran carried with them pebbles, stones, sand—and the air was silent, the lands were empty for as far as the eye could see.

The kin could see far indeed.

There were no demesnes here, although there were Lords; there were no souls. Mandaros did not control the only gate to this realm, and the kin were free to gaze upon the souls of those who had not yet made their Choice; who had not yet traveled the length and breadth of their many, many lives. And the souls of the undecided were both an offense and a dangerous curiosity.

He looked at the rigid form of the woman beside him, seeing beyond the fragile network of skin and vein and flesh. She was pale, pale gray; if darkness lingered, it lingered so far away from the heart that he knew she was a lifetime or two away from her last journey to the Hall of Mandaros. And while Mandaros reigned, while the Kings reigned, while the world turned and changed in ways that were less conducive to the fear and the hatred, the loss and the bitter, bitter anger that consumed the spirit, such a soul as this would never be theirs. Or be his.

Ah, but the Lord had his plans, and the Lord could see far beyond the span of a single human life.

The kinlord's lips lifted in a subtle smile. Because he knew, as did the Lord, that the span of a single human life—less—was all that they had, if they were to succeed. What Allasakar had done, the Oathmaker could do again in a matter of decades.

If the Oathmaker and the Lord stood across a field of battle, both at the peak of their powers, there was no contest. But they would not stand at the peak of their powers; or at least the Lord would not. Not now. To exist in this world at all he had had to sever the connection between the hells and the mortal plane before he was fully prepared. He was, as the kin, required to form a body out of the substance of the plain itself—and to build a body to house the power of a god was no simple task, no easy feat. Once, it might have been.

Before the sundering.

But the lands of man fought and pulled against the immortal; to create the avatar itself was a task not to be hurried—when one had the luxury, and the knowledge. They knew now. They had not known then. Thus even with the plans of the Lord of the Hells. Crippled or no, he was strong. And crippled or no, he wore the mantle; he was the Lord of them all.

The Lord they had chosen to follow.

She stirred, as she stood beside him, drawing his attention.

"Welcome," he said, his voice once again soft, "to the Shining City."

She did not blink, did not react.

He cast again, cast swiftly, bound her tightly without ever lifting a hand.

"Askeyia a'Narin," he said, "fear is not your friend here. **You will not feel it.**"

And because it was something she desperately desired, she obeyed the command in his words.

Such a human weakness.

The City had been carved out of the rock of a mountain that seemed to exist for only that purpose; its face, where its face could be seen was sheer and sharp, as if the rock itself had been shorn and pulled new from the ground.

It was the first thing she noticed, that the rock was new, that the city was rock. That there was, from this vantage, no life at all, no greenery, no color, no bird on wing in the open sky.

Allasakar. She could not speak the name; it had been forbidden to all but the boldest of children for so long that she could not clearly remember the first time she had heard it.

The last time was still too clear.

As if to deny it, she turned her face to the window and the world it framed. Nothing moved; if not for the wind through the open frame, it might have been a painter's vision of isolation. But the wind was cold and sharp; it stung the skin and dried the eyes. More, it could not accomplish. Askeyia a'Narin was, after all, a healer-born. She adjusted to cold, and its damage, with the same conscious effort it took to draw breath—which was to say, none at all.

She could not banish the fear.

Lord Isladar came, frequently, his displeasure a crease at the corners of black eyes, or a tightening of the lips. She was afraid of him; she could not hide the fear, and the more she tried—and she did try—the more it called him. He would come, stand by her, a statue that spoke a word, or two, or three. Then, satisfied, he would nod and speak soothing words, of a kind that were forgotten the moment he uttered them.

She would speak just so, she knew, to an injured child. Or an animal, half-mad with pain.

A dusk, heralding the northern, frozen night, had come;

after it, after a night so long that she dared not close her eyes, the dawn had followed.

And the dawn, in this thin, dry air, was glorious.

The sun rose, framed by the stone sill; hands that barely felt like her own gripped its edge; breath stopped a moment. For the first time since she'd arrived in this terrible place, she did two things.

She accepted that this was no dream, no capricious nightmare. And she prayed.

There was, in this room, a bed; it was wide enough for two, she thought. Like the city that spread in silence far beneath the open window, the bed was gray and colorless—and as she approached it, as the sun's rays crested the window's sill, she realized that it was of a piece with the wall.

The headboard that grew out of the wall itself was tall and plain, except for a single small detail, a symbol that she did not recognize, but felt oddly comforted by, in its center. A circle, made, she thought, of chain, with a flower at its center. But the flower was unlike any flower she had seen; its petals were wild, unmatching. The first was a thing that seemed to flicker and burn, a leaf of flame, the second, a lily's petal, the third a long, flat leaf—she thought it cornlike. There was a fourth petal, but it had been pulled from the flower, as if by wind.

She reached out to touch the symbol.

"I would not, were I you."

Her hand stopped a hair's breadth from the stone; she did not look up, but his shadow fell across the bed. Swallowing, she pulled that hand away and buried it in the folds of her skirt.

"I have brought food."

Silently, she turned; he set it down. And then he stared at her for a long moment, displeased. "Askeyia a'Narin," he said softly, "why do you dispel my magicks?"

She shook her head numbly, her hair tumbling into her eyes and away at the force of the movement. "I—I don't—I'm not—"

He shook his head. "The room," he said softly, "is warded; from without, no one should sense your presence. But this is the Shining Court." He frowned a moment, and then added, "Askeyia, you have no friends in this Court."

She nodded.

"Neither do I. I am *Kialli*. The *Kialli* do not know friendship in any way that you would understand it. It is a mortal flaw—an impulse that draws the weak together and binds them fast. We are, none of us, weak; we seek power, and the power that we seek overlaps in all things.

"You are a part of my plan, of my Lord's plan; my enemies may well seek you. If you do not stop this, those who seek will find." He did not touch her; did not move at all.

"I—I don't know what I'm doing. I don't know what you want me to—to stop."

"I have cast this spell ten times. You—" and then he froze, his frown of a piece with the wall, gray and hard, but only half as cold as his narrowed eyes. "I see," he said softly. "This is most unfortunate."

What? she wanted to shout. *What is most unfortunate? What am I doing?* But she was afraid of the answer, and she said nothing, and this time he left at once, speaking no words at all, and making no gestures above her upturned face.

The tower was of the stone itself. The mattress, heavy rolls of cotton under broadsheet, was not, and the light warmed it. She sat. She sat in the silence of this terrible room, seeing the dawn give way to day.

It fascinated him, this unconscious rejection of his shadow. As if it were just another minor flaw, some petty injury like the scraping of skin or the breaking of a nail, his shadow, his hard-won *Kialli* cloak, was cast aside. He was certain a greater spell would hold her, just as a greater injury would call her attention; he could afford neither for the mere trifle of masking her fear; not when so much lay ahead that required true power.

He stood beyond her door, listening to the rhythms of her mortal body. Hearing the breath, the passage of air into lung, the flow of blood in vessel and vein. Hearing, beneath that, other workings. He had stayed outside this door for the passage of a day and a half, gleaning the information that he required to cast this final spell. It was unlike any spell that the kinlord had cast before it; a subtle spell—a spell that the healer herself might have used.

And because of its nature, the cost was high. The shadow struggled everywhere against his command as he

drew it in; fought him as if it were sentient, as if it realized the perversion of its truest purpose.

Two battles, then. The casting of the spell. And the
keeping of it. By sheer force of will, he could hold the
spell in place, and it was necessary; it was her life.

He chose that moment when the night was strongest,
and the moon dim. He touched the door, paused, and then
spoke; his sigil burned a moment in air before his hand
passed through it. Let another Lord speak his name in this
place, and the door would grant no passage unless they
could defeat the sigil itself.

She was awake. Which was unfortunate.

The window framed her; the wind chilled.

"Askeyia," he said. "**Come.**"

But she knew, he thought—or some part of her did. She
stood as if she were part of the mountain peak, frozen,
immobile.

"Askeyia," he said again, ill-pleased, "if you fight me,
this will be . . . difficult. Fight or no, you will fulfill your
role. Come." He held out a hand but he knew, as he did
so, that the gesture was futile. She could not give him
what he demanded; not willingly. It was not in her nature.

And that was, again, unfortunate.

He could not wait; his plan required her presence, and it
required his power, and the two would slip farther apart
as the night waned. Without another word he crossed
the room, taking a step, less than a step, so great was the
shadow he cast.

She screamed, he silenced her.

Then, in the darkness of tower and pale moonlight, he
surrounded her with the effort of days, submerging her.
He forced her to drink, to breathe. And as he felt the
shadows slide down her throat, as he felt them take root in
her heart and her lungs and the vessels that carried her
talent-born blood, he closed his eyes.

For she was not—quite—ready for the evening's work,
but he had her body now, and he brought it, quickly, to
its time.

The screams could be heard across the breadth of the
Shining City. The kin, lesser and greater, froze a moment
and then shivered in this familiar wind. The fields of the
Hells were behind them, yes—but they were carried

within as well. They had chosen their place so long ago the lesser kin could not remember the choosing. The greater kin did, but even they, like their lesser cousins, were drawn by the sounds of terror, of pain.

Through the empty streets they came, leaving the mockery of buildings, of manors, of dwellings that had ceased to have meaning for them. They came as if called, as if commanded, as if drawn by a spell they could not ignore.

And they came to ring the tower in which the Lord of the Hells reigned. There, in bitter silence, they accepted the crumbs from his table, for they knew that the mortal trapped within would never be thrown to them.

It was a rape, yes, but of more than the physical body; the demands of the Lord reached farther than the magicks of his most subtle servant could have guessed. In the darkness of tower and stone and shadow, her life was the beacon that drew him, and it had taken all of Isladar's craft to preserve her mind and her life.

He did not hide from her the fact of her violation; could not—although had it been in his power, he would have.

Had she been other than healer-born, he might have been able to force her to see the Lord as the kin saw him, and against the face of such majesty, of such power, she would have willingly offered what had instead been taken.

And had she been of weaker blood, the act itself would not have had to be repeated, over and over, until the course of the evening itself had stripped her of the use of her power. But he knew the moment that those defenses flagged, and when they did, he knelt as the choked and raw noises she made died into a lull, the weakest form of applause that a soul could utter.

"My Lord," he said, speaking clearly enough to make his voice heard, but no more than that, "it is done." Waiting was as natural for the kin as drawing breath was for a mortal—and it was infinitely more necessary if one waited upon the Lord. Impatience was rewarded, in its fashion.

"Bring her back to me," the Lord replied, "when you are finished."

Isladar nodded, still waiting, and at last the Lord bade

him rise. To rise, otherwise, was also rewarded. Isladar had stood by the side of his Lord since the Hells first opened before them; he was the only one of the *Kialli* who had occupied the Lord's space so closely to remain within it. The others had perished in the charnel wind, their screams loud enough, for an instant, to quiet the whole of the Hells. The will of the Lord.

He took the healer-born girl, lifting her tightly curled body in the span of two slender arms. He did not shift her; if he had had the power, he would not have touched her at all. Perhaps it was best this way. Without power, there was no shadow to linger in her eyes, across her skin, in all the wounds and openings.

She did not come at night, and night would have been merciful. The darkness, with moonlight's weaker silver, would have hidden much: bruises, scrapes, tears and rents in cloth and the surface skin beneath it. It might have hidden the odd angle of the leg that had not yet been set. More merciful still, it might have blinded her to the terrible emptiness of the young girl's expression—or better, to the young girl's *familiar* face.

But the sun was high and the sky as clear as the skies in the Northern Wastes almost always were. She could see everything; every detail. Nothing at all was spared her.

I am Evayne a'Nolan and Evayne a'Neaamis—but I swear to you, Father, that I will be a'Neaamis no longer if— Her hands hurt; she glanced down and saw that they were bleeding. Her own nails had pierced skin in the moment it had taken her to draw breath and think. She was, by her own reckoning, fifty Imperial years of age; her hair was a white-streaked darkness, her skin, weathered as even the rocks were weathered by the passage of time and the scouring of sand, be it carried by wind or water.

The path of the otherwhen took her where no one desired to go, not even she; of late, it led her from death to death, and she was tired. For more than thirty years, she had walked it at the whim of immortal father and Time, and if it had been a hated path in her youth, it was now just a path, a part of her life.

But her life itself was dedicated to war, and in the service of that war, she was a lone soldier; she paused a

moment to fight here and there at the sides of those who
were allies, but she did not linger, no matter how much
she might desire it. And perhaps, just perhaps, she had
come to see the wisdom of that forced choice.

There had been little rest in the past few months, and
she was certain, although no battle's sound reached her
ears, that there would be no rest here, for either herself or
the girl. But the girl was not dead yet.

At least there was hope.

As if she could hear the intake of breath, the girl who
lay curled upon the stone bed lifted her hands in a gesture
that was half plea and half defense; her lips were thick
and swollen, the side of her face, purpled by the blow—
by several blows—of a large hand.

And yet, even this disfigured, Evayne a'Nolan recognized Askeyia a'Narin. Levec's student; a child, an
almost-woman with a soft heart and a naive desire to see
great deeds done. Of Levec's many students, Askeyia was
one who hovered, hoping against hope to catch some
snippet of dread destiny, as if it were a disease. Not even
in her coldest moments would Evayne have pointed out
that this, this meeting, was one such thing.

She had never seen a healer this injured who still lived;
it was against their nature, and their instincts.

"D–don't—" the girl said piteously, "don't." But it was
weak and fragile; the sound a mouse might make when it
had been in play too long between the paws of a cat.

She, who had seen much, looked away.

She did not recognize this room; it was barren of any
detail that might have given it light, or a sense of comfort
or warmth. No; light came from the window, and the
window was a thing of stone. She turned, as if the need
for light was greater than any other impulse, and stared
out; stared down.

When she turned back to the injured girl, she was as
gray as the stone itself. Evayne's robes were blue, always
blue; she spoke a word, frowned, and spoke another, a
stronger one. In the haze of the light by the window—for
she stood by the window itself—the midnight richness
seeped skyward from the magical weave, leaving her in
white, all white.

Because she knew where she was. And she knew that
the white would be a comfort, even if it was a lie.

"Askeyia," she said softly, speaking for the first time since she'd entered this tower. She did not seek the crystal ball by which she was known as *seer;* she did not need it. She knew the *when* and she knew the *where;* the glance outside the single tower window told her both.

The girl looked up at the sound of the voice; she was not so broken that suspicion was her first reaction. "E–Evayne?"

The older woman swallowed and then smiled falsely. "Yes."

"What are you—what are you doing here?" Hope. "Have you come to—have you—did Levec send you?"

Levec doesn't know where you are. But she did not say it. Instead, she crossed the room, leaving shadows that were only the castoffs of light. She caught the girl in her arms and held her, and after a moment of stiffness that told Evayne more than she would ever ask, the girl relaxed and began to sob, very like a child, into her robes.

Those robes caught the tears and kept them, a bitter memento. Evayne spoke a word; saw the green glow of her mage-light halo Askeyia, her momentary ward. It was a spell better used in the presence of physicians, for it told her much about the condition of the body upon which it was cast. The spell came more easily than words would have.

And it gave her a bitter, bitter answer.

Askeyia was chilled by the fevers brought on by too great a use of power in too short a space of time. That, she expected. Her leg was broken cleanly, but poorly set; her face was bruised but whole, her vision had been hampered somehow by the strikes to the side of her face. These, and more, Evayne cataloged in an instant.

But it was the last thing that was the most terrible, because she understood it all then.

Askeyia a'Narin was pregnant.

She must have tightened her grip, for the girl looked up, the matted darkness of her hair scudding the underside of the seer's chin.

"Evayne?"

No. No, I will not do this.

"Evayne, what is it? What's wrong? Is he coming?"

I will not do this. The fifty-year-old woman, who had seen battles that were far darker and far more real than the glory of legend bit her lip until it bled. Held the girl, held Askeyia, a moment longer, as if her arms were bower or cradle—or armor. She lowered her face into the crook of the girl's neck; blood there, sticky but dried.

She had not been brought to rescue Askeyia.

The silver lily that hung round her throat bit into her collarbone; she did not move, thinking of what its maker would have said to her for what she was about to do.

"Askeyia," she said, in a voice so husky the word came out a rumble. "Forgive me. But I cannot take you from this place. The Lord who rules it has a grip that is far too strong."

Lies, all lies. She hated them. Because she knew, now, the *how* of Kiriel di'Ashaf, the dark, wild child that did not—in this year, at this time—exist. And she was glad that she had not known it sooner.

But Askeyia was gullible, even in fear.

"You are caught in a war, Askeyia. And you are a healer." Swallowing hurt; the words stuck. "You're—you're with child."

White-faced, the girl drew back, covering herself, pulling the scraps of dress together as if—as if the night just past had not passed. As if it never would. Her eyes were wide and dark and round.

And Evayne raised a hand, gentle with the girl as she could not be gentle with herself. "No, child," she said, although the Askeyia that she remembered did not care to be called a child. "Remember your talent. Remember your birth. You are healer-born. If the child you carry is not to your liking, you need not carry it to term."

"But I—"

"No, not tonight. And not tomorrow, if I am a judge of the power that you've used. But the night after, if you desire it, you will have your freedom from—from what you bear." She saw Askeyia's shoulders slump. Relief, of a sort.

"If you do nothing," the seer continued, "the child will never come to term." She stopped speaking a moment, and looked beyond the gray of wall, to whatever lay without. "Askeyia, I never told you who I was, and you asked. You always asked." She had hoped the girl would smile, but there was about her a watchful fear that Evayne was certain would never again leave her face.

"I was raised in Callenton."

At that, Askeyia's brows rose. "In Callenton? That's the town over from—from where I was born. Evanton. I went there once, with my father, in the summer." Her eyes clouded then, as she thought of the father who had sent her to the safety of the mighty healing houses in Averalaan.

"My father was a blacksmith, and until his death, I was only a strange-looking child. After his death—ah. After his death, I was a stranger, a foreigner. You know how cruel children are before they discover that they aren't children anymore.

"In Callenton, I came into the power that brings me to you." She very gently reached into her robes—her white robes—and pulled out a glowing sphere that pulsed in her hand like a heart. In it, silver clouds turned in upon themselves, roiling. Waiting.

"A man came to me, to teach me of my gift. I did not know who he was, but he knew me well, and he offered me great mystery, great adventure, glory. It required a sacrifice, of course." She shook her head, staring at the surface of the seer's crystal. "I was not as brave as you, Askeyia. I was timid. He told me that I would have to walk a path that no other man, or woman, had ever walked before. That I would walk it alone and that it would take me across decades and centuries. That, once I had chosen, I would be bound; I could speak of nothing that had not yet happened. Offer no warning. But if—*if* I did all these things, I might avert the crowning of the Lord of the Hells upon the mortal lands. I told you, Askeyia, that I was timid. What would you have done?"

Askeyia straightened her shoulders then, although her arms were still tightly wound across her body, covering her breasts. "I—" She looked at her lap. Swallowed. "I would have said yes."

"I said no."

"But you—"

"And that night, that terrible night, the demons came. We had no soldiers, Askeyia, except for one man who fled the Empire to forget the Dominion Wars. We had no mages. There were no god-born children to lead us or protect us.

"And he came back to me at that moment, and he asked me again if I would follow his path.

"And I told him yes. Yes, because everyone that I loved—precious few, but *precious*—was there."

"W—what happened?"

"I don't know," she told the young girl softly, more honest now than she had been in decades. "I've never been allowed to go back. I cannot choose where the path takes me. But it takes me where I need to be. I did not know that it would bring me to you." She smiled, but the smile was a bitter one. "I've lost them all. If I were to go back to them now, they would never recognize me. My life has been given to the fight, and taken by it."

"And will it work?" Askeyia said softly, as if asking the end of a story.

"I don't know. But I have to try. What happened here, what happened to you—it's not the worst thing that *will* happen if the Lord of the Hells rules all. Askeyia a'Narin, you carry his child."

"I won't for long."

Evayne swallowed. "If you do not carry this child to term, we stand no chance of winning this war."

The silence. Oh, the silence.

Of the two, it was Evayne who looked away, casting her gaze stoneward.

"And if I do? If I do, can you tell me that we *will* win? Against a *god*?" Her voice was thin and high and strained. But it was not mad, it was not hysterical.

Evayne started to speak, and Askeyia cried out, "*Look at me!*" and the words died on the older woman's lips.

"No," she said, the lie that was so distasteful defeated. "I cannot say that with certainty. I can only say that she is hope, and she is our hope, as she is his."

"She?"

"If you have this child, this child will be a girl. And she will be all that she was born to be."

"How can you ask this?"

"Because, Askeyia, she will be his daughter, but she will be yours as well. It is only hope, yes. But it *is* hope."

"And for me?"

"I promise you that you will suffer no more in the birthing than many others suffer naturally."

"And will I go home? Will I be free?"

Evayne rose, and in rising, she took the weight of her

answer with her, carrying it, burdened by it. She saw the clouds rolling in to either side.

"No," she whispered. "Just as I will never be. I cannot force you, Askeyia, and I would not. But if a healer's vocation is to save lives, you will be the greatest healer the world has ever had, known or not.

"And I promise you, before the end, you will be known."

She heard Askeyia begin to cry as the path closed in about her, taking her from the desperate young woman, and leaving her with the burden of what she had asked, of what she would ask.

She was Evayne a'Nolan.

II: ASHAF

15th of Wittan, 412AA
The Terrean of Averda, the Green Valley

She would always remember that he came at the break of dawn. Not at full morning, when the serafs were out in the fields, sun burnishing their forearms with color and the glow of sweat seen at a distance, but when the darkness had not yet been broken, and an old woman could take the time to sit beside the earthen shroud that lay over so many of her once-bright futures. It happened that way sometimes.

She lifted a goblet carefully, searched the still, dark surface of its liquid, and then spilled the contents, drop by careful drop, over the graves. The wine was almost finished for the season, and she'd little taste for it otherwise; it was folly to drink alone, a type of weakness that she'd sometimes longed for but never truly approached.

Harvest was around the corner; a day, maybe three, away. She'd seen enough of them to know that it would be a good year, Lord willing. The Tor'agar would be pleased.

Ashaf kep'Valente had much to be thankful for. She served a Tor who was just, if at times harsh; she had her health, her sight, her teeth, and the kind of strength that years of labor cannot destroy. Not labor.

But other things hurt, and over time it became harder and harder to ignore them. She was tired. The Lady knew it, if no one else did. She wanted to see her children again, and there was only one way she could ever do it. One way.

"Ashaf kep'Valente."

She looked up from the Lady's blessing, although the sun had not yet robbed the sky of all its hidden shadows, its quiet darkness. And she saw him for the first time.

He was neither young nor handsome as Ashaf reckoned either, but in his face she saw the conjunction of cool distance and absolute certainty that spoke of power. He did wear a fine and heavy cloak, out of season in the Averdan summer. It was the colors of harvest, gold and green and brown—but it felt black to her, and that was unsettling.

Had they a new Tor? It would not be the first time she had found out this way. But it would be the worst, and it would be painful; this Tor was a good man, a known one.

This stranger, she thought, although she did not know why, would be neither. Ah, age and family made a coward of a woman. Bow and scrape and beg and give way, if it kept you alive for your family.

But she had no family now.

Her eyes fell at once to his collar, his breast, but he wore no sun with rays to mark his importance among the clansman.

"No," he said quietly, "I am no Tor or Tyr; if you bow to me here, it is at the desire of your courtesy, no more."

"And have you come to find the Tor, then?" She rose, standing implacably between this stranger and those graves, as if by putting herself there she could guard her heart. As if she knew, even then, that it was necessary.

"No," he said quietly. "Your Tor has little of interest to offer me." He paused. "You are not a very curious woman, are you?"

She shrugged, wondering if she had time to raise a shout and call the men from the field. Wondering, in truth, if it was worth the effort. Perhaps the Lady heard her prayers, and if this was not the method she would have chosen to end her time and toil, one couldn't argue with the Lady. Sometimes the answers to your prayers were answers, like them or no, and once asked, very little could be taken back.

When he saw that she wasn't about to tender an answer, he smiled, the expression shrouded and somehow dangerous, although she thought he meant it to be friendly. She would learn the error of that, and many things, in time. "I was right," he told her. "The Averdans are different. Ashaf kep'Valente, I have come to purchase your service."

"Then you do want to speak with the Tor," she said

firmly, thinking that he would take her from this place, these tangible, buried memories, and not much liking it.

"Perhaps. Perhaps not. You are the first woman I have met that I think suitable for my needs. But I will not take your service if it is offered unwillingly."

At that, the daylight broke; the Lady's time passed. Ashaf kep'Valente snorted and settled into things practical. "You aren't from the Dominion," she said boldly, "if you think that service and willing are one and the same. You buy me, I work. You don't, I work." She shrugged. "But it's not up to me to jump through your hoops either way. You talk to the Tor, and if he's willing, he'll give me the orders." She straightened her shoulders, first left, then right, and wiped dew-moistened hands on her apron, knowing what answer the Tor would tender. Or believing that she did. "Now, I've work to be about."

"Indeed. As have I."

But his eyes were the darkest brown she had ever seen as he caught, and held, her gaze. "I think we will speak, you and I," he said, and for a moment she felt like a young woman again. And she hadn't much liked being young, with no freedom, and choices that were so painfully few. Age had its precious value.

He came that evening, again at the bridge between darkness and light; dusk. Ashaf was not surprised to hear the knock at the sliding door of her one-room home. Her husband had built it, with the Tor's permission, when they'd birthed their third live child. He was proud, said the Tor, of their fecundity; he hoped that their children would serve the clan as well as their parents had.

Oh, her husband had been so proud of the praise offered. And proud, too, of the fact that he could live, almost like a poor clansman, in a home of his own. Perhaps it was his hubris that angered the Lord above, although it had not angered the Tor. She would never know.

You are maudlin, she told herself. *The Lady's night is going to be a long one.* She rose, took the steps necessary to reach the screen. There, silhouetted against the darkness, she saw him for the second time. No face, no clothing, no voice—but she knew him by the shadows his lamp cast against the opaque cloth. She hesitated a moment, wondering whether to feign sleep, and knowing at the same time that he had *heard* her quiet shuffle to this entranceway.

She opened the screen.

"Ashaf kep'Valente," he said, and he bowed. He held a lamp that was burning brightly, some reminder of the Lord's power in the Lady's night. But she thought that he held it for her benefit, and not his own, for his eyes were the color of starless night.

She had always been taught that the golden-eyed pretenders were the demon changelings born to earth, but she felt at this moment that gold was life and night was death; the echoes of the Leonne wars.

And she was sun-scorched if she was going to let this man intimidate her in her own home, this one remaining artifact of her past life. "I don't believe I know you," she told him stiffly. "And strangers don't cross *this* threshold."

"Very well," he replied, bowing with such perfect grace she felt old, ungainly, ugly. "I am Isladar."

"Isladar of?"

"Just Isladar." He rose, lifting the lamp in his left hand. "As you will be just Ashaf, if you so choose. Have I satisfied the guardian of this abode? Might I be given leave to enter?"

There were old stories about creatures that could not enter, unless invited—but then could not be forced to leave before they had exacted their terrible price, if they could be forced to leave at all. She hesitated a moment, and then, feeling foolish, stepped aside. It was clear that this man had power, much of it unseen, a thing made not by birth and blood and rank, but by something other. If he were Widan, if he wielded the full night of the Sword of Knowledge, he could strike her down with a gesture, and destroy the timber and wood and cloth of her husband's making. What point in ill manners?

"But bring the lamp," she added. "We don't get a lot of tallow, and we don't waste what we have."

"Even so."

He stayed the evening, whiling it away as if he were a chisel, and time a rock or a piece of wood. But he asked her for nothing. Instead, he asked about this place, this one-room dwelling. She demurred, saying little; she did not know this man enough to want to share the few precious memories she did have. He did not seem displeased, and turned his discourse to the question of wood, of the type of wood that could be found in the Averdan valleys, and of the finishes applied to this tiny home. She listened politely, thinking that morning was going to be hard; she was not a young woman anymore, to speak and while away the Lady's hours without suffering during the Lord's.

As if hearing her, he rose, lifting his lamp and his light and his regard, as if each were somehow a cloud. "Ashaf kep'Valente," he said softly, bowing. "The stars are out; the night is not a dark one. I thank you for your company this eve."

She began to kneel before him, as if he were the Tor, and stopped; then she said, "And I thank you for yours. It is not . . . what I expected."

"Oh? And do you, Ashaf kep'Valente, know what it is, exactly, that you *did* expect?" And the darkness was in his eyes, and along the glittering edge of the teeth in his sensuous half-smile.

She could not speak then. Words would have marred his menace, and she greatly desired to use them, but she felt his power again, and it made her feel young, and in youth, she had known the value of silence, of remaining hidden. The Lady's smile was dark this eve.

He stared at her a long while. Then he said, "Might I return to visit you again?"

"Could I stop you?"

"With a word." He lifted the lamp; its light lengthened his face and darkened the shadows around it.

But she nodded. "As you will." And turned, feeling old, knowing that the menace and the strangeness, the sense of hidden power and danger, did not change the fact that he had not hurt her, although he had every opportunity to do so.

When, she thought, *did I become such a lonely old woman?*

The earth that lay beneath the silvered moon was silent, and the silence was all the answer that she had never wanted.

* * *

As a concubine in the court of the Tor's father—a man who returned to her in nightmares for years after she had been "discarded"—she had been envied by the other serafs in the village; they knew that she would be taken from their toil and hardship, and given a wife's name, and a wife's place, at the side of a man of power; that she would live in luxury, and never again have to face the heat of the Lord's face, the chill of the wind. And she had thought so herself, as she was taken and cleaned and clothed and oiled. One night, two, and the illusion was gone, although appearances had to be maintained. She learned her manners, her diction, the nicety of movement and the tricks by which the Tor might be pleased. She learned to sing and play the samisen. To dance. She would not dance now.

In the harem, she had never slept well. There was always, beneath the surface of sleep, a certain knowledge that, at any time, the Tor—or the cerdan he thought to reward—might come upon her unawares. She bore the old scars, some visible, most hidden; time under the Lady's skies, with a gentle man whom the Tor's son—upon taking the clan's title—had seen fit to grant her permission to marry, had slowly masked and eased the viscerality of those memories. There had been little love lost between the new Tor and the old.

But that husband had passed, like the pain, and under this night sky, her sleep was as harsh a thing as it had once been during those years.

Ashaf dreamed, and her dreams had never been kind.

The sound of the chimes woke her, or she thought it was chimes; a hint of music lingered in the air. There was no light in the room; she lay on her side on the worn, wide roll that had served her for too many years. And she heard the voice.

But where Isladar's voice held the menace or danger of the not-quite-known, this voice held something familiar. And besides, it was night, and it was a woman's voice, and after all, night was the Lady's time.

"Ashaf."

She was disoriented by the nearness of the word; thought, for a moment, that the harem enclosed her again, and a wife had jostled her to give her a few minutes of warning, granting her time to prepare, if such preparation were possible. Kesli had done it, often, before her untimely death. Kesli. She sat up quickly, stiffly, pulling the sleeping silks up to cover her shoulders and breasts.

Except that there were no silks; there was a blanket of rough cotton twill. She was home. Home.

"Ashaf."

"Who—who is it? Who's there?" She hated the sound of her voice, when it came; it wobbled so much she knew she was making a child's display of fear.

"Not a friend," the voice replied. "Do you mind if I bring a little light into this place?"

"Not the Lord's light," Ashaf said, quartering herself with the sign of the Lady's moon.

"Not the Lord's light, no." And light came, and it was the Lady's light, a soft, silver glow that did not destroy the privacy of night colors, but did allow a woman to see by.

Two women.

Not a friend, Ashaf thought, repeating the stranger's phrase to herself as she stared at the pale contours of this other woman's face. She wore blue, a dark midnight blue that made her seem one with the Lady's intent; the hood framed her face, hid her arms. There were shadows about her and within her; Ashaf recognized them at once, for they bowed her as well: old pain. Old fear.

"Who are you?"

"I am Evayne a'Nolan."

"a'Nolan? You are a Northerner, then."

"I have no home," the woman replied gravely, "But if names are important, then, yes, I was named in the North."

"Names are important." Ashaf rose. "It seems this is a night for visitors."

"It is night," the other woman said softly, "and in the South, night is the time of possibility."

"Possibility." She paused. "You told me that you are not a friend, yet I do not feel you to be an enemy."

"If a man is driving a wagon, and the weather is poor, and he does not see the child that runs out into the road, the child is still dead. That man, if you are the mother of the child, is no friend, although he intended you no ill. An accident."

Ashaf felt the cold, then, but this Evayne did not stop speaking; she merely paused a moment.

"And if a man is at the till of a ship, be it Northern or Southern, and it is being pursued by pirates or vessels of war, and a child falls overboard, and he *sees* this clearly, but raises no cry because to stop is to lose the lives of the rest of his passengers—although there is no guarantee that the ship will escape, regardless—that man is less your friend. And that accident becomes a choice.

"And that choice . . ." The woman in midnight blue lowered her face a moment. "I have made that choice. And I have come to you to ask you to make a choice as well."

"What choice?"

"I will not tell you, Ashaf; you will know it soon enough."

The older woman snorted. "Speak plainly."

"Very well. I would come to you in dream, but your dreams are so distant and so troubled that the path has brought me here, instead, where words are harder and much more solid.

"Ashaf kep'Valente, if you choose to leave your home, you will journey to a place that defines darkness, and you will see, in the time remaining to you, things that will make the days of your youth seem easy by comparison."

Ashaf waited in silence, knowing that such an obvious choice was not that: obvious. How could it be, and be called a choice at all? She was patient now.

"And if you choose to leave your home, you will be a warrior, but you will be unsung, and the war that you fight will have no reward for you. Make no mistake; you will die before the battle is fully joined. You will never see its end, and you will never know whether or not your life and your effort made any difference at all. No one will find your body; no one will say the rites by which the Lady's blessing is conferred. Your story ends here, in this village; there will be no one to tell it, to carry it on, to bring it to light."

It was the stranger who paled as she spoke, her eyes darkening, her gaze falling; Ashaf kep'Valente thought that this Evayne would feel more at ease speaking of her own death. She waited, still, feeling detached.

"But if," the stranger said, and Ashaf thought, *ah, now it comes,* "you choose this task—and it must be willingly chosen—then you will begin the battle, and you will define some of the rules by which it is fought. You will step into a war that started before the birth of man—before the birth of the Firstborn—and your presence will count for much. With or without you, the battle is coming, and with it, the darkness that clan Leonne fought so long and so hard against."

The clan Leonne. The clan that, by right of battle and bloodshed, now ruled the Dominion of Annagar from beside the waters of the Tor Leonne. Clan wars were clan wars, and they happened; Ashaf had seen two in her life. The lot of a seraf changed little, except when the raiding and reprisals were fierce—in which case, the serafs died. When the war was over, they had either the old master, or a new one, and they toiled, as ever.

But Leonne was made by no petty clan infighting. Ashaf knew the old stories, although she was simple seraf. That the founder, Leonne, had been given the Sun Sword by the Lord himself; that he had fought to preserve the Lady's domain, in the name of the Lord. And that, of course, he faced the priests of the so-called Lord of Night to do so. Children's stories. True stories. So often, they were the same, if you know how to understand what lay beneath the words. "I don't understand."

"Don't you?"

"You're telling me if I choose to go on Lady knows what journey, that I will be forgotten and unmourned."

"No, Ashaf—you will *never* be forgotten and unmourned."

"And I'm to do this to save the—the world?" The old woman laughed. "I am not a warrior, Evayne a'Nolan. Even in my youth, I could not wield a clansman's sword. You ask me to fight? Then the darkness of the night had befuddled you."

"Has it? There are territories over which battles are fought in this world in which no sword is raised."

Ah, yes. How could she have forgotten, who had fought—and lost—so many? And why was it that to win was to prepare for another battle, but to lose was to lose all? Oh, she was tired, was Ashaf kep'Valente. It was only when she was weary that the dead were so strong.

"You wish me to make this journey."

"I wish you to know and understand that the price of it will be, in the end, your death." There was no softness at all in the words.

"And if I don't?"

"I do not know. Perhaps another woman will be asked to make the choice that I ask of you." The stranger was silent a long time. And then her face softened; she lifted a hand a moment, as if to touch the older woman's face. She stopped, lowering the hand, letting the gesture linger only in her expression. "I can promise you this: You will never have to bury her."

And then, before Ashaf's eyes could sting at the words and the memories they invoked, the stranger took a step into the room's shadows—and silver light, pale and luminescent, swallowed her, returning her, perhaps, to the Lady's Moon.

She missed the dawn, but met the day when the shadows cast were still long and slender. The fields were full of moving bodies; women toiled with their scythes in their personal plots in the common before being called to serve upon the Lord's lands at the sides of their husbands. This Tor'agar granted them that much. His father had not. Small children gathered tied stalks; older children knotted and bundled them. During this month, this, the only time of year when the Lady's hand was felt during the daylight hours, there were no idle hands.

Not even, she thought ruefully, her own. Her back was strong, her arms stronger; she would be missed. And she did not care to offer excuses, either of the two that she had, for her absence. She scurried with haste to the edge of the Lord's field, knowing her own part of the common serafs' plot would be tended by the younger women in the village. Age granted her that unspoken right, but she hated to take advantage of it now when in her dotage she might truly require it. Unself-conscious in her movements, she rolled up her sleeves, inviting the sun's touch as she ran.

"Ashaf!"

"Na'Carre," she said, smiling broadly at a slender, too tall youth.

He blushed, almost ducking under the hand that ran through the sun-bleached tuft of his curly hair. He was a young man now, and no child, to be so called. When had he grown so? Last year, and he had blushed and smiled, joining her a moment to brag about his new exploits, his ability to trap small game in the forests outside of the Lord's fields and the serafs' common. He brought her an almost recognizable pelt, a gift of sorts, proof of the truth of his words.

She stopped a moment to look at him, and his mother, Valla kep'Valente, thwacked him soundly on the shoulder for being what he was: a youth yearning impatiently for the imagined grace of manhood.

She had been just such a youth except, of course, she had desired to be woman and wife.

"Ashaf," Valla said, falling into step beside the older woman. "Are you well? It's not like you to sleep so late."

Not, Ashaf thought, during harvest. "I slept poorly," she told the younger woman, wondering if she had ever walked with such unself-conscious, easy grace. "Yesterday was the start of the harvest season; I rose too early."

"Ah," Valla said, her own face taking the shadows a moment. Every seraf had her dead, be they mother or sister or child. Or father. Or brother. Or husband. "We said our rites. My youngest—Tia—she wouldn't mind me. Crawled all over the graves as if they were hillocks made for child's play."

"The Lady," Ashaf said wryly and sadly both, "is *the* mother. She understands; the joy of children is no disrespect to either her or those who now rest in her keeping. Believe that, Valla."

The younger woman smiled and nodded, just as Ashaf knew she would. Ashaf, having lost so much, had done what she could to fill her life; she was old enough now to be considered wise—at least by the women. They came to her, when they could not or would not go to their own mothers, and she let them come, taking a pain and a pleasure from their youthful company. The what-ifs of her own family.

Her arms ached, but the smile across her lips, habit and

more, was pleasant and warm enough. "Now come. We've no time for talk; as it is, we'll be under the headman's eyes. Look at the sun."

She loved the harvest season, and as she watched it unfold, she wondered what the cooler weather would bring. Rain; probably too much of it. Averda was the Lady's land; there was no doubt about it. And those who called the Lady the weaker of the two were fools who deserved to live in the harsh, wind-blasted desert plains. If the sand made men, she thought, it scoured them so clean only their swords and their will remained. And swords and will were a poor home and a poor haven for life.

Here, with green and gold and red all about, she thought she could be happy. No, she did not think it; she felt it, a deep and even peace that came from working with life, for it. There were drummers on the fields' edge, and a man who played the pipes as if the pipes were a sweet, youthful voice. She did not recognize him, and that was odd; she recognized all of the village serafs on sight.

"He's pretty, isn't he?" Valla said, catching the black strands of hair that had worked free of her confining knot and tying them up again.

"Do you know him?"

"I? No." The younger woman laughed. "But I would if Arrego weren't so jealous!"

"Valla!"

"He's Voyani," she replied, as if that explained anything. Or everything.

It explained much.

In the Dominion, there were the clansmen, and there were the serafs. The clansmen were free, and where they had power and the will to protect their holdings, they gathered serafs, branding and naming them. If they were powerful enough, they chose to merely name; the name was enough. Ashaf kep'Valente bore no scar, no brand. She understood that she was owned by a powerful clan, and perhaps she was even blessed by the ownership; today, under this sky, with the smell of the earth in her nostrils, the soil beneath her nails, the harvest beside her bent back, she felt so. And she knew it as the Lord's will, and the Lady's. Some served. Some ruled.

But the Voyani were as old as the land. They traveled,

many upon the horses of the open plains, and many not; they moved in groups, and they defended each other as fiercely as blood-born clansmen. But they took no serafs. They owned no land. They carried no war with them.

It was said that they were not averse to robbing the clansmen they found who were poor and unable to defend themselves properly, and Ashaf knew it for truth. Yet they were suffered to survive, and survive they did, trading and bartering and carrying information from one Terrean to the next. They even moved out of the Dominion from time to time, seeking the merchants in the Northern Empire. It was said that some, one or two, settled there, like so many of the poor, free clansmen who could make no mark for themselves in the Dominion. The North took the weak ones, and accepted them; the Lord let them go. The Lord had no use for weakness.

It was also said, although she did not know if it were true, that serafs who escaped their clan could travel with the Voyani and find both home and freedom in Essalieyan. She and her husband had spoken of it in whispers when their first child was born. Perhaps the Lady had heard them. Perhaps the Lady had been angered by it. Perhaps the Lady had chosen to keep the children within her reach.

Too much darkness. During the Sun's dance. She shook herself. "Why are the Voyani here?"

Valla shrugged.

"Which family?"

"Hers. Yollana's."

Ashaf felt a little chill in the sun's heat. She raised a hand, adjusted her hat, feeling the edge of the wide brim as if its presence were a comfort. "Has she come to trade?"

"I think it's too early for that. We're just starting our harvest."

"Then what?"

"Yollana," Valla replied, lowering her voice. "is moon-touched. She goes where she goes. You know that. I've even heard that the Tor—"

"Enough," Ashaf said, raising a hand and touching the moving lips of a careless young woman. The gesture brought the silence that she hoped for—and demanded. Whether it was true or no, it was never safe to speculate, beneath the day's open sky, about the habits and the secrets of powerful men. The wind carried careless words farther than arrows and spears.

Yes, she knew Yollana well. What girl, with a heart full of foolish dreams in these, the richest lands of Annagar, did not? What girl, with such a heart, could resist the trek over fields and hill, before night had fully set, to offer the mysterious Voyani woman what little food or item she could find in order to procure both a blessing and a hint of the future?

She had already faced Yollana once, in the year before her first marriage to the man of her desire. She could remember, clearly, the icy night of Yollana's face, the darkness of unblinking eyes, as Yollana had promised her that she would have her heart's desire. The first intimation that her heart was a thing to be feared. She would have others, but like so many things, the first was a scar that time did not diminish.

That year, she had discovered that nightmare and dream come from the same place. And it was nightmare that returned her to it, time and again, stripping her of the strength of wisdom and experience, paring her down to a girl's fear and helplessness.

Her arms ached, and her back, as the minutes dwindled into a stream of time; hours passing.

Things happened, when they happened, in threes. Three visitors: Isladar of no clan, Evayne of Nolan, and now Yollana of the Havalla Voyani.

I am too old, she thought. *I haven't the strength.* But she wiped her dirt-crusted hands on the thick cotton drape of her long skirts and shielded her eyes against the sun's fall. She could see the Voyani wagons at the crest of the gently sloped hill beyond which her house lay. She knew that she would go around them.

And that it would make no difference.

Dusk was the time of shadows.

Night, and the Lady's moon was brilliant against the speckled backdrop of cool, dark blue. Day, and the Lord's face turned a merciless, necessary heat upon the greens and the golds, the reds and the browns, the earth's colors. But at dusk, with neither Lord nor Lady in ascendance, the light and the darkness intertwined and every possible path was a step into the unknown.

She could not sleep.

And sleepless, she left the sanctity of her single-room dwelling to stand a moment in the wash of a sky that was caught, in crimson, between two shades of blue. Beneath that sky, crossing the footpaths that had been worn by time and the steady movement of sturdy heels, was a lone figure, illuminated from behind by the lamp that hung across her left shoulder by the shaft of a long pole. The figure's face was in shadow, but she did not need to see it to feel the apprehension of recognition.

Fate.

Ashaf waited numbly as the figure came closer.

Yollana, the wisewoman of the Havalla Voyani.

But here, she felt a strange thing: not fear, as she had expected, and not even resignation, although its touch was heavy upon her unbent shoulders. No, she felt kinship; the kinship of those weary with the burdens of the responsibilities they have chosen—and wearier still with the loss of them.

The Yollana of her youth was gone in that instant; her perfect midnight hair bleached everywhere by the touch of harsh sun and time. Her pale skin was lined now, although not furrowed; it was no longer translucence defined. But if she did not have the slenderness of youth, she had the muscled, sturdy appearance of one who has been tried and tested without breaking.

As if she had expected no less, Yollana looked up from the ground's even slope as she at last approached the house, nodding at the younger woman who waited. Her eyes were the eyes that Ashaf remembered.

"Well met," the Voyani wisewoman said, bowing low enough that the folds of her voluminous shirt obscured the wide, red sash across her midriff.

"And you," Ashaf said softly. She waited a long moment, and then looked away. "I have no water to offer."

"I do," Yollana replied, and she lifted the skin from the folds of her wide skirts. Those skirts could hide many a thing: water, gold. A dagger. "Will you drink with me?"

It was formal; an offer of sorts. But of what, and for what, Ashaf could not guess. She nodded quietly. "Night is coming," she said. "I should sleep soon." But she turned quietly and opened the door to her home, inviting by gesture this third visitor for whom she felt such ambivalence.

The lamp was bright enough to illuminate the four walls of her life; to cast a shadow around the sagging cotton mats upon which she lay night by night; to show the marks and stains and scratches in the wood of the small table before which she knelt to eat. To pray.

She crossed the room and knelt there now, taking from a small shelf beside the table the delicate clay bowls that had been a gift from her husband and placing them upon the worn wooden surface. After a moment, Yollana joined her, unhooking the lamp and placing it on the floor by her bent knees. They stared at each other a moment in uneasy silence; it was the Voyani woman who spoke first.

Yollana's smile was crooked. "You've aged," she said. She took the skin from her belt, uncapped it, and poured. She was skilled, and it was clear from the way that she watched each drop that she had traveled in the Lord's heartlands.

"And you," Ashaf replied. "But more gracefully."

"Voyani blood." Carefully lifting a bowl, she offered the sweet water to Ashaf.

Ashaf took it and lifted it to her lips, accepting the visitor's gift as if there was nothing unusual about such a visit. "All blood is red," she said softly. Then she stopped; the water that touched her tongue was sweet and cool—it was almost as if she drank water's ideal, and not the water itself.

At that, Yollana smiled broadly. "All blood, yes. I give you my word under the Lady's moon that I will spill none of yours this eve."

Ashaf laughed bitterly. "And that is meant to comfort? Oh, no, Yollana. I know the Havalla Voyani well. You are subtle when you exact your price."

History stood between them; history and the piercing clarity of the memory of a young girl long gone.

"We have all met our heart's desire," Yollana replied at last, speaking to a past that had never, and would never, fully die. "And most of us have survived it. If I had warned you then, what would you have done, you a seraf of the clan Valente?" She lifted a hand. "Don't answer.

We both know that you would not have chosen to believe me. You were sixteen, Ashaf kep'Valente." Her smile was oddly crooked. "I was sixteen once. I know the age."

The younger woman's face twisted a moment, and then relaxed. "I survived," she said softly. "And for a time, I flourished. It is gone now."

"Yes. You have lost two lives."

She started, as if in pain, and then said, "I have lost more than that."

"You have mourned and buried more," Yollana replied, as cool this night as she had been almost thirty years past. "But the two that I speak of are yours." Yollana's words were carried by a cold, sharp wind; they pierced the skin and more.

I have lost two lives, Ashaf thought, feeling the strange truth of the words as they echoed, unspoken, between them.

Things were done in three. She exhaled slowly, feeling the dread of the moment give way to weariness.

"Why have you come, Yollana? It is not the way of the Voyani to seek out the serafs—or the clansmen, for that matter. You hide in your tents and your wagons, in your stalls and beneath the masks you wear upon your stages. If you want gold, I have none to give you. If you want food, there are richer women than I.

"And if you wish to tell a fortune, you must find someone who is fool enough to ask you. I have already been bled. I will not hold my hand beneath your dagger again."

"This night I cannot see the answer to the question of your future written so clearly across your face. You were beautiful in your youth, Ashaf; you were known for it two villages in any direction. It did not take the mystical skills of the Voyani ancestors to know what that beauty presaged."

"I will not speak about my past," Ashaf said. "And I have not asked you about my future." She spoke calmly now, and clearly, meeting eyes that had once been dark and icy and yes, mysterious.

She was surprised when Yollana turned aside, her eyes flickering with some emotion that made her seem human. Made her seem, for a moment, as much a seraf as Ashaf, and not a woman of Voyani freedoms. "No. But I have come in search of your future, whether you ask it of me or no."

"What?"

"I have crossed the plains, Ashaf kep'Valente." She looked down at the still surface of the almost untouched water in her bowl. "I have stood beside the waters of the Tor Leonne, and I have gathered them."

Ashaf grew still; her bowl was half empty.

"You have lost two lives, and you stand upon the threshold of a third. I cannot influence your choice, and I would not; I could not bear your burden; not then, and not now.

"I come to perform no act of magic, no act of mysticism. I have left my tents and my wagons and my family behind. Tonight, we are two women beneath the Lady's Moon." She raised her head and the lamp's glow caught and whitened her chin, making of her face a stark relief.

Ashaf looked out and saw that at least some of her words were true; dusk had passed, and the secrecy of darkness held them. She looked down at her half empty bowl, as if deciding, as if afraid to decide.

The water was sweet as she lifted the delicate clay to her lips. *From the Tor Leonne,* she thought. *For me.* So did the Serras drink in all their finery, surrounded by serafs and cerdan.

But she knew, from her time in the harem, that the Serras were only a little more free, and only a little more honored, than the serafs themselves. The will of the Lord whose waters were so sweet.

"Why?"

"Because you have haunted my dreams for three nights. Three nights beneath the Lady's Moon, I have dreamed of the death of the Havalla Voyani—and more, the death of the Dominion." She drew breath; her lips thinned as if she were attempting to hold the words back. No Voyani woman spoke her mind so freely to strangers—not for free. And among the Voyani, Yollana was more mysterious than any.

"Did you have these dreams," Ashaf asked, as if the revelation were as natural as the turn of seasons in the valley that had been home for the only parts of her life that she cared to remember, "before you journeyed to the Tor Leonne? I have not heard that the Tyr'agar freely grants the Voyani permission to take what the lake holds."

"Yes," Yollana said starkly. "Three nights." She moved then, unbending at the knee and rising as if freedom of action could soothe her.

"You saw me."

"I saw you."

"Where?"

Yollana averted her gaze and did not speak.

"Yollana."

"I will not lie to you this eve. I will never lie to you again." She fell silent, and it was a moment before Ashaf realized that Yollana did not intend to answer. It seemed to her, as she watched the Voyani woman, that Yollana's actions were a mixture of nervousness and, oddly, pity. She should have felt fear, but she felt almost nothing. Almost.

"Why have you come?" she said, asking for the third time, realizing as the words left her lips that the third time was the significant one.

"To bring you this water," Yollana replied, quietly placing the skin upon Ashaf's humble table. "The Havalla Voyani will be in no one's debt."

The answer made no sense, but the set of Yollana's lips, the shadowed lines across her brow, made it clear that she would answer no questions about such a debt. They stood a moment in silence, and then Yollana shook her head, sending graying curls across the curves of her face, her shoulders. "You will forgive me," she said, almost wry in tone. "But I am not a gentle woman. Not a sympathetic one. I am not good at these offers, these gestures. I raised Voyani; I define what the Havalla are." She reached into the folds of her shirt and pulled something from between her breasts. As she lifted it, it caught the light and sent it out in a fan of intense color.

"Take this," Yollana said, and if there was a request in the two words, she hid it well. "Take this, and wear it. Travel this village, these lands. Speak to the people who make this your home. Visit your graves, your fields, your hills; find the shade in your forest, the cooling waters in your brook and small river." She let it fall; Ashaf gasped until she saw the glittering chain that stopped it from reaching ground. A necklace or a pendant of some sort.

She reached out an open palm, and Yollana carefully dropped the stone—for it was a stone, a clear one, like a diamond that would beggar even a Tyr—into her hand. At once, it flared with a deep, blue light; the light ran the length of her arm, shrouding it.

Magic.

"What—what does it do?" Her voice was, momentarily, a girl's voice—the girl that she had thought long gone. Dreamer. Seeker of wonder.

"It is the Lady's magic," Yollana replied, "not the Lord's. It will not protect you; it will not defend you. Where a blade is raised or spell is thrown, you will find no solace in it."

Ashaf smiled wryly. "I did not ask you what it wasn't. I asked you what it is."

"It is a keeper," Yollana said. "Of memory. Of affection. Of place. Wear it, as I have told you to wear it, and it will take some of what you feel and hold it within depths that you cannot even imagine. Wear it, and you will feel exactly the peace or the joy or the quiet—yes, or the sorrow—that you felt when you first donned it."

"Why?"

"It is a piece of home," Yollana replied gravely. "Many of the Voyani women wear them, because the heart—our hearts—so seldom find a home, and when they do, we cannot remain there."

"But this is—this is—" Ashaf fell silent, realizing two things. For the first, she bowed low. "You have honored me," she said softly.

Yollana's face was in shadow as she bent to retrieve the lamp. Ashaf slid the chain over her head with shaking hands, letting the stone fall to rest against her skin. What should have been cold was warm; what should have been hard was smooth and almost soft.

Honored? Yes. But she knew, as the Voyani woman attached the lamp to the pole she carried, that Yollana did not expect to see her again. Did not expect that anyone would. The Voyani did not surrender the secrets of their hearts to anyone.

What had Evayne of Nolan said?

Your story ends here, in this village; there will be no one to tell it, to carry it on, to bring it to light.

* * *

The next day, at dawn, Ashaf kep'Valente rose and walked to the graves in which lay the remnants of the second life that Yollana of the Havalla Voyani had spoken of. She knew now when it ended—had almost known it then, so bleak was the day, and the year, and the year that followed. The last of her children. Her son.

You were to find your joys, she thought, as her hand smoothed out drying strands of once green grass. But her joy, such as it was, was here, if she could let go of the memory that ended it.

And sometimes she could; sometimes she could see his youth—all of their youths—and his innocence, although she expected that the latter was the kindness of aged memory.

As if this were her last day here, she knelt before the grave, these graves—but she could not sit for long; the tears came, and it was not tears that she wished to capture.

Valla kep'Valente was waiting for her this second morning. Valla, with her delicate chin, her raven's hair, her intemperate words. She was like a child, and unlike; she spoke her mind as it pleased her, and often with great surprise at the results.

The pinks were fading from the sky, and the men had been fed; it was time to tend the fruit of the fields. They walked together, and to Ashaf it seemed that everything—the colors of the valley fields, the smell of the cut stalks and turned earth, the movement of birds and men, the sound of the river—was heightened. Almost new. She looked from side to side, as if a wonder long dead had found new life.

"Ashaf? Ashaf, have you heard a thing I've said?"

"It's—it's a lovely day," Ashaf said, blushing.

"Which means no." Valla's face was caught a moment between a smile and a frown; the smile won. "It is a beautiful day."

"Is that Riva?"

"Yes. And that monstrous son of hers."

"He's not monstrous," Ashaf said softly. "Or he will not always be. He is reckless. When your own are that age, you will understand it better."

"My own," Valla said, with the arrogance of loving ignorance, "will not survive if they choose to become like

Eric. It's Riva's own fault." She shrugged. "Give the child no child's name, and what happens? He knows no mother's calm."

It was common wisdom. "Na'Eri," she said quietly, turning the words around in her mouth. "Be kind."

Valla's brow lifted a moment. "You weren't so forgiving when he broke your door."

"True enough," the older woman said. "But the door was fixed."

"I worry about you, Ashaf. You've been sleeping well?"

"No," Ashaf replied cheerfully. "Very poorly. Come; the shadows are lengthening and the overseer will take our names."

He didn't, of course; and she knew he wouldn't. Although he was a clansman in theory, he had spent his life here, in this village, among the serafs. He had played with them, bullied them, and been bullied by them; he had lain with them, and broken their hearts, and had his heart broken. He had wed here, under the Lady's Moon, with the permission of the Tor'agar—the same man who had given Ashaf a husband and her freedom.

The freedom of a seraf.

He was also a good ten years younger than she, and twice, when his daughters were ill, had come over the hillocks, his lamp and his fear burning high. And she had followed him to the biggest house in the village, to tend to his children in the silence of sickness, of terror. How could she do less, when she understood that particular helplessness so well?

"Ashaf. Valla. You're late again."

"Daro," Valla said, kneeling meekly.

"Daro," Ashaf said. "At my age—"

"At your age you set about Michale with a broom and reddened both his ears." But his good-natured smile was broad enough; it had been a good year, and the harvest would please the Tor who ruled them all, whether his serafs were late or no. "We'll fall behind without you, Ashaf. You set the good example."

"And she terrifies those who don't follow it!" Someone else, his words carrying in a loud, happy boom. Michale.

She set about her work, feeling the long stalks of wheat

as they lay, new, against her dry hands. The children came to help her, although she needed little help; they came to thresh and stomp and squabble while they worked. That was the way of the young.

The way of the village.

She felt a sharp pang, seeing them all. And she did not name it because she did not have to. She could have chosen any home when the Tor'agar who had been her husband met his just end beneath the Lady's Moon. It was truth; his son had been almost a son to her, for all sons were reared in the harem until they came of an age deemed suitable by their sires.

But she had chosen to return to this village, as if by coming back she could reclaim what had been lost: dreams. Innocence. Trust.

And she had, for a while.

There was a warmth at her chest, a warmth and a softness, as if a child lay pillowed against her breast. And she realized that she cared very much for these people, and this place; that not only her dead, but her living, were here in numbers.

"Ashaf?"

It was Daro, his black hair swept in an unruly knot above his forehead. His wife loved long hair, and although it was not at all practical, he kept it so as not to have to listen to her complaints. Or so he said; there was an affection in Daro that was strong and deep and not afraid of the gibes of men.

"I am sorry," she told him softly, setting a callused hand gently against his shirt.

"And I am worried. It's not like you to miss the call three days running. Are you ill?"

"Do I look ill?"

"No. But I know you, Ashaf. You'd have one hand in the Lady's before you'd admit that anything was wrong."

"Then why," she said pointedly, "do you waste your breath and time asking?"

"Because if I get close enough to ask you over this din, I'll be able to see for myself." The concern lingered in his eyes, and she surprised herself by setting all work aside.

"Come," she said, and he followed, just as he followed her the evening his daughter's fever had—barely—broken.

* * *

They climbed the highest of the hills that the forest shielded from the outside, and sat there, looking down upon the men and women who toiled in such high spirits below.

"We'll finish early," she said.

He nodded.

"Is the Tor happy?"

"You'll be able to ask him yourself," Daro replied. "He's traveling this season, and intends this village to be his last stop." As he spoke, he cast a sidelong glance at her, the question in his voice unmistakable.

As always, the news that he would visit warmed her. He was not her son; she reminded herself of this again and again, although in truth she needed no reminder. He was the Tor'agar Danello kai di'Valente; he held her life, and the life of this village, in a hand that could just as easily curl into fist as open in offering.

But he held her in regard, he flattered her, and in the privacy of the tiny home that she would not leave, he spoke to her as if they were still prisoners in the same harem.

And that, she thought, *was the first life, and it is over.*

"Do you love this village?" someone said, and when Daro replied, she realized it was her.

"It is my responsibility."

"And you understand responsibility well," Ashaf replied softly. Proudly. "This is a village unlike any village in the Dominion, and it was made by the Tor'agar and by you. Give me your word, in the presence of the Lord, that you will guard it when I am gone."

"I have given just that word," Daro replied wryly, "to the Tor'agar himself." He laughed as he saw her expression shift into sternness. "But I am a wise man. He is in the capital. You are here.

"I give you my solemn word that I will guard this village in your absence. The Lord sees all. May he scorch me if I lie, or prove false to my vow. But, Ashaf," he continued, more seriously, "I don't want to have to do it without your help."

"No," she said softly.

The sun was warm and high.

* * *

She returned home while the sun was still ascendant, casting a shadow across the graves that she and her husband had made. That she had made alone after his passing, changing the shape of the earth with spades and tears.

Moving, she came to stand by the graves so that the sun cast her shadow away from what lay within them. The day had softened the edges of the loss, as it sometimes did, and she could sit here a moment, speaking silently the names of her children and her husband as if they were litany. Nothing lived within them, of course; nothing that could answer the words she did not speak aloud.

But she had stayed here, by the side of the dead, because it was here that their memories were strongest. She let them come; all of them. But she held the tears until dusk, offering them to no judgmental, unsympathetic Lord, and no Lady who, mother or not, had seen fit to part her from her family.

He came that night.

She should have known, and perhaps in some way she did, for her sleep was restless and easily broken. Yet it was not the sound of his voice that wakened her, shouting through the screens; nor was it the sound of his hand against the wooden beams.

She rose in the silence of insects and wind through the valley's tree branches—the silence of the pause before breath, of the stillness in a crowded room after the shattering of a precious crystal glass. Something had called her from sleep, but no trace remained of its sound except her certain knowledge that it was there.

She rose and went to the screen that separated the world without from the one within. The moonlight was bright enough to be visible, but not bright enough to see by. Darkness, light—it made little difference to Ashaf. Every inch of her home was more familiar to her in the darkness than most places were in the day.

Little difference? Ah. Not this night. She felt that she wanted the light, or rather that she should; she struggled a moment with tallow and wick before she brought its flickering glimmer into the night.

And then she remembered—and was surprised that she could forget for even a moment such a fact: That the harem had never been given over to night's darkness; lights abounded, proof to the wives—and their children—that the Lord's will ruled in the harem of the Tor'agar at all times. Very few were the people who had dared to speak against this more than once, although it made even the Radann—the men whose worship of the Lord of the Sun defined their lives—uneasy. "The Lady's time will come," they would say, muttering among themselves in their cloisters.

And it had. When the rites had been said over the newly turned earth. Oh, she had smiled then, her face veiled and masked, her anger hidden. The only joy she was allowed to show were her tears, and she shed them freely, knowing that the clansmen would not understand—and that her sister-wives would.

She stared at the candle until the image of its light had burned itself, blue, into her vision, and then she carefully blew it out.

The screen was heavy this night, as if her reluctance added weight and stiffness to its movement. She put her shoulders behind the action; they had borne greater burdens than this.

Moonlight silvered the grass and the leaves of the tall trees beyond the village. Starlight, starcloud, and the deepest of blue filled the sky. Somewhere, there were men and women who understood the beauty of things that were glimpsed, not seen. She smiled wryly. Dreams.

And then the smile dimmed. The sight of sky was lost.

"Ashaf kep'Valente."

She stared at the dark, dark robes of the man who stood before her door as if he were a stranger. There was something about his face, something about his eyes, that she had not seen during their dawn meeting, or their twilight one.

He spoke a guttural word, and from the folds of his cloak a lamp fell, swinging as if in a heavy breeze although the night air was still. She was not surprised to see that no hands held it, although it was suspended in air. Not surprised to see that his eyes were all blackness, his face almost white.

It was the Lady's night.

"Isladar of no clan," she said. She did not bow or kneel. "Have you come to offer me a choice?"

At those words, spoken in such a quiet tone, he raised a dark brow. She had surprised him, and from his reaction, he was not a man who enjoyed the unexpected. But he nodded after a moment.

"Then enter," she said, standing aside. "Enter into the home of Ashaf kep'Valente for this third night."

"Ah." He smiled grimly. "This is the third night. You are superstitious, Ashaf. It is . . . charming." His cloak shifted; in the light his lamp cast she could see that he carried something beneath it. "I will accept your offer."

"I have water," she said. And it was true.

"Water? Ah. I forget. In the South there is the custom of water as an offering of either hospitality or respect. It is not often pursued in the Averdan valleys."

She walked to the table, the small, scarred table that was so much a part of her life she couldn't clearly remember a time that the house did not have it. Oh, she knew when it had arrived, but knowledge and memory did not always speak the same language.

"Sit," she said quietly as she retrieved her bowls. They were shallow; she saw this clearly in the glow of the lamp that no hands held. "You are not Widan."

"I bear no Widan's mark," Isladar said agreeably.

She lifted the skin that Yollana had left her and poured, sparingly, into both bowls. The first, she offered to Isladar, and the second, she took for herself. She lifted the bowl, waiting; he lifted his.

And then, as he brought the edge of the delicate clay to his lips, the waters taken from the lake of the Tor Leonne began to steam.

His brow rose again, and then his lips turned up in a genuine smile. "I think," he said softly, "that the hospitality of this house is both too fine and too dangerous for one such as I." The smile vanished as quickly as it had come. "Very well, Ashaf kep'Valente. I will not ask you how you came by this water; it is of little import and little consequence. This evening, I wear no disguise; I hide nothing."

"You do not speak all the truth," she said, which was as close as she had yet come to accusing a man with great power of lying. She felt no surprise at all that the waters did not pass his lips. Fear, yes—but not a visceral fear. A subtle one. A deep one.

"No one does." He nodded politely to her. "If we are to travel together, you and I, we must travel this evening. Already, I have been gone too long."

"What is the choice that you offer me?"

"To remain here, in this little village, as Ashaf kep'Valente. Or to travel with me, to a North that you cannot possibly imagine." He rose, and threw back the folds of his cloak. In the light, in his arms, there lay a small, poorly swaddled child. The child was crying; its face was almost purple with effort. But Ashaf heard no sound at all. She looked up, once, to see Isladar's face; such an expression could have been carved out of stone, so unmoved, and unmoving, did it seem.

"What are you doing to the child?" She rose as well, her arms already extended.

"I? I am merely silencing her cries. She can breathe."

She. Her. Ashaf asked for no permission as she took the child from Isladar's arms. At once, the child's pitiful cries filled the room. They were not strong.

"How old is she?" Ashaf said, all sternness.

"She was born," Isladar replied, "Upon the fifteenth of Wittan."

"The Lady's dawn," Ashaf said softly. "The harvest." She looked down into the child's face. The infant's face. "You don't know anything about children." It wasn't a question.

"I know a great deal about how to twist a person," he replied affably. "But not one so young, no. I see to her feeding."

"And who cleans her?"

He shrugged. "Does it matter? She is cleaned. She is healthy."

"And she's hungry."

"She is always hungry." Isladar frowned.

"No, I mean, she's hungry right now. And I don't have much to feed her." She stopped a moment, staring into the child's purple-red face. It wasn't lovely, and it was, and she felt it sharply as memory stung her.

"Where is her mother?"

"In the Hall of Mandaros," Isladar replied. And then he smiled coolly. "I forget. Annagarians are . . . quaint in their beliefs, and entirely incorrect; you do not know who sits in judgment. Her mother is quite dead."

Motherless.

This is not my child, she told herself, as she began to bounce her up and down while she gave thought to milk and liquid rice and who she might ask for either. Then she stopped again, and stared down at the waters of the Tor Leonne as they lay in her shallow drinking bowl.

She sat carefully, holding the child with the ease of years of long practice, before she lifted the bowl. No, she thought, too young yet.

"I would not, if I were you," Isladar said softly, although he made no move toward her.

Ashaf lifted her chin, met the blackness of his eyes with the solid brown of hers, and then turned her attention away from his gaze, his words. She rose, walked to the mats upon which she slept, and beside them found a clean cotton shirt. Dropping the edge of this into the water itself, she waited a moment. Then she lifted the wet cloth, and laid it, cool, against the child's lips.

A second, two, and then the infant began to suck. She cried out once, twice—a third time—and then she relaxed as the waters of the Tor Leonne took the edge off her hunger. Rising again, balancing child and shirt, Ashaf came to the table and picked up the Voyani skin. She filled her bowl, and fed the child, knowing that the girl would sleep soon.

Infants this young slept and ate and dirtied themselves in both the Lord's and the Lady's time. They did not see, they did not hear, and they did not crave the company of their mothers.

And so it was that Ashaf knew, by two signs, that this child was no normal infant. First, the satiated child raised her reddened, newborn face to gaze upon the person who had offered her the waters of the Lord. And second, as those eyes met Ashaf's, she saw that they were liquid gold. They had been brown when Isladar had placed the child in her arms. Infant brown.

But the waters of the Tor were special.

Demon child.

Ashaf paled, but she did not drop the child, or in any way frown as the infant's lids closed slowly over those damning eyes.

"You're a demon," she said softly, not to the child, but to Isladar.

"I am a demon," Isladar agreed.

"The waters of the Lord would not even bear the touch of your lips."

"Indeed."

"And this child—is this child yours?"

Isladar laughed, and the laughter was like a slow, deliberate cut. "Not mine, no."

The Radann did not suffer the golden-eyed children to live. And often, did not suffer their mothers to survive such an ill-omened birth.

But . . . but the child had taken the waters of the Tor Leonne. Had even, after a moment, been comforted by them, as any child would be. Surely, if the Lord's waters burned at the very closeness of Isladar, they would have harmed the child had she been of such evil birth.

Her arms tightened a moment as she gazed down at the sleeping face, seeing in it so many sleeping faces, so many sleepless nights, so many memories that had nothing at all to do with the baby herself. "What is her name?"

"It is not important," Isladar replied evenly. "Either you will accompany me, or you will not. If you will not, it is better that you do not know."

Knowing the answer before she asked the question, Ashaf said, "What is the choice that you have come to offer me?"

"You know it," he replied. "But I will say it, if you feel it must be said. You may remain here, with your memories and your people and your dead, or you may travel with me—a long way, and not a pleasant one—and when we arrive at your new home, you will be given sole care of the child until she is of an age to learn. Then," he said, seeing that she intended to interrupt him, "I will teach her. To read, to write, and to use what powers she may be gifted with. But when she is that age, while I am teaching her these things, you will teach her, Ashaf kep'Valente, to be human."

Her arms tightened again as she stared at a now sleeping infant, thinking that the golden-eyed were demon-kin. Thinking that they must not be suffered to live. Thinking that, for a demon's child, this one was warm and light and scrawny, like any new life, any new possibility. Arms tightened, hands shook; she had held

each of her own, her own precious burdens, just so. Each
of them, wizened with new life, free forever from the element of water, the body of the mother. Had she begun
each life with a prayer? Had she begun each new possibility in both pain and in hope, and ended each—

Ah. She stood, babe in arms, history surrounding her
like a shadow family. Thinking, because she could not
stop from thinking it, that Evayne of Nolan had said this
one, this only, important thing two evenings past.

You will never have to bury her.

~mmmo

ANNAGAR

~mmmo

CHAPTER ONE

Serra Teresa di'Marano was uneasy, and if she was very careful, and kept her thoughts upon the festive celebrations, she hoped not to put a name to that unease, for things named were things with power. And she knew well that it was hard to rise above those things in life that held power.

Her lips, turned up in a gracious smile, and her chin, lowered just enough that she might not meet the eyes of the gathered crowd too boldly, were steady, but these were the perfected surface of manner, of grace, of social standing. And of these things, by necessity, the Serra Teresa was master. Her hands, folded around the handle of an ivory fan, sat in the lap her bent knees made; she wore a white silk sari, fringed in a deep, sapphire blue, with golden stars and moon and sun embroidered across the swath of the perfect cloth.

She was thirty-two years old, long past the first blush of the youth men found so pleasing, yet even so there was about her a beauty that endures, and the poets made much of the fact that long into the twilight of her life—should the Lady will it—she might capture more than the lust of men by her mystery and her strength.

Strength. A chill touched her beneath the skin—a night chill, here, at the sun's height. She could hear the howling of the desert wind.

"Teresa, you must be so proud. The children of Marano have voices worthy of the Lord himself!"

Proud? Ah, yes. It was Serra Teresa's gift to the festival to find those voices—young voices, as pleased the Lady—within clan Marano that she thought noteworthy, and to train them so that they might, in their unblemished innocence, in turn please the clansmen who gathered in the Tor Leonne for the Festival of the Moon. If, she thought wryly, such unblemished innocence existed, ever, outside of the boundless realm of a poet's heart.

"Worthy of the Lord? But this is the Lady's Festival." She smiled perfectly, gracefully, hoping the momentary unease would pass. Then, remembering herself, she said, "Lissa, when we are not in the harem, you must remember to use the honorific."

"Yes, Serra Teresa."

Lissa en'Marano, youngest of Ser Sendari par di'Marano's sub-wives, was perhaps the Serra's favorite; she therefore spoke with affection as she offered her correction. Had any of the important clansmen—the Tors, or the Tyrs, although none of the latter were in attendance—heard the comment, she would have saved the correction until they returned to the harem, but upon return, would have been much stricter.

And perhaps she showed a little weakness now. But it was the Festival of the Moon, or it would be in three days, and she felt the pull of that singular night of freedom already taking root.

Or she felt the unease growing.

The voices of the children were superb. An eight-year-old boy, Na'sare—Ami's son—sang the praises of the Tor Leonne and its magical founding, while the seven children at his feet—three boys and four girls—added harmonies. A child's song could never attain the full range of emotion that an adult's could, but there was a softness, a sweetness, a delicate rightness to the voice that one lost as one aged. And in the telling of legends, with their ideals, their valor, their optimism, what better voices to sing?

It was cold, in the heat of the day; the notes reached by the thin, pure voice chimed a warning. She raised her fan; she was Serra Teresa, and the showing of unease was not for a woman of her age and her responsibility.

The Tyr'agar Markaso kai di'Leonne ruled them all, demanding their service, and their death, when that death was deemed necessary, as his clan's due. His line had ruled unbroken for hundreds of years, untouched by desert wind and change of rain and shifting season. It was, or so the songs said, the will of the Lord. The Lord respected power.

As did the Serra Teresa.

The clan Leonne, led by Leonne the Founder, had vanquished their enemies and rivals, and before the slaughter of the servants of the Night Lord—he whose name was never mentioned within the Dominion—they came to the Tor, seeking the blessing of the Lord of the Day. For some said that the Night Lord was the Lord of the Day, given dominion in darkness as well as light, and they wished a sign that they did not act against the Lord.

Yet it was not the Lord who gave the sign, or at least, there was no sign during the sunlight hours, rather it was the Lady, worshiped only in a secret way that often ended with death when the worshipers were discovered, who by her powers and mystery created the lake beside which the Tyr'agar and his family—and all of their descendants—ruled.

Water was the source of life and of blessing; thus was Leonne answered.

And it was thus that the Festival of the Moon began—with the tale of the Tor. And the Tyr.

The clansmen raised their whips and their crops in approbation as Ami's son, delighted by the gravity of their approval, bowed low. He held the dying note of the setting sun nonetheless, and Serra Teresa smiled in spite of herself. The smile froze.

Unease?

The harpists shifted, silence descending as serafs moved with grace—and speed—to take the instruments that the Northern bards had inspired from their masters and return to them the more traditional samisen. The children, nervous, looked over their silk-swathed shoulders to her; she nodded gracefully, flicking the fan in her lap either left or right as she reminded the youngest of how they were to arrange themselves.

"The clansmen are pleased. Look! Tor'agar Leo kai di'Palenz just nodded! This is a coup for Marano." Lissa again, soft-voiced, her excitement coloring her words. The folds of her sea-green sari hid the quickening life she carried; she was still small enough that she was allowed out of the harem's confines.

"You recognized the Tor? Very good," Serra Teresa

said. She meant it. Lissa was new to the harem, and she
had come from the lowly family of a seraf who worked the
lands Marano held; her familiarity with the clansmen—
and their leaders—was not yet all that it should be.
Frowning, she added, "but the title, Lissa, is Tor'agnate."
The lowest of the ruling clansmen's ranks. "Above the
clan marking, the sun—it has only four rays. No, don't
squint, it is very unbecoming. There are four rays, not
six." Her smile was gentle. "Leo di'Palenz is one of the
Tor'agnati of the Terrean of Raverra; his title gives him
the right to . . . ?"

"Four rays in the rising sun."

"Good. He serves the Tor'agar Carlos kai di'Morgana."

"Who is allowed to wear six rays above the rising sun."

"Better." The Serra's smile was soft and almost openly
affectionate—a rare public display. But it was hard, with
Lissa, to be anything less. "And he serves in turn?"

"The Tyr'agnate . . ."

"It is a good guess," she said softly, for it was, but
Raverra, of the five Terreans, had no Tyr'agnate; it was
the heartland, and it was ruled by the Tyr'agar. "But in
this case, the Tyr'agar himself is their liege lord." She did
not add, but could have, that his crest was everywhere in
evidence within the city of the Tor Leonne, and the Tor
Leonne proper: the sun ascendant, with ten full, distinct
rays. There were only two men in the whole of the
Dominion who were privileged to wear that rank.

The man who ruled the Radann, the warriors of the Lord.
And the man who ruled the Dominion.

Crestfallen, Lissa nodded, but her smile brightened as
the clansmen settled into the mournful musicality of the
samisen's long notes. "Na'dio!" she whispered.

Yes.

Serra Diora di'Marano, halfway between four and five,
was slowly and gravely rising. Her porcelain face had not
once slipped in unbecoming smile; of all the children
who had sought the comfort of her fan-signal, Diora
had not once, this concert, been among them. It was because of her extraordinary ability to retain her sense of an
occasion's gravity that Serra Teresa had chosen her own
niece to sing the last of this cycle: The song of the Sun
Sword.

She felt the cold; it was sharp and sudden, like the wound a clean blade leaves.

Her hands were slightly whiter around the knuckle as she lifted the fan.

"Oh, Teresa," Lissa said, honorific forgotten again as she gazed upon the child that meant more to her than almost anyone else in the harem. "Look at her."

Serra Teresa could see nothing else. This slender-boned, high-cheeked, large-eyed child was perfect. Her mother's daughter. Dark hair fell, unfettered by the pearls and pins, by the braids and twists, that graced an adult's. She wore a white sari, edged in the same gold embroidery that Serra Teresa's more elaborate silks showed. Her hair touched her cheeks like a shadow as she bowed to the quiet audience, and a whisper shook the clansmen as they saw, for the first time, the child of the Serra Alora en'Marano. Her brother's wife.

Alora. Four years dead, and already the shadows of her passing could be seen—could be felt—in the face of her child.

Unease? No.

Value nothing too highly, especially not your own life, Na'tere. Her grandfather's voice, stretching out from a past that was almost beyond memory's grip.

Why?

Because it will make a coward of you. A coward. Only an oathbreaker committed a graver crime—although there were many who would argue that fear was the more unmanning of the two. *Care too much, and you lose the power to act because every action you take will cause a loss. Every one.* He was dead now, dust; he had failed in the clan test because he had been too proud to acknowledge that he could no longer ride with the riders. And he was the only man in the clan Marano who called her Na'tere after she reached the age of five.

And even at five years old, she had not been naive enough to think that he cared so much about her, although she felt secure in his indulgence, for she was a girl. A girl.

A boy, and she could have ruled Marano; she knew it, and thought it without much rancor; it was a truth written upon wind, and by wind scattered.

Serra Teresa was thirty-two years old. Unmarried and childless, she saw to the harem of her brother, Ser Sendari par di'Marano. Adano, the kai of the clan, had a living wife, and no need of his sister's aid. At least, she thought grimly, not in the affairs of the harem. With her brothers, she had a polite and reserved relationship; they served the same interests, no more and no less.

She had had no suitors—at least, so Sendari and Adano claimed. She knew better, of course, but knew also that no suitor was grand enough to take her from the clan Marano, whether she wished it or no. So. As a woman, she had no place in the rulership of the clan; unmarried, she had no husband, no children and sister-wives of her own to guide and instruct and protect. She existed, like something outside of the natural unfolding of time, for poets to make a mystery of.

What did she have?

Loyalty to the clan, of course. Loyalty to the two men who protected her from the life she might otherwise have led. Loyalty to Sendari's harem, and even affection for some of the sub-wives she herself had chosen for her brother's use. But care? No. She had listened to her grandfather well, and the event of his death had driven home the truth of his words. A valuable lesson. Very little of the activities that defined her life had the ability to move her.

As if in denial of that, the sun flashed bright across her hand. She looked down to see it: finely crafted, so beautiful in design, so expensively jeweled, that it should have been a husband's morning-gift. A ring. Sendari had asked her once where that ring had come from, and she had demurred; Adano had not even noticed. The only woman who would have answered was dead four years and more, in childbirth, or so it was said.

Diora was Alora's child.

Serra Teresa di'Marano listened, breath held, as her heart kept an awkward, uneven time to the samisen strings. And then, as Diora di'Marano began to sing in her clear, soft voice, she froze completely.

There was a strength in her voice that no child—no natural child—could ever have. It wasn't possible; it shouldn't have been possible. Diora—her Na'dio—was only four.

But like knew like, and in that instant, she knew that

her niece, the child that she had never had, and would never have, bore the curse.

Serra Teresa di'Marano was afraid, and she had named the fear.

She found Sendari by the Lady's shrine. The moon's face was almost full in the clear night sky on the end of this first day of the Festival. He was not the man she wanted to see—or rather, she wished to see no men at all, and of them, he the least. Her private supplication to the dead and the lost could not be spoken in his presence, and she wished to be free of the words, even if only the Lady and the open sky could catch them.

But she was patient, the Serra Teresa; she knew how to wait.

"Serra Teresa," Ser Sendari said, bowing very low.

"Ser Sendari." It was always thus with them, and perhaps it was better so; false affection, or worse, true affection, weakened one. Had they not both learned the truth of that, time and again? She bowed in return, and held the bow, not grudging him the respect. Although he was two years her junior, and Adano four her senior, she favored Sendari.

He was, after all, following the path of the Wise. The Sword of Knowledge had opened its doors to his study, and he had become a blade in their service; he missed only the final tempering, the edge gained by the test of fire. Already he had learned to twist elemental fire to his use; to call it to hand, and to light the lamps and the contemplation fires.

"What brings you to the shrine this eve?"

"Festival night," she replied. "It is the custom."

He glanced around as if to make a point; the pavilion was empty.

But she did not offer him another explanation, and he did not demand it; what good would it do? She could not be made to answer a question that she did not wish to answer.

He had night thoughts of his own, perhaps. Sendari had always been a deeper man than most.

A strong breeze blew through the pavilion, scattering the shadowed petals that lay there like a fragrant blanket.

An echo of the wind's voice, the wind's touch. So much had been taken from them.

"I heard that Diora acquitted herself well this day."

Was there a question beneath those words, and was it sharper than Sendari's wont? Or was it imagination, was it her own fear? "Your daughter sang well."

"I heard that the Tyr of Oerta himself offered her a blossom from the height of the Tor Leonne's trees."

"That," she said, the smoothness of her voice edged with a rare severity, "was exaggeration. I hope you did not hear this from a source you consider reliable."

"It was not garnered from any of my sources," he replied. Silence, heavy, between them. Then, "I will take the test of the Sword two days after the Festival, before the Lady turns her face into shadow again. I will face the fire of the sword-sworn, and I will prove myself equal to their power." His smile was caught by the round glass lamps that quartered the shrine as it fell into her silence. "I have surprised you, Serra Teresa."

"Yes," she said softly; there was no point in lying. He knew it, and she, and there were no other witnesses to keep count.

"And angered you."

She did not answer him; her anger was his guess, and if it was shrewd—if it was, indeed, correct—he did not have to hear it from her lips. But she knew, then, why he waited by the Lady's shrine. It was for her, may the wind take him.

The ring on her finger was cool; she gripped it a little too tightly, hiding the hand in the submissive posture and hoping that he would not notice. But he was Ser Sendari; he noticed much. Too much.

"She does not look much like her mother."

"Appearance," Serra Teresa replied, "is all guile; the Lady's mask. What lies beneath, only time will tell."

"Serra Teresa," he said gravely, turning his face to the moon, "you will speak freely; you do not need to wait upon my questions or my prompting; I do not require you to hamper your speech to suit mine."

"You mean, for this evening," she said, and if there was a trace of bitterness in the words, he did her the grace of ignoring them. "I am, after all, only a Serra."

"You are Serra Teresa di'Marano," her brother replied coldly, "and we both know what that means."

A threat? She met it without flinching. What did it matter, after all? Sendari was par, not kai, the younger brother, not the oldest one—and her life was thus not his to end. Only Adano had that privilege, and Adano had not felt the need to travel to the Tor for the Festival of the Moon. Once a year—for the Festival of the Sun—was enough.

She did not reply, and at length he spoke.

"Yes," he said softly. "Even that vow, I will break." His face was grave as he turned to her. "I have surprised you again, Serra Teresa."

"Yes." She bowed. "What will become of Diora if you fail the test?"

"She will go to Adano."

"Adano has daughters of his own; three—and not one of them is a match for Diora, in either beauty or ability. And, I believe, he will soon have two sons."

"Does it matter? I have no other issue; she has no brothers to protect her. She will go to Adano, and he will do as he will do. If I fail. And I do not intend to fail."

"Have you been at a testing before?"

"No." He knew that she knew the answer well enough; no one who did not, by right of combat, wear the Sword of Knowledge, had seen the testing. He lifted a hand. "I know how few survive, Serra Teresa."

"And you will take this risk?"

Silence.

"Under the Festival Moon," Teresa whispered, turning to face her brother.

"No—now, Teresa."

She let the anger show then, and it was clear and cold, like the lake of the Tor Leonne. "You gave her your word."

"Alora?" He smiled softly. "A third time, sister. A third time, you have been caught off guard. And if I, a mere supplicant, can surprise Serra Teresa three times in the space of an hour, can I not surprise the addled and arrogant minds of the Wise? I will be Widan Sendari by sun's rise of the third day."

Alora. He had not spoken her name aloud for over four years. It was understood, between them, that the name of

Serra Alora en'Marano died when she had, her head
cradled in Teresa's arms, her babe mewling pathetically
for food. Sendari allowed no mention of her.

We both took oaths, she thought, anger warming the
surprise. "It was an oath given to a woman," she said,
each word cold and hard. "You are not strictly honor-
bound to keep it."

His face showed her nothing, nothing at all. But he had
been expecting this, and she, she was still off guard, as if
she were no more than a girl on this moonful night.

"It was given to a wife," he answered. "Why do we
argue, Serra?"

"Why indeed? You are Ser Sendari, and you will meet
the test of the Sword whether I will it or no—a dead
woman's words notwithstanding."

"And you," he said, the words as sharp as hers were
cold, "will protect my child if I fail the test. You have the
means to do it, Teresa, and you will do it." He paused.
"Or does the breaking of one oath warrant the breaking of
another?"

She said nothing to that; nothing at all. "I wish you the
Lady's favor and the Lord's strength," she said, bowing
very low. She turned, then.

"We both loved her," Sendari said, as if he could not
resist a fourth strike at the heart of the woman who was
his sister. "And we have both paid."

She acknowledged the truth of that in silence, her hand
around the ring that Alora had given her to bind her to the
oaths they had sworn years before the birth of Diora.

So be it, she thought, as the anger took root. *I will protect my niece from everything, Sendari. I will give her the
life that was denied me, even if it does not serve Marano's
interests.*

Because I swore to protect Alora's child.

Because I so swore.

There was worse news to come.

"Teresa!"

Morning bright, Lissa pranced across the threshold of
the sleeping room, looking like the coltish young woman
she was, and not the demure wife she should have been.
My weakness, the Serra thought, although she felt no real
regret. She sat up, artlessly pushing the sleeping silks to

one side of the mats upon which she made night's repose. She occupied the wife's chambers, and these rooms, no one but the sister-wives visited, not even dignitaries.

A sister-wife could be asked to entertain her husband's guest, and in any event, had to be trained in the arts necessary to do so discreetly; a wife could not. Not without insult to the clan of her birth; not without casting doubts upon the legitimacy of the husband's bloodline.

"What is it, Lissa? Do you feel the baby?"

"The baby?"

"I see," Teresa said wryly. "What is it, exactly, that you have come to tell me?"

"There's a foreigner in the Tor!"

"There are many foreigners in the Tor," was the indulgent reply. "It *is* the Festival of the Moon."

"Yes, but this one's special. He sang the morning anthem. I mean," she added, not noticing the sudden tension in Teresa's face, "that he petitioned to sing it, and he was allowed. By the Tyr'agar himself!" She took silence as encouragement because she was young, and continued. "He has hair like golden ringlets, Teresa, and he wears it like a crown; he's tall and lovely, and his eyes are bluer than the waters of the sea." The sea, of course, was poetic notion to young Lissa, who had never seen it.

"I don't suppose you heard the name of this paean of earthly beauty?" She should have reminded Lissa that singing fulsome praises of the beauty of a man not one's husband was a dangerous and unwise activity. Should have, but couldn't; the harem was barely a part of her thoughts. It had been crowded out by sudden fear.

"Yes. His name is Kallandras of clan Senniel." Lissa paused. "And he's asked for an audience with Ser Sendari. I think he wants to sing for us." She clapped. "A coup for Marano—to have the man chosen by the Tyr'agar begging to sing in our court!"

"Yes," Teresa replied absently. "Has Ser Sendari seen this Kallandras?"

"Not yet," was the quiet reply. "The request has just come, and Ser Sendari is in his chambers." She lowered her voice conspiratorially, as if she truly believed a whisper to be a secret. "He practices the Craft. Mellora saw him at it when she tried to visit. He told her we are not allowed to disturb him; not even the serafs are to enter to clean." At this, she wrinkled her nose.

"I see. Come, Lissa. Help me dress, and quickly. You must lead me to the young man before he decides that Marano is not a suitable clan to make such a petition of. We don't want him to go elsewhere."

Did I do this on purpose? Teresa thought, as Lissa practically scurried across the great room, decorum forgotten, to save Marano this assumed loss. *Did I train you to be so guileless, so transparent, that you might never be a threat to me?*

Or was it a different weakness, some love of an innocence that never lasted long enough? She did not know, and it did not matter; the deed had been done, and she would not undo it.

In the quiet of his chamber, with the curtains drawn to shed as much of day's light as possible, Sendari par di'Marano sat in contemplative silence. The fires were banked; he was exhausted. But he had accomplished much for the day, although there were no witnesses to it.

No man could call himself a follower of the Sword of Knowledge who did not display at least the talent of calling flame to earth; Sendari had taken to it quickly, much to his father's displeasure.

His father, Tor'agar Vendiro kai di'Marano of Mancorvo. The oldest son, Adano, was much like their father; proud and windburned riding the plains of Mancorvo upon the finest horses the Dominion produced. He lived to fight, and to him a battle, with its attendant savagery, its viscerality, was all the freedom that he wanted or needed. A man's life. A *man's* life. Vendiro had been proud of Adano, blessed by him.

Of his younger son, he had had little enough good to say; Sendari was competent at arms, but he did not have the flare for it, nor the aggression. His fights in the ring were always of a more cunning nature—the strength of intellect over mere muscles. He had bested men his better with the scimitar. He had bested Adano, once.

He bore the scar of the battle after it, although it had paled into a silver line across his brow.

He rode—the clansmen all did—but again, not well,

and he bore horses little enough love, although his mannerisms showed none of his distaste for their presence or their use.

No; he read, and there was little enough kept by the clan to learn on. He volunteered service to clan Lamberto—the ruling clan of the Terrean of Mancorvo, and his father's liege lord—although again, the learning to be gleaned there was scant. Mareo di'Lamberto was cut from the same cloth—the same bolt—as Vendiro di'Marano; they had no patience for the more sedentary arts. Reading. Writing. Music. Of course, they had their court, and of course, that court had poets and musicians of great renown—but money, and the graces of their chosen wives, could buy what their inclination did not lead them to.

When had he first found the fire?

He could not remember the date, and that surprised him; he could not clearly remember a time without fire's voice. He had had it, certainly, upon the eve that he had first met Alora.

Alora.

It was such a bitter name; the saying of it conjured flame where he thought none remained.

Promise me, Sendari, he heard her say, the tone of her voice soft and pleading, although the iron beneath it was strong.

Anything. Anything, Alora—although they will think me unmanned to say it. He was used to being thought of as less than a man, and he was—he knew it even now—maddened by her in a grimly glorious way.

Do not walk this path any farther. We have what we need; you have your harem, and it is a fine one; you have your position with the clan Lamberto; you have your lands and fine horses for the sons that we will have. You are counted among the Wise; you do not need to have the Sword's edge.

They had had no sons. The plans of youth were often ended thus.

If I do not take the test of the Sword, I will never be Widan. I will be nothing but par di'Marano and you will be nothing but the wife of a second son.

That is all of my desire. You will be, she had said, and

her words cut and cut, *Sendari, and you will be alive, and you will be the only man that I have ever—*

He could not hear her say the word, not even in memory; it forced him up from the comfort of his cushions in a frenzy that was part anger and part humiliation at the lack of control. He did not want to think of Alora—but he had to. He had to. For he had given her his word, and by breaking it, he was breaking a vow that would have been more sacred than any vow given by man to the Lord, had she but lived.

Yes, curse her. Yes. Even knowing what he did. Had she lived, she would have held him, and he would have been powerless before her, and powerless before the clansmen.

But she died. She died, and the grimness of memory and longing and loathing had not yet buried her. If it ever would. He would be Widan. Before, had he taken the test and failed, there was a lifetime of Alora to be lost.

And after?

He had had few friends among the clansmen and the riders. But he had made one, Ser Alesso par di'Marente, a man of vision and a man who, in Sendari's objective opinion, was more than a match for his brother, his father, or the Tyr'agnate who ruled them both. *Take the test, Sendari.*

No. I will do what I can to aid you. I will find you a suitable Widan, if that is what you require. But I have—I have chosen not to take that risk.

He remembered Alesso's anger. *She weakens you, Sendari. She weakens us.*

He should have lied; he lied to every other man. But not to Alesso.

Yes, my friend, he'd said. *And it is a weakness that is stronger than any other weakness that any other man has been unmanned by. I love her.* It had been Moon-night, and he had spoken freely.

Flame flew in the confines of the chamber of contemplation, wild in its hunger to consume. And then lightning joined it, charring and bright; wind came, and beneath that wind, a shadow. The man who would be Widan had the fires, yes—but he had more, the range of his knowledge broader and deeper than any of the sword-sworn suspected.

It was a storm that was over quickly, that exhausted his reserve without pushing it too deeply.

There were no witnesses. He was glad that the preparations leading up to the test of the Sword required an absolute concentration, for he would have been forced to kill any seraf—or concubine—who had been present for such an inelegant display. Which would anger the Serra Teresa.

Ah, sister, he thought, with little love but with great respect, *had we been born in a different time, you with your voice and I with my craft, we would be living in Tor Sendari.*

And what, his sister said, although it was memory, only memory, *of Diora?*

Diora was laughing. The sound of her voice, raised in merriment with the children of concubines, stopped Teresa a moment as she stood in the long, open hall. Her niece was usually so grave and so serious that she had the bearing and sophistication of a much older child, with a desire to be all that the clan demanded of its women.

Serra Teresa di'Marano would never have said it aloud, but she loved the sound of Diora's laughter, and as age took it from her, she missed it more and more. She stood, savoring it, hearing the way laughter matched what lay beneath voice so completely.

Then, squaring her shoulders and straightening the fall of deep green silk, she began to walk again. She might train Lissa to be guileless, but Lissa was only the daughter of a seraf; Diora was blood.

As she entered the circle, a seraf rushed to attend her. "Serra Teresa," the woman said, falling at once into the submissive posture, knees against the tiled floor.

"Olena. The children seem happy."

The woman paled slightly. "It is the approach of the Festival Night," she said, her voice steady. "I think it has infected them with its spirit."

"That must be the explanation. The children of Sendari are usually much better behaved than this."

"Serra," the seraf said. "Do you wish to speak with them?"

"I wish only to speak with Serra Diora. If you would have her escorted to my chambers."

*   *   *

"You sang well, Na'dio."

Diora, grave and wide-eyed, nodded in agreement with
her aunt. "Thank you, Ona Teresa." Her eyes, so dark a
brown they were almost black, were unblinking; Serra
Teresa could almost see her unmarred reflection in their
surface.

How to begin? She was a master at the manipulation of
men and women, but children—children shifted like
leaves in the wind, blowing this way and that at the behest
of the adult to whom they last spoke. To tell her that it
was to be "our secret" was a thing of the moment, and
Serra Teresa was not naive enough to believe that a four-
year-old girl, no matter how serious, could hold on to that
concept for as long as it would take.

Especially not as this particular young girl found such
favor in her father's eyes.

How to begin? How to tell her to lie, now and forever,
to the man who was her father, to the women who were as
mothers to her?

Stop, she told herself firmly. *You will do as you have
always done: What you must.* Schooling her voice, she
began to speak.

"Na'dio, you are special. No, do not bow your head,
and do not be pleased. You are special in a way that no
woman should be." Her tone was harsh, accusatory; she
saw Diora stiffen and then pale. Good. "Your father is one
of the Wise."

Diora nodded.

"He is not of a powerful clan, and he is not kai. He
cannot afford to be dishonored. Do you understand?"

She nodded again, so serious that Teresa believed that
she did, in fact, understand.

"When you sing, what do you feel?" She watched as
Diora tried to put into words a singular feeling that could
never be contained by them.

"Good," her almost-daughter said at last. "Happy." The
child frowned. "Or not happy. The Sun Sword is not a
happy song."

"No, it is not. And there are very few 'happy' songs,
Diora. Only the serafs sing them."

She bridled, did this child of Alora and Sendari,
looking for a moment so much like her mother that Teresa

fell silent. The most terrible wounds were always caused in this fashion because, unexpected, they were impossible to defend against. She knew that Alora would not have allowed what she was about to do; it made it hard. For a moment. But she was the Serra Teresa di'Marano.

"I do not speak of the songs, however, but the singer. You can sing so that men will listen, will want to listen. No. Do not be proud of it. It is a curse," Serra Teresa said.

"Why?"

"What man wishes a wife who can, with a word, control his actions? And if there were such a man who was strong enough to believe that he could overcome his wife's power, what other men would be certain—could be certain—of it? Which Tor would follow such a Tyr, which Ser would follow such a Tor?

"Can a clansman be ruled by a woman?"

"No."

"Indeed."

"But I would never try—"

"Of course not, Na'dio," Serra Teresa said, hearing the truth in the intent, and mourning the intent that could not survive the harsh reality of adult life. "But I know it. You know it. Who else will know it?"

She said nothing, her brow ever so slightly creased. She was thinking. "Ona Teresa?"

"Yes?"

"Is this why you never had to leave Father?"

"Why—"

"You have the same song," Diora added quickly, her little voice almost an accusation, if such a thing were possible. "You never had to get married. You never had to leave Marano."

Never had to? The flash of hope in Diora's eyes was sharp and painful; innocence, and worse. For Diora knew that Teresa had the voice.

"You must never speak of this, Diora," she said, and her voice was as cold as the desert night. "You will anger your father greatly, and you will send me to the Lady's path far sooner than I wish to walk it."

Diora's cheeks grew pale; she knew that Serra Teresa spoke of death. Yet this one night, she did not fall silent; did not retreat into obedience as a good child must. "But you are a woman, and you are not hated. You honor our clan. Father says so."

"Have you—have you spoken to him of this? Have you told him that you can hear my song?" How long? How long had she known? The world shifted in Serra Teresa's perspective, as it had several times in her life. Each of these times, she had shed a little of the ability to hope. It was not different now.

"No. He's—he's been very busy."

What was important? Survival. And what was survival? Ah, the answer to that changed with the years. But she knew what the first step was, although she regretted it even as she took it.

"Diora, you will not sing again until after the Festival of the Moon."

And Diora, child of her blood and Alora's heart, had no choice but to obey, for Serra Teresa was indeed cursed and blessed both by the voice.

The foreigner was not as young as Lissa's enthusiasm might have led one to believe, although he wore his age well. In all other respects, Serra Teresa found her description to be accurate. And Serra Teresa, unlike the young Lissa, had seen the sea several times in her travels at the side of either Adano or Sendari.

He was not too tall, this man, and not too broad of chest—a feature which many women admired. Indeed he was slender and fine-boned, and his skin was pale, whereas many of the Northerners spent too much time under the sun's glare.

He also, she saw, knew how to bow gracefully.

It was almost a pity that she was going to have to have him killed.

"Serra Teresa di'Marano," he said, his voice the very epitome of respect, admiration, and deference. "I am Kallandras of Senniel, and I have come to request an audience with Ser Sendari par di'Marano at his earliest convenience." He spoke in fluent Torra, with an exotic inflection to the words that made him seem interesting rather than ill-studied—a foreign prince and not an ignorant barbarian.

She did not want to speak; she did not want to give herself away to this foreign man, for she knew, as Lissa did not, that there was no clan Senniel. There was, in the foreign tongue, a Senniel College, and it was a place in which those with the voice were schooled in song.

And detection.

She did not make haste to bow in return, for it was not necessary; her station did not demand that she treat him as an equal; indeed, it demanded that she do otherwise, although as the ranking woman—and the only member of the clan present—she was required to offer hospitality.

Her cerdan watched her closely, waiting for a subtle signal; she gave them none, and they relaxed a little. Weapons, readied, were lowered; they would not be returned to sheath until the man had left.

When a man not of the clan Marano came to visit the rooms the son of the Tor'agar occupied, and only women were there to greet him, there were always cerdan, obviously armed, in attendance. They stood between the visitor and Serra Teresa, although they were subtle enough to stay to the walls and mute their open contempt for things Northern. Had they not been, they would not be the Serra Teresa's guards.

The bard—for this is what the Northerners who came from Senniel called themselves—waited upon her reply, and she realized, grudging it, that she would have to tender one. Years of experience told her two things: first, that Senniel College trained minstrels, and not all of those who sang had the voice, the second, that this bard did. She could hear it in his words, and he had spoken few enough of them.

She was no novice herself at the intricacies of voice, and although she paused a long moment, when she did reply, all nuance, all trace of fear, was completely absent from her words.

"I am Serra Teresa di'Marano. I have heard that you sang the Lord's anthem at the opening of the Festival." She paused, saw that he had no interest in interrupting her, and cursed him mentally. "It is an honor that is rarely given to outsiders."

"I am not a stranger to the Dominion of Annagar," he replied, again flawlessly. "And I am not a stranger to song—even a war rally such as the Lord of the Sun requires."

Hospitality demanded that she continue with pleasantries. She was Serra Teresa. "You are no stranger to our language; you speak it as if you were born to it."

"Do I?" He smiled, and the smile was an odd one. Serra Teresa knew that it was voice alone that commanded and demanded, yet she felt herself smile in response as she met the blue, blue eyes of this golden-haired danger.

"Of course," she said. "Or do you accuse me of exaggerating for the sake of courtesy?"

"I have heard—all of Senniel has heard—the words of the poet Feranno. I do not accuse you, Serra. I merely observe."

She smiled then, because she knew the words of Feranno's poem by heart; written for her at the age of sixteen, it immortalized her beauty, the joy of her grace, her elegance in motion and stillness—and, of course, her song.

The cerdan were appropriately angered by the man's boldness; he did not have youth as an excuse, and he had no permission to pay court to the Serra, without which, his behavior implied, she was nothing but, at best, the daughter of the lowliest of the clans. But Serra Teresa lifted her fan slightly, as if at a breeze, although in the confines of the chamber the air was still.

Northerners, ignorant of the customs of Annagar, used flattery without care; they spoke freely, as young boys will, and because of this, they touched places in the heart that only the very young normally touched. *Perhaps,* she thought, *I am overhasty. Perhaps his presence here is coincidence. I did not see him at the ceremony yesterday.* It surprised her, but she accepted the fact that she did not wish to kill this man.

Glancing to the side, she could see the stiff jaw of Ser Armando, the senior cerdan in the room. He met her eyes, and while he did not relax, the very slight tilt of her chin was a dismissive shrug, a sign that she did not deem the stranger offensive, or at least not mortally so.

"Please, accept my humble apologies, Ser Kallandras of Senniel. If Ser Sendari par di'Marano knew that such an illustrious and important man had come to seek his audience, I am certain that he would speak with you at once—but he has left us strict instructions that he is not to be disturbed except in case of grave emergency, and we, his sister and his wives, do not have the authority to interrupt him for anything less, no matter what honor you might confer."

"It is I who must apologize," Kallandras replied, as graceful in seeming as a well-trained clansman. "For I would not have had you disturbed had I realized that you were alone here. But I must ask you to take a message to Ser Sendari, if it will not trouble you too greatly."

She nodded, not trusting her voice.

"Tell him that yesterday I heard his daughter sing, and it is she I wish to discuss."

CHAPTER TWO

There was something wrong with Serra Teresa's voice, but until he was escorted from the premises by cerdan who were, at best, coldly suspicious, he did not suspect what it was.

In fact, until he sat in a circle of contemplation, the harp in his lap, and Salla, the lute by which he had made his name, in her case, until he began to tap the strings in a series of building harmonics, drawing music from them, until he began to sing wordlessly, the answer eluded him.

Because in song, the voice often had its clearest expression.

And Serra Teresa's voice was completely devoid of expression.

Oh, the rise was there, and the fall; the quality and tone and texture of her voice were nearly flawless, and although he had not heard her sing—and suspected that he would not—he could well imagine that Feranno, poet of extravagant words and more extravagant sentiment, had in this single case no cause for exaggeration. But beneath the surface of the words she had spoken, there was an impenetrable distance, as if windows had not only been closed, but barred and boarded against those who might happen, while walking past, to look in.

And who, he thought idly, the strings playing the question back to him in different variations, cloaked their voices so carefully? Who could hear the nuances, the cracks between words in which a person might reveal the unspoken impulse behind the spoken word?

The mage-born. The seer-born.

Or the bard-born.

Kallandras was the most unusual bard that Senniel College had ever produced. He knew it, and acknowledged it with the curious flatness that he acknowledged most facts about himself: It was true, but of little interest. At thirty-two, he was no longer a remarkable prodigy as a bard-master—but he had earned his name and his title at a far earlier age, to the consternation of many of the older members of the College. Time had done its work, healing their annoyance; pride had done the rest, for Senniel's fame was spread far and wide on the wings of Kallandras' grace, youth, and beauty. And his song. His song.

It was his song that had moved the Tyr'agar Markaso di'Leonne. Not to tears—never that, among the clansmen—but his lovely wife wept openly in a rare public display, and she was not in gesture or tone reprimanded. Kallandras understood the subtle nuance of voice very well; had there been shame, or anger, in the Tyr'agar's voice, he would have known it, although no one else might, for the Tyr was not a well-schooled man in that regard.

How could he be, in the Dominion of Annagar, where the bard-born were scattered about like a lost tribe, their talents untrained, their abilities uninvoked? And, if he were honest, feared. He was lucky, in his way; Senniel trained the bard-born, but it did not segregate them, and he could conceal his power well beneath facade.

He knew how to use his youth, and when it began to fade, he knew how to use maturity. Neither of these were gifts the College fostered—but he had spent his time in many courts, and with many a noble, and he observed everything keenly.

It was the second day of the festival, and the sun had barely reached the height, as the Annagarians reckoned midday. He told the time by the shadow he cast along the circumference of the inlaid stone circle. The Tor Leonne was beautiful at this time of the year; a little cooler than during the Summer Festival—the Festival of the Sun—but also more prone to the rains that made the ground fertile. The trees here were small compared to those that grew in standing rings in the heart of the city of Averalaan where Kallandras of Senniel made his home, but in their season, they blossomed with both flower and fruit, gracing the Tor Leonne with a height of color and a sense of fecundity that were a stark contrast to the Dominion's desert regions.

During daylight, Kallandras often smiled; he smiled

now, the expression lending youth to his face, and a semblance of innocence. They were masks, but much in the Dominion was—Kallandras had been to Annagar before. Once, as a bard.

And before that . . .

His smile did not falter, but the music did; his talent, when he did not consciously control it, betrayed him, voicing what lay beneath the surface of face and manner. Desert longing.

And now was not the time, not the place, to express it. Stilling his hands by habitual force of will, he set the harp aside. Serra Teresa.

"What are you wearing on Festival Night?" Lissa's voice was soft and thoughtful as she massaged Serra Teresa's shoulders with oils and a very delicate perfume.

"Lissa," was the quiet reply, "you've asked me that for the last three festivals that we've attended."

"I know," the girl—it was so very hard, at times, to think of Lissa as a woman—said brightly, "but if I don't ask, and you change your mind and decide it's all right to tell me, I'll never know."

"I am," Serra Teresa said dryly, "hardly likely to change my mind, as you say, about such a custom. It would defeat the entire purpose of the Festival Night." She smiled. "I will wear a mask."

"Everyone will wear a mask," was the almost tart reply. Lissa did not—quite—have the flawless manners required of the harem. "But I think I would know you anywhere."

"Then you must guess, as any man or woman, when you see me pass."

"I would tell you," Lissa said, her voice so light the words did not sound wheedling. "I would tell you if you asked me."

"You most certainly will not." The Serra smiled indulgently. "I would never ask." The words were unnecessary. She enjoyed the saying of them for precisely that reason; they were a luxury, and if they revealed anything, it was the very real affection she felt for this particular concubine on this particular day.

The bells chimed, delicate in their insistence. Lissa rose at once, but Serra Teresa caught her wrist, sorry for the intrusion, and yet, sharpened by it. "I am expecting someone," she said quietly. "You must go now, by the back ways, to the Inner Chamber."

"But—but Ser Sendari is not to be disturbed—he won't—"

Affection for the girl was marred by impatience at the slowness of her wit. "Lissa, Ser Sendari will not be in the Inner Chamber. Go there, and wait for me. Speak to no one."

Wide-eyed, the younger woman nodded, and then her brows rose. "Are you—are you—" she dropped her voice into a shaking whisper, "is it a—a—guest?"

Oh, Lissa, she thought, impatience forgotten. Lissa often worried about the Serra Teresa; she often told her that she was the most beautiful woman in the Dominion, and that someday, she would make the most wonderful wife—as if, somehow, the fact that she had no husband was a mortal offense, and a deep hurt occasioned by the whims of foolish men.

"Yes," she told her young companion, "it is a guest."

"Oh, Teresa! But who?"

"You know as well as I that no man save Sendari is allowed, by law, into this chamber. Dear heart, it is not the dangerous entanglement that you believe; I am a Serra of clan Marano—who would insult my station by a presumption of that nature?"

"But the cerdan made no announcement . . ." Her eyes were full of romance and romantic notion. It was odd, but there were those who came from humble backgrounds who could cling in such ignorance to the folly of that naïveté in a way that those exposed early to power never could. Odd, and charming.

"The cerdan have no reason at all to stop this guest."

"But I don't—"

"No, Lissa, and that is why I am so fond of you." Lissa bowed her head in genuine pleasure, for Serra Teresa rarely said as much as this. "Now. Hush, and go quickly."

The person who entered the Serra Teresa's chambers was tall and slender. A sari of a pale yellow, edged in orange, brown and gold, fell from across the left shoulder to the ground, hiding all but the tips of delicately woven slippers. The day was cool; over the sari, a hood and shawl were wound, and they, too, were of a pale color.

Serra Teresa sat in the half-circle chair in which she often passed her judgments when disputes among Sendari's wives came to her attention. She did not enjoy it, as the mat cushions were softer and of a more pleasant texture, but it gave her the advantage of height, and the presence of formality, both of which she desired. The room was almost deathly in its stillness; there were no serafs in attendance, and the Serra was rarely without.

Her visitor noted this in silence. "I have come as you requested." The figure bowed low, the hem of the silk touching the shadows cast by bent back.

"You serve the Lady," she said, making a quiet question of the statement.

"We all serve the Lady in our fashion," was the reply. It was true, but the assassins were her dark face, her final judgment—the death to her season of birth and growth. "What would you have of us, Serra Teresa?"

"There is a man in the Tor Leonne, a foreigner of some import. I wish him dead."

"Method?"

"Unimportant."

"He is a foreigner. Will this not cause difficulty?"

She shrugged. Because it was not an assassin's concern, advice, however oblique, was rarely offered. But thrice now, in subtle fashion and however indirectly, this same assassin gave his muted opinion, and for this reason, she favored this one, perhaps because she had no other link of familiarity, not even a true name. "They will have their difficulties soon enough, I think; such an assassination will be the least of their concerns." She did not fear to say too much.

Silence in the large chamber, a silence heavy with the significance of what the Serra had said. "Come. Time is of the essence." She rose, leaving the comfort of the chair behind, and walked toward the assassin, her face composed.

She had no fear, perhaps because she had been called upon, twice before, to render such a delicate service in the stead of Adano di'Marano, or perhaps because she knew that the confidentiality of these particular assassins had never been broken. Or perhaps for other reasons, some need to be known that even she could not fully understand or control. It was, after all, the season of the Festival Moon.

The figure lifted a hand, freeing it from the confines of sari and shawl. It was a man's hand, not a woman's, although in bearing and gait he might easily have fooled even the Serra. He had certainly fooled the cerdan.

Serra Teresa stood, lifting her face so that she might meet his eyes, that they might be on a level. His eyes were as dark as hers, night meeting night beneath the closed dome of the roof in a silence undisturbed by breeze or stream or speech. But the wind—she felt the wind's howl trapped just beneath the base of her throat. Not fear.

In five places, he touched her face, anchoring his hand with his fingers and his thumb. She did not close her eyes. He did. It was not an act of capitulation; between these two, there was no contest. But she wished to see the lines of his face as he somehow skirted the edge of the who that she was, seeking the information that he needed: the name, and more, of the victim.

Kallandras of Senniel College.

She was not prepared for what she saw: The widening of eyes grown completely black, the twisting of lips, the expression, silent, that usually accompanied a roar of anger or pain, an animal reflex. He pulled his hand back from her face as if burned by what he had touched, but although he moved with force, none of it was applied to her or against her.

Before she could speak, his face fell into an expression of neutrality, in the same way that folds of cloth fall into straight lines when lifted and pinned.

"I assume," she said softly, surprising herself with the wryness of a tone which she did not feel, "that this means you will not accept the contract."

"I would accept it if it meant certain death," he replied. "But I am merely a servant to the will of the Lady."

Although his face was still shuttered, she heard all that lay beneath it in the space between his words. Pain. Anger. A sense of loss, of betrayal so profound not even the slaughter of kin by kin could encompass it. It was so strong, she wondered idly if she would have heard it without the unique burden of her gift. Seeing his face, she doubted it. She doubted it very much.

You knew him, she thought. And because she was Serra

Teresa, she was wise enough not to ask, although the curiosity was almost as strong as any she had yet felt. She and Sendari had that in common, if little else besides blood.

"Thank you for your time," she said softly. "I have troubled you needlessly."

He bowed, but did not speak again, hearing the dismissal in the words for what it was. But as he stood, he said softly, "I wish you well, Serra."

Of that, she felt certain, although he had never said anything so heartfelt before. This Kallandras, this bard, was an enemy of the brotherhood.

Yet he was alive, somehow, protected by the Lady.

The sun was high, and it was not the Lord who could answer the questions that Serra Teresa wished to ask.

A man could only push himself so far before he exhausted the reserves of power—whether physical or intellectual—that were required for any arduous task. Ser Sendari acknowledged this in the darkness of his chambers. This room, and this room alone, had a door, styled after those that closed the great vaults in the Tor Leonne. Elsewhere, the hangings divided his temporary home, lending the air those sounds of movement and speech, both the subtle and the impossible to ignore, that were the heart of life.

He had had his fill of silence and study. Tomorrow was the night of the Festival Moon, but tonight was still a Festival Night, with all that that implied. Wrapping himself against the chill of the full evening, he paused once to gaze into the depths of the room which had become his personal battleground.

Books lay open, scattered with precise care to reveal just those elements that he needed; they were his keys, the sword that he must learn to wield. A goblet, half-empty, an earthen mug and a pail of sweet water, a platter with some sort of foot. A cushion. A stool. The trappings of power.

He smiled as he shook his head.

He left the residence by the seraf's entrance, to avoid Teresa and his wives. He did not wish to answer their questions, and he felt a twinge of guilt at avoiding his responsibilities to them. But in truth, it was not the frivolous company of the young and the beautiful that he desired this eve; he wished companionship of more substance.

On a Festival Night, it was there.

Merchants came to line the streets of the city; to tell fortunes to the foolish, to offer solace to the weary, and to sell their many, many wares. Those clansmen that were, after all, little better than serafs themselves, built awnings beneath which they served wine and water, spiced fruits and other delicacies under the face of the turning moon.

Upon the crest of the hill, the palace could be seen—and it was in the palace, the Tor Leonne proper, that the clansmen who mattered were ensconced for the Festival. There, the reputedly magical properties of the lake were enjoyed by those who curried favor or those who had been born to it.

Ser Sendari had not been born to it. Even if he survived the test of the sword—and in the privacy of his thoughts, where no face could be lost, he was willing to admit the possibility of failure—and became Widan, he would still be nothing more than par di'Marano to Adano's kai. All of his effort, all of his power, all of his finely honed knowledge would serve Marano, and therefore, Adano.

Ah, Lady, if only Adano had been the second son.

If. If only. He frowned at the direction of his thoughts; they were pathetic and unworthy. The Lady's presence was obviously heavy on his mind. And why not? It was the Festival of the Moon, after all. He turned his gaze away from the lights upon the hill; the Tor Leonne was not for him this night.

Not this one.

Musicians played in the streets of the Tor Leonne, some good, some bad, and some, Sendari thought, who deserved the Lady's harshest judgment. Men's voices were raised in loud and boisterous song, and the drunken boasts of old soldiers destroyed the quiet that usually settled over the city at night. The young men were out roving, and one or two lives were certain to end in some imaginary contest of "honor"; the young boys were out, listening with rapt attention to the sounds of their first Festival. Eating the fruits and the confections and the sweet foods, drinking poor wine and sweet water, watching the comings and goings of clansmen whose deeds they hoped, one day, to rival.

He could hardly remember the days when he had been such a child; they were another country, and the ways to it had long since been destroyed. But he found it unexpectedly poignant to see two young boys together, the younger self-consciously aping the actions of the elder, the elder cautioning the younger and attempting to keep him safe. To watch them, thinking of the days when par and kai had such very different meanings.

Sendari could not pause for long, however; the crowds were thicker, and they surged around him, moving him forward inch by inch. Shaking off the webs of youth, he began to move in their direction.

He found a place to sit beneath the awnings of the silvered trees, a spot which, imbued by the lively atmosphere of the Festival, lost all of its lovely mystery. A fountain, old and slow to move at any but Festival time, gurgled at his back as he sat upon its marble shelf, thinking. And trying not to think.

Alora.

Adano.

Diora.

The Festival of the Sun made the Tor Leonne an easier place to rest one's feet and gird for battle. Not so this Festival, a half-year away. Moon-touched, he thought night thoughts, too melancholy to be properly grim, which would have been more acceptable to a man of Sendari's character.

"Sendari!"

He started to smile before he realized that he recognized the voice; there were some things that were lodged in places deeper than conscious memory. Lifting an arm, he curved his fingers in greeting.

Captain Alesso par di'Marente, looking very much a child of the night, lifted a goblet in return. "Wine?"

"Not from that vineyard," Sendari said, grimacing as his friend shrugged and half-emptied the glass.

"Then I'll drink yours."

"I'd guess that you already have."

As he tilted his head back, his hair gleamed as if the back of a raven's wings were brushing the nape of his neck. He was a tall man, and his bearing was one of quiet confidence. He could wield a sword better than most of the warriors that Sendari had seen take the Festival Challenge, and he could handle a mount as if the line that separated horse and rider could be severed at will. Sendari knew this, and accepted it without rancor.

Because Captain Alesso par di'Marente was also a politically canny man, one who understood power. Or rather, he thought, one who understood that power was not necessarily the ground gained by standing like a common oaf and planting one's sword into another's chest. Not necessarily.

"How will you spend the Festival Night?"

"I? In study, old friend. I have much to learn, and it is, after all, a night like any other. You?"

"I shall spend it as always, in the arms of those women who could never come to me willingly otherwise. Come," Alesso said, tossing the goblet aside. "I've had enough of the Festival crowd."

"Oh?"

"I want peace and a moment for thought."

Sendari laughed.

"What?"

"You, Alesso. When it is quiet, it is too quiet; you must drink or ride or fight to escape the consequence of a moment's peace. But here—here, where you should be in your element—you want peace, and you ask me why I laugh?"

Alesso di'Marente smiled, a sure sign that he had had enough drink for the evening. "If you wish to remain here, remain here."

"You lead, di'Marente."

"As always."

Peace was not, in the end, the quiet that Sendari usually associated with the word. Nor was it the meditative stillness, the silent companionship in which friends need not speak to be understood. Alesso's smile, rare, had obviously not been due to drink alone.

"I should have known," Sendari said, panting slightly from the exertion of the forbidden climb.

"Yes," Alesso replied quietly. "You should have."

They stood together, gazing at the Lady's face as the

waters of the lake of the Tor Leonne rippled it. Music came from across the lake; the sound of muted merriment.

"We're not young men anymore."

"No."

Silence. Sendari did not need to tell Alesso what their transgression here would mean; he knew it. He always understood the risks of the tasks he chose to undertake. And yet he did not shy away from risk; indeed, as he grew older, he grew both less cautious and more cunning.

"I've heard a disturbing rumor, Sendari."

"Ah. You as well?" Sendari listened to the lap of waves against rocks and rushes; it was such an uncommon sound in the South that he had to stop a moment to savor it. "Do you know when war will be declared?"

"The war?" Alesso shrugged. "After the Festival, no doubt. But it wasn't war that I spoke of."

"What else is there to speak of—or not to speak of? It is in the air, Alesso. The Tyr wishes to advance beyond the cradle of Averda; it has been two summers with very poor harvests in the plains, and he is pressed hard on all sides by the ramifications. There are reasons why I wish to take the test."

"That is the rumor I wished to discuss."

"That—ah." A momentary surprise, and a slightly longer annoyance, flitted across Sendari's features. The decision should have been a private affair; he had spoken to no one save Teresa about it. He knew how she felt about Alesso di'Marente; it was not from her that the information had come. From who, then? What weakness was there in his household? One of his wives? The serafs? He wanted to ask, but let it drop as he met his companion's dark gaze. "I should have known. How long?"

"How long have I been watching—and watching over—you?" Alesso looked into the darkness that the full moon kept at bay. "In one way or another, since you were eight." Alesso himself had been ten, an older boy whose daring greatly impressed the child that Sendari had been. The adult that he had become. This continuity, unlooked for, between his childhood self and his adult self caught him off guard, as no doubt Alesso had intended.

"Why?"

"Why," was Alesso's response, "will you take the test?

Years ago, when invited to do so by Widan Cortano himself, you refused."

Sendari knew that Alesso already knew the answer, and he was angry a moment; the sound of the waters calmed him by slow degrees. "Does it matter?"

His companion spoke again. "She is truly gone."

"This is not the night to discuss her," Sendari said softly, a warning in his voice.

"There will never be such a night," was Alesso's reply. "Tomorrow, when the Festival Moon is at her fullest, you will wander the streets like any other stranger, reveling in your choice of freedoms.

"She stood between us a long time, old friend."

"And still does," Sendari surprised himself by saying. "Do not speak of what you do not understand."

"Then let me speak, instead, of what I do understand.

"You will take the test of the sword, and you will survive it. You will be marked as a Widan, in the service of clan Marano. Your kai, Adano, will offer your services to the clan Leonne, and with your cunning, your rise through the ranks of the counselors will be swift."

Alora's ghost melted into the recesses of his night thoughts, leaving him space to smile. It was a thin smile. "Will you always plan my life, Alesso?"

"Plan? Not I. I merely predict."

Silence again. Uncomfortable, the unsaid between them like a veil or a wall. Sendari gazed at the lake, listening for the sounds of the streets that seemed so far removed they might be imagination.

"Let me ask you a question, Sendari. Let us pretend, for the moment, that the Lady's Moon holds sway. Let us take no responsibility for the things said here, between us; they are moon thoughts, night thoughts. They exist outside of the natural order; they will travel no farther."

Sendari raised a hand to stem the tide of words; Alesso stood silent for as long as it took that hand to fall, shaking slightly, to Sendari's side.

"Have you never considered killing Adano?"

Because Alesso was his friend, and because the pledge that had been uttered was so unusual for Alesso, Sendari did not respond the way honor—the way blood—demanded he should. The insult in the question would have been death for a lesser man; it darkened Sendari's cheeks.

With anger.

With shame.

"You take your risk," he said at last. "And I take mine. Of course I've considered it. Adano cannot lead Marano where I could have led it, had I been born first."

Alesso might have laughed, had he been another man; there was no triumph at all in his expression as he met, and held, Sendari's dark eyes. "And yet Adano lives."

"Corano kai di'Marente lives as well. Or would you tell me that I am alone in my desire?"

"Oh, no. Why would I tell such a useless lie to you?" he asked, placing his cloak against grass and rock alike, as he stared at the moon's reflection as if, Sendari thought, it were a mirror. He spoke to the moon's face, to the waters of the lake, to the wind that carried no man's words. But he spoke in Sendari's hearing, and that was enough. "I could have killed him. I almost did, twice. It would have been so simple. And then I would be kai, my brothers par; Marente would be mine, and it would be a great clan."

"It is not inconsiderable now."

"No? But neither is Marano." Alesso's smile creased the line of his profile ever so slightly. "But the risk is high, old friend." And it was. Blood did not shed blood in the Dominion of Annagar without great danger—but the worst of the kin crimes was the killing of the kai. Only a handful of times in the history of the Dominion had such a crime occurred, and because of it, the rule of the Lord of Night had finally been brought to an end.

By the clan Leonne. Wielding the Sun Sword in the name of Justice.

"And is it only the risk?"

"Is it only the risk that holds your hand?"

"Mine?" Brooding silence; after a moment, Sendari joined Alesso on the incline, sitting more carefully. "No. Not risk alone. But I had—"

"Her."

"Yes. I have already shown myself open to weakness of that nature."

Alesso ignored the pointed comment. "The others, I would kill. My sisters. My younger brothers."

"Would you?"

Grim smile. "Let us not put it to the test, then. But I believe that I could, if the cause were right."

"But not Corano."

"No. And what does that leave me?"

"The rank you attain in the service of your kai—or the service of the Tyr, if you are so offered."

Alesso spit.

Had he been a different man, Sendari would have joined him.

"One weakness. Am I to be judged by history for one weakness? I think not. There are always other options; there are always other opportunities.

"We are not beasts of burden, to be prized and sold. I am Alesso di'Marente. You are Sendari di'Marano. Take the test. There is nothing left to stop you. Take the test, make yourself known." The older man stood suddenly, raising his face to the moon. "And I tell you, Sendari, that if we so dare, our children will not be of Marano or Marente."

Sendari was silent, swept away a moment by the breadth of the captain's vision.

"They will be di'Alesso and di'Sendari."

Diora's fingers stretched across the samisen's strings as if it were a loom and she the threads from which whole cloth would be made.

Serra Teresa watched her at a discreet distance. Watched her mutely touching and pulling music from a samisen when she had no song of her own to offer. The Festival was not yet finished, and a child—even a child with Diora's will—could not so easily shake the compulsion that she had placed upon her. Not easily, no. The risk was there. But although Diora frowned as if in pain, she made no song.

Serra Teresa felt a satisfaction and a profound self-loathing that mingled poorly; she made her way back down the halls of the small residence that Ser Sendari occupied, thinking that she had seen deaths less wrong than this.

And then she set it aside. It was the day of the Festival Moon.

There was much to plan.

* * *

Kallandras received the message in the rooms that were reserved for visiting dignitaries. It was carried by a seraf who spoke so softly and so smoothly, his voice was almost without inflection. A sign, that.

As much a sign as the fact that the message was written, and tied in three places with strands of golden twine that might have been better used for silk. The Annagarians did not trust the printed word for anything but unwieldy treaties; they rarely consigned messages to it, choosing instead those serafs, or cerdan, whom they trusted to be their mouthpieces. He stared at the scroll, wondering idly who had sent it, and why. There was a wrongness about it that was not immediately evident. And it should have been. It should have been.

Oh, it had been a mistake to come here. Annagar was not Essalieyan; it was seductive in its stark simplicity, its complex dance of death. For in the midst of this wellspring of life, in the center of the Tor Leonne, death made a man powerful—the death of his enemies. Kallandras understood death too well.

Sioban would have listened had he demanded she send another in his stead. He smiled softly, thinking of the bardmaster. Perhaps she would have listened. Perhaps not.

I send you into the heart of pitched battle, and you sing your way out—there's no other way to explain just how much you can survive. There was, of course, a question in the words, but it was casual. She knew that he wouldn't answer it; he knew that she accepted the ignorance as gracefully as anyone who led could. *And I don't give a damn about explanations. I send you, you return; I send out another, and I worry at it for the months that he's gone. I'm old enough now not to need that worry if I don't absolutely have to carry it.*

There's rumor that the troops are gathering along the border; there's rumor that the Tyr'agar needs a war. The Festival of the Moon is coming. Go to the Tor Leonne. Find out. Find out the truth, Kallandras, and sing it home.

At the ebb of the day—as the Annagarians reckoned it—the air was pleasantly cool; the chill of the night gave way quickly to the bite of the sun. In Essalieyan, it grew hot, but never so hot as in the southern clime; and it grew cool, but again, never so cold as in Raverra, the Terrean which held the Tor Leonne. The winds in Essalieyan—unless one were a seaman—were part of the weather, no more, no less. But in Annagar, the winds scoured a man's soul and swept the life from the land, some harbinger of either the Lord's or the Lady's displeasure. The wind blew the Lady's name across the stretch of sands and empty waste, reddening his cheeks.

Today, the air was deceptively still. The day was pleasant. There was no rain to mar it. But there was a storm on the horizon; by what was not said, what was not done, what was unsigned, Kallandras could feel it gathering in the air. War, he thought. But not now. Not for at least one more day.

The Festival of the Moon was a sacred thing to the Annagarians, a wild night, a hidden place in which one could say all that one felt without fear. And he thought the Annagarian court, with its strict rules of behavior, its silence, its manners, might destroy itself completely without that single evening of freedom. And he, bard-born, but trained by the brotherhood of the Lady, to wear any mask, and to mask any desire from all but his brothers themselves.

His brothers.

Throughout the history of the Dominion, even during the dark years in which the Lord of the Night sought to eradicate the Lady's following, the Festival of the Moon had been celebrated. Not so the Festival of the Sun—but then again, the Festival of the Sun had been forgone for the call to war, something the Lord was certain to appreciate. The Lady. The Lord.

The universe of the Annagarians was divided into these polarities, as if the gods that they worshiped were real. They weren't, of course; Kallandras, as a bard who studied legend lore, knew that the only true god to have held dominion in these lands was the Lord of Night—Allasakar.

He did not speak the name aloud. It had been seven years since he had—almost—gazed upon the face of that death, that god; he did not wish to recall it clearly, although he was not a man who turned away from the terrors the darkness held.

The priestly Radann listened to the whisper of the Lord of Day; listened hard enough that they occasionally heard things. Something. But the god-born children who became the guiding priests of the Essalieyanese Churches were butchered here at birth, for it was commonly understood that these golden-eyed children were changeling creatures of great evil.

And it was also commonly understood that the women who bore them were unclean, and fit only for that death as well.

Ah, Lady.

Kallandras' musing, followed appropriately by the directionless hum of strings, stopped abruptly. He set Salla aside and quietly picked up the rolled scroll.

There, in a hand that he did not recognize, was a message that was short and pointed, yet for all that beautifully penned.

If you wish to discover the truth of the Tyr Leonne's intent, come alone to the Eastern Fount of Contemplation one hour past the setting of the sun.

It was not signed.

CHAPTER THREE

The night of the Festival Moon.

Lissa was pale.

She did not speak, and while the other wives supped and preened and prepared their masks and their saris for this single flight of freedom in the open streets of the Tor Leonne, she grew whiter still, until even the eager anticipation of her cowives could not be sustained.

"What is it, Lissa, what's wrong?"

"I—I don't feel well." The girl smiled wanly at the oldest of Sendari's consorts, Alana en'Marano.

"The sickness, is it?" The matronly woman caught the young girl's hand and held it tightly. Her face rippled in a frown of concern, and although it was smoothed away quickly, Lissa caught its import.

"What's wrong?" she whispered.

"Nothing. Here." Alana poured sweet water into a goblet and held it under the young girl's lips. "Drink this. Illia, stop flattening that pillow and be useful. Go at once and fetch the Serra. Tell her we've gone to the chambers."

"The Serra left orders that she was not to be disturbed."

"Wind take those orders, Illia, this is important."

"But she—"

"Go and get the Serra."

Illia did not demur again. Sendari, had he been here, would not have demurred—not when Alana used that tone of voice. The slender young woman vanished at once, racing down the open walkways as if she were a child.

Alana turned to Lissa again, all annoyance draining from her face. And that, of course, made things seem more frightening, for Alana was not known for the sweetness of her disposition. "Lissa, I think it best that you retire to the sleeping chamber. It is warm and crowded here."

"It's—it is hot."

"Come. Give me your arm, girl, and lean on me. You weigh nothing as it is; I can bear your weight a little while."

"Serra—Serra Teresa."

Unmasked and barely dressed, the Serra Teresa looked up, her expression completely neutral. "Illia," she said softly. "Are you not yourself preparing for the Festival Night?" Her words were cool, which was a bad sign; they could get colder still, which would be worse.

Illia knelt to the floor, pleasing in her fluidity and grace, and most intent in her humility. The serafs to either side of Serra Teresa backed away, bowing as well, but less deferentially than Illia did.

"Serra," she said, her tone much more even. "Forgive me for interrupting you. I did not think it wise—but Alana insisted."

"And Alana is now the Serra?"

"No, Serra."

"Good. I will speak with Alana myself. Later."

Illia knew a dismissal when she heard it, which was a very good thing. She flattened herself against the cold floor again, and when she rose, she left without a word.

Serra Teresa's momentary anger faded at once, and she felt something akin to shame, which was distinctly unpleasant and completely uncalled for. Her orders, after all, had been quite clear. It was essential that, this eve of all Festival Nights, no one see the mask she chose, or the clothing she wore. No one, of course, save the serafs who served her alone.

Ah, the sun was down, had been down; the sticks burned low and short, taunting her with their time, their lack of time. She could apologize to Illia on the morrow, and to Alana—but she could not stay to sort out the difficulties of the harem this eve.

Not this eve. They were in place, and awaiting her, and the foreign bard would be waiting as well. She could not be late. Lifting her arms, she nodded at the seraf.

"Bind them," she said. "Bind them as tightly as you can." He was at work at once, as was his companion; they worked in the silence of her thoughts, her fear. She was not in the first blush of youth, nor would she be again; her body was full and not easily hidden beneath the trappings of the clothing that she had chosen. But she bore the pain, and the indignity, very well for a Serra.

How will you spend the Festival Night?
In study. I have much to learn.
Masks.
Diora, wrapped round in the loose-fitting robes of childhood, smiled when she saw him.

And Sendari knew that she was a serious child, even a grave one; her smiles were seldom given, and like any rare thing, prized highly by those who understood them. No one understood them better than he.

Her hair was dark and fine, and so busy were the wives with their own preparations that no one in the harem had thought to catch and pin it into ugly, twisted braids; it hung straight from her head to the blades of her shoulders as if she had stepped out of the lake of the Tor Leonne and been dried by moonlight.

"You aren't wearing a mask," she said gravely.

The lines of her chin changed slightly as she spoke; he thought if he stared at her face hard enough, and long enough, its image would become as deeply ingrained in memory as the words and the gestures by which incantations were focused. Upon which his power was based. "Neither are you." He bowed, and her smile deepened, her large, dark eyes crinkling at the corners. Spells were simple compared to the complexity of life; he could retain them and recall them at whim. But Na'dio—every time he thought he finally understood her, she changed. One day, he would come home to a marriageable daughter.

But not tonight. Tonight was his. He shook himself, smiling down at her upturned face. "If we are to go out in the streets of the Tor Leonne, we must have masks." From the folds of his robes, he drew them out, one large and one delicately small. The latter, he untied gently and held out. "Come, Na'dio. The evening will be short enough; will you miss any of it?"

"No, Father." Her smile was the widest she had yet offered him as she saw the feathers and the golden, round-ed beak beneath them. She had asked for this face, and he had remonstrated with her quietly for her boldness.

A wiser father than he would not have rewarded that

boldness in any way. But it was the night of the Festival
Moon, and her smile was brighter than the Lady's face,
sweeter than the most carefully aged wine, more valuable
than the Northern jewels.

For her? He thought ruefully, as he tied the mask se-
curely around her face. "Hold still, Na'dio. The mask
must be properly fitted or everyone will know who you
are."

"Can I help with yours?"

"I think you are not quite tall enough," he replied
serenely. "We will let the serafs attend to me."

Kallandras found the Eastern Fount of Contemplation
with little difficulty, for he knew the city of two decades
past very well, and it had not changed much in the intervening time. Not much at all, really, beneath the blanket of
lit shadows that was the Festival of the Moon. His youth
was here, and the yearning for it was so sharp he almost
felt that he was sixteen years of age again, with all of the
attendant loss. He smiled and bowed, fixing his mask in
place and pulling his hood over the flattened golden curls
that would mark him, immediately, as a foreigner.

Passing as an Annagarian was not difficult this one eve.
He could speak like a native, and at that, a native of rank,
if he so chose, smoothing away the cultivated blemish of
Weston accent. What was hard was passing from place to
place without being caught up by revelers who started
their drinking the moment the Lady's face allowed.

He carried neither harp nor lute, in keeping with the
Festival's spirit. But he carried no sword either. If tonight
was a night for the Annagarians to celebrate their hidden
selves, it was no such thing for Kallandras. What was
hidden, was hidden, and it was not the Lady's Moon
whose light could reveal it.

The Eastern Fount was still, but the Circle of Contemplation had been cleared and cleaned, and its brass line
polished to a shine for the Festival. Found on the outskirts
of the streets that led to the Tor Leonne proper, it was
relatively deserted; there were one or two people who
had, like the bard, taken refuge for a moment from the
noise and the gaiety in the city.

He waited, and watched; time turned.

* * *

She was late.

To dress properly, to acquire clothing appropriate to both station and size—it had taken longer than she anticipated, a thing which rarely occurred. But Serra Teresa did not panic, and did not race through the streets in unseemly haste. Either he would be there, or he would not.

The Eastern Fount was at the edge of the Tor Leonne; she had chosen it for that reason. The gates were open to the Festival Moon, although the circles of contemplation were almost entirely empty. Three men stood in the darkness, two speaking together in low tones, flagons at their sides, and one—one sitting quietly in the circle.

She would have known the bard anywhere, although until she saw him sitting thus, she hadn't been certain. He was so precise in his choice of place; he sat dead center, and his legs, crossed just so, made him look like a sculpture, and not a man at all.

There were three lamps that burned quite high, and in their glow she could see that his clothing was of the shadows. He carried no harp, no lute; she did not see a sword. But she had misgivings as she saw him sitting.

She missed a step.

Stumbling, she caught his attention; he raised his face, and she saw that he wore the fool's mask; his lips turned up in a smile wider than an actual face, his nose, bright red and large, his skin paler than death. It was sewn into a hood, that his hair might be hidden from view.

We choose what we reveal, she thought, self-consciously touching her own mask. Steel, thin and almost featureless, was cool beneath her fingertips. If her eyes gave life to the austerity of her chosen facade, she could not know.

He rose, offering neither bow nor word; she met him halfway across the courtyard, bowing on the outside edge of the Circle of Contemplation. Then, silently, she raised her left arm, snapping her hand as if flicking away an insect too small to be seen.

"I am sorry," she said. Knowing that no matter how she shaded or lowered her voice, no matter what accent she layered over it, no matter which language she spoke, he would know who she was, she chose not to try.

"No," he said, "you are not."

She shrugged. "Then I am not. I have some regret."

"And I some curiosity." The bard's eyes—she could see them now, recessed beneath the curve of his mask—never left her, although to her right and left the two men who had been conversing so pleasantly now stood. Where they had carried flagons, they now carried short bows; these were strung and readied.

She was impressed by their speed and their silent grace. "I have no time to answer your questions. This is not the way I had hoped to spend this one night." She smiled, her cheeks touching the contours of a mask not rounded to contain such an expression. "You will have the opportunity to ask the Lady."

"I fear," was his neutral reply, "that the Lady will not answer my questions."

The Serra stepped away from him then, distancing herself from the men who would perform the act. "Kill him quickly." She stood prepared for his voice, for the power that made of mere words an unavoidable command. Against her, he could gain little purchase, but against these, much; it was for that reason that she could arrange no absent killing, no normal death. She could speak against his voice, layer her own command over his; hold him back for just long enough. The cerdan knew how to handle their weapons.

They lifted their bows, but instead of calling upon the power that made him so very dangerous, he shook his head softly and said the strangest thing.

"Life is so ironic."

She wanted to walk, and carried herself with all the bursting pride of a child who has not yet been injured enough to understand how harsh the world is.

He wanted to carry her, but he did not insist; the streets of the Tor were tiring for a child of Diora's age and size, and in the end, satisfied by her brief display of independence, she would retire to his arms or his shoulders to seek a safer—and a higher—vantage from which to view the world.

In the darkness of the moonlit night, it was impossible to tell whether she was boy or girl, and her voice, the words that she chose, did not give her away. Nor did the clothing she wore, or the mask.

Na'dio, he thought, as he held her small hand, *if only you had been a son.* There was no anger in him, but the sorrow was profound, and it grew with time. Diora was a bright child, a grave one; she was, he knew, very much like her father, but at an earlier age.

A son could have studied the Widan's art.

"Father, look!"

He caught her arm quickly, although she no longer needed the restraint, and then looked between the gaps in the gathering crowd before them. Blades rose and fell, catching torchlight and lamplight so briefly they glittered like rippling water. In the circle, ringed with gold-inlaid flares, two men were dancing, their blades circling each other's bodies so closely it appeared certain that one, or the other, would soon bleed.

Diora raised her arms, and he smiled softly, acceding to the unspoken request. He reminded himself, as he lifted her and deftly slid her up on his shoulders, that her weight at this age was not inconsiderable. And it didn't matter.

"They aren't fighting, are they?" she asked; his smile deepened.

"No," he said softly. "They are blade-dancing. And they are very good."

"Why?"

"Why are they good?"

"Why do they dance?"

"Because," he replied, knowing that she wouldn't understand it, "they wish to celebrate their lives, their living." She did not interrupt him when he paused both for breath and to gather his thoughts. "See the blades? They rise and they fall, always, in constant motion. These two have danced together for a long time; if they had not, they could not dance masked. They know, or hope they know, where each other will step, where they will circle, or where they will slash. If they are mistaken, they will fall, either together or separately."

"Oh."

"This close to death, Na'dio, and one feels life keenly, because one holds it so tenuously." She said nothing, and he could see, in his mind's eye, the furrowing of her brow, and the slight widening of her eyes, that spoke of concentration. "Whether or not we dance like this, we all dance," Sendari said. "And in the end, one way or another, we all fail."

She was silent; he knew that she didn't understand, but she was already well enough trained that she would not question him. Teresa's hand.

"Do they love each other?"

He frowned. To be wrong was one thing. To be completely surprised was quite another. He could not even understand the source of the question. The test of the sword was close enough that he felt each failure to anticipate keenly, be it at the hands of a Widan or the words of a four-year-old child. "What is love, Na'dio?"

She reached out with her slender arms and wrapped them around his head like silken bands, pressing the mask's edge into his face. "I love you," she told him, stroking his hair.

Beside him, one of the dance's witnesses looked up, his mask catching light and sparkling with it. Serene, as he could not have been had it been any other night, Ser Sendari di'Marano tilted his shoulders and pulled his daughter from them, folding her tightly in his arms, unmindful of who might see him, unconcerned with the contempt they no doubt felt.

The dancers danced, and he, hugging his young child tightly as he spun away from them, teetered on an edge no less terrible, and no less sharp.

"And I," he said, "love you, Na'dio."

"More than Lissa or Illia or Alana? More than Ona Teresa?"

"More, my vain little girl, than any woman or man in the whole of the Lady's night."

"For always?"

"For always."

"No matter what?"

"No matter what. Although," he added, mock severe, "you are such a perfect child that I know you will never do anything that could possibly displease me."

She hugged him, he hugged her, the moon shone down upon them both. He knew, then, that he would remember this night more sharply and more cleanly than he did his spells and his incantations and his elemental wards. The heart was such a dangerous country.

"Come," he told her, as he saw the height of the moon

against the backdrop of stars and darkness. "The skyfires will start soon."

The arrows flew.

And they flew wild.

His arms were suddenly extended, although when he'd lifted them, she couldn't say; he moved that quickly. Light flashed, a spark, iron against the grindstone. To either side, the men who had stood, armed, crumpled, their robes billowing in a huff as if suddenly emptied.

Serra Teresa froze, then, waiting.

And he bowed. "I," he said softly, "*am* sorry."

"Yes," she said, hearing the truth in his words as if it came from a very great distance. "Are they dead?"

He did not answer.

"What will you do?"

"If you mean, do I intend to kill you, then no."

Silence, stretched thin. Then, in the deserted fount, Serra Teresa di'Marano very quietly lifted her mask, setting it, like a helm, upon her head.

"I'm afraid," the bard said softly, "that I can do you no like favor." As he spoke, he, too, lifted his mask; she did not understand the words, although the nuances told her more than he wished her to know. Or perhaps they told her what he wished her to know: that he was hidden and driven.

"Why," the bard asked, "did you try to have me killed?"

"You knew they were waiting here," she said softly.

"Does it matter? You tried, and it failed. Why, Serra?"

"Because," she said flatly, knowing that he would hear a lie if she offered it now, "you are a bard of the Northern Colleges."

His eyes narrowed. "And bards are normally worthy of such a death, in such a political clime? I think not. **Tell me the truth, Serra Teresa.**"

She clenched her teeth but felt her lips move; the force of his voice was astonishing. This was not a man whose voice, in the end, she could have contained—not even for the time it would have taken two men to fire an arrow each. A waste. "I tried to kill you," she said, fighting each word, "because you are a bard." It was no different; she had intended to tell him the truth, but was humiliated at the lack of choice he left her.

His eyes widened. "The truth," he said, all power gone from the quiet of his voice. "I confess, Serra, that I hear the resentment you bear us in your voice, but I do not understand it."

"How could you?" she replied, free from his compulsion, but no longer free from her own. "How could you?" She turned, the dead to either side momentarily forgotten; her eyes were flashing oddly in the burning light.

"Tell me, Serra. If you will it. It is the night of the Festival Moon, after all." He smiled grimly. "You know that I came to gather information, or you would not have tempted me with such a message. But that does not concern you."

"No."

"Then what?"

He was young for a bard of his stature. Young and distant. His eyes, wide and blue, held no acquisitive attraction, no contempt, no fear, no desire; he was Lissa's Sun Lord in the dead of the Lady's Night. Afterward, she would wonder—often—why, but she felt, as she met those eyes, that she could trust him with what she had to say.

Say? She opened her lips a moment, but the words fell away. "You are a bard," she said softly.

"Yes."

"Sing, then. Sing softly for me."

He raised a pale, perfect brow, and then he nodded.

She thought it a kindness until she heard the song that he chose.

"The sun has gone down, has gone down, my love
Na'tere, Na'tere child
Let me take down my helm and my shield bright
Let me forsake the world of guile
For the Lady is watching, is watching, my love
Na'tere, Na'tere dear
And she knows that the heart which is guarded and
scarred
Is still pierced by the darkest of fear
When you smile I feel joy
When you cry I feel pain

When you sleep in my arms I feel strong
But the Lord does not care
For the infant who sleeps
In the cradle of arms and my song
The time it will come, it will come, my love
Na'tere, Na'tere my own
When the veil will fall and separate us
May you bury me when you are grown
For the heart, oh the heart, is a dangerous place
It is breaking with joy, and with fear
Worse, though, if you'd never been born to me,
Na'tere, Na'tere, my dear."

It was an old song, sung only after the last rays of sun were shining palely in the night sky, when it was safe to speak of both love for a child, and the terrible hope for that child's future. So very many died.

Serra Teresa cried, because the bard's voice was so very, very pure that it brought back the years that age had stolen from her, when cradled safely in her father's arms, she could sleep. Yet it was not for herself that she'd asked for this song, and she swallowed those tears, finding her voice, *the* voice, with which to join him. Serra Teresa di'Marano sang as the bard did, word for word—except the child's name she used was Diora's.

She saw his eyes widen as she sang, because in song she could not hide her curse and her gift. There was freedom, at the last, in that, for she did not sing during Festival Season, for fear that the bards would hear—and would speak of—what that song held.

Lifting a hand as the last of the notes died away, she began to speak. "It was at the Festival of the Sun. I was twelve. Part of the chorus of the opening day. He heard me."

"He?"

"His name was Robart; a bard from Morniel College." His eyes, when she met them, were perfectly still; they gave nothing at all away. "He was older than you are, Kallandras of Senniel, but far less wise. He had never visited Annagar before." She let the words trail away into silence, and then realized that she was waiting for his question, for the display of curiosity which would make the continuation of her story socially acceptable. But it

was the Night of the Festival Moon, and she needed no
permission, need practice no grace.

"My father, of course, feigned delight—but he did not
act against Robart immediately. Instead, he invited him to
our home in Mancorvo. He told the bard that such a
talent—mine—was obviously much rarer in the Dominion
than in the Empire, and offered to help Robart search the
Terrean for children such as I—children whose voices
could be trained to evoke emotion, and more. Even inti-
mated, I believe—although I was not privy to all of their
conversations—that he might petition the Tyr'agar for
permission to found a bardic college within his domain."

"We wondered what had happened to Robart."

She had the curious feeling that he spoke more for her
sake than his own.

"Oh, he searched. He found two children, but they were
both boys."

He did not ask her what had happened to the boys.
Meeting his eyes, she knew that he knew, that he understood the Dominion better than many of the people who
were born to it. *Who are you?* she thought, not for the first
time. He was like no Northerner she had ever met, and in
her time in the Tor, she had met many.

"Robart trained me until my father felt I had learned
enough." She was quiet a moment, thinking. Then, "I was
sixteen years old when he died. I understood what it
meant better than he, and I think before the end he heard
what I could not tell him in my voice. But he thought he
could survive it, somehow. He was not a wise man.

"When I was seventeen, five offers from clans of
varying note had been made for me; when I was eighteen,
another ten. My father refused them all. When I turned
nineteen, there were more; it was not until I was a full
twenty-one years that I was considered either too old, or
too valued, and the offers ceased.

"I remained with Marano, serving either my father, or
after his death, my brother."

"I wondered," he said quietly. "For you are di'Marano,
and famed for it."

"I am Serra Teresa," she replied. "I have no husband, I
have no wives, I have no harem and no place in which my
will rules; no place of my own." She started to turn away,
because she did not wish him to see her face, and then

stopped because she knew that her voice told him more than the expression of a well-schooled Serra could ever give away. "I have no children."

"No? But you have sung that song before."

"Yes."

Silence.

"Serra, you did not try to kill me in revenge for Robart. He paid the price for his intervention, and I hear the regret in you for that death."

She smiled, almost rueful. It was not a genuine expression. "No, Kallandras of Senniel, I did not."

"Then why?"

"Because, you will tell my brother that Diora is bard-born; that she has the voice. And he studies the path of the Wise. He will know that for her voice to be heard so clearly, so early in her life, she must be a power."

"Yes. And a power such as the voice rarely takes. But if she is not trained—"

"She will be Annagarian, and she will have the life that she was born to, and she will be happy."

"Happy?" was the single, moody word. Serra Teresa heard the doubt and the bitterness and the scorn that weighted these two syllables. "Did it not occur to you merely to tell me that my own life would likely be forfeit should I choose to reveal what I knew?"

"No. Because to tell you that, I would have to tell you what no man in Annagar knows, save Sendari and Adano: that I, too, have that gift. You would have knowledge of Marano that would damage us greatly should you choose to reveal it at the wrong time, or to the wrong person." She lifted a hand, as if to implore.

Emerald caught the light, holding it a moment. Gold. The white flash of diamond. She raised her eyes to the face of the Festival Moon, and because it was Moon-night, she said, through gritted teeth, "I am no oath-breaker. What I have promised, I will do." The set of her face grew grim indeed; it changed her so much that no man would have recognized her, even though he knew her well. Only the serafs might, and they did not speak.

The bard turned away, looking not to her, but toward the moon's face. "I will not pursue this," he told her quietly.

"In exchange for what?"

He smiled. "What I want, Serra, you could never give me. But . . . I hear the winds of war, and the storm is gathering. Where will it start?"

"Mancorvo," she said flatly. "They will come through the passes."

"Impossible."

"It is true. The Widan have been summoned, and they will provide the necessary protections to guard the cerdan. A small force will begin systematically raiding and destroying the villages there."

"The whole of the Sword of Knowledge would have to be wielded in order to guard those passes."

"Yes," she said starkly. "And because it is Festival Night, I will tell you that the Tyr'agar is a fool for the command; he weakens the Dominion, and his own hold over it, because the Widan are not young and the passage will tax them greatly."

"And?"

She nodded. "The main body of the Tyr's army will gather in the cradle of Averda. They will wait until word of the slaughter of your people has had time to reach the right ears, to galvanize the Twin Crowns. Your armies will be directed away from the main body of the Annagarian army because the Kings and The Ten will not be able to ignore the damage the raiders do." Her voice was ice. "The Essalieyanese are weak of heart in matters of death."

He shrugged; there was no offense at all in the still lines of his face as he turned it skyward, exposing the pale line of his throat. "Look," he said softly, and she did, although there was no command in the word.

Skyfire.

He carried Diora in the circle of his arms, instead of perching her upon his shoulders. He wanted to see her face, but if he could, he could never give her this night of fire. Yet wonder lasted so short a time in the face of a child.

The streets of the Tor were crowded; wine and ale and water were splashed in careless libation at the Lady's feet—which for this one night were the whole of the Dominion. Storytellers, like merchants selling their wares, drew their tales to an overhasty end, breaking the circles and gathering their mats so that they might also watch this night of wonder, this gift of largesse from the Tyr'agar and his Widan.

Magic was in the air, and the silence that watches from behind the eyes of lives that are almost stripped of wonder. Sendari watched the clear night sky, thinking that in two days, the Widan he faced would not be wondrous, but terrible. Thinking that, in two days, he might leave her, as he always did, but this time with no certainty of return.

"Father," Na'dio said, and he realized that he was holding her a little too closely.

"Look up," he told her, knowing that there was never any certainty of return, no matter what the day, what the occasion. "Look now. It starts."

"I don't see anything."

But he could feel the winds rising, subtle in their current; the air itself seemed to twist with the pull of the Widan's art.

"Look," he said again, pointing while he balanced her weight with one arm.

This time, a rain of pale blue fire streaked the night sky as it fell. Because he held her as close as he could, he heard her intake of breath above the delighted murmur of the crowd. He wished again that he could see her face, her eyes, the child behind this mask.

Fire, red and green and gold, blossomed like living flowers with their brief, brief lives. Beauty burned itself into Na'dio's memory; he knew it by the silence, the stillness, the awed watchfulness. Ah, there—the plains eagle, golden-taloned, green-eyed, a hundred times larger than life as it passed above the crowd and dispersed into darkness.

Na'dio cried out in wonder, lifting her hand to follow its descent. As just such a child, he had watched his first skyfires on just such a night. But he had not perched upon his father's shoulders; his father was a warrior, and even upon the Night of the Festival Moon, his heart was given to other things. No, Adano had stood beside him, stalwart, amused, and protective.

Always protective; always aware that to be head of the clan was to be its defender. Had Sendari been considered weak because of his fondness for learned study? Only one

man had dared to make jest of it in Adano's presence—
and he, their mutual father. The memory of that time had
scarred his heart; they were brothers, and the betrayal of
such a man was not—quite—within him.

He pressed his child close again, hearing in the loud
and noisy whistles, the sharp breaths, the glad cries, a
type of silence that settled where such pale noise could
not disturb it.

Forever, he thought.

But Alora's eyes were closed beneath the weight of
both earth and four empty years, and she had promised
him no less.

The stallion came next, and then, mythic, the dragon
that spoke with the voice of the wind. More flowers, the
Lady's tree, the mask of the night sky. He did not want to
let his child go; he did not want to end the night that had
begun with such a terrible vulnerability.

But the end was coming; he saw it, felt it, as the last of
the great fires cut across the sky in a swath of angry red
and gold: the Sun Sword. The weapon by which the
Tyr'agar proved, yearly, his legitimacy. It was said that
no man could wield this Sword who did not have the
blood of the clan in his veins; as Widan, he would discover the truth. As Widan—

"What is it, Na'dio? What is wrong?" He felt her tense
and shrink, as if the sword edge itself was descending
upon her upturned gaze. "I have you," he whispered.
"You are safe."

But she shook her head. He could not see her face; he
did not need to. The leap of muscles, the little tremors,
told him what he would find there. Why? "Na'dio, you
have nothing to fear from the Sword of the Sun. It is not
even real. Look, Na'dio, look. It fades as we watch it."

Her arms twined tightly around his neck; the mask
pressed softly into his shoulder. It was late, he thought;
she was tired.

But he felt the edge of worry, stronger because of the
night. Diora was no coward, and no meek child, to be
afraid of the sight of a sword.

"We will go back," he told her, regretting the words as
he spoke them. "It is too noisy here, and I do not wish to
share you with anyone but the Lady."

* * *

When they returned to the dwelling which Sendari di'Marano had procured for his personal use during the Festival, they found Illia and Irina waiting for them, their knees pressed to the floor, their hands in their laps, as if they were kep'Marano, and not en'Marano. Illia's face was pale but still; Irina's was tear-streaked and puffy. Sendari found neither pleasing.

He removed the safety of his mask, his features already hardening into the lines that time had etched there. He set his daughter down almost as an afterthought, the pang of their separation superseded by this unwelcome interruption.

"Speak," he said coolly. "What has happened? Why are you not in the Festival Streets?"

Irina pressed her head into her knees, but Illia spoke.

"Sendari," she said, as was her wife-right. "It is Lissa."

He thought he saw her flinch, but her expression was cast in a neutral alabaster that gave little away, which showed her quality, the quality of her training. Before he could speak, the child at his side interrupted him, the feathers that hid her face bobbing in agitation.

"What? What's wrong with Lissa?"

"Na'dio," Sendari said curtly, "go to the sleeping chamber and join the other children. I will attend to this."

But Diora—his Diora—did not move. "What's wrong with Lissa, Ona Illia? What's wrong with her?"

"Diora," Sendari said, his voice now quite cold. "You are to go to the other children now."

She froze in place, and then turned, lifting her masked face to him. "It is Festival Night," she said, half grave and half angered. "And I am still wearing my mask."

Irina looked positively shocked, but Illia, again, did not notice any infraction. Any correction. It was Festival Night. And her defiance was under the Lady's dominion. But Sendari was not pleased by this turn of events.

"Na'dio," he said, kneeling, "I ask you, as I have no right to order you this eve, please—"

The bells rang, shattering the silence.

Irina began to cry in earnest, and even Illia blanched. Sendari rose, lecture forgotten. "Take me," he said sternly. "Now."

The fires were over; night settled against the horizon like a blanket, or lovers' silks. Serra Teresa di'Marano rose and quietly pulled the mask down to once again cover her face. "Who are you?"

"Who are you?" He pulled his own mask down, hooding his hair and then completely obscuring the line of his jaw, the set of his pale features. "It is Festival Night," he added softly, "But I am not Annagarian, and if I follow a face of the Lady, it is not the moon's face. I do not believe that we will meet again this Festival." He bowed. "But I am honored, Serra Teresa, for you have, indeed, the voice that the poet Feranno once ascribed to you with such a poverty of praise."

She was pleased in spite of herself, and the smile that she offered him was tentative, almost pained; she forgot, for a moment, that he could not see her face. *Teresa,* she told herself, *you are far from girlhood; leave it be.*

He bowed; as his head dipped, she lifted a hand, as if to touch him.

A scream shattered the stillness of the Eastern Fount, as cruel as the howl of the winds over the empty dunes.

That scream carried a name.

Lissa.

CHAPTER FOUR

"Serra?"

The bard's hand was on her arm, his arm around her shoulder. She looked up, searching his nonface, seeing only the red nose that was so ugly in the darkness. Had she stumbled? Had she fallen? The air was chill.

"Serra Teresa."

She pulled herself free as the cry faded. Tears coursed down her cheeks. They were not her own.

"Serra, I am sorry—but I fear that you must make haste. The enclave of the Mancorvan cerdan is across the Tor, and I do not think we have much time."

"What—what—"

He caught first one arm and then the other, pulling her to face him so that their masks touched. "Serra Teresa. Teresa. That cry—I have only heard that voice once before, but I would recognize it anywhere."

She knew, then, that she knew it, too. *Diora*. The name set her free; she pulled away from the weakness that gripped her and stood.

"Who is Lissa?"

She shook her head, curt now, controlled. The evening was behind her. And ahead—ahead lay the Lady's will. "Lissa en'Marano is the youngest of Ser Sendari's wives."

"I will leave you," the bard said softly, "for I have far to travel this eve, and much, I think, to accomplish. Lady. Serra. I wish you well."

But she was beyond the pleasantry of a simple wish. The fount, chosen because it was empty and distant, now seemed to mock her with its dead. Lissa. Diora had screamed Lissa's name, and she had, across the Tor, heard it. "Wait!" she said, casting the voice as Robart had taught her so many, many years ago.

"Yes?" The bard did not stop, but his voice did; she knew that he alone could hear her words, and she alone his.

"You heard Diora."

"Oh, yes," he said quietly. "I do not think any of the bard-born in the Tor Leonne did not hear that cry this eve." His words paused as his body disappeared entirely from view. "But I will say this: If there are other bards in the Tor, they will not know who it was that they heard. You know, Serra, and I." Again a lengthy pause. Then, as if he were a disembodied spirit, some sending of the Lady's will, "Someone, I fear, is dying."

She ran. She who had not run to make her first appointment with death this eve, did everything that she could to make certain that she arrived in time for this second, and unplanned, meeting.

She could hear Diora weeping as she shoved the gates open and ran through the courtyard, the sky-open halls, and the hangings that were meant to convey a sense of privacy in lives that had so very little of it.

Serafs scattered before her; she rode an ill wind, and they did not wish to be scoured by what she carried in her wake. It was well known among Sendari's serafs that the youngest member of his harem was also the Serra's favorite. Well known, as well, that this Lissa would not be the first wife to die beneath the open winds of a moon-filled sky.

"Ramdan."

The oldest of the serafs that personally served Serra Teresa bowed quietly at the outermost edge of the chambers. He held out a hand, and she placed her cloak and hat in it, pulling her mask from her face and throwing it to one side as if its touch burned. He was not an old man, not yet, but he had the dignity that a gulf of years granted, and he wore it well. She knew, as he rose from his bow, the items she had given him in his hands, that he had waited here in perfect silence for her return. He had an uncanny sense of her movements.

"What has happened?"

"Lissa en'Marano has taken ill."

"Ill?"

"Alana en'Marano believes that the child she carries

has died. The young woman bleeds, and the bleeding does not lessen."

"Thank you."

"Serra, if I may be so bold?"

She allowed very few of her serafs to interrupt her—and never during the course of a normal evening. But the Festival Moon raged above; she did not even feel the icy regard that such evidence of poor training usually invoked. "Yes, but be quick."

"The healers have been called."

Her face almost broke then, in the bitter parody of a mocking smile. "And do you think they will come? Lissa is not the Serra, and they did not come for her." Ramdan's seraf face was utterly impassive in the face of her naked grief. He knew that she spoke of the woman whose name had been forbidden the clan.

"They came, Teresa."

Serra Teresa turned to see the haggard lines of her brother's face. Of Sendari's face. He held up a hand, palm out—a gesture of denial. "Don't," he said softly. Coldly. "There are things that even the Festival Moon cannot forgive." He turned away. "She is . . . not conscious, I think. Go to her, if you must. Say your farewells." She saw him struggle with his own advice. "It would," he said, failing it, "be fitting, after all. It was you she wanted in the end."

And he, too, spoke of a woman who was not Lissa.

But it was Lissa who was dying. Lissa who, chosen by Teresa, was not loved by Sendari. Sendari had only loved one of his wives; he chose to indulge the rest with a distant affection.

We all protect ourselves as we can, she thought, drawing herself up, hiding herself once again behind the mask of her face. *The heart is a treacherous country.* "Where is Diora?"

"With Lissa. She will not be moved."

"With your permission, Ser Sendari, I will tend to Lissa."

"And with yours, Serra Teresa, I will tell the serafs that we are to have late visitors. If," he added, his control less than hers, "they can even be found."

The silks and the cushions were covered in blood. Lissa was white, whiter than the ivory and the pale, perfect lilies that adorned the lake of the Tor Leonne. Her hair, dark, seemed a shadow that clung to her face, her forehead; her eyes were closed. Beside the youngest of the wives, the oldest sat, holding limp hands in two strong ones, and praying for the Lady's mercy.

Diora—Serra Diora—looked up from her weeping; the act was a physical thing, not a simple matter of fallen tears. Not the act of a fine Serra; not the display one expected of a woman of the clans.

Moon-night.

Serra Teresa walked to where Lissa lay, and touched Alana's bent shoulders. The older woman looked up, her eyes reddened with weeping as well.

"Ona Teresa?"

"Na'dio," Teresa said. "Must you stay?"

Mutely, Diora nodded. And then, swallowing as if something large and painful was caught in her throat, she whispered, "she wants me to sing."

"She did, love," Alana said, "but she won't hear it now."

"She will," was the child's grim reply. "I told her I would sing. I promised. I'll *make* her hear me."

Alana turned a weary face to Serra Teresa. "It's been like this," she said, nodding grimly and sadly at the young child. "She won't leave. I've told her to sing, and be done—but she won't sing. She insisted on waiting for you."

Mutely, Serra Teresa met the mutinous, the hungry, gaze of her niece. Thinking, then, that she was so very much Alora's child. Knowing that the geas that she had been bound by—the promise not to sing during the Festival—was about to be snapped by something older and stronger: Love, and the pain of its imminent loss. Worse still, knowing that Diora could have snapped that compulsion but had chosen to wait. To wait for her.

What did it matter now?

"Forgive me, Na'dio," she said, "for I have wronged you and Lissa both. Sing. Sing, and with your permission, I will sing with you."

Tears started anew in the young girl's eyes, and Teresa thought she could see her reflection, shining palely, in them. Had she ever been so young, to forgive so transparently and so easily such a wrong?

What, she wondered, was worse—to love and be hurt, or to love and have to hurt? For she had done both, and would again. *Sing,* she thought, and it was almost a prayer.

Diora knew two songs well.

In her little girl voice, a voice that had far more strength than it should have, she began. "The sun has gone down, has gone down, my love . . ."

The moonlight was strong in the harem of Ser Sendari di'Marano.

As she found her voice, Teresa gently pulled Alana away, and taking a seat, not beside, but behind the prone Lissa, she very gently cradled that young woman's head in her lap, stroking damp cheeks with the palms of her cool hands.

For the heart—oh, the heart—is a dangerous place.

She had sat just so, with Alora, just so; she had sat in the dark of a night, waiting for the healers to come. Waiting, wild with fear. Singing.

Alora had asked her to sing. Her voice broke, and broke again, as if it were a stream meeting rocks almost large enough to dam it—almost, but not quite. Because Alora had asked it of her, a last favor.

She never loved Lissa in that way, but the past met the present, making of each a harsh and terrible place.

Diora finished the last stanza alone.

The cerdan walked in, swords drawn, four abreast. The oldest man, bearded and grim—although whether it was with the nearness of death or the interruption of the evening's festivity, was not clear—bowed to her. These chambers were, after all, in the absence of a proper wife, her demesne.

"Ser Laonis di'Caveras has come at the request of Ser Sendari to view Lissa en'Marano. With your permission, Serra."

"Granted."

The cerdan bowed, quickly, putting up his sword—although, very properly, not sheathing it—before he moved to the side to take up his post along the walls. She noticed, of course. Even at times like this, she noticed the small details that spoke of good training, of grace under pressure.

Especially at times like this. For, looking at the cerdan, she could keep the pretense of hope alive for a few seconds longer. If, after all, hope of such a painful nature was a boon, a thing to be craved, to be clung to.

The healer waited.

And she, as the presiding Serra in these hidden chambers, had no choice but to look at him; to meet the dark gaze that rested beneath heavy brows, a lined forehead.

"Ser Laonis," she began, but he lifted his hand curtly, forestalling her. She dropped her head at once in acquiescence, and he crossed the room, his pale robes a cold, bright halo.

"If you would, Serra?"

"Of course." Gently, carefully—and quickly—she lifted Lissa's sweaty head from her lap and slid across the cushions, pulling herself free from her chosen burden.

The healer's serafs came up behind her, and at his direction, began to unwrap Lissa's blood-soaked sari. He intended to examine her, but Serra Teresa could hear the hardening in his voice, and she knew that he expected a death this night.

Knew that he had no intention of stopping it.

"Na'dio," she said, catching her niece by the shoulders and pulling her away from Lissa and the healer. "You have sung your song. It is time, now, for you to retire."

"No."

"Diora di'Marano. You are in the company of clansmen."

Diora said nothing, her silence defiant and determined. Teresa knew that she could send the girl on her way with a single word. But she had already wounded with words once this Festival, and she could not bring herself to do so again. Not while the moon reigned, Lord forgive her.

The healer rose, grim-faced, his eyes shuttered. "Serra," he said, bowing low.

"Ser Laonis," she replied, waiting.

"Lissa en'Marano has suffered a miscarriage. She is hemorrhaging."

"Will she recover?" She laced the words with a bright hope that she did not feel, with a trust that she could not feel, and with a fear that kept her knees locked, her chin high.

His face softened. "Even if the bleeding is stopped, she

has lost too much blood. She will sleep in the Lady's arms before the night is ended."

That was the answer. That had to be the answer. Teresa knew that her voice could not compel this man to the act that would save Lissa's life; no bard's voice could force that much, for that long, from anyone. Swallowing, she nodded.

But Diora spoke into the silence of his words. "Can't you heal her?"

"Na'dio—"

"He's a healer, Ona Teresa. Can't he heal her?"

"She is too close to death," the Serra said quietly.

"But she's not dead yet!"

"No. Na'dio—"

"But everyone knows that the healers can bring someone back if they're not dead. Everyone knows it!"

"Na'dio."

The young girl turned to face the older man. "Why won't you heal her?"

"I am a clansman," the healer replied icily. "Little one. Understand this: To bring this—this half-wife—back would mean that I would have to become her. I am a rider. She is barely free—and she is a woman. Would you have me be unmanned?"

"Yes," Diora said, her voice as icy as his had become. "What difference would it make?"

Ser Laonis flushed with anger and shock; Serra Teresa, watching him, did the same, although she knew that Diora did not understand the full import of her insult. She had never seen Diora so poorly behaved. "You are lucky," he said, "that it is the Night of the Festival Moon. You are lucky that you are a child, and you do not know what it is that you say."

"I do know what I say," Diora replied, with the steely gravity that was so unusual in a child of any age. "You're just afraid. You're a coward—and Father says that no real man is ruled by fear."

Ser Laonis spit upon the floor and turned to his serafs. "I did not come here to be insulted by an unmannered child. Serra Teresa, you will inform Ser Sendari that in future I will not come to his summons. You, bring water and cloths; I will wash, and we will leave."

"I'm afraid I cannot allow that."

All heads turned and four steel blades flashed in the light of a dozen lamps.

Perched in a window that faced the interior courtyard, clothed in shadow and bearing the exaggerated features of the clown, sat a man that only Serra Teresa recognized.

Kallandras of Senniel.

"What is this?" Ser Laonis said softly. "Treachery?"

"I assure you, Ser Laonis," Serra Teresa said, answering his question although it was not directed at her, "that the clan Marano intends no treachery this eve. This man—this reveler—is not one of us."

"Then you will, of course, have your cerdan deal with him." It was a command; Ser Laonis was personally powerful enough that he could give such orders and expect them to be obeyed.

"I?" Serra Teresa said, staring at the mask, at the glimmer of blue behind the open eyes. "But I am not Ser Sendari, Ser Laonis; the order to kill can only be given by Sendari unless there is a threat to my life or the virtue of his wives." She paused. "Is that not so, Karras?"

"It is, Serra," the cerdan so addressed replied, bowing.

"Then, stranger, have you come to threaten either my wives, or myself?"

"No, Serra Teresa, I have not."

His voice. His voice was night and darkness and a wild, wild wind. It chilled her, and she was old enough to be chilled by very little in the Dominion. Diora came to her side, unbidden, and stood within the circle of her skirts— except that she did not wear skirts this eve.

"Why have you come?"

"Not," the stranger replied, "to answer the questions of women, even such a one as the fabled Serra Teresa di'Marano." He lifted a hand then, and the light that flashed off cerdan swords was dull and harmless compared to the light that glittered upon his finger.

"Ser Laonis," the voice behind the mask said, "you have been granted a gift by the will of the Lady, and it is the Lady's night. Will you not use it?"

"For one who is not even full wife? You have already heard my answer. I will leave. Do not hinder me, or the clan Caveras will never again tend a Marano, on the field or off it, for as long as either clan lives."

"That," the stranger said gravely, "is a very long time, Ser Laonis. And who can say with certainty that the winds will not have carried your name so far from the lips of man that the deeds this night will be long forgotten?"

Ser Laonis stiffened, for although he was not born to the voice, he heard the hint of the stranger's music, and it was dark. "Who are you?"

"It is Festival Night. I am a servant of the Lady, no more and no less. We all are." The light upon his hand grew brighter, like a Widan mark gone awry. "Do you think that this youngling was meant to die? I think not. This is the Lady's night; if she wished to lower the dark shroud, she would have called Lissa en'Marano on any night but this one."

Serra Teresa felt something so sharp and so painful she thought for a moment she had been stabbed. And she had, but by hope. The bard's voice, it seemed, could touch even she.

"Your gift is a gift of the Lady's, not the Lord's; you will use it, as she desires."

"And you speak for the Lady?"

"Yes," the stranger said, jumping lithely out of the window's stone frame. "And I speak with the voice of the wind." His feet did not touch the ground, and light limned him, carried by the beginnings of the storm.

Alana drew the Lady's circle across her left breast at the mention of the wind; the serafs, terrified, fell to the ground at once. All, that is, save Ramdan, who stood behind his Serra in a silence born of years and determination.

Ser Laonis di'Caveras paled until his face was the color of the light that danced around the stranger.

"This is the night of the Festival Moon, and the Lady's face is upon you. Choose, Laonis, and choose quickly."

"I serve the Lord," Ser Laonis said, but he took a step back, raising his voice to be heard above the wind's howl.

"And will you live in the heat of a sun that knows no cooling night? You will live in a desert, Laonis, and the night's peace will be denied you."

"Who is she?" the clansman cried. "Who is she, to merit this?"

But the stranger had no answer to give the healer. Instead, he looked to the Serra Teresa, nodding his head before she could see the expression in the deep-set eyes of the mask—of the many masks—he wore.

He understood loss. He understood love. He understood what a bard had cost her; understood that she could not, cleanly, hate the man, that she had grown attached enough to someone who understood her gift and its compulsion that she still mourned his death beneath the surface of her ever-present resentment of the fact that his well-meaning interference had taken from her the life that she'd been groomed and trained for—the one chance that she had to be more than a "child" in someone else's harem. And he understood what Alora had given her in its place, and what Alora's loss meant.

Alora's death. And she had never mentioned Alora's death.

Was she a simple child, a simple girl, to be so moved by understanding? Was she a weak and simpering innocent, to crave so desperately a thing which made her so vulnerable?

Could she meet his unflinching eyes, without acknowledging the depth of this gift? The wind, she knew, would never mean again what it meant to the rest of the Dominion. His coming had cleansed its howl; had shown her the heart of the storm.

He spoke with the wind's voice, and she answered with her own, wordless.

Beneath her hands, Diora stirred, hearing in the ululation of her aunt things felt that came from a person far older and far more wounded than she. She looked up, her small hands reaching out for the clenched fists of the woman who had been, in all things, her mother. She who had sought protection from the wind, sought now to offer it.

Alora.

Diora.

Tears spilled down Teresa's cheeks, and she let them fall, unheeding. Let the voyani catch them and make of them a spell; let the clansmen speak of them as weakness, as infirmity, as age.

She offered them to Kallandras.

And he turned the wind in the palm of his hand into a sword that Ser Laonis di'Caveras bowed before. There was not a man in the room, nor a woman, who would not have bowed to that voice, that will, and that threat; not even she.

As if to mock her, and to steady her, the Lady chided her gently for such arrogance; for there were always those whose very nature abhorred a retreat from their given vows. She stepped back and hit the broad chest of her most trusted seraf, a man she had owned for almost all of her life. And he, unbent, would be unbending, a shelter of sorts whose steadiness should have required no reminder.

The healer of the clan Caveras moved with the gale, his feet hurried against the silks and the cushions. Alana en'Marano huddled against the ground as his shadow passed above her; Illia cowered against the wall, beneath the light of the lamp that the wind's force did not touch.

"Send . . . them . . . away," Ser Laonis said, his teeth clenched tightly over the words as he forced his head round and glared at Serra Teresa. "Leave!" he added to his personal serafs. They were well enough trained that they stayed their ground in the storm, but his words cut them free and they flew.

The Serra looked at the Marano cerdan and then she nodded. Because she stood in the chamber of the wives, and not in any other room, they were obliged to obey her unspoken command. Obligation or no, they were wise enough to treat as commands each of the carefully worded requests she made of them; power has many faces, and not all of them wear obvious rank.

The cerdan sheathed their swords, shaken, and left the chambers, escorting Alana and Illia in their midst. The Serra stepped away from her seraf with a dignity that she did not feel, and he, too, she sent away—for if the healer did not wish his own serafs in attendance, he would most certainly not want hers.

Ramdan hovered until the healer's shaking white hands touched Lissa en'Marano's body, pushing the stained silks aside in a blind search for skin. Then he bowed to his Serra and walked quietly out of the room, his hair tossed by wind, his hems flapping in the gale.

Serra Teresa, Serra Diora and the masked stranger whose hand burned with a cold fire watched as Ser Laonis sank into the healer's trance, his hands stilling against Lissa en'Marano's white, white skin. Wind turned to breeze, and the breeze gentled his face, brushing away strands of his hair. His eyes were closed, his brow creased; sweat caught the light and softened his features.

Serra Teresa had never seen a healing so close to the edge before. In truth, she had only twice seen healers called, both times for Adano in his tumultuous youth. He would not speak of either now. Watching Ser Laonis' face become slowly more unguarded, she thought she understood why.

"Diora," she said, pitching her voice above the wind, although it was quieting. "It is time for you to leave us." She thought that Diora might demur, and was prepared for it, but the child raised her face without argument.

Serra Teresa bent down and hugged her niece tightly, planting a kiss upon either upturned cheek.

"Will he heal her?" Diora whispered into her aunt's ear, the voice, that special gift, undampened by wind.

"Yes," was the soft reply. There was no doubt in it.

She felt the tension leave Diora's body in a rush, as if it were water and Diora a broken vessel. She tightened her arms instinctively to catch her almost-child's sudden weight. "I'm very tired," Diora whispered.

And why wouldn't she be? She had spent herself fighting the compulsion placed there by a woman trained in the voice. Teresa lifted her, thinking it odd that her weight was so slight.

"Kallandras," she said, again folding her voice in privacy, although she doubted very much that anyone but he would hear it.

The white mask turned toward her, in silence.

"I must take my child to the sleeping chambers. Will you watch?"

"I will watch," he said, his voice smooth and completely uncluttered by expression, "for as long as is necessary."

She had never seen a healing so close to the edge before; had never been so close to having her curiosity satisfied. But Diora's arms were around her neck, the trust—and the need—in them implicit, a just weight. Perhaps this was the Lady's way of granting the healer some small measure of privacy, some peace from the voyeurism of the curious.

Or perhaps it was a test, a choice between the desire to be comforted and the desire to comfort. Only beneath the

Festival Moon could she have been given two such choices in peace. She kissed the top of Diora's head, knowing the gesture for the luxury that it was.

But as she walked away, child in arms, she called upon the voice and sent it to the man who had brought the wind. "Why?" she asked him softly, knowing that he would hear all of the questions that single word contained.

The sound of her feet against the stones was her only answer for a long moment.

"I don't know."

It was almost a stranger's voice, and she understood in that moment why he was so guarded—for she heard a wild keening beneath the surface of those words, an enormity of loss that dwarfed any that she had ever felt, and she knew then that this was as honest as she wanted him to be.

He did not stay to the end, for he knew what Serra Teresa did not: that a healing of this nature, when one walked so close to death's edge, brought together two people in so complete a fashion that to sunder them again brought the healer only pain.

And the healed.

He had no desire to see such pain; it was a distant mirror that nonetheless reflected too much, too clearly. But his word, once given, he would not break again; he remained in the harem's open chamber until Lissa en'Marano's prone, red body began to rise and fall with the movement of easy breath.

He watched her hands tremble and flutter weakly, gaining strength as the seconds passed. And he watched those hands close around the neck of the reluctant healer, as if to hold him there forever. The healer's eyes, he could not see, and the healer did not move.

"Lady bless you," he said softly, gaining the window.

He sat there a moment under the Festival Moon, the sounds of merriment and freedom as loud as high waves against the sea wall of his home.

"They will kill you on the morrow," she said, her voice clear and strong although the sleeping chambers of the children surrounded her.

"I know," he told her. "There will be war this year, as

there was a decade ago; we will survive it now as we did then. We will fight our way to peace over the bodies of the fallen, when neither side can afford to support such an effort; there will follow treaties, and there will be trade. And perhaps, then, you might come to Essalieyan and visit the college of Senniel."

"Perhaps," she said, but her tone said *never*.

"Teach her, Serra. Teach her as much as you dare. It is terrible to grow up with such a gift in isolation."

"As I can, I will." She paused. "I will not forget this evening."

"Nor I. May the memory not be a trap."

They were both silent a moment, and then Teresa said, "It so often is, isn't it? Lady watch you."

"And you."

He pushed himself off the side of the building and into the courtyard, rolling into the cover of shadow so reflexively it was almost more natural than breathing. He found Salla and his harp, fit one snugly over his shoulder and the other beneath his arm, and then bid a silent farewell to the Dominion of Annagar, and the vibrant streets of the Tor Leonne.

He had hundreds of miles to travel and an army to pass around to deliver his message. It was time to move on.

CHAPTER FIVE

Sunlight.

Bright and crimson with first light; the Festival Moon's ascendancy was over. The streets shrank into their normal lines, their hard-edged, dusty reality; people hid their masks, or buried them, or kept them as heart's ease against the coming days. The Lord held sway, and the Lord's will was no feckless freedom, no weakness, no childish utterances; in the Dominion, strength ruled.

The people of Annagar understood strength well.

In the morning, Serra Teresa rose as Ramdan played the chimes. She saw her mask on the cushion beside her bed and held it a moment, weighing its value. Then, gesturing, she handed the slender, simple face to her seraf. "To be kept," she told him.

"And the clothing?"

"To be discarded."

He bowed and then stopped as she lifted a perfectly graceful hand.

"No—keep it. Keep it for me." She seldom changed her mind; it was an open sign of hasty decision—or indecision.

He bowed again.

It was her custom to start the morning with the samisen or the harp, and the morning after the Festival of the Moon was, in theory, a morning like any other. But he knew her well enough to bring no instrument on this particular morn; the night cast its shadows, and there was only one way to dispel them.

Her clothing was laid out for her, and after washing and gentle oiling, she felt ready to leave the night behind.

The brass bell outside of her personal room chimed. Ramdan bowed and left her, returning with a graceful haste.

Sendari, she thought.

"Ser Sendari wishes the pleasure of Serra Teresa's company at her earliest possible convenience."

"And he will be?"

"In the Chamber of Contemplation."

"Very well." She adjusted the swathe of the sari's silk and pulled the braided strands of her dark hair forward. Then, as a well-schooled Serra must, she obeyed her brother's command.

He did not bow when he saw her, and that lapse of grace was rare. So, too, were the circles under his eyes, the color of his face. His clothing was disheveled and dusty, his hands dirty, his lips cracked. She should have been shocked.

"Ser Sendari," Serra Teresa said, bowing very low.

Too low. His eyes narrowed at the implied criticism of his own lack of greeting. "Serra Teresa," he said, curtly. "I apologize if I have not yet had time to attire myself in the usual fashion—but I have received a most unsettling . . . message."

She waited; he kept her there, and silent, a full five minutes, as was his right. The night was gone, the moon dimmed; she was once again a woman, and he her superior. He began again. "The message was carried by a seraf of the clan Caveras. Does this mean anything to you?"

"No, Ser Sendari. Perhaps it has something to do with Ser Laonis?"

"Indeed it does." He clipped each word so sharply it almost sounded as if he were spitting. "And do you know what the gist of the message might be?"

She tired of his game, and her part in it, but she knew how to play it forever. "No, Ser Sendari."

"Lord burn you, Teresa—this is not the time!"

No one in the room moved; indeed, Ser Sendari's serafs froze in startlement at his outburst.

"At your command, then." The Serra drew herself up. "Have you been to your wives?"

"No—but I now know that Ser Laonis, for reasons that are entirely unclear to me, chose to heal Lissa."

"Yes."

"Do you know what the risks of that healing entail?"

"Yes, Sendari."

"Do you know what it costs?"

"No."

"Well, my clever, clever sister, let me tell you. Ten thousand soldi, payable immediately."

The lines of her face did not change at all; they had frozen in place. "Immediately?"

"That is what I said."

"I am not completely aware of the financial condition of this family." This was almost true. "Is this of grave difficulty?"

"That is," he replied, through teeth that were obviously clenched, "twenty times what we paid to procure Lissa, as you well know. If I could sell all of the serafs I have with me, and most of my wives, I might be able to raise two thirds of that price—but not in one day." He said it because in his sleepless exhaustion he was not completely certain that she knew it; he should have been. "How did you come to allow this?"

She said absolutely nothing.

His voice carried what lay between the words. For the Serra Teresa, the healing had already become a triumph of life over death, of hope over despair; for Sendari, it was a reminder of what lay between them, behind him. Of his failure to convince a long-ago healer to walk the same edge for his wife.

That healer was dead two years, in a riding accident in which he had instantly broken his neck—one of the few accidents a healer of any note could not survive. He had never told her, and she had never asked, if he was the hand behind that death, or if it was merely the Lady come in her time. Whichever, it was clear that that death had not assuaged the earlier one.

After a moment Ser Sendari straightened his shoulders. "Enough." It was not an apology—not quite. But it was as close as he could come in the presence of another. "I have sent a rider to Adano, and I have asked the aid of Captain Alesso di'Marente."

He did not need to tell her that Marente would be reluctant to intervene if Caveras made it clear that Marano was to suffer; very few crossed healers without paying a high price.

She bowed then. "With your permission, Ser Sendari, I wish to retire to the harem."

"While we have it," Sendari muttered darkly, but he nodded.

She found Alana outside of the morning chambers, ringing her hands in a most unattractive and unbecoming fashion. Her hair hung loose, and although it had been washed, it had not been braided or pearled; she wore a sleeping shift, and not a proper sari, and her hands and feet seemed rough and dry.

"Teresa!" Alana lifted her head and straightened her shoulders as she saw the Serra approach.

"Alana. Does something trouble you?"

"Yes, Serra." The relief in the oldest of Sendari's wives was evident; the Serra Teresa was here, and there was very little in the harem that did not bend to the Serra's will. Her hands fell to her sides, although Teresa was not certain that Alana was even aware of the change in her posture.

She should have been more severe, but it had been a long night, and there were no guests, no outsiders, to see such a poor display of schooling on Alana's part. "Tell me," the Serra said quietly.

"It's Lissa," the older woman replied, bringing her hands up and then, as if only suddenly aware of the motion, forcing them down again. "She's—she won't eat. She won't speak. Illia thought it was the baby—it's her first, and you've seen how it is, to lose the first. But I've just come from seeing her myself, and it's not the loss of the child."

"What is it? Was the healing not complete?"

"I—I don't know, Teresa. She won't speak."

"Stand aside, then. Let me go to her."

Serra Teresa had seen death before, her grandfather's first among them, but by no means the last. She knew what a corpse looked like, and knew what a difference there was between a living man and a man whose lips had passed their last breath, although that difference might be measured in seconds.

She knew that the healers, should they so choose, could call a man back from that last breath. And she had never seen it done, never once, although the clans had the money for it. But until she spoke, on that first morning,

with Lissa en'Marano, until she saw the shattered gray-
ness of the young woman's usually bright face, until she
saw the lift of eyes, the slight tip of head, the nuance of
gesture that was not—quite—Lissa's, she did not understand why.

*To bring this—this half-wife back, I would have to
become her.*

He had told them the truth.

"Lissa," she said, and stopped as Lissa en'Marano
came into view.

The girl's face was mired in tears; her hair, unwashed
and untended, was matted to her shining skin. Her eyes,
wide and dark, were unblinking and reddened, and they
looked into a distance that was so far away, Teresa
thought that walking all her life, she might never bridge
the gap. Beside her, trays of food, untouched, and a full
pitcher of clear, sweet water, showed that the serafs had
been unsuccessful in their attempts to feed her.

There were no serafs now.

"Lissa," Serra Teresa said again, her voice less stern.
"Alana says that you will not speak with her. What ails
you?"

The girl did not answer.

Teresa walked quietly across the room, kneeling on the
foremost of the cushions against which Lissa lay like a
broken doll. "Lissa," she said again, but this time, the
word carried her concern, her authority, the fear she felt,
and the desire to protect this youngest of the wives.

If it carried compulsion, it was a compulsion that
no magic could reproduce, no stranger's voice. Lissa
en'Marano turned to face her.

She opened her mouth, but she did not speak; the words
were too large for her lips, or so it seemed to Serra Teresa
as she watched the girl struggle. After a moment, she gave
up entirely on the words, and instead opened her arms and
pulled the girl in as if she were still a child in the harem's
private chambers. Lissa stiffened a moment against the
brace of her arms, and then she collapsed there, crying in
a way that no woman of any worth did—loudly, gracelessly, noisily.

At another time, she might have brushed those tears
aside and explained to her that tears could be, if they were
absolutely necessary, an embellishment to a woman's

beauty—a hint of the vulnerability that some men found so appealing—if they were done gracefully and minimally. She knew that Lissa was beyond listening. Later, perhaps.

Or perhaps not.

"Lissa," she said, ignoring the stiffness in her neck and her shoulders, "please. Only tell me what ails you, and I will do what it is in my power to do to help."

Sobbing, choked and quieting as Lissa raised her head, was the only answer that Serra Teresa received for several minutes. She brushed strands of hair out of a wet, wet face, pulling it back, attempting to return to Lissa some of the beauty and the clean simplicity that she had been chosen for. Lissa did not resist her, but Teresa thought it might be because she simply didn't care. She waited, sitting within the circle of Lissa's privacy.

Then, words breaking as if they were vessels dropped a long distance onto the peaks of rocks and barren ground, Lissa said, "He left me."

Teresa knew better than to interrupt the words with questions. One of the most important lessons she had ever learned in life was when to wait.

"He's gone. Teresa—it was so dark and so cold—I was so tired—I wanted someone to come for me—I thought they would come—"

She knew that she would need cleaning herself; knew that the work of her serafs would be undone by such close contact with Lissa. But what, after all, were serafs for? She held the youngest of Sendari's wives as tightly as she could. Because no one else could do it. And because, yes, no one was there to witness it.

"But they didn't come. It was so dark. And then—and then I heard it—I heard singing—I thought it was my mother's voice, when she was young—but I couldn't feel her—I was cold—"

"Lissa, Lissa, Lissa."

"And he came instead. I didn't know who he was. And I thought he didn't want to—I thought he didn't want to find me—he was angry—but he called me, and he was the only one there—"

"It's all right, Lissa. It's all right."

"And then he touched me, and I knew." She was crying now, and her voice was heavy with loss. "I knew he would bring back the light. I knew he could keep the darkness away. I saw what he was, Teresa. Do you understand? I saw him on the *inside*. He was afraid of being me. Of being with me. He was—I was afraid—and he saw that, too. You told me—you told me I wasn't to trust anyone, not even Sendari. But it was so dark, and I was alone—it was different there. It didn't matter.

"He had to know who I was. I—I answered all the questions. But they weren't questions, they weren't—I told him, but I didn't have to speak. And then he answered me, and he was afraid of me, and then he was happy—I didn't care, if he was frightened and he was a clansman, he was like me—

"He's gone, Teresa. He knew everything about me. He understood everything I am. He promised to bring me back—here—and he left." She raised a tear-streaked, swollen face. "And he's not what he looks like, he's not. Do you know when he first learned about his gift? He healed a dog, Teresa—and it wasn't even his, but it was hurt. It's been so hard—to not heal, to leave us to die—he hates it—he has to—"

"Hush, Lissa." Teresa covered the girl's moving lips with her forefinger, pressing them gently. "Of that, you must never speak. Do you understand? Believe that there are reasons why all men hide their true face, whatever that face may be." She put her arms around the young girl again, and began to sing softly. And she sang sleep, with all of the power that she had, gentling it with the love and the loss that she now felt.

Would it have been better to have Alora alive, but to lose everything else about her? To have her either live as an empty shell, or to live in the harem of another, with no allegiance to the oath rings and the promises that had been her earlier life?

Even now, she could not say for certain.

Ramdan returned to her, and bowed, interrupting her musing, which was just as well. The serafs had finished anointing her hair with the hint of a summer fragrance; she gestured them aside as the chief of her serafs lifted his head.

"Ser Sendari will see you," Ramdan said gravely. He offered her a hand and she rose. Together, Serra and seraf, they walked down the halls toward the chamber of contemplation that Sendari had made a fortress within his residence.

"Are the preparations made for our leave-taking?"

"Yes, Serra."

"And the horses?"

"Ready as well."

"Good."

"I realize it is unusual," Serra Teresa said, "but it is not without precedent. It is not the clansman, but his wife, his sister or his mother, who procure—and bargain for—the women of the harem."

Sendari gazed at her with narrowed eyes. "Teresa," he said at last, "there is something that you are not telling me. No, don't waste your breath with nicety and graceful comment; speak frankly, if you will waste my time speaking at all. I have one day beyond which the test of the sword waits. If you believe that you can maneuver around this healer—and by extension, the clan—I will trust you."

"I see that the moon has not left you, Ser Sendari," she said, speaking as frankly as was her wont when so commanded.

"Oh? Then you see with night eyes, Serra Teresa. We have obviously received no reply from Adano," he added crisply, "but Marente cannot move if Caveras desires no interference."

"It was not unexpected."

"No." He turned. "A seraf from Caveras is waiting by the fountain."

"Has he been waiting long?"

"A matter of hours."

"Good. And our time?"

"We have until sunset, Teresa." His gaze fell to rest upon the contemplation patterns he had etched into the wood of the floor by dint of his personal flame.

"I wish your dispensation, brother."

"To do what?"

"To deal, in this matter, as I see fit."

"You deal, dearest sister, as you see fit without my dispensation." Grudgingly, he added, "but for form's sake, I will grant it." Silence descended awkwardly around him, a shroud and a defense against Serra Teresa's gift. Her curse. He turned on his cushions, upsetting the goblet that rested at his feet. Water spilled, spreading a wet darkness across the mats before he could stop it.

But she was gone; the door—the only solid door in the quarters—was closed upon both Teresa and their conversation. He would have liked to start it again; to speak like a civil man. To tell her that he knew that she could hear the rawness of the day and the night in his voice. That he hated to be so vulnerable. Especially to her. Because she knew it, anyway, but it would give him the pretense of choice in the matter.

Grinding his teeth, he tried to force his thought to conform to the channels of the Widan's art. He would not seek her absolution.

And not because she was merely a woman; there was nothing, in the end, that was mere about his sister, and he knew it. It was because Teresa's hands and Teresa's lap were the cradle of comfort for Alora's dying. Not his.

He would send her back to Adano. Alana en'Marano could run his harem without his sister's interference. And he would find a new wife. A real wife.

Alora.

Fire blackened and scorched an uneven circle around him, a barrier of flame.

Ramdan and four of the Marano cerdan accompanied the Serra. She chose Karras di'Marano because he was so very straight and narrow that he could not be intimidated; he chose his companions. They did not need to know where Ser Laonis made his dwelling within the Tor Leonne because his seraf led them quickly through the sparsely populated streets, winding ever upward until Teresa realized that he was leading them to the Tor Leonne proper. She paled slightly, although her complexion, kept from the harsh grace of sun by veil and hat, hid it well.

It was good that the serafs sent to find a healer had been sent on the night of the Festival Moon. Such intrusion, such effrontery, on any other night would have marked Marano. But of course, it should not have surprised her; if Caveras was not a clan of import, Ser Laonis was still worthy of the attention of Tyrs—and worth that respect to those who might, in future, need the gift the Lady had granted him.

The cerdan that guarded the gates were no ordinary cerdan, although their posts made of them less than the legendary Tyran of the Leonne clan, the oathguards who, alone in the Dominion, were considered completely trustworthy by the Tyr'agar. Few were the men who were invited to take that oath, and even fewer were the men who, once invited, accepted. The oathguards were tested under the eyes of the Lord, and those who were found wanting did not survive.

Or so it was said.

The Serra Teresa di'Marano bowed at a discreet and respectful distance as her cerdan approached the gates. They were stopped by cerdan who bore both the crest of the rising sun and naked blades as evidence of their pride in their office; they were richly attired, but more, perfectly composed. Training was something that the Serra Teresa appreciated.

"Who seeks to pass?"

"The Serra Teresa di'Marano."

"For what purpose?"

"She is summoned by Ser Laonis di'Caveras."

"And who will bear the responsibility for her passage?"

"Ser Laonis di'Caveras."

"You may pass."

The cerdan bowed to each other, their swords glinting as the blades caught and held the sun's face a moment. Serra Teresa di'Marano rose slowly, her eyes upon the perfectly tended road that led, if one followed it from start to finish, to the presence of the Tyr'agar himself.

Ser Illara kai di'Leonne, she thought, as she made her way past the cerdan who stood now at respectful attention, *will one day be in need of a wife.* At eight years of age he was an awkward boy, but he would, if he survived, be Tyr'agar, and as heir to that position, he was already much sought after by women who wished to be the wife to the largest harem in the land.

Many of these women were Serra Teresa's age; a few were older. She had no desire to join their ranks, thinking it unseemly, if not unwise. But Na'dio was four, and Na'dio was already in grace and elegance a child who far surpassed the gangly kai di'Leonne. It was perhaps time that Serra Diora di'Marano began her training in earnest. Time that the attention of the young Ser Illara's illustrious mother was drawn to a child of such exquisite seeming with a few carefully placed words.

For if such a family made such an offer to Adano or Sendari, they refused it at their peril. Yes, even if Sendari suspected—or knew—he would still be forced to give his child to the Leonne clan. Diora would be safe from her gift.

"This way, Serra," Ramdan said, speaking so softly his words might have been the rustle of the tall-stemmed flowers that grew in such restrained numbers to either side.

She did not acknowledge his words; indeed, no one did, which was as it should be. He was a shadow, something the light cast down across the path the Annagarians chose to walk.

The lake of the Tor Leonne lay like the very mirror of the Lord, placed so that his power might seek it in contemplation, and the Serra Teresa stopped to quietly admire not the light across its surface, not the play of the waves, not the grand but small boat which floated serenely beside the single dock, but rather the sound of the lapping water against rock and sand and reed. She loved this part of the Tor Leonne best of all for its aural illusion of peace.

And it was an illusion; as she listened, she could hear the bark of a familiar voice. Ser Laonis was ordering his cerdan and his serafs to prepare for the guests that were coming. The supplicants. She allowed herself a small smile. At this distance, she could hear the chaos beneath his barely controlled words—the anger, the fear, the impatience.

Ten thousand soldi.

Had he first ascertained the relative modesty of Sendari's worth before making such a demand? She thought he must have—for had Sendari the money, he would have paid it without demur. One did not, could not, anger a healer; they were rare.

If Sendari paid, that would be the end of it.

And not the end, she thought, that Ser Laonis desired.

They walked until the building came into view. It was sudden, the view, as if trees, like curtains, had been pulled back by a deft and expert hand.

A seraf waited upon the platform that served as the entry for honored guests. She was very young, and obviously trained for her presentation, for she was exquisitely lovely. Gold adorned her ears, her throat, her slender, birdlike wrists; she wore pale blues and greens, although she was of an age where a full sari was considered too adult. Soon, Teresa thought, she would be a sub-wife in a harem. Perhaps even Laonis'.

Ramdan bowed once to his Serra and then crossed the perfectly placed stones that led to the platform. He mounted it and knelt at its edge, bowing in turn to the girl who waited.

"Serra Teresa di'Marano has come to speak on behalf of Ser Sendari di'Marano."

The girl's brows rose, and Teresa frowned; the look spoiled her composed delicacy.

"Tell Ser Laonis that Ser Sendari felt that it was a matter of the harem, and not the clan—but that should Ser Laonis wish it, Ser Sendari will come himself."

The seraf rose and stepped back, sliding the screens only wide enough to allow her room to step between them. Ramdan continued to kneel; the wait was long.

But the girl returned, and this time she was perfect; her face betrayed nothing. "Ser Laonis will speak with Serra Teresa in the chamber of contemplation."

He was an older man. The past night had been as unkind to him as years to another; his hair was streaked with gray, his face lined, his eyes dark. Serafs had taken care to disguise the look of malaise, but it lingered, obvious to anyone of Serra Teresa's perception.

He sat before a small table, and upon it there were fruits; grapes so pale they were almost white, and a wine so dark it seemed black in the confines of the slender, silvered goblets. Cushions, orange, red, and yellow, were heaped in a circle around the table; Ser Laonis sat upon them, and he sat heavily, although he was not an overly large man.

"Please, Serra Teresa." He gestured, and she walked— with grace, with care, with perfect decorum—to the cushions. Kneeling, she took her place across from him, the small table a symbolic wall between them.

"Wine?"

"Thank you." She touched the slender stem of the goblet and lifted it a moment to her lips; it was cold, although no ice, no hint of that Widan's trick in this clime, was in evidence. Then, as if fortified, she lowered her head, hiding her eyes beneath the fan of her lashes. "Ser Laonis," she said, her voice soft, "I do not wish to be unseemly or overly bold. But as this concerns a matter of the harem, perhaps you wish me to discuss this with your wife?"

"I have no wife," he told her quietly. "You have come to discuss matters of the harem, and you are, no doubt, much like my own mother in such an . . . arena. I would not have you hampered, and I will not judge you poorly."

"You are gracious, Ser Laonis di'Caveras."

"I can afford to be."

Silence a moment. "I spoke, this morning, with Lissa." He turned to his cerdan, and the young seraf who stood in attendance. "Leave," he told them curtly. It was clear that they were used to such commands, for they obeyed without demur—and with great speed. "I would ask you to dismiss your own cerdan. And your seraf."

"Done," she said softly.

One man and one woman in a small quiet room.

"What," the man said, "did she say?"

"Very little," the woman replied. "She is well-schooled."

His face was pale, and grew paler still; he lifted his goblet, raised it to his lips, and set it aside untouched.

"We received your summons," she said.

"My summons?"

"Yes. Accept my apology for our tardiness. Ten thousand soldi is a sum that is not inconsiderable for our family."

"Indeed."

Silence.

"Ser Laonis."

"Serra Teresa."

"May I begin again?"

"Please do."

"I did not know, when we summoned you, that you would heal my Lissa." She raised her goblet and touched the beaded drops of water along its sides, their chill more attractive to her than the wine.

Stony silence.

"I did not know—nor did Sendari—that some stranger on Festival Night would come, speaking with such a voice." She paused. "I wish it were night, now."

"But it is not."

"No." She, too, set the goblet down; this rise and fall was a type of breath for both of them. "You know that we do not have ten thousand soldi." She raised a hand before he could reply.

His acquiescent silence was shocking in a clansman.

"Because we do not have the ten thousand, we cannot afford to save Lissa's life."

At that, a smile touched his lips, albeit a bitter one. "I think it late for that," he said dryly, showing a hint of the man that he might once have been, and might become again when this shadow left him. If it did.

"*I* chose her," she said abruptly. "I chose her when she was a child the age of your lovely young seraf. I have trained her well, but I have protected her against much, and she is not yet wise." She watched his face, the lines of it hardening.

Grudgingly, Ser Laonis said, "I doubt that Lissa will ever be completely wise. She is not you, Serra Teresa, and she will never be so, no matter how much she admires you. Yes," he added grimly, "I do know how much she admires you. And why."

"This is not a simple matter of pretense," Serra Teresa said softly, "although perhaps my guileless Lissa would say otherwise. You are not a boy, Ser Laonis, but a man— a clansman."

"And a clansman should know how a proper Serra behaves—how she must behave, whether inclined that way or no?"

"Indeed."

"Very well. Serra Teresa, you will honor my intelligence by speaking to me as if you have some. Intelligence," he added sharply.

"At your command, then," she said sweetly. "What do you intend to do with Lissa?" His surprise was a pleasure, and it should not have been. Chiding herself inwardly, she waited for him to speak.

"I will, although it is no business of your own," he said evenly, "make her my wife."

It was the Serra's turn to be speechless, the healer's turn to be pleased—but the pleasure was brief. "She is worth ten thousand soldi to me. You are quite right. I made certain that my price was beyond your reach. Had you come up with the gold, I would have raised the price as a penalty for your delay. There is only one thing I will take as payment for my service to your clan."

In silence, Serra Teresa raised the goblet. She could pay attention to silver and wine instead of the healer's face, and the desperation in the voice beneath the words. Lissa was born a seraf. Lissa was another man's concubine, another man's pleasure. To take her—and to take her, not for play, not for dalliance, but to wife, to make her a Serra—he could not do it.

Could not, and yet he intended no less; the truth was there, raw, in the words.

She had heard such a rawness before. In Sendari's voice. And in her own.

"Lissa is not in fit state to come to you," she said softly. "Ser Laonis—"

"Do not say it."

"I must say it, for Lissa's sake. There will be no easy home for you in the Dominion; if you were not healer, there would be no home. Perhaps, had she never been Sendari's, things would be different. But she has."

"I know it."

"And what would you do then?"

His smile was a very odd thing. "Find a home, if that's what must be done." The smile dimmed. "I tire, Serra Teresa, even of a woman of your grace and wit and beauty. You will send me Lissa en'Marano, or I will beggar Marano into serafdom and retrieve her from the blocks."

This, too, was truth.

"I will send you Lissa en'Marano," she said, rising.

Diora cried.

Neither Serra Teresa nor Ser Sendari could comfort her; only Lissa could have done that, but the young concubine's eyes were glistening as if with fever-sight. She was with them in body, but she had already left them.

Why? Diora asked, and asked again. *She's our wife. Why is she leaving?*

Because, Serra Teresa told her gently, *Ser Laonis saved her life, and we could not afford the price of it. Diora, she will be happy where she is going.*

I wouldn't be. I wouldn't be happy to leave.

Na'dio.

Serra Teresa and Ser Sendari had suffered loss before; those losses had scarred and hardened them, inuring their hearts to such a leave-taking, if not their pride.

But the first loss was always the hardest; always the worst. They stood by, the father and the aunt, watching. Diora was old enough to learn, and the Dominion of Annagar demanded that she learn well, for if the first loss was the hardest, it was also just that: the first loss. There would be others, always; loss and loss and loss. And death.

But Serra Teresa underestimated how quickly the young child could learn.

Neither she nor Sendari ever saw Diora cry again.

But Serra Teresa kept her word to her own dead, and to a strange bard, and if Diora did not cry, she sang, she spoke, she whispered; if she did not plead, she cajoled with a lilt, a smile, a little laugh that sounded like the tinkling spill of cool water against marble.

They played the samisen and the harp, and although Diora di'Marano never sang again at a Festival, they both watched those foreigners who dared to come after the winds of war had passed, searching for a familiar face.

Wind, Serra Teresa would say, *sing.* A dare, a risk, a heartfelt gratitude—all of this, in these two quiet words.

But she would have cause to remember, in the years to come, that the voice of the wind was the wind; only in the hands of a golden-haired foreigner could its terrible course be turned, blind, toward mercy.

CHAPTER SIX

The Sword of Knowledge was aptly named; a double-edged, dangerous weapon in a world where weapons were an absolute necessity, it cut—it always cut—two ways. Yet on this single night of his life, the moon just off full, the air still hot and dusty with summer's strength, Sendari di'Marano knew that it was not the desire for knowledge which drove the Widan. It was, as in the rest of the Dominion of Annagar, a struggle for power, for supremacy. Different weapons, of course; weapons arcane and personal. But no matter how disguised the struggle was, no matter how misunderstood by clansmen who measured their strength by the size of their lands, their horses, and the swords that they carried, the struggle was there. The Widan were wise in the ways of many things, but they were men.

And the Lord demanded, of men, his due.

"So," the man seated before him said softly. "You have been invited three times to take the test of the Sword." Sendari par di'Marano bowed as he acknowledged the truth—and the veiled edge of accusation—in the voice of the man known, among Widan, as the Sword's Edge. His hair was a black-streaked white, his beard as long and fine as any such vanity possessed by another Widan, and his hands were remarkably pale, unblemished by the stain of labor or the touch of sun. He dressed finely, in Southern silks, and he sat upon a stone throne that was as old as this building itself—a monument to the struggle of man for knowledge and power.

Yet it was not his presumption that was first noticed—although the Widan had no ruler, no leader, no undisputed head—rather, it was his eyes that caught and held the attention, for they were a shade that traveled between the color of pale sky and light-touched steel, and they missed nothing.

"And only on the third have you chosen the course."

"So it would seem."

The shadows stirred; there was a magic here that was thick and heavy and completely impervious to the spells of understanding that Sendari knew. But he knew enough to sense the wards and sigil that bore the signature of Cortano di'Alexes.

The worth of a man in the Dominion was measured by the power he held, by the relative power. Cortano di'Alexes was worth any ten of the Widan; perhaps any twenty. It was hard to say, because he chose—as they all did—to veil their power in the world that did not walk the Sword's edge. The clansmen were suspicious enough to be dangerous if they gathered in their angry enclaves.

"Then I will not ask you why you chose to make this journey; it is enough that you have. You embark upon a journey that will kill you or free you. Turn back, turn even to glance, and you will lose the road for this turning.

"But you will not lose your life."

"I will not," Sendari replied gravely, "lose my life in any case. I am Widan."

"The winds will judge, or the Lord." Cortano's smile was soft. Unpleasant. "Do not," he repeated softly, "look back."

And then, as if to enforce this rule, the Widan came with a swath of silk and carefully bound his eyes, turning and winding the midnight blue across Sendari's brow until no light at all reached him. Quiet, he waited until they were finished; he had seen the beginnings of this ceremony many, many times. He had never once seen its end.

Tonight, that would change. He followed the Widan until he heard the grating of stone against stone—a creaking, ponderous sound that spoke of weight and years both. A musty, dank wind rose about him, disturbing the hem of his robe.

"Now, Sendari, you walk the Sword's edge," Widan Mikalis said. "You must blunt or sharpen its blade by your own choice." Had Mikalis' voice ever come from such a remove? Sendari thought not, but he was not surprised; vision played a part in every conversation between men. Robes rustled. He faced the unknown, blind.

And a smile touched his lips. If it was bitter, what

matter? He stepped into darkness, and with no man to lead him, who was there to witness the tale his face told?

The blindfold itself was symbolic—to one wise in the ways of power, it made no difference. Spells to heighten other senses had given Ser Sendari par di'Marano the lay of the land through which he had passed. He traveled, confined on all sides by worn rock, the particular scent of aged water becoming stronger with each step he took. At his back the Widan-Initiates followed; at his front, no guide but the tunnel itself. And the tunnel was distinctive enough that he knew, without question, that he could find this place again without the aid of those who knew it well.

What he could not find again was the mystery—yes, it was definitely there—of this first traveling. Tonight, he would take the test, and it would kill him or elevate him.

It was not uncommon to misstep while blindfolded— for no hands were offered him in guidance or fellowship—but it was not considered a good omen. Therefore, Sendari chose to use some small portion of his power to proceed with grace and certainty. He wondered, briefly, how much that vanity would cost him.

The blindfold was removed, unknotted from behind, and taken from his face with an ease that spoke of practice. The darkness beneath closed lids gave way to shadows half-warm with light; magelight. And a light that bore no signature that he could discern. He knew the marks of the Widan well.

"Yes," the Widan at his back said softly, as reverently as one of the Wise could speak, "this is an ancient place. It was chosen by the founder for that reason."

History.

Curiosity caught him a moment; none interfered. There was in this curiosity something that hallowed a man; that made him, that drove him to greatness. A man sighed; the sigh was caught and echoed by the cavernous ceiling above these narrowly spaced, natural walls. He thought he recognized, again, the voice of Mikalis di'Arretta.

"A test," that man said. "Of the Widan's heart. It burns in you, Sendari."

But Sendari was no longer listening. The rock beneath his hand was not cool, but it was not warm; it seemed to *tingle* with an internal force of its own. There was, in the unnatural light here, a hint of otherness, something tantalizing. It reminded him of something that he was certain he had seen before, although he could not immediately recall what.

"Widan-Designate," another voice at his back said quietly, and with some amusement, "now is not the time. Pass the test, and the ways will be open to you; you may study them at your leisure." The momentary warmth faded quickly.

"This is the foot of the path. If you will face the test of the Sword, continue; if you will not, return. You will have no other opportunity to change your mind."

He did not recognize the voice immediately, and when it came to him, it came as a part of a collection of facts. Marcaro di'Ravenne, a man whose study drew him, time and again, to the Northern plains. A man who, therefore, Sendari had little measure of. Was he a threat?

The Widan-Designate chuckled. Of course he was. They all were.

The Widan themselves were not a brotherhood or a fellowship; they were a circle steeped in the mysteries of knowledge that had come, fragmented and obscure, from a time before the Dominion of Annagar had made its mark across the continent.

We are men of knowledge, Sendari thought, as his eyes grew accustomed to the scant light in the hall before him. *We are not men of superstitious ceremony.*

And if that were true, if ceremony held no significance, there would be no blindfold, no tunnel, no test.

"Choose."

Had he not chosen yet?

The road not traveled lay before him. He gazed at it, at the surface of rock that had been almost worn smooth with the passage of time. Thinking, because he could not help but think, of her. Alora.

In a darkness devoid of sun or moon or star, time ceased to hold him; if it passed above, either quickly or slowly, it mattered little. Here, in the darkness that Widan light lessened by slow degree, he was suspended above—or beneath—the world in which he lived.

And she was there, a memory that was so strong he thought he had but to turn to give her flesh and form.

And to turn was to forsake the test.

This strong, after four years and a bitter final betrayal. He reached out, as if still blindfolded, and gripped the cold surface of worn rock with shaking hands. Let the Widan following at his back think him weak or doubtful. Let the men watching feel it even more strongly. It would work in his favor; all underestimation eventually had, and besides, he was no longer a child, flushed with the anger of another man's casual mockery of all that he could not do.

Doubt did not shake him or sear him; anger did. At her, yes, and at himself. But was it not always this way, when one opened the heart too wide? She could not deprive him of power as she had once done; she was dead. Her time had passed. As if to mock him, a gust of hot wind blew across his face, coming from the palely lit darkness ahead. She was his road not taken, and if he would have given all to take it again, he did not turn aside.

Night thoughts.

Dark thoughts.

Take the test, Sendari. Alesso's voice; the voice of sanity and reason. And if *his* voice were sanity and reason, the Widan were in a sorry state indeed. Were all supplicants so tried before they made their final choice?

He waited for the summons, but the summons did not come.

Instead, he saw her daughter. His daughter. Diora. There, in the shadows, her four-year-old face turned up to him in perfect trust, perfect confidence. Moon-night had passed, and what had been open was hidden—but it was very much alive. Thus was his heart hollowed and hallowed with care.

I will not fail you, he told this apparition. And then he grimaced; what thought was this, at such a time? How could one *not* fail a daughter, in the end? In the darkness of this moment before death, he was almost brutal in his honesty. Because, in the darkness, he could be.

Diora was chattel, and as such, a thing beyond his control. That he loved her was not at question, but was also irrelevant. For he had watched the daughters of more powerful men given to—or taken by—other powerful men, and he knew that a father's whim and determination afforded little comfort. Give her to a husband, and she was his. But keep her . . . keep her, and she became like Teresa.

"Choose," the voice said again.

Sendari par di'Marano took a step forward, releasing the cavern's jutting face. He followed it with another, and then another, each step becoming more certain. He had come this way, for this reason alone: to take the test.

Because to take the test *was* to betray her, and her memory, and if he could do that—if he could do that, perhaps he could finally leave her behind. He was so very tired of the peculiar pain, unseen and omnipresent, that had driven him so hard for the last four years.

As he stepped into shadow, light flared, a wild, brilliant light that Sendari was certain bore the trace signature of the Widan Cortano di'Alexes. He cursed; the curse was taken by the cavern's too-perfect acoustics and magnified.

No more than a curse escaped him, for as the light came, blinding a moment in its clarity, he saw where the tunnel had taken him, and he was, in spite of himself, awed. The tunnel itself had fallen away completely; there was no more confining wall, no steadying rock to either side. Instead, there was an expanse of space that would dwarf the valley plains—something that went on into darkness both on the left and right. His eyes could not penetrate the distance, and he did not try for long. He used the brilliant magelight as his guide.

The roof of this cavern was almost beyond sight, and the floor; there was rock, and somewhere below it, a winding bed of water made itself heard in a rush that sounded very like the howling of the desert wind.

The banks of the river were rock, as hard and cool as the walls of the tunnel he had followed—but between them was a gap of darkness so long that light could not illuminate it.

Across the divide, a lone man stood.

Cortano.

Sendari par di'Marano bowed.

The cavern caught the words of the Sword's Edge, sharpening them, if that were possible.

"Three times," the man said softly, "we asked. The first, I asked personally."

Sendari nodded.

"But you saw fit to refuse, Widan-Designate. The Lord's law governs even here: To refuse a man of power has its price. *I* am your test, and I am your opponent."

Sendari waited, cool as the stone that surrounded him. Many of the Widan-Designates never passed the test of the Sword—but many did. In a straight contest between a Widan of experience, and a Widan with less, there would be no contest; no test at all. He did not let fear unman him or unnerve him. Fear for himself, fear of his own death—these had never been the force which drove him.

"Very good," Cortano said softly, after a few minutes of silence had passed. "There is steel in you, Widan-Designate; and I believe the steel is a fine one. I am your test, but if you survive it, I will be your temper." He turned, his robes dark in the light, his left arm outstretched and pointing. "There, Sendari. Look."

The Widan-Designate followed the line the man's arm made; it ended in a bridge, a natural outcropping of rock that seemed to have grown from either side of the chasm to meet in its center, seamless and whole. There were no rails to this bridge, and indeed, as Sendari studied it, he saw that it was widest at the foot of either side, narrowest at its curved midpoint. Not a comforting structure, although one certain not to break with the mere weight of a man, not to creak and rot with the passage of time.

"Your task is simple. Only cross the bridge, and you will be declared Widan."

"In what time?"

Cortano's smile could be seen across that gulf that separated them. "I will wait, Sendari. You will either cross it or perish in your own time."

"How generous."

"A man in my position can afford to be," Cortano replied.

There and then, Sendari vowed to become at least Cortano's equal in the wielding of the art. He did not give voice to the momentary anger; it would only expose the weakness of his reaction. Instead he walked to the foot of the bridge, his steps slow and measured. There were tests to be performed here before he so much as stepped onto the rocky platform. Meticulous, focused now, he performed each in its turn.

The bridge was as it appeared, no more and no less. No

spell of seeming was laid upon it to make it appear whole; no spell of displacement; no disguise which might make of this bridge a thing of cloth or string—or air. It was, from his brief exploration, of a piece, although what might form and mold the rock in such a fashion, Sendari could not say.

And what he did not know was always a source of both curiosity and irritation. Knowledge, to Sendari par di'Marano, was like drink to a man long grown accustomed to its taste and its comfort. He rose.

Cortano, impassive now, waited, his arms by his sides.

Sendari stepped onto the bridge.

There was no light, no flare of fire, no obvious attack. But the bridge itself was treacherous enough; if it was of a piece, it was not a smooth piece, and his foot found purchase, heavily soled as it was, with difficulty. He took another step, removing the foot that anchored him to the tunnel side of the chasm. Found his balance, although the bridge was narrower than it had first seemed.

He looked up, as he took his third step. Cortano smiled and gestured. The lights went out.

No evening sky was as black as this darkness, although Sendari was certain that the darkness was natural. They were buried deep within the folds of the earth itself, and the earth hid—and held—its own. No Lord touched this place with the fiery light of the sun, nor Lady with the soft, silver glow of moon. This was a place beyond their concern and their dominion.

The Widan's home.

Sendari froze and then, with the darkness as cover, he crouched, finding the face of the rock with his fingers, as if truly blind. Instinct, perhaps, or some fear of falling older by far than the man himself, caused his hands to grip its worn edges, its hard folds. Had his first impulse been to call the light, to heighten the senses, he would have perished.

For within the chasm itself, coming from his left and building in force, he could hear howling, the prowl of an angry wind. What had Cortano said?

The winds will judge.

He had just enough time to tighten his grip, to flatten himself into the contours of the bridge itself, before that judgment came, tearing at the flaps and folds of his robes, pulling his hair, twisting his beard up and into his sightless eyes. Sand, scouring, was carried in the heart of the wind—if the wind could be said to have a heart at all—he could feel it scrape across his skin. Thus were mountains worn to facelessness.

He could not speak; the words were torn from his lips and scattered against the rock face of the chasm's walls. He could not gesture; he could not use those elements of nicety that had become part of his ritual when, locked away from prying eyes and babbling voices, he had summoned fire and bent it to his will.

No, all he had was will. Will.

Clinging, blind, his hands warm with blood and pain, Sendari di'Marano began to force that will into channels of his desire. Fire was his strength, and there was no call for it here; no way to use or invoke it. He could not destroy the wind. No living man could; even the Lord tolerated its presence in the Dominion. But destruction was not the only form of victory; indeed, in this struggle there was only one form that victory could take.

He strengthened his grip by slow degree, pulling on reserves of power to augment sheer physical strength—of which there was little enough. He could not still the wind's voice, but he could—if his will did not continue to falter and flail like a disobedient child—glove his hands against the grinding tongues of sand. He did not try to stand. He did not try to deny the force of the wind in that fashion.

Pride forgotten, Sendari di'Marano began to crawl.

He had run this gauntlet before, after all.

Not physically, of course.

But the wind had come one shadowed night, and taken, in its wake, the only thing that he would have held onto with everything that he was. The only thing that he *had* held onto in such a fashion until that moment. He would have done more than crawl to keep her. He had, pleading with the healer until he could not speak for tears. The shame of that single moment burned and stung his cheeks more than the sand-laden winds ever could. And it had been for nothing, although the healer had paid. She died, and he waited while she did so, seeking a blind, instinctive comfort in the arms of his sister. Denied even the ability to hold her and take what comfort he could from that.

Ah. Blood. Anger. Pain.

Jealousy.

Yes. He knew it. Teresa knew it. It was ever between them, and he thought that it would remain so. Because he could not let it go. Would not.

The rock beneath his hands was hard; he gripped it, he forced his hands to become a part of it; he supported himself by the strength of his fingers. The wind pulled him up; his chest skirted rock-ridge and came down with a bruising thud. Ah, fire——he used it just a moment, precisely and perfectly, to sheer the straps of his sandals into ash. Thus freed, the leather fell away, claimed by the gale, and he set about fastening his toes, his soles, the skin of his feet, to the rock itself.

He crawled, bloody-minded in his determination.

If her death had not bowed him, if her death had not demanded his own, nothing could. Not one thing. If he crawled across the bridge, he crawled; pride would suffer, but no more. He had but to gain the other edge of the chasm and he was done.

Close, now. He could feel the bridge's incline become decline. He wrapped his arms around the whole of the bridge's thinnest points, as if it were a stone tree, and he a child determined to climb what was, in the end, just beyond his reach. Will shored him up, and power; he kept his grip and his focus as he moved, surely, across the divide.

He was not prepared for the fire.

It lapped up the sides of the bridge like water, but where it struck, it *burned*. Elemental, wild, the heart of fire, not fire's civilized core, red flames tried to take his hands. He cried out, but he did not move, for to move was death. Here, the wind helped; it tore at chunks of flame, throwing it, damping it, dulling its heat.

He did not study the flame; he knew it was Cortano's. And he knew, at this point, that he had to unmake the fire before it made of him a thing of ash and bone. He had controlled the flame, and flame's voice, before——but never when another Widan chose to wield it.

No matter.

Sendari par di'Marano brought his teeth together, cutting off the cry that sounded only vaguely like his own voice. Anger shored him up; the will and the focus that he had brought to bear to crawl this far across the bridge that spanned the crevice was nothing compared to the will that attacked the fire.

Because fire was *his*. Because it was the one thing, the only thing, that he had left after Alora. Because he could not believe the arrogance of a man—of any man—who would think to use his strongest gift against him.

He was *Widan*. He was Sendari di'Marano, and he was the pawn—and the victim—of no man. He took the flames, forced them away from his skin, and then guttered them, viciously, as if they were indeed alive.

Cortano brought them back, but weaker, and he crushed them again, using power—finding power—that he did not know, until that moment, he possessed. Flayed and bleeding, his hands held fast, as if they were separate from him, with a will and a mind of their own.

And then, fires to either side, he began to crawl. The wind raged; the fires crackled; Sendari snarled. He was Widan. He was Widan, and he had been denied too much in his life. This was within his power. This was within his control. And what was internal, what came from within, no one could break, be he even Cortano di'Alexes.

Be he the Lord of the Sun.

Sendari par di'Marano inched his way across the divide, and came, upon raw hands and bloodied knees, into his title.

The wind stopped its howl as his first hand cleared the bridge; silence reigned in the darkness that, Sendari realized, he had never once attempted to alleviate.

"You are not afraid of the darkness," Cortano di'Alexes said.

"No."

"Good. You are not humbled by it either. You will need both of these traits in the future. Rise, Sendari di'Marano, if you can. The worst of your life is behind you. You are Widan, and you have joined the Wise."

The light returned; Sendari flinched as it made clear the extent of the wounds he had taken to come this far. But he rose slowly, finding his feet as he turned to face the opposite side of the bridge. There, bearing witness, were the men who had the right, by this test, to wear the Sword of Knowledge.

He could not clearly see their faces, but he knew, although the distance was great, that not a single man begrudged him his victory; his victory reminded them of their own.

"Tomorrow, if you desire it, you may return to the tunnels. And you may cross the bridge; the wind howls only once for each man who seeks entry here."

"The wind," Sendari said softly.

Cortano's eyes were a glittering, almost unnatural blue. "No," he said, "it is not mine."

"Then whose?"

"A mystery, Sendari, that we have never fully apprehended. Perhaps you will be the one; perhaps not. The founder gave us these tunnels, and this chasm, and he decreed that no man with too much pride or too little caution could walk the edge of the Sword well. This was his test."

"And the fire?"

"Ah." Cortano's smile was cool. "I am the Sword's Edge, Sendari. When I make a request of you, think twice before refusing it."

Sendari par di'Marano returned to the surface of the world a Widan; if he returned in robes made ragged by rock edge and sticky by blood, his triumph was not lessened, for he had survived. The chasm had not claimed him, nor the wind, and if he had not chosen to stand against the wind's fury—well, did it matter in the end how a man survived such a test, if the survival itself was all that counted?

The day had passed, and the dusk; there was moonlight across the waters of the Tor Leonne, rippled and uneven, but no less bright for the darkness. Hands washed in the waters of that lake and bandaged in soft cotton, Sendari stood a moment, turning this way and that in the cool breeze as if he were no more substantial than an eagle's fallen feather.

He had faced death, but the world did not look new; it looked, measure for measure, like the Tor Leonne that he had grown accustomed to over the years: Grand and perfect, but so distant, so far away, the ripples of his greatest triumph might never touch or disturb it.

I am Widan, he thought, as he began to walk. *I am Widan Sendari par di'Marano.* The night sounds of insects touched him, as far away as the Tor Leonne itself; the quiet buzzing of mosquitoes, summoned no doubt by the scent of the blood, dry or no, that lay across his sleeves. His hands themselves, he did not bend or curl; they hurt, and they would pain him for some time yet—if they ever fully healed.

Pain of this nature *was* nature.

Tomorrow, his legs would be stiff, and his arms, his shoulders, his back. He was not a young man, to crawl across a bridge so long or wide with only his physical strength and a touch of the magic that was his pride. He wanted a bath, someplace warm and restful to retire to.

Some part of him did.

But it was night, and the moon was just off full, so close the eye could hardly discern the difference, although spell could. When he found himself standing outside of the small harem that a man of his station was given room for in the Tor Leonne, he knew why he had come. The Moon's face had turned her light upon him, guiding his steps while his thoughts, defenseless, were elsewhere.

And now he stood before the cloth hanging that separated the man from his wives and his children. Wives. He had no wife, and that, he thought, would have to change. This life would have to change.

No light came from around the hanging itself, and in such twilight shadows, even the light of a single candle would make itself known by its flickering. He reached out with his bandaged hands, saw them, pale and indistinct against the hanging whose colors night had temporarily taken from the eye.

Freedom? He hesitated a moment, thinking that he had passed his test, that he had survived, and wondering, as his hands seemed to move of their own accord, wondering bitterly, how many more tests he would have to face, how many more he would have to undergo before he finally failed and the winds swept him into their endless turmoil, their eternal death.

Numbly, he pushed aside the hangings. He took a single

step and stopped, his toes a candle's width from the mats that lay across the floor in perfect order. In the moonlight, he could see that the women were sleeping; indeed, he could hear Alana snoring, her breath heavy and rumbling. There were animals in the North who slumbered as heavily and defended their own as viciously; he thought it with a stab of affection, a prickling unease.

Illia lay beside her, head tucked into her arms, legs curled against the cushions she had piled atop the mats. Between these two, the youngest and the oldest of his wives, were two children; in the darkness, he could not tell who they were, although in theory they were his.

His eyes searched the sleeping quarters, and then he sighed, a gust of breath at once heavy with relief and disappointment. She was not here.

He turned, let the hanging fall to one side, and began to walk down halls that seemed interminable, suddenly, in their length. He wanted rest now; sleep—a celebration of his victory required more energy, and more pride, than he now had. The only movement in these halls and walks was the flicker of torchlight and lamplight; these burned low, and they would not guide him home for long before they were guttered.

Yet they served their purpose, and that was, in the end, enough. Perfection would have to wait, as ever, the start of another day.

He shoved the hangings to his private rooms aside; he did not desire the company of his wives, and in any case, he did not trust Teresa to arrive after he had had a chance to change his robes and comport himself in a manner befitting a Widan; he thought rather she would find him, sleeping in stained and torn clothing, his blood soaking through the new cloth that bound the back of his hands, as vulnerable in his exhaustion as any of the children there.

A man was allowed his vulnerability in his harem, among his wives, but Sendari would not expose himself to Teresa in this fashion; indeed, he had all but decided that he would send her back to Adano.

He took a step forward, into the darkness of his rooms. The outer chamber was austere, almost empty; the inner chamber likewise, except that the mats were laid, and cushions delicately arranged against the eastern wall;

beneath these cushions, sleeping silks with which to protect oneself from the evening's chill—for the nights in the
Tor Leonne could be almost unpleasantly cool.

He walked between these two rooms, his legs growing
heavier, his pain more severe. In the morning, at the rise
of the Lord's light, he would celebrate.

Alesso di'Marente would be the first outside of the
Sword of Knowledge to know of his victory and his
title—if, Sendari thought with a minor frown, he did not
already know it—and they would celebrate as friends, as
clansmen, as men of skill and power.

He lifted the second hanging, slid between it and the
wall, and then let it go.

Let it go to flickering candlelight—had he been so
tired, so bleary in his travel, that he had missed the
narrow frame of flame around the door?—in a near dark
room. The mats were down, and two cushions had been
taken from their place by the wall. Not pulled or dragged,
but chosen with deliberate care, so that the pleasing pat-
tern by the wall itself, altered, was not destroyed.

Teresa's handiwork, he thought, in one way or another.

But he did not feel the anger that he should have, in this
place that was, by his stricture and his rightful rule, forbidden to all but the serafs who were to clean it.

Because across those two pillows, not two feet away
from the falling, rolling wax of the candle itself, lay
Na'dio. Her eyes were closed, her hands beneath her
cheeks; such a child, he thought, the Lady must love, for
in sleep, beneath the darkened sky, she was so very perfect he felt another stab of affection, pure and clean, a terrible weakness.

Was he free?

No. For this child was Alora's child. *I made an oath to
Alora,* he thought, as his hands curled reflexively, and
stiffened just as reflexively, *but I made no such oath
to Diora. She is not the same weakness. She is not a
weakness.*

He wavered a moment on the threshold, and then he
whispered her name—not to wake her, but to say it,
because he felt that he had to say it. *"Na'dio."*

It was enough, Lady's judgment, enough; the child on
his mats stirred, and her eyes flickered, in odd counter-
point to the flickering of the candle's insistent, tiny flame.

Her eyes, as dark as night, but larger somehow, brighter in spite of their color.

He watched her wake, and then, paralyzed, watched wakefulness transform her face as if it were a sculptor. He saw her momentary disorientation give way to shock, to round-eyed wonder, and finally, utterly abandon itself to a fierce joy.

"Father!"

He should have told her that his hands were injured, his chest scraped and scored by rock, his arms and legs bruised by their rise and fall—the wind's work—against solid stone. If he could not, then at least, at very least, he should have told her that his hands were raw and the flesh near scored from them by the bite of an elemental mage; that they were almost done bleeding, but to move them, to use them, was to open the mess—it could hardly be called a wound—again.

And he knew it, but as she lifted herself from the mats, shoving her slight weight up by the palms of her whole and perfect hands, he stiffened, bending at the knee, removing the distance of age and height that separated a man from his child. He caught her as she hurled herself across the room, staggered with the weight of her, the unexpected burden, took a strangled breath at the strength of her grip round his neck.

And he laughed, although the laughter was a pathetic, choked sound. "Na'dio," he said. "I have barely survived the test of the Sword—will you strangle me for my trouble?"

But he wrapped his arms around her, catching her and lifting her, his hands stretching and bleeding at the motion. Because there were moments that a man must take, when he could take them—or find them—at all. And this, precious, unlooked for, was one.

CHAPTER SEVEN

3rd of Seril, 426 AA
City of Amar, Terrean of Mancorvo

All things must end.

All things, be they valued or hated beyond measure. Such was the will of the Lord and the Lady. But the endings were bitter indeed, and often resisted by those who could not, or would not, submit themselves easily to the whim of another master.

He thought all of these things, on this fine, clear day, the sun reigning, without attendant clouds, in the heavens. But the man who faced him quietly, even deferentially, noticed none of the clouds which had already begun to gather beneath the surface of the Widan Sendari di'Marano's eyes.

"Understand, Widan Sendari par di'Marano, that your daughter, the Serra Diora di'Marano, will be wed to the *kai* Leonne; that her children will be his children, and that her sons will rule the Dominion in their time.

"Thus it is that we," and here he nodded quietly to a woman that must, Sendari thought, be one of the harem elders of the Tyr'agar himself, "have come to travel to the Marano domain, seeking to make an agreement between our Tyr—and yours."

The reminder was not lost upon Sendari. "I am . . . overwhelmed," he said, sounding no such thing. "It is rare indeed that the clan Leonne seeks to marry so far beneath it."

Although his words were humble, his tone was not; the man who had been sent to facilitate negotiations stood stiffly a moment in his uncertainty. "It is rare indeed," he said at last, "and I'm glad to see that you appreciate its significance." His hair was streaked by time, his face worn; both gave him the blended look of authority and wisdom that was so prized by the Tyr'agar. He did not dress as a court noble, he dressed as a rider—which was just as well; his travels brought him to Mancorvo, and in Mancorvo, things courtly were considered beneath those who sought to prove themselves worthy of the regard of the Lord.

"And how is it that the kai Leonne—or the kai's father—happened upon the daughter of a humble par?"

"You will find, Ser Sendari," the negotiator said, choosing his family title over the coveted Widan, "that there are few indeed who have not 'happened' upon the daughter that you have guarded so zealously. She is famed throughout the Dominion for her beauty; the poets carry her words to the farthest reaches of the five Terreans and back."

"The daughter of every clansman of note is so famed," was the cool reply.

"Indeed. And it is not fame alone, but experience, that moved my master's hand. Your brother, Tor'agar Adano kai di'Marano, offered the service of his sister, the famed Serra Teresa—and she, in turn, brought her niece to light in the Pavilion of the Dawn.

"The sun rose upon these two women, and with them. I tell you now, Ser Sendari, that not a clansmen remained unmoved who were privileged to hear their voices and their song; they are matchless in their gifts."

He paused, as if the sudden outburst were almost embarrassing. In truth, it was, and entirely inappropriate; it gave away much of his bargaining position, and much of the Tyr's desire. "It is clear that you understand her worth," he added coolly.

And Sendari thought, *Teresa,* and the word was a dagger, a stab of anger so visceral he was afraid, for a single moment, to speak. The moment passed, and quickly; one did not keep the appointed representative of the Tyr'agar waiting. "Yes, Ser Alexi, I understand her worth. I will retire now, to consider in full the enormity of the honor that you have done the clan Marano."

"Consider it," the negotiator said, bowing. He did not have to add, *and quickly.* It was understood. Such an offer could not be refused.

* * *

"Sendari."

"Adano."

The two men sat in a quiet room; a seraf knelt by the far wall, a pitcher of water at her side. When either man chose to lift the cup set before him, she would unobtrusively rise and fill it; she was trained by Serra Teresa di'Marano, and because of that, knew no gracelessness, no artlessness, when serving the Tor'agar and his chosen guests.

The Tor'agar was, in all things, a clansman that the Dominion could be proud of. His hair was still dark, and his shoulders broad; no part of his face had ever been broken, although he had seen combat time and again during the wars. He rode as if riding were more natural to him than walking, and he wielded a sword as if it were an extra arm; he wore armor more readily than silk. He was, by all accounts, handsome, and he was, rarer, loyal to those things that he valued and respected.

His brother.

His Tyr.

The man he faced was shorter, slighter in every way; he wielded a sword poorly, and barely deigned to ride. His face was longer and narrower than his brother's, and he wore a beard, as if to hide a weaker chin. Yet there was, between these two, a similarity of appearance, some echo that spoke of their birth.

"Sendari," Adano said again, meeting his brother's gaze with a directness that spoke of affection, authority, and blood. "This man, Ser Alexi—he is valued by the Tyr'agar. He would not have been sent otherwise."

"I know it."

Silence, uncomfortable, uneasy. There was so much that these two—a man, a true man, of the clans, and his weaker, wiser brother—had chosen not to say to each other over the years. Their silences were folds of comfort into which they might drop, places in which understanding reigned, rather than prejudice and fear.

And that understanding, Sendari saw, had been stretched, like a fine and unmatchable cloth, to breaking; it was not a magical thing, after all, but a thing made of man, made of two men, made when those men's roads had diverged decades past.

What, for the sake of an old affection, would he do?

"Sendari, when you chose—when you chose not to take the test of the Sword, I accepted your decision. It would have weakened Marano to lose you, and I did not think that the loss was worth the risk. I also understood at that time that there were . . . reasons why you might choose as you did.

"If you have reasons for doing so now, I must ask you, please, as brother—put them aside. Marano is under the Tyr's eye, and his eye is not particularly kind when he has offered honor and been offered insult in return."

"And if I cannot, as brother, as you so quaintly say, put 'them' aside?"

"Then I will ask it as Tor'agar, and your kai."

"And if I politely decline your request?"

"What would you have me say, Sendari? That I would see clan Marano brought down? You know, as well as I, that I could order you to do as I say—but that has never been our way, and I have no desire to be forced to it. I do not wish to order you as if you were common cerdan." He paused. "But I will not beg.

"We both know, for the sake of Marano, the Tyr'agar cannot be refused."

But two long days later, Ser Alexi kai di'Orro still waited. And three days.

At the end of the fifth day, road weary with dust and sweat, and unaccompanied, although his position commanded, literally, the armies of the Tyr, came General Alesso di'Marente.

"She is a daughter, Sendari; you value her too highly. No, this is not meant as criticism. It is fact, and as Widan you cannot turn from truth. As always, the decision you make is yours alone. But the clansmen see you as weak with every hour you wait." The General Alesso di'Marente was not so young a man as he had been; the sun had burned some of the color from his hair, and the wind had worn fine lines into the contours of his eyes, his jaw, his lips. But it was not the passage of time that had hardened him or angered him; not the turn of the sun or the march of the seasons. Loss, in battle—the first war between the Empire and the Dominion in decades—had cut a swathe in his pride that, over a decade later, still showed in his face. Those lines, etched, made his face seem a thing of stone—unyielding.

If Sendari had faced the test of the Sword, Alesso had faced the test of the field; the former had been granted a title above the sway of clans and birth; the latter, by dint of strategic brilliance, had also improved his lot, but by greater degree, turning a rout into a retreat, and destroying the most famous of his enemies: the Black Ospreys. To Alesso, it was a Pyrrhic victory, a shadow victory shared with the Tyr'agnate of Averda. The failure drove him, although in the eyes of the clans, he alone had emerged not only unscathed, but elevated in stature.

In the eyes of the Lord, the men who sat in the heat of the summer day, surrounded on one side by artfully arranged rocks and on the other by plants that had a touch of the desert's defiance in their spines and quills, were not equals.

The Lord valued combat above all else.

"On the contrary," Sendari replied, eyes lidded in that half-open expression that spoke not of fatigue but rather of great anger, "They will think me strong. Not one of them would dare to take the risk that the offer be withdrawn."

"Those who do not know your past might mistake your hesitance for part of the bride-price negotiations—but *I* know the truth, and Cortano knows; there will be others."

"I am not inclined to care what they think."

Alesso rose, angered. "And my regard, Sendari?"

The serafs were nowhere to be seen. Water had been brought, and something to blunt the edge of the hunger that might occur between meals; both had been left in the stillness that lies between two proud men.

Sendari should have noted their absence for what it was, for Alesso rarely argued where any ears but his could hear what was said. "I am not the keeper of your regard."

"Your actions define it."

"Then judge me," Sendari said, rising as well, so as not to give Alesso the advantage of too much height, "by those actions."

"If you choose to act at all."

This was not the first time that these two had argued; it

would not be the last. They were like brothers in that regard, although no blood bound them. "Alesso."

The General subsided a moment. "You are my closest . . . adviser," he said, when he could speak again. "And I will not lose you because of your oversentimental attachment to a daughter. She is not your son, old friend, and if she were, she still would not have the value of a kai; you are the second son of the Marano clan."

"Even Adano has urged you to think clearly upon your action."

"I am *Widan*, Alesso. It is unlikely that I would think any other way."

Silence again, heavy with the struggle to leave things unsaid. To speak things in anger gave words a power and a history that friendship weathered poorly; and for all that they disagreed, the friendship between these two men was genuine and worth much to both.

"Sendari," the General said, bowing. "She is only a daughter."

The Widan bowed in return, stiffly. "Yes."

"But even so, ask yourself this: Would this match not be the very thing that she would have desired?"

Because Alesso so rarely acknowledged his previous wife, it took Sendari a moment to understand who that "she" was. And when he understood it; when the words had sunk, like water, between the cracks of a dry and parched land, he rose, his face the desert's face for just that moment.

The dead did not remain buried.

"You are . . . unkind, Alesso."

"Yes. But not to you alone." He turned, but did not leave; not yet. His hand sought the hilt of his sword and found it. Almost, Sendari thought, as if to still himself, to steady himself. "I despise weak men," the General said.

"Understood."

"And the Lord offers only contempt for their struggles.

"She weakened you, old friend, and I cannot decide whether or not I, in my turn, desire to face that weakness or no. But dead, she controls your life. Even in this."

"In this?" Sendari felt anger's echo, a thing much weaker than anger itself, but no less haunting. "Why? You are right, Alesso. Diora is only a daughter.

"But I believe I might drive a hard bargain for her

in such a way that her value will be known across the Dominion."

The General did the Widan a courtesy; he did not turn until a moment had passed in which the Widan might carefully school his face.

28th of Seril, 426 AA
The Tor Leonne, Annagar

Some scars healed.

Eleven years after the test of the Sword, the Widan Sendari di'Marano's arms were the pale, white color of fire-touched flesh. Gone were the blisters, the cracked skin, the rawness of blood brought by heat too close to skin's surface; all that remained were these marks, like an oiled parchment. And the rank. Widan.

Wise.

He stood, clenching his fists, the morning sun bleaching the water of all color until it resembled, in his eyes, the shade of the scars on his arms and hands. White.

"Sendari?"

He looked down at the feel of small hands across his chest; delicate hands, and cool, as if they had been washed in the waters of the lake that he gazed upon. They hadn't, of course; the waters of this lake were special, and given to only a few for such frivolities. This was, after all, the Tor Leonne itself, the seat of the power of the Dominion.

There was only one woman who came to him thus, only one who was not wise enough to know when to leave him alone, and when to approach. The Serra Fiona en'Marano.

Passing the Widan's test gave him a patina of power, an aura of authority, that belied his rank; the clansmen came, with their marriageable daughters or sisters, to pay their respects.

And he wished a wife, a clansman's wife.

Not one who would ask him to make promises that she herself could not keep.

Younger than the concubine whose service to him had been the price of her life, the Serra Fiona had been lithe and supple, and prone to a self-importance that time had not yet worn the edges off. It wasn't pleasing, but it pleased him to indulge it in some small way. He knew that she would suffer for it in the harem, for although it was technically her harem now, and his concubines her sister-wives, he knew that her place among the women who had not been her choice was still delicate. In eleven years, these women had not forgiven her youthful arrogance and her attempt to rule what had never been ruled: the harem of Widan Sendari par di'Marano's previous wife.

Previous wife.

"Sendari?"

He caught her hands, pulling them round his chest and pinning them there, so that she might feel that she had his attention. He was not a man who wished his wife to be a counselor or a coconspirator. He wished his wife to be pliant, and obedient, and graceful; he wished her be desirable, to dress perfectly, to play the samisen as a woman alone could play it; he wished her to be pleasing in all things, but pleasing in a way that did not, in the end, touch more than the senses, did not warm more than the body. He had suffered enough at the hands of the Lord's whim, at the howl of the desert wind. He would not willingly suffer more.

Her hands slid, playful, down; he caught them, feeling a rare annoyance. "Fiona," he said softly. A warning.

She was well enough brought up that she heeded it, retreating as delicately as she could and gathering her silks about her shoulders—but he knew, as she hid the ivory of her skin from sun's light and her husband's eyes, that her pride had been pricked.

His concubines would suffer for it. Youth could be so petulant. But the rest of the concubines could take care of themselves. And if, for some reason, they could not defend themselves against the wrath of a rejected wife, they could no doubt turn to the Serra Teresa for guidance and wise counsel.

For Teresa was among them, albeit as visitor, and where she went, she reigned. Even Fiona did not raise voice against her.

Left alone, Ser Sendari di'Marano contemplated the magnificent waters that defined the Tor Leonne. Thinking that fire—the sun's face—was the Lord's aspect, and water, the Lady's; thinking further that the Lady's aspect was the heart of the Dominion, its seat of power, if not its regalia. Thinking that the anger of the Lady must, in the end be far deeper than the anger of the Lord, for it was the Lady who, time and again, demanded the due of life.

At night.

It was morning, now; the sun should have offered comfort as it hung in the summer sky. But its travel over the waters reminded him unaccountably of scars, of scarring, of loss.

Loss.

The Serra Diora di'Marano was to be married in three days time. He had refused no less than six offers for her hand, finding some pretense, some excuse, that might shield her from the interest of the clans for just a day longer, or a week. His wife was his wife, and as all men, he did not trust a man not to treat his daughter in as dismissive a fashion as he treated the lovely Fiona—and the certain knowledge that his daughter, his intelligent, cunning, perfect daughter would be so regarded angered him and worried him both. She was of an age where as yet had no desire to leave the harem that had been her home for all of her life—and he . . . he was still her father.

But the seventh offer was an offer that he could not refuse. And even so, he had delayed his response until he stood upon an edge very different than the Sword's—and one far more dangerous.

Did it matter? He was here, now, obedient and richer for that obedience; he had drawn the attention of the Tyr'agar himself, both for his negotiating skill and for the golden sword that he wore upon his breast; and his daughter was there—somewhere among the many pavilions designed by Leonne the Founder to grace the lakeside in such a way that they might see no other, granting not the illusion of privacy, but something rarer in the Tor Leonne: its substance.

His daughter.

And not his daughter anymore.

He stared down at the pale skin that covered his hands, remembering the test of the Sword, and the reason he had taken it; aware that he had passed another, and at no less risk. What he did not know, as he stared at the waters, was whether this test, like the last such test he had taken, had empowered him—or whether it had robbed him of some meaning, some strength that was hidden from the eyes of the clans.

* * *

The Radann Fredero kai el'Sol stood in the courtyard of
the edifice that had been built, at the behest of Leonne the
Founder so many years ago, when the dark years had
come to their close with the death of a Tyr whose name,
and whose clan name, had been carefully expunged from
the texts by which history was learned. Leonne the Founder had been a man both blessed and chosen by the Lord
as his warrior; it was to Leonne the Founder that the Sun
Sword was given.

The Radann—the men who spent their life's devotion,
and their lives, in the service of the Lord—had been commanded to follow the lead of Leonne the Founder, and
they had, in faith and strength, stood beside him, wielding
their own weapons against those who sought to deny the
Lord his dominion.

It was the time of legends, of their making.

The courtyard attested to that, with its fine arches
of stone, its flagstones, its interior sculptures, each of a
piece of stone, and each created by a man who could
bring, to stone, a semblance of eternal life. There, the
sword bearer, and to his left, the crown bearer; to his
right, the vessel bearer, and across from him—across, the
symbol of the Lord himself: The many-rayed, magnificent sun.

The time of legend, Fredero thought, had long since
ended. Leonne the Founder had been a great warrior. His
blood could barely be seen in the man who now wore the
Sword's crown: the Tyr'agar Markaso di'Leonne. Markaso
was a dour man and cold; he spent too much time in the
sun—Fredero lifted his hands in a propitiary benediction
at the thought—and too little with the sword, too little
upon the horse, too little with the war council that was
built beneath his feet.

Danger, there.

He bowed his head a moment, and said a customary,
solitary prayer; it was no plea, of course, for the Lord did
not listen to the pleas of men. Rather it was a promise, a
form of negotiation.

The Sun's weight was heavy, this day, and the Radann
kai el'Sol did not know why. But he felt it was inauspi-
cious, this chill within on a day so clear and so full of
promise.

Where was Jevri?

As if the impatient words were spoken aloud, an old man came briskly into view, followed by a half-dozen young servitors, each of whom carefully handled the hem of a long train. They were obviously ill at ease, these men; they were sworn to the Lord's service, and the Lord's service—in their mute, but nonetheless obvious opinion—had nothing to do with the carrying of exquisite garments. Serra's garments, of course.

They were far too wise to state their opinions, although not one of them was terribly good at acting. Fredero rarely chose his servitors for their ability to dissemble.

"It's about time," he said testily.

The oldest of the men—by at least three decades—managed to turn a bow of respect into a shrug. "It is timely," he replied. "We have not yet seen to its fitting, however."

"Servitor, need I remind you—"

"Only if it will put you at ease. Among the six of us, we've already heard it so often we've lost the desire to learn how to count."

Four of the five young men looked shocked, but they kept their eyes firmly upon the silk that they carried—a misstep might stain it, or cause it to tear, and that would be worth, if not their lives, their positions at the least. Besides which, while they revered the kai el'Sol as the Lord's Sword, they knew that his relationship with Jevri el'Sol was almost a familial one.

Not familial, of course; no man could petition the Radann for entry without first disavowing all ties of blood. Fredero kai el'Sol had been known, in his youth, as Ser Fredero par di'Lamberto—brother to the man who ruled the Terrean of Mancorvo. The Lambertans were known, across the Dominion, for their honor; the Lord was willing to accept his service before he'd observed his first rites.

Jevri, it was said, had journeyed with him. No one asked the cantankerous older man if such rumors were true; at best, he'd box their ears a time or two for neglecting the Lord's work to satisfy their idle curiosity.

Jevri was like a fond uncle in the lowest ranks of a great clan—linked by blood and name, but not by circumstance, to the seat of power. The kai el'Sol was its forbidding patriarch.

But every patriarch came from someone's harem, at one time or another. And what ties there were between Jevri and the kai el'Sol were ties that the two men understood well—and that no other men sought to interfere with.

"Does it meet with your approval?" This, the only genuine question that the old man had yet asked.

The Radann Fredero kai el'Sol walked quietly around the garment, squinting as a touch of wind caught silk and turned crystal into unexpected light. He knew that, as a dress destined for the Serra known throughout the Terrean as the Flower of the Dominion, it had to be perfect. And he knew, as well, that no man upon the Lord's earth could create such perfection if it were not Jevri.

"Yes," he said softly. "And Jevri?"

"What?"

"The Tyr'agnate Mareo kai di'Lamberto will be present, with his Serra. And the Serra Carlatta di'Lamberto will attend as well. She has always loved the glitter of ceremonies such as these."

Jevri showed a rare smile then, one that Fredero echoed although he knew it was a vanity.

In another life, another time, the Serra Carlatta di'Lamberto had been his mother. He knew no family now, but the Lord—yet he retained an affection for the past that had started him upon his exalted road.

Exalted?

He smiled wryly as he waved the men, with their garment, out of the open courtyard. Wondering, curious as all men must be, about a woman known to all as the Flower of the Dominion, but seen in the end by very, very few.

The Flower of the Dominion sat in the shade and the shadows of the Pavilion of Restful Repose. The samisen lay, strings still, in her lap; she was silent, as if the playing alone had given her voice.

"Na'dio," the Serra beside her said, and the young woman bestirred herself. "Tell me."

"It is . . . nothing, Ona Teresa."

"Nothing? Then come, play for me. In three short days,

I will no longer have the pleasure either of your company or of your voice."

And her company *was* her voice; they both knew it. They were hidden, these two, in ways that even the most carefully graceful, the most exquisitely mannered, of Serras were not, for they shared this mutual gift and curse: that their voices, when brought to bear, could sway men of action momentarily to their will.

Shade kept the sun from the silks that they wore; shadow made of the Serra Diora's hair a midnight darkness, a black that seemed almost blue. For three more days, she would wear maiden's hair, long tresses unadorned by complicated combs and adult adornments.

Three days. Less.

The sun had already begun its long descent.

The Serra Diora di'Marano began to strum the strings of the samisen, but she did not sing, and the music itself became a natural sound, a thing that melted into the background, rather than drawing one's attention.

"Na'dio?"

Her aunt was almost never this insistent; she traced the strings with the tips of fingers slightly hardened to their use, and then stilled them, unwilling to speak, or afraid to. Because to her father, her much loved father, she could offer a lie that would calm nerves and ease fear; to her aunt, she could not. For Ona Teresa heard everything that lay hidden beneath her words—just as she heard, in her aunt's voice, the same. They were vulnerable to each other, and the Serra Diora did not wish her aunt to know how much she worried.

How much she did not want this marriage, this union that the Serra Teresa di'Marano, by dint of will and subtle politicking, had brought to be.

Diora knew that the Serra Teresa's life had been blunted by her own desire for a harem, if not a husband, for a life with sister-wives of her choosing, children of her birthing, a world of her making.

Diora did not desire these things, and did not understand how a woman with her aunt's subtle mystery and power could. She loved the harem of her childhood greatly, although she had never truly warmed to her father's chosen wife, and all of those women—every one—would be taken from her by a man that she had met the requisite two times: Once during the Lord's dominion, and once during the Lady's.

There had been no touching, of course; there were far too many outsiders for that. But the Ser Illara kai di'Leonne—the kai, the heir to the Dominion—had found her comely enough, and by his nod, and the nod of the Tyr'agar, she knew that she was very close to being betrothed. In the Lord's sight, she had played her harp, and in the Lord's hearing, she had given voice to her song, speaking not of a woman's charm, or a woman's love, but of a great warrior's deeds: Leonne the Founder.

It was untraditional. It was unfeminine. Unbecoming a meeting of a young woman and a young man who might, if the young man's clan granted approval, marry.

She had thought, perhaps, that that might be the end of it, but no—the Tyr'agar, or perhaps his son, had proved insistent.

Meeting during the Lady's dominion had been a muted affair, although the ceremonies surrounding it had been more precise. She could recall, clearly, the Tyran with which the kai Leonne had been surrounded; she herself had been guarded by the Tor'agar Adano kai di'Marano— her uncle—and her father, Widan Sendari par di'Marano. Her aunt had taken the palanquin at her side, and Serra Fiona had been chosen as her father's companion.

Although her father's words were gracious, perfect greetings, they were not friendly; she could hear, beneath their rare musicality, reluctance, anger, worry. Perhaps, just perhaps . . .

But the Serra Diora was her father's daughter in almost all things; she was no fool. The Tyr'agar's offer was no offer, and to refuse it—she forced herself to sound pleased with the union whenever her father could hear her speak.

And because she was young, she believed that she had fooled him completely. She had no desire to destroy his clan, or to be the cause of his clan's destruction; she was fond of Ono Adano in her own way, although she detested his son.

"Na'dio."

The Serra Diora di'Marano lifted her head and let the strings lie. In truth, the samisen was a mournful instrument, and she greatly desired the Northern harp; it was the companion of her youth, and her youthful lessons.

Of the many lessons she had learned, this was first: to speak without being heard; to pitch words so that they traveled to one listener, and one alone, no matter who else might strive to catch them. "I do not wish to be like Fiona."

The Serra Teresa was too well-mannered a woman to show her derision. Her smile was gentle and graceful. "You will never be like the Serra Fiona."

"He has his harem," Diora continued quietly. "And his concubines. I did not choose them. I do not know them. They don't know me. How will they feel, when I come to the heart of their dominion, to rule?"

"They will feel," she said, "as Alana did when Alora, your mother, first arrived."

"And that?"

The lips of the older woman turned up in a rueful smile. "They will resent you, and fear you, depending on the strength of their security in their husband's affections." The smile dimmed. "This husband will not be a mere par to a Tor'agar; he will be *the* Tyr'agar, when his time comes, and with the Lord's blessing.

"Truth, Diora?" The older woman paused a moment, staring into the glimmering light that could be seen through the windblown leaves from their place upon the Pavilion of Restful Repose. Diora could almost taste her hesitation—and she knew that she would not like what she heard, for Ona Teresa rarely called her Diora, and only when her mood was heavy or grim. "Very well. I will give you truth.

"For the concubines of a Tyr'agar, life is more . . . difficult. The Leonne blood runs in the veins of all those who are born to the husband—to *your* husband—and the blood itself is legitimate, whether it is recognized as such, be the children born of concubines or no. Leonne has ruled these lands for hundreds of years—but the crown has not always been passed from Tyr'agar to kai in a straight line. There have been factions. There have been internal revolts.

"In fully one third of all cases, when the kai Leonne becomes the Tyr'agar, he has his male half brothers executed. It is not done lightly, but it is also not done by a man who is secure in his power.

"The current Tyr'agar has lost one war, and that, badly; he has lost lands, and respect, and he is . . . ill-loved. His son, Ser Illara, is young, and perhaps he will remove the shadow under which his father has placed his clan by his failure. But perhaps not. It is likely, in my opinion, that he will have his brothers killed in one way or another by the time he takes the Tor Leonne."

Diora said nothing although she made her own vow: not to meet these brothers if her aunt was correct. Not to like them.

"It is quite likely that you will be feared and hated in your turn—because yours sons will displace their sons, and perhaps, in the end, murder them."

"I'd not—"

"And *if* that is what it takes for your sons to survive, you *will* see it done. Trust me, Diora, Na'dio—there is no connection so strong as that of blood to blood, and of the blood connections, none so strong as that of a mother who protects her children."

"And they would not kill me?"

"They would not dare. You are the Serra. Their lives are measured by yours, once you are given the harem—or wives would too often die mysteriously.

"But when my mother—"

"Hush. You know what I mean, when I speak." Diora saw her aunt's ivory hand curl a moment, as if at a spasm of pain. "And your father is not the Tyr'agar; your father is so far away from being a man of import that it didn't matter."

"It seems so—cold."

Serra Teresa frowned.

"Diora," she said, the word sharper than was her wont, "you go to the harem as woman, not as child; do not expect any in the harem to treat you as anything else. You will not *be* a child, you will be *my* niece, and there is no better training than the training I have given you.

"Win them over with your gift. You know how."

But in Father's harem, I'm loved, Diora thought bitterly, *through no artifact of gift or curse or will.* But she did not speak it. Because she knew what Ona Teresa would say: that love was for children, and only for children. It was, of course, another lie—because the Serra Teresa di'Marano had loved the Serra Alora en'Marano as dearly, as deeply, as had her husband. Diora knew it, and knew that her father knew it as well; she did not know if Ona Teresa understood just how much of her loss she spoke with, on those rare occasions when she mentioned the Serra Alora en'Marano, dead these fifteen years.

But of course she must know it; she had trained Diora to listen, and to listen well, to the voices of the men and women that surrounded her; to understand, clearly, that those voices spoke in a far deeper and a far truer way than the words in which they were wrapped and covered. *We all have weaknesses,* she thought, looking at her aunt from the corner of her eye as the shadows darkened her face.

"Na'dio," her aunt said softly, the edge gone from her voice as if it had never existed at all although the sting of its cut still lingered. "The desire to be loved—it is a false desire, a madness, a weakness. If you let it, it will control your life, and it will lead you down roads, in the end, that even the damned don't travel." So soft, her voice. So soft and so completely certain.

The Serra Diora began to play the samisen in the wake of that terrible certainty.

1st of Emperal, 426 AA
The Tor Leonne

The Radann kai el'Sol was not allowed to see the Flower of the Dominion; nor was Jevri, his servitor. While the kai el'Sol was disappointed, he was not surprised. The man whose genius had been brought to bear in the creation of the dress itself was beside himself with frustration and not a little annoyance.

"What do you mean, we *can't* see her? Who's going to do the final fittings? Who's going to take the dress in, or take it up, or alter its train, or—"

"Jevri, *I* have no objections to your presence. I believe the Tyr'agar himself has no objections, as she is not, technically, a member of his family until two days hence. But the girl's father and the girl's aunt have insisted that she will remain within the harem—and bound by harem conventions in the strictest sense of the word—until the day of the wedding itself."

"But he's not even a ranking clansman!"

"He's Widan," the Radann said, with just a hint of distaste. "But more, he's protective. This marriage and this match—it will make his family; I'm certain he's intelligent enough to see that for himself. He doesn't want anything . . . untoward occurring. She is heavily guarded now, all of the time. There are those who might—just might—consider taking inappropriate action to deflower the Flower; it would be more of a blow to the Tyr'agar and his family than a simple assassination, especially were word of it to come out after the wedding. Ser Sendari simply seeks to protect the interests of his clan, as any prudent man must."

"I don't care about his clan—the work—the time we've spent—"

Fredero laughed. "I assure you, Jevri, the dress itself is obviously a work of art. There's nothing that can be done to it that will rob it of its glory."

The Serra Diora di'Marano did not like the Tyr'agar. She did not trust him. Neither of these reactions surprised her; she rarely liked or trusted any of the clansmen. She had not expected that the man who ruled them all would be an exception, and she was not disappointed.

The mats beneath her knees were hard; she became aware of this because she had been kept kneeling for some time. To show her, she thought, her place and her value to the clan itself: beneath those who ruled, but tolerated in their presence. It was less than she had hoped for, but more than she might have been granted before the wedding. She said nothing; did nothing; was in all things pliant. When she was asked to rise, she would unfold slowly, taking care to move as gracefully as if in delicate dance; she would make her way to the foot of the platform upon which these two—the Tyr and his wife—looked down upon the waters of the Tor Leonne, there to find cushions that matched the pale color of the silks she wore, and she would wait until one or the other, the Tyr or the Serra, bid her play or sing.

Or so she told herself; by the fall of shadows in the sun's light, she had been kneeling thus for the better part of an hour, kept waiting, as if she were a seraf. Her hair, she knew, looked like child's hair in its unadorned fall. Like child's hair, or like the hair of a wife in the harem, one not suitably attired for public consumption.

That had been Teresa's choice and in truth Diora favored it—she wished to be as unassuming as possible in the eyes of the clan Leonne. And if the Tyr'agar Markaso kai di'Leonne, the man who by right of blood and law wielded the Sun Sword and bore the Sword's crown, was a careless man who was too used to the authority of his clan's title, his wife, the Serra Amanita en'Leonne, was not. She was sharp as good steel, and if she was not young, she was still comely enough to merit her chair at the side of the man who ruled the Dominion.

The minutes passed, and Diora knelt, silks protecting her from the sun's open kiss, her back turned toward the nearly flawless sky.

"Sendari, you look as if you've swallowed fire."

The Widan stiffened slightly, and then struggled to control the lines of his face, forcing them into a forbidding neutrality that well-suited his title. He also forced himself to bow, albeit it shallowly, to the man who had spoken; rank did not demand it, but respect did, and in all things, even as his daughter below, Sendari strove to be respectful. He hated it, of course.

"Widan Cortano."

"I believe I see your greatly favored daughter. Or at least her back."

Too perceptive, the Sword's Edge. And cutting, as befit his status. There was much about him to fear—the scars upon Sendari's hands were reminder enough, if he needed it. He was not a foolish man; even before he had honed his power, expanded it, increased it, he had known that Cortano di'Alexes was a man to respect. And to fear, if it came to that.

"The Tyr'agar," Sendari said, through teeth that would not, quite, unclench, "is a busy man."

"Oh, indeed. Of course he has summoned no clansmen into his presence while the Flower of the Dominion crouches, unfurled, at his feet. I had heard that you were difficult to negotiate with. I see," the Sword's Edge added, offering a rare and unwelcome smile, "that it was truth."

They stood upon the pathway that led to the Pavilion of the Dawn; it was covered, carefully, with the natural growth of trees, but those trees provided shade for a very particular time of day—a time that had passed with the hours. From here, it was easy enough to see the Pavilion of the Sword, the pavilion from which the Tyr'agar could view the waters of the Tor Leonne with ease and comfort. An ease and comfort that were denied—were publicly denied—the daughter of the Widan.

"Come, Sendari. He will not give the girl leave to rise while you watch."

"He doesn't know I'm watching," Sendari replied, the words a snap of irritation. His lips closed over them, but not before they escaped, and he became tight-lipped and silent.

"Of course he knows it. There isn't a spell of conceal-ment cast in the Tor that he doesn't know about." It was Cortano's turn to smile thinly. "The Sword of Knowl-edge, after all, serves the Sword of God. I'm surprised at you; it took some courage to negotiate the terms that you did with the Tyr'agar. I hear you've become, among other things, one of three personal advisers."

"Indeed."

"It is not a title I myself hold," Cortano continued softly.

"You did not choose to marry and beget a daughter who would catch his errant son's attention." The Widan cast his long gaze across the waters to see the stillness of unmoving silk before he allowed himself to be drawn away.

"I? No. I have little patience for women."

Sendari shrugged. "I have little patience for serafs and their handling. I have little patience for the details of a house. I have a wife who sees to these things while I see to my art."

It was an old argument among the Widan, and comfort-able enough; certainly more comfortable than the sight of a daughter made to kneel, as if she were a mere seraf, for hours on end.

"Indeed. And note that I have been delving, and you have been standing, half-cloaked, on the edge of a lake, watching a woman's bent back." The Sword's Edge

frowned, running his hands through the length of his beard.
"Leonne is arrogant."

"The prerogative of one who rules."

"Indeed."

Moonlight, welcome moonlight. The Serra Diora, boxed
in on all sides by the confines of a garden far finer than
any the Marano clan had ever owned, breathed freely for
the first time that day. The stone beneath her legs was
cool, as was the breeze; there was no Tyr above her, no
humbling etiquette to follow by which the whole of her
father's clan would be judged.

Alana and Illia had massaged her back and bathed her
with scented water while the moon rose in the darkening
sky; they had offered her food and water, although she
declined both, and in the end, sang her cradle songs while
she lay, close-eyed, upon the mats in the harem, this unfamiliar place which was to be the unwelcome substitute
for home for these coming two days.

Teresa did not come to her, and for this she was grateful; Teresa was not like Alana or Illia, in the end; there
was very little about her that was soft, that understood
how to be gentle.

*Because this gentleness that you value is illusion. For-
get it, Diora, forget about it. You will be the wife of a
Tyr—and this softness is* not *what a Tyr's wife must have
if she is to survive.*

Yes, Ona Teresa, she thought, as the moon's face illuminated her own. *Yes.*

But she thought: I will choose my own wives and my
own harem, and we will make a lie of what you've told
me, and it will be our secret. Knowing, as she thought
it, that it was a girl's thought, not a woman's thought, and
that it was foolish, willful, childish.

But her arms ached, her back hurt, and the songs that
she had heard tonight were songs that, in two short days,
she would never hear again; she told herself stories, as she
had often done, to comfort the fear of the responsibility
she faced. Did it matter if the stories were true or not?

No; it was only their comfort that she required, and she
was not stupid enough, not even for a moment, to actually
believe in them.

* * *

"It is not a good sign," Teresa said softly to Alana. The sun was at its height, but clouds had come in from the east, rare enough in their beauty that they could not be disliked, for all that they were a dangerous portent in the matter of a Leonne wedding.

"No," Alana replied. Neither woman spoke of the obvious clouds. Their eyes, from the height of a gently sloped hill, were held by the standard of the clan Garrardi. Just arrived, less than two days before the wedding was to occur. The Garrardi clan ruled the Terrean of Oerta, and if they were not the richest of the ruling clans, their lord, Eduardo kai di'Garrardi, was still Tyr'agnate. To come, so late in the season, for a wedding of this nature was unfortunate.

The more so because, as both Teresa and Alana knew, his offer had been one of the six that Ser Sendari had, with so much difficulty, refused. They were both glad of it, for in the matter of husbands in the Southern lands, the choice of a good one and a bad one was literally the choice between life and death—unless one were, perhaps, the Tyr'agar, marrying a daughter out of the clan. Such a man, one could not afford to offend with a death.

Ser Sendari was not the Tyr'agar.

And Eduardo di'Garrardi was not a man famed for his even temper or his good use of the concubines that he did have. He had no wife; he had never deemed any woman suitable or worthy, until he had first seen the young Serra Diora. There was only one man he could lose her to in safety.

It had not been an insignificant part of Serra Teresa's decision to . . . encourage the interest of Ser Illara and his clan in her niece. The other, of course, had been the fact that Sendari could not refuse the Tyr'agar. As her father, had he been so approached, could not have refused him.

"My eyes aren't what they used to be," Alana said softly, "but I'd say he looks displeased."

"I would have to agree. It is unfortunate."

"Ser Jarrani came early," Alana offered, her voice weaker than was her wont.

At that, the Serra Teresa smiled warmly. "Yes. The *Tyr'agnate* Jarrani kai di'Lorenza did indeed come early. As did the Tyr'agnate Ramiro kai di'Callesta." The richest of the four Tyr'agnati, and the one least liked by the clansmen for his trade and barter with the Northern Empire.

"Lamberto?"

"*Tyr'agnate* Lamberto, Alana. We are not in the harem." It was a reminder that the Serra should not have had to make.

Alana shrugged. "That we're not," she said, unrepentant.

Worry and fear are no excuse for graceless discourse, Teresa thought, but she did not say it; Alana was coming of an age where such brusqueness was considered almost acceptable. Almost.

But not in the Tor Leonne. Acknowledging this without apology, Alana continued. "The Tyr'agnate Mareo kai di'Lamberto came two days past. Late as well."

"Yes. But his delay can easily be blamed," could in truth be blamed, "upon his great hatred of the Tyr'agnate Ramiro kai di'Callesta. The fighting between the Averdan and Mancorvan cerdan has grown increasingly costly, and I believe that both of the Tyrs have privately petitioned the Tyr'agar for intervention."

Neither would receive it, and Teresa believed that Ramiro di'Callesta knew it; she was certain he observed the request for form's sake. If Ramiro had been forced to deliver his lands to his Northern enemies, he had also inflicted the greatest damage upon their armies; the Tyr'agar would prefer to see him politically disadvantaged, strategically occupied.

The loss of the war was still a bitter blow to the Dominion; the loss of the lands in Averda and Mancorvo, a painful one. Although it was not spoken of directly, that loss was laid at the feet of the Tyr'agar and the clan Leonne. Annagar was not, like Essalieyan, a land of over-abundance; to lose those fertile fields had been costly indeed.

And it was not, of course, just lands that were demanded; not just lands that were given. As a sign of future intent, the Tyr'agnati, and the Tyr'agar, had been forced to surrender one member of their family into the keeping of the Imperial Court.

The demon Kings called it a "hostage exchange," and indeed, there were hostages in the Tor Leonne—men and women whose very presence was a slap in the face of the

Dominion. But of these, at least, Teresa was secretly glad, for it meant, on rare occasions, a glimpse of a man that she might, in another life, have called friend.

Kallandras of Senniel College.

It was a complication that she, of the Voyani, did not have to make.

Many also cared that we, or—and she said, interrupting. Were like our own to ignore forever drew anoccasion. Teresa thought that she did not care. Blais was coming in an age where their brokenness, was considered almost acceptable. Among

But not to the Tor Leonne. Accords for the without anything. Voyani can make it. The Voyanne Marent, for all subjects some reduced, her trust as well.

Yes. But the oldest own party, the hardening, foolish you be flatment open hand near the of the the Tyr created Hanno of Callesta. The fighting boys out the Averdan and Mancorvian cannot has drawn to be a simply closely and belches that both of the Tyr have privately antici pated to offer them everything.

Neither would preserve the and belief. Believed that Ramiro di Callesta knew it; she was Teresa be against the eastier for later doubt. It cannot but been though to deliver his favor to his wretchen and how he had also imbued the greatest of more then only.

Teresa Candid prefer to see this possibility the had seen sympathetic occasion.

The does nothing yet and still to interview to the Dominion, the loss of the Lords in Averdan and Mancorvia because one. Although it was not spoken of directly, the loss occured at the tactless, the Tor they and the Leonne Numerous as not like Lussalyen, a land of ego committed to force them. Knowing they had been there balked.

And it was not just these, just those that were the mandan that time their chance. given for a distant time the of the Tyr agreat. And he forages and deterning to surrender the members of their family into the keeping of the important house.

The dominan Forus will take a thought explained, and indeed there were someone in the T'a Leonne someone without whose very presence had slip in the face the

CHAPTER EIGHT

"She is a pretty young thing," Marrana ATamalyn said quietly. "Not, if I had to guess, her most notable trait, although it's certainly likely to be the most commented on." She lifted her head and brushed strands of hair from sun-lined cheeks. "It's good to see you," she told her companion as she lifted the decanter in which water had been left. "We do not see visitors nearly often enough."

Her guest very politely lifted his goblet to his lips; in truth, he was thirsty, and the offer was welcome. Brushing golden curls from his eyes, he smiled and the smile removed years from his face. "I assure you, ATamalyn, the honor is mine."

"Well, if you insist." She paused, lifted her own goblet, and narrowed her eyes. "But I must say, Kallandras, that you don't often show this oblique an interest in this sort of affair."

He smiled again. "I've met the young woman in question a handful of times. Each and every time she seemed a child. To come for an Imperial wedding and to discover that the bardic college did indeed translate the name and the title correctly—well, it makes me feel my age."

"And that?"

He laughed. "Now, Marrana, is that delicate? Is that becoming?"

Her arched brow was the politest answer she tendered, although it wasn't the only one. Marrana ATamalyn had served two full years as hostage in the Tor Leonne; in another year, her tenure here would be ended, and another chosen to take her place. Neither she, nor her companion, envied the person who would become a hostage in this court; they both knew the Dominion well enough to understand that they were foreigners in a land that viewed all but blood ties with suspicion.

Essalieyanese, in a land where the Imperial Kings were called demons because of the heritage of the blood that bound them so tightly to just and wise rule.

"Are you here to play?"

"I believe," Kallandras said, "that honor has been granted me."

"Or requested of you?"

"No," he said, the blue of his eyes trapping the light beneath a somber expression, "I made the offer. It is my gift, on a day of such glory." He paused, hovering around an explanation that he did not owe her. In the end, he chose to give it anyway. "I wished to come. To see the Serra Diora and her aunt. Marrana, I know it's hard for you to be here. To me, this is desert land; I expect it to kill almost anyone who passes through it, in one way or another."

"I wish," she told him softly, her voice momentarily aged, "that I, too, could see it that way. Maybe, if I were only here for a month. But these lands—I think that this is what Essalieyan would have been without the Kings.

"I'm not a particularly upstanding woman, Kallandras; I have my own past, and it's certainly colorful."

He smiled; it was true, and more to the point, still worthy of song in Senniel College.

"But I pray now. I pray that these—not the Tyrs, of course, but almost all of the rest—find, in their time, Kings of their own who will rule with wisdom and justice.

"Do you know what they do to the god-born here? What they do to the women who bear them? The children they burn alive, and the mothers as well—if they're lucky." She ran a hand over her eyes, lifted her fan and brought it up, as a shield, from the momentary ferocity of her expression. "My apologies, Kallandras. Of course you know. We all know it."

"It's oft been observed that knowledge without experience is like a body without a heart; it doesn't live. I understand, Marrana." He reached out then, and lightly touched her hand. His gaze grew distant. "It's hard. Even I have been tempted to interfere."

"Not half as tempted as I," was the quiet, bitter reply. "And probably ten times as successful."

"Marrana, what do you gain by judging yourself this harshly?"

She was silent.

"In the Empire, you are a woman of power. You will return to the Empire with a clear understanding of what that power means, for good *and* ill."

"I feel as if I'm a girl again, Kallandras," the older woman said. "You're from Senniel. You might remember the life that I led as a girl."

"I remember the song, ATamalyn." It had not been a pleasant life. It had barely been a free one.

Although the hostages had some leeway in discussing economic ventures, they had little power; if they had freedom, they were not held in regard. They did not speak about the gifts of the talent-born in the Dominion. They did not speak of magery, or of gods, or of politics. And they did not—could not—interfere in the matter of slaves, of slavery.

This, Kallandras knew, was the silence that was breaking the back of Marrana ATamalyn.

What he didn't understand was why it concerned him. Age, he thought; perhaps it was just age. Age or no, it discomfited him. While the sun shone in the thin-walled building that housed most of the Imperial hostages, he drew out his lute and began to play.

He was rewarded by the bark of Marrana ATamalyn's laughter—a harsh, unfeminine sound. A welcome one.

In the heat of the early day, Kallandras of Senniel College very quietly and very precisely sang all fifty-five of the verses of "Marrana's March." And every chorus in between.

When he left the quarters of the Imperial hostages, he had spoken at least a few words to all of the ten, and stopped to play with the families of men who had chosen to bring wives and children with them. He had imparted news to those hungry for home; the news was mundane enough, in its fashion, but the very banality of it seemed to wake these men and women to a certain hope. He noted with satisfaction that in the quarters of The Ten there were no serafs.

But he departed as the sun reached its height, promising the youngest that they would hear him sing upon the day of the wedding between the kai Leonne and the mysterious Flower of the Dominion, a woman said to be so beautiful that the kai Leonne had been struck, as if by storm's lightning, upon first glimpse of her.

The men rolled their eyes, and the older women; the younger women were rapt in their attention.

"Bards," Marrana said, snorting. "A bunch of sweet-voiced liars."

Kallandras smiled and bowed, retreating into the exposure of Southern sky, and then retreating farther into the shade of leafy bower. The path that wound its way to this building was not so finely tended as all other paths within the Tor Leonne, but it was still pleasant and easily traveled. Easily rested upon.

Salla was in his lap almost before his back touched bark and his thighs cool ground; her strings were humming faintly as his fingers danced harmonics in the stillness and solitude of the Tor.

Or perhaps, he thought, as the winds shifted, just stillness.

"That was well sung," he heard a woman say.

"If I'd known," he replied, pitching his voice so that it would carry only to her ears, "that you were listening, I most certainly would not have chosen to play each and every verse."

He could hear her smile, although he knew that he wouldn't see it; not today. There was about the vibrancy of her voice a special glow—something that spoke from the heart to the heart, yet at a great remove.

"Contrary though it might be, I must disagree. But I was willing to listen to each verse, and each chorus, as you call them in your Northern style. Gently done, Kallandras."

"Gently done? I've been accused of many things in my life, but seldom that."

"Perhaps. But very few would think a man who calls the winds themselves would be gentle."

"Very few know that I call the winds, Serra Teresa." The light caught the diamond that bound his finger. He had tried to remove it once—and only once. For nothing less than the Lady's absolution would he ever try again. Power, it seemed, had its cost.

"Ah."

Their oldest mutual memory. The most dangerous one, when each stood on the edge of a different abyss, everything laid bare, every emotion so clear that it could not be mistaken, could not be dismissed. No matter that those emotions had been stripped of history, of context—they existed, primal, a force which events drove one to, as if all emotions waited for such a collision, such a communion.

And such communion was almost always painful, yet it held a bitter joy, a dark one. For a moment, a messy, vulnerable moment, one wasn't alone.

Kallandras of Senniel, Kallandras of a brotherhood that was older than even the famed bardic college, understood isolation too well.

He changed the subject. "Were you watching?" He had known that she might hear his song and even be amused by it, for those who could sing with the voice could almost always hear it when it was unguarded, but he also knew that her talent would not grant her the benefit of Marrana ATamalyn's words. He had the irrational urge to protect the ATamalyn's words from the ears of the clansmen; to protect her weakness, her vulnerability. As if such craving—for justice, for wisdom—was weak. No matter. Without those words, his song had no context by which it might be judged compassionate; indeed, without context, it might have been mockery, albeit gentle.

"I? No, Kallandras of Senniel." Her voice carried a genuine regret.

"Then one of your serafs?"

"No," she said again.

He smiled, although he guessed she wouldn't see it. "Am I never to walk the Tor Leonne without the watchful eyes of one clan's spy or another's?"

"Never," she replied. "You are known here, and feared, in your fashion."

"You are too serious, fair Serra."

"It is a serious occasion, a wedding of this stature. There will be no Festival Moon for us."

"But at least there will likewise be no Festival Sun."

She laughed, and her laughter was the musical, light

grace that he associated only with Annagar. Only with the
Serra Teresa and her perfect niece. "You know us too well
to be a stranger, Kallandras. You know death too well to be
a Northerner. And yet you understand Marrana ATamalyn too well to be a clansman."

"You flatter me."

"Do I?" He heard the trace of lovely bitterness in the
two syllables. "Is it flattery to be told, however gracefully, that you seem to have no place?"

"Ah, but I belong to all places, surely."

"Is there a difference?"

Silence. The play of wind through golden ringlets,
and in the distance, through silks of a very fine sari; the
same wind, beginning to end, touching them both in different ways.

"Serra Teresa," he said, knowing then that she was
ensconced in a harem where the open sky did not trouble
her brow, "it would be my honor if you would choose to
join me in the palace of the Imperial hostages."

"At the request of?"

"Marrana ATamalyn, of course." Men and women did
not meet openly, and they did not meet alone, when they
were of a clan that ranked as high as Marano. But such
was the way of people, great or small, that they found
ways to meet that defied no rules, and broke all.

"I think," she replied, after a long moment, "that I
would like that. But I think it unwise, Kallandras of Senniel, to meet under those auspices. I will be watching the
ceremony from the Pavilion of the Moon, and after it is
complete, and the dusk has given way to the Lady's
dominion, I will retire to the Eastern temple. Meet me
there, by the Fount of Contemplation."

It was not until after he was certain that she no longer
listened that he laughed, thinking of the last fount, the last
meeting beneath the face of the watching moon.

And then the laughter died abruptly as he thought about
what she had—and had not—said. The Serra Teresa
di'Marano was a woman of the clans before she was anything else; she would not betray her family, or her
family's plan. But she had told him something, when she
had decided to speak at all, although only when the music
of her words had faded did he choose to understand it.

He was being watched.

And if she knew, so intimately, the details of such a small meeting as his meeting with Marrana had been, then she was privy to the results of the surveillance itself, or some part of it.

Which told him much indeed.

Thank you, Serra, he said, but only to himself. This type of gift, by its very nature, demanded no recognition, allowed for no display of gratitude.

"I do not understand," the Widan Sendari said—and the saying of those four words was no simple task for a man who wielded the Sword of Knowledge, "what your interest in this particular Northern minstrel is."

"No," Cortano replied quietly. "You do not."

The silence between them was the silence of struggle, common among the Widan, who disdained the more vulgar displays of conflict. Which was just as well; the open clash of the Sword of Knowledge was often deadly, and in a way that drew the unwanted attention of the clansmen.

At last, Cortano smiled thinly. "He is gifted, Sendari, in the way that the Northern minstrels sometimes are. He bears watching for this reason."

Sendari di'Marano was gracious enough to accept this concession for what it was; a peace offering—and a partial truth. More, he would not be trusted with; or so Cortano's neutral expression suggested. He did not know if the Sword's Edge was aware of the Serra Teresa's power; there should have been no chance whatever of that, but it seemed . . . odd that Cortano would ask Sendari to play the unwelcome part of spy at this time.

Or perhaps this was a test—another test. There had been so many of them, beneath Cortano's watchful eye.

"Very well," Sendari said quietly. "If you deem it necessary, he will be observed. But a question, Cortano, in return for the burden of the surveillance."

"Ask it."

"Is this at the behest of the Tyr'agar?"

The Sword's Edge smiled in a fashion that reminded Sendari, immediately, of his informal title. "No." The finality of the single syllable stopped the questions that had already begun to follow. "And I have now told you more than I wished you to know. Give me no cause to regret it."

It was real.

The offer, its acceptance, its consequence.

She had known it, of course, from the moment the cerdan who bore her palanquin had crossed beneath the arched gate of the Tor Leonne proper. Had known it before that, when her father, stiff and gray as if he'd suffered a fatal wound, came to tell her how proud he was of the fact that his daughter, above all others in the Dominion, had been chosen worthy to wed the kai Leonne, his voice all the while carrying so much anger and apprehension that she thought even one untalented must be able to hear it.

And the arrival of the golden chains by which she might adorn herself, the sapphires and the emeralds, the rich, deep red of ruby and the sheen of opal—these, too, had made the reality of her future more solid.

It was as if each little detail had become one step in a path that led to the clan Leonne.

And the dress itself was the edge of the precipice.

She saw it, as if from a great distance; saw it, as if it were a weighty stone that had been dropped into the center of a deep, still pool. Or of a deep, still harem. Her father's wives.

They could not believe the fall of the fabric itself, and long before Diora was allowed to stand—still and perfect upon a pedestal designed for dressmaking—the harem of Sendari di'Marano was a moving hush broken by little whispers and the awed gush of breath that knows the confinement of no words.

Illia spoke first, handling the garment with more care than she handled a babe. "I have never seen a dress so fine." It was true, but she spoke again, as if she knew the words were too meager for such a gift. "Look at the silk, Alana. Look at these—they're pearls. And here—" Silence again, as she lifted the hem of the dress to the light that came in from the open screens. That light was trapped by crystal, and cast against the walls and the mats of this most private room.

"Yes," the Serra Teresa said quietly, and they all turned at once at the sound of her voice. "They are diamonds from the Northern mines. A gift from the Imperial hostages to the woman who will one day be consort to the Tyr'agar himself."

Alana bowed, as did Illana; Illia dipped her body in a graceful bend at the waist, but she held the dress, and this was not so public an occasion that its safety was less important than her manners.

Only the Serra Fiona remained distant at the approach of the Serra Teresa.

"How do you know that they're real?" Illia asked, as much to break the uncomfortable silence as to satisfy her curiosity.

"I was there when Sendari grudgingly handed them, stone by stone, to the Radann kai el'Sol." Her smile was less than kind, but not less than perfect. "And the Radann kai el'Sol has Lambertan blood, even if he chose to forsake his clan's name to join the priesthood. Those stones are these stones." She crossed the room gracefully. "I am not certain which I prefer, the Northern glitter, or the Eastern pearl."

For the first time, the Serra Diora spoke. "You prefer the diamond," she said gravely, "because it is clear and hard and perfect; it will not break or crack with time, and in the light of the Lord's Sun, it shows its heart, and its heart is fire."

The Serra Teresa's dark brows rose in genuine surprise. "And you, Na'dio?"

"You tell me," she said.

"Na'dio." Alana's stern voice was not unlike the sound of a fist striking wood.

But the Serra Teresa seemed unperturbed by her niece's near sullen display. "You prefer the pearl, because it comes from the water, and its sheen is soft as silk; because each pearl comes from its shell, unique; because the pearl takes its sand and its salt and in the deep of a water that holds its mysteries from us, it makes a thing of beauty. You love the pearl because it is delicate."

"Yes."

"And that is the way of your blood, Diora di'Marano. That you love what is delicate. What you love, and what you are, these are different things. If you must chose what to *be*, learn from the diamond; the pearl will avail you nothing."

And then, to Diora's great surprise, the Serra Teresa bowed, as if in deep respect, and left the room. She did not wait to see the dress, or to see it fitted.

The General Alesso di'Marente did not trust the Sword of Knowledge. He trusted the Widan Sendari, but made of him an exception. Men who wielded the power of the mysteries were men who made of themselves daggers or blades—and at that, blades without hilts, without handles, things too dangerous to wield—and too tempting to permanently destroy.

They could not be tempted with lands and titles; not in the same way that true clansmen could. Their power, Sendari often said, was knowledge, and they bartered with it as if it were land. Or water. Or horses.

This was more true, he thought, of the Sword's Edge than it was of any other Widan.

But Alesso was curious. And because he was, he had accepted the offer extended him by Cortano di'Alexes, the man who, in Sendari's estimation, was the most powerful—and dangerous—of the Widan. To accept his offer, however, was a grueling affair. The sun was high, and hot, and there were no awnings beneath which a man might find shade in the open courtyard. There was also no fount, no water within easy reach, no cushions or mats upon which to rest.

There were no serafs in the courtyard, and the men who stood to either side of the open arch were armed only with the ruby-edged golden sword that marked them clearly as Widan. The man to the left was scarred by fire's hand, but the man to the right was as tall and proud as any warrior born; Alesso did not wish to try their temper—or his patience—by ignoring their decree.

And their decree was, ignobly enough, that he must wait, without, like any common clansman. He waited, but his patience, such as it was, was completely destroyed by the exercise, and when at last the Widan Cortano di'Alexes emerged, in person, to greet him, he offered a brusque bow and no words at all.

Cortano raised a peppered brow. "It is . . . good of you to wait," he said, his expression completely neutral.

"Yes," was the terse reply.

"I am about to make my rounds of the Tor Leonne, General. I would appreciate your company."

"You have it," Alesso said evenly, "for as long as your company interests me."

Not an auspicious beginning.

But the sunlight in the harsh and austere courtyard gave way to the bower of trees meant to shield the inhabitants of the Tor from the sun's harsh heat, and as they approached the lake itself, a breeze blew across it, cool and fresh. The General won his war, and after a moment, sunlight glittering safely off the surface of rippling water, he spoke.

"We will, of course, be watched."

"Of course." The Widan shrugged. "But I know the Widan set to watch us, and I believe he will hear little enough of what is said."

"I see." Pause. "May I ask who that Widan is?"

"You may, but I will not answer. The identity of a single capable Widan is not of concern to me today. Nor should it be of concern to you, General Alesso, unless what I have to say does not meet with your approval."

"A threat. How . . . unwise."

The Sword's Edge offered the General a rare smile. "I am seldom called unwise, General. It is almost amusing to hear the word and realize it is spoken to me." The smile dimmed. "Almost." He knelt, hiding his expression; his beard fell into the momentary lap his knees made as his hand reached for, and entered, the lake. He did not rise, however, but left his hand in the water as if it were a lily or an anchor.

"If you wished to wage war against the Empire," he said softly, "And I speak, of course, purely hypothetically, what is the first step you would take?"

Alesso said nothing for a moment, thinking about the replies he could make. About the cost of those replies, if this conversation were, indeed, monitored by a Widan who reported to the Tyr'agar—or worse, by a Widan who might enable the Tyr'agar to listen. "I do not think," he said, distantly, "that I would wage war against the Empire."

"The clansmen desire it."

"The clansmen always desire it. For centuries, the demon Kings have ruled lands that are ours by right. For a decade now, they have ruled more, at great cost to us. But it was tried once. You must be aware of it, Cortano; you were a part of the failed mountain expedition."

"It was not a failure on our part," the Sword's Edge said, bridling as any clansman might. "But it was costly; the timing was poor. Many of the Widan perished in the crossing."

"And the Empire's mage-born scholars were a match for the Sword of Knowledge, battled-honed or no." An insult. A calculated insult.

The Sword's Edge kept his face turned toward a lake that moved just a little too much to reflect it. "True enough," he said at last, but coldly. "I ask you to think on this, then. If you were the Tyr'agar—if you could reach that high, and hold what you did reach—could you wage a war and win it?"

"I am not the Tyr'agar," Alesso said softly. "And I would not be one."

"Ah. Then I fear I have misjudged you. Of the three Generals, you were the only one that I felt had the steel necessary to replace the Leonne Tyr as ruler of the Dominion."

The silence that followed was the silence of shock; Alesso di'Marente held himself rigid a moment, his hand on the hilt of his half-drawn sword.

"You are not a child, General. Spoken blasphemy carries no weight unless it is heard, and the Lord of the Sun most certainly will not pluck the words and carry them to the waiting ear of his vengeful and petty Tyr." The Widan rose abruptly. "Do you think this is a test of loyalty? You are beyond those tests here. As am I. Markaso di'Leonne is a weak man, a weak Tyr; his bloodline has never been so diluted.

"Marente is not a strong clan. It would have been, under your rule."

"Enough. I've told you—I do not wish to be Tyr'agar." He paused, weighing his words, weighing the Widan's, coming up with no balance that could be easily read. At last, grudgingly, he said, "I do not have the blood."

"You speak of the Sun Sword."

As it wasn't a question, Alesso did not trouble himself to answer. His hand did not leave his sword.

"Legend has it that the Sword itself will be true to the

bloodline as long as the bloodline exists." It was Cortano's turn to pause, to weigh words; Alesso thought he saw the gathering of caution in the older man's face. Until he spoke. "But Leonne is a small clan. It has been harrowed by its own twice in the last three generations. It is not widespread, and the sons—there are few enough. Let us be plain, Alesso: If the clan is obliterated, the Sun Sword will take a new master."

"And you are certain of this?"

Cortano smiled softly. "The Widan specialize in the knowledge of the antiquities. I am as certain of this as I am of anything."

The sun across the water had never been so bright; the General covered his eyes and turned away from the lake. Then, slowly, his hand grew slack and fell to his side.

"It is not possible," he said. "We could take the Tor, with the right allies, but the strike would have to be quick and complete."

"It would have to be delivered without warning, yes."

"Let us speak then, in your precious hypotheticals. If we were to remove Leonne, the most likely outcome is that one of the Tyr'agnati would step in, after a brief and bloody war, to inherit the waters of Tor. I am not willing to risk the life I have for the benefit of another clan."

"No." Cortano shrugged. "And I am not willing to waste the life I have in the political machinations it would take to ensure your position over the waters. I will give you my support should you manage to secure that title for yourself.

"But I have allies that would be interested in the rulership of a military man, and it is for that reason alone that I have chosen to approach you. Of the three Generals, you are the only one who, in my opinion, has any chance at all of waging a successful war against the Empire.

"If you would agree to wage such a war, I am certain that *they* would provide you with the political aid you might require." And as he spoke these words, the Sword's Edge turned to face the General.

His eyes were as sharp and clear as blue diamonds, and as hard. "Make of this what you will, General Alesso di'Marente. But make your decision quickly."

"I will," the General replied, "make my decision in my own time. If I am to be Tyr'agar, I am to be a man who is not beholden to a Widan, be he Sword's Edge or designate."

Cortano nodded, expressionless.

The sun crept higher into a sky that was bounded by lake and mountain and endless blue, its light changing the shadows cast by two powerful men, alone, on the edge of the waters by which the ruler of the Dominion was known.

Sendari watched his daughter from the distance of years and a bitter fatigue. He knew her well enough to know that she was not happy—but happiness, as Alana was wont to say, was for children, and in a short time, the Serra Diora di'Marano would become the Serra Diora en'Leonne—the woman emerging from the child like a chrysalis. And what might he say to her then?

In the heat of the Emperal sun, he thought her fair and dark; the shape of her face reminded him, like a heart blow, of another face, on the verge of the same delicate balance between child and woman. Yet Alora had never seemed a child to him, no matter that she was sweet and joyful in her quiet, fierce way. He had seen, in his wife, the steel by which men were made great; it lay beneath the front of her heart, and it was unbreakable.

But not, alas, invulnerable. Not immortal.

Fiona did not come to him, and for this, he was glad. She did not relish the attention that was paid to Diora, and while she was happy enough to have his daughter finally leave the harem, she was obviously jealous of that daughter's destination. Women were such strange creatures, at times.

He found himself thinking this, while he, a man, was inexplicably drawn across the courtyard that separated him from the harem of wives made noisy by planning and apprehension, by the hope for joy and the fear of its failure.

He remembered his own wedding night; remembered the ceremony that was held before it. Blushed, to think of his daughter involved in such a human exercise. Froze, to think of what it might be, otherwise. She was not his to protect. The time for that had passed.

The sun was sinking; this was the last day that Diora was to be di'Marano—his daughter, not the kai Leonne's wife. Did that not mean something? Did that not give him the right to be her father, this one last time? He opened his lips to speak, but the only word he could frame was a silent *Na'dio*.

She looked up, met his eyes across the distance that he had closed, and was still closing, and bowed her head prettily. It was not what he desired. The moon was a madness that illuminated his thoughts, casting aside the heat of the blistering sun, the face of the warrior Lord.

He did not realize, until he came to stand before her, that he had come to her seeking, of all things, comfort. Did not realize how deep that need was until she spoke, and at that spoke a single, precious word.

"Father."

Not a question. Not a plea. Not, he thought, a benediction. "Na'dio."

He opened his arms then, and in the light of the Lord's day, he held her tightly. She was restrained, well-trained; she held herself stiff a moment, but when he did not let go, she relaxed, returning his embrace as if she, and not he, were the parent who offered comfort.

And in the height of the second day of Emperal, the Widan Sendari di'Marano knew that he would lose his daughter, his Na'dio.

Of course I'm going to lose her, he thought irritably. *She marries into the clan Leonne.* But he could not shake the shadow, and in the end, he held her more tightly for it. Thinking of Alora. Of childbirth. Of death.

Wondering what might have been, had his wife never borne such a child as this at all. Remembering that, on the dawn of the worst night of his adult life, he had hoped to hate the girl left in the wake of Alora's bloody death.

Even in that resolve, he had been weak.

And the Lord hated weakness.

It was customary, when the Tyr'agnati gathered, for the Tyr'agar to summon his Generals. Although there were four Tyr'agnati to his three Commanders, the message was not lost upon any of the men who chose to attend at the whim of the ruler of the Dominion: that these three men were loyal to the Tyr'agar, and that they, among them, commanded armies that could be turned at any time against a wayward Tyr or a rebellious Terrean.

It was a loosely followed rule that the Generals held no lands; that they were taken from the ranks of the par— close enough to the power in a clan to understand what power meant, but far enough away from it that their military demesnes could not be deemed a threat to the clan Leonne.

The Tyr'agar Markaso kai di'Leonne had chosen to break this rule once, at his own discretion. And he, as most of the Leonnes through history, had been given little cause for regret. His Generals served him, and they served well.

But today, the sun's face burning the sky a deep blue, one of those Generals turned his face to the Lord's chosen ruler and saw the shadow he cast upon it. The Tyr'agar was not a man in his dotage; the waters of the lake kept the Leonne clan as healthy as age allowed. But he was not a man in his prime; his face bore the wind's lines, and those lines had been etched farther into flesh by failure, by a string of failures, some larger than others.

He was not a warrior of any note, although his sword hand was competent enough; he was not a man who rode well, for he rarely had cause to leave the Tor Leonne, and upon the plateau where the seat of his power rested, there was little enough room to truly run a horse. He was not tall, not in any way prepossessing; indeed, the only thing that spoke for him at all was the blood which, by the Lord's law, granted him the right to preside over the lake as if it were his own.

The sun rose; the Tyr'agar spoke, quietly, with the Tyr'agnate of Averda. And with every word that left his mouth, with every nervous movement of hand, of limb, Alesso saw a man grown smaller and feebler in stature until he was just that: a man, a man whose brow was ornamented with the Sword's crown—a simple circle of sword's steel bent round by the hand of the Lord and placed upon the head of Leonne the Founder centuries past. A sign, or so the Radann said, that the warrior clans of the Dominion were to forgo the opulence and decadence, the baubled weakness, of the North.

Yet this Tyr wore Northern gems upon his fingers as if they were a part of his hand; called for Northern harps, suffered Northerners to live in the Tor Leonne at the whim and command of Northern Kings. This Tyr was weak enough that he had seen fit to cleanse his clan of brothers who might have contested his rule and his competence.

Surely, he thought, as he studied this suddenly foreign, slightly obtuse man, *this cannot be the Lord's choice.*

"General Alesso."

"Tyr'agnate."' The General bowed. "You seem ill-pleased."

"Do I?" The Tyr'agnate Eduardo kai di'Garrardi cast a sidelong glance at his unexpected companion.

"You have not joined your Tyran—or your peers—in the usual celebratory festivals that are opening up like wild plants across the breadth of the Tor."

Eduardo shrugged. Bending, he picked up a smooth, flat stone. He held it in his palms a moment, as if absorbing its heat, and then, before the General could interfere, skipped it across the surface of the waters of the Tor Leonne as if the lake was a mere lake, a thing of common mud and weed, like any other lake in the Northern heartlands of the Dominion.

Alesso di'Marente raised a dark brow, but said nothing. He stood with his hands behind his back, and if they curled in momentary anger, the gesture was unseen.

The Tyr'agnate of the Terrean of Oerta was a tall man. He could not be said, in a classical sense, to be a handsome one, but his face, sharp and narrow as an eagle's, nonetheless had the force of expression and the leanness of line that spoke of power, of a man of power. In all things, Eduado kai di'Garrari was either absent or first.

He clothed himself like a clansman when he went among the clans, and like the Tyr'agar himself when he came to the Tor Leonne, and he rode a horse that was finer than any horse the Northern plains had bred in living memory: Sword's blood. Alesso appreciated all of these things, but distantly, dimly; he saw in them a man whose love for finery was, in itself, that most dangerous of things: A manipulable weakness.

But it was dangerous to the Tyr, and not to the General, and the fact that the ruler of Oerta had deliberately arrived within a hair's breadth of open hostility made that foible an attractive one. The Tyr'agar was not a man well-loved.

"Your early absence was cause for some concern," Alesso said quietly.

"And you've been sent to enforce my good behavior?" Eduardo laughed. His hand found another stone; there were many of them upon this particular, narrow path, each flat and smooth—a temptation to the young. And the unwary.

The General caught the Tyr'agnate's hand before the stone flew. They regarded each other a moment in a tense silence.

It was Eduardo who spoke first. "You bear him no great love and no great loyalty. Were it not for you, our losses would have been greater, our capitulation far more complete." He spoke, of course, of the war. But that war was seldom openly discussed—and then, not within the Tor Leonne proper. Not if a man were wise.

Eduardo kai di'Garrardi was not a man said to be wise by any measure, but he was canny, and because of his recklessness, unpredictable, which made him dangerous.

Alesso took the compliment as if it had never been offered.

And Eduardo did not choose to take the implied criticism of his silence. "And the clansmen know it as well. He keeps you as General because he has not yet hired assassins capable of killing you. And he might, one day, choose to pay the price of the—"

"Enough." If the war was not spoken of in the Tor, there were things that were never spoken of, no matter where a man might stand. "Eduardo—Tyr'agnate—you do yourself a disservice by this reckless behavior."

"And you are now to fill the role of wife, to tell me how I must behave in the presence of clansmen?" He wrenched his wrist free and flung the stone with an easy, deadly grace. Thrice it skittered across the surface of the lake, but the fourth time it touched water, it sank.

"No, not that." Alesso looked at the lake, and then at the man who stood beside it in such foul humor. He had carefully studied the intricate complexities of the relations between the clan Leonne and the clan Garrardi, and he could see nothing—nothing at all—that would account for this hostility. Perhaps some internal argument, some disagreement over a major trade route. Certainly, the Tyr'agnate Jarrani kai di'Lorenza seemed content enough in the presence of the Tyr'agar for the moment, and it would be Jarrani who would benefit from Garrardi's loss, if it came to that.

Yet he was certain he would know of such a major breach between the two clans, and there had been no hint of it.

He wished, of course, some certainty that this was not a momentary anger, a fleeting hostility. "I would not attempt to hold the reins of the ruler of Garrardi. No sane man would."

That pleased the Tyr'agnate's vanity, and he subsided a moment.

"But I would agree, cautiously, with your assessment. He has cost us both much." Without speaking another word, the General turned his head toward the path that led, between trees and shrubs and carefully scrubbed rock, to the dwelling that housed the Imperial hostages.

Eduardo kai di'Garrardi spit.

A good sign. Or it would have been, had he not spit into the lake itself. Alesso di'Marente was not a superstitious man, not a man driven to cowardice by the edicts of the Radann and the edicts of the Lady. He lived by the law of the Lord, and the law of the Lord was the rule of the powerful over the weak—for in such a way, the Dominion was made strong.

But to spit into the waters of the Tor Leonne was worse than to spit upon the Sword's crown, for the waters and the ownership of the Tor that protected them were the measure by which the ruler of the Dominion was truly known.

Those and the Sun Sword.

"It may be, Tyr'agnate, that you and I will have words at our leisure in a more suitable clime."

The Tyr'agnate's eyes narrowed into edges as he met Alesso's neutral expression. And then, shrugging, he bent and picked up another rock. "As you say," he said softly, and Alesso thought he caught a glimmer of a smile across the face of the Tyr.

General Baredan kai di'Navarre might as well have been Tyran for all the use he would be to Alesso. In fact, Baredan kai di'Navarre was one of the few heads of a clan, even were that clan of little import in the political field, whose service the Tyr'agar had chosen to accept. He had come to the Tyr'agar, and the clan Leonne, as a young man in the time of the Tyr'agar Carlos kai di'Leonne; he had given his blood oath, and been taken into the ranks of the Leonne oathguards, the Tyran upon whom the clan Leonne depended. There were no oaths more sacred than these—not even the oaths that bound the Radann to their Lord, separating them, in the only honorable fashion, from the families whose blood gave them both life and a name. None, Alesso was certain, had been more fervently offered than those by a young Baredan di'Navarre, and if that youthful fervency had been dimmed by the harsh reality of experience, his honor still bound him to the words that had begun his distinguished career. No longer Tyran, he was General, and of the three, second to Alesso in terms of the men he commanded, and second to none when it came to holding the Tyr's ear. Unlike General Cormano, Baredan had acquitted himself passingly well in the Imperio-Dominion war; he had the respect of the cerdan who served beneath him.

He had the respect of the Generals who served at his side. A pity, that. Something that one could genuinely regret, for Alesso was one of those Generals. He observed his friend's interaction with the Tyr'agnate Ramiro di'Callesta on the pavilion at the height of the gentle slope.

The two men met openly, of course, upon the Pavilion of the Sun; it was bowered and sheltered from the sun's full heat, and the water offered in silvered pitchers was water drawn from the lake of the Tor Leonne itself. Those waters were always cool, no matter what heat strove to warm them; they were always refreshing. And they were offered to dignitaries of import. The Tyr'agnate Ramiro di'Callesta was such a man. The richest, even with the loss of his lands by the humiliating Imperial treaty, of the four Tyr'agnati, he was by far the most cunning and the least predictable.

It was the task of the Generals—General Alesso di'Marente, General Baredan di'Navarre, and General Cormano par di'Valente—to protect the interests of the clan Leonne, and their duty often brought them into subtle conflict with the Tyr'agnati, the four men who, by birth and dint of maneuvering skill, ruled just beneath the

Tyr'agar, beholden to him by vows that were, in Alesso's opinion, worth the blocks they were cut into.

And no oath seemed less tenuous than the oath given by Ramiro di'Callesta—the man who had been most hurt by Leonne's ill-considered and poorly planned war. Baredan understood this, but not with the precise intellectual gleaning of Alesso or Sendari; to him, it was instinctive. It came like breath and with just as much thought. Of the four, he favored the most dangerous with the pleasure and privilege of his company.

Callesta was the most dangerous clan in the Dominion, and only its position—at the border of the Empire itself—had stopped Callesta's complete political dominion over the clan Leonne for its catastrophic failure in its war effort. If Alesso had proved himself to be the most capable of the Generals, Callesta—*this* Callesta, not the father who died upon the field—had proved himself to be the most canny of the Tyrs, bound by no strict rules of honor, no outmoded warrior code, no rigid Radann's edicts.

Of the three Generals, Alesso knew it best. It was under the command of the young Ramiro di'Callesta that General Alesso di'Marente had made his mark. They were tied by that, and separated by it as well; men of power became wary of men of power. It was a fundamental truth of the Dominion, and neither sought to deny its effect.

As he approached the pavilion, the Tyr looked down and smiled. "General Alesso." The smile was genuine, as was the smile that Alesso di'Marente returned. They clasped arms, as men do, and then drew back, regarding each other with an almost open appraisal and a mutual satisfaction. Time had robbed them of little. Yet.

He could not use this man.

He could not trust this man.

Of the Tyrs, Ramiro di'Callesta gained most by the rule of a weak Tyr'agar, for he was subtle enough to manipulate a man who did not take the advice of what counsel he had well.

Beneath the sun of the open sky, upon the Pavilion of the Sun, of the Lord himself, he met the eyes of these two men without flinching. Baredan di'Navarre. Ramiro di'Callesta.

And he knew that he would have to have Baredan assassinated. Ramiro di'Callesta was a canny man; war would take him before the assassin's blade—but such a war would leave Averda open for division, and Averda was the most fertile and the most prized Terrean in Annagar. He considered, briefly, an alliance with the Callestan Tyr; the winds took the thought. Ramiro and Alesso were alike in too many ways, but Ramiro di'Callesta's bloodline had a history that predated the founding of the Dominion—and in the Dominion, blood counted for much. Too much.

Winds take you, Cortano, he thought, as he smiled. *Winds take you. The Lord won't.*

On the day before the wedding which had drawn these diverse men together, Alesso di'Marente took the first step upon the path that would lead him to greatness or obliteration. Took it without moving, without raising sword, without lifting voice. Oh, he knew there was more to the war than these two men; far more. The path that would lead to the lake was a shadowed path, one that would never clearly be discerned if approached with timidity.

He was not a young man, but he was not an old one; he could see the length and breadth of the future unfold before him as a series of obstacles, of challenges, each of which must be met.

And more clearly than that, he could see the Sword's crown, the Sun Sword, and the rippling perfection of the lake itself as it lay beneath his feet.

One did not pray to the Sun Lord.

One vowed.

Alesso di'Marente committed himself upon that day, at the sun's height.

"Some men will tell you what they like," Alana said quietly as Diora knelt on the mats before her feet. "Some won't."

"That's helpful." Illia's voice was thin with sarcasm and tension. She rubbed oils into the palms of her hands and then carefully, evenly, spread them down the length of Diora's exposed back, starting first with shoulders that were hard and tense. "And you won't have to worry about *men;* just *man.* One. He'll not give your services to a visiting dignitary; he'll not expect you to warm the arms of a man he wishes to reward or comfort."

Serra Diora di'Marano said nothing.

"Na'dio?"

She nodded, the dutiful daughter, and rose as Illia stepped aside. Her skin was white and flawless, but it was cold, and the pliancy of a feminine body had been replaced by steel. "Na'dio,' Alana repeated, her voice almost a croon. "Please. You have nothing to fear."

Diora bit her lip—a habit that she'd thought lost to childhood.

Illana en'Marano turned her unusual honey-colored hair away, and Illia, bold and beautiful still, cast her gaze toward the cushions that lay, unused, against the far wall.

"It's not true," the girl who stood in twilight said. "Because if I had nothing to fear, none of you would be afraid. And you are. You all are."

"That's nonsense," Alana said, gruff now because she was old enough to speak gruffly. But she was the only one who spoke, and the two words were forced and heavy.

"You've been here for two weeks," Diora continued, her skin white as clouds or lilies. White as the dead. "You have your serafs, you have your days in the open sun. You've spoken with the wives of the Tors and even the Tyrs upon occasion, because each and every one of them has attempted to find out more about *me*." She lowered her head, tilting her chin toward her pronounced collarbone. "And I know you. I know you, Illia. I know you, Illana. If Fiona would tell me nothing at all about Ser Illara, it would not surprise me; there has always been distance between us.

"But not you. You are all my mothers. You've asked, in return for the information about *me* that you've given, whether that information is true or no."

"Na'dio, it is not nice to accuse your mothers of lying." Alana's voice was as dry as fallen leaves. As light, as empty of life.

"No, and I hate to be in such a position that I must do so," was Diora's grave reply. "But you've *asked,* and you've *heard.* Will you tell me nothing?"

"You've met Ser Illara," Illia said, her voice almost completely devoid of expression. "Yet you have never chosen to tell us what your impressions were, and of all of us, with one exception, you've always been the most perceptive; you are Teresa's kin."

Silence.

It was Diora who broke it, because only Diora could. "I have only seen him twice." Lifting her chin, she accepted Illia's hand and stepped upon the pedestal, light and lithe in movement because such movement had become natural to her. She waited for the dress to be brought, her eyes dark and distant, a window into a summer storm, a thing of heat and wind and death. "He is a man like his father."

"Ai." Alana bowed her head a moment, and then lifted it, wiping her brow with the palm of her hand. Wiping her sari, staining the silks dark with sweat. There were no serafs here; their husband had forbidden the intrusion, and in a perverse way they were grateful for the lack. Illana picked up the heavy fan and began to push the still air around the room in a gentle mockery of breeze. "He's not a gentle man," the oldest of Sendari's wives said. "But he's not a brutal one. He's a man. If you're lucky, he'll take to the fields of the lower plains with his father's Tyran, and he'll leave you to your harem."

"I think," Diora said quietly, "that he's killed a wife. At least one. It's in his voice, in the way that he watches them." She was not thinking, not clearly, to speak so plainly. But she spoke as the buttons of the dress were, one by one, undone, and the silks laid across her standing body as if they were a clansman's shroud.

"You've seen his wives?" Sharp question, that; Illia's voice had thinned in the way that the Serra Teresa least liked.

"Yes—but at a distance. One of them—younger, I think, than I—is with child." She closed her eyes, recalling that chubby face, the shadows beneath the eyes, the pallor of skin gray with unease, even fear. Had he beaten her? She could not be certain; could not ask. She was, after all, a Serra, and the business of a Serra was not the way a man treated the women he owned. "I do not think he is pleased by it."

Silence, longer. At last, Alana said simply, "He saw his uncles slaughtered as a child. He sees a threat in his brothers—and that threat is real. He has killed two wives."

Illia's intake of breath was so sharp Diora almost

laughed, although the well of laughter would have been a bitter thing. She was a Serra; she held her peace.

"Why did you not tell me?" The second youngest of Sendari's wives said to the oldest, her pale cheeks flushing with an unbecoming anger.

"What good would it have done? He will not kill *this* wife, and this is the only wife that we must concern ourselves with."

"How?" Diora asked, the single word forced from between pale lips.

"Na'dio, it is not necessary."

Diora heard two things when Alana spoke. The first, every wife in the harem understood: that she would not speak further upon the subject, no matter what entreaties were made or threats offered. The second, what every wife in the harem feared: that the deaths had been unpleasant, slow affairs.

"Why?" she asked softly.

To her great surprise, Alana caught her hands, both of them, and pressed them together between her own, holding them as if they were an injured bird; hard enough that she might stop them from flailing or fleeing, yet gently enough that she might offer no injury, no hurt.

"The kai Leonne has reason to fear his brothers. They fear him; they fear that he will choose his father's course, and have them executed when their father at last passes on.

"His life is not secure. Men who fear for their lives react harshly. He believed that these two, his wives, were in the employ of his brothers; he could not prove it, and therefore could not demand his brothers' deaths. But he sought to end the threat that his wives may have posed. Na'dio, he will not harm you. Because your life and his life will be inseparable; if he falls, you will fall. If he rises, you will rise. Your children will be his heirs, and it is their blood that will claim the waters and the crown and the Sword."

Diora left her numb hands in the hands of the oldest of her father's wives, the oldest of her mothers. "They weren't guilty," she said softly, only the barest hint of a question in the words.

"Does it matter?" Alana replied. "You have seen serafs killed all your life for their mistakes and their folly—or the mistakes of their masters. Did those deaths hurt you?"

Her hands, now, were a cage, not a nest. "Did they weaken you? Did you notice them at all?

"They *are* serafs, in every possible way. Honored, if their husband is honorable, and doomed if not."

"Alana—" Illia began, but Alana's glare silenced her.

Diora was cold. And perfect. She lifted her chin, raised her shoulders, arched her back ever so slightly. And she met the angry eyes of Alana en'Marano, hearing what had not been said.

That Sendari's wives were no more free, no more privileged, and no more protected than Ser Illara's. That they had been given no more choice in their fate and their disposition than his wives. That she, and she alone, was granted a measure of safety because of who she would be.

A clanswoman. The wife, not the concubine, not the sister-wife.

"Safety," Alana said grudgingly, "is for the dead." She released Diora's hands, and those perfect, fair hands fell at once to the young woman's sides. Then she turned and stalked out of the room, as graceless as a clansman come newly from the field.

Come injured from that field.

"Forgive her, Na'dio," Illana said unexpectedly. "This is so terribly hard for her." She lifted a string of tiny, perfect pearls that, end to end, was as long as her arm. "She thought—she hoped—that Sendari would never have to see you married. He refused the *Tyr'agnate* of Oerta." She reached up, and Diora bent, stretching her neck for the clasp of cool gold. "She has lost one son and two daughters, and the daughters of a concubine are always born for barter."

"But she thought you would be safe. And you will be. But it is not—it is not what she desired. You know that Alana has always worried."

Illia brought combs, jade combs, of a green that was almost blue it was so dark and deep. She wound them round with flowers, small white blossoms that had been carefully preserved in the waters of the Tor Leonne for just this purpose. She found a small footstool, and gained its squat height. There, she caught the long, fine strands of Diora's shining hair and began to bind them.

And Diora di'Marano turned her face to pale screens that hid from sight the waning of the day. For on this day, no sunlight was to touch her skin. She was to be given, unglimpsed, in all her finery, to the clan Leonne and the kai Leonne in the time between the Lord's dominion and the Lady's. For that was the time of men, and of the meeting of man and woman. They brought rings for her hands, more gold, the shimmer of opal on bracelet, the twine of worked metal in links wide as her delicate wrists.

She bowed her head, lifted her arms, spread her fingers, striving now to regain the calm and the poise for which she was known.

Wondering, as she did, where Ona Teresa was, and if she would see her at all before she was taken forever from the heart of Widan Sendari di'Marano's harem.

Dusk came quickly, a fall of stately hue across the horizon. The concubines of Sendari di'Marano had become quiet with that peculiar anxiety a mother shows for her children; only the Serra Fiona was graceful and perfect as befit her rank. She had, with the inattentive consent of her husband, procured a sari of such quality that she hoped in some way to stand out among the gathered clansmen, once they had had their fill of the so-called Flower of the Dominion.

But even she had to stare in a wonder so spontaneous it was, for a moment, devoid of envy, as the doors slid to either side of the great room, and the Serra Diora di'Marano stepped at last into the open air, Sendari's concubines carrying her train. Her head was bowed, and in the light of the dying day, the pearls seemed flat and unremarkable, nestled as they were within the sheen of her black, black hair; she was delicate, graceful—in all things, the embodiment of her title.

Awe gave way to movement; the Serra Fiona di'Marano was meant to accompany her husband, and he had stepped forward, reluctant and heavy, as if the years he had lived had somehow doubled at the sight of his daughter. He did not glance at his wife or his concubines; he did not so much as acknowledge the men with which his daughter was surrounded. They stepped to either side of her to allow him passage, and closed once he was within their circle. They were Adano's Toran, and Adano, one of the five Tor'agar who served the Tyr'agnate Mareo di'Lamberto, could be seen down the slope of the hill, waiting, his clan's crest a brilliant splash of color on a high pole.

"Sendari," Fiona said, as gently and reverently as she possibly could. "It is time." But her voice was laced with the first display of anxiety; there would be no palanquins and no horses for this walk, and the clan Leonne waited.

Ill-omened, to start the ceremonies too close to the Lady's time, or too close to the Lord's. But if they did not hurry, they would suffer those omens, and the clan Leonne was unlikely to be gracious.

He stepped toward his daughter and away from his wife, wondering for just a moment why he had chosen Fiona, she chattered so. He was awed, as Fiona was; as awed as the Toran that his kai had personally selected for his daughter's protection. But his awe was not a man's awe; not a woman's awe; it was the terrible wonder of a parent who sees, truly that his flesh and blood is *not* his flesh and blood any longer, but a thing separate, a thing unknown, a thing lost.

Na'dio, he wanted to say, but he opened his mouth upon a different word, two words. "Serra Diora."

Did she flinch? Did she stiffen? He could not be certain, and he realized it was because, indeed, the sun had fallen.

"Widan Sendari," she replied, waiting.

"I would be honored if you would allow me to escort you." He did not, could not, speak the words that he felt; there were no words for that.

But she seemed to hear them anyway, as she so often did, his perceptive, his beautiful daughter. "Father," she said, softly, so that even the Toran would have had to strain to catch her words, "I would never choose another."

They began to walk. He felt a perverse pride when he saw the pale face of his oldest concubine and realized that she held her tears at bay. She had become, on occasion, an embarrassment, and the Serra Fiona had petitioned him, twice, for her removal. He resisted her, for the moment, and he thought that he would continue to do so. Because Alana understood what Na'dio was to him; she was almost that to Alana. They were, in this, of a mind.

He heard the waters before he saw them; they walked a path that revealed the lake only at the last moment. The

Tyr'agar had chosen the dwelling for that reason: it would shield his kai's chosen bride from the prying eyes of lesser clansmen until she reached the platform of the lake. Then, and only then, would they see what he gifted his son with.

What Sendari gifted the kai Leonne, however reluctantly, with. The Flower of the Dominion.

There was a hush in the air, an expectancy. The night was coming. Had night ever fallen so quickly? He wondered, unwilling to hurry his step. Unwilling, at the same time, to slow himself, for fear that she would pay the price of an ill-aspected union. And angry at himself for the suspicion. He was *Widan*, not common clansman. He knew better.

"Father?"

He had stopped, at the bend, the water yards away— and the clan Leonne. The smile that he offered her would have to do, and in the lowering light, he thought it might.

But she answered it by reaching up, quietly, and passing her arms round his shoulders. Pressing her head, with its awkward combs and pearls and jutting pins, into the center of his chest, as if to catch the sound of his heart. As if to bring herself as close to it as she could one last time.

He held her, moving quickly, catching her a moment in his arms. She raised her lips to his cheek, touched his wizened skin. Of their own volition, his arms fell away. He heard the good-bye that she had not spoken; was stunned by it.

In the terrible fog of the dusk, he let her go, as if he were not Sendari, but rather a man who observed him with a distant contempt.

Alana passed him, and Illana, carrying the train that trailed, like white shadow, above the greenery. He felt Fiona's hand at the crook of his arm, a gentle, unobtrusive pressure. He almost slapped her, but mastered the anger at her unwanted interference.

Because, of course, she was right. He followed, quickly, the Toran forming up on either side now, two walls, and not an unbroken circle. He saw his daughter's glorious robed back disappear around the bend, and then he heard it: the intake of thousands of breaths, the awed hush of a crowd.

He ran, then, quickly; came in time to see that even Ser

Illara and the Tyr'agar themselves were dumbstruck by his daughter. The kai Leonne took a dangerous step forward.

The Radann kai el'Sol moved more quickly. "Not yet, Ser Illara," Fredero kai el'Sol said, his voice soft and yet completely implacable. "For she *is* the Flower of the Dominion, and you will not wrong her in front of the entire Dominion by acting as husband when the ceremonies have not been observed."

The kai Leonne's frown was a momentary thing; a shadow cast by a cloud passing quickly above in a strong gale. His hand fell to the side as he nodded his assent, but his eyes did not waver.

Those eyes—that expression. Sendari reminded himself that he was Widan; that this was the way of men and women. But he had never seen his daughter—could not see her—as Ser Illara did, as an object of desire, as a physical possession.

"Be steady, Sendari." Teresa's voice. Teresa's disembodied voice. A welcome interruption, which said much.

At least, he thought, *I have the courage to face this. Where are you, o perfect sister?* He straightened himself, found his pride, and wrapped himself tightly in it. He would not waver again. The deed had already been done when he had given his assent to this union. Acceptance came. Late, but it came.

He walked quietly past Alana and Illana and found himself at Diora's side. There, he caught her ringed hand in a firm grip, lifted it, and said, "Radann kai el'Sol, I present to you the Serra Diora di'Marano."

The Radann kai el'Sol bowed gravely; the sun and the lit fires that surrounded the platform in blown glass globes caught the light of the hilt of his sword, *Balagar,* as he did. The sword, passed from kai el'Sol to kai el'Sol since the choosing of Leonne by the Lord of the Sun, was a thing of legend—a reminder that in the world of men, legends still walked.

Turning slightly, Sendari saw that the Tyr'agar was also girded round with a sword, and he knew, as he saw the intricate, ancient sheath, that the haven of the Sun Sword was empty this eve.

This symbol was *the* symbol of Leonne power, this and

the lake, water and fire. The crown was a bauble, an after-thought. To own the lake was a simple affair. But to own the Sword? To own the Sword, one must *be* Leonne. Or so legend said, but it was a well-preserved legend, and Sendari knew that fully three quarters of the clansmen believed it to be true.

As he passed the hand of his daughter into the hand of the Radann kai el'Sol, a curious emptiness filled him, and because it filled him, he did not recognize it immediately for what it was. He watched, as rapt as the clansmen that surrounded the platform and the lake itself, as the Radann kai el'Sol speckled Diora's perfect forehead with droplets of the water of the lake; as he brushed her eyelids with the kiss of life. He could not hear what the kai el'Sol said; nor could he hear what the Serra Diora di'Marano replied.

But whatever it was, it was enough; the Radann kai el'Sol reached out for the sword hand of the kai Leonne, and he stood a moment, bearing the right and the left hand, the man's and the woman's, while he watched the last rays of the sun color the lake and the sky with a glory that its height could not achieve.

CHAPTER NINE

Touching the Radann kai el'Sol felt completely natural, like touching an uncle, or one of the Marano Toran who could, with honor, offer her aid when entering or leaving her palanquin. Her hand could rest in his, could stay there in safety, with no stain of dishonor, no risk of insult. Her fingers, thin and white and ringed, closed around his palm like a delicate trap, the instinct, the need for familiarity, tightening them almost before she realized that she had made her first mistake.

The blush rose in her cheeks; she lowered her head prettily to hide her momentary shame. She was Diora di'Marano, and she was the pride of the moment; she could not—*would not*—in front of so many of her clan's rivals be anything less than perfect. It was a little thing, of course, this clutching, this momentary blind desire for things safe and known—but he would understand what it meant, and she would.

He waited while she composed herself, and when she lifted her face to meet his eyes, his expression was distant, respectful—in all things proper. Yet he waited that extra moment before he began, and she thought, although it might be years before she was certain, that his hand tightened just a fraction as it held and covered her own.

And then, holding her hand, holding the hand of the Ser Illara kai di'Leonne, he stepped back between them, and thence behind, drawing them toward each other and placing the hands that he held—and the hand that held his—together.

Touching the Radann kai el'Sol was like touching the warmth of the god he served.

Touching Ser Illara kai di'Leonne was like touching the heat. For the second time in less than an hour, she startled, shying ever so slightly. Where the Radann's hand had been firm, the kai's was tight.

The roar of the clans erupted around the lake, and the lake's hills and man-made valleys carried the sound, echoing it, giving it a depth and a height not normally reserved for human voice. The kai Leonne smiled, but the smile was not warm; it was not even triumphant; it was a quick thing, like the strike of lightning in the Northern rains—a natural occurrence, and a terrifying one.

She did not move—it would have been the wrong thing to do—but to be still she had to lock her knees and stiffen her neck and shoulders, giving her body a graceful, regal line, evoking a perfect distance.

It was not to his liking; she saw that immediately and had almost no chance to correct herself; he was upon her, around her, his hands upon her face, her neck, his own face so close to hers, so impossibly close, she thought she would never again be free of the smell of his breath, of the heat of it.

She heard the clansmen cry out again in glad approval at this, her first kiss, the first touch of a man who meant her the harm that men meant, but who had the right, by marriage, to offer it.

And in spite of herself, in front of the gathered clans, she was like kindling to his fire, and when he drew back, her body followed his as if the diamonds and pearls so painstaking beaded into the edge of her dress had become attached to the setting of his very fine robe. His smile was not kind, but it was not unkind; it was an expression, she would realize later, that was very much his own, and unperturbed by her, unresponsive to her.

One or two of the clansmen called out a suggestion, an encouragement, that again brought the blush to her cheeks; the Radann kai el'Sol brought his hands together in a thunderclap, demanding silence—or at least, respect. He was a tall man, and a forbidding one, and even in the poor light, he saw well enough to know who had spoken. Or so it seemed to Diora.

The Tyr'agar came to stand before her, momentarily displacing the son. "You *are* lovely," he said softly, too softly, the words devoid of warmth. "A pity, really, that you were born a Serra and not a seraf, or I would never have gifted so fine a creature to so unappreciative a son."

He bowed, and then caught her hand as he rose; where his son's grip had been tight, his was gentle—but it was more of a trap, for she could not pull away from this man, of all men in the Dominion.

"Welcome," he said, in a voice unnaturally loud, "Diora *en*'Leonne. Welcome to the clan Leonne. May you honor us all." And his fingers, beneath the protective curve of the palm of her hand caressed the flesh there lightly, gently. She saw the Lady's Night descending in his eyes as he leaned forward and very properly offered her the kiss of the clan leader, a light press of lips to forehead.

She turned to her husband, to her new husband, and saw his narrowed eyes upon his father's profile, and her heart, like the sun, began its descent.

The Serra Teresa di'Marano did watch the ceremony. But she did not choose to view it from the vantage of the lake, surrounded by the clan that had birthed her; nor did she choose, as she might have, to accompany her almost-daughter upon her final journey as a di'Marano. She watched the ceremony from the vantage of the smallest shrine to the Lady, nestled as it was upon a hill, and hidden behind a veil of slender trees. The shrine, she had graced with the strength of her prayer almost as soon as the sun had begun its descent; she paused now, as the Tyr'agar accepted her Na'dio into his clan. It was done.

Lady help her, it was done.

She clasped her hands together to still them; they shook terribly, and it mortified her, but she could not stop them. The sight of the ring, the single remaining evidence of her binding oaths, did not help. She almost removed it. Almost. It was far too fine for the rest of her apparel; it stood out, the one imperfection in an otherwise unquestionable affectation.

The finery of Marano did not grace her this eve, although it was her right. She wore a simple sari, albeit one of a very fine, very expensive color—a color that was, shade for shade that of the coming night, a deep blue untroubled by moon or star. She was the Serra Teresa di'Marano. She was alone. And she knew what she should be, what she must be, on this very special day. Perfectly composed, dignified, graceful—elegantly happy.

But her heart was as empty as Sendari's had become;

she had realized it sooner, that was all. What she could offer was not fit for the clans, and it would trouble Na'dio to see it so openly.

She stood alone, which was less of a risk at her age than it had once been. Faithful Ramdan, she had sent away, and he, being seraf without compare, had condemned her decision with perfect grace: by obeying it. She was fond of him, in her fashion, but he was not blood. And blood was everything.

Ah, a lie.

A lie, on this fine summer eve.

Alora had not been blood.

Fires sprang to life in the air above the lake, reflected by the waters—the Sword of Knowledge, announcing itself, openly, to the clansmen, at the behest of the Tyr'agar. She heard, again, the hushed awe of the clans and smiled with quiet pride—for the silent awe was dim and short compared to the gasp that Diora di'Marano evoked.

"Serra Teresa."

She did not turn; she did not need to. That voice, she would recognize anywhere. "Kallandras."

He was a shadow in the shadows; she felt it although she could not see it. "You missed the ceremony."

"I heard your song."

"I know." He paused. "I would rather it had been a different one."

She knew what he meant, and after a grudging moment said, "Why? Why sing a cradle song for one who is about to leave childhood behind?"

"Because," the bard replied with his perfect, perfect voice, "that is often the time when one most needs to hear one. Such a song speaks to the heart."

"A child's heart, surely."

"All hearts, in part, are children's hearts. Hers, as yours, is secret now. Hidden."

"Do you need that, in the North? The hidden heart?" She did not deny the truth of his words, because he was gentle; because he was unlike the clansmen, unlike the concubines, unlike Teresa herself.

"Every man and woman has a hidden heart. Or two." She heard the shiver of strings, a light, a fleeting melody, and turned abruptly. His face was shadowed from the moonlight by the shrine; she had brought no lamp with

her, and thought that, this eve, no lamp might be lit; the
fires below were brilliant.

"This is not the Fount of Contemplation."

"No," she replied, twisting the ring upon her finger,
staring at his barely seen face.

He sat lightly upon the Lady's altar. It was a shock, to
see him sit so; she felt the stiffness of her widened eyes
before she could control the expression. Or before she
remembered that she did not need to; the Lady defended
herself, and the Lady's lands were not the Northern lands,
the Lady's followers, not the Imperial lords who were
demon-ruled and glad of it.

"Did you do this?" he asked her. When she returned
silence, he gestured broadly toward the lake itself. The
sounds of merriment drifted toward them, carried by
the breeze, the gentle face of the wind. "Did you . . .
influence the Leonne clan in its decision, the kai in his
choice?"

It was never safe to say all. Never. But to lie to a man
who could hear the lie clearly in her voice, no matter how
she might disguise it with clever, pretty words? "Yes."

"Serra, why?"

How can you ask me that? she thought, but she could
not give voice to the question. Oddly, she felt betrayed.
And then ashamed. These things followed each other
quickly, naturally, stumbling together into a single, wordless whole. In the darkness of the Lady's night, she knew
that she wanted to be understood by someone who did not
hate her, envy her, fear her. Someone who was not
Sendari.

Someone to whom she did not have to give understanding in return. *Lady,* she thought, *are we all to be
such children, always such children, at heart?*

"I gave my word," she said quietly, "To the Serra
Diora's mother."

"I had heard that the Serra Diora's mother died in
childbirth."

"Yes. Died." Her head fell a moment, a sharp dip of
motion; she held out both hands, palms up, before her
face in the darkness. "But she knew that the child was
coming. And she knew that the child was a daughter."

"Who was she, Serra Teresa? Who was Diora's mother?
I hear of her in every word you speak, and yet you have

never named her." He paused, and then added, "I see her shadow in the face of the Serra Diora's father; I see that shadow fall between you, in a land where the only ties that count are blood ties."

The Serra Teresa laughed, a bitter, silent laugh—as ungraceful, as ungracious, as she had yet been. "The only ties that count?" She lifted her hand then, unfettered by the ties that he had so carefully invoked, and as the mage-fires flared above the lake below in an incandescent display of color and pageantry, the emerald that Alora had given her—a stone gained by dint of plea and subtle misdirection from the man who was her husband—caught light, held it, fractured it.

"An oath ring," Kallandras said softly.

"And what do you know of oath rings? What do you know of the oaths that bind them, you who walk unhindered in any land you pass through? You have your voice, you have your training, you have your own name—"

She stopped; he had not moved a muscle; not spoken a word. But he lifted his hand, and she had seen just that gesture once before—it was a gesture that a decade did not erase from memory; rather, it sharpened and heightened. A ring lay there, clearer than diamond, and harder and wilder.

"No oath bound that ring to your finger," she said, when she could find her voice.

"The breaking of oaths bound it there," he said coldly. "And to truly break an oath, one must first *make* the oath."

Humbled, she lowered her hand; he held his aloft a fraction of a second longer, as if a strong wind pushed against his palm and then subsided. "It is an oath ring," she told him. "But not of a kind that is common in the Dominion. Oath rings are plain, a simple band, sometimes less—the twining of hair, the weave of silk knots. Those who wear oath rings—they are the Serras and wives of the clansmen.

"In the North, you speak of love, and even in the South, we hear it sung. We dream, as girls, that love will come and take us, treasure us, make of us women who can rise above the lives the Lord has decreed."

"There is the Lady," Kallandras said softly, so softly that, were she not cursed, she would not have heard.

"Yes. The Lady." She turned from him, her face a face now, not the mask that came so naturally to her.

"I was not his Serra. I was not his wife. I had no part to play in his harem." Her hands fell to her sides; she stood a moment, stiff, head bent, the weight of memory preventing all movement. "I had no part to play in any harem; I was too old to be a child in my father's harem, and too much of an asset to my brother to be granted a life of my own. You know this."

"Yes."

"I went to Sendari a year after his marriage. Adano— our kai, our much respected kai—sent me." The bitterness was now beneath the surface of her words; her words were like glass, smooth and hard and slippery. But they were as transparent, to Kallandras, as the globes of the lamp upon the waters.

He rose; she did not see his movement or did not care.

"Adano wanted Sendari to take the Widan's test. To face the Sword of Knowledge. He had spoken with Sendari about it. Spoken harsh words, in the end; Sendari would not be moved, although he loved—and loves—our kai much.

"Sendari knew, when he saw me, that I carried the word of the Tor'agar. He knew that I was sent because of my gift; knew, the instant I stepped from the palanquin, that I was Adano's threat; the only threat he would offer."

The ring was green in the darkness; green and blue. The color of water, the color of life.

"He was pale; I remember that. I was no happier."

She waited for some sort of comment, some condemnation—something to speak after or to speak against. He gave her his music instead. It was almost enough, but she waited a moment longer. "You are a Serra; he is par. You understood your roles."

"Yes. But understanding is not forgiveness, and neither Sendari nor I forgive much.

"He could not send me back without disobeying the Tor'agar—a slap in the face which he knew would force Adano to respond. But he could not allow me to speak with him alone."

"And you would not do this thing before witnesses?"

"No." There was scorn in the word; it left her voice as she remembered that she spoke not to a clansman, but to a

Northern minstrel. "To do this before witnesses would be to shame Sendari in such a way that it would hurt the clan—and perhaps his chances for success in the test. They would not know the power of my voice—they would only see that he had submitted to the demands and the desires of a woman, a mere sister, in plain view of the Lord.

"He ordered his cerdan to have me placed, immediately, within the small harem that his Serra had gathered.

"It was his right. As brother, he had—and has—precedence." She raised her hand again, lifted it as if to touch the hand of a person just beyond reach. The tips of her fingers stretched out into darkness and fell. "I don't know if he thought it would be punishment to me. I don't know if he thought of me at all, or of Adano and Adano's anger. He is canny, and when he is absolutely controlled, I hear only hints of his feelings in the words that he covers them with.

"So I entered his harem.

"Had I been with the Tor'agar, nothing would have happened. Adano's palace is large, and the rooms within his personal quarters plentiful. I had very little to do with Adano's Serra, his wives, or his children. My rooms there were separate; I had cerdan to guard me, and serafs to serve me, and samisen and harp for company. I was occasionally asked to play for his guests, when his guests were those he did not trust; I was asked to play for his guests when he wished their influence to favor him.

"I was sent to tell Sendari to take the test.

"But as I said, I had no opportunity.

"What I did not realize was that I would have little privacy either. I had no separate rooms; I slept in the hall where his wives slept; I was given the silks that they were given; I was expected to eat when they ate, and to sleep when they slept. I was not expected to entertain my brother's guests in the more earthy fashions, but in all else, I was subsumed by the harem itself, under another woman's rule."

"I cannot imagine," Kallandras said dryly, "that anyone could rule you, be he man or woman."

"You have not lived in the South for long enough."

"No?"

"Have you?"

He offered no answer. She spoke. "I was angry, at first. Angry at Adano, for sending me to force from my brother what he would barely let me force from his horses; angry at Sendari for refusing to follow what seemed at that time to be the only reasonable path; angry at myself, for not realizing immediately that Sendari would neutralize me in whatever fashion he could without bringing harm to our brother's clan. To our clan. Because I was not a young girl, then. I was a woman."

"You are not old now."

She was not in the mood to be flattered by him, although she heard the truth in his voice. "But I found myself liking his wives—the concubines. The Serra herself, I did not meet for the first five days.

"Alana, in particular, I found appealing; she was like one of my father's wives. Not the Serra—not my mother; she was far too perfect. Alana was graceful, yes, and lovely, but she was plump and if she suffered in this life—and she did—it ground the edges from her, rather than sharpening them.

"She knew that I was trapped in the harem, although she didn't understand why, and she knew that I was . . . a stranger. To all harems. I had no sister-wives. She made hesitant overtures, peace offerings in the name of her husband. And I refused them, politely, every one."

"Why?"

"I don't know. I wouldn't, now. Can you tell me that you understand the motivation for your every petty deed long after the motive has died?"

"Yes."

"I am not so . . . unlucky. I remember that I was not as . . . graceful as I could have been." She bowed her head; the seraf's hood dappled her forehead in soft folds as she seemed to retreat into it.

"But it changed when I saw her."

The shift in her voice came as no surprise to Kallandras; he listened, because he had been trained to listen, and because it was easier than speech. Even Salla lay silent in his lap; he could not trust himself to touch her strings. The Serra Teresa's loss *was* loss, and it reminded him, always, of his own. She was so very near to it now.

"She was beautiful, Kallandras, to me and to Sendari—

but she wasn't beautiful in the classical sense. I am, and I was. Not Alora." There was no false modesty and no pride at all in the words that she spoke. There was distance, but not from him. "Her eyes were dark and large, but not round enough; her chin was too square, her lips too full, her face was wide. But these things together, in her face—they were melody and perfect harmony. She was short. I remember that she was short; I thought—I remember thinking—that Sendari's vanity must have forced him to search hard to find a woman who would, by comparison, make him seem so much the clansman in stature. It was not a kind thought, but we were not kind to each other, my brother and I.

"She said, 'You must be the Serra Teresa.' "

"I said, 'You must be the Serra Alora. I've heard . . . much about you.' "

"And she said, 'And I've heard that you were born with a gift that you hope to wield against my husband.' Just that." She shook her head, seeing the past, Kallandras thought, more clearly than she saw the celebrations beneath them both. "He *told* her."

"She was his wife," Kallandras said and for the first time, understood what Alora di'Marano must have meant to Sendari.

"Yes. But not Adano's. Not *mine*. And while I watched this woman who was no part of me, she spoke again."

Alora said, "I have asked my husband not to take this test of his, this test of the Sword. I have no need of such proof of his power, and I will not take the risk. I wish children, his children, and I wish my wives; I have no other needs. If you have come here at his kai's insistence, then speak to *me,* Serra, because if you ask him, if you *tell* him, he will refuse you."

"And you rule Sendari? He obeys your commands?"

"We rule each other, although I don't expect you to understand that." Her eyes were like black lightning in a sun-browned sky. "I don't expect any of the Marano clan to understand Sendari. They never have before." She turned and then turned back, always in motion, flickering like fire, or like cloth turned by wind. "But I understand him.

"He's given me his word, Serra Teresa, that he will not take this test."

"If you know of my gift and my curse, you know that his word won't matter."

"No, Serra, I don't know that. You think you do. We are willing to test this, this eve. If you can break him, he will do as his kai demands; if you cannot, you will leave, and he will no longer live under your threat."

"You are . . . bold for a Serra."

"And the desert fox is bold when he defends his mate."

Silence, then. The Serra Teresa di'Marano watched the Serra Alora en'Marano, wondering how it was that Sendari had managed to find this woman, how it was that she had managed to survive the courtship, how it was that the Lady had offered the solitary younger brother a companion whose love she would have heard in every word even had she not been born to the voice.

"You mean this," she said because she felt she must say something.

"Yes."

"How did he find you, Serra Alora?"

"Ask, rather, how did I find your brother? There is little love between you, or you would see him clearly."

"There is too much love between you, or you would."

"And whose sight, whose vision, is preferable?"

Teresa's frown was momentary; a ripple across a perfect face. Then, smoothly, and because it was the only truth that mattered, she said, "The Tor'agar Adano kai di'Marano's."

"Did you?"

"Did I?"

"Meet your brother?"

"That eve, yes. You never met Alora en'Marano. You could either dismiss her as unfeminine and ungraceful, or you could listen to her. In the end, there was only one choice for me. Sendari and I are . . . alike. It pains me to say this; I believe that he would die before such an admission left his lips."

"And did you use the voice?"

"Oh, yes, Kallandras of Senniel. I did."

He was silent. She expected no less. She had, after all, been taught by Robart of Morniel College, and she knew that, to him, this overt use of voice was anathema. Worse. She would argue, at times, the sun settling into the Lady's dominion, that the subtle use was no less a violation of his odd code of justice—but influence, to Robart, was not the same as force.

In the Dominion, Robart, the only men who have influence are men who wield force; the one is just a promise of the other. It had been meant as a warning, but Robart did not understand that; not then. By the time understanding came, it had been far too late; he had already been broken by her father's machinations.

She waited for some sign of Kallandras' disapproval, some withdrawal. Instead, he said, "And did it fail?"

"Fail?" Turning, she saw that he stood, and that his lute lay upon the Lady's altar, untouched. "I do not understand you, Kallandras of Senniel."

"No. But it is not to understand me that you speak."

"And tell me, oh, wise Northern bard, why do I speak?"

He did not answer. Instead, he said, "Did you fail, Serra Teresa?"

And she said softly. "Yes."

She thought that Alora would be triumphant, but there was no triumph in Sendari's wife; instead, the first display of weakness; a sparkle in the eye, a glimmering blur that spoke of tears, no matter that they did not fall.

"You will return to Adano," Sendari had said, his voice as abrasive as sand-laden wind, and for all that it was quiet.

"Wait, Sendari." Not her voice. It was not in her to beg for any favor—be it even the ear—of her brother, of either of her brothers.

They both turned, as one person, to Serra Alora en'Marano. "This thing, this task, your brother set it. The Serra Teresa is a Serra, and one of whom much good is said. She could not refuse Adano. You can; you have that privilege. Let her stay with us."

"This is not what you said five days ago."

"Five days ago I had not met your sister. It is not just her gift, husband, that sets her apart; without it, she would still have influence. She has about her the Lady's eyes, the Lady's expression. Have her stay in our house. with us; Adano does not need her influence—or the protection such a woman might offer."

"My brother will not allow it."

"Will he arm himself to retrieve her? Tell him only that she wishes to stay—or better, have her send such word—and he will think that she stays in order to better influence you."

"And if she does not wish to stay?" Teresa heard the refusal in every word her brother spoke, and beneath it, his reluctance, yet she was certain, no matter what she heard, that he would not say no to this woman, to this strange, unlovely, fiercely beautiful, dark-eyed wife.

Those dark eyes turned to Teresa, followed by face, by form; it was hard to say what Alora en'Marano did because her eyes were, for their depth of color, bright, almost shining; they seemed to be the whole of her face, some poet's window into a soul that Teresa was suddenly not so certain she wished to gaze into.

"Would you?" The Serra Alora asked softly. "Would you stay with us, be part of my harem?"

"*Your* harem?" her husband said, with just a hint of a wry smile, a hint of vulnerability.

"She can't be part of yours," Alora said sweetly. "The laws of Lord and Lady forbid it."

"But your harem *is* my harem, wife."

"Yes." The sweetness fell away from her face in an instant; she was, Teresa thought, a thing of steel, a thing of terrible danger. "And I would do everything in my power to protect it. I love my harem, and you, and my wives, and their children." He did not see fit to correct her designation of ownership. "I would keep the Serra Teresa if only because I see you in her, Sendari, and I know that, if she learned to love them, too, she would protect them no less fiercely than I."

But there was more than that. At least, Teresa thought there was; she had never felt so uncertain, in her adult life, about the difference between what she heard in a woman's voice and what she desired.

"She offered you what you could not have," the bard said quietly, his voice an instrument. "A position in her harem as one of her wives."

"Was it so wrong?" she asked Kallandras, her fingers folded around the emerald.

"For her to ask it? Or for you to desire it?"

"Either."

"No, Serra. Neither. But were I your brother, I think in the end I would have found the courage to face my wife's disappointment. She said it: You were, and are, alike in many ways. Thwarted by birth, and either of you a match for—a master for—the brother who rules you.

"She understood you both too well."

"She understood us both," the Serra replied woodenly, "and we both needed that from her. I . . . stayed. I used my influence with Adano, and I stayed.

"She didn't fear me. She didn't fear my gift. Not even Sendari could say that."

"No. She couldn't fear you if she could love you."

"I know," was the bitter reply. She spread her hands. "In the North, you have such odd, such unnatural ideas about marriage. And love. About acts of love." Folding her hands as if they were the wings of a momentarily unsettled bird, she continued. "Here, in the South, we are different. There is husband, and Serra, and harem. A husband belongs to the Lord and the clans; a Serra belongs to the husband. And the harem she builds belongs to the husband as well, in theory—but it is her place. There, she might find the love of a woman's heart, a refuge among her equals.

"To be unmarried, among the clans, is to be denied that love. Do you understand this?"

"Serra Teresa, you don't have to justify your actions; not to me."

"And to who if not you? Alora is dead."

"I am not Alora en'Marano." Kallandras' face was pale in the moonlight. He fell silent as merriment, discordant in its cheer and ebullience, wafted up on the breeze. "But I would guess, if I were forced to make one, that Sendari di'Marano shared the Northern, the unnatural view."

"He came upon us," she said, her face as pale as his, as perfect. "She knew, better than I, the look on his face; he said nothing. Offered no word. Left us, let the curtains fall.

"But she left me to run after him, down the long hall. I can still hear the echo of her steps, the heavy rhythm of

her breath, the sound of his name as it rebounded, unanswered, against the walls. I do not know what she said
to him. I do not know how he replied.

"But I know that she hurt, and hurt him; I wept for her
sake, Bard—but for his pain, I think I was glad. And it
was wrong. And I have paid." Again, her hands fluttered.
"Alana and Illana thought Sendari had taken leave of his
senses, if he'd had them at all; he grew up in the harem of
our father; he understood what it meant to be a wife. They
made it clear, as they could, because they loved Alora in
their fashion, as they loved each other.

"He loved her. It burned him. Until I came, until
I stayed, he had never realized how much of a trap it
could be."

"Her death brought no peace."

"No. She died birthing her child, her daughter. *My*
daughter, the only child I will ever be allowed. Had she
been a son, I could hold her, and keep her."

"Tell that," Kallandras said softly, "to any clanswoman
whose son fought in the Imperial war. Averda's lands are
rich with the gift of the fallen."

"Then if I could not hold her, I could hold the hope."

"Serra Teresa, you are of Annagar. What is hope to you
but the breeze that presages the wind?"

"She died," Teresa said, as if she had not heard a word,
"and she called me, because she knew that I would not
hate the babe who was killing her. Who did kill her. She
called *me* because she needed comfort, do you understand? Because she needed comfort from someone who
would not be so shattered by her dying that he could not
give it.

"Do you think me harsh in my judgment? She called
him, Kallandras. I saw." She would not weep, but she did
not need to; he could hear the storm in her voice, the rawness, the momentary wildness. "Perhaps she meant more
to him than I; perhaps not. I do not know. I cannot say.
But he loved her as a man loves, and I loved her as a
woman—and in the end, he took the comfort he needed,
and I gave the comfort *she* needed. In the end, she chose."

"And it was a hollow victory, for you."

"Yes," the Serra said, acknowledging the rivalry for
what it was. "But do not judge me harshly. It was all I
had. He turned from us slowly, inexorably; turned from

the harem that she gave him, from the daughter that he loved.

"We were alike, he and I, both gifted in our fashion. His gift called him, and he went gladly."

"I do not judge you at all, Serra. I have not lived your life, nor will I. I have lost, you have lost, but my gift sustains me in some small way, while yours has been used to bind and cripple you." He came to stand beside her, touching her with words, only words, as he gazed down upon the lake.

"Will she have what I did not have?"

"Who can say? You gave the Serra Alora your word. You've kept it. Take peace from that."

The wind rustled the leaves of the trees that gave the shrine its privacy. Kallandras stiffened, and his eyes went wide, as if he were seeing something in a distance that Serra Teresa knew, instinctively, her eyes would never breach.

"Serra," he said, his voice touching her ears, and hers alone, with just a tendril of fear, "I have been followed carefully since I arrived in the Tor. I have been listened to, tracked, and I believe, tonight, I will be hunted. If I can come again to the Tor for the Festival Moon, I will certainly travel, but I believe it might be a while longer before we meet again."

"And will we?"

He was gone, a blur of shadow and movement so fast that she thought there should have been crashing, the breaking of branches, the disturbing of plant and standing stone. There was silence and the silence was one of wind.

CHAPTER TEN

The first night, the Lady was kind to Diora en'Leonne, in her fashion. In the two Southern Terreans, it was common to sheet the bride to prove to the clansmen that she had come unsullied to the marriage—but in the Northern Terreans, and in the heartlands, such custom did not prevail. For one, there were too many clans who had been embarrassed by it in the past—almost always for political reasons, because there were ways to blood a sheet when the bride had proved somewhat flawed, and it was further considered coarse; an invasion of a man's harem, and a man's privacy. In the three Northern Terreans, the only blood a clansman's Serra was expected to shed was the blood of the afterbirth, and that was not the affair of a single night—or rather, not the affair of this single night.

Therefore, Diora en'Leonne had little to prove to the clansmen who grew mellow or wild with the free flow of rich wine and thick ale. Her husband had less to prove, and when Diora was at last given leave to retire, he remained with the Tyran, drinking as the night waned.

It was the Serra Amanita who, responding to the unspoken and nearly unseen directive of her eldest, rose to lead the newest member of clan Leonne away, and if she was not gentle—and Diora suspected that years and the wind had long since driven all trace of softness from the Serra who ruled the most important harem in the Dominion, neither was she cruel or unkind. Her eyes had the redness of tears held back, her breath the scent of plum wine, the gentlest of the wines, and the thinnest.

"Follow," she said, and Diora en'Leonne obeyed. Strictly speaking, of course, there was no edict that commanded obedience from the wife of a clansman to his mother—but laws of the heart were as strong as the codes that controlled the clans, perhaps stronger, and Diora knew better than to offend the Serra Amanita.

Serafs came to gather her train as she walked away from the lily-strewn waters of the Tor Leonne; they trailed her steps like perfect, silent shadows, remarkable for the absence of noise their movements made. In spite of herself, Diora was impressed, even pleased; these serafs, Teresa herself would be proud to have trained.

They accompanied her to the palace that stood taller than any other edifice upon the plateau, and as they approached, Diora saw that the palace, fine and grand, was built in such a way that the apartments faced the lake; the seraf quarters and the cerdan quarters looked away.

She entered into a courtyard, passing beneath a gabled roof, and between two standing statues who bore, across their hearts, the emblem of the Tyr'agar's personal guards: the oathguards. The Tyran. They were forbidding, she thought; fierce of feature, larger than life. A warning, that those who intended harm to the clan made themselves formidable enemies when they crossed this threshold.

She, who should have found it comforting, found it oddly unsettling. A girl's fears. Unworthy of a Serra of her husband's rank.

Ser Illara kai di'Leonne had been granted quarters near the heart of power; his rooms were only slightly smaller than the rooms his father occupied and no less grandly appointed. The screens here were traced with ebony and jade, and gold was everywhere to be found in the detailing on the wooden beams, metallic imitations of the rays of the light that the Lord cast.

Everywhere, they numbered ten. And ten, of course, meant only one thing: Radann, kai or par el'Sol, or Tyr'agar. The men favored of, and by, the Lord.

She held her breath as the last screen slid open, although until she saw it, she didn't know that it was the last one. It opened into a hallway, not a room, and the hall was long and wide. Paper lanterns hung from beams in the ceiling, and to either side of the hall were small doors, each closed to create the illusion of privacy.

"The harem," Serra Amanita said quietly. "Cross this threshold, Diora en'Leonne, and you have entered the heart of your responsibility. You are young, but you have handled these past three days with grace and diligence, and you are, as promised, comely.

"The clan Leonne will rest, in time, upon the shoulders of your husband. If he falls, you will fall; if he rises, you will rise.

"I apologize," she continued, without any trace of regret, "for choosing some of the Ser Illara's wives for you. You were not in residence at that time, and Illara is a man, not a boy; he has a man's needs, and better those needs be tended by wives than used against him by outsiders. Do you understand?"

Diora nodded. She knew that, married to the Tyr's son, she would come to a harem half-built, and not by her choosing. But her throat was dry.

"I, too, stood upon this threshold. I, too, faced a harem that was not mine." She turned then, catching Diora's glance with the unblinking darkness of her gaze. "It is mine now. Understand, Diora en'Leonne, that you serve your husband, and after him, *my* husband—but the women within these walls serve your husband, and after him, *you*. If they do not please you, and it pleases your husband, have them replaced. You will be given the necessary resources." She paused. "I chose them," she said, her gaze distant, "but they are not mine. I will take no offense at any decision you make. You are the Serra here." She bowed her head then, and Diora returned the gesture with a full kneel, dropping her forehead to the mats.

"These serafs are my gift to you, child. Use them as you will."

When Diora rose, the Serra Amanita was gone.

She knew that the Tyr'agar's wife was not her friend, but in some things, she had just declared herself an ally. In the Dominion, one did not confuse the two, if one truly found friends at all. She looked at the three serafs; they were women, not girls, but they were perfect.

"Come," she said, taking a deep breath. Serafs at her back, catching the train that she would never wear again, she entered her new home.

To traverse the hall took time, and before she had reached the great room at the end of the hall, she could hear the muted sounds of hurried movement; feet that fell

a little too heavily, words that were loud enough—just—
to be considered shouts.

And then the screens were beneath the hands of her
serafs, and with a nod, they rolled noiselessly open. In the
dress that was a gift from the second most powerful man
in the Dominion, the Serra Diora en'Leonne first looked
upon the women who would be her sister-wives, should
she choose to keep them. There were five, a small number
for a man of Ser Illara's rank, and a large number for a
man of her father's.

The first, and the loveliest, was tall and slender; she
wore almost as much gold as Diora herself did, and her
eyes were as cool as the desert night. She held, in her left
hand, the shoulder of a small child; in the harem, it was
difficult to tell when young children were boys or girls if
one did not know them; they were dressed in a similar
fashion. The child was no exception; although the child's
hair had been cut to just above the shoulder, the face
was pretty enough that Diora did not choose to hazard a
guess. She thought the child perhaps four years of age and
was surprised; no one had warned her that the Ser Illara
already had one child.

"I am Samanta en'Leonne," the woman said. Diora listened to her voice, to what lay beneath the words, as
closely as she had ever listened. And she was born to
listen; she could hear all the nuance that even Samanta
was unaware of. Fear. Anger. The loss of fleeting hope.
Envy. "This child is my seraf; he was purchased for me
by my husband at my request."

Diora smiled, but the smile had none of the natural
grace or warmth it should have. The child, she thought,
was definitely Samanta's; his look was too much akin to
hers for there to be no blood between them. Not Illara's?
How unusual. A man did not often like to be reminded of
the past, or pasts, of his wives.

"Samanta finds favor in the eyes of Ser Illara," another
woman said softly as if in warning. Turning, Diora met
the gray eyes of the oldest woman in the harem. There
was truth in her eyes and her voice, and clarity. This
woman, Diora was certain, would make a fine singer; one
whose voice would be strong enough to carry almost any
legend's full dramatic weight.

Her hair was silvered and fine; it fell in long strands

down the gentle curve of her back, held by simple combs and pins. She knelt to Diora, where the first wife still stood in stiff defiance. "I am Serena en'Leonne," she said. "I am the elder here. Illara was my keep when he was young, and the Serra Amanita feels that it is always wise to have, at the heart of a harem, women who know all of their husband's faces. We do not share the nights, he and I—we share his childhood."

Truth. All of it. Affection and beneath it, certainty in that affection. She did not, seeing the woman who would be this harem's Serra, see a threat, either to her own position or to her place in her husband's heart. Much like Alana, really.

"But he listens to her," the first wife said, half-grudging.

"And Samanta does not." Another woman stepped forward; she was, Diora thought, a year older than Diora herself, if that. Her body was slender and supple, and her face quite lovely, but these traits, Diora expected in the younger wives of the kai Leonne. What was remarkable about her face was its lack of harshness; she seemed, as she bowed very prettily, to be too gentle, too happy. Wives were seldom either, but there was something about this one that reminded her of her youth. "I was worried," she told Diora gravely, "when we learned that Illara had finally found his Serra."

"And now?" Her own voice was far less calm, far less pleasant.

"And now, seeing you, I cannot believe you could mean us harm. I'm Faida en'Leonne. I come from the Terrean of Mancorvo, a gift from the Tyr'agnate Mareo di'Lamberto."

It astonished her, to hear the words leave Faida en'Leonne's mouth. Because Faida believed them. Meant them. She exposed herself with such ease and so little knowledge it almost took Diora's breath away.

How can you trust me? she thought, perversely pleased by this woman's naiveté.

"You are—"

"I am the daughter of one of his son's wives." Again she smiled, hesitantly but not fearfully.

And Diora knew who she reminded her of, although it had been many, many years since she had last seen her: Lissa en'Marano. Gone to another clan, and another man, so unfairly, so completely, when Diora herself had been too young to understand her loss. If she even understood it now.

"Faida trusts everyone too easily," the fourth woman said, her voice low and throaty. Yet if the words were critical, beneath them, and around them, she could hear an affection so fierce it could not be questioned. And a warning, implicit in the words: That those whom she trusted were being watched by a woman less trusting and more dangerous. Her first impression of Ruatha en'Leonne: ferocity in affection.

She was almost of an age with Faida, but her eyes had that shadowed look that spoke of hardship seen and felt, of a life lived in shadow, and raised by shadow's whim. Or perhaps, Diora thought, the shadows were only bruises.

She would see them, in her time in the harem. She hoped that she would not see worse.

"Ruatha," the fifth wife said, and she stepped out from behind both Faida and Ruatha. "Faida is often right in these things."

"But Faida still chose to shield you, you idiot," was Ruatha's near-hiss of a reply.

"And how shall she shield me? This *is* the Serra's harem. I am her sister-wife. And as wives, if we are so blessed, we will all bear his children. Even she."

"Yes," Ruatha said, all fire, all awkward anger, "but *her* children will live."

Diora was certain, then, that the shadows were bruises; no woman could be so unpleasantly outspoken and escape them. She was surprised that the Ser Illara kept such a wife as this, although she was lovely in her fashion, and intense as the high sun or the desert storm.

"I am Deirdre en'Leonne," the last of the kai Leonne's wives said, "and when the rains come, I will bear our husband's first child." She knelt, awkward and yet oddly graceful, the rounded swell of the child she carried within evident beneath the fine, cool silks. "Welcome to the harem of Ser Illara.

"Tell us, Serra Diora, what you expect of us."

The Serra Diora nodded almost regally, and then said, "I would trade information with you, Deirdre en'Leonne."

"With me?"

"Yes. I will tell you what I expect—and what I hope

for—in my sister-wives, and you will tell me what he
hopes for, and expects, from me."

Deirdre turned—they all turned—to the placid and
tranquil face of the eldest wife. Serena en'Leonne earned
her name; her expression deepened without darkening. "I
think," she told the wives quietly, "that you might be
about your business for the eve. Deirdre, you've outpaced
sleep for far too long given the precious burden you carry.
Ruatha, tend her, and then yourself; it is likely that Ser
Illara will have dignitaries he wishes to keep happy before
dawn."

"It's almost dawn now," Diora heard herself say.

"Ah. You are right, Serra. Deirdre, we will trust you to
put yourself to sleep. Ruatha?"

Ruatha was tight-faced and pinched, but she nodded and
melted into the screens and the shadows the lamps left.

"Samanta, I think you should send Tianno with Deirdre.
You are still a jewel in Ser Illara's harem, and I believe that
your setting, this night, is in the garden."

She should have taken control; she felt it slipping from
between her hands as Serena spoke. But she found that
she did not want to fight for it. If she could fight
this gracious, this older woman at all. The thinnest edge
of fear sharpened her words; Diora thought it might cut
deeply if examined too closely. She did not.

"And what of me?" she asked, her voice as light as she
dared make it.

"You, my dear, I would be honored to have join me.
Come, share the waters of the Tor with an old woman
who will be of little interest to those that your husband
will bring." She rose then, leaving cushions and silks in
her wake; Diora saw a flash of their color as the lamplight
reflected the sheen of near-perfect weave. "Serra Diora?"
Serena said, extending a hand.

Diora reached out hesitantly, and then brought her palm
to the older woman's and twined fingers with her, as if
she were a child. As if Serena were the sharp-tongued
Alana.

Don't compare, she told herself sharply, as she allowed
herself to be led toward a low table in the corner of this
grand, domed room. *These women are themselves, they
cannot be the harem of Sendari di'Marano. If you're to be
happy at all, you'll judge them by their own standards.*

But she longed for the familiar.

The Serra Diora di'Marano felt something that she rarely felt. Fear. She knew her hand trembled as it rested within the protective custody of Serena en'Leonne's—and she hated it, but she could not make it stop.

"You are safe enough from his guests, Serra. And you are so well presented, so well garbed, that I cannot give you advice or help there. I have truly never seen a bride so perfect grace the Tor, and I have seen many."

"Thank you, Serra—Serena. But there are very few such weddings in the Tor Leonne."

"Tyrian weddings? No, you are right. There are few. I make my comparison rather with the Lord's Consort. And there is a Lord's Consort yearly, at each Festival of the Sun." She smiled, and the lines at the corners of her eyes became evident. "The Lord's Consort is gifted with a sari early as fine as this, and she sits upon the platform of the Sun, tended to and protected by no lesser guards than the Radann themselves.

"She is said to be the Lady's substitute, for the Lady is ultimately too wise to forsake her Dominion to be honored in such a fashion at the height of the Lord's power. He is compelling, and he is attractive, and he is necessary—but he is in all aspects a man, and she knows that she alone, of all of us, is given the choice. She will not put herself into a man's power, no matter the honor offered. But that is what is said. What is done is simply this: A woman is chosen, for her beauty and her grace, and given the seat of honor in the Lord's name for the Festival's duration.

You will see this yourself, if you've not seen it yet, for you've joined the clan Leonne, and the Festival of the Sun is the Leonne festival.

But you have been chosen as the bride of the kai Leonne; you will never be chosen as the Lord's Consort. Alesso would never allow it."

"And tonight, Serena, I will be Ser Illara's Serra."

"Yes, I think so." Gray eyes were steady and unblinking a moment as the older woman met the younger woman's eyes and held them for the second time that eve. "You are younger than I thought you would be," she softly said. "But one is young at one time in a life or another. Come. Take the waters with me, Serra Diora.

Tomorrow, or perhaps the day after, we might speak at leisure about your husband."

Was there disapproval in her words? It was hard to tell, and Diora knew how to listen. Quiet, she took the cup that Serena en'Leonne offered, thinking that it was very hard not to call this woman Serra. Knowing what Ona Teresa would say of that.

He came to the harem after dawn's first light. Serena wisely refused to let the wives sleep until their husband returned to the fold, for only when he finally returned would they know what their duties were to be. Wine, she said, in a tone that implied that this was a well-traveled discourse, flowed freely on occasions of this magnitude and the clansmen were affected by it according to the Lady's whim.

The Lady's whim in the Lord's time could be dangerous; Diora was reminded of this when the screen ground open and Ser Illara strode in.

He brought with him four men; she did not recognize their faces immediately, although one of the four men wore the sun rising with eight distinct rays—the emblem of the Tyr'agnati or their kai.

"Ah, my lovely new wife," Ser Illara said, the words running together almost indistinctly.

She should have tensed, but tension seemed beyond her, and instead, she bowed gracefully, perfectly, groundward.

"The jewel of my harem. The Serra of the kai Leonne." He stepped forward, casting a long shadow in the light of fixed lamps on the wall.

The serafs, unbidden, opened the eastern doors, and the light of the growing day entered the room, a more welcome stranger than these. Diora looked carefully to Serena; Serena was likewise bowed to the ground, her hair carefully arranged in a spill over concealed shoulders.

"Well, wife, have you nothing at all to say to your husband?"

She rose, but not quickly enough for his liking; his hand caught her hair, fingers burrowing into combed and pinned strands as if they were dirt and rock, and a scalable edifice. She offered no resistance; indeed, felt no desire to resist. It frightened her, or it started to; she could not hold onto the fear itself; it was elusive.

But she thought, and oddly, *It is good that Deirdre has left us.*

"Samanta!"

"Kai Leonne," Serena said, lifting her face from the mat and unbending slightly. "Samanta en'Leonne awaits the pleasure of your guests by the Dawn Pavilion in the garden."

"Oh. Good." He turned, overbalanced because of Diora's weight, and righted himself without quite tumbling. "Callesta—she's yours, if you want her." He turned back to Diora, drew her to her feet ungently, and pressed his lips against hers, baring his teeth beneath them.

It hurt.

He laughed; she heard the wine speaking with his voice, and waited, thinking, knowing that there would be more. There was. He caught her hair again, turning her face to the day, to the Lord's light—exposing it for his guests to see. "You wanted her," he said, to one in particular.

The man who wore the eight-rayed sun.

She thought for a moment that he would hand her to the Tyr'agnate; she raised a hand—the first gesture that she had made at all since he'd pulled her to her feet. Fluttering, the hand fell at once to her side; she held it both stiffly and carefully, as if it were a trapped butterfly.

Wondering, as she did, what was *wrong* with her. There was a thickness to her tongue, a slowness to her movements, a lack of focus, a lack of awareness, that the Serra Diora did not suffer. Poison? For a moment, her heart beat more quickly—but it was only a moment. A calm was upon her, a distance, that she could not breach.

"I don't think," the Ser Illara said mockingly, "that she suits you, Eduardo." He laughed. It was not a kind laugh.

Of course, if I wanted it, she would accept you and be gone.

But then we'd never know, would we, whether the child she'd get would be mine or yours—so I rather fear that you will have to accept your loss, in this.

But here: A small taste.

Before she could move—before she could even begin to realize what he was about to do—he caught the wound

cloth of her silk sari and pulled it, hard, burning the side
of her neck and her shoulder with its speed as he tore it
from her and held her by the hair.

As if she were a horse, and he wanted to show a man
her teeth. She flushed; she could not help it. But more
than that she would not do. Humiliation, after all, was a
thing done by two. It required a victim, and she was
a Serra with dignity greater than this.

But not much greater, if she were truthful.

Not in front of him, she thought. *Please.*

For she knew who he was. *Eduardo.* Eduardo di'Gar
rardi, the Tyr'agnate of Oerta. Her husband pulled he
head back, forcing her to arch her back to retain he
footing. She knew—what young girl did not—what thi
would do to the shape of her breasts; what it would revea
to the witnesses. His hand ran across her nipples, a delib
erate provocation of a man that Diora could no longer se
and a proof of ownership.

"It would not shame her, to accept my attention," th
Tyr'agnate said coldly. Diora could hear the heated ang
in his voice, the danger, the threat—and yes, the desire.
am Tyr'agnate, and you are kai—a man who, *in theor*
will rule."

Silence, then. A long stretch, a bitter one.

"I am the kai *Leonne,*" Ser Illara said at last. "Heir
the Dominion, not the least of its Terreans. No kai Leon
since the founding has not taken the Tor, although
ruling clans of the Terreans have come and gone lik
weak political ally. It would shame her and it wo
shame *me,*" his tone made clear which of the two was
greater crime, "and this is all of her that you will hav
see that it's not enough—but perhaps you'd like to sp
time with a concubine as you will *never* have the Se
Close your eyes, Tyr'agnate, and pretend."

He pulled her up, by the hair; pins finally tumbled
darkness fell around her shoulders and her exposed f
lending her modesty that he did not wish. And the
kissed her again and pulled her away to his pers
chambers, the sun shortening the shadows cast agains
finely brushed cloth of the mats, his gait making of h
graceless, lumbering creature.

* * *

"You handled that well," Serena said, as she rubbed oils and salves into the reddened skin of the Serra Diora's throat and shoulder. "The night of such an event is often difficult. Ser Illara is not a bad husband," she continued, as she paused to moisten her hands, "but when he drinks, he is greatly diminished. Do not judge him harshly."

"I am his wife," Diora said, into the cushion that separated her upper body from the mats below it. "I will not judge." She started to roll over, but Serena held her firmly in place.

"Not yet, Diora. I am not yet done."

"I don't remember," the younger woman said softly, as if Serena had not spoken. "This bruise, and that—I don't remember the getting of either."

"And you wish to? You are brave, Diora, or foolish. Treat it as the Lady's mercy."

"But this was done in daylight."

"Yes, during the Lord's time. It is not always so. The Festival of the Sun will have this effect upon your husband as well, although as he grows older, he may gentle." Her tone made it clear that she thought it unlikely.

"Did you do this, Serena? Did you cause this?"

"Cause?"

"I felt . . . heavy. Unable to move. I didn't even want to avoid him."

"He is not a husband who likes struggle, although there are those who do." Serena rose.

"Serena? The question?"

"There, young Serra. The rawness will vanish in a day or two; I suggest that you remain within the harem until it does. They paid a high price for you, the Serra Amanita and the Tyr'agar, and although Ser Illara can, of course, do with you as he wishes, they will not be pleased at any obvious abuse.

At the mention of the Tyr'agar, Diora stiffened. But she did not ask Serena the question that hovered just behind her lips. Could not ask it. "W–where are you going?"

"I?" The oldest woman in the harem paled. "I am going to see Ruatha en'Leonne. She . . . entertained the Tyr'agnate, and I fear that he was less considerate than your husband in his use."

"Can I help?"

"An odd question, but a well-meant one. Ruatha is the

most difficult of Ser Illara's wives; I believe that the Serra Amanita would be happy to see her removed. But if she is a not a good wife, she is a good sister-wife. She is not like you or I, Serra Diora; she hopes, she dreams, of one day being treated as if she were once again a much-loved daughter, and not the property of a clansman.

"I am not certain that she will be happy to see you."

"She won't be."

"She might. Come, if you still desire it, and tend Ruatha en'Leonne with me."

To her surprise, she did desire it, and not until they stood outside the small chamber that Ruatha now occupied did she realize that Serena had not answered her question.

General Alesso di'Marente sat beneath the shadowed eaves of a sun shelter built by the Widan for the Widan; it was made of stone, but curiously smooth and cool, even at the height of day. There were four posts that supported the peaked roof, and upon each post, in relief, were symbols that he did not recognize, although he was learned enough to think them elemental in nature.

He was not a patient man; by dint of will, he had learned to wait, and if he was not gracious, there were few enough to witness the lack. It was not, after all, for the Tyr that he waited; he did not need that level of composure.

No, it was for a man who had made an offer a few short days past that would, if accepted, decide his fate. Would, if successful, mean that he would never have to wait, in the sight of the Lord, for another living man should he so choose. And for freedom of that nature, he was willing to suborn his impatience. The shadows lengthened; the sun had reached its zenith and now sought the comfort of the Western plateau.

Still, he waited. The Tyr'agar and the clan Leonne had retired into the inner sanctum to recover from the previous day's ceremony—a gaudy, drunken affair with, in Alesso's opinion, just enough excess to please the boys who had yet to take their ranks, but not so much that those selfsame boys would have to be censured for the damage they caused. A delicate balance, and one of the few that Markaso di'Leonne was good at striking.

One of the very few.

A seraf came to offer him water or wine. He accepted, politely, setting the goblet to one side while the heat of the day caused beads of water to gather on the face of the polished silver. Something bothered him, and when the seraf returned carrying fruits and moist breads, he realized what it was: for a seraf, the man's movements were ungainly, even awkward. The deference was there, but it was there in all the wrong ways.

"You," he said, the amiability of a long wait gathering around his words before he spoke, "who is your master?"

The man frowned, a quick expression that fell away from his face so smoothly it was clear that he was used to dealing with ill-tempered men. "My master," the man said, "is Cortano."

"And you are a seraf?"

"No." Bending, the man placed the tray he carried beneath the sun shelter's proffered shade. "No more than you."

"Are you Widan?"

"Widan-Designate," he replied, speaking cleanly and clearly and without resentment. "And in four years, should my master so choose, I will have learned enough to be offered a place upon the path that leads to the test of the Sword."

"I see. He must trust you."

"Must he?" The man bowed. "I defer to your superior understanding of politics, General Alesso. For myself, I assume that he understands that my fate is tied to his success, and that I, as Widan-Designate, will respond accordingly.

"If you have any further needs, I will tend them as I am able. The Widan Cortano extends his apologies; he bid me tell you, if you inquired, that he is waiting for an important associate, without whom your meeting is destined to be fruitless."

"I see." He took a breath. "He is aware that I have been waiting for almost half this day?"

"Indeed. As has he."

"Very well. Tell your master that I will continue to wait."

The man bowed, as if the reply had never been at question. But the sun's shadows were long indeed before that wait was rewarded, and as the inches grew, so also did

Alesso's determination that the results of the meeting be worthy of the increasingly humiliating wait. The Lord did not favor those who waited, like serafs, upon the will of another.

But the Lord did not countenance men of no ambition, or men whose gross desires overmastered their ability to plan well. Caught, as he often was, in a dance along the edge of the Lord's unspoken commandment to warriors who followed his ways, Alesso drank the sweet water left in the goblet beside him.

To his great surprise, he found that he was drinking from the waters of the Tor itself. He laughed; Cortano's serafs—or perhaps his students—were bold indeed, or foolish; not even Cortano was, by Leonne law, allowed this liberty.

Refreshed, amused, he kept his vigil.

And it was rewarded.

Cortano di'Alexes appeared, from the depths of the darkness beneath the haven, as the last of the light fled the garden and the evening sky's pink gave way to a blue that would deepen into blackness punctuated by stars. At his side, robed like one of the less affluent Widan, a tall figure walked.

One sweeping glance around the garden told him that the Widan-Designate had vanished; there was no moving life that was not smaller than his hand. His hand touched his sword and wavered there a moment before firmly gripping the hilt; he did not know why, but he felt the presence of a physical danger, a sudden threat.

Cortano di'Alexes nodded at his minimal gesture. "I believe," he said to his companion, "that I have won this wager."

His companion nodded. Reaching up, he pulled back the cowl of his robe to reveal a face that was as pale as that of a Serra born to harem and never ungentled by the touch of the Lord. But a Serra's face could never be so unpleasingly edged, so harsh in feature, so shadowed in look. And a Serra's hair could never be so utterly, completely black.

"General," this stranger said, as Alesso's grip upon his sword tightened further, whitening his knuckles until he could see the bone beneath the skin.

"Alesso," the Sword's Edge said, still well-pleased, "May I introduce Lord Isladar?"

"Lord?"

"Indeed."

Not a title that any man would dare to take in the Dominion. "You may. You may also explain what the subject of the wager that I have won for you was."

"Ah. That? A trifling thing, no more. Lord Isladar and I have, on many occasions, debated the proper use of magic and glamour. I believed that, for this meeting, he should use a binding spell that was more than merely physical; he believed that appearance would carry the day, as it has so often in his travels." Cortano's sideways glance was almost smug—if an expression so undignified could cross that Widan's face.

"Indeed," Lord Isladar said softly. "Cortano felt that you were of a finer mettle than most of the mortals I deal with. He was, in his suspicions, correct. You are not a trusting man, General."

"No." The General almost drew his sword; he wanted the comfort of its edge between him and this associate of Cortano's. "Cortano," he said, his voice deceptively soft, "when this Lord uses the word 'mortal' in that fashion, what does he mean?"

"I mean," the subject of the question replied, "what you fear I do, General. There is a reason that we do not willingly walk in daylight." With a gesture that was sharp and final and curiously like the downward slash of long blade, Lord Isladar let fall the deception of which Cortano spoke.

Bathed in early moonlight, he grew an inch or two; his shoulders were less broad, his hands longer and finer. But it was his eyes that were striking, his eyes that were dangerous; they were a black without end. He smiled faintly, as Alesso di'Marente *did* draw his sword, and the smile was edged with the glimmering of sharp teeth. Unnatural teeth.

Alesso was a man of action. A man. The years when he had been locked within his father's protective harem and coddled with children's tales had long since passed; but having been lived they left traces that time alone could not erase. He was not a religious man by the lights of the

Radann, but he was a man who was entirely immersed in the culture of the Lord. He knew what he faced.

This creature was a servant of the Lord of Night.

"Cortano," Alesso asked softly, "what have you done?"

"I? Very little, General. But if you think that I had the power to summon this creature, you honor me perhaps a little too highly. I could not call Lord Isladar, and if I did, I could not hold him. He is of the *Kialli* among the demon-kin, and the mages who could bind and use the *Kialli* have long since crumbled to dust in the annals of our poor history."

"But they did exist," Isladar said. It surprised Alesso, to hear him say it; he was not a creature that the General would have thought willing to speak of a weakness or a loss, however far in the past it might be.

Almost as if the words were spoken, the creature smiled thinly. "I am not like the kin in many things, General Alesso di'Marente, and it would do you well to remember this. If mortals live brief lives, if their lives are tainted by the concerns of the merely mortal, they are not less dangerous for their lack of years."

"He is trying to tell you, in his oblique way, that the kin are both ruthless and arrogant, and that he feels their arrogance toward mortals is unwarranted in many cases."

"Thank you, Cortano," Isladar said dryly. "But I believe that you requested my presence for a reason."

"Indeed."

"And that reason?"

Cortano did not choose to answer the question; he turned his appraising glance upon Alesso, and Alesso felt as if he stood unshaded beneath the glare of the high sun. "Alesso, this creature is not the only one of his kin to walk our lands in recent years. He is not the only one who *will* walk our lands in the future, and he is not the most powerful, although I would say he is the most dangerous."

"Thank you, Cortano."

"Certainly the most easily flattered."

"Cortano."

"Very well. I told you that I had allies. These allies wish the Dominion to be a force and a power in the new world. But force and power or no, either you will rule it, or they will. Their time is coming; not even the foreign demons—" and he lingered over the word, as if appreciating an irony that was not immediately clear to the General, "—will be able to defeat the army they have begun to build."

"If 'they' are 'destined' to rule, what purpose will I serve?" Alesso's blade was steady. He was aware, as any man of power must be, that a man who had no purpose was usually a dead one.

"We are," Isladar said softly, "unprepared to deal with the Empire of Essalieyan in a suitable fashion at this point. We do not wish to alert our enemies to our presence until such a time as that alarm would do them no good.

"We are not yet at that stage." He paused, weighing his words, or so Alesso thought. "General, the man who rules this Dominion now is a man who has once declared war upon the Empire, no more and no less. He failed because he did not have the necessary tools—or the will—to carry a war to successful completion.

"We wish to see war carried to the Empire again, within the course of this year."

"Impossible."

"Is it? Impossible in your current state? Yes, I agree. The Tyr'agar could not lead an army to victory if it was handed to him. The clansmen are not loyal to him; his loss hurt him much in that regard. But we are prepared to offer you our dedicated, and our *hidden,* support.

"I am aware of what the words Lord of Night have come to mean in the Dominion," he added quietly.

"And you would do this just for the war?"

"No. In time, the worship of the Lord of Night must return to these lands. This will occur in any case; your choice this night does not affect that fact. But I assure you that the will of the priests will be suborned to the will of the Tyr'agar, if that man is a man of our choosing."

Alesso was silent for a long time. At last, he said, "And am I that man?" And he sheathed his sword.

"If you make wise choices, yes, you will be that and more. The Empire of Essalieyan is a land that is vast and more appropriate for the ministrations of the kin than the Dominion. We can make our treaties, General; that the Dominion will be free from the predation of the kin for so long as your blood rules."

There was a glittering in the eye of the demon that

matched the glittering in the eye of the General; for a moment, only the two existed, and in the falling night, they did not look so distinct, so different.

Alesso thought, *You are lying to me about everything but your need for this war.* He smiled. Cautiously, he said, "Tell me, Lord Isladar. You speak of 'we' and 'our.' Who is this 'we'?"

"The Shining Court, General. Newly risen, and destined to be the council from which all power in this world is granted. Cortano di'Alexes is one of its founding members."

The Sword's Edge smiled. "You might become one of its most influential if you choose to support us."

"The clan Leonne will have to perish."

"Of course."

"Any interference in the politics of the Dominion, other than our own," and here, Alesso nodded to the Widan Cortano, "are expressly forbidden."

"Agreed. You will find that most of our number have little interest in human politics, except as it affects the eventual disposition of the humans in question." His smile was unpleasant.

"You and your kind will remain *unseen* until I have been installed as the Dominion's ruler. There must be no word, no hint, of your existence, or my part in it."

"Indeed."

"I will choose my own adviser or advisers, and they will be under my protection."

Silence. "If we feel the choice of adviser unwise—"

"You will live with it. It will be considered a part of the politics of the realm."

"Make your choice, General."

Ignoring the ambiguity of the reply, Alesso pressed on. "And I will want some proof that you are indeed capable of all that you have offered or implied."

"Of course."

CHAPTER ELEVEN

Wittan, 426 AA
The Tor Leonne

It should not have surprised the Widan Sendari di'Marano, but it did. Alesso was a man who lived to surprise. Whether or not the beneficiaries of such pleasantries, Sendari thought, survived his little surprises was another matter entirely—and one not open to debate at this moment.

I intend to assassinate the clan Leonne and become Tyr'agar—but I would be happier to know that you stood at my side. The words still hung in the air between them, chased weakly by those that had followed: details, plans, logistics.

He should have known, though; Alesso rarely asked for the use of magery as a protective measure against unwanted eavesdroppers. He could be relatively certain that the Widan would not detect this use of magic; Sendari was, after all, one of the Sword set to watch for all signs of magic's use within the Tor Leonne, and was hardly likely to report himself.

Markaso di'Leonne, the Tyr'agar, very wisely chose not to trust the Sword's Edge; they were, he and Cortano, in almost every aspect, unalike, save in that they ruled their chosen domains. Because he did not trust the Sword's Edge, he ill-trusted the Sword of Knowledge, but no Tyr ruled who did not, at one time or another, employ the services of a mage; he used three, informing each of them in a slightly different fashion of the events they were to oversee and forbidding each from consulting with the others. Thus he attempted to trap those who might work against him in some fashion, however small.

The Widan, for their part, did their work without speaking to each other; it was wisest. The Widan were known across the Dominion for their unusual obsessions, their fixations on areas of knowledge that no true clansman would consider noteworthy. They were not always known for their ability to maintain the complexity of a lie, and Sendari, as his two compatriots, had decided it was wisest not to put oneself in a position where one would have to.

If one had the choice.

He turned to stare out at the lake, for it was by the lake that they now stood, the waters rippling in the fading wash of sinking sun and dusk breeze. They had climbed to this spot, or one much like it, when they had been younger men.

This time, as adviser to the Tyr, the climb was not so dangerous for the Widan; as General under the Tyr, even less so. But the lake held some of that moment's forbidden exhilaration—and fear. Just as, no doubt, Alesso had intended. He did very little without some forethought.

"Do you remember the Festival of the Moon?" Alesso spoke softly, his gaze intent, his arms crossed and propped over a bent knee. The winds had added creases to his forehead and the corners of his eyes, and darkened his skin enough that the rainy season could not pale it.

War had done the rest.

Sendari nodded, almost solemn in reply.

"Then you have been answered, as I have. Come, Sendari. You have Adano, and I, my own brother. But I want more for my sons—for *my* blood—than the name Marente, and the service to an increasingly distant kai. Why do you hesitate? You cannot love the clan Leonne."

"No more than you," the Widan replied, bristling slightly. "But you are talking about an act that has been attempted, several times, in the history of the Dominion—without success."

"We have allies that the nameless clans did not."

"Your Shining Court."

"The Shining Court."

"And you trust them?"

"Not at all. But I trust that they need me, and for the moment, that is enough. Let us take from them what *we* need."

"If we give them the Dominion, they will have no need of us."

"Indeed." The General smiled. "So we will not give them the Dominion."

"If, as you say," Sendari replied, his face tight with the effort of remaining expressionless, "the kin will be on our side, and within the Dominion, I do not see that we will have the choice."

"Think, Sendari. Let us wage war with the Empire; it will be a war that we *can* win, a war that we must win if I am to consolidate my rule. It will be a weak thing, at best. Essalieyan won the war that the Tyr brought against it, no? And we are still the Dominion, if diminished.

"Let us win, and not win, in the same fashion. There is a reason that the Shining Court fears the demon Kings and their followers. When we have won the lands that we need to win, and we have fulfilled our necessary function, might we not go to the demon Kings with a tale of how our own ranks were infiltrated by the kin? By the men and women who call themselves *Allasakari*? I assure you, the Imperial court *will* listen. Do not forget the events of sixteen years past."

"We do not, now, have a good report of those events."

"Sendari, enough. Either you will support me, or you will not."

"And if not?"

"Then not," Alesso replied, his brows creasing into a single line. "Or would you like me to offer you threats that our friendship renders meaningless?"

Silence, then. It was Sendari who turned away, as always, to stare out upon the waters of the Tor Leonne. "No; if we argue, we will argue in earnest, as we always do. Do not make mock threats."

"I do not want to do this without you," Alesso said quietly. "We have been through much together. Come. Be my Widan. Be my eyes and ears within the Sword of Knowledge; be my conduit into the Shining Court. I do not have your skill or your ability—no one who has not passed the Sword's test does. But I need both. And unlike most men, I have access to a Widan I can trust. Sendari—would you not be *the* Sendari—the man who founds his line?"

"Yes," the Widan said, but distantly, indistinctly.

"Then what is wrong?"

The Widan's silence was long and painful, but it was unexpected. Therefore it took Alesso a moment to recognize it for what it was. His face darkened; he rose, taking his foot from its perch on the smooth rock. "I offer you an opportunity that most of the men situated within the Tor Leonne would kill for, and you think not of the offer itself, but of *her*." He turned, folding his hands behind his back; Sendari knew that he was on the verge of walking away.

But they were like brothers in their anger; bound by things invisible that were also strong.

"She's dead, Alesso."

"Her daughter still rules your life. *Still*."

"She is married to the kai Leonne. Part of the clan Leonne. What you speak of—it would be her death. You would no more consign your own to death than I."

"I would consign a married daughter to the fate of her clan," the General replied heatedly. "I would not throw away the opportunity to rule the Tor for the sake of a mere girl."

"And that is why you are General, and I am merely Widan. Alesso—I will not speak against you, and you know this. But to act against her, to be the hand that kills her—I cannot do it."

Without another word, General Alesso di'Marente walked away, his steps a little too loud to be as measured and as cold as he would have liked. Sendari turned back to the lake. They had been friends many, many years; they knew each other well.

The argument was not yet over.

She wanted to be liked. It surprised Diora, just how much of a hunger it was, how much of a need. Made her acutely aware of the fact that she had never felt the need before. Even when the Serra Fiona had come into her father's harem, she had not been displaced; what she needed, she received.

Behind the screens of the kai Leonne's harem, her world became five women, and then, quickly, four; Samanta en'Leonne alone rejected what she attempted, time and again, to offer, choosing instead to focus the force of her attention upon their mutual husband. She heard the fear and the dislike in Samanta's voice, and she accepted both as the truth that they were.

But in Serena, she found the voice of an august authority, a woman whose knowledge of Ser Illara's likes and dislikes, and the roots of either, was invaluable; in Faida's voice, she found happiness and acceptance; in Deirdre's a cautious optimism, and in Ruatha's, anger, more anger, and fear not for herself, but for those whom she made her world.

She had given up on Samanta quickly, but she could not give up on Ruatha, although time and again she was ungently rebuffed for her attempts at building some bridge between them.

"Na'dio," Serena said one day, almost two weeks after Diora had been introduced to both harem and husband. "Ruatha is a wild child, a girl who was too hurt by her previous owners to be wisely brought here. Bluntly, my dear, she was a mistake. I've noticed that you've decided to let Samanta be; might you not also leave Ruatha to her own devices?"

"I can't," Diora said quietly, responding to the familiar diminutive that Serena alone seemed comfortable using.

"Why, Na'dio?"

"I don't really know." The younger woman turned restlessly from the small table upon which sweet water sat. "I think it is because Samanta—Samanta loves Illara in her fashion. She is like, very like, serafs I have observed; she thinks of him as a partner, as a husband. She is not friendly—either to you, or to me—because she feels she does not need to be; she came here by his favor, and she retains it; she is beautiful, Serena."

"Yes. She is."

"But I was taught differently, I think." Diora rose, restive; she found her Northern harp and began to play it almost absently, a balm for restless fingers, restless spirit. "I was taught that a husband's interest is transient; that if his interest is in beauty alone, then his interest will wane, like the moon—but it will never return. To be a partner, one must be an equal; equal to the politics that a husband will face, equal to the enemies, subtle and obvious, greater and lesser.

"If you are unfortunate and you have a husband who

desires the advice of no such wife, it is still unwise to place one's faith in favoritism, unless that is all one has.

"That is all, Serena, that Samanta has, and I see the time coming—I hear it in Illara's voice—when she will not even have that."

"Which tells me much about you, Diora. But it does not answer my question."

"In Ruatha, I hear a different disdain, a different resentment, a different anger. You're right—she was not the ideal wife for a harem, any harem, but certainly not so important a one as this will be. I can dismiss her from my husband's harem. The Serra Amanita has said, clearly, that she will take no offense, and will further give me the resources by which I might replace her with someone more suitable."

By her stillness, she knew that Serena listened. "And?"

"I don't want to do that."

Motion—breath—returned to the eldest wife in the harem. Diora smiled, albeit slightly bitterly.

"You see? You care about Ruatha; you do not want her sent away."

"You are perceptive, Serra Diora."

"I have to be. I will be honest, Serena, as honest as I know how to be. I look at Ruatha, and I see her, hovering over Deirdre as if she were Deirdre's oathguard. She would lay down her life for Deirdre and the unborn child she carries. I have seen such ferocity before, I think—or perhaps I've seen the effects of it, enough so that it compels me. I don't know. But I want to reach her. You care about her. Faida does. Deirdre does. I think I might, if I were allowed."

"And is that all?"

"Yes." But as she began to sing, she knew that she was not, was never, entirely truthful. What she wanted was to have, measure for measure, that ferocity of affection. For herself. She envied Faida and Deirdre Ruatha's love.

It took Alesso three days to distance himself enough from his anger that he might again seek Sendari out; the longest it had ever taken was four months. But a friendship that has never been tested in the fires of anger has never been tempered. Sendari waited in the three days of silence with the patience that Alesso had never mastered.

And when Alesso finally came to the modest quarters that the Tyr had granted one of his three personal advisers, he greeted the General personally, ordered the serafs to make the room ready in his absence for entertaining a guest of import. Teresa had trained these serafs; he did not trouble himself to make his desire explicit. They brought sweet water and wine and midday food, and they left, melting behind the screens that granted the General and the Widan the privacy their conversation demanded.

Alesso did not choose to avail himself of the cushions that lay upon the mat before the low table; for that reason, Sendari also chose to stand, although he preferred the comfort of the bright, soft accoutrements.

"I have given you reasonable time to consider my offer," Alesso began, without preamble, his hands clenched behind his back.

"And I appreciate the time you've given me," Sendari replied, cooling. They glared at each other for a moment, for long enough, in fact, that Sendari fully expected Alesso to storm out of his presence a second time.

But Alesso turned away and began to speak again. "If she is without child, if she is *kept* without child, then she will be returned to your harem."

Sendari was silent for a long time. "Alesso," he said quietly, "I have never tried to force you to make a choice you cannot make. Your boundaries are your boundaries; mine are mine. She is what she is to me."

"You gave her to Leonne."

"Yes. But to imply that giving her to Leonne was giving her to death is foolish. Leonne has reigned for longer than almost any of the clans in the Dominion; its line is unbroken. If any clan could provide a promise of safety, it was Leonne."

"If she were dead, Sendari, you'd be free."

"Free to follow you?"

It was the General's turn to offer silence as a response. At last he said, "Yes," but softly. "You have a keen eye, a keen ear, and some personal ambition—but that ambition would never extend to me, to mine. You are Widan, I am General—but we are alike, in our fashion. I will do this without you if I must."

"You don't need my protection, clansman."

"No. If it were protection I wanted, I would never have made this alliance. But we *can* do this, Sendari. Take the Tor and slide out from under the grip of our allies." He held out his sword hand. "Tonight, I tender my final reply to Cortano di'Alexes. I have no doubt that I'm being observed."

"No. Nor I." Sendari stared at the proffered hand, and then met the gaze of the man he called friend. "I accept your challenge," he said softly.

8th of Marran, 426 AA
Tor Leonne

Birth was always a terrifying experience.

She did not remember when it had become so; did not remember when she understood the difference between the peculiar, extenuated cries of pain that heralded new life—or early death. There were herbs and mixtures that aided a woman birthing a child, but at times, Diora thought that childbirth was a type of theft: a life for a life.

And no guarantee that the new life, fragile and bereft of mother, would survive either.

In the harem, the wives learned many things. Serena, the eldest, had seen many births; had seen the deaths that followed, or the lives. She had held many a child when she had been a wife in the harem of the Tyr'agar—and she had attended the mourning ceremonies in the twilight between night and dawn for those that had simply not been large enough or strong enough to survive that painful entry into the world.

Diora had seen births, but always at a distance; a huddle of wives around their sister-wife, saris stained with sweat and heat and a tense excitement, an unspoken anxiety. It was obvious to Alana when the birth went well and when it threatened to go poorly, and it was Alana's voice that often prevailed above the happy or agonized cries of the women whose bodies were undergoing these final, fateful contortions. Alana was not here. And Serena was not Alana, but she was wise in the way that older wives are, and far more gently spoken.

She was not so fascinated by the pregnancy as the younger wives were: in particular, Faida, Ruatha, and yes, Diora herself.

As she had not done since she was a small child, she would often stop and shyly ask Deirdre if she might—gently—touch the swell of growing stomach. Deirdre was not so shy or modest—not when her husband was not present; she would just as shyly consent, and they would stand a moment, joined by the life that both women could feel moving beneath their hands. She was no seraf, but she felt compelled to help; to aid Deirdre when she rose, to offer her food when she would take it; to pour her water from the lake that was clan Leonne's by birthright. They all did, fluttering like so many hungry butterflies around the blossom of a single flower. And perhaps because she was willing—was compelled—to offer this aid to Deirdre, Ruatha accepted it, if grudgingly, for what it was.

They spoke for hours at a time about names. As the child of a concubine, the choice of this baby's name was entirely the mother's; if Diora had a child, the naming would be done by the father—or perhaps the father's father. She knew this, but knew also that her child would be honored and exalted above all.

And if she hadn't known it, Ruatha made it clear.

"Why do you do this?" she asked, the third time that Ruatha interrupted their playful musings with just such a grim reminder.

"Why do I do what?"

"Why do you always insist that there be this distance, and this difference, between us?"

"I don't insist. The clans do. *You* are the Serra, we are only wives."

"We are all his wives, Ruatha. And at the moment, it is Samanta who holds Illara's attention and favor—not I."

"You could have it, if you wanted it."

Diora shrugged gracefully. "I want my harem," she replied softly. "I do not play Serra behind these screens. I do not tell you what to wear, or how to dress, or what to say or do. I do not plan your lives and your days; I do not lecture you or admonish you.

"And I do not attempt to take from you the things that bring you joy. If I am Serra—and I am, and I cannot change that—do you think I had more choice in it than you? We are all what we are by the Lord's decree, and if I have higher rank, it is because of who our husband *is*, not who I am."

Ruatha started to speak, and Faida pressed a gentle hand to her lips, silencing her. "Diora," she said, "forgive her. She is protective, and she is afraid."

"Of what?" Diora asked although she already knew the answer. She wanted it to be spoken. She wanted it said; things said had substance enough to be faced if one knew how.

Faida had the grace to flinch and look away; Diora thought that she would let Ruatha speak after all. But her hand did not fall from Ruatha's lips, and after a deep breath, she spoke, bringing her dark, unblinking gaze to the fore, as if it were a shield. Odd, that vulnerability could be such a shield. It was not the way of the clansmen.

But, of course, they were not men.

"Deirdre and Ruatha are close. The child that Deirdre carries could belong to any of us—except you. We were happy, when we found that her waning had stopped, until we spoke to our husband.

"He was not happy, Diora. He was, I think, even angry, although he did not speak of it." She drew breath, closing her eyes a moment; when she opened them, they seemed even larger. "The Tyr'agar killed his brothers when he took the crown and the Sword upon his father's death. They were cleanly killed, but they were killed."

Faida had not been alive when the Tyr'agar took the Tor.

"Yes," Diora said, knowing it for truth, although she, too, had not been born at that time.

"We believe that Ser Illara will also kill his brothers when the time comes; already, two have died by accident—riding accidents, both. Serena says nothing when we ask her, and when she says nothing it means a great deal."

"I am not certain, myself," Diora whispered.

"If Deirdre's child is a girl, then she will stay in the harem, and be a part of it, and no brother will displace her and be her death. But if she is cursed and her child is a boy, his life depends on your inability to bear our husband sons.

"It is hard for Ruatha to hear you speak of naming, of

birthing, of caring for a child that your own children may well be the death of."

"And for you, Faida?"

Faida said, "If Deirdre does not mind it, I do not mind. This child is her child, and her joy, and if you can add to her joy, that is enough for me." She let her fingers brush the lips of the angriest of Illara's few wives as her hand fell away.

"What do you have to say to that, Serra?" Ruatha said, trying, for Faida's sake, not to bristle so obviously. She failed, of course, but Diora expected no less.

"I hope, for all of our happiness, that Deirdre's child is a girl. Let us make our offerings tonight at the shrine of the Lady. We must take new incense and braziers there anyway."

When Deirdre slipped and fell, no one was in attendance. Her serafs found her, although how much time had passed, they could not say. What they could say, what they did say, was this: She was alive, but not conscious, and her left leg was broken.

They found Serena first, of course, but Diora was with the elder, and when she rose, in a silver-haired flash of pale worry, Diora followed, hesitating only long enough to tell the serafs to bring Ruatha to the site.

The site was the garden half-wall; Diora was uncertain as to how a woman might slip and fall unless she were foolish enough to climb or balance upon that wall. And Deirdre was many things, but that foolish? Serena's lips took on a gray cast, and then a white one as she pressed them firmly shut.

And Serena's silences were loud indeed.

"She is alive," Serena said, "but I fear that the child's safe delivery may be costly, if it's possible at all. Diora, Marjora, help me move her—*do not touch the break.* Put your hands beneath her shoulders and here, beneath her back; slide her onto the carrier."

"Should I bring the men?" the young seraf asked nervously.

"No. We will have to take her to the birthing rooms and hope that she wakes."

Diora touched her sister-wife's brow; it felt oddly clammy; the glow beneath the skin had been replaced by a distant gray. She did not like it. "Serena," she said, as she struggled gracelessly to put her weight into the lifting, "is the baby going to come?"

"I believe so, yes."

"If her leg is broken—"

"Diora, enough."

"No," someone said, "answer the question." Ruatha stepped up to the carrier, coming over the half-wall as if it were a pasture fence and she still a simple seraf girl. Her chest was heaving; Diora had heard that expression a dozen times, but had never really appreciated it until that moment.

"I will answer the question," Serena said quietly and without rancor, "when we have the leisure. We do not have it now, Ruatha; do not hinder me. If you care for Deirdre at all, take hold of one of the poles and keep it as steady as your strength allows."

Ruatha swallowed the words; her cheeks were red with the effort of running and of silence both. She turned to Diora, saw that Diora struggled with both of the poles that supported the stretched cloth upon which Deirdre lay so silently, and stepped in to take the leftmost one. Then, the four women bore Deirdre back into the screened world of Ser Illara's harem.

Faida met them; the oldest of the serafs had taken the time to find her and to call her to the birthing room. She had time to gather the waters of the Tor, and she readied them carefully, not knowing how they would be used. It gave her—and the serafs who hovered anxiously in the birthing room that had never been used by any of Ser Illara's wives—something to do.

Oh, Diora thought, *Illara would be angry to see them all like this.* Her own brow was beaded with sweat, her hair matted to her forehead, her sari crumpled and, she thought, stained. Serena and Ruatha fared as poorly for their effort, and Faida looked no better, for all that she had not been called to carry Deirdre; she looked worse; her hair was long and unbound, like a child's hair, and her eyes were reddened and swollen.

She went at once to Ruatha and then hovered; she wanted comfort, but dared not to ask for it until their precious and heavy burden was placed—very, very carefully—upon the mats. Serena would not let them use the cushions for fear of the leg itself.

"Come, Ruatha, if you care for her. Help me. Her leg must be repositioned, or it will heal poorly and she will limp."

Faida blanched, and Ruatha bit her lip. It was the first time that Diora had ever seen her hesitate in quite that way, and it came to the Serra that her sister-wife, her angry, hardened, defiant Ruatha, was afraid.

"Ruatha," she said quietly, "if you cannot help, I can. I've done it before, for my father's son. It is not a dangerous task, and if Deirdre is unconscious, and we move quickly, she won't feel it at all."

"But—but how can she birth a child if her leg is—if she must keep the leg still?"

They all looked to Serena, and Serena said nothing; she knelt by Deirdre's side. The serafs brought her the splinting she required, and the cottons and the silks with which to bind them in place; they left them on the floor and moved a discreet distance away.

"Why doesn't she wake up?"

"Faida," Diora said softly, "not yet. I promise, I will wake her when this is done."

Serena's glance wavered a moment; she lifted a hand to wipe her brow and a seraf stepped forward at once with a cloth. "Na'dio," the older woman whispered, "help me, if you've done this before. It has been—long enough, and I am greatly wearied."

"The sari," Diora said quietly.

"Yes," Serena replied, hesitating. "It was costly."

"I will see to its replacement. It must be cut away. We cannot move her to unwind the silk."

Serena nodded, looking faintly relieved. They cut, carefully and precisely, so that both leg and the round curve of Deirdre's belly were revealed to the light of the waning day.

Very carefully and very quietly Diora examined the leg, seeing it as if it existed in isolation. It was oddly angled, but no bone jutted through skin, or just beneath it, as it had done with her brother. She was afraid for just a moment, and suppressed it as she could, but the fear of failure lingered: If she failed, and Deirdre limped, she would be ruined as a wife for a man of the kai Leonne's importance; the flaw would be too obvious to hide beneath the folds of perfect silk. Grace and beauty were everything in the harem of an important man, and if beauty could be judiciously added by paints and jewels and combs and cloth, grace could not so easily be faked.

But to do nothing was to guarantee failure; it was the weaker course. Clenching her jaw, she nodded to herself, and then, carefully, she set the bone, straightening the leg, pressing her hands firmly into skin and muscle in a search for the awkward hump of misaligned bone. It was hard; the flesh there was swollen and dark with bruising, and unlikely to get better before it got worse. But it was not the most difficult thing she had ever had to do, and she remembered, for the first time in almost two months, that she was the Serra Diora, niece to the Serra Teresa.

She splinted the leg, and bound it as tightly as she dared, remembering Ona Teresa's admonishment about the free flow of blood from one part of the body to another.

"Well done, Diora," Serena said.

She started, remembering that she was *en'Leonne* now, but not diminished for all that was true. Had she forgotten? Turning to Faida, she said simply. "Please, go and bring me my harp."

It was such an unexpected request that Faida's brows creased unpleasantly over the bridge of her nose, mirroring her confusion. But she nodded and acquiesced, not because the request was an order from her Serra, but because it gave her something to do.

Serena rose; Ruatha offered her the waters, and she drank them almost greedily. Then she did what Diora could not do; she examined the unconscious Deirdre looking for signs of the child in the turn of her flesh, and the feel and color of it. She took almost as long as Diora had to set the leg.

"The baby," Serena said at last, and Diora heard the strength of the fear in those words more clearly than she had ever heard fear in Serena's words. She realized, with a start, that she was deliberately listening for it; that she was using her gift, when she might need the strength of it for later.

"Serena?"

Dead-eyed, the older woman turned to the harem's Serra, her gaze bypassing Ruatha as if it dared not rest upon her for even a second. As if it might burn. "The baby is coming" she said, "And the leg—she cannot move it."

"Then she will not move it."

At that, Serena offered her a bitter smile. "You've never seen a birthing, Diora. There might be some very small chance that we could deliver her of child if this were her third or fourth—but it's her first, and the pain is always greatest, the labor hardest, with the first."

"No, Serena, *you* don't understand. If the movement will cost her, she *will not* move." Gray eyes met brown ones, and it was the gray that fell away.

"You give me hope, Serra Diora," the eldest wife said faintly. "Because I almost believe you."

"What—what will you do to her?" Ruatha spoke as if speech were not voluntary. The words were punctuated with a brightness of eye and a quickness of breath. "No matter what you do for the leg, you can't bind it whole when it's that newly broken. And you can't bind *her* if she's to give birth."

"I will . . . sing," Diora replied. "When Faida brings me my harp, I will wake Deirdre, and she will be in pain."

"We have the waters," Serena said, "both of the Tor and of distance; she will have both, together. Ruatha," she added softly, lifting a hand and then letting it drop, as if remembering just who Ruatha was. "More than that, we cannot do. Believe that we care about Deirdre as much as we are capable of caring, and bring me my philters."

Her hands shook as Faida delivered the harp into them. Sweat came from heat and nervousness as she settled herself down upon the flat mats, taking only enough care to find a position which was comfortable for the body, not the eyes. This was her harem's most private place, this birthing room; if she could not be herself—whatever that meant, in this place—here, she could not lower her guard anywhere.

And even the greatest of warriors put their shields up and went home when the time was right.

She smiled almost bitterly at that analogy, wondering why she had chosen it; it wasn't particularly fitting this night, of all nights—for if she lowered her guard, she did it at the very moment that she lifted her greatest weapon, in a land where the Serras did not wield a weapon more

graceful or deadly than a dagger. Did she trust these
women?

No.

But she wanted to.

She could hear Ona Teresa's admonition; the warning
of years, of a decade and a half, never wavering and never
changing. *Never tell anyone, Diora. Not even your father.
Especially not your father.*

Had that driven a wedge between them, she and her
father? She did not know; he had grown stranger and
stranger as he had traveled the Widan's path—less the
man that she remembered loving so completely, more the
powerful clansman. But she could say, of all living men,
she trusted only one, and that man, her father, Sendari
di'Marano.

But she had not trusted him with the knowledge of
her gift.

Could she, she thought, trust them? Ruatha with her
sharp tongue, her poor discretion, her quick anger, Serena,
the distant woman who had helped to raise Illara and might
well choose his interests over his wives', Faida, soft-
spoken, quiet, and too trusting by far. Of the three, she
thought Faida was the most dangerous, because she would
act without intent.

"Diora," Serena said softly, "wake her soon."

She began to play. Softly at first, a Northern tune that
she had learned from no less a man than Kallandras of the
mythical Senniel College. But as the Northern tune passed
from her fingers to the strings and from the strings to the
ears, she continued, seeking her own tune, giving the
strings the imperative that lay beneath the wordless, perfect harmony she sang.

She opened her eyes, for she closed them often while
playing; things seen were less subtle than things heard,
but they caught the eye's attention almost before one realized one's attention had wandered. And to sing like this,
to use her gift to command, required a focus that was as
sharp as a blade's edge; once she had it, it could not easily
be wrested from her, but gaining that ground was not
simple.

She saw Deirdre laid out against the mats, her body
exposed, her chest rising and falling rhythmically. The
silks that had been so expensive now lay at her side in a

rent and jagged bundle; small red beads were scattered across the floor, catching light like drops of hard liquid.

"Diora?"

Almost imperceptibly, Diora nodded at the sound of the voice. She wove her awareness of it into her song, and as she did, she felt that she understood Serena en'Leonne perfectly; she was a distant mother, a woman who loved her sister-wives and dreaded their loss enough that she hid behind the veil of age, distancing herself where she could.

As if it helped. As if it ever helped, this forced distance, this fear of pain. She sang a gentle benediction to the tense and waiting woman, and then she turned her words, and all that they held, to Deirdre.

Deirdre en'Leonne and her almost-born infant.

Who was Deirdre en'Leonne? Was she black-haired and brown-eyed and delicate of frame? Was she lovely, was she supple, was she the woman who danced, within the harem's confines, more sensuously now that she carried the promise of life than she had ever danced without?

Was she a mother, if not these things, a woman who would sing the cradle song in the dusk after the passing of the Lord's dominion, holding child as burden and blessing and broken heart while praying, all the while, for the Lady's mercy, or was she a wife who hoped to gain her husband's favor, and his mother's favor, by giving him a son—a son that might not be, might never be, superseded?

Or did she desire instead, a girl, a girl she might keep as her own until the day that she was old enough to be presented, as a gift, to the harem of another Tyr?

All those things, was Deirdre, but she was more than that. She was more than woman; she was girl at heart, hidden from the critical eye of all save those who loved her enough to indulge her. She could not read, of course; few women could. But if read to, she would listen, her face wreathed in the serious lines that Sendari di'Marano would have approved of in a daughter.

She was not Serena, and yet, of the three women—Faida, Ruatha, and Deirdre—it was Deirdre who was the anchor, the hidden, quiet strength. Ruatha had the ferocity of desire and protectiveness, and Faida the singsong quality of her open joy; it was Deirdre who bound them and held them together.

Diora wondered when she had noticed this, or if it came

to her only now, as she sang a song of Deirdre's life, a song made of words bound together by the strength of her voice. By the strength of a love that she was almost afraid to reveal, that she had no choice but to reveal if she was to wake Deirdre and bind her.

If she was to touch what no longer slept within the rounded hallow of her body.

The song broke twice. She picked it up each time, and the third time it faded, she was ready.

"Wake, Deirdre, wake; Ruatha is waiting, and Faida, and I."

Deirdre's eyelashes lay heavy upon her pale cheeks. Diora spoke again, and they fluttered; a third time, and they opened wide. She turned her face at once, propped shaking hands to either side and began to rise. Ruatha was at her side immediately, with waters from the Tor. And with the waters that Serena called the waters of distance. Something to dim the pain.

Diora smiled, but the smile was difficult to offer; she was listening more intently than she had ever listened to anything in her life. "Serena," she said at last, "I hear the child." She closed her eyes to gather strength and distance.

Serena nodded.

"I can . . . sing calm," she told the harem eldest. "I can sing stillness, and it will be done—but you *must* explain it to her first—why it's necessary. If she doesn't know, she won't be as—it will be harder, for me."

Serena nodded, the lines around her thin lips white with pressure. But she spoke gently to Deirdre en'Leonne. She touched the leg, the curve of the stomach, the matted stickiness of her sister-wife's brow. Her voice, low and inseparable from the tone of the music Diora played, seemed to calm the young woman.

And in calmness, her best chance lay.

"How long?" Serena asked the woman who played the Northern harp.

"As long as it takes," Diora replied, almost as fierce in her answer as Ruatha might have been. But her answer was followed by a momentary silence, and then a forced and quiet question. "How long *will* it take?"

"I don't know. Hours, Na'dio. At least, I think, the full half-day. This child will be born under the moon's face, in the Lady's time. Can you. . . sing . . . for that long? She will need our help in all things; she cannot put weight on that leg, and she will not be able to curl or crouch as she should."

Twelve hours. "Yes," Diora replied, although she had never done it before. "And longer."

Faida came to offer her water, and she stopped only long enough to drink it; she found the waters of the Tor Leonne to be the only balm for her aching throat, her tired hands. She cursed silently; had she been Ona Teresa, she would have been able to dispense with the harp—but when she did not have the focus of the strings and their beautiful song, she did not know how to offer a gentle command. She could speak, but the power in her voice was almost binding; even Kallandras said that hers was a voice to rival his own had she but been given the opportunity to hone it.

She vowed she *would* learn; she was learning, in bits and pieces, all the time. Lady's whim.

But she could not learn quickly enough for *this*. Like all else in life, the lesson would come too late for Deirdre.

The sands ran. She could see their even trickle as the glasses were turned and turned again. The lamps were lit, that Serena might see better; Deirdre herself seemed preternaturally calm. She answered every question that Serena asked.

But it was not until the moon was high that Serena rose and buried her face in her hands.

Diora was tired. She thought, at any moment, her voice might crack.

"Serena?" Faida said, making of the name a question.

"The baby is turned," Serena said. It lies feet first, and I fear—" She fell silent.

"Are they out?" Diora asked, although the speaking of the words was costly. She stumbled; her fingers seemed to collide with each other as her hands gave in to cramping.

"Are they out? What do you mean, Na'dio?"

"The feet."

"Not yet. Very soon."

"Feet are bad?"

"Now? Yes."

She was *so tired*. She had never been tired in her adult

life; the weariness was like a drug or a poison. It made her hands heavy. As they fell against the strings, she thought she had dropped them, that they were no longer a part of her body.

She thought she could not keep playing; her hands were numb and prickly. She could not command with any subtlety at all unless she did. Rising, stumbling as if the weight of her own body was completely unfamiliar, she spoke two words.

"Turn over."

She could see the sudden bulge, the twisting, in Deirdre's body, as the infant *obeyed*. Deirdre made an animal sound, a grunting in the well of her throat. Diora picked up the harp again.

Two hours later, she heard it: the baby's cry.

Her eyes were closed; she did not see it come, candlelit and wet, into the world, head and shoulders cradled in the hands of Serena en'Leonne. To hear it was enough. To hear its voice, the whisper of its cry.

Faida's cry was louder, sweeter; she leaped and landed at least once in sheer joy. Serena was weeping; she could hear this, too, almost as clearly as she could hear Deirdre's exhausted and happy plea to hold—

her son.

A son.

She stopped playing when someone pried the harp from her hands. Without the harp to steady them, they shook; they shook terribly. The room was filled with a bitter wind, a cold one. *A son.*

But, no, it wasn't the wind; the screens and the hangings did not whisper at all with the breeze's voice. *What was it?* she thought as she attempted to rise. Her legs buckled, awkward and stiff beneath her; they would not carry her weight. She fell; she could not even put her arms out to stop the mats from striking her.

But someone else offered their arms instead, and she took to them, like a child lost in the grip of a terrible fever.

Ah. A fever. Something about the word was familiar. A warning, perhaps, about fevers. Something Kallandras had said. "Don't let them see me," she said, pressing her face into the warmth and the softness of another woman's cheek. "Don't call them. Don't let *anyone* see me."

And she heard, to her surprise and amazement, the voice she least expected to hear. "I won't. I promise." Ferocity, truth, and blessed protectiveness.

Ruatha's voice.

The chill took her, and the darkness; the lights dimmed. *I want to see the baby,* she thought, *but perhaps they won't let me because it's a boy.*

As if she had spoken—and perhaps she had, the person carrying most of her weight drew her to where Deirdre sat. To where Deirdre held a small, reddened little infant, face almost lost to the swell of his mother's breast.

"Look, Diora." Candles made twin trails of light down the cheeks of Deirdre en'Leonne; she had never smiled so radiantly in all the time that Diora had known her.

Mother and child were the last thing she saw before she gave herself over to the darkness of exhaustion. And the mage-fevers that, Kallandras had warned her, could strike anyone born with the gift if they attempted to do too much, for too long.

Three days she shivered in darkness with an uncontrollable chill. Serena did not come the first day, nor did Deirdre or Faida. But Ruatha was there almost constantly, holding the waters of the Tor Leonne in a solid silver mug. It was a common thing, and Diora knew it—but she had broken two glasses of Northern crystal because her spasms came and went in a completely wild and unpredictable way, and she did not wish to break another—of any sort.

Besides, crushing silver was almost impossible, and if she pressed the vessel as tightly as she could between clenched palms, she could hold it. She found Ruatha a comfort and hated to see her leave, be it only to personally fetch more of the waters of the Tor—yet she also felt perversely guilty because if Ruatha was with her, she was not with Deirdre, and she remembered enough of her days in her father's harem to know that after the first euphoria had faded into pleasant glow, the mother was often tired and in need of aid.

But when she mentioned it, Ruatha shook her dark head. "She doesn't need me," she told Diora gravely.

"She has her son, and she has Faida with whom to share joy, and Serena from whom to take advice.

"I am not a mother," Ruatha added, staring a moment at hands that seemed, for all her strength, curiously unblemished and unhardened. "I don't know how to share what she has to offer. I'm happy that she's happy. I would kill to protect her baby." She raised her head, met Diora's eyes with eyes that were just as dark. "But you *need* me. So I'm here."

Awkward silence filled a room that would have been still if Ruatha had not picked up the large fan and begun to use it to send a gust of warm air across Diora's fevered face. Diora broke it because she was the better taught of the two. "You wouldn't have done this before."

"No."

"Why then? Why now?"

Hair fell down her shoulder and silk-clothed back as Ruatha en'Leonne shrugged tightly. "I don't know. What you did—we all saw it. We haven't spoken about it. Serena won't let us. But even if she didn't forbid it, I don't know that we would. You were—you seemed like the Lady's hand, Diora. Faida says you were sent to us by the Lady as an act of mercy." She smiled awkwardly, looking at the fan and not at the woman to whom she spoke. In anger, she was direct and forceful. But here—it was almost as if she dared not meet Diora's eyes, not because of what she might see in the harem's Serra, but rather, because of what Diora would see in her.

"I told her we deserve you. Or maybe she does. I'm not—I haven't been kind. To you. I'm—I didn't know what you'd do."

"Ser Illara?"

"He's been—occupied. Samanta is desperate because Deirdre's given him his first son; she has something to prove, and we've let her. We—Serena, that is—told him that you were unwell because of the heat, and that you did not wish to disgrace yourself by being less than the Serra that he had the right to expect. Or something like that. He seemed to accept it, so we've all been left alone.

"Especially Deirdre."

"But the baby," Diora said softly. "The baby is a boy."

Ruatha met her eyes again. "Yes," she said, oddly gentle. She reached for Diora's cup, filled it, and then moved closer, placing the back of her hand across Diora's forehead. "Diora—you're too hot. Are you certain—?"

"Yes. If they come," Diora replied, feeling lucid but oddly detached, "they'll call the healers. If the healers come, they'll know what it is that I—that I suffer. They'll know what the fever means." Ah, no—Ruatha was right. She could feel the cold building within as her hands started to shake and droplets of precious water flitted across the sleeping silks like wasted tears. "That I'm gifted, somehow. The Lady's gift or the Lord's—it makes no difference. If they know, they'll take me away, or they'll give me to the Radann for cleansing, or worse, they'll make a weapon of me, and nothing more than a weapon."

The words stopped as her teeth began to chatter. Ruatha brought blankets and pried the cup from between her hands before the water was completely spilled by her short, jittery movements.

"Sleep," Ruatha said. "There will be no healers here."

Diora believed her. And because she did, she slept peacefully.

Two days after that, Diora rose for the first time. She was exhausted by the fevers but hungry; her search for food brought her into the largest of the rooms: the harem's center, where Serena en'Leonne usually held court. But it was not Serena who occupied the place of honor beneath the artist-rendered golden sun on the high ceilings above; it was Deirdre, and in Deirdre's arms, wrapped tight and bound into stillness—which looked uncomfortable at best—was the babe.

"Na'dio!" Serena rose at once. "Where is Ruatha?"

Diora smiled. "Asleep. And she should be. I don't think she's slept for close to six days."

"She'll be angry if you left while she was sleeping," Deirdre offered, a tired smile tugging at the corner of her lips.

"Oh. But she was exhausted."

"Well, yes." Deirdre looked down at the bundle in her arms; arms that were, now, a mother's arms, and strong enough to carry the weight for as long as the Lady allowed.

"Diora," Serena said, beckoning quietly.

Diora smiled wanly, but she did not look away, not yet. She had eyes for the mother and the child, as if they were not quite real; as if they could be taken from her in a moment because they had crossed a threshold that she herself had never even approached. Deirdre *made* this life.

"Would you like to—to hold him?"

She said yes before she spoke; her arms made an awkward cradle as she approached Deirdre en'Leonne, she who seldom made any movement awkwardly. Deirdre smiled, but Diora heard, clearly, the catch of her breath as she placed her newborn son into another woman's arms. Any other woman.

"Hold his head," she said, although she knew that Diora had grown up within the confines of a clan's harem, and had seen infants before.

"Does he have a name?"

"Danello."

"Na'dani," Diora said quietly. The child slept on. "He's beautiful, Deirdre—although I don't think he looks much like you yet."

"No. Only tell me he doesn't look too much like our husband, and I'll be grateful."

Diora laughed—but Serena clearly considered this inappropriate. "Na'dio, Na'Deir, that is *quite* enough. Your husband is the man who will rule the Tor, and he *must* be treated with respect, gravity, and dignity. Is that clear?"

"Yes, Serena," Deirdre said, not in the least repentant.

Diora had the grace to blush. But when she gave Na'dani back to his mother, she whispered, "He's already far more beautiful than our husband could ever be."

Which, of course, set Deirdre to giggling, which in turn set Serena to frowning. Life was returning—*would* return, if Diora had any say at all—to normal.

She joined Serena by the screen doors that had been opened to let in light and a view of the rippling lake a full building's height and more beneath their feet. They sat in the silence the view created, feeling peaceful, hopeful.

Diora spoke first, but that was often the case when these two sat alone. "I need your aid," she told the older woman quietly.

Serena waited, listening to the muted whisper of the waters as they moved between rushes and lilies, over rocks and plants and a bank of sand. This was the voice of the Tor Leonne, because it was a symbol of life in a land that seemed to care so little for it. The Lady's gift to men bred by the desert winds.

"If I have no child this year, no one will notice," Diora continued, speaking so that only Serena might hear.

"True. But next? I think next year, it would be remarked on, and not in our husband's favor."

"Then I would have that child next year, not this one."

"Why, Diora?"

The younger wife glanced over her shoulder at Deirdre en'Leonne and the babe she held so close.

"Because I believe that my child will be the death of that one. Not now, not for many years—but it is coming. It always comes when the Tyr feels his hold on his clan is weak." She spoke now with the Marano voice, her father's crisp and dry precision informing every word.

"And what will waiting a year or two do?"

"In a year or two, many things can change, Serena. Before the Lady came to these lands, the Lord's lands, it is said by many that there was only the desert and the desert winds. Nothing stands against those winds when they howl across the open plain.

"Yet the Lady stood. And if not for the Lady, there would be no life in Annagar."

"So it is said, yes. And you see yourself as the Lady come to the Lord's Dominion?"

"To bring life, yes. Or to preserve it. I believe that I can change our husband, Serena. I believe that I can help him rule—that I can, in a year, maybe only a little longer, make him confident enough that he need not raise my son to be quite so . . . cautious."

"Delicately put, Na'dio. You could offer to have no children at all."

"But, as you say, that would hurt our husband's reputation, and I have no desire to do that. His loss of face would no doubt be blamed, by Leonne, upon his Serra, or his wives, and his heir would be, would have to be, the child of a mere wife, a concubine.

"And even if I decided to have no children, and he was forced to choose among his wives' children for *one* son to elevate, do you not think that single son would have to be far more ruthless to survive? Each and every one of his brothers would know that if it were not for a slip of the finger, a mistaken gesture on their father's part, they would be ruler of this vast domain instead of merely elevated serafs, or Tyran, if their brother so desired.

"Oh, no. If that were to happen, I would say that the son so chosen would be foolish indeed not to have the rest of his brothers killed because *he* would have justification in so doing."

"And your child would never need to take such drastic action."

"No."

Serena offered Diora a measured smile, one of the few. "You are wise, Diora en'Leonne; wiser, I think, than many have given you credit for. I will aid you in this endeavor for the course of a full year—although there is risk in the timing. Illara is . . . a young man, with a young's man's sense of himself. I believe he already considers it a slight that you do not carry his child."

Diora shrugged elegantly. "I will bear the Leonne heir in time. and I will make that child and this house stronger than either already are."

"I believe, having delivered Danello into his mother's arms, that you will do just that," Serena said. But there was something in her eyes, some distant sadness, some lingering sorrow, that Diora could not understand.

"Be careful, Na'dio," Serena said softly. "Remember that the heart is a dangerous land, and there is not one more painful to have to leave once it is full entered."

But Diora did not hear her elder; she had already turned toward Deirdre, her ear caught by the slightly off-tune hum of a cradle song. Dusk was approaching.

CHAPTER TWELVE

Month of Scaral, 426 AA
The Tor Leonne

The preparations for the Festival of the Moon once again changed the face of the Tor Leonne. Where the Festival of the Sun was powerful, political, the Festival of the Moon held a hint of the Lady in everything; in the flowers planted in beds by the palace and the pavilions, in the blossoms, that came as if by unspoken decree to pinken the skirts of the red-leaved foreign trees, and in the loons that stopped to water in the lake itself.

Masks were made and masks sold, and in the streets of the lower city—a city that the wives and the Serra of the kai Leonne were never privileged to see, wines were being pressed in preparation for the festival of the following year, and the previous year's vintage, for the less discerning of the revelers, being carted through the streets.

No Tyr missed the Festival of the Sun, for it was by its nature a gathering of men who claimed power. But Moonnight was different, a door into the hidden world, a place where the power they spent their lives, and their family's blood, building afforded them no purchase. The Tyrs who chose to make this trek—and this year there were only two, the Tyr'agnate of Oerta and the Tyr'agnate of Sorgassa, had begun to arrive with their retinue. Diora saw their approach clearly because she recognized the banner of clan Lorenza, with the rising sun and its clearly marked distinct rays bordering its lowest edge, and the horse of the Tyr'agnate Eduardo kai di'Garrardi. She prayed, although it was full noon, that she would not have to look upon his face at any closer proximity than this—but it was Festival time, and much about the Festival was unpredictable.

The Tyr'agnate was the only unpleasant ripple in the tide of the day. Her husband, Ser Illara, had come and gone several times, sneaking past his wives when he thought they might otherwise be occupied to gaze upon the face of his infant son. The child was young and had only very recently started to smile, and the father—the angry and sullen father—had become captivated in some small way by that display of unaffected joy.

If joy it was. No one could quite say what would make Na'dani smile—and many things had been tried, most with so little dignity it might seem the Festival of the Moon had already arrived within the harem's heart and merely waited the chance to spread its wings wide over the rest of the Tor.

Deirdre was happy, if nervous still, and Ruatha took great pains to absent herself from her husband's side when he chose to visit this previously unwanted child. They held their breath—Deirdre, Faida, Ruatha, and Diora—as if it were drawn by a single person, waiting. Hoping.

The Serra Amanita also chose to visit the harem, but where her son was cautiously affectionate, she was quite cold; it put them all on their best behavior immediately, her visit, and it did not let go of them for days afterward. Her shadow was long and dark when it fell.

It fell heavily.

Of the women of the harem, only the Serra Diora en'Leonne was requested to avoid most of the revelry of the Festival itself, and she found this a bitter, bitter blow—although it wasn't unexpected. During a Festival night, many things, unasked for, could happen—and some things must *not* involve the Serra of the kai Leonne. The Tyr'agar could not, of course, command her absence—it was the Festival of the Moon, and she was no criminal— but his request held the force of law. Of the Lord's law. Of all the men in the realm whose bloodline must be unquestionable, it was his.

Still, if she was to acquiesce graciously to captivity, she was given her choice of companions, each of whom would then bear the weight of a similar "request." She hovered between selfish and selfless, and settled upon selfish with both guilt and hesitation. She wanted Ruatha and Faida and Deirdre to remain at her side. Deirdre was still often tired; for a small and completely immobile infant, Na'dani seemed to rule as much of her life as she let him. And, given her reluctance to place him with even the serafs who had been trained in such things, that was much.

Faida and Ruatha, on the other hand, had much more to lose, for the Festival of the Moon was the single night of absolute freedom that any of them might know. But they agreed willingly enough, setting only a single condition upon their voluntary captivity: that they might plan their own small celebration within the Leonne garden. Such permissions as were required were not withheld.

Unfortunately, such permissions not being withheld, they went about their plans with zeal and determination—and without Diora. They knew her strengths well; they did not speak in her presence and if conversation turned, in a sudden pivot of words, to the Festival Night, they would fall just as instantly silent.

The plans of the great and the powerful had never been of as much interest to Diora as the plans of these three women, these sister-wives. Had the days ever passed so slowly?

22nd Scaral, The Festival of the Moon, 426 AA
The Tor Leonne

It had started here. Sendari often thought it would end here, by the lake, with the moon full and hanging in a clear, cool sky. He knelt to touch the water's edge, remembering the shallower ponds of a boy's youth, where mosquitoes nested. They did not nest here, although perhaps it was because the dragonflies that hovered over the lilies were more efficient.

He doubted it.

He was a man of knowledge, and not a man of mindless superstition; he did not, as many of the Widan did not, believe in the Lord and the Lady. But this lake . . . this lake tested his lack of faith, and in the darkness of night, much to his great bemusement, it often won.

He stood alone this eve. Last year, just one year past, he and Na'dio had skirted the edge of the lake together. In the moonlight, the waters were shimmering, pale light into which one might descend forever—a door into the

Lady's realm, a place of peace. Her hand was on his arm; he could feel it still, resting delicately against the raw silk robes he wore; she bowed her forehead into his shoulder and spoke a moment of childhood. Her childhood.

His own was far enough behind him that hers did not evoke it—but the days of *her* childhood woke in him memories that only the moon stirred now. He let her speak, interrupting seldom, before time's passage called them to descend into the city.

But even then they had been forced to part ways, she to go to the demiwall to join the gathered spectators, and he to join the Widan in their display of finery: the fireworks by which the Festival was celebrated, the single gift which the Sword of Knowledge offered to anyone, be they Tyr'agar or common clansmen. He had thought, then, that this year, this year he would escape that duty although his fires were the brightest and his dragons the most fearsome, so that he might have some time with his daughter on the one night when it was not a weakness to do so.

But that was before the clan Leonne had made an offer which he had been either too wise, or too cowardly, to refuse. It was done. Even if Alesso's plans prevailed, it would not be undone; he wondered how much of a wedge it would drive between them, and if that wedge might be removed over time.

Or if she would continue to be a part and parcel of offers that he, as father, could not easily refuse. There were hints of that now; he faced them squarely, hearing the barely veiled desire in Eduardo di'Garrardi's voice. Hearing the anger at being first refused so that the Flower of the Dominion might be passed, untouched, to the kai Leonne.

You have already given her in marriage to one man, Alesso said. *And she is known throughout the Dominion for both her beauty and her song. If she is desired, and she will be, might she not be given to wife again?*

Yes.

It was too dark for Alesso to cast a shadow, but a shadow was cast across the lake's surface, and the waters, where the shadow touched them, seemed to bubble as if at sudden, scouring heat. He turned, angered, knowing who he would see.

Isladar, self-styled Lord. "Well met, Widan."

"What are you doing here?"

"I have been summoned for the revelry, I believe."

"I do not profess to have much of a sense of humor."

"Very well. This is the night of the Festival Moon, but it is not coincidence that our Lord sought this night for his own purpose and his own worship. More than that, oh, scholar of the antiquities, I shall leave to you to better understand."

The *Kialli* lord was dressed like a man, albeit a tall and slender one. Sendari found him profoundly beautiful for moments at a time—when he could see with human eyes, and not with eyes trained to magic's use. "You are not so respectful as your Sword's Edge."

"You have nothing I desire, Isladar."

The kinlord smiled. "Nothing at all? Ah, I fear at the moment that there is truth in what you say. A pity. Of the two, desire and fear, I have found in my experiments and studies that desire is the stronger leash. Fear is unreliable."

"I do not fear you."

"You do. But you do not let the fear control you. You are wise, Widan, but that is to be expected."

"You came for a reason?"

"Ah. Yes. It appears that, this eve, we are to meet with the General, and three . . . guests. I was sent to accompany you."

"You were sent to find me."

"Yes."

"Very well." Sendari turned, grudging the demon his company on this night, this night of freedom. "Do you know who these companions are?"

"Ah, yes. The Tyr'agnate Jarrani kai di'Lorenza, the Tyr'agnate Eduardo kai di'Garrardi, and the Second Captain of the Tyran."

Sendari's feet failed him; he stumbled in the darkness, sliding against grass and the occasional rock as he attempted to right himself. "A Captain of the *oathguards*? Has Alesso lost all sense?"

"No. You forget, Widan, that my vision is clearer than either yours or the General's in at least one regard. That man, be he one of your ever-so-honorable oathguards or no, has almost chosen his final home. He is ours."

By *ours,* Sendari knew that the kinlord did not refer to the conspirators.

"You don't seem pleased."

"Of course I'm pleased," Sendari said, lying and hating the fact that this creature was well aware of it. The Tyran were the only men who swore to serve another man loyally, placing their honor above the value of their lives. They were chosen because they were trusted. Odd, that. The Tyr'agar trusted his Generals to a point, and the Sword of Knowledge not at all; therefore Sendari did not consider the planned betrayal by Alesso of the Tyr he served to be an evil act.

But the Captain of the *oathguards*? He wondered if Alesso felt the same shock and the same almost naive sense of disappointment. Naive? Yes. He took a breath, freeing himself from the voice of a child, of a simpleton. "It will make the task simpler."

"Yes. He will be your most effective weapon; I do not believe that the *Kialli* will be necessary at all."

"A pity. The *Kialli* will be necessary indeed. We've discussed this, Isladar. The last of the line Leonne is not in Annagar; he's a hostage in the keep of the Imperial Kings. His death is in your hands."

Isladar nodded gravely. "Come, Widan. The night will wane soon enough, and we have need of it."

The Serra Diora en'Leonne stared at the face of a dozen masks, thinking, as she caressed the feathers of an eagle, that she had worn masks all her life, some lovelier and more complex than this, some gaudy, and some so austere even Ona Teresa could find no fault.

And yet tonight she wanted no mask, felt she needed none. This was her harem, and these, these were *her* wives. Oh, they were Illara's as well, but Illara was there, by the lake, beginning an evening of pleasant drinking that might—or might not—turn ugly by dawn's light. She thought it might not although she could not be completely certain.

The serafs waited for her to make her choice; she touched the feathered mask again and then lifted it quickly, knowing that, if she did not choose, they could not leave. Their evening was already passing.

"The rest," she told them, "are yours; take the ones that

you most like and keep them. This is my first Festival as a Leonne—I want you to remember it kindly." These were fine masks; expensive, jeweled here and there to catch the light, furred, rendered in exquisitely rich paints. As gifts, they were not grand—unless one gave them to serafs.

Speechless, the younger girls gaped—their first display of poor training, but forgiven because it was the Night of the Festival Moon—while the older women quickly and practically set about the task of choosing among the masks. They knew that Diora spoke honestly, and waiting would only mean that the masks they most liked might be worn or chosen by another. In ones and twos the serafs who served the Serra Diora's harem vanished through the open screen doors that cut her off, this night, from the world that lay hidden for every other day of the year.

She began to walk toward the garden and Serena appeared, as if by Widan conjuring, at just that moment. "Will you not join me a moment, Na'dio?"

Diora laughed. "You were sent to make certain that I do not arrive before they wish me to."

"You wound me," Serena replied, but her smile and her tone revealed a heart momentarily at peace. "But I am not quite so calculating. Na'dani is beginning to wake, and he *will* fuss, this night of all nights. A baby's life *is* a Festival Night, whether it be this date, or the next, day or night, dusk or twilight.

"And you, my dear, my most favored Na'dio, have a very special gift for easing Na'dani's night pains. I thought you might—Ah. He is awake now."

Diora heard the truth of this for herself although Na'dani's cries were so much weaker and thinner than the vaguely remembered cries of the children she'd grown up with. Hurrying across the wooden floors, she followed Serena into the cradle room, preceding her to the cradle itself, the cradle that had already begun to shake from side to side as the babe kicked and swung his arms and legs in wobbly circles.

It was, of course, her song that settled the babe, and they all knew it. She did not need to touch him; indeed, she did not need to stand in the same room; she could sing him to sleep while curled in the warm prison of her husband's arms, and the babe would hear her voice as if there was no distance between them.

And there was no distance.

Because she loved this child as she could not remember loving a child before him. She loved to touch him, to hold him; the smell of him was more of a wonder than the waters of the Tor Leonne. His tiny body made her arms feel strong, and she loved nothing more than this: to be able to stand, child in her arms, song on her lips for his ears alone.

> *The sun has gone down, has gone down, my love*
> *Na'dani, Na'dani child*
> *Let me take down my helm and my shield bright*
> *Let me forsake the world of guile*
> *For the Lady is watching, is watching, my love*
> *Na'dani, Na'dani dear*
> *And she knows that the heart which is guarded and*
> *   scarred*
> *Is still pierced by the darkest of fear*
> *   When you smile I feel joy*
> *   When you cry I feel pain*
> *   When you sleep in my arms I feel strong*
> *   But the Lord does not care*
> *   For the infant who sleeps*
> *   In the cradle of arms and my song*
> *The time it will come, it will come, my love*
> *Na'dani, Na'dani my own*
> *When the veil will fall and separate us*
> *May you bury me when you are grown*
> *For the heart, oh the heart, is a dangerous place*
> *It is breaking with joy, and with fear*
> *Worse, though, if you'd never been born to me,*
> *Na'dani, Na'dani, my dear."*

He was, of course, asleep before the last of the words left her lips. Asleep, she thought, before she had finished the first stanza of the song. Her arms were her cradle, and she promised, with full heart, that she would protect him as if he were her own child because he was the child of her heart, the first.

She laid him down almost reluctantly as Serena watched; there were tears in the older woman's eyes. "You would not know that he's not yours," she said softly.

"I feel that he *is* mine," was Diora's half-guilty reply.

"But surely so much can happen to make a life so short, does it matter how many of us love him?"

"Only if you believe that the winds are jealous," Serena said.

"Not tonight. Tonight, by the Lady's decree, we do as our hearts desire."

"Yes, we do," Deirdre said softly.

Diora had the grace to blush almost guiltily. "I know he's not really mine," she said weakly, lifting her hand from the side of the cradle as if the hand itself, and not the woman it belonged to, was reluctant to let go. "It's just that I've never—"

"It's the Festival Moon, Diora. And I see that you haven't yet donned your mask."

"You aren't wearing one either."

"No—but we decided there'd be no point anyway. You've never forgotten a voice if you've heard it speak more than two words—there's no chance at all that we could fool you. You've made honest women of all of us; there's hardly any point in lying." She smiled almost ruefully and changed the subject. "I hate it when he cries and there's nothing I can do. You calm him. And you'll protect him. If anyone in the harem can, it's you." For a moment her words were sharp with the intensity of the unspoken plea. Diora took a step back at what she heard in the voice itself and then, in quick succession, two steps forward—for the same reason. It was awkward, but vulnerability did that.

Deirdre gently turned her face away. "I've never been so afraid, Diora. It's him. I—"

Silence. The touch of skin beneath two palms, two unblemished, unseasoned palms. Dark eyes met dark eyes beneath the Festival Moon. Deirdre relaxed a moment into the warmth of those hands, and then brought her own up to ring the Serra Diora's wrists.

"But Na'dani's had his attention for the moment, and before he decides he's hungry, we'd like some of yours. Come."

Serena smiled at both of them, almost as if she were mother here, and they her daughters. "I will watch over Na'dani. You are both young and energetic; go before the evening is wasted."

* * *

Deirdre led her into the Leonne garden—the garden that was protected, on all sides, by the walls of the palace itself. There was a pond here in which small colorful fish swam beneath green lily pads and their white tufts. There were standing stones, smooth and worn with time, that might have once borne a slightly different shape, a different surface. The twisted shapes of dwarf trees, the darkness of their leaves stretching up and out like elderly hands, stood companion to the stones, and of the two, it was difficult to say which had stood longer: the stones or the trees; there was about both the aura that spoke not of beauty, nor, in the end, of peace, but of survival and endurance. Around these, no flowers had been planted, no gaudy colors displayed. The stone and the crippled trees spoke most powerfully when they spoke alone.

But it was not for this, in the evening's shallows, that the two women came, and if Diora stopped, as she always did, to pay her respectful bow to these monuments, Deirdre dragged her away before she could sink into the contemplation of what they meant.

Ah, the road took them, pulled them, and they followed. Birds came, although they were few, and often easily startled; insects lived within the earth and above the still water, humming with a noise of their own. In the darkness, life itself seemed to celebrate the lack of the Lord's heat, the Lord's fire. The shadows were cool.

The garden was large; from its center, the walls of the palace were memory unless one looked for them. It was to this center that the winding roads led, and if their path was a lazy one that passed by stone and water and artfully arranged flower, no one complained.

They walked hand in hand, these two women, these two Leonne wives. The moon's full face was high and bright and easily seen; its light shone like silver warmed by time's passage. Moon shadows flittered in the breeze as the foliage bowed; almost, Diora did likewise.

But Deirdre pulled her along until she saw the glimmer of lamplight in the garden's heart. There were no serafs here; she saw two women, recognizing them at once by their gait. Ruatha and Faida.

They wore saris that were simple with pale shades that the lamps, not the moon, brought to light. She thought them too graceful to be here—thought them, for a moment, mourning Leonne wives from centuries gone, come to dance where the living might listen to their sad plight with either pity or terror.

And who listened to the tales of wives but wives?

She shook her head; the vision passed, and she stood, her suddenly cold hand in Deirdre's warmer, larger one.

"I have her," Deirdre said, lifting that hand. "She would have been all night near Na'dani's basket if you hadn't sent me, Faida."

"Well, you'd have been there all night as well," Ruatha replied cheerfully. Deidre frowned, but the frown was a mask; beneath it there was far too much amusement and affection.

Faida ran across the path, her feet unfettered by sandals. She swept Diora into a hug, and then pointed up, and up, and up; her hair hung to the hollow of her knees as they stared together at the face of the Lady's Moon. "Diora," she said. "It's the Festival Night."

"I know."

"We—Ruatha, Deirdre, and I—are your equals, for just this night."

"You are more than my equals," Diora replied, gravely and seriously, "on any night."

"The clans don't recognize it."

"The clans are not your sister-wife."

"I told you," Ruatha said wryly.

"You are spoiling Faida's speech," Deirdre reprimanded gently, prying her hand free from Diora's.

"Yes, you are."

"It *is* the Festival night," Diora replied in her own defense. But she fell silent as she realized that she was, of all things, nervous. Nervous before these women, whom she trusted. Trust. It did not come easily to a Serra, to a woman of the clans, if it came at all.

"What was I saying?"

"As if you'd forget. You've been practicing all day, Faida."

"Ru, let me finish.

"Tonight, under the Lady's Moon, we're all equal; we can be who we'd like to be; we can say anything without fear of reprisal." She dropped her gaze then, to her feet, to the shadow the moon cast around her body.

"Faida . . ."

"You say it if it's so easy!"

Ruatha laughed then, and Deirdre laughed, and Diora knew by this that Faida had probably insisted, in her undeniably sweet way, that the gift of first speech be hers.

"What she's trying to say," Ruatha en'Leonne said, coming forward at last to join her three sister-wives where they stood under the lambent light of the moon, with the moon as witness, "is that we each have gifts for you—but if you accept them, they demand as much back in return." And as she spoke, she drew from her neck one of the many golden chains clasped there, and on the end of that chain were three rings. They were jade, Diora thought, although in the darkness it was hard to tell. "Faida and Deirdre won't say no to me; they wouldn't dare."

"It would break her heart," Deirdre added, "and there's nothing quite so unhappy as Ruatha's tears." She lifted her ringless hand, the Lady's hand, as Ruatha slid the first of the rings from the chain with remarkably steady hands. She put it on Deirdre's finger, and Deirdre let the hand drop.

Faida raised a hand, and in her turn, bore the ring that had been such a slight weight around Ruatha's neck.

Then the three of them turned, as nervous, Diora thought, as she. She knew oath rings when she saw them, even if the darkness obscured them. And she knew that an oath ring was a binding made of love and determination and loyalty; it was blessed by and of the Lady, and one did not accept or wear one lightly. But she had never heard of oath rings given in this fashion: as one woman to three. To swear an oath of the heart to one woman, one accepted a daunting responsibility. To three . . . she was silent.

No one thought to raise the lamp to better examine Ruatha's rings; it was what they signified that mattered here, and if one needed lamplight to see it, they would never mean enough.

Diora en'Leonne, the Serra of the second most important man in the realm, found that she could not speak. There were words trembling on her lips, but her breath could not be moved to utter them.

For a long moment, they stared at her, and then, shaking far more than Ruatha or Deirdre or Faida, Diora en'Leonne lifted her hand.

Faida and Deirdre cheered, a loud sound, even a childish one, and certainly not a noise that wives of important clansmen were supposed to be familiar with, but Ruatha only smiled. At least Diora thought it a smile; the shadows made it hard to tell.

Here, one had to see with the heart.

"They aren't very fine," Ruatha said. "We didn't want to ask our husband for help. We wanted them to be ours."

Deirdre lifted a necklace that was also strung with rings; they were different, cooler to the touch, but they numbered three as well. To each of her sister-wives, she gave one, placing them in line with Ruatha's upon a single finger. Faida, the first to speak, offered a ring to each as well, her hands the steadiest of the three.

"Diora?" she asked quietly. "Are you crying?"

Diora shook her head: *Yes.* And then, while they watched in shock—and before Faida joined her in tears— she, too, reached into the folds of her sari and drew from it a single, slender chain. It had belonged to her mother, or so Ona Teresa had claimed. And she had made fitting use of it.

Around the flat gold links hung three rings. Each of the three caught the lamplight in the garden and played with it, scattering light across the plants and the path and the small stone table upon which was placed food, water, and a screen to protect both.

"You knew!" Faida's voice was heavy with disappointment and accusation.

Diora found her voice although she let the tears continue to fall. "No. I didn't. I call the Lady herself to bear witness—I did not know. But it *is* the Night of the Festival Moon, and I thought that maybe—that this one night I could ask, I could dare to ask, of *you*—"

The rings were very fine. They were jeweled, and the gold was Lord's gold, heavy and pale. Each ring was identical: at its heart, emerald, and to either side, pearl.

"These were cut from the same stone," she told them. "I want—"

But Ruatha shook her head and lifted her hand, signaling for Diora to place this ring, this accepted gift and requested faith, above the two she already bore. And Deirdre followed, and Faida.

And then they embraced, an awkward press of arms and

legs and bodies pressed into too small a space, and no one
cried more than Diora. No one laughed louder, either,
when they heard the wailing cry of Na'dani approaching
them in the gilded darkness of this Festival Night, as he
was carried to his mother by a slightly weary Serena.

Dawn came, a fringe of welcome light on the horizon.
Diora woke with it, apprehensive. But the rings on her
finger were real. Waking at this edge of the Lord's dominion did not take them from her. No moon magic,
these, but magic nonetheless. She brought her hand to her
face, closed her eyes, and let the cool feel of gold and jade
and silver touch her cheek.

And then she, born to the voice that was gift and curse,
froze.

There was no sound in the garden. The bowers of the
trees above did not shake in the wind; the crickets did not
sing; the insects did not buzz. And beside her, on blankets
that were slightly too rough to be truly fine, her sister-
wives did not breathe.

She might have cried out in terror, in fear—but before
she could break the silence with the sound of her voice,
another woman did.

"They sleep a . . . magical slumber. They will awaken
unharmed and unchanged, but what I say must be said to
you alone.

"Well met, Serra Diora. I've heard much about you."

She turned at once, and in the dawn's growing light
saw a midnight shade: a woman, robed in a blue so deep it
should have looked black. Should have, and didn't. She
wore a hood, and as she spoke, the hood began to curl
back on itself until her face was revealed.

Not a young woman, this. Older, she thought, than
Serena en'Leonne, for all that her hair was black as midnight shadow. Diora carried a dagger, as so many of the
women born to the clans did; she drew it.

"I mean you no harm, Serra Diora."

But her voice—her voice told a different tale.

"You are not telling the truth," Diora replied evenly,
planting her feet in the garden's path, standing between
this stranger and her sister-wives. Living her vow, so soon
after it had been made.

"I am telling the truth," was the heavy reply. The

woman's eyes were unblinking. "I am Evayne a'Nolan, and I come to offer the only warning I am able to offer you, here, so close to the heart of their power."

That *was* true. Diora let the blade's flat reflect the rising sun as she met this woman's odd, pale eyes. They were not gray, nor blue, nor green, nor brown; they were the color of purple lilacs. Caution decreed that she maintain her guard, but some instinct caused the dagger to waver.

"I believe that you mean me no harm," she said at last. "But you know of a danger to me, or you believe you do, and you think it will kill me."

"In a manner," Evayne replied, and her voice was bitter with grief and something that Diora would have called rage, had it not been so quiet. "I have little time, Serra Diora. Listen to me now.

"There will come a time, well before the next Festival of the Moon, when the heart of the Dominion will be struck by the howling winds. I cannot tell you what exactly occurs; I do not know it."

A lie.

"But I will tell you this much: You cannot prevent it. There is nothing at all that you can do that will change what is to occur. It is a tide, a current. Fight it, and you will be both exhausted and destroyed. Ride it—ride it, and you will have your chance to right what has been wronged, in a fashion."

Truth. Absolute and unshakable.

"What do you speak of? What wind? What event?"

The stranger paused a moment, as if listening. "You will know it when it comes. There will be no mistaking what it portends. Listen to me," the woman said, her voice so intense it could not be ignored. "To survive, you must be a rock that the winds cannot shake. You will be hurt almost beyond measure; certainly beyond your own. Hide the pain, Diora en'Leonne. Hide it well. If it is seen, if it is known at all, you will join them; you do not deal with fools but with cunning men, with men of power."

"What do you mean? Join who? Who do you speak of?"

"Do not move, Diora en'Leonne. When the time comes, no matter what you see, or hear, in spite of all you feel— *do not move.*" She lifted her head, testing a wind that

Diora could not see or feel. "They will find me, if I linger even five minutes. Child, I *am* sorry."

The figure in blue bowed; the hood climbed up her face as if it were alive. She gestured and took a single step toward Diora. The air swallowed her whole.

Noise returned to the garden; noise and life.

But the sun was cold where it fell upon her sleeping wives; her heart, as she gazed upon those perfect faces, sleep-gentled and vulnerable, felt as if it belonged, for a moment, to some other woman, to another body; as if it— as if it were becoming a standing stone, or a tree cut and bent and twisted into a shape that was its own, unique.

For she had heard death in those words, death in each and every one of them.

And it was not for her.

WAR

CHAPTER THIRTEEN

8th of Morel, 427 AA
The Tor Leonne

> *When riders gather in silence, the storm follows.*
> *—Mancorvan proverb*
> *Danger is more than one powerful man in a quiet room.*
> *—Averdan proverb*

Three men sat in an empty room.

Before the dusk had settled across the shoulders of the night's cupbearer, but moments after the multiple lamps had been blessed by the priests and lit against the coming shadow, they met, as they had planned, in the Tyr's contemplation rooms.

There were no cushions or palanquins, no divans, no benches; no serafs danced in attendance, no women brought trays of delicacies, flasks of wine, or warm wet towels with which to wipe away the sand and sweat of the day's exertions. Each of these men was allowed a personal escort of between four and eight cerdan at all times; it was not only an honor granted by the Tyr, but also a symbol of their rank. Not a single guard stood among them.

The pleasing strains of quiet samisen music carried from across the lake that had been the gift of the Lady to the Tyr'agar over two hundred years ago. If they looked into the distance, they might see the family of the Tyr before night's repose.

General Alesso par di'Marente looked. "The night is clear," he said as the lamps along the lakefront began their bright glow.

Widan Sendari par de'Marano touched his long, fine beard. It was a habit of his, a gesture of contemplation

and concentration. Or of nervousness. His face, placid
and still as the lake's waters, showed no hint of which as
he gazed at the profile of the most powerful man in the
Dominion of Annagar. "Alesso," he said quietly.

"There is no turning back," the General replied. His
eyes, like the night, were darkening, and if his hair
showed the slow march of time, that time did not touch
the angular lines of his face. "Baredan and Cormano are
dead."

"You have proof?" The third man, silent until now, also
turned his gaze upon Alesso di'Marano. Tyran Calevro
kai di'Horaro clasped his hands loosely behind his back
as he met the eyes of his ally. They were cold.

"What proof is needed?"

"They're Generals, not common cerdan. You cannot
assume that they will trust any trap you've devised."

"They received an urgent summons—carried not by
any common cerdan, but by the Tyran. They answered it."
He paused and then turned once again to gaze across the
lake. "Why would they not? The Tyran are the most honorable men in the Dominion. They know no treachery."

Tyran Calevro kai di'Horaro flushed an unflattering
purple. "Alesso, I warn you—"

"Calevro." The Widan spoke. "General di'Marente has
not been in error once since we ventured down this path.
You do him a disservice to question him." His voice was
the voice of the most respected of the Tyr'agar's Widan
counselors, at once calm and commanding. "Come. We
gather tonight to witness the beginning of a dynasty."

But the Second Captain of the oathguards was not so
easily turned aside; his was the greatest crime, of all
crimes committed here. He would not have it committed
for no reason. "The army?"

"The armies are in place," Alesso replied, without
turning back. "The city will be ours, and the Terrean."
Another light, caught in the shape of an eagle, flared to
life above the pavilion upon which the Tyr'agar sat with
his wife and his oldest son. "And after the Festival of the
Sun, we will own the Dominion."

"If all goes according to plan. We do not own all five of
the Tyr'agnati."

Alesso was angered a moment. "They will come. What
choice will they have? If they hear rumors of the

Tyr'agar's death, so be it. More than that, they will not have. They will be on the road, with their courts and their finery."

"But the—"

"But what? It is the Festival of the Lord—they will come."

"And if they do not?"

"Calevro, you try my patience. This moment is ours. Savor it. The game is about to be won."

The Tyran fell silent, and when next a man spoke, it was Widan Sendari. "Alesso?"

"Ah, look. He gathers his daughters to him. How fitting." The General's smile was soft; in another light, it might have seemed tender. "What concerns you, Widan?"

"My daughter."

"Serra Diora will be quite safe," the General replied. "As long as she does nothing at all to interfere."

"That was not our plan—"

"It is necessity's plan," the General replied. "She is canny, the young Serra. And wise beyond the ways of women, as her father taught her to be." He turned away from the Tyr'agar's family, to face his allies for the last time that night. "But if she shows her loyalty to be to her husband's clan, she will die with the rest of them.

"She must, old friend," he added softly, reaching out unexpectedly to grip Widan Sendari's slightly bent shoulders.

Her father was silent. Serra Diora was known across the five Terreans as the Flower of the Dominion. And she was wise, but also cunning in the ways of women. Was she not as she was raised to be? She was the daughter of the most cunning man in the Dominion. Exquisite—even in a father's eyes—and dangerous. Ah, dangerous.

"She is your daughter, Sendari. Trust her."

He murmured her name so softly the samisen's strings carried it away from the ears of his allies. A mercy.

From across the lake, the screaming began.

She was the most beautiful woman in the Dominion of Annagar. The poets all said so.

Her hair was the color of a night so dark and soft that a man could only dream of experiencing it. She was tiny and yet, once seen, she filled the whole of man's vision with her perfect grace and her lithe, supple movements. Her voice was the bell's voice, her hands were ivory made flesh; her nose and her lips and her chin were the subjects of countless poems. Even the bards of the North carried her name—and her fame—to the ears of undeserving, unhorsed barbarians.

She sat, her legs folded perfectly beneath her, her head slightly bent so that the tip of her chin might hover delicately above the folds of her blue silk sari. Gold adorned the line of her jaw, trailing like a liquid spill from her ears.

She was so perfectly composed one could almost miss the spray of blood that darkened her lap and speckled her bare upper arms. One might miss the slow, deliberate breaths, the clenched hands.

Eight men, wearing the uniform of the Tyran, held their swords a moment, staring openly upon a face that very few had seen. They were tense; the kill had not yet settled and they glanced from corner to corner, waiting for their companions to join them.

They made no move toward her, and she, no move to rise.

No move at all, save breath, and breathing, by their orders, she was allowed. It was difficult; to kill her, one risked the wrath of the Widan Sendari, but to disobey the General was likewise unthinkable. A poor choice for simple oathguards.

The harem of Ser Illara Valens kai di'Leonne was a wing unto itself, with rooms and fountains and courtyards to better display the women that the heir to the Dominion had chosen for his own use. There were places to hide here, places behind which a mother desperate to protect the life of her young child might find a moment's respite.

There were guards in the harem—but not any lowly cerdan, with eyes too round, or a mouth too apt to spill the secrets of the beauty of the women therein. No; the Tyr'agar had decreed—and who would have thought to argue—that the harem, with its women and its valuable children, was far too important to be trusted to common men. The guards he had offered his oldest son—the guards that had been accepted—had been oathguards. They held the title of Tyran: the only men whom the Tyr trusted. Their life's work had been the safety of the women and children of Ser Illara.

Their night's work was almost done.

How long could the slaughter of unarmed women take? Screams and cries echoed throughout the rounded, acoustically exquisite harem. Sobbing, pleading. The Tyran did not take their time—but it was clear that they did not hesitate to indulge their baser urges before they continued with their work; who would be left to speak of it? And against whom was it an outrage? Ser Illara kai di'Leonne was dead. The Tyr'agar was dead. These women belonged only to the little families that they had been gathered from, year after year; families who had no voice and no power.

Serra Diora had been wife to Ser Illara; a woman of power. She folded her hands in her lap as she listened. Her face was grave and lovely and demure.

A child's scream, cut short almost as quickly as it began. Not hers. She had borne the heir no children in their short marriage.

Had she, she would be dead.

Heavy steps upon marble, upon silk. Cushions thrown and scattered. Cries of discovery, both victim's and victor's. Feet away from her straight back.

"Diora!"

Serra Diora looked the very statue of the Dominion's most beautiful woman. The child had been found. She closed her eyes as she heard the terrified fury of his mother's voice; the slight scrape of small dagger against sheath. The cry of denial.

Then, silence. The child himself made no cry.

"Tyran di'Barento." The man closest to the harem's wide, beautiful doors stood forward at the formal request of his man. He was young, tall, proud; his face was unscarred, and his hair a gleaming turn of Annagarian black.

Tyran di'Barento.

"Bring him."

The Tyran obeyed his commander; the body of the child was carried, like so much baggage, across the shining floor. Tyran di'Barento lifted the head that rested at such an odd angle, gazed at it. Nodded. "The last."

"The women?"

Di'Barento shrugged. "What is done, is done." But his eyes narrowed as his gaze came to rest upon the Flower of the Dominion. Dropping the corpse of the babe to one side, he bowed; the bow was low and respectful.

"Serra Diora di'Marano, if you will allow it, we will provide you escort to your father's side."

Serra Diora di'Marano sat on the flat silk mats in her father's waiting chambers. From before her bent knees, oil scent carried on the breeze; the lamp had been placed there by the Tyran, that she not be left in the darkness. She knew Widan Sendari would be awake, but wondered, briefly, if Serra Fiona en'Marano had slept through the slaughter.

Diora had taken the time to change, donning a simple white sari and taking none of the jewelry that had been gifted her by Ser Illara. But there were rings on her fingers: three, each simple, none worthy of her station. No one sought to part her from them, nor would they have been easily surrendered—but even these she would give up with silent, perfect grace should the need arise.

She knew how to wait.

How to wait, when waiting was all she had.

In time, the Widan came. He was girded not for war, but rather for the business by which he had become known throughout the Terreans. His shirt was fine, although night's hand bled it of the full richness of its color, its luster. He wore a cloak, caught in two places by the worked gold of the Sword of Knowledge; rubies glimmered along one edge, a warning to the foolish. On the third finger of his right hand, the sun in splendor; on the third finger of his left, the crescent moon. Symbols of his office, of his value to the Tyr. Only his footwear was unusual; boots made his tread heavy and unpleasing. As his toes crossed the circle of the lamp's reach, she saw the russet stains that had seeped into pale leather. These boots, he would not keep.

"Serra Diora," Widan Sendari said, bowing his head and shoulders in quiet respect. "I am pleased to find you well."

"And I, you, Widan." Like a fan, her hands folded delicately as they lay, palms down, in her lap.

He stared down at her, from the vantage of height and

the power of rank, the lantern's soft glow the bridge between them. His fingers crossed the width of his beard, stroking it absently. She seemed a spirit, an otherworld vision, pure white against the muddied shadows. And she spoke not a word.

Ah, she was Diora, and she was still his daughter. He walked past her kneeling form. "Come, Na'dio," he said, the words quite soft. He slid the wooden screen open abruptly; it stuck on the rails, adding a reality that the moment did not demand.

She rose as he lifted the door, feeling its weight. She did him the grace of not offering her aid. Why should she? Her training was perfect; she could not be separated from it. And no true woman made a man feel weak and awkward in his own dwelling. Ah, there. He had it. He would speak with the serafs on the morrow, and if the door troubled him again, he would have them killed.

Beneath the curve of his waiting arm, Diora stood.

Night opened before them, and beneath its watchful eyes, fire across the lake. Fire on the lake. The waters were burning.

When she was young—and Na'dio was the only name that she answered to—they had come to the Tor Leonne upon the eye of the Festival of the Moon, father and daughter. On Moon-night, masked in the veils and facades of the Festival's height, a man in his prime and a four-year-old child wandered the streets of Tor Leonne, caught up in the scents of spice and rich sweetmeats, of masked women's perfumes. She had asked him, then, why they had to pretend to be other people.

He could still feel the brush of the eagle's feather against his cheek as he bent down to catch her in his arms and raise her to the heights of his shoulders. *They don't pretend to be other people,* he told her gravely, as a shameless, reckless young woman ran a hand across his chest, touching the darkened skin beneath the simple silk shirt before the flow of the crowd carried her away. She wore a tiger's face, but her voice was a kit's.

Na'dio had chosen the night-hunter's mask, with its round, feathered visage and its wide eyes. He had fastened it with care, and this, too, he remembered, for the feel of the ties was not unlike the touch of his beard between his fingers.

But they're all wearing masks.

Yes. And because they wear masks, they can be who they are, who they would like to be. As the Lady decrees, he added softly.

As the Lady decrees, she replied gravely. Even then, she had been so grave.

And the Lady decrees that you be my Na'dio this eve, and not Serra Teresa's perfect lady. Come.

He did not put her down—had no desire to put her down—although on any other evening, it would have shamed him to show so open an attachment to a daughter. Together, they mounted the slope of Tor Leonne. The Festival of the Moon was at its peak. Caught in the passions of youth, or the memories of it, men and women made the shadows noisy with their hope and their merriment and their brief, brief loves.

Only when Sendari reached the railings of the Pavilion of the Moon did he lift his child from his shoulders, and then it was only to hold her, while his arms could take her weight. And that, on Moon-night, might be forever.

See, he said softly. *There is light in the darkness. And because it is dark, the light will be more beautiful than any light you have ever seen.*

She listened, rapt in her interest, complete in her trust of his promise. It was Moon-night. Ah.

Fireflower bloomed in a brilliant spray of blue petals hundreds of yards above their suddenly upturned faces. Muted whispers, awe, a sudden hush. Blue gave way to crimson, and that to green, and before any of the three colors had faded, a ball of golden seed scattered in the night wind, brighter than the face of the moon itself.

He held her close; he heard her intake of breath, her cry of sweet glee. And he wished, that one year, that he might wear this mask—and she her own—forever.

But Widan Sendari was a wise and cunning man, and the dream of the Festival Moon was little better than a sleeper's delirium; the time had come and gone, and during its passage great powers had been made—and greater power broken. He looked down at her upturned face, seeing the woman his daughter had become in her silence and stillness.

Na'dio, he thought, but he did not say the name aloud again. *When was the last time you called me Father?* It was a full two quarters and more before the Festival of the Moon, but if she resided within Tor Leonne, he thought he might even find the freedom in which to ask her.

The fires were bright enough to give a glow to her eyes.

During the height of the following day, the serafs toiled to clean the blood from the Tyrian platform, supervised by General Alesso di'Marente. He was grim and silent, a man preparing for war now that the first battle had been won.

Or so he seemed to Radann Fredero kai el'Sol.

The day was cold. The evening's work had been done quickly—too quickly—and efficiently. The dead lay in neat rows, their heads set close to the bodies they had fallen from, if they had submitted to the Tyran.

"This was foul work," the General said, his expression smooth and diffident and utterly chilling. "Would you not agree, kai el'Sol?"

He could not speak. He gazed upon the Leonne dead as if sight alone might wake them.

"But I am certain that our investigations will lead us to the . . . assassins. Obviously, in our endeavors to apprehend the killers of the clan Leonne, I have been forced to close the Tor until further notice. No one—be it seraf maid or Radann el'Sol—is to leave these grounds without my permission. The cerdan have been given orders to shoot to kill, and the mages are keeping the periphery patrolled."

"Sound precautions," Fredero heard his voice as if it were a stranger's—and at that, a stranger that he took an instant dislike to, but could not, for shock, dismiss.

"Thus ends a proud line. It doesn't appear that the Tyr'agar offered resistance at all. But Leonne was beloved of the Lord, and it is right that the Lord's rites be offered to the clan. I trust you to see to this, as the kai el'Sol."

Fredero nodded; refusing to allow the stranger to speak with his voice again.

"Oh, and, kai el'Sol? There will, of course, be a new Tyr'agar crowned by the Radann at the Festival of the Sun." He offered a boon, this General, this killer: He turned and walked away, sparing Fredero the effort, the terrible, treacherous effort, of having to speak his compliance.

And then he was alone with serafs who still scrubbed and oiled and cleaned. Alone with the spirit-emptied bodies of the dead. The light in the open eyes had been guttered by the wind.

But something reflected the sunlight unevenly, and as he approached it, searching for some sign, some meaning by which to decide a course, he saw it clearly.

Kneeling, gently rolling the headless body of Markaso di'Leonne to one side, Fredero kai el'Sol reached out to lift the Sword's crown from its place beneath the large man.

The crown has fallen. He rose, carrying the burden of the truth in the object itself. The dead were dead. But this? They had passed it to him to decide.

And this day, this first of days, no decision came to him; he had not pulled his sword and attacked the General openly, warrior to warrior, the wrath of god against the desires of a traitor.

I am only a man, he thought. *But the Lord is impartial. Power is the law in the Lord's land.* The crown was heavy in his hands as he walked, slowly and proudly, to the temple.

But the serafs at his back began to speak, and he knew what they said, for he had seen it himself in the silvered glass: His hair had gone gray between dusk and dawn; age had fallen upon him like the decisive blow of a sword. Like the judgment of an angry Lord.

There will be a new Tyr'agar crowned by the Radann at the Festival of the Sun.

Serra Fiona en'Marano sat with her forehead to the sleeping mats in the bedchambers of Widan Sendari. Her hair was a spill of dark brown, artfully interspersed with strands of pearls and a touch of magenta silk that incidentally matched the throws and cushions beside which she waited. She was many years her husband's junior, and as such was considered to be a fine prize; Serra Alora en'Marano had died in childbirth many years before.

Serra Fiona only wished that her cursed daughter had died with her.

The Widan had few concubines, and most of these were

gifts; he treated them well, as befit a man of his import and station, and in return, he expected them to serve his interests when visitors came, and to follow the dictates of his wife. In the harem, Serra Fiona ruled both wives—and their children—with a quiet that was usually reserved for the grave.

Unfortunately, with the return of Serra Diora, her position within the harem had been subtly changed, and she did not like it one bit. Her son, Artano, was kai—but Sendari had not seen fit to bring him on the road from Mancorvo; he remained with his father's brother, Tor'agar Adano kai di'Marano. And had he been present, Fiona knew, Artano would have been ignored in all the real ways in favor of Serra Diora—a daughter returned to her clan. A *daughter*. Her son was a fine youth; almost eleven, and already riding like a clansman. And Sendari showed pride in Artano—when Diora was elsewhere.

"Serra Fiona," the Widan's voice, rising on her name, was her signal; she rose with grace, sitting back on her knees while she continued to wait, her face schooled enough to keep what she felt from tainting its lines. He knew it, of course; he knew far too much about her for her moods, whether masked or no, to be truly hidden. But he was proud of her ability to keep her face smooth and free from the sullen moods that many another less-well-trained wife was prone to.

He sat in repose, the trays of the morning meal half-empty around him. His beard was a peppered spill across a chest that had softened only slightly with age. Lifting his arm, he signaled to the waiting seraf; the man bowed quickly and silently—such a quiet surety of motion was what the Widan most prized in his servants—before leaving his Ser's presence. He bowed once at the screen door, stepped across its threshold, knelt, and then slid it quietly shut.

"You found him," Sendari said, as he met the blue eyes of his young wife. It was a compliment.

She was not to be put off so easily, however. "Widan Sendari," she began, stopping as he lifted a hand.

"Come, Fiona. Join me. It has been many days since I have had the pleasure of your company."

"As you wish, Widan," she replied. Her movement was a study in stilted grace, but her face was lovely. She

crossed the silk mats like an angry cat, stopping at last to
kneel in the cushions by his feet, her back quite stiff.

He laughed, his eyes shining with genuine pleasure.
Touching her bare shoulders with the flat of palms, he
stroked her skin before unwinding the silk sari she wore
in one quick and easy motion. She did not respond at all.

"You are enough to quell a man's ardor, Fiona,"
he said.

"Not," she replied coolly, "the Widan Sendari's." She
had to lift her chin ever so slightly as his nose and lips
traced the underside of her ivory jaw.

Again he laughed—and this she found most infuriating—before he caught her tightly in his arms. Another
man might strike her, dismiss her, force her—but not
Sendari. No. His answer to her subtle defiance, her cool
anger, was always this slightly indulgent amusement—the
same, kind for kind, as he tendered his concubines' children. One day, one day, she thought, she would like to see
him angered.

She was younger than he, and not terribly wise.

And if she chose to withhold the delights of a lady's
pleasure, he chose to evoke them; it was an uneven battle
from start to finish, for Widan Sendari did not enter into
any game that he felt he might lose.

Later, tangled in his arms, pearls from a broken strand
rolling into the silken folds beneath her back, she was
allowed to speak her mind. It was always this way with
Sendari; the act of loving gentled him for moments at
a time, and if one knew how, one could work around
him then.

"It is the Serra Diora Maria di'Marano," she said softly,
her chin against his chest. She felt his muscles stiffen
beneath her face, and she stiffened in return.

"What of her?"

"You have placed her in the harem, Sendari."

Silence. Then his hands tickling the small of her
back—and exposing it to the air. "So I have."

"She is not a concubine."

"I believe I'm aware of that, Fiona."

"She is not your wife."

He laughed. She hated it. "No, she is certainly not my
wife. And if she were not my daughter, I swear by the
Lady's darkest night that I would not take her if she were

offered to me." The laughter faded; she felt his beard brush her hair. "She is my child," he said quietly.

Children did belong in the harem of a powerful man; children, wives, and concubines. Fiona was very glad that he could not see her expression before she replied. "She is no child. Her place is not among us."

"Oh. And is it you, Serra, who will decide the place of my kin?"

She felt the edge in his voice as keenly as if it were a dagger held far enough from the skin that it did not draw blood—but barely. "Sendari, please." Her voice was much meeker. "They do not listen to me while she is present. She is used to the harem of—"

"He is dead. It is finished. She has lost much," he added quietly.

"And I? Am I to be seraf to her desire?" In spite of herself, she pulled back from the comfort of his chest and his chin. The breeze was cool; hours had passed, and the serafs had left the sliders open.

"No," he replied, catching her by either arm. "You will be seraf to mine." He pulled her close again.

Serra Fiona was not to be moved.

"Very well. I will tell you something, but if I hear it repeated in any quarter of my house, I will have your lovely tongue removed." He caught her chin and forced her face up; her blue eyes—striking in their color in this land—met his dark ones, and she shivered slightly. "I am fond of you, Fiona, or I would not have taken you to wife. I am pleased with your talent and your wisdom in quelling the disputes among my women and their children."

She nodded, too nervous to be flattered.

"Serra Diora will no longer be part of the harem after the Festival of the Sun."

There was silence as she counted: Three weeks and two days. "Will you—will you send her away?"

"Women," he said, all anger gone from his voice. "She is not your rival, Fiona. But no. I will not send her away. She will be the Flower of the Dominion, and she will blossom at the Festival of the Sun. The Lord of the Festival will be the man who claims her, who plucks her from the Tor Leonne and takes her back to his Terrean."

"If I were General Alesso, I would keep her."

At that, his smile dimmed and cooled. "Then let us be

glad that you are not Alesso. Come; I am not yet tired, and you are the reward for years of planning. I will enjoy you while I am able."

But she held back until he threw up his arms in mock frustration. "Very well! Very well! I will call Serra Teresa to the Tor Leonne."

"And Serra Diora?"

"Can live with her, under Adano's auspices. It will bring peace to an old man's house. Are you well-satisfied, my little cat?"

He was rewarded by the radiant confidence of the smile she showed him only when she was happy. It was odd, with Serra Fiona. In her happiness, she was most vulnerable.

And he, too, was pleased; Serra Teresa was already on the road from Mancorvo.

"I look forward to the Festival," Fiona said, as she curled into his chest, "especially this year. There has been no music, no dancing, no poetry; there has been no color since the—since the night. The Tyr'agnati will bring it with them. They will be coming?"

"Can they refuse? It *is* the Festival."

"But there is no Tyr."

He kissed her fiercely. "Yes. But there will be, by Festival's end; and he will be a stronger Tyr than we have had for centuries."

Serra Teresa di'Marano came to the Tor Leonne with serafs enough to beggar a Tyr'agnate. She rode on a palanquin carried by cerdan who wore the Marano-marks, and although the palanquin's curtains were properly drawn against the eyes of the commoners who toiled in the streets of the Tor Leonne, there was something in their shimmering fabric, their jewel- and pearl-embroidered raw silk, that was unseemly for an unmarried woman.

It was said that Serra Teresa was a woman of cunning and intelligence—and as such, she was far too valuable to the Marano clan to be married out. It was said that there were offers for her hand from no less a clan than Leonne itself, and whispered further that it was on behalf of the Tyr'agar that those offers had been made. It was even said that the loneliness, the lack of male companionship, had driven her to the shadow of the Lady—but he who carried that rumor carried it at his own peril. The Marano clan was not without power.

And she was at the heart of the Marano clan, although she held no title.

Merchants stopped a moment in the street, if they were coarse enough, to gape at the procession—but while the unadorned circle upon the palanquin's height declared her to be a woman traveling without her lord, no one was bold enough to usurp the right of passage from her train, although it was within their right to do so. Law was theory in the Tor Leonne; power ruled.

Up the winding road the cerdan walked, bending under the weight of the palanquin with an easy grace and a certainty of motion that spoke of long years of practice. The serafs, with their many chests and bags, toiled up the slopes at a respectful distance, and behind them came the riders.

They were only three, but even a witless child could see that their horses, stallions all, were worth as much as the rest of the procession combined. Only the Terrean of Mancorvo produced beasts of such a rich, deep brown, but even for Mancorvans, they were fine—for they came from the field runs of the Tyr'agnate Mareo kai di'Lamberto, and if Lamberto produced poor horses, they did not disgrace themselves by offering them for sale.

Whispers followed the hush, and in them, the name. Marano.

Upon the plateau of the winding road rested the palace of the Tor Leonne, and there was no palace in the whole of the five Terreans that was grander. Gold and copper caught the muted light of cloud-strewn sky and scattered it back through the boughs of trees laden with delicate blossoms and early fruit. By Tyrian decree, nothing grew, and nothing stood, which was taller than the residence of the Tyr, yet even so, the palace itself seemed deceptively small as the roadway curved toward the Tyrian gates.

The noise of the streets of the Tor below were muted by the hush of wind through leaves, the fall of windblown petals; here, the birds cried in a splendid isolation that was at once wild and contrived.

The Tyr'agar was a man who wanted the heart of nature to unfold in its season before his eyes. Where else could

one wander in perfect safety without ever having to look
upon another man? Nowhere but here. And it was said
that the Tyr availed himself of the wonders of that privacy. Or he had.

The gates were open, as they always were at the
morning's height, but there was only one procession that
wended its way toward them. Cerdan stood at attention,
wearing with pride the uniforms—line for line—that they
wore in the service of the clan Leonne. The rising sun
glittered at their left breasts as they came to stand, four
abreast, between the ancient columns upon which the
open gates were hinged. Beneath that sun, ivory, a blend
of linens that fell heavily over red silk.

The cerdan that led the Marano procession stepped forward and bowed; the hems of their robes brushed the
smooth, stone way as they held the crescent of their
swords groundward in the supplicant posture.

"Who seeks to pass?" The oldest man present spoke,
his voice deceptively quiet.

"Serra Teresa di'Marano." The Marano cerdan did not
rise; they stood upon the soil of the Tyr'agar—the man
who ruled at the whim of the Lord—and here, of all
places protocol ruled.

"For what purpose?"

That Marano cerdan who had answered first glanced
awkwardly over his shoulder, as if seeking counsel. At
last, his voice muted, he said, "To visit the court of the
Tyr'agar." It was not ritual. But what ritual was left when
the Tyr'agar's clan no longer existed?

The older cerdan did not betray emotion; he was the
perfect vessel for a Tyr's will. "Who will bear responsibility for her passage?"

"Widan Sendari par di'Marano."

The older man bowed deeply and stepped to one side.
"Pass."

They met in the Pavilion of the Dawn.

Sera Diora left her attendants and the men that guarded
her, and although she moved gracefully, even regally,
with no sign of undue haste, she reached the side of her
aunt in a moment.

She wore azure, and Serra Teresa silver and while, and
as they embraced briefly, the colors of their two silk saris

blended together in a perfect harmony that the Tor Leonne had not seen for almost ten days. Attendants and guards studiously turned their glances aside, but not before seeing the most beautiful woman in the world show a brief glimpse of the child she might once have been to the open skies.

Serra Teresa took her brother's daughter gently aside as the serafs made haste to arrange the firm mats and colored pillows that they were to sit among.

"Ramdan," she said quietly. "Bring the samisen."

The seraf so addressed was the oldest of all men present; his hair was a white crown with hints of the gray that might once have been black. But his eyes were clear, and his back unbent; he moved slowly but as if age were a mantle of dignity, not a weakness.

"Sendari says that you will be my companion," the Serra told her niece, "until the Festival of the Sun."

Diora sat, folding her legs delicately beneath her and taking great care to spread the folds of the sari so that it might remain free of wrinkles. She nodded, wordless, and Serra Teresa rewarded her with a smile.

Ramdan placed the long, slender samisen into his Serra's hands and stepped aside, falling away like a shadow from the brilliance of the two women who sat in perfect repose on this warm summer day. Serra Teresa gazed a moment at the strings and then touched them gently, pulling a quiver, but not a full note, from the movement.

"Do you still play?" she asked her niece.

They both knew the answer, but Diora smiled. "Yes, Ona Teresa."

"And would you play for me? The day has been quite long, and the week harsh, and I do not recall another's touch as sure as yours, or another's voice as pleasing."

Diora's blush was a pleasant fan of color. She was, in all things, Serra Teresa's most apt pupil.

"Ser Artana sends his regards to his sister."

"And his sister," Diora replied quite coolly, "returns his regards." Her fingers brushed the strings beneath her hands.

"Na'dio," Serra Teresa said, using a voice that only her niece might hear, "you think that things will never change between you. But he is your family, and you are both young."

"Yes, Ona Teresa," Diora replied dutifully. But there was an edge to the words, fine and sharp, that only those with great familiarity might note. As if to acknowledge this, Diora spoke again. "He did not come to the Tor Leonne with my father."

"No."

"I should have known, then." Her voice was soft and pleasant, her face, quiet and placid. "How could the Widan Sendari travel to the Tor Leonne for the Festival of the Sun without his kai—unless he thought the risk to the family too great?"

"Diora."

Silence. The samisen answered for her.

But Serra Teresa frowned as she watched her niece's fingers in their play across the strings. "Diora, what do you wear?"

Music. The refrain to a hymn of a clan long dead in the Tyr'agnate wars.

"Diora." The word, sharper now, where Serra Teresa was never publicly sharp.

The Tyr'agnate wars replied; the clouds parted; the breeze carried the warmth of the summer day, the smell of lilac.

"Diora."

"Rings," the younger woman whispered, fighting the compulsion without any sign of the struggle. "Three."

Serra Teresa stared at her brother's daughter for a long moment, and then she smiled, but the smile was laden with sorrow. "You are your mother's daughter," she said softly. "Those rings—they are oath rings."

The strings stilled as Diora laid shaking hands against them. She turned to her aunt, her eyes unblinking, her face still delicately smooth in its lack of anger, its lack of sorrow.

Training, Serra Teresa thought, warred often with youth.

"They are oath rings," the younger woman said, straightening her shoulders and lifting her chin before she gave with dignity the information she knew Serra Teresa could compel. She touched the first ring, a plain band with intricate knotwork etched across its length. "This is Faida's." The next, silver, where the first had been gold, caught light as she lifted it; it was free of design, but set into the band, where they might not catch at cloth and hair, were two small stones, one sapphire and one night-heart. "This is Deirdre's." And the last, jade, a tiny ring with no marking and no stone. "This is Ruatha's."

"And the matching rings?"

"They lie buried beneath the dirt in a mound outside the Tor Leonne where any seraf can walk with impunity." She paused. "I heard rumors that serafs had, indeed, begun digging."

On another day, Serra Teresa would give a lecture on a true Serra's ability to rise above common rumor and gossip. "What oaths, Diora?" Serra Teresa whispered. "What oaths did you swear?"

Diora lifted a hand; three rings caught the light and sent it scattering as if it were dangerous. "They were private oaths, Serra; I took a vow upon it. I will not allow you to force me to break that vow." She turned her unblinking, defiant gaze upon the most dangerous woman in Annagar, and she waited.

Quiet reigned beneath the open sky. Then, gently, Serra Teresa took the samisen from her niece's lap. "Na'dio," she said, as she began to play the Water's song, "do not wear the rings upon your fingers."

Diora did not reply, but she folded her hands delicately in her lap.

"If you will allow me, we might make a chain for them, and if not a chain, we might braid them into your hair. But they are not fit for your station."

"I have no station."

"You are the daughter of Widan Sendari par di'Marano—and if he has his way, my dear, you will be Serra Diora Maria *di'Sendari*."

The birth of a clan. Diora understood all then.

Serra Teresa caught Diora's hands, unsettling the samisen to do so.

But Diora was stone. She had to be.

"It is not a woman's world, Diora. Do not seek to play a man's game in it."

"Yes, Ona Teresa."

A lone Serra sat unattended in the Pavilion of the Dawn beneath a sky of dusk and coming shadow. If serafs

attended her at all, they were hidden in the confines of the
pavilion, that they might not be an unnecessary distraction. The woman's dark hair caught the fading sun's light,
as did the sheen of her silks. Her hands were smooth and
unadorned—almost a child's, they seemed so soft and
perfect.

Yet it was not the sight of her which had drawn General
Alesso from his steps across the breadth of the Tor
Leonne; no, it was the song which she pulled from the
mournful strings of the samisen that lay perfectly balanced in her lap. Such a voice as she sang with, Alesso
had never heard, and he felt, with each word, each syllable, that he was the gong being struck, and struck again.

The serafs at his back knelt noisily against the grass
and dirt, bowing their heads at the heels of his boots.
They even started to speak, to ask him what he desired,
but they were well-enough trained to fall silent immediately at his gesture—which was good as he did not feel
the desire to replace them.

Minutes he stood thus, listening, straining in dusk's
light to see enough of the young woman's face to know
her. Then, at last, he turned to the serafs who groveled
beneath him. "That Serra," he asked softly, "who is she?"

Silence, and then a young woman raised her forehead.
"It is—it is the Serra Diora en—di'Marano." She swallowed, but the General had already returned to his contemplation of the sweetest song in the Tor—perhaps in
the Dominion itself.

When at last—almost an hour later—the music faded
for the final time, the stars were gathered brightly above
in a deep, clear sky.

So it was that General Alesso heard for the first time
the song of Serra Diora, and he came away with a profound and uneasy understanding of why she was called
the Flower of the Dominion. He did not speak of her song,
but he did not forget it. He would never forget it.

The Widan Sendari rose to greet Serra Teresa, leaving
behind his serafs, his attendant wife, and his work.

"Serra Teresa," he said, catching both of her hands in
his and pressing them tightly. "It was good of you to
come so quickly at my summons."

Serra Teresa curtsied deeply and perfectly, bending at

the knees as if this simple movement were an art. "Our brother has graciously allowed me to pass from the capital to aid you in a most trying time."

"He has, has he?" The Widan's bark of laughter was short and sharp. "Ah, well. Adano will have Marano; he is kai, after all; I am par. Will he have you, Serra Teresa?"

"That is a matter," Serra Teresa replied quietly and meekly, "for the Sers of the clan to decide. I will, of course, abide by their decision."

"Of course." Sendari's face darkened a moment. "Fiona, take the serafs and leave us for a moment. I will join you in your chambers."

The young wife made haste to bow, not so much out of fear for her husband's displeasure, but out of fear for Serra Teresa's disapproval. For Serra Teresa embodied the art of the feminine graces, enough so that she recognized instantly where they were lacking.

Serra Teresa stood in compliant silence while the room was made, by each departure, a more secluded, a more private, space. Food and wine were left behind by the serafs who were most accustomed to dealing with the Widan's requests, but the screens were pulled fast, and oils were left in full lamps, in case the darkness came unexpectedly upon the two.

"Sit, Teresa," Sendari said. "Sit and tell me the news."

"As I said, Adano was willing to part with me for the moment. But he was only barely willing; things have become . . . difficult." She paused, then reached out for the delicate stem of a silver goblet. "Sendari?"

"Not for the moment, Teresa. What do you mean, difficult?"

She took a breath, and let it out at once. "News has traveled, Sendari. If you will forgive me, I must be blunt. Tyr'agnate Mareo kai di'Lamberto will not be attending the Festival of the Sun, as previously planned. Nor, I believe, will Tyr'agnate Ramiro kai di'Callesta."

"They must have been turned back on the roads," the Widan said softly.

"They were, as you know, already in transit with most of their court. Turning back was difficult, and rumor has it that it was not done without some cost and some . . . fear." Very, very few were the Tyr'agnati, in the history of the Dominion of Annagar, who had refused the trek to the Tor Leonne—or the Tor Paravo before it—for the Festival of the Sun. Not and survived.

"Impossible."

Serra Teresa nodded her head in acquiescence to the wisdom of the Widan. "As you say, Widan Sendari."

"Teresa, do not play these games with me. Not now."

"Very well, Sendari—but remember, it is at your command."

His smile was bitter indeed.

"I know the truth of di'Lamberto's refusal because I was there. Both I, and Adano, had gratefully accepted the request to accompany Mareo di'Lamberto as part of his court at the Festival of the Sun. We were on the road. We turned back." She paused. "Ramiro di'Callesta is far more cunning, and it may be that he will absorb this news and seek power in the Tor Leonne—but I fear that he may well feel that power, if it is here, will be his to lose, not to gain. He was not, after all, offered prior warning."

Sendari's face went completely slack as he stared into the surface of the sweet, dark wine, seeing perhaps a reflection, perhaps a crimson spill. "We expected some news to escape," he said at last. "The slaughter of a clan—even one so small and self-contained as Leonne—does not pass without comment."

"It is not just news of the Tyr's death, nor even the death of his kai. It is not of the slaughter of his children, nor even the slaughter of their wives, and their children."

Widan Sendari said nothing, but when Serra Teresa wordlessly offered him the goblet again, he accepted it. "More than that," he said softly. "No one has left the grounds. No seraf, no cerdan—and no member of any of the clans. No message was delivered by magic; the Sword's Edge himself made it impossible with the aid of his allies." His eyes became cold points, and his voice was sharp but completely even. Thus did a Widan gird for battle. "What news was carried?"

"The news that the Tyran betrayed their Tyr at the behest of General Alesso."

That news. To di'Lamberto—a clan known for its love of, its loyalty to, honor. Mareo di'Lamberto was not a political creature—in fact, if he'd been a man with lesser territory and a smaller army, he might have been called a fool. He would, without thought, turn back in disgust, Festival or no. Consequences or no. "No more?"

"It was enough." She paused. "And Adano is still alive."

If Adano was alive, no mention of the treachery of clan di'Marano had passed through the Tor. Sendari rose, the lines of his face hardening further into anger. "Baredan," he said icily. "General Baredan di'Navarre."

"I believe that it was, indeed, the General," Serra Teresa said. "Of the three, he has always been the eagle."

"Where was he traveling?"

"To Averda, although that is only a guess."

"Then you do not know for certain of Ramiro's refusal?"

She did not dignify the question with a response. The moment stretched, and when it was broken, it was broken by the Widan.

"Thank you, Serra," he told her quietly. It was a dismissal, but it did not anger her; she knew where he was going—and why.

But she was Serra Teresa. "Widan," she said, as he reached the screen. He paused, unused to interruption of any sort, from anyone, be they man, woman, or seraf.

"Yes, Serra Teresa?"

"She is Alora's daughter. In every respect."

His brows gathered a moment before it became clear to him who she spoke of. Diora.

CHAPTER FOURTEEN

21st of Morel, 427 AA
Essalieyan, Avantari, the Palace of the Twin Kings

Midnight.

The moon, full, hovered above the bay with a clear and watchful eye. Sea salt was in the air, carried by a breeze both high and warm through the streets of *Averalaan Aramarelas*. The stars were glittering, the sky clear; there was no sign of thunderstorm across the perfect horizon.

Yet it was the lightning strike that woke Valedan di'Leonne as he lay sleeping in the open spaces of the Arannan Halls. Something heavy fell across his legs and convulsed there, writhing. A man.

A dead man.

He woke with a cry, or he would have—the shock was so complete he could force no breath from his lips. Instead, he threw himself off his sleeping cushions, pulling his legs and thighs out from beneath whatever—whoever—it was that had fallen so heavily.

"Valedan," a voice said in the darkness. "Do not move."

He didn't recognize the speaker, and he could not have said why, later, he felt compelled to obey her—but he did as she commanded, locking his knees rigidly to stop their shaking. A ring of pale orange light, an inch wider than his feet on all sides, appeared across the ground.

Fire consumed the cushions that had been his sleep's comfort for the last eight months as the dead man rose, limned in red, red light.

Valedan found his voice.

The creature's lidless eyes flickered over Valedan a moment as the young man stood frozen ten feet away. But when he spoke, it was not to the boy. It was to the shadows.

"Do not interfere in what is not your concern, and you may be spared."

"And are the half-named kin to decide what is, and what is not, my concern?"

Fire flared, the heat almost scorching. Valedan crossed his forearms in front of his face as the intensity almost forced him back. But he did not move. He did not lift his feet. Because he knew, without knowing how, that to lift his feet was to die here, consumed by flames as hot as, or hotter than this. Having seen the cushions, he had no illusions whatever about how long he would last.

"You know the kin," the creature said, as the last of its human seeming melted away. Great wings unfurled, uncomfortable beneath the ten-foot ceilings; long, obsidian arms glittered in the unnatural light of fire. Horns, black as pitch, and pale, long teeth filled out the contours of its face. The creature gestured for light, and it came; the room was harshly illuminated.

"Yes." Bereft of shadows, a small figure in robes the color of midnight nodded her hooded head.

"Then know this. You will not be killed by half-named kin. Be honored."

The woman lifted her hands to her face and pulled the folds of her hood down. Her hair was dark, and her skin very pale; her eyes were an unnatural shade that glittered no less dangerously than the demon's teeth. "I will not," she said gravely, "do you the honor of dying. Please forgive my manners."

Almost casually, the creature bent down and lifted a slab of rock with one crooked talon. Shattered bits of stone scattered across the floor as he gingerly balanced it a moment in the flat of his hand. It was half a good man's height and width.

Lightning struck again, and this time Valedan could see the source of it clearly: the hands of the robed woman. He began to murmur a prayer to the Lady; it was the Lord's time soon, but it did no harm to whisper Her name in the darkness. Valedan had no more time to react; the stone shattered, as if it were glass or crystal. Sharp shards of rock flew in all directions.

Not a single one of them hit.

"Very good," the creature said, its voice growing deeper and heavier by the word. "If I had the time to play, little human, I would take it. But duty calls." He turned, pivoting neatly on feet that should have been far too large for such a delicate maneuver, and sent a stream of liquid fire from his fingertips.

To Valedan.

Lady, he thought, numb.

But the fire split, passing around him in a narrow, narrow circle—a circle that gleamed momentarily orange in the bright light. Where the fire struck rock, rock melted. Valedan had never seen such a working as this, although he had met mages and the barely remembered Widan in his time.

The woman was chanting softly.

"I *am* impressed."

"It's easy to impress a demon," another voice said, coming out of nowhere. "They're such arrogant creatures they expect so little."

Ebony muscles caught rivulets of fire as the creature pivoted again, moving almost faster than the eye.

But not faster than the blade that left the hand of the slender, blond man who stood in the arch of the open window, insect net in pieces in his left hand.

The death roar of the demon literally shook the halls— more so because, until the creature tried to remove the blade from his chest and failed, it did not realize that it was a death roar. But blue-and-gold light lanced up wherever the haft or the blade of the knife came in contact with ebony flesh, and in the end, the fire that had been its mantle was guttered.

Only when the last of the twitching had passed did the woman look up to meet the eyes of the fair-haired man. "You took your time."

"It is not so easy as all that to steal weapons from the Astari on a moment's notice," the man replied coolly. "You might have come to me sooner."

"If I had the choice," she said pertly, turning to face Valedan, "I'm not certain I would ever come to you at all." Then she gave a low bow. "I don't believe you've met me before, Valedan di'Leonne. But I know of you. I am Evayne a'Nolan, and in return for this eve's work, I ask a favor."

He owed her his life. And because he was young, he said, "Anything."

But the man in darker clothing removed the ties that bound his hair so tightly, freeing coiling strands of gold and silver. Only then did Valedan recognize him: Kallandras of Senniel, the favored bard in Queen Siodonay's court. "Be careful what you promise her," he told Valedan softly. "She will collect without mercy."

21st of Morel, 427 AA
Annagar, The Tor Leonne

Widan Sendari di'Marano was not pleased; that much was clear by the tight set of his lips. If one was not familiar with him, one might be able to lose sight of it in the length of dark beard, the dignity of the Sword of Knowledge.

General Alesso di'Marente had known the Widan for almost twenty years; he could not ignore the slight furrows in brow and the corners of dark eyes. "Widan Sendari?"

"General di'Marente." The Widan bowed formally—too formally. "I request a private audience."

"I see." Turning, the General spoke two words. Serafs and cerdan alike vanished behind the screens as if they were mice. "This is important." It was not a question.

"Yes. And private."

"Sendari—" The word, terse, was cut off by a tightening of lips identical to the Widan's. "Very well." With a curt wave, the four Tyran who stood at the corners of the room were also dismissed. They sheathed their weapons in perfect unison, and bowed to the man at the room's center.

Silence held a moment as Alesso di'Marente rose to greet his ally. "Speak," he said, his voice low with warning.

"It might interest you to know that Lamberto—and possibly Callesta—will not be attending the Festival of the Sun at the Tor Leonne this year."

The expression upon the General's face became guarded. "What do you mean?"

"I mean," the Widan replied, measuring his words, "that Mareo di'Lamberto and Ramiro di'Callesta have heard word of the events that passed here; they will not trust you, and it is likely that even Ramiro, canny as he is, will refuse the pilgrimage." He paused. "Nor, General, do you have the authority to command them."

"No," Alesso replied, almost genially. "It is the Festival itself that will give me that right, as you well know. How did you come by this information?"

"Serra Teresa di'Marano."

"Serra Teresa? I see. And she?"

At this, Sendari's brows drew down; his fingers stroked the length of his beard as if it was a cat's tail. "Baredan di'Navarre."

The General's eyes narrowed at the name. "Impossible," he said flatly.

"Is it?"

"I saw the body myself. Baredan di'Navarre is dead."

"You will have that body exhumed," the Widan said. "I would see it myself."

They stared at each other a moment, two men of power with anger between them. It was Widan Sendari who spoke first. "My pardon, Alesso," he said, and if his voice was cool, it was sincere. They were not friends because they knew no conflict, but rather because they knew how to gracefully survive it.

"Serra Teresa is not known for fallibility," Alesso replied, relenting as well. "It is foolish to waste our strengths against each other. If Lamberto and Callesta will not come to the Tor Leonne, we will carry the war to them. The armies stand ready," he added softly. "As do our allies. We hoped to take the Terreans without the cost of war—but no true power comes peacefully." He smiled, and the smile was the coldest expression that had yet crossed his face. "Mancorvo and Averda will not stand together; they will fall, and easily, upon our field."

Sendari closed his eyes and took a deep breath. "Yes," he said quietly. "It is so. But still, I would see the body."

"Very well; if it is not Baredan's, there is more at work here than we would like. I will call the serafs."

"I counsel against their use in this; I would summon the Tyran instead."

But Alesso grimaced. "They report to di'Horaro, and we will hear Calevro's opinion soon enough. It is late, old friend, and I would see to this in peace."

Sendari did not demur again.

* * *

Widan Sendari was dressed for the darkness. If not for the gleaming length of his beard and the glint of the Sword of Knowledge at his breast, he might have been mistaken for a simple seraf. Alesso came in court garb accompanied by the silent serafs that had been a part of his personal service for many years; they were few indeed. They brought shovels and spades and worked to the steady flicker of lamps until their skin glowed in the dim light, and they did not speak a word.

Sendari wondered if they still had their tongues, but chose not to ask. It was unseasonably chill and damp; the breeze was biting. *I am old for this,* he thought, and that chilled him further. He seldom felt his age.

But perhaps it was not age. Indeed, if he were honest, it was not age. Diora did not speak to him at all. Oh, the words were there, and the tone of voice, for her voice was always perfect—but beneath the words was a distance so vast he thought—he thought—

A cold, red glitter caught his eye, and he turned his attention to the Sword of Knowledge. Blood. Night was the time of omens.

"There," Alesso said, his voice a night whisper.

The ground was shallow; the bodies interred here were not meant to remain. In less than two hours the grass had been carefully rolled back, and the dirt beneath removed. It was a testament to their fear of Alesso that the serafs immediately jumped to pull the corpse from its shallow earthen créche; it was night, and one did not disturb the dead beneath the eyes of the Lady without invoking her displeasure. Even Sendari raised a palm in warding before he realized what he had done. The Widan were not superstitious. They were men of knowledge.

But a man's heart and child's heart had something in common, and knowledge alone did not save one from that commonality.

Alesso noticed everything, but chose to raise a brow and offer a sardonic smile. "I believe," he said softly, "that your skills are now required."

The Widan nodded, gesturing for the serafs to lift the lamps that stood upon the ground. The lamps were dim for precise work; he looked at their slender cases and grimaced. "Hold them well," he told the serafs, "and do not be surprised by anything that occurs."

They could see the glint of the golden sword at his chest, and they nodded quietly, knuckles whitening as they obeyed his command. He smiled and then raised both hands, palm up, in a sudden flicker of motion. The oil in the lamps began to burn unnaturally bright; the flames leaped, tongues touching open air.

There. Good enough. The body.

He recognized the slack face at once, although death lent it a certain grisly complexion. "The Lady's ceremonies were performed?"

"By whom?" Alesso replied sharply. "Of course not." But his eyes narrowed as the Widan's question took root; Sendari asked nothing without purpose, not even trivial questions about the weather.

"Observe," the Widan said, walking over to a corpse that was, in the right glare of the Lord's light, only that. "There was no blessing, no supplication, no protection." Kneeling, he gently touched the contours of the body's cheek and jaw. "But the worms have not begun to feed; there are no marks." His grip tightened suddenly, like a vise—the serafs jumped back as if they expected movement, causing the light to waver.

General Alesso's face was completely neutral; a bad sign. He crossed the grass and came to stand beside the kneeling Widan. "Then what," he said, gazing down at the corpse, "is this?"

But the man kneeling on the grass had become the Sword of Knowledge. Power was a game to be played, but this—this was life's blood. Alesso grimaced, but subsided; he had seen this fevered concentration before, and doubted very much that Sendari di'Marano heard anything but the questions that were running through his Widan's mind.

A spectator, the General watched as the Widan passed a hand over the corpse's face; the lids, closed to that point, rolled open over sightless eyes. "Here," he said softly. Before Alesso could speak another word, the Widan carefully, and expertly, pulled the eyes out of sockets that no longer had use for them. The serafs made sounds akin to wind through hanging leaves and the lamps dipped again in their hands as they freed a palm momentarily to ward against the Lady's displeasure.

Only the General remained unmoved.

"No. Watch."

But the Widan's words were unnecessary. Blinded in such a visceral fashion, the whole corpse seemed to lose the patina, not of life, but of having lived at all. Skin turned slowly to wax, and at that not a smooth coat, but the drippings of a hastily melting candle; Baredan was of a class in which tallow saw little use. Beneath this blotched and blobby layer was a mask of wood with hollows for eyes and a cut hole for a mouth; in fact, the body was entirely of wood. It, like the skin, had the look of something constructed in haste, for the arms and legs were not of equal lengths, and they were rough-hewn, not sanded and ground to a finer finish.

The Widan's hands curled around the eyes, knuckles white; his expression fluctuated between triumph and anger.

"Tell me," the General said, his voice the essence of command.

"It is Voyani magic."

"Voyani?" The first surprise that Alesso had openly showed in the long evening. "But they barely have competent herb-lore!"

The Widan approached the wooden dummy. "Here," he said softly, his grip around the eyes still tight. "Over the 'heart.' This is a Voyani mark. Brush the wax from the forehead, and you will see it there as well. It appears that one at least of the Voyani is trained in the old ways."

Alesso drew a dagger and dulled its edge against wax and wood grain. When he had finished, he bent down to inspect the crookedly carved emblem of the quartered moon.

"He must have done them a service," the Widan said thoughtfully. "For I have only read of rumors of this magic, and it is from a time when the Voyani were not known as the wanderers."

"Can we use them?"

At that, Sendari laughed. "It is my intent to begin studies into that very question."

"Then allow me to save you from wasting your time."

Both men spun at once in the direction of the voice, and for the first time in the evening, the serafs did cry out, their voices a thin, short wail. But the lamps did not waver; instead, they were drawn to the chest and held there as if they, glass and wick and burning oil, were the only shield the night offered.

"The Voyani magics are tied to the Voyani themselves; those eyes were imbued with a life-gift. You will not be able to duplicate it, even if you happen upon a willing victim." The creature that stood before them was neither man nor woman; it was tall and slim and black as pitch. But its eyes were red, and its teeth white, and they glimmered in reflected lamplight as it spoke. "Forgive me for this intrusion. My Lord sends his greetings from the Shining Court."

Alesso said nothing, but he wished that he had taken Widan Sendari's advice and called for Tyran instead of his serafs. Silence extended a moment around them like a heavy fog; when Alesso spoke, his anger burned it away as if it were Lord's light itself. Yet he did not raise his voice.

"Why have you come here?"

"To tell you," the creature said, ears flattening slightly, "that Volkar-Assarak failed in his . . . duty."

"Do not play games with me," the General said softly. "Speak plainly if you will speak at all, and speak quickly."

Power recognized power; that was the rule of the two Dominions. The creature took a step back, retreating from both the light cast and the man who stood at its forefront. "The boy, Valedan di'Leonne, is still alive."

Sendari and Alesso exchanged grim glances. "Rectify it," the General said at last.

"My Lord Assarak bids me to tell you that we will do as we can—but that Volkar-Assarak failed to be subtle."

"They are aware of what he was." It was not a question. The creature did not answer.

Again, the General and his counselor exchanged a measured glance. "They will have their cursed god-spawn spread across the palace like lice." Alesso spoke through clenched teeth. "Very well; he lives. It appears that we will have to do this the difficult way.

"Tell Lord Assarak that due to his failure, we require the aid we were promised. In ten days, we ride to war."

It was a dismissal, and had the creature been anyone else—be he noble, Tyran, or seraf—he would have died in the next minute, for he failed to obey the unspoken command. He did, however, bow quite low.

"My Lord Assarak regrets that that is unfortunately impossible at this time."

"What is this?" Alesso said, speaking so softly even the Widan strained to catch the words. "Treachery?"

"There has been an . . . upheaval in the Shining Court. The forces that you were promised no longer exist." If such a creature could, this one swallowed. "However, Lord Assarak, and Our Lord, wish to assure you that it will be a mere matter of human months—seven, perhaps eight—and that force, doubled in power, will be at your disposal and your absolute command." The creature paused, bowed again. "But Lord Isladar wishes to point out that, if you wish to dispense with pretense, you may have some thousand of the lesser kin as part of the army itself. They require no provisions, will keep an easy pace with a mortal forced march, and they will cut a swath through your enemy that your enemy will be powerless to prevent."

"Not so," the Widan said quietly to Alesso.

Alesso frowned at the very name. "Isladar," he replied, "knows well that neither we—nor you—can yet afford so open a display; to take a thousand kin through the Dominion would turn the Dominion against us; it would not be—yet—enough. If we cannot have the Lords—and the kin who can take some human guise—we will not have the kin.

"In time, we will worship the Lord, both in light and darkness; there will be no Lady. But the lands will not accept His law. Not yet. And it is best that he remember this. Leave. We will take counsel here and respond to the Shining Court."

The creature bowed again, and the darkness took it, weaving so black a cloud around its body that the lamplight could not pierce it at all. Alesso stood under the open sky—the Lady's sky—his jaw white. "Sendari," he said. "We have much to discuss. Come." Turning to the serafs, he added, "Remain here. I will send someone to have the puppet removed, and then the grave must be filled again."

As one man, they bowed.

Widan Sendari par di'Marano was a master of the subtle skills; he walked the edge of secrecy better than any of the Widan, living or past. He knew it; it was a source of quiet pride, a balm against the angry father of his youth. But it was more than that; it was the certain veil, the unpierced safety in which discussions between men of power could be held.

He called upon his powers rarely, for their use was not small, and any who knew the art's effects could say for certain that the art had been called, and be suspicious of it. Other forms of secrecy, other dances, other misdirections—these appealed to his wisdom and his understanding of the rules of simplicity: Never use an army where a dagger will do.

But there were some discussions which by their very nature presented so great a risk that the suspicions of those who might watch were of negligible import by comparison. He called upon the veil now, raising it in layers that twisted the sound into the expected venue of conversation should a listener stumble upon them in the darkness.

"I knew we could not trust them, but I did not realize that they would betray us before we had had a chance to fulfil our bargain."

Widan Sendari di'Marano watched his oldest friend in the silence of shadows and flickering lamp. He was not at home in this darkness, and his mind turned, again and again, to the Voyani artifacts—those two eyes—which rested in the confines of his Widan's robes.

"Sendari." It was a command.

"You miss so little, Alesso. Very well. Let me give you my full attention." He drew breath and exhaled; the lamp flickered as his breath passed by, a little gust of wind. "I believe that what the creature told you is true."

"Which part?"

"All of it."

Alesso was silent as he absorbed these three words. "This would be the prefect time to turn upon us."

"Yes." Sendari shrugged. "And were I them, I would

choose it. Let a shifter take my place—or yours—and lead the campaign against the North, and see to the refashioning of the Lord's worship in the Dominion entirely as it, or its kinlord, sees fit. There is risk in it, however."

"And that?"

"Who brought the Allasakari to their knees?" The question offered was a quiet one because the answer was not a name which Alesso di'Marente wished to hear, let alone speak.

He spoke it. "Leonne."

"They have faced the winds once; they will seek a wall behind which to face them again. We are that wall, of course."

"Of course." But there was more to it than that; they both felt it. Oh, it was dark, and the moon was at her height. Alesso gave the Lady her due. "The Shining Court."

"Yes."

They stared at the flames, rather than seeking the doubt in each other's eyes. Of the two, Sendari had always found it easier to express doubt. Of the two. They were both proud men.

"There has never been a gathering of so many of the kinlords." A question, but accompanied by no rise in voice.

"No," the Widan replied. "And it worried me, in truth. But those who study demon lore say that the kinlords spend eternity as we do: attempting to enlarge their dominion." His smile was quite grim as his fingers found the length of his beard. "It is why I believe the creature; the kinlords must be warring among themselves. Nature exerts its influence."

"The Allasakari said that they summoned the kinlords."

The Widan stared into the fire for a long time. "I told you, Alesso. They did not, by the test of my spells, lie."

"And yet we do not believe them."

"No."

The General smiled, and it was a wolf's smile. "And we told them, old friend, that in exchange for the assassination of the entire Leonne clan and the action of the kinlords in securing our rule, we would wage war against the Northern empire. And under spell, we did not lie."

Sendari nodded. "No." But he stroked his beard

absently. "What a game, Alesso. What a gamble we have taken." Silence, heavy and dark. "We consort with the enemies of the Lady. We have promised the rule of the land to the Lord."

"So we have," Alesso said lightly, shrugging the words off. "And we told no lie, according to the spells of the Allasakari priests."

"He ruled for over a century before the coming of Leonne," the Widan said mildly, the warning in his voice unmistakable.

"We know this." Alesso stood, which was usually a signal of conversation's end. But he turned, his face seeking the soft glow of moonlight through thin screen. "Did they attempt to assassinate the boy?"

"I believe yes," was the reserved reply.

"You are not certain?"

"No. I cannot be."

"Why?"

"You know it as well as I. You dare not touch the Sun Sword until that boy is dead, and if he is not dead . . . the Sun Sword was a weapon that the kinlords feared. One of the very, very few." Sendari gazed into the depths of the fire. His hand sought, and found, the eyes of the Voyani simulacrum. "If they do not wish the blade brought into play, they will keep him alive for as long as it takes them to prepare their own schemes."

"Yes."

"And that leaves us with the problem of the boy. And the interference of the kin in the capital of the Kings."

Vergo kep'Marente emptied his bladder in the bush, taking care to keep to the shadows cast by the full moon above. Then he carefully wrapped the length of his shawl over his peppered hair, and slid farther into the cover of the rock gardens. He had served the General Alesso di'Marente for all of his adult life, and knew well the nuance of that powerful man's expression; the glance that he had passed over the four serafs who had faithfully obeyed all of his commands was one of regret, however distant.

And Vergo kep'Marente was a seraf without parallel. If death were the only threat, he was prepared to meet it and accept it as his master's will. Thus did the serafs prove themselves worthy for the true life in service to the Lady—for the serafs knew, as the clansmen did not, that it was service that the Lady most valued—and most rewarded.

But if he served the General, he sought to serve the Lady as well, and under her moon, General Alesso di'Marente had all but spoken the forbidden name. No matter; he had made clear his intent to lead the Dominion once more into the fold of the Lord of the Night, and this—this Vergo kep'Marente could not allow. Not without some attempt, however unworthy it might prove to be, to come to the Lady's earthly defense.

He gained the high ground, clinging to low wall and standing stone, and paused a moment there as he heard the sound of heavy boots upon the paths. Closing his eyes, he murmured a supplication just before the cries of dismay were cut off by the work of swordsmen. Then, touching his head to the soft ground, he moved more quickly.

The serafs knew how to navigate the Tor Leonne; from the peak of its heights to the depth of its valley, they walked in near invisibility as the clansmen and the riders conversed and dallied. Vergo knew the Tor better than almost any man, and he knew, from his service to the General, exactly who occupied each of the guest houses and rooms. Quickly then, quickly, he ran, until the lights of the evening hours shone from across the lake. Then, composing himself, he walked with the supplicant dignity appropriate to his station. He paused only once, to look at the face of the moon in the still water beside the bridge. Starlight. Silence. The Lady was in her glory. For every night of his adult life upon the plateau of the Tor, in cool wind and hot still night air, he had come to gaze upon the face of the Lady, and this small pause brought routine back to a night that had lost all semblance of things normal. He whispered a prayer and felt the easing of the cords between his shoulder blades as he gazed upon light in darkness.

Quieted by this beauty, and the reminder of his purpose, he continued to the domo.

Serafs did not announce their presence by use of the brass clappers; if a message was to pass to one clan-born, it passed from seraf to seraf, and thence from seraf to cerdan. Vergo saw no reason to change this routine. He

was a seraf, after all, and not yet worthy of note—not yet
a hunted fugitive.

Not yet. And perhaps not ever. If the General was not
careful, he would not question the Tyran. They would
come, with drawn and blooded blades as evidence of their
obedience. He would inspect the crescent swords, ask if
the serafs were properly buried, and then thank the Tyran
for their service—and their loyalty.

But the Widan was different, and if the Widan were
there, he might think to ask: "How many?"

Vergo's time was the Lady's time now; his life had
ended at the command of his master, and only the grace of
the moonlight and its shadows had preserved him. But the
Lady's grace was her own to bestow, and no man—no
wise one—could demand that it last beyond her whim.
Let him only speak; let him only deliver his message.
Then fate might take its course.

He knelt upon the coarse mats outside of the closed
sliding doors, blowing on the lamps so that their flicker
might be seen through the textured screens. Then, in a
silence of breath and heartbeat, he waited.

The doors slid open a crack, and the face of a young
seraf—a girl on the verge of womanhood—peered out
from around the door's frame. Vergo privately thought
this girl had been brought from the training halls too
early; this was not the appropriate posture for a seraf to a
woman of Serra Teresa's consequence. Or Serra Teresa's
exacting standards. But he was seraf, not Ser, and it was
not his position to criticize or advise.

The girl stepped out into the night, slid the door shut
behind her, and then knelt upon the mats in front of the
door. Her hair was dark and fell in a single braid across
her shoulder.

He touched his forehead to the wooden slats and then
raised his head. "I bear a message from Ser Alesso
di'Marente for Serra Teresa di'Marano, if she would
hear it."

The young girl bowed her head to ground in return and
then rose. "It is late," she said quietly.

"Indeed. And my master apologized for the distur-
bance, but the message is most urgent."

"Wait, then."

As she slid the doors open again, he caught the scent of

something sweet and light wafting across the breeze. He had had daughters, of course; some had even been accepted as concubines to the clansmen, both of Marente, and farther afield. To his great surprise, Vergo felt a bitter pang as the young seraf disappeared—for it was at this age, with one foot firmly planted in childhood, and one in womanhood, that most of his daughters had been taken from him.

Ah, but that was a graceless thought. A useless one. And only beneath the gaze of the pale moon, from which such things could not be hidden, would a man think it. Lady's grace, he thought, bowing his head; he must be close, indeed, to the end of his life. At least none of his daughters had been given to Garrardi.

The young seraf returned, accompanied by no cerdan, no other seraf. She knelt upon the slats, but this time her bow was very correct. "If you will follow me, the Serra will hear the message you bear."

Serra Teresa di'Marano was not a young woman—and because she did not have youth to hide behind, the night made her powerful. Or at least so it seemed to Vergo kep'Marente as he knelt at her feet in the orange flicker of lamplight that somehow felt strange. She sat upon a divan, cushions to either side, her hands resting against raw silk as if it were the arms of a throne. Jewels glittered upon her fingers, multiple rings in silver and gold against which the light played.

The young seraf knelt immediately to the left of, and behind, the Serra. Vergo noted the complete absence of cerdan in the Serra's quarters; the lack did not comfort him.

"You are Vergo kep'Marente," the Serra said softly.

Vergo was well-trained; he knew how to school his face in the presence of a woman of quality, and he did so now, although surprise made his heart dance. "I am, Serra."

"And you bear a message from Ser Alesso?"

"I do."

"Then speak it freely."

He hesitated a moment. "Serra," he said, his voice a shaky whisper.

She raised a dark brow.

"Are you—do you—" Shaking himself, he straightened his shoulders. "It is said that you are a follower of the Lady's mysteries."

"And this, Alesso sent you to ask? I think not, seraf." Her expression was odd; she stared at him long in the dim silence before speaking again. "Ser Alesso did not send you."

It was almost a relief, to hear the words from her lips. "No, Serra. The Lady of Night did."

"I see. Personally?"

He had the grace to blush, although the shadows hid it. "No, Serra. But I live at her whim."

"And, at this moment, at mine. I grow impatient, seraf. Why have you come?"

"To tell you that Ser Alesso and Widan Sendari serve the Lord."

"That is hardly news."

"And they intend to return the dominion of night to his keeping."

Her face, at that moment, became stone; her eyes, a glittering darkness, an ebony. He thought her the very picture of the Lady, for not in youth did the true power of a woman reside.

22nd of Morel, 427 AA
Annagar, The Terrean of Averda, Callesta

General Baredan kai di'Navarre saw the sun begin its ascent over the last of his prayers, and rose, unbending his knees. For each of three days he had wakened in darkness to begin this ritual, beneath a sky shorn of roof and beam. No one else would bespeak the Lady for the safe ascent of the Tyr Leonne, and it was clear that the clan now resided beyond the Lord's reach or care.

All, he thought, save one, Lady be bountiful in her infinite mercy.

He spilled wine, dark and rich, in a half circle at his feet; the ground drank it in as he waited. No serafs attended him, but for the moment, none were wanted. Had they been, there would still be none. He had left the Tor Leonne in haste enough to preserve his life, but little else of his fortune. Not since his youthful days as a common cerdan in the Tyr'agar's armies had he traveled so poorly.

But it was in those days that he had distinguished himself
in the eyes of the kai di'Leonne, and for all the years of
his service thereafter, he served the kai—and then, when
the time came, the Tyr—with pride. With honor.

Markaso. He was younger then; the winds had carried
him far from youth.

When the sun had fully crested the horizon, and not
before, Baredan opened his lips on a different prayer: one
for the clan Navarre. He had thought to do without, and
grimaced; it seemed, in dark times, that there was never
an end to prayer.

He'd sent word, of course, once he'd cleared the Tor
Leonne; had it not been for the coming Festival, he would
have been found with his clan. They lived in the heart of
the Terrean of Raverra, and there was no question in
Baredan's mind that that Terrean belonged to Alesso. Let
warning only reach them, and he would serve the Lady
for life.

As it was, he had escaped by dressing as a seraf,
answering the Tyran's summons to the welcome gate, and
racing in search of his "master" at their behest. He had
always been a good lord to those who served his clan. His
wife's advice. He had chosen to take her advice in such
matters—the serafs were, by and large, the concern of the
women—but he had never been so grateful for her
wisdom. Ten serafs had seen him pass in his hasty disguise. Any one of them might have spoken—and gained
much for it.

He hoped they did not lose in equal measure for their
silence.

Bardur had been waiting for him with tack and bridle in
the stables. The stables. He grimaced. More than one loss,
this war. And it would be war.

Michaele. His kai.

"General di'Navarre."

He turned, surprised. A respectful distance away, unattended by even the most trusted of his Tyran, stood the
man who had been the second most powerful in the
Dominion. Tyr'agnate Ramiro kai di'Callesta. His dark
hair looked peppered, and the winds had carved their lines
into his brow, the corners of his eyes. But his eyes were
still the hawk's, piercing in their clarity.

He knew the Tyr'agnate on sight; not a man whose care

had been the protection of the Tyr'agar did not. Men in power were always a threat; they had to be watched.

And who watched the watchers? Bitter thought, that. He was sorry that the ceremony of placation required so much wine; he had a sudden thirst for it. "Tyr'agnate kai di'Callesta."

"Call me Ramiro. I have no doubt that you have called me worse."

"Not in audience," Baredan replied, smiling. It surprised him; he had not smiled in weeks.

"This is no audience," the Tyr'agnate replied. "It is a chance meeting of two solitary men who seek the blessing of the Lord of the Dawn."

Ramiro di'Callesta sought no one's blessing. Again, Baredan felt his lips tugged up.

"Walk with me."

A command. Baredan nodded; he felt no need to assert his authority here. He had, after all, very little of it with the passing of the Tyr. His knees were still damp from the dew, his cloak's edge wet; what further proof of the day's supplication could be asked for? And a man who had been on his knees in such a fashion was not a man to command this Tyr'agnate. If any man was.

The lands of Averda were the richest in the Dominion. Almost anything could be grown here; there was even an abundance of fruit in the wild, untended by anything save the sight of the Lord. A man could grow soft here. Baredan cast a sideways glance at his companion's profile. It gave nothing away.

He cursed his luck quietly.

Tyr'agnate Mareo di'Lamberto was the only man of the Five he trusted—the only man whose honor was above question. But he was also known for his hatred of the Essalieyanese, and Baredan di'Navarre intended to cross the borders between their countries. To ask, although it galled him, for their aid. He could not do so without the knowledge of the Tyr whose border he crossed.

And perhaps, knowing that the last di'Leonne might survive in the foreign court, the Tyr'agnate of Mancorvo would accede to Baredan's request. But perhaps not—and if not, the flight was over, the war stillborn. It was too great a risk; Mareo could not be moved once he had reached his decision.

Mareo, however, was not his concern; this man was. He did not know Ramiro di'Callesta well. Averda continued to trade and barter with the foreign merchants and their kin; the roads were kept open, the taxes paid.

The grasslands stretched out before them as far as the eye could see, changing only in color and texture in the valley below. A crop of some sort.

"Do you know your histories, di'Navarre?"

It was not the question he expected. "Military histories, yes."

"Good." He paused, bent down, and lifted a small weed from beneath his toes. Frowned a moment, before crushing it and letting it fall back to earth. "Then you know of the clan wars that ended only with the rise of the clan Leonne."

Baredan nodded. "A bitter time."

"Two clans were razed to the ground. Not even daughters were spared." Ramiro folded gloved hands behind his back as he came to stand at the edge of the gentle slope that led valleyward. The sun cast his shadow, stilettolike, down the slopes. "The villages were burned and burned again where people were foolish enough to rebuild; the serafs were slaughtered like pigs."

"It was war," Baredan said.

"Ah, yes. Of course." He lifted his chin slightly. "And your lands have not known war for a very long time. But mine have; I was born to it."

"I fought in the Dominion-Imperial wars."

"So you did." Ramiro's smile was an odd one. "As did I. We were both younger men then. We found our glory."

He fell silent again, as he watched the valley below. Serafs toiled in the fields, digging and weeding; here and there, children pushed their way against the tide of stalks that towered over their heads, bending them wayward in their wake. "I do not want a war," Ramiro said at last. "I do not expect you to understand why."

Baredan froze under the heat of the rising sun.

"If I do as you desire, you will take a small cadre of my men—my Tyran—and you will ride in haste and speed to the court of the Imperial Kings, holding a writ with my seal and my guarantee."

The General said nothing. He had made no formal

request, but he acknowledged, by his silence, the perception of the Tyr'agnate.

"In the court, if all is as you hope, you will find the lone member of the Leonne clan still alive. And what will you have when you find him?" Ramiro turned from the fields below to face Baredan di'Navarre. "You will have the son of a concubine, raised to full clan status solely as a sop to the foreigners' idea of acceptable hostages. He will be no more than seventeen turnings, and over half of them will have been spent in the courts of the foreign Kings." His gaze was intent and unblinking. "And what will you do with such a boy?"

"He is less than one year off his manhood," Baredan replied through clenched teeth.

"Or many. He was not raised in the Dominion. Or are you naive enough to expect blood to run true?"

"If you are not inclined to aid me, then I ask that you do not impede."

"Which is why you came to Averda instead of passing through Mancorvo."

"The Mancorvan border is almost impassable; you know that as well as I."

"Yes," Ramiro di'Callesta replied. "Or better." There was anger in the two words, but they did not rise to the surface. Old wounds, between these two Tyrs. "But you have not answered my question, Baredan—and I will not answer all of my questions for myself. If you find the boy, what will you do?"

"We don't even know if he's still alive," Baredan said softly.

"Not an answer, but I will tell you this: The boy, as of a threeday of hard riding, is still alive." Ramiro's smile was sharp as a knife's edge. "Although word is slow to escape the Tor Leonne, we have managed to ascertain one important fact: Alesso di'Marente has not dared to touch the Sun Sword." The smile was gone as quickly as it had come. "The boy?"

But Baredan was silent a moment as the full import of the Tyr's words took root. He had not thought to know the full truth one way or the other until he reached the foreign court. Hope caught in his throat a moment; he forced it down, down. Care was needed here. "I will carry word of the massacre to Ser Valedan kai di'Leonne. By the law of the Lord of the Sun, he is the Tyr. If he wills it, I will join his cause, and we will return to the Dominion."

"The army is Alesso's."

Baredan grimaced, but shrugged. "He does not control the whole of the army."

"The first and the second," Ramiro replied grimly. "The third was scattered across the Dominion on fool's errands. Those that cannot be turned will be easy fodder for the rest."

"It is not so easy to break an army as that. They were my men, and they will remain so."

At that, a brief, sharp smile touched the Tyr's lips. "Very well. So you think to stand against Alesso di'Marente with some part of the third?"

"Averda and Mancorvo have their cerdan."

Ramiro of Averda raised a peppered brow, and then, of all things, laughed. The wind carried the sound of his voice to the valley below where one or two of the serafs looked up, shielding their eyes against the rays of the rising sun. Seeing only two lone men, they went back to their travails without the proper obeisances.

"It may have escaped your attention, kai di'Navarre, but the cerdan of Averda and Mancorvo spend much of their time fighting each other. How do you propose to put two such men as Mareo and I upon the same side? I tell you now, he will not bend." The mirth was slow to fade, but when it did, it was gone. "No, the time has come for truth, and I will have it.

"What do you intend, Baredan?"

Say it, the General thought, staring into the valley as the wind whispered through the tall stalks below. *He already knows.* But he found it hard; he had not yet spoken the words aloud, and they were tainted everywhere with the feel of treason, of treachery.

No. The treachery was not his alone; the Lord's laws were clear. Ser Valedan kai di'Leonne awaited him in Essalieyan.

"I will ask the foreign Kings for aid," he said softly, so softly that he could barely hear the words. "If they offer it, we will ride to Annagar with an army to rival Alesso di'Marente's."

Ramiro's face was completely neutral as he listened to the General's quiet words. "You were wise indeed not to attempt such a passage through Mancorvo. Three days hence, kai di'Navarre, you will ride North with my personal representative."

The General's eyes widened.

"You do not know the foreigners except by spy and diplomat; you do not speak their tongue well, and you do not understand their laws. We have personally negotiated the fees and taxes for the trade routes between Averda and the Kings' court; they know us, and we, them. My representatives have their trust—if such a thing is ever given. They have been," he added, with a slightly edged smile, "as you well know, a source of Averdan trade."

Baredan knew it; all of Annagar did. It was whispered— or, after drinking among the unwise, spoken out loud—that Tyr'agnate Ramiro di'Callesta paid the price of honor for the sake of money—and at that, foreign gold. "Come. The morning chimes are about to be sounded, and we are expected."

All things moved at Ramiro di'Callesta's command in the Terrean of Averda. Breeze carried the sonorous notes of the domo's silver bells.

Lord's light came in through the clear, clean glass, casting no obvious shadow. Beneath it, unfettered by the presence of human hands and human garb, the Sun Sword sat atop a golden bier, a curved perfect crescent of gleaming light. Layers of metal had been folded and kneaded together to produce its blade—but which metals, and by what process, no swordsmith in the Dominion could now say. The hand that had crafted this sword had crafted it in secrecy, and the secrets of its making had been taken into the Lady's darkness when he departed the Lord's dominion.

She knew the last time that she had seen this Sword worn—remembered clearly the last time that she had seen it drawn. Her wedding. She'd thought to see it carried, in time, by the children she would bear.

It was almost too much.

But no; no. She took a breath, a perfect breath. The Sword. There were always legends, and when they failed, histories. The people of the Dominion of Annagar knew these two things about the Sun Sword: that it could not be returned, unblooded, to its scabbard, and that it would not suffer the touch of one who was not of the clan Leonne while any son of that clan lived.

Fools believed it wholeheartedly; the wise demurred. But the Widan cautioned those who would test the truth of old histories to think carefully before they made their gamble. So other legends rose: that even the Widan, who crafted the light of the Lord into fire that could be held and thrown by mortal hands, feared the touch of the Sun Sword.

Serra Diora was not a fool, yet she was not counted among the wise. Sandalwood burned in the braziers set out at the foot of the stairs that led to the Sword, and she dutifully added a handful of sticks, kneeling and bowing forehead to ground twice, once to the east and once to the west. She drew her sari up from her back, arranging its folds so that it might cover her hair and obscure her face. Then she rose and began to mount those stairs. There were three, and upon each, she stopped to fuel the braziers and to bow. Then, the last time, she rose and took the final step. The Sword was but an arm's reach away.

Two scabbards lay before it.

The first was a work of its own: The sun in splendor rose in gold and pearl and amber, casting a long ray from the scabbard's mouth to its gold-tipped point. Diamonds glittered along its edge, and rubies; white fire and red heat. This was the scabbard the Tyr'agar wore during the Festival of the Sun, and it was by this scabbard that the Sun Sword was known to the clans—for the blade was not drawn unless the kai Leonne was foolish enough to join the Lord's challenge.

The second scabbard was an unadorned, black sheath, with a tip of the same metal as the blade. It was never used, but in it, the Sword had first arrived at the Tor. Or so legend said.

But Serra Diora knew better; she knew that this scabbard, this common, unworkmanly piece, was the sheath in which the Sun Sword rode to war.

"Na'dio," someone said softly.

Turning slowly, she met the gaze of Serra Teresa di'Marano. "Ona Teresa," she acknowledged carefully, turning her gaze once again to the sword.

"You were late in coming," Serra Teresa continued, although she did not approach the stairs. "And I thought I might find you here." When her niece did not answer, she frowned slightly. "Na'dio," she said again, and although the voice was still gentle and pleasing in tone, it was laced with command. "These are not the manners that I taught you. Come. The Pavilion of the Dawn is now free for our use; the party of the General has moved on."

In the shade provided by the pavilion, the two Serras sat. Their serafs attended them briefly, arranging cushions and pillows and the small blocks used for food and wine in silence. Then, having served, the eldest of Serra Teresa's serafs once again placed the samisen by her side. She nodded gracefully, and he responded with a perfect, deferential bow. Then, turning, he mutely ordered the serafs away.

The sun was a little too bright, and a little too high, but such was the price for retreating to the pavilion after the dawn hours; the Serras willingly paid it in return for the privacy it granted them.

They had met thus for three days, but on this third day, Serra Teresa did not pass the samisen to her niece. Instead, she settled it carefully upon her own lap, gazing down upon its still strings with a distance that music's contemplation seldom invoked.

"Ona Teresa?" Diora said softly, after some minutes had passed in the silence of wind and flowers and rising sun.

"Hush, child," her aunt replied. Taking the samisen, she began to play.

Diora knew the accepted canon; her aunt played no pleasing melody, no proper lament, no summer meditation. Yet as the younger Serra listened, she heard the teasing of form and shape in the way Serra Teresa blended notes, one into the other, as if they were silk, and she a weaver. It had been long since she could sit thus, listening to a musician of such skill perform.

It did not last.

The music continued, but Serra Teresa's silent concentration did not. "Serra Diora," she said, the two words as distant as her expression.

Diora lifted her chin slightly, pulling both shoulders back. It was habit, and she corrected her posture at once, but not before her aunt had raised a dark brow reprimandingly. "Serra Teresa." The words were perfectly pitched; they carried to Serra Teresa, and no one else.

The woman playing the samisen smiled briefly, with perhaps a hint of pride in the younger woman's achievement. But they did not speak of these things, even in the hidden voice. "Tell me," she said, "of the Tor Leonne."

They could play games, and sometimes they did, for words were weapons, and the use of them was a skill to be honed in subtle conflict. But they knew each other's measure well; Serra Diora was silent for a full four minutes before she at last chose to speak.

"General Alesso di'Marente returned to the Tor Leonne six weeks ago. His presence here is not unusual, and preparations for the Festival of the Sun had already begun. He arrived with cerdan and serafs in numbers greater than even yours."

At this, Serra Teresa raised a brow. "Na'dio," she said softly, "It is almost vulgar to notice such things." The tone of her words held no sting—held, in fact, no remonstrative disapproval. Her fingers did not falter; the song filled the air as her niece continued to speak.

Diora smiled. "Yes, Ona Teresa. General Alesso di'Marente arrived at the Tor Leonne with many cerdan and many serafs in attendance."

"Better."

"General di'Navarre and General di'Valente arrived with their usual following. Widan Sendari arrived with Widan Antorio; they journeyed in haste."

"I believe I know Sendari's movements. Were there others of . . . interest?"

"I believe so, but I cannot say with certainty," Diora replied, her expression as remote as her aunt's, although she did not know it. "I had no word before the slaughter." Her eyes were wide as she spoke, unblinking in the brightness. Her hands lay perfectly cupped in her lap, but they were utterly still; she might have been a statue with moving lips. Stone. "They did not raise blade against me."

No one must know how you feel.

Diora carved the words out of stone with effort, giving them no more power, and no less, than words of minor import held.

Music answered where Serra Teresa would not. Minutes passed as the silence thinned, and although the distance remained upon Diora's face like a scar, she began to speak again. "Afterward, there was fire upon the lake. It burned for three days. General di'Marente called it a sign from the Lord. The Tor Leonne was closed at once; only those serafs and cerdan personally approved by the General have been allowed to leave or enter. Because it is, of course, a time of great trouble for the Dominion; there is no Tyr'agar. General di'Marente has begun a thorough search for the hands involved in the slaughter." Silence again, heavy with accusation.

"Very good, Na'dio." Serra Teresa's voice filled with the approval reserved for the young in the privacy of the harem, away from the eyes of men.

Diora should not have found it comforting. But she did; she did.

Her eyes were heavy with the weight of water's sting, and she looked across the short space between herself and the woman who had been mother to her for most of her childhood. And she saw, for just a passing second, a glimpse of sorrow so profound, and loss so new, that she fell suddenly silent, as if struck.

"Na'dio," Ona Teresa said, not masking her words, not struggling to hide what lay beneath them as Diora did.

"The Captain of the Tyran was found to be involved in the deaths—surviving serafs attested to the fact that the Tyran indeed were responsible for much of the slaughter. He was executed the morning after the assassination. Tyran Calevro di'Horaro, the second, now holds the title until the Festival of the Sun."

Serra Teresa nodded. "That, I did not know." She gazed at the daughter she had never had. "Na'dio," she said. "There is more."

"There is always more," Diora replied. "The Festival of the Sun will be sparsely attended this year."

The older woman smiled, and the smile was a broad one; were she less graceful, she might have laughed aloud. But she did not. "You tell me my own news," she said. "And by it, prove that there are no secrets in the Tor."

No secrets? There were always secrets. The Widan had taught her that and taught her well. "Serra Fiona en'Marano is most grateful that you arrived at the Tor. It has freed her to spend much needed time in preparation for the Festival of the Sun."

"Ah, yes," Serra Teresa said. "I had forgotten. General di'Marente has no wife."

Serra Teresa had a memory as sharp as the Sun Sword's edge. "The Radann are in their temple; they bespeak the Lord at the height of the sun. For the first time in many, many years, they may be called upon to choose the Tyr'agar."

"For the first time."

As one, both women turned a moment and looked to the North. To the North, where, beyond the plains and the valleys, their ancient enemy lay: Essalieyan.

CHAPTER FIFTEEN

11th of Morel, 427 AA
Essalieyan, Averalaan Aramarelas

The city rose out of the sea mist like a nightmare.

Spires, tall and dark against the night sky, towered like the unnatural peaks of the Northern Wastes.

The Wastes, she knew well. Empty, silent, cold; the great cats hunted there, where food seemed scarcest. The rocks were gray and brown and white, except in the brief, brief spring. She felt a keen desire to return to them.

But they would find her there; they would know where to look, and how to hunt.

"Kiriel," her companion said softly. Everything she did seemed soft, slight, cautious. "This is Averalaan."

Kiriel shrugged; her companion frowned. They had played this over and over until it seemed a rote by which they were to learn—or teach—something.

They stood at the height of the sand hills on the bay, and watched as the sun rose slowly, burning away the dawn mist.

Evayne looked across the water to the isle, and then back. The young girl at her side, dark-haired and pale-skinned as any night creature, also stared, unblinking, at the length of bright ripples that played across the horizon, as if reaching out to touch them.

Kiriel.

She felt a pang that she had not thought to feel; of all of her people—and she thought of so many of the path-chosen comrades as hers—Kiriel was the one she pitied least, and therefore felt most comfortable with.

But not this eve.

The girl who had escaped the City in the Northern

Wastes was a wild creature, eyes reddened, cheeks flushed, hair a stream of shadow. There had been blood spilled— some of it her own—and worse; her eyes held that tale in their perfectly black depths. Depths which, Evayne knew, were only half-illusion.

"The god-born walk freely in the City," she said quietly.

Kiriel shrugged.

The sky, flushed with dawn, grew brighter; Evayne thought for a moment that if her companion disappeared with the last of the shadows, it would be somehow fitting.

She did not.

"You don't speak much." Midnight-blue robes curled up around her face as her hood rose; the robes themselves had been restive since Kiriel had come from between the passes to join them.

Kiriel shrugged. Then, as if it were drawn out of her, she added, "I've nothing to say."

"Very well. Let me explain the rules."

A dark brow rose as the young woman bridled.

"These streets are not the streets you grew up in. The strong do not kill the weak, either for display or to gain ground. Magic is not used without writ and consent, except in enterprises that the Mysterium supervises. Weapons may be worn, but not drawn without provocation."

"And who," the young woman said brittlely, ignoring the barrage of names and items to cut through to the heart of the matter, "enforces these rules?"

"They are enforced," Evayne said coolly. "Or do you think the City was built in the Northern Wastes because the climate was perfect for it? There is power here, Kiriel—do not test yourself against it. I promise you, you will fail."

It was, of course, the wrong thing to say, but once said, it could not be withdrawn. Evayne had no desire to try. "Here, they will not search for you if you do not make yourself known. Your coloring is . . . unusual." At this, Evayne did smile. "But in Averalaan, it will only make you striking, not strange."

Silence, long and almost painful. Kiriel had never looked young to Evayne, and the glimpses of youth in the lines across her brow were a cry for comfort that could not be answered. "Where—where will you be?"

"I don't know. You are not the only child to walk under

a god's shadow. I have lived with that burden a long time."

At this, black eyes narrowed. "You lie," Kiriel said.

"Do I?"

"Your eyes."

"Could be as much illusion as your own," she smiled wryly, and added, "were you not who you are. Yes. My eyes are not the gold-ringed black of the god-born. But I do not lie, Kiriel. I do not believe I have ever lied to you."

"Why do you speak of me as if you know who I am?"

"Because," Evayne said softly, "In some other place, and some other time, I will." Dangerous to say, that, but the geas did not bind her lips. "If you wish, I will take you to a place that will offer you safety and food in return for your service."

Kiriel shrugged.

Evayne sighed and began to walk down the slope toward the demiwall. There, along with the fishers, they would meet the main road that led into Averalaan.

"Evayne!"

The violet-eyed woman stopped and turned. "Yes?"

"You dropped something." Light glinted off platinum as Kiriel rose, holding a ring—a slender, unadorned band—between her fingers.

Although she knew what she would see, Evayne still raised a shaking hand to her face. There, in the morning light, three gemstones caught and bound rays of sun. Three: Emerald, Ruby, and Sapphire.

Myrddion's rings had a destiny of their own; they *chose* their bearer. Evayne was their steward, the woman who had freed them to begin their long work; she had no say in where they went, or to whom. Nor did she always understand why.

She lowered her hand and then looked up the slope to where Kiriel stood with the fifth of the five rings of Myrddion; the fifth, reputed in legend and bard-lore to be the most powerful. The shadow that Kiriel cast seemed long indeed; of the Five, it was Kiriel alone Evayne was not, and had never been, certain of. Even Kallandras, bard-born and death-trained, she had trusted from the moment he first made his choice: For no game, no whim, no power struggle, could drive him from his brothers to her side.

Why did I not see this? she thought. Although she had seen very, very little of Kiriel in her life thus far, she had seen enough to know that Kiriel's hands were as unfettered as her throat, her ears, or her hair.

"Evayne?"

It was not her choice, in the end; it was Myrddion's. And she could question, she could guard, she could watch—but she could not hold a ring from its intended. "Keep it," she said, as neutrally as she could, although her left hand curled tightly around the three that remained under her stewardship. "It is yours."

But Kiriel heard the fear and the doubt in the older woman's voice—the first fear and first doubt that she had yet heard there. It made her smile softly as she slid the ring effortlessly onto her left hand.

Such an expression was not an unfamiliar sight for Evayne, but it chilled her nonetheless. "Come, Kiriel," she said, her face betraying nothing. "We have far to walk."

They came at last to the bridge across which lay *Averalaan Aramarelas,* and there Evayne paused to pay the toll. The men who stood guard at the foot of that bridge wore the comforting familiarity of the crown over the crossed sword and rod, and she paid their toll cheerfully, which caused a slight raising of eyebrows; rich or poor, no one liked an obvious form of tax.

But the journey had been one of silence, none of it companionable, and Evayne mistrusted the way that Kiriel's eyes darted to and fro across the human crowds as if searching for prey. She had seen such expressions before, and it never boded well. If she could reach her destination quickly, so much the better.

The younger Evayne would have given Kiriel the benefit of the doubt; after all, Kiriel had never been in a large city before—not one teeming with human life in such a variety of guises. The dark-eyed gaze might have been a sign of avid curiosity; it might have been a gesture of apprehension; it might have been the reflex of a woman used to defending her life against all manner of attack.

But it was none of these things. It was hunger. For what?

She gave you her word. And the value of that word? Evayne cast a sidelong glance at Kiriel's profile. Were it not for the icy set of her jaw, the narrowing of her eyes, she might have been beautiful—but she was cold for it; she exuded the type of danger that only a fool would be willing to tempt.

And in a city this size, Evayne thought ruefully, there were fools aplenty. She just prayed that none of them were thieves—for Kiriel's reflexes were easily a match for the most professional of cutpurses. And Kiriel's temper was not to be trifled with.

"You're worried," Kiriel said.

"You should be used to it," was the crisp reply.

Kiriel's smile was as sharp as her sword. But it was not so malicious a smile as that first one by the bay had been. Shrugging, she began to follow Evayne across the bridge. She stopped once, at the peak, to gaze into the moving water below.

"Have you seen the ocean before?"

Shrug. And then, so softly that Evayne barely heard it, she said, "No. But she told me about it."

"She?"

There was no reply, and Evayne, who regretted little at this age, regretted that single spoken word.

They came to the manse on foot, but only Evayne knew how unusual it was for visitors to arrive that way; Evayne knew who The Ten were. She glanced across at her dour companion and found that the isle's buildings, vast and beautiful though they were, were not enough to draw attention away from the sparse and thinning crowds.

She knew that this city was not the city that Kiriel was used to. The daily affairs of the Essalieyanese would be almost incomprehensible to her. But she knew well that Kiriel would not betray her ignorance of the lives of the passersby by asking anything so simple and direct as a question. Not yet.

"We come to the House in which you will find a place. Follow me," she told the younger girl. "But do not speak. The guards will lead us into the courtyard while they wait on The Kalakar's word."

Of all The Ten, Kalakar was the most straightforward

in its handling of security. The men at the gates were soldiers, not House Guards, and although some concession had been made for dress, the colors—silver-edged gray and a brilliant, dark blue—were those of the uniforms of the Crowns' defenders. It made Evayne smile softly. That concession, no doubt, had been the decision of the House Council, and not The Kalakar herself.

But perhaps not; The Kalakar understood ceremony when ceremony was necessary for the good of the army.

The men at the gates raised a hand in both greeting and command; Evayne stopped, and gently placed a hand upon Kiriel's shoulder to prevent the younger woman's unfamiliarity with Essalieyanese gestures from causing a minor incident. But Kiriel was still.

Of course. The men were armed and armored; this, she understood.

"State your name and business."

"I am Evayne a'Nolan, and I have come, albeit belatedly, at the behest of The Kalakar."

The man snapped out a curt order to a runner behind the gate. Before he could leave, Evayne raised a hand, the gesture almost an exact duplicate of the gate guard's. "She will not be completely familiar with my name. But give her this; by it, she will recognize me." Gold glinted in her cupped palm. Seeing its color, the guard stiffened in anger.

Then, seeing more, he stilled. His gaze was sharply focused as he met her violet eyes. "Karlson!" He took what she offered, closing his callused fingers almost gingerly around it.

"Sir!"

"Take this to The Kalakar at once. You will find her in the drill hall."

At that, Evayne did smile. "She hasn't changed much, has she?"

"Not for me to say, ma'am." But the guard looked at her long and hard, as if coming to a decision of his own. "Primus Greyhame," he said. "I've heard about you."

They were led into the courtyard, and from there, onto a wide, flat terrace that was beautifully adorned with trellises and summer blossoms. Leaves and petals provided privacy of a sort from common traffic.

Kiriel touched them carefully and slowly, as if by doing so she might memorize their texture, their color, their scent. Evayne said nothing at all as the young woman explored; it was the first sign of natural curiosity that she had yet seen. But it did not escape her notice that her charge's right hand was always upon her sword hilt.

"A'Nolan," someone said, and Evayne turned in time to catch the low bow of the young runner at the gate. Karlson? Yes, that was the name Greyhame had shouted. He was young, this man; but so many of them seemed to be too young these days. "The Kalakar will see you. Please follow."

"My companion?"

"She will see *you*. Refreshments will be brought for your companion if she wishes to remain upon the terrace."

"Very well." She turned to Kiriel. "Wait here. Do nothing." There was no request in either statement.

If Kiriel resented command, there was no sign of that anger across her pale features.

When Evayne entered the drill hall, she was amazed at just how much noise a hall could contain. There was blade work being practiced here, and more; she could see the glint of field-plate as she cleared the narrow, ancient doors. Sweat hung in air already heavy with midday sun, but the sea breeze was sharp and cool as it passed through the many open windows, blending the scent of salt into the human mix.

"Kalliaris' Curse!" A young man's voice, with enough frustration behind it to force it above the din. It was followed quickly enough by laughter.

"She's got you again, Michale—and she's armed with a god-cursed ladle!" Another man's voice—older, surer, a mix of amusement and annoyance.

"I'd say god-blessed," Evayne said wryly as she cleared the shoulders of the gathered spectators and glanced down into a slightly inclined basin. A quick glance told her all she needed to know; a young woman in an apron, with—yes—a ladle, sat firmly upon the chest of a young man twice her size. Her knee was pressed a little too heavily into his throat.

"Kalakar?" The dark-haired, clean-shaven soldier—a

Primus by his markings—stepped up to the rim of the basin.

Following the direction of the man's gaze, Evayne shifted slightly. Standing on a narrow platform that was separated from the pit by height and nothing more was a lone woman in serviceable gray and blue, with a feather— a kestrel's feather—embroidered across her left breast in silver thread. She was not a young woman, although still Evayne's junior, and the furrows in her brow hid the scars across her forehead from view. Momentarily.

"Primus, I thought you said these were the trained corps?"

"I thought they were," was the rather grim reply.

"Then Kalakar is in trouble; if Carla had chosen to attack in earnest, the bearers would be bringing him out of the pit. Continue."

"Sir!" Fist struck chest.

"I think," Evayne said softly to her guide, "that it is safe to interrupt now."

"Then you don't know The Kalakar," the young man replied under his breath. But he straightened his shoulders in good humor and nudged his way gently toward the platform. For a young man, he was a sizable one—she really hadn't noticed it because his demeanor was not a large man's demeanor—and he cleared a good path for Evayne to follow.

And so The Kalakar saw Evayne a'Nolan for only the second time. Their eyes met, blue-gray and violet, the pale shades of steel and gemstone. It was The Kalakar who bowed.

"So. It *is* you."

"It's been a long time."

"For me, yes. But you've hardly aged a day."

She'd aged a month, at first guess, but did not choose to speak it. Instead, she stared at this woman, seeing in her expression a bridge between the younger Verrus, the older Commander. There had been very little continuity in Evayne's life, and even now, with regret and resentment far behind her, she still looked for the signs of it.

The scars across The Kalakar's forehead had faded as much as they ever would; those across thighs and fore-arms were well-hidden. A month ago, Evayne had scrubbed The Kalakar's blood from her own cheeks, her hands; the robes, of course, took care of themselves.

"I've missed this," The Kalakar said, as she lifted the signet ring that the young runner had brought her as proof of Evayne's identity. "But I'm well enough known that it wasn't necessary to have a new one made."

"You waited for me to return it." It wasn't a question.

"Yes. That, and—as The Kalakar—they've given me a better ring." Grim humor, but humor nonetheless, transformed The Kalakar's face, brightening it and sharpening its details. By no stretch of the imagination was The Kalakar a classically beautiful woman; she was large-boned and square-jawed and her hair—what little there was of it—was fine and pale. But there was strength about her, and among the defenders, she was a legend for the loyalty that she expected from—and gave to—her men.

Evayne knew, firsthand, the truth of those stories. Loyalty had not been a luxury to Ellora Decravet AKalakar upon the Annagarian fields; it was not a luxury now. It was bred into bone and blood.

"I owe you my life." Blunt.

"You would have been safe if you had abandoned the three companies."

"I've heard it said," The Kalakar replied, grinning ferociously. "But I am safe. And I didn't leave them. They were mine."

"And still are. If I'm not mistaken, the Primus looks familiar."

"Just as damned pretty as the day we first signed him on, too." She grinned. "But not quite as earnest."

They were silent as the young Sentrus was rescued from the kitchen help, dragged to his feet, and sent into a more traditional combat.

"Why have you come now?"

"Do you mean, why have I come at all, or is the timing significant?"

"Both."

"I will answer the second first. Yes. The timing is significant. There will be a call to an execution in the capital of *Averalaan Aramarelas*. Refuse to join it, no matter what tidings come that might otherwise cause you to support such an action."

"I've reason to believe in your advice, Evayne of

nowhere, and I will take it as I can. I suppose it would be a waste of words to ask you just what in the Hells is going to happen?" Before Evayne could finish drawing breath, The Kalakar continued. "As I thought.

"What of the answer to the first question?"

"I wish a boon."

"Granted."

"And you haven't heard it yet? You are trusting for a woman of your rank and station."

"I'm a damned good judge of character. What is it, exactly, that you want?"

"A moment of privacy. May I?" She lifted her hands.

"Hold." The Kalakar turned and looked up to the near-empty galleries above, lifted her hands in a quick two-cut jab, and then nodded in satisfaction. "Yes."

Evayne smiled and began to cast the net of silence within which she could speak in peace. Very few were the mages who could breach her spells now, and not one of them was upon Kalakar grounds. The Kalakar's mages were less subtly trained.

"In the courtyard, upon the southern terrace, is a young woman. She is my height, and my weight, but she wields the blade so well she could take on the King's Challenge and win."

A pale brow rose slightly. "You think highly of her."

"I think highly of her ability."

It was a difference that was not lost upon either woman. "Go on."

"I wish you to take her on."

"Pardon?"

"I wish for her to become a part of the Kalakar army."

"Kalakar doesn't have an army."

"Very well; if you will preserve that myth, the Kalakar House Guards."

"Why?"

"Because you need her, and because she needs you."

"Ah. We finally become cryptic."

There was a measured pause before Evayne spoke again; when she did, she chose her words carefully and spoke them slowly as if each one were reluctantly yielded. "The kin are hunting for her."

The woman who was, in private, Ellora AKalakar,

missed a beat. The narrowing of her eyes was a chill shift of expression. "Who sent them?"

Silence. Evayne's lips became a thin line as she turned away momentarily.

"Why?"

"That I honestly do not know. And I wish I could tell you; it would ease my mind."

"Where is she from?"

Evayne met the older woman's eyes, opened her mouth to speak, and then shut it again. In spite of herself, her admiration for a woman who was, perhaps, not the best of rulers, kept meaningless words at bay.

"I see," The Kalakar said softly. "Do you trust the girl?"

"Do I? Does it matter? You are The Kalakar, and it is under you that she will serve. She will meet your standard, and pass your test, or she will not."

"Not true," The Kalakar replied. "You asked it as a boon—and for your aid in the massacre of the Averdan hollows, I have granted it. But you've told me enough, seer." Turning, she called down to the Primus in the pit. He looked up, surprised at the interruption. "I've matters to attend to, Gavren; the mettle of the men of the Blue Linnet will have to be settled tomorrow."

She turned crisply back to the blue-robed woman who waited in amused silence. "This girl is on the visitor's terrace?"

Evayne nodded almost ruefully. "And it appears," she said, her voice growing softer, "that you must greet her on your own."

Because she had seen it once before—and that once at such a dark time that the memory was indelible—The Kalakar said nothing as the light of day and the play of shadows beneath the open ceilings seemed to swallow the older woman. Then, gripping the signet ring tightly in the palm of her hand, she smiled.

She was not a woman who liked to be in debt; not a woman who balked at the chance to repay old debts and have done.

To the air, she brought her forearm across her chest in salute both to the past and the future. And then, that taken care of, she strode quickly out to the courtyard; curiosity was her worst weakness.

* * *

If Evayne had been worried that The Kalakar might
see the unprepossessing size of the girl and dismiss her
as unsuitable for the soldier's trade, her fear was unfounded.
Although in height and weight the dark-haired young
woman seemed slight, she pivoted into a defensive stance
that was so sure it spoke of either years of experience or an
instinctive natural ability—or both. She wore armor, a fine-
linked shirt with plated joints at knee, shoulder, and elbow.
But the links were of black metal. Not painted, for paint
would catch the light and this seemed to drink it in. Something was familiar about the workmanship—and it was
something that Ellora did not like, although it was not obviously Annagarian or, worse, Allasakari in make; those she
knew well enough to spot at a hundred yards.

Slim, steady fingers rested upon the pommel of a
sheathed sword. It was not bonded. The sword itself was
both long and wide; it looked, sheathed, to have a
Southern weight to it, but not a Southern curve. Ellora
wanted to see it—although, Kalliaris willing, not from the
wrong end.

There was danger here; an old soldier's instinct sent a
chill, wordless whisper down The Kalakar's left ear.
She'd only ignored it once. Learned not to, damned
quickly.

The girl sized her up as well, returning her measured
stare with a tight-lipped defiance. But she didn't speak.
After five minutes, it became clear that she wasn't
going to.

"You're not from around here." It wasn't a question.

"No."

"Good."

At that, the young woman raised a dark brow.

"You've just committed three serious protocol errors,
and you're only a civilian." She paused. "First: I'm *The*
Kalakar. There are ten important Houses, and I rule one of
them. You bow when you enter my presence, and you
wait until I've acknowledged that bow before you rise.
Second: I'm your elder—by a good number of years—and
were I not your superior, manners would still demand that
you at least lower your head. Third: You are the supplicant here. I've granted you an audience, which means I'm
willing to hear you speak. If you want something from

me, you ask me—you don't wait for me to ask you. Is that clear?"

"Am I?"

"Are you what?"

"A supplicant?"

It was not what Ellora expected to hear. "Aren't you?"

"It depends."

Definitely not what Ellora expected. "This," she said dryly, "should be interesting. There's food here; do you mind if I join you?" The irony in her tone, heavy enough to crush a lesser man, didn't seem to bother the younger woman in the slightest.

In fact, it didn't seem to be apparent to her. At all. *I must be getting subtle in my old age.*

"What exactly does it depend on?"

It was obvious that Ellora was not the only woman to be nonplussed. The girl opened her mouth to speak, but, having nothing to say, clamped her lips into an uncomfortably narrow line. Her eyes, narrowed as well, searched the older woman's—but when she didn't find what she seemed to be searching for, she relaxed. Which is to say, her knuckles, white around the sword's hilt, took on color as her grip loosened. She did not let go.

"Let's start again," Ellora said. "Why have you come to my House?"

"She brought me here."

"I see. Did she say why?"

"She said I would find service and food here."

"Perhaps she didn't make it clear that the service was to be offered to Kalakar by you. In return for which, you receive food and shelter."

"What . . . service?"

"Do you know what an army is?"

The girl nodded, once again oblivious to the heavy sarcasm in the older woman's voice. "Good. Service to Kalakar—to me—would take that venue. You become a Sentrus in the Kalakar House Guards. You follow my commands, you follow my rules, and you defend the interests of my House. In return, you become a part of the best army in the Empire; you become a compatriot to the men and women who define the term loyalty. There is no finer force."

The girl was silent for a long time, weighing the words

that she'd been offered. Then, quietly, she looked up at the woman who ruled the House. It was, Ellora thought, as if a mask had fallen from her face and been replaced in haste; something looked out of those dark, dark eyes that seemed haunted. And hungry. And Ellora very much doubted that this stiff, defiant young girl wanted to reveal either. Yet it was in that brief glimpse, awkward and unspoken, that Ellora understood why Evayne had come.

Yet again, The Kalakar was to be surprised.

"You don't want me," the young woman said softly. It was not an accusation; it was a confession. Ellora had thought to hear neither.

"Pardon?"

"You don't want me. These House Guards—these Kalakar guards—they are yours. I think they are . . . important to you."

The girl didn't know. Ellora looked at the not-quite-neutral expression on the young woman's face. "Yes," she said, leaving sarcasm and irony behind. "To me, they *are* the House.

"The woman who brought you here didn't tell you about Kalakar." There was no question; the answer was obvious.

"No."

"Then I will not. Words are easy; they prove nothing. But let me say this: I'll take you on your own merits if I'm convinced you have any. I won't ask about your past; I don't care about what you did under someone else's rule. What I care about is Kalakar, and the House Guards. Give me your word that you will live and die as a House Guard, and I will give you my word that you will have the protection that I extend to any of my people."

"And what of them?"

"Them?"

"The House Guards."

"What do you mean?"

It was the younger woman's turn to be frustrated, but the frustration didn't prevent her from speaking. "You can give me your word—and I'll trust it—but you can't give me their word. The rest of the House Guards. Are they going to want to die because you tell them that I have to be protected?"

"I don't know your name, young lady," was the terse

reply, "but I do see your ignorance, and I forgive it. Barely. You may insult me as you see fit—but the men and women of the House Guards are above your reproach. Wear their colors, wear their name, and you *are* a House Guard. You will not have brothers or sisters who mean more, or to whom you mean more. They will raise their swords in your defense, and they will lower their shields only when they've fallen. Do you understand?"

"No."

To be brought up short so many times in such a brief conversation was refreshing. At least that's what she told herself as she unclenched her teeth and tried to smile. "No?"

"I know that you mean what you say. And I know how to fight." She swallowed, and for the first time since The Kalakar stepped onto the terrace, she lifted a shaking hand from the comfort and security of a sword hilt. "Tell me how to wear these colors. Tell me what I must do."

"You can start," The Kalakar said, rising, "by telling me your name."

"Kiriel," the girl said. Then, hesitantly, "Kiriel di'Ashaf."

The Kalakar frowned. "That's the Southern variant," she said stiffly. "In Averalaan, we style it A'Ashaf." Pausing, she looked down at the set lines of the younger woman's jaw. "Do you speak Annagarese?"

"Some." Kiriel lowered her head. "It's from the Valley."

"Averda." The Kalakar knew, from the tone of the young woman's voice, that she would not speak about the teacher of that language.

"Well?" The Kalakar rose as the two men entered her study. Papers were scattered from one end of the room to the other, although most were concentrated on the surface of a desk that was—beneath everything—something of a personal heirloom. The maids and the servants did not clean this room—at the command of The Kalakar, no one touched it—and the scent of dust was strong enough to carry over the smell of burning oil. The study had one window, and at that, a small one; The Kalakar disliked working where passersby could watch her.

The younger of the two men, Gavren AKalakar, gave a

crisp salute. Had he a different personality, he would have been the regiment's heartbreaker; he had a face which could be used as a model for the statues of the gods. Had, in fact, been used, at least five times. Battle—the action he had seen—had been fierce and intense, but somehow, perhaps through the grace of a protective god, that face had always emerged intact.

The Kalakar nodded at the younger man. He did everything so crisply and cleanly he had never once been up on drunk and disorderly charges—and rumor had it that more than once it was Gavren who had had to fend off the unwanted attentions of starry-eyed villagers rather than the other way around, much to the amusement—and envy—of his cohorts. She believed it and privately wondered if *any* of those starry-eyed maids had ever gotten what they wanted. "Speak."

"She almost broke Stavro's arm. She did break Corin's ribs." As Primus Gavren AKalakar noted the darkening set of The Kalakar's face, he raised a hand. "I do not believe that she injured either Sentrus intentionally."

"She broke Corin's ribs by accident?"

The Primus nodded quietly.

"Corin's no Michale."

"No; he knew she was trouble the moment she set foot in the pit. We all did. She's not a pretty face—well, she is that—but she's too damned cold for it. Doesn't play to her size either."

"You didn't like her."

Primus Gavren exhaled. It always came down to this, no matter how professional he wanted to be. The Kalakar was, he thought ruefully, a lot like his mother, Lady lead her to peace. You couldn't lie to her—in fact, you usually didn't get enough time to try.

She laughed before he could answer. "I love it when you think, Gavren—you do it so slowly." Genuine amusement took any sting out of the words as the man who was generally acknowledged to be the regiment's own Karatis reddened.

"There's nothing about her to dislike—" he began, but The Kalakar waved him to silence and turned quietly to the older man who stood to his left. "Well?"

Vernon AKalakar—the Verrus known to the Kalakar House Guards as the Iron Fist—frowned. As this was his usual expression, neither Gavren nor Ellora was particularly concerned. He was an older man; the only man on the Council who had more military experience than Ellora herself. It showed; his face was lined with a network of sun-bleached scars, and he was missing the tip of his right ear, but he stood with the quiet confidence of a Verrus. "I don't know why you accepted her, Commander, but you must have had your reasons. It's clear that she knows how to fight. Clearer still that she knows how to kill. What's not clear to me—and I was there—is that she knows how not to kill." He raised a finger to his chin; he often did while in thought.

"Corin is still alive," The Kalakar pointed out dryly.

"In a test situation, where there is no serious threat." Vernon AKalakar was not known for his sense of humor. With, Ellora thought wryly, damned good reason. "She's trouble."

"And that means?"

"If you must keep her with the House Guards, you keep her with the Black Ospreys."

Gavren's dark brows disappeared into the line of his hair. "You want to put a girl who's not yet adult with them?" Pause. "Uh, sir." Fist, with no conviction, struck unarmored chest.

The Kalakar looked to her adviser. "The Ospreys?"

Vernon Loris AKalakar nodded quite grimly.

"I was afraid you'd say that."

"You knew I'd say it."

"Well, yes." She sighed. "But you know what Duarte's going to say. Luckily, I'm the Commander—and you're the Verrus. You tell him."

"Yes, sir." Respect was in each of the two words, but Ellora had no illusions; she would regret this sooner or later. Later, as usual, was preferable.

Primus Duarte Samison AKalakar was a man in his prime—which is to say, just shy of forty and not pleased with the prospect of crossing that decade. It wasn't age; his training in the Order—surrounded by men and women who had not reached the peak of their powers until their sixth decade—took the sting out of encroaching mortality. But as he rolled up and out of the dusty basin, hands sprouting a thin, thin ribbon of blue flame, his back creaked ominously.

Hiding in the basin beneath the cover of thatched mat and a thin veil of dust-held hiding had been part of the plan. The Ospreys, replete in their light armor with weapons drawn and readied a hundred yards away were also a part of Duarte's plan—although he wasn't part of theirs.

The voice of the Verrus—a whip's crack of a shout—froze the Ospreys in place, and the delicate balance of the training run was shattered. Which meant, of course, that an hour eating dirt and dust with the rest of the worms, an hour sweating and baking under the cloudless sun, with a back that was getting—admit it—too old for this sort of severe test, had just been thrown away. Cursing under his breath, he stood; if it was over, it was over. There wasn't any reason to leave his cheek buried in the dust.

He narrowed his eyes and swore as he glanced at the Ospreys. Those sons of bitches were carrying armed crossbows—something The Kalakar strictly prohibited in practice. Vernon was going to have their balls. No, not just balls. Fiara was right in there among them, which only proved that women had just as little common sense as men—at least in the Ospreys.

"Good show," muttered Alexis, wiping her chin and scanning the horizon with narrowed blue eyes. "Get up, Auralis. It's done. Vernon's blown it."

At another time, Duarte would have remembered that he loved to see Alexis angered—it made her vibrant, lovely, and absolutely deadly—but at this moment, he was annoyed enough himself to miss the opportunity.

Cursing, he seared the grass off the edge of the dust bowl, announcing his presence to the rest of the Ospreys. They'd gotten better at this sort of game; half an hour, and they'd have been discovered. Of course, in fifteen minutes, Auralis, Alexis, and he would have singed their left eyebrows off, but still. Things happened in a training run.

"Duarte, the unit hasn't recovered from the last bill The Kalakar tendered for damage done to her scenery." Auralis, unperturbed as always, rose as if dust couldn't cling to him, folding his arms lazily across his chest. His hair, long for a soldier's, hung at his back in a single copper plait. "Well, what have we here?" He whistled softly, ignoring Alexis' glare, which wasn't easy.

Verrus Vernon, uniformed for the warmer weather, walked with a young woman by his side—a stranger to the House Guards. It was privately said that Auralis knew every woman on the grounds, some more intimately than others. Whether it was truth or no, it was clear that he hadn't seen *this* dark-haired, slender girl before. Smiling broadly—with a pause for a wink at Alexis—he jumped out of the basin, stamping out the last of Duarte's flames as an afterthought.

"Vernon!"

The Verrus—a man who liked to stand on formality if ever there was one—stiffened. But as Auralis had, just this past month, been busted from Decarus to Sentrus, he hadn't much to lose.

"Primus Duarte!"

"I'm coming, I'm coming." Duarte, still trailing a cloud of dust from the edge of the grass-green cape he wore crossed the hollow and came to stand in front of the Verrus. He had carefully schooled his expression and now only looked annoyed, rather than murderous. Still, he managed to make the fist to chest salute look almost respectful.

It was more than the Verrus expected.

"I see," Vernon said, looking over the heads of the Ospreys who remained standing, like a poorly formed shield wall, a hundred yards away, "that you were in training. I apologize for the interruption, but—"

"Kalakar's orders." It was always The Kalakar's orders. "What have we done wrong this time?"

"I don't know—but I'm certain that Verrus Korama would be most interested in the details should you care to divulge them. Today that is not my concern."

"What is?"

The Verrus looked very much like the fist for which he was named. "I don't," he said, in a steely cold voice, "see crossbows on the field?"

"No, sir."

"Good." Verrus Vernon looked down—he was unbowed by age, and had always been a tall man—upon the young girl at his side. "This," he said to her, "is Primus Duarte."

Duarte looked at the girl, meeting her gaze as if it were a blade's edge. The hair on the back of his neck rose, and he took a step back. It had been at least ten years since someone had, in a confrontational setting, forced him back a step by their sheer presence—and this youngling, weapon bonded, for the Mother's sake, had just done it without opening her mouth.

He didn't know why, and Duarte was not a man who liked ignorance, especially not his own. The girl was Alexis' height—maybe less; she was slender, although the dark mesh of her armor and underclothing might hide muscle bulk. Her face was very pale, her eyes as dark as her hair. Her chin was neither pointed nor squared, her cheeks high, her forehead perfectly smooth with youth. But her sword was long; had he been the arms master to equip her, he would have suggested something lighter.

Alexis was at his side in a minute, and he caught the glint of steel—unsheathed—in her hand. "Not now," he told her softly, his words as sharp as her blade.

Looking across at Vernon, he caught—of all things— an almost sympathetic grimace. He didn't need sympathy from the Verrus. "Who is she, and why is she important enough to interrupt our exercise?"

"She is Kiriel di'Ashaf, and she is, by The Kalakar's command, a member of the unit under your command."

"What?"

"She is, by The Kalakar's command, a member of the seventeenth."

"That's not the way the seventeenth works," Alexis said, her voice cool and clean as she glared at the young woman. "If The Kalakar—"

"Alexis. Not now."

She subsided grimly. A thought came and went as Duarte glanced briefly at her: although older, she was not so unlike the stranger, except that her anger, and her unsheathed blade, made her somehow seem the less dangerous of the two.

"Verrus, this is unusual. The nature of the seventeenth is subtle and doesn't adapt easily to any external influences that are not hostile." He kept his tone as neutral as possible, which was tricky. "But if The Kalakar so commands, you know that I—that we—have never been disloyal."

"Disobedient, maybe," Auralis said, stepping forward.

"Disobedient, certainly." It was Duarte who spoke, but Auralis didn't choose to hear him. He was in mid-bow— mid-Southern-bow—and as the sun caught the sweat along his back and chest, he looked like a bronzed statue, an ideal depiction of a man, not a real one. He offered a hand, and after a moment, the young girl accepted it; nor did she seem surprised when he turned her hand over and carefully lowered his forehead to her inner wrist.

"Kiriel di'Ashaf? There are very few from the South who petition The Kalakar; you are the first in many a year."

She did not answer him, which brought a smile to Alexis' lips—the first one since the Verrus had interrupted their session—but instead gazed out beyond his broad shoulders.

Duarte knew that she was staring at the Ospreys. Counting them, measuring them by the easy way they stood, weapons half-readied, in the distance. He thought, however, that it should have taken longer for her to gain their full measure—for he had no doubt that in her brief glance, she had.

Turning lightly on one foot, she bowed to the Verrus; the movement was stiff and unnatural.

"We don't bow here," Auralis told her almost gently. "We salute. You are no longer considered a civilian; you are a Sentrus, and when you greet—or take your leave— of a Verrus, you strike the center of your chest with your left fist."

"Right fist if you're left-handed," Alexis added, grudgingly.

Smiling strangely, she did as they told her, humoring them as if at play. The Verrus nodded briskly. "I wish you luck, young lady." His expression made it clear that he wasn't certain who would need it more—she, or the Ospreys. Vernon was not usually an expressive man.

She remained standing almost motionless until the Verrus was out of sight. Then she turned again to look at Duarte. "These are yours?" she asked, taking in the Ospreys with a graceful gesture.

"They're The Kalakar's," he replied, eyes narrowed.

"I see."

"And you?"

She smiled at the question; it was clear she'd expected no less. "I serve The Kalakar," she said, and her dark eyes were bright.

Duarte Samison AKalakar felt every hair on the back of his neck rise, and he silently cursed The Kalakar in each of the four languages he knew.

CHAPTER SIXTEEN

Serra Amara en'Callesta was no longer in the flower of youthful beauty; she had borne two strong sons and three beautiful daughters, and at the Lady's mercy, all but one had survived into adulthood. A night thought, that—but evening was fast approaching, and the Pavilion of the Dusk, positioned so that one might feel the solitary wonder of the Lord's decent, made way for such musings. The living could never hurt you as profoundly as the dead. And the dead were legion.

Serafs attended her in silence, and she allowed it; Tyr Ramiro often told her that she was far too patient with their maunderings and their ponderous service. But as wife of the Tyr'agnate, she was allowed her pick of serafs, and chose only those whose company soothed and eased her.

It was said, among the clans, that she had never once suffered a seraf to be put to death, and if that was not precisely true, she did nothing by action to refute it; thus she held claim to the title Amara the Gentle—and she held it fiercely.

"Amara?"

She did not need to turn; the voice, soft and pleasing, could only belong to Eliana en'Callesta—the youngest of the concubines in Tyr Ramiro's tightly knit harem. Youngest and, without question, most beautiful. Amara appreciated beauty and grace—but more, she had the uncanny knack for seeing its potential; Eliana had been taken from her family—a seraf's family—at the age of eight, with her second teeth barely in. It saved money, to be so perceptive, and while Averda was the richest of the five Terreans, prudent management, where it was possible, was to be valued.

Prudence. She almost sighed. There were times,

although only under the Lady's Moon could such things even be thought, when she felt closer to Eliana than she did to any of her sons or daughters—for Eliana would be hers to keep, no matter the whim of any other clansman; she was the property of Ramiro's harem—and the harem was Serra Amara's.

"Eliana. Have you come to keep an old woman company?"

The girl's laugh was musical, bewitching; it wove a spell of pleasure by its utterance that evoked a response as genuine as the girl herself. "I have come," she said, "to keep company with Serra Amara if she will have me."

"And the Tyr'agnate?"

Eliana's full lips turned down in a slight frown. "He is alone again this eve. We thought he might be drawn to the Inner Chamber, but he will not be moved."

"We?"

"Sara, Deana, and I."

"It is this business with the General," Serra Amara said. "Come, Eliana. Sit by me; it is dark and the Lady's fingers are running through my thoughts." It was true, of course, but also untrue. The young girl took her place upon the silks, and rested her head upon the older woman's shoulder.

"Tell me," the Serra said.

"The General is like other men, and unlike. I told him that the Tyr'agnate—and his wife, the Serra Amara en'Callesta—had been called away to attend to their kai, and that I would be pleased of his company. He followed me to the Outer Chamber willingly enough."

"And?"

"He was gentle," she said as if it surprised her. "He—" she hung her head a moment, and hair the texture of silk and the color of gold curled around the hollow of her neck. "He did not desire me."

"That I do not believe."

"No?"

"I saw the way he observed you at the meal, Eliana." She sat forward, and a seraf handed her a goblet of sweet water. "But it says enough of his character that he did not accept what was offered." She watched in silence as the nets were drawn across the pavilion's face to keep insects at bay. Serafs, like shadows, were bitten as they worked, yet they never once complained. "He did not mention the incident to Ramiro," she added quietly.

Eliana lifted a shoulder so gracefully it could hardly be called a shrug. "And the Tyr is not angry with my failure?"

"No. But he isn't surprised either; Baredan is one who would speak after loving. He practices caution as he can." She smiled. "Tell me of the General."

"I think he values loyalty," was the quiet reply. "What he says, he means. Do you know that—" she paused, silent, as Amara waited. The moon was brightening above them.

"Tell me," the Serra said, making of the command a request. "Whatever it is, I will not laugh."

"I took him to the Outer Chamber. He sat upon the bench by the fountain, staring into the water in silence. He wanted no music, no food, no love—but he asked me to talk. Just speak. It was odd, Amara; he is not like Ramiro."

"No."

"I spoke, at first hoping to please him, to rouse him. But he stopped me, and asked me to speak, instead, as I would speak. I didn't know what to say. He asked me questions, and I answered them."

"Questions?"

"About Averda. About my life in the harem. About Serra Amara the Gentle. He did not ask me for any secrets, and perhaps I spoke too freely. I don't know why he wanted to hear me."

With such a voice, and such a disposition, Amara would have been unsurprised had the man been anyone but the General. But why? Baredan di'Navarre was a man, no more.

"He spoke of war, Amara—but not the specifics," she added hastily. "He said he had come a long way. He—" she lowered her face a moment. "He rode his horse to death to reach Mancorvo. It hurts him."

"I did not know."

They were silent a moment, in respect for the loss that would, in almost any other circumstance, be considered a grave crime.

"I had very little to say, after he told me. But I spoke of things that please me—no, of things that make me happy.

As I did, he looked at me. He said I was beautiful, spoke the way a man will. I thought, then, that he might lay with me—but he did not. Instead, he turned to the fountain, and he said, 'Lady, grant me a sign.' "

"He said this during the *day*?"

Eliana swallowed and nodded. She raised a pale face to the moon's light and accepted the goblet that Amara held. "A butterfly landed upon his shoulder."

"A butterfly?"

"Yes. And it was black and crimson."

"You have rejected Eliana, Sara, and Deana, Ramiro. And I hear, also, that you have turned aside Aliane and Maria." Serra Amara en'Callesta stood in the door of the vast chamber, raising her voice so that it might be heard by the man who sat kneeling in the sparsely furnished room. She wore deep, deep blue, a silk to match the color of her eyes; her hair, still dark after the passage of so many years, was bound by pearls and sapphires: the handiwork of the women of the harem.

"Did you also hear," the man kneeling said, without turning to greet his wife, "that I sent Carelo and Alfredo about their business, with little regard for their advice?"

"Oh, indeed, Tyr'agnate, I have. And the kai was most understanding, given what his father was like at that age. Might I enter?"

"And could I stop you if I wished it, Gentle Amara?"

"With but a word."

"That word would not be 'no.' "

"Ramiro, you make me sound like a Voyani shrew."

"A mistake, my love." He rose swiftly, turning with the speed of a hunting cat upon his waiting wife. "And if I am very good, I hope not to suffer its consequences."

She laughed as he swept her into his arms; he was the only person who could make her laugh out loud, unmindful of the social grace her station demanded.

"Why do you send me children at a time like this?"

"Because it is too tiring to come to you myself without exhausting you first. I am not a young woman any more."

His laughter left a smile upon his lips as he touched his wife's cheek, tracing its line to the tip of her chin. She knew him well enough by now to know that it was the first smile that had rested there since his quiet morning walk with Baredan di'Navarre two days past. It was vain, and she knew it, but she took her secret pride in the ability to evoke such a response where no one else, be they youthful, powerful, or beautiful, could.

But she also knew him well enough to know that the smile would dim, and then vanish as if it had never been. "Come," he said quietly. "The serafs have been and gone, and we will have peace within."

"Peace? This, I will see." Her own smile vanished beneath the weight of recent history. "The Festival of the Sun," she said to her husband.

"I know. Baredan di'Navarre believes that Alesso is no friend to Averda—but he will be an enemy in blood if we refuse the call to the Tor Leonne. And Mareo di'Lamberto has so refused." Either Amara or Ramiro could have pointed out that, with no Tyr'agar, there was in truth no call, for only the Tyr'agar had that right, and there was none. But the Radann were already mediating with the Lord of the Sun in ceremonies that were older than the Tor Leonne itself, for it was the Lord of the Sun, centuries past, who had first declared which clan would rule the Dominion. The Radann were the ears and eyes of the Lord, and it was said that Alesso di'Marente was the sword behind their necks. There would be a Tyr'agar, one way or another, at the end of this Festival. And the fact that his power had not been respected beforehand had a cost they both knew well; which of the clansmen, in matters of power, stood on nicety of form?

Serra Amara knew that if Callesta chose the Tor, and the Festival of the Sun, Mareo di'Lamberto would be isolated. And most probably destroyed. "You do not think that you will travel to the Tor Leonne."

"No."

She exhaled heavily, although it was bad form. "Good. If Alesso di'Marente had intended to share his power with you, you would have had word—or invitation—before the fall of clan Leonne."

He laughed. "You trust no one, do you?"

"I trust you."

"You trust me," he replied, "in affairs that do not interest you."

She placed an arm around his waist, and he an arm across her shoulders; they knew each other's bodies well enough to be comfortable walking thus. The large, empty chamber receded, and the small, sparsely decorated room opened up. This was Ramiro's heart, this singularly uncolorful room, with its lacquered chests and reliquaries. Here, scrolls and bonds and papers, old as the clan's founding, were placed, and here as well were the rings and the sigils, the shield and the sword, upon which Callestans swore their adult oaths.

Or, in the case of Serra Amara, their marriage oaths. She smiled, but sadly, as she saw these chests—and then the smile dimmed completely as she noted that the last— the black-and-gold chest in which the sword rested, lay open, its red silk reflected like too-bright blood against the blade's curve.

"You've decided," she told her husband, as she left him to kneel before the Callestan sword.

"Have I?"

"Mancorvo has taken the lives of a hundred of our serafs in the past four years. We have ordered our cerdan across the border, and we have brought back their serafs to replace those lost to us. We have killed and been killed; the nightfires have burned throughout all but the harvest season.

"But not once, Ramiro, except upon the day our kai proved himself, have you considered such actions so bitter that you opened the swordhaven."

"You think you know me so well, gentle wife."

Piqued, she rose and turned, leaving the naked blade at her back. "And am I so wrong?"

"I opened the swordhaven," he told her softly, "because Baredan di'Navarre is not a man I would dishonor with a dagger or a common blade. He is a man."

She was speechless, and then she turned again to look at the chest, at the sword that waited within, unsheathed. Ungirded. "You have not killed him."

"No."

"I am slow, Ramiro. This game of war—it is no longer my game. Tell me what you are thinking." She drew close, because he wanted it, and put her arms around him, wrapping herself tightly to the pillar that he had become.

"That I should kill him. That he will start a war that will destroy Averda, and possibly Annagar, by delivering it into the hands of the Empire; that he will prove to the rest of the clansmen that I am as Mareo di'Lamberto says: a lackey of the bloodless Northerners, with no sense of loyalty or honor."

"The Lady," his wife said softly.

"Yes. It is night—and I have never been comfortable with night decisions."

"This was not a night decision," she said.

He smiled into her hair, bending as if from too tall a height to kiss its darkness. "No; the decision to kill Baredan di'Navarre was made two days ago, after dawn, while the sun rose."

"You admire him." It was not a question.

"Is it so obvious?"

"Not to Baredan, no." Amara pulled herself gently from her husband's embrace. "But to me, now. You could have sent him northward with your Tyran. They could have killed him easily, with no witnesses, and disposed of the problem he poses. Instead, you are here, with the sword of Callesta unblooded." She paused. "And you sent Eliana to him, as a final gift, a last night."

"Yes."

"But he would not take what she offered, because he would not dishonor you."

"Yes, curse him." He turned from his wife to the sword, and she walked quietly to the hard mats at the farthest edge of the ornate circle in which the clan's history lay protected. There she knelt, with a grace that spoke of experience.

"You could have offered her openly."

"And what test," he replied with grim amusement, "would that have been?" He reached down and his hand rested, open-palmed, above the haft of the sword. Twice it wavered, and once it touched the twined cotton grip around the hilt, but it did not close there. "I told him," he said, whispering because he knew his wife could hear the words, "that we would travel together.

"I have not taken this sword from this room since the end of the Imperial wars. If I take it, it will become known."

"Yes, my husband." She placed her hands in her lap, the very picture of demure silence, for she knew, as well as he, that he could not return it to this room unblooded.

Lift it, and he was committed to war, no matter how short and one-sided. Or how long and bloody.

But demure or no, he knew his wife's measure. "And what would you counsel, my delicate wife? If I am not to go to the Tor Leonne—what does that leave me?"

She lifted her chin, it was the defining line of a strong face. "A seventeen-year-old boy with the blood of a Tyr'agar weak enough to be destroyed in one evening's short work." She paused. "And a clansman you admire, who will pursue and support that boy to the best of his ability."

The corded muscles of his arms tightened; the edge of his chin touched the hollow of his collar. "I am a fool," he said, as his hand closed.

Light caught the blade; Serra Amara gasped in a voice twenty years younger than she as he raised it high and spoke a single word: *Callesta.*

Carelo kai di'Callesta was his mother's son in appearance, but he had his father's youthful impatience and his father's temper. The last of which, many said quietly, was not so bad a thing. Those who knew of Serra Amara by hearsay said it because a Tyr'agnate who is too gentle is merely weak, and a weak Tyr'agnate cannot rule a border Terrean. Those who knew Serra Amara quite intimately said it because such a temper was not to be trusted with the wise rule of a border Terrean. Those in between felt that it was better that the son mirror the father in as many ways as possible as a matter of principle.

"Kai di'Callesta," Serra Amara said, the formality of the address a sign that she had grown weary with argument, "the Terrean cannot be run solely on the basis of your fear of the good opinion of other clans."

"Serra Amara," he replied, matching her formality with a stiffness all his own, "I do not intend any insult to the way the Tyr rules the Terrean. But what you have told me is—"

"What I have told you, I have told you at the behest of the Tyr," she said, before he could, indeed, insult his father. Although they were alone in the stone gardens, serafs toiled under the sun of the Festival season, and how many of those serafs reported directly—and secretly—to Ramiro, she did not know. But she was certain that there was at least one, and she did not wish her son to endanger himself by openly insulting the Tyr. That, Ramiro would not accept without intervention, whatever he might choose to hear in private.

He understood her warning, and fell silent, but barely. In that, he was like his father as a youth—and that man, Amara remembered well, although the years had gentled the memory. "Carelo, before you decide upon a course of action, know this: I support your father's decision."

"And what would you have me say?"

"A good question." She rose. "I will leave you with it, but will add this: There will be war, one way or the other."

"If we went to the Tor Leonne, the war would be with Mancorvo—and Lamberto would finally be crushed!"

"Lamberto," she said evenly, thinking privately that her son spent too much time with his riders, and not enough with his wife, "will be a target for the new Tyr'agar. There is no question of it. But think: He cannot be more of an enemy to Averda than he already is, and Mareo di'Lamberto will accept no offers from the Tyr'agar. At worst, Lamberto will fight two wars, but I think it likely that the raids between Averda and Mancorvo—should we desire it—will end rather abruptly."

"Serra Amara—"

"You are too trusting," she said coldly, resuming her seat.

Stung, he flushed.

"The General Alesso di'Marente controls perhaps half of the armies of the Tyr'agar."

"More, if Baredan di'Navarre is to be believed."

She shrugged delicately. "More, then. Do you think fear of these armies is enough to have the Tyr'agnati proclaim him Tyr'agar?"

Silence.

"Carelo, you will answer me."

Grudgingly, Carelo shook his young head. He was, Amara thought, such a striking man. "No."

"No, then." She gestured; a seraf appeared at her side in an instant with a goblet and a fan. She took the fan herself and sent him on without speaking a word. "We know, from the reaction of Mareo di'Lamberto, that Mareo was not one of the Tyr'agnate who supports Alesso's bid. We know, because we are as surprised by Baredan di'Navarre's news as Lamberto was, that we are also not one of the clans upon whom Alesso's success rests. Think," she said, allowing frustration to texture her tone.

"You think," he said slowly, "that Mancorvo and Averda are to be among the spoils of the new Tyr's reign."

She almost clapped her hands, but stopped, closing them around the stem of her goblet instead. Young men could be so headstrong. "Yes."

"Why?"

"Because, my son, he must have felt confident of the support of two fourths of the Tyr'agnati—in no other way could he be proclaimed Tyr'agar; the four would war among themselves for that right." She paused. "Therefore, it is clear that Oerta and Sorgassa support him."

"But we can't stand for long against the armies of the Tyr'agar." Here, he showed a glimmer of the pragmatism that had become his father's strength. Young Alfredo, his brother, was just as likely to stand against impossible odds with honor as he was to act intelligently.

"Not if things remain as they are, no."

"Then let us enter our own negotiations with Marente, while time remains. Averda is the richest of the Terreans. Let him lose one of the three he holds instead."

"Possible." This time, there was respect in the word. "However, negotiations rely on two things. One: that we have something that he wants. Two: that he has something that we want. What do we have?"

"We have Averda."

"And will we give that to his rule? I think not," she said softly. "What else do we have?"

"Legitimacy."

"Yes. And it may be that in the months to come he will need it. If, indeed, he does not choose to field his army the moment the Festival of the Sun has ended.

"What does he have that we want?"

"Mancorvo."

"Promised, I believe, to someone else."

"Then nothing. We wish to rule our lands as we have, in peace."

"There will be no peace," she said again. "Because in order to negotiate, two parties must be at equal strength, or at equal disadvantage. Unless the situation changes, I would say that Alesso di'Marente does not feel the need to bargain. It is rumored that he holds the Radann, and they may very well be forced to bless his rulership at the Festival—which means he does not need legitimacy.

"We have Averda, and he wants it. It is as simple, for the moment, as that."

Carelo kai di'Callesta bowed his head, this time with genuine respect.

"Na'care," she said, knowing that he hated the name, but feeling fond enough to use it anyway. "You should spend more time with your lovely wife."

He straightened his shoulders, striving to look anything but the young Tyran. "We should begin to plan. Where is the Tyr'agnate to be found?"

"He is currently inspecting the defenses along the southern border."

"Without me?" Carelo bridled. Which was as Amara expected; the border defenses were, after all, his command.

"Carelo, he left you in charge here. What better way to show his trust could he have chosen?"

The son had the grace to redden, and when he rose and walked away, his mother cast her gaze out to the standing rocks in the sparse, empty space. She was disappointed.

Until she heard his voice again, at her back. "Serra Amara."

"Yes?"

"As we do not intend to negotiate with Marente, you expect that we will have to face them on the field."

"Astute."

"Then you neglected to tell me how exactly it is that the Tyr'agnate expects to be able to withstand the General's armies."

"Ah, Na'care, Na'care," she said, unmindful of who might hear the pride in her voice, "we will make a ruler of you yet."

She did not, of course, expect him to like the answer.

Radann Fredero kai el'Sol,
Please accept our apologies for our inability to attend the Festival of the Sun this year. The Radann in the Terrean of Averda have been instructed to perform the proper rituals, and while we fully understand that these

rituals, so far from the Tor Leonne, are no replacement for your exalted services, we feel in this clime that we must make do with their lesser grace.

We would, of course, accept your invitation, but it has come to our attention that Mareo di'Lamberto has not, and it places us in a delicate situation. As you may be aware, the difficulties between Lamberto and Callesta have grown ever more bitter; as of late, we have lost a village, and during this season we cannot afford to lose another. As Lamberto will remain within his Terrean, we do not have our traditional guarantee that, for the Festival of the Sun, hostilities will cease, and we cannot leave our Terrean open to attack by stripping it of its most able leaders.

We hope that you will understand our difficulty and speak a word on our behalf to the Lord.

The loss of the Tyr'agar is a blow to Callesta, but the clan Leonne was small and perhaps not as strong in influence as it might have been; the Dominion lost much in the wars under the Tyr'agar's direction—Averda knows the truth of that better than any Terrean. We have no desire to rule the Dominion, nor would we accept the position were it to be offered to us. Yet we do not believe that any of the current Tyr'agnati would suit better; if there is to be a Tyr'agar, it is not from within the four that he is to be found.

The Radann have always given wise counsel, and it is our belief that in such times, their counsel will, of course, continue to be a wall against the wind. Should you desire it, we would be pleased to enter into deliberations with regard to the seat of the Tor Leonne.

    —Tyr'agnate Ramiro kai di'Callesta

"Well?" Alesso di'Marente set the scroll aside.

"He's committed it to writing," the Widan Sendari said. He lifted a goblet and a seraf, a young boy with perhaps too much energy, filled it.

"Yes. And if it were written to me, I would accept it as an offer."

Sendari shrugged. "There is no doubt that Baredan di'Navarre traveled to Averda. Ramiro di'Callesta has never been a stupid man."

"No. Unfortunately."

"He does not choose to expose himself by presenting himself to you directly at the Festival of the Sun. We both know, in his position, that we would do the same."

Alesso frowned. "Yes."

Sendari set the goblet aside untouched, and began to stroke the fine, long line of his beard. "He is no Lamberto, to stand on points of honor."

"Do you think he would be satisfied to serve me?"

"If his other choice was annihilation, yes." Sendari's smile was dark. "Alesso, we gambled, and in this case, it failed. We will still own the Tor; even Ramiro di'Callesta acknowledges as much in the letter to the Radann. Yes, it would have been better to have killed him at the height of the Festival. But that was asssassination, and this is combat. You made your name in the latter, and not the former."

"Oh?" was the moody reply. "Tell that to the clan Leonne." He reached out suddenly and grabbed Sendari's goblet; wine sloshed over the rim, staining the cushions beneath his crossed legs. "I am not a patient man, old friend. I see the need to act; I act. But in this—" He lifted the cup to his lips and upended it.

"Enough, Alesso. Enough. Yes, we should have ridden to war. And we can, if you judge the armies enough."

"They will not be enough." Alesso lifted the goblet with an angry wave. It was filled. Quickly. "Oh, we could win a war against two Terreans that will not stand together. But not without cost. Not against those two. And after the war, what? You know where Baredan has gone, old friend. You know what he was seeing." Fingers were as white as aged silver against the goblet stem. "The sun-scorched child of an ugly concubine. Legitimized and sent North to be forgotten."

"Yes. Ser Valedan."

They were silent a moment. "The Sun Sword," Alesso said grimly. "Our cause will be hurt if I cannot wield it. Cannot the Widan—"

"No. And you know it. A blade that can cut through the shadows that surround the kinlords will not be put off by our magics." His brow furrowed, for the problem was an old one, and oft-asked. "Perhaps if the Widan worked in concert—but I believe that we could not keep knowledge of that from the clansmen, and that will hurt you more."

"Then we've no choice."

Sendari said nothing. It was the prudent course. But he sat back uneasily against the sky-blue cushions, his throat too dry to drink.

"Tell Tyran Calevro to make the Tor Leonne ready for the public execution of the Northern hostages. Tell him to make their deaths quick but bloody; they must be a insult—worse—to the Northerners." He rose. "Then set a few of the Northern merchants free. Let them carry the tale."

"They will slaughter all of the hostages, Alesso."

"That is the plan," was the cool, dry reply.

"The Tyr'agnati will have no choice but to call for blood, and most certainly the Northerners—"

"The Northerners back away from war like beaten dogs whenever the opportunity presents itself." He paused. "But of course, when it is explained that the deaths were caused by a terrible political unrest—when we send the heads and the rings of those involved—they will bluster and ask for concessions. The hostages are not blood-kin, remember."

"They may back away from war," the Widan conceded, "but it is we, in the end, who ceded the lands in Averda to them. Weigh carefully. We cannot take the Dominion to war while we do not own it. Too much will be too unstable, and if the war is won by a General who is not Alesso di'Marente, we have lost the Dominion. Perhaps it might be better to forget about the boy and take the armies you control against Mancorvo and Averda."

"No, old friend," Alesso said, although he did not turn to face the Widan, "we will order the death of the Imperial hostages, and then we will wait. They will kill the boy, and I will wield the Sun Sword, I will hold the Tor. Only then will we call the war; for then we can take the cursed Shining Court out on a very short leash. But they had better," he added, throwing the goblet to the ground where the sweet wine was lapped up by the wooden planks, "be all that they say they are. And more."

Lady's last shadow.

Baredan di'Navarre stood in the darkness, waiting. It was cool in the valley, but not cold, and the sound of the insects sitting atop stalks of corn and wheat began to abate.

Sashallon, he thought, and it hurt. The horse that he rode for what was in all probability the most important ride of his life would be a stranger. As if the wind could hear his thoughts, it turned, bringing the scent of horses to him.

"General kai di'Navarre."

He recognized the voice in an instant, and bowed, although the bow was an act of generosity, not a dictate of custom.

The young girl, Eliana en'Callesta, returned his bow with an agile grace that made him feel truly old. At her side, with a glass lamp swinging in the brisk breeze, stood an older seraf with a neutral expression. His shadow fell across her feet. Eliana was not a woman who should stand in shadow.

Had he ever looked so perfect? Had he ever walked with such a complete confidence in his youth, in his own beauty? At that, he smiled ruefully. He had never been a beautiful man; not even his wives said otherwise. And there. She could bring a smile to his lips without speaking a word.

"Eliana," he said quietly. "Have you come to see an old man off?"

"Not an old one," she said. "But an honorable one. There are so few left in the Dominion." She spoke gravely, and the gravity made her, of all things, more beautiful. Holding the folds of her sari with her left hand, she reached down with her right and pulled out a long-stemmed flower. It was crimson, and beneath its closed bloom, there were thorns. "Serra Amara sends this to you," she told him softly.

"And I would not refuse a gift from Serra Amara the Gentle." He took the rose carefully, but in the dawn's poor light it was not easy to see what was stem and what thorn; the gift drew blood.

"A wise man indeed."

General Baredan di'Navarre smiled. "Tyr'agnate," he said, dropping carefully to one knee. And then, from a vantage much closer to ground than Baredan was comfortable with, he saw it: the sword of Callesta. Another man might have passed over it, for its sheath was not ornate. It was black, bound and knotted from top to bottom in linen and silk, with gold tip and gold mouth. What set it apart was the crimson mark in its center. The mark of Callesta.

"Do not," Ramiro di'Callesta said, "kneel before me. You are not beholden here, kai di'Navarre."

Baredan di'Navarre nodded grimly, but surprise still tightened his lips, silencing him. The sword. The sword of Callesta. He was certain it had not seen the Lord's light for at least a decade.

"Yes," Ramiro said, stepping to one side to allow his cerdan—no, his Tyran—to pass.

"Then I will ride," Baredan said, "with a lighter heart."

"And I," another voice said, "will wait with a heavier one." The Lord's light colored the sky; Serra Amara the Gentle wore a thin, thin silk against the line of her jaw as protection from the wearying sun. "General Baredan, we charge you with the safe return of our Tyr."

"With the—" He showed his surprise then, and Amara did not judge him weaker for the display; it was dawn, and in the moments when the Lady handed reign of her dominion to the Lord, it was hard to know where one's thoughts were best placed. "I am honored, Tyr'agnate di'Callesta."

The Tyr nodded briefly. "We will take an escort of a dozen." He turned to face the cerdan who waited with his wife. "The Terrean, in my absence, will be guarded and governed by my kai in my stead. His word is my word."

One of the Tyran stood apart, and bowed quite low. "Tyr'agnate." When he rose, Baredan thought he saw the likeness of the mother in his face. Ser Carelo kai di'Navarre.

The Tyr'agnate nodded as if satisfied, and continued. "Ser Alfredo di'Callesta will, however, be given command of the Western border patrols. It is time he assumed some of the responsibilities of Averda."

"Tyr'agnate," the kai said, bowing again, his face a perfectly composed mask.

"Come, Baredan. We ride with the sun's rise. The borders will almost certainly be watched."

He took no serafs with him because his mood was poor and he could ill afford to lose another; he had been forced to discard too many, and their experience and training was already missed. Even in the quiet splendor—the carefully cultivated appearance of tranquil, undisturbed wilderness—even in the presence of the lake of the Tor Leonne, his anger festered.

But the Festival of the Sun was to commence in less than ten days. Each pavilion, each viewing platform, each guest house and each hidden path, had to be tended, manicured, readied. This first year of the reign of Alesso di'Alesso, everything must be perfect.

He cursed the need for that perfection in silence, for at every stop he made, serafs and cerdan abounded, carrying bolts of fabric, hammers, nails; toiling with their wheelbarrows and their dirt, flowers, and spades; seeking, in each change, the blessing of the wives of Marano and Horaro, the women who, in the absence of a ruling clan, sought to better themselves by making the Festival of the Sun in their image.

Of course, when they saw Alesso di'Marente, they made haste to leave their labor, and of course, they made haste to bow, lengthening their stay and their work as they groveled. His power was not certain enough that he could afford to have any of them killed out of hand, although were he to do so, today would have been the day.

He cursed the Shining Court. Baredan di'Navarre was what he had been chosen to be: cunning, untrusting, untrappable—the Annagarian warrior. Just how cunning, and how suspicious, even Alesso had not begun to guess, and they had been friends a long time. He admired the General, even as he planned to crush him, for there was enough of the warrior in Alesso di'Marente that he truly appreciated a worthy rival.

Unreliable allies, on the other hand, were not accorded the same respect.

Wage war against the Essalieyanese, and you will have at your disposal kinlords.

And these?

He had watched the Lords in action. In the heat of the high sun, he felt a momentary chill, and he lifted his face to the Lord's. Wind touched his forehead.

What did the kinlords do in their millennia in the hells? They fought for dominion. And that fight, that desire for power, Alesso par di'Marente understood.

He nodded grimly at three serafs as they knelt gravely before him, their hands slightly dirt-stained, their presentation poor. Of course, presentation when one was digging and building could not be perfect; he passed them by, pretending not to hear the sigh of relief the youngest gave.

Yes, the kinlords battled. But it was not for the glory of killing and dying that Alesso Di'Marente struggled. It was for this space of wilderness, this near-perfect retreat, this crown of the Dominion.

I will be the greatest Tyr'agar that the Dominion has ever known. Or I will be the last. At this moment, neither sat well.

He did not know what he was searching for—did not, in fact, realize that he had been searching at all—until he came across the distant sound of mournful samisen music. He stood within a small stand of perfectly landscaped trees, and as he turned, the wind brought the notes to life, carrying an unmistakable voice.

No serafs attended him, by his strict command; nor did the cerdan that he normally brought with him. He regretted his decision, for their absence made of his approach an insult, and he did not wish to insult the Flower of the Dominion. Yet he approached as if drawn, seeking the words that the distance blurred.

Beneath his vantage, the Pavilion of the Dawn—well past its best viewing hours—lay protected against the sun's harshness by a simple, gabled roof; the screens had not been drawn. Upon the serafs' platform were two men and a young girl; they sat at ease, legs bent beneath them, heads bowed. The wide, round hats of the Southern Annagarians were bound with bright ribbons; they wore them well.

He followed the path that the trees hid until he could see beyond the serafs, and there he stopped, for Serra Diora di'Marano was singing. Her lashes were a dark sweep of perfect curve against her fair skin; her hair, unpearled and unfettered, hung down her shoulders and back as if she were a young child. She wore midnight-blue and ivory, and gold caught the light at her neck in strands that bound it perfectly.

He could not name the song she sang, and he was not unlearned. But the song brought him a measure of peace that he had not felt since . . . since last he heard her sing. She brought back youth, and the brashness of it.

He was a man, under the Lord's sight; a warrior who had proved himself upon the fields of battle against the Lord's enemies. The Tor Leonne—the Tor—was his, and in a man's home, a man's domain, he could do as he pleased if he had the strength to defend that action. General Alesso di'Marente had that strength.

The serafs looked up as he approached. The oldest of them, gray-haired and slender, rose in the seraf half-crouch, moving forward a graceful step to kneel in the soft dirt before the pavilion. The youngest, the girl, rose as well, stepping into the pavilion's shadows.

General Alesso par di'Marente stopped a foot away from the seraf when it became clear that the seraf did not intend to move for the clansman. Alesso wore the rayless sun above the crescent sword—a military symbol, a symbol that only clansmen were allowed to bear.

Had he not thought it would displease her, he would have killed the seraf outright; he considered it, before bowing very correctly instead. "Tell your Serra that the General Alesso di'Marente wishes the privilege of her audience."

The seraf bowed at once, his gray hair blending with bent stalks of grass that, like the man, had passed their season of soft newness. Then he rose and retreated. But he did not retreat to where Serra Diora sat; he moved father back, disappearing from view into the cooler recess of the building.

Alesso had just time to curse quietly under his breath before the seraf returned to once again resume his position upon the seraf platform. "The Serra Teresa di'Marano grants the audience the General Alesso di'Marente requests."

Widan Sendari di'Marano was a troubled man. "Serra Teresa, you must be mistaken."

"You are the Widan, Ser Sendari. If you insist, and you walk the path of the Wise, who am I to demur?" She lifted her lavender fan and spread it wide, waving it through the air so delicately her hands seemed involved in an intricate dance. "Yet to my unlearned and untrained eye, I would say that Alesso di'Marente has shown his intent."

"Alesso is not a mere boy, to be overwhelmed by a woman's face or figure." He froze. "Or voice."

The air cooled. "Speak plainly, Widan Sendari di'Marano."

"You have not interfered?"

"Make the accusation, if you will make it; if you will not, leave it be." Her cheeks were colored slightly; they gave a pleasing blush to her appearance. But they also gave warning, and if the Widan did not take warning well, he took it.

"It is not like Alesso," he said roughly.

"It is exactly like Alesso," she replied. "You have interest and affection in the women that she chose for you, and in the woman that Fiona has chosen since. But you are not a poet, Sendari, and you will never be one; you have never had a young warrior's heart." Her eyes narrowed; the fan stilled, and she studied its perfect crescent, its jade ribbing. "Or did you have another plan for my niece? For I will concede that it is unlike Alesso to work against a plan he himself has devised."

"Indeed." He stared at her; she did not meet his gaze. "Speak," he said at last. "Speak plainly, at my request."

She lifted the carafe of sweet water and poured it for him. "I do not interfere in your affairs, Widan. But if I were so inclined, I would not beguile Alesso di'Marente or in any way draw him to my Na'dio. He has already killed two wives."

"One died in childbirth," Sendari replied, too sharply.

"Very well, then."

"What exactly did he say?"

"What did he say? He said very little. But he approached without seraf or cerdan."

The Widan darkened slightly. "And?"

"He chose to speak with my serafs, and they carried his message. But he meant it, I think, for Diora. He sat with us for two hours, and during that time, Diora sang and he watched her."

"Just that?"

"Yes. Only that." She paused, setting down the carafe and lifting the fan again, the effect one of grace and muted satisfaction. "He did not look at another thing under the Lord's sky."

The Widan rose heavily, as if age were settling more

quickly than he had ever expected it would upon his shoulders. He did not know if Teresa knew it, although he suspected that she did.

Serra Diora Maria di'Marano had already been promised to the Tyr'agnate Eduardo kai di'Garrardi of the Terrean of Oerta in return for his pledged support of Alesso di'Marente at the Festival of the Sun. And she had been promised, with the very reluctant approval of her father, by Alesso di'Marente; for without his approval, Garrardi had vowed to withdraw not only his support, but his silence.

A dangerous game, that. But well-played.

CHAPTER SEVENTEEN

28th of Morel, 427 AA
Averalaan, Avantari

"This was the third attempt on Ser Valedan di'Leonne's life in less than three weeks!"

"We're well aware of that."

"How is it that, in three weeks, your security has been so poor that not once, not twice, but thrice, the boy's life has been endangered?"

Commander Sivari had a headache that would not go away. The portly, loud, and theatrically enraged Annagarian seated—if the up and down, back and forth motion could be dignified with the word—before him had been in his office for no less than three quarters of an hour, sweat-draped vermilion silks flouncing about as he gesticulated.

It was a pity, the commander thought idly, that weapon skill and endurance faded with age, but the ability to sit behind a desk and write out commands did not. The desk was a front line that he had grown to loathe over the years.

". . . and we demand justice!"

Prattle. Frothing. Abuse.

"The Imperial Court accepted us as hostages—you've accepted the responsibility for our safety and our well-being. Are you listening?"

It was a pity. Most of the Annagarians that Sivari had met were a quiet and controlled bunch; people who preferred a silken, understated threat to a blather of incoherent babble. That type of Annagarian, he could deal with. Besides which, Ser Oscari was cerdan, not hostage; guard, not valuable noble.

"Don't just sit there, Valedan, speak up for yourself!" The large man pushed the younger one forward in his seat.

Unfortunately, the young man wasn't expecting the blow, and righted himself only by flattening his palms against the surface of Sivari's desk. Sivari's crowded desk.

"No. Don't touch them. I'll tend to them later." He tried to smile, but his face was too stiff from maintaining a studied, neutral expression through the older man's babble. "Ser Oscari, if you wouldn't mind?"

"Wouldn't mind what?"

"Wouldn't mind leaving us to speak."

"Leave? Why should I? No one's tried to kill the boy when an Annagarian's been around—or hadn't you noticed that?"

"That's not true, Oscari," the boy interjected, his voice a study in quiet deference. "Serra Alina was there the third time."

"Serra Alina is a woman. I am a clansman!" The older man shook his head and rolled his eyes. "You see?" he said, jabbing the air in front of the Commander. "This is what comes of sending a boy too young to the North! He forgets himself! He forgets our customs!"

"The customs of the Valley," Commander Sivari said quietly, "are not the customs of the rest of the Dominion." Besides which, he had thrice had occasion to speak with Serra Alina, and she had a temper which, while cool and polite and perfectly hidden beneath a composed and elegant exterior, exposed Oscari's for the bluster that it was.

Ser Oscari di'Vanera drew himself up to his full height. "And just what," he said, "do you mean by that?"

Or perhaps it was just the merchants. "Ser Oscari," the Commander said, "I mean that you are cerdan, not Tor or Tyr. It is your job, and your right, to protect your clan. Of which," he added, his voice a trifle chillier, "Ser Valedan is not a member."

"We're all Annagarian here," the large man said, although the wind was out of his sails.

For the life of him, Sivari could not understand what Ser Fillipo di'Callesta—brother to the reigning Tyr'agnate—valued in the extremely annoying Oscari. But Oscari was of Fillipo's retinue. "Yes, you are all Annagarian. I do not dispute that. But you have been in my office for nearly an hour, and I have had no further details, no better description, from young Valedan here." He raised a hand as Oscari began to spout anew. "Ser

Valedan. This is a matter not for the Kings' Swords, but the Kings' Diplomats. Please. Ser Oscari."

He began the mental countdown, starting at thirty and not at the customary three. When he reached the two-second mark, Oscari finished whatever it was he was saying and stomped out of the office, threatening Sivari with some ailment, and the wrath of the Tyr'agnate's brother, neither of which Sivari found particularly worrisome.

"Does the man never shut up?" he asked.

"No," was the quiet reply.

Commander Sivari smiled. "Ser Valedan di'Leonne, you must forgive my poor manners. I am not happy with the breach in our security."

The boy nodded seriously; it was hard for Sivari to remember that he was seventeen years of age. Oh, he was the right size for it, he certainly had the build and the face—but he lacked experience, and it showed.

"But, Ser Valedan, we find it unusual that in the first two incidents, the assassin was a conjured creature. Do you understand what this is?"

"A demon."

"We are aware that you are from the clan Leonne."

At this the boy nodded. Sivari was well aware that his mother—what was her name?—filled his head with nonsense about the Great Tyr, but the boy seemed to have survived such nonsense intact.

"We do not wish to start an incident with the Dominion."

"No, sir."

"Can you think of any clan that would benefit from your death, either directly or indirectly?"

"No, sir. But Alina says that if I die, the Tyr'agar would have to respond by killing all of you." His expression was quite pained. "I mean, all of the hostages in the Tor Leonne."

"Which, if it did not start a war, would certainly damage relations and trade between the Dominion and the Empire. Who would most gain by it?"

"I don't know."

"Valedan, that isn't a good enough answer. The first time, maybe. The second time, barely. But this is the third attempt. Two of the Kings' Swords were killed, and four injured. Do you understand? The time for ignorance has passed." The Lord of the Compact was riding the Kings' Commander, in language that had grown increasingly chill.

"Oh, indeed it has," someone said.

Commander Sivari looked up. Standing with his back against the closed door was Devon ATerafin, his dark hair silvered slightly with passing time, his face a set study of utter neutrality. Sivari knew better than to ask how he had come; Devon was uncanny in his ability to move . . . quietly. "What is it?"

"You won't like it."

"When you deliver the news, I never do. What is it?"

Devon turned to the young man who was seated in front of Commander Sivari's desk. He fell to one knee before him, bowing his head in the Southern style. "I bring you word," he said, as the dark-haired young man seemed to shrink back slightly, "from the Tor Leonne.

"The Tyr'agar is dead. The members of the clan Leonne who resided within the Tor are dead; not even the daughters or the wives were spared. Ser Valedan kai di'Leonne, you are the clan now." He paused, and then lifted his head. No Averalaan winter was as cold as the ATerafin's expression. "You are a fortunate young man," he said softly, the words more of a threat than a statement. "You will stay in the Arannan Halls. There is an armed guard, and two shadows, who will be at your side constantly from this moment on. You will accept the company of a mage of our choice, and you will accept the company of a bard that Senniel sees fit to appoint. You will follow the orders of those attendants and guards that we assign—while you remain in *Averalaan Aramarelas*— in all things. Is that clear?"

The young man paled. "My father—my father is dead?"

Sivari closed his eyes a moment. "ATerafin," he said, lifting a hand. "The boy has had his shock. The rest can wait."

"No, Commander Sivari, it can't." He walked over to where Valedan sat. "Ser Valedan kai di'Leonne, the merchants of Terafin have just arrived home from their journey to Raverra. They were detained in the Tor Leonne for seven days.

"During those seven days, the Imperial hostages were

slaughtered in the public square. Not even a child survived." His jaw tightened, if that were possible. Ser Valedan di'Leonne stared up at him, his eyes a blackness of shock, of a man who has heard so much, so quickly, that he refused to understand any more of it. "If the enemies of your clan have not succeeded in their past assassination attempts, they will now be aided by most of The Ten.

"Come. I will escort you back to your quarters."

"Kalakar! Kalakar!"

A young man she didn't immediately recognize came tearing across the green. She frowned as he stopped, chest heaving. He was one of the servants, not the soldiers. The frown deepened. The servants were chosen for their ability to live up to the expectation of other noble Houses. Running, arms flapping, feet kicking up clods of loose dirt nearest the flower beds, this young man looked anything but able.

"I believe," The Kalakar said dryly to her companion "that's me he's shouting for."

"I believe," her companion said, smiling ruefully, "that you're right." He rose gracefully and set his glass upon the edge of the demiwall. "It was really far too quiet a day." Verrus Korama was as unlike Ellora as day to night; he was slender, almost sylvan; she was heavily boned and built. His temper was mercurial, yet superficial; hers was slow to wake, but when it did, it left its scars, both in her memory and in the memory of anyone who witnessed it. Where she was prone to execution, he was prone to mercy; where she was given to dry, earthy humor, he was almost too proper for a military man. He was the only one she knew who didn't drink.

And if she had to choose one man out of the entire regiment to save, it would be Korama.

"Whoa, there," The Kalakar said, as the boy stumbled to a halt. "Take a breath, and take a rest."

The fair-haired servant flushed. "Vernon Loris said you were to have this."

She frowned. Korama stood. Vernon did not use civilians as messengers where a military man would do. "Be quick, then." She held out a ringed hand, and the child— or so he seemed in height and manner—immediately placed a curled scroll into it. The weight gone, he collapsed to his knees, breathing a little too quickly. The grass was tall enough and dry enough to protect his clothing from dirt, which was just as well; the formidable woman in charge of the servants' laundry and uniforms bullied even The Kalakar on occasion. And the boy was wearing white and gold. Household, and at that, inner House.

"You didn't tell your staff where you could be found, did you?" Korama spoke quietly against the breeze.

As the answer was perfectly obvious, she didn't bother to give it. Instead, she looked at the seal, pressed into silvered wax, that lay across the center of the scroll. Terafin.

Kalakar and Terafin were not enemies, but they were not friends; they moved in circles that overlapped seldom, but when they did, the two Houses clashed as any of The Ten did. The fine hairs rose on the back of The Kalakar's neck; she felt the lightning's lattice in the air, and knew the storm was about to start in earnest.

The scroll was the bolt.

She broke the seal, and unfurled the vellum carefully, seeing the ink and the turn of the letters before she looked at the words they formed. The hand that had penned the message was none other than Amarais'.

"Kalakar?"

It was such a short message. Three sentences.

She could not keep herself from crushing it. She knew why Vernon had chosen—wisely—to send a servant in the stead of a House Guard. "Boy," she said softly.

"Allan, Kalakar."

"Allan. Is a reply expected?"

"No, Kalakar."

"Good. Please leave us."

"Yes, Kalakar." He stood quickly, wiping his hands on the front of his pants. She watched him turn and leave, less frantic in his pace than when he'd arrived. It was easy to watch him. Her eyes did it automatically, too numb for a moment to move, to look at the business at hand.

"Ellora?"

"It's Madson," she told him, her face a mask.

"Madson? Madson's in Annagar, isn't he?"

She lifted the hand that held the crushed scroll. Lifted it, moving her arm as if it could not be bent at the elbow.

He took the burden from her.

"Cormaris' Crown," she heard him say. And then, silence.

"We cannot overlook this!"

"Vernon—"

"We don't even have his body—we have nothing left but this!" Verrus Vernon Loris AKalakar threw the remnants of the scroll onto the center of the table in the meeting hall. "Do you know—"

"Vernon." Korama raised a hand. "We all fought in the Southern wars. We know what they do with the dead."

"And the living. Do you know what kind of death he had?"

"It isn't necessary," Korama said.

But The Kalakar lifted a white face. "No," she said quietly. "I don't."

"I took the liberty of speaking with the Terafin merchant myself."

"That *was* a liberty, Verrus. Have you spoken to anyone else about this?"

"No, Kalakar."

"Good. You will not."

"Yes, Kalakar." Vernon's lips were a single white-gray line.

"But you *will* tell me," she added, so softly her words hardly carried.

"They cut off his legs at the knees and made him try to walk."

She said nothing.

"He should have refused and died with dignity, but he couldn't; they told him if he could walk, they would spare his children." Her silence slowed him where her anger could not. "We have to act, Kalakar. We have Annagarian nobles littered about the isle as if they own it. Hostages," he added, his voice blurring on the word. "Make them pay."

She said nothing again, but she stared at the signet ring upon her hand as if it burned.

Serra Marlena en'Leonne rent her silk sari—or tried; the fabric was, sadly, stronger than her hands—and wailed like a newborn child. The kohl and powders that adorned the whole of her face caked and gathered in the lines that age and wind had worn there. The veil, she had torn off in shock and anger, that the Lord might see her outraged face and know that wrong had been done.

Valedan sat a discreet distance from her heaving shoulders, uncertain of how to offer comfort to a woman whose husband lay dead an empire away. Especially not when he had been, even at that distance, the center of her world.

"It was treachery," his mother said, the words muffled by the thick palms of her hands. "Treachery. Markaso was a great man, a great man. Only treachery could have felled him."

He nodded awkwardly, staring at her back, and the pale roots of her dark, dark hair, too numb to say anything at all. The only thing he felt, besides this unnatural awkwardness, was guilt: guilt at the lack of loss he felt for the shadowy figure of his father.

The Tyr'agar had been an older man when last they met. He remembered this well, for they did not meet often, and the blurring of years—the passage of time— was not lessened, as it had been for his mother in his eyes, by their constant companionship. Finely robed in gold and silver, with black and white and blue embroidery, sword-girded and heavily booted, the man who ruled the Dominion of Annagar returned from war to his harem. His eyes were dark and narrow, and his beard thin; he was wide—broad-shouldered, tall, but thickening at the middle if truth were to be told. And there was no warmth in him.

He greeted his Serra, and in turn his wives, and then paused a moment to praise Ser Illara, his kai. Valedan, and the rest of his half brothers and sisters, waited quietly, even meekly. To speak out of turn was dangerous, especially for the concubines' children. At six, he had known it clearly. Yet his father never struck him, never beat him, never hurt him.

Because, his mother said, he was a great man.

What had he said, the stern and terrible man who ruled the Southern Dominion? What words had he offered to those who waited in such meek silence?

Serra Marlena and *her* son.

Oh, it stung. Even now. Especially now. He rose; he

wanted peace, and this place, this courtyard with its blind-folded stone boy in the center of its lone fountain, had been his one certain retreat. Until now.

He and his mother had traveled with two cerdan to the heart of the enemy's empire. To these very halls, to live and breathe the salty, tangy air of the open sea in a land where horses were beasts of burden and women ruled and blood-kin were less than nothing among the families of the powerful. Because his father, the great and powerful Tyr, needed the aid of those loyal to him, of those he both loved and trusted as his own kin, in a land where treachery abounded. Or so his mother told him.

But certainly those second sons and bothers that the Tyr'agnati had sent were not so valuable to the men who remained in the Dominion. He realized it now, at seventeen, when at eight things had seemed so much clearer.

"Markaso," the woman beside him sobbed, and he saw her a moment, unkindly, as she was: too old, too lacking in the fine self-control of a suitable wife, too unlovely for the man that his father had become. She sent letters, of course—but who answered them, if they were answered at all, he did not know.

The hangings to the courtyard were shoved to one side; they flapped heavily against the smooth stone walls as Serra Alina di'Lamberto—the only woman to be sent as hostage to the Northern Kings—stepped into the room with her servants. Valedan remembered her because so many people had been privately proud of Tyr'agnate di'Lamberto for defying the Northerners while acceding to their demands for surety. A woman was, in the end, of no value to a Tyr. He would not have released a son or a brother. To get one, the Northerners would have had to obliterate the Terrean of Mancorvo. They chose, in the end, to accept.

Serra Alina had been given time to dress, but little time to prepare herself for public appearance; she wore no gold, no jewels, no adornments, and the sari that fell so exquisitely was of a simple, pale blue, with no embroidery, no obvious sign of well-crafted artisanship. She was pale, but composed, and although she was of an age with Serra Marlena, she was slender and tall and stern. Too stern, his mother told him, which is why she had never been married off. What man would have a woman so hard in his bed?

He rose at once and bowed correctly.

"Ser Valedan," she said, bending at the knee. "The Kings' Swords have . . . graciously offered me escort to these halls. For my own safety." She paused. "They are rousing the rest as well, I believe. Will they all be brought to the Arannan Halls?"

"I—I don't know, Serra Alina." She was so unlike his mother that many found it hard to answer her; to Valedan she was a sword; not to be feared, unless he faced its moving edge.

"Ser Valedan, I will not stand on ceremony here." She rose from the scant half-bow and her servants hastened to straighten the folds of fabric that fell at her back. "What has happened? Why does Serra Marlena weep so?"

"It's—it's the Tyr'agar."

The Serra grew still, although until she did, he would have thought her incapable of being more steely. "What has happened to the illustrious Tyr'agar?"

"He's been murdered," Serra Marlena said, raising an angry, reddened face. "Murdered, they say—by treachery!"

"Who is 'they'?" Serra Alina stepped past Valedan and caught Serra Marlena by the shoulders. "Who is they, Serra Marlena?"

"The N—Northerners. The diplomats."

"Valedan. Tell me."

He thought he heard the faint edge of disgust in her voice, but he could not be certain. "The ATerafin, Devon, brought news. From Terafin." He swallowed as Serra Alina left his mother's side and came to stand uncomfortably close to his own. "The Tyr—and the clan—have been killed. "And—and—" He swallowed. "And all of the Essalieyanese hostages."

"All of the Imperial hostages."

"Y—yes."

"Lady of Night." The Serra grew white, whiter than alabaster—whiter than the blindfolded stone face of the thin boy who stood in the center of the courtyard's fountain. He thought she might crumple. "Who carried this news?"

"A Terafin merchant. He witnessed the killings. They were . . . they were public."

"Who authorized the deaths?"

"I don't know."

"Was a Northerner responsible for the death of the Tyr?"

"No," a new voice said. They both looked up at once. Standing in the open door, the hanging's heavy cloth bunched up in a mailed fist, stood the Imperial princess, Mirialyn ACormais. A sword belt hung round her narrow waist, and beneath it lay a chain shirt and hauberk. Her hair was tightly bound, and although she was not a young woman, Valedan noted that the roots and the length were of a color. "If Northerners had killed the Tyr, would they have then had the chance to murder each and every member of the clan Leonne? Not even the children of the concubines were spared." The daughter of King Cormalyn bowed; metal clinked as she rose. "I will not enter farther, Serra Marlena, Serra Alina. But this night has changed your life in *Averalaan Aramarelas*. Do not sleep heavily."

"Wait, ACormaris," Serra Alina said. The princess paused, caught at the edge of the threshold that had never once been a barrier before. "Our deaths. Will they be public sport?"

Valedan drew breath so sharp the sound pulled the hair on the nape of his neck. Of course. The Northern hostages were dead. He hadn't thought. He couldn't think. Or he didn't want to. But Serra Alina's words gave him no choice. He turned a face now as pale as hers to the quiet princess.

"Serra Alina—" Princess Mirialyn seemed as pale as the Serra, although that was natural; she was fairer in color. "Do not act rashly, but wait. I will—I will do as I am able." She swallowed, and Valedan felt the first deep chill of real fear. Mirialyn ACormaris was known for her fearlessness and her honor, yet even he could see the apprehension in her unblinking eyes.

Serra Alina bowed. "Serra Marlena," she said without turning, in a tone too quiet to carry to the door, "you humiliate us all by this . . . public display. Do you wish to dishonor your husband's choice? Cease this crying at once. We are Annagarian; the men will be here soon."

* * *

She woke from sleep with a scream. Not a muffled scream; not the cries, pathetic and whimpering, that so often accompany nightmare. No, she screamed, and across the narrow hall, in a set of rooms occupied by the quietest of the men who served her, Teller sat bolt upright, his own dreams and sleep thrown off so completely he might have been waiting, awake, for this moment.

He was halfway through the door when they collided, he a slight and slender man, and she, a slight and slender woman, both in their nightclothes, both running as if the lives of their loved ones depended on it.

"Jay?" He caught her shoulders, held them in the brace of fingers that were used to waking her from the seer-touched morass of nightmare. "Jay!"

She met his eyes in the half-lit halls, and he knew at once that this was no waking nightmare; her gaze, framed as it was by eyes both wide and round, was here, and not in the half-world between dream and wakefulness. He almost took a step back at what he saw there. Because he hadn't seen it for years and years, and that youth was not a youth he had any desire to recall so clearly, in the dark.

"Where's Avandar?"

Things had to be tough if she wanted him.

Another door opened in the narrow hall, and a woman peered out from behind it, tentative, as if she might interrupt something that she'd rather not. "Jay? Is that you?"

"It's us," Teller replied. He met Finch's shadowed gaze and shook his head; saw her relax even before he began to speak again. "Jay's—"

"Jay's fine." Jewel Markess ATerafin said. "But if Jay doesn't move quickly, a lot of other people aren't going to be. Where in the hells is Avandar?"

"He is," came the dry reply, "not in the hells. You summoned me?"

"Summon is about right," Finch murmured, thinking of how well he fit in with the canon of other summoned creatures. Avandar might live with them, he might serve the same woman they all served, but he wasn't one of them. The fact that he was mage-born didn't keep him out—they'd all met one or two that they could tolerate, maybe even like—and it wasn't that he was a domicis, and used to running the lives of anyone who happened to live under the same roof, or in the same wing of the building, as he did. It was his chilly arrogance, his aloof distance, his almost open contempt for anyone—anything—that didn't meet the hidden criteria by which he meted out his approval.

Stealing a glance at his profile, she was chagrined to meet his piercing gaze. He was a striking man—not the sort of man that she would have ever guessed would be a servant to anyone else's whim or desire, be they King or even God. But he had chosen the life of a domicis, and he fulfilled it, if not graciously, then well.

Jewel, used to this exchange, ignored it. "Yes, I did. Wake Morretz. Tell him we need to see The Terafin at once."

"We?"

"I."

"Very well."

Jewel sat in the near darkness of mage-light. Amarais Handernesse ATerafin—The Terafin—sat as well; there was an intimacy in the setting that spoke of the years of trust between them. Morretz, the domicis of The Terafin, stood behind her, his brass hair pale in the shadows, his blue eyes untouched by the darkness. Avandar, the domicis of Jewel, stood beside her, arms folded almost lazily, hair dark, eyes dark, demeanor cool. They were a study in opposites, these two men.

The women ignored them.

"Jewel," The Terafin said. "It is late."

Jewel nodded and drew breath. "The Ten meet in the morning."

"Yes. It was," The Terafin added dryly, "to be a secret meeting."

"They'll vote to kill the hostages."

The older woman stiffened. "We," she said coldly, "will vote. This is not a matter open to House Council discussion, Jewel. It is a decision that I have made, and I favor it."

"Unfavor it," the younger woman said, heated where The Terafin was cool. Morretz cleared his throat, and Jewel subsided, sitting back into the rests of her chair without realizing that she'd begun to leave it. "Terafin," she said, and then, "Amarais."

"This is a seeing."

"Yes."

"Tell me."

"If we kill the hostages, we will lose the war."

Avandar's head swiveled to the side. "You made no mention of war."

"I didn't have the time."

"It's a long walk from your rooms."

"I don't owe you explanations, Avandar. Or is hearing the truth at the same time as The Terafin not good enough?"

He said nothing at all, but stepped back, bowing as if the gesture were a reprimand.

"Do you think the Southerners intend war?" The Terafin waited a moment and then reached out to the side, gesturing. Morretz nodded, and the lamps flared eerily, brighter in their burning although the height and the width of the flames did not increase. In the new light, the older woman studied the lines of the younger woman's face as they blended with sweat and strain and certainty. She had come to this house a young woman of fifteen or sixteen years; she had grown much, in the intervening seventeen years, both in power and in wisdom. Her temper, however, had not changed greatly. "You cannot call the vision back."

"No, Terafin." She did not add that she was not certain she would if it were possible. Was it imagination? Was it more? For she thought she saw the shadows at The Terafin's back stirring with unwelcome, unnatural life. "I don't know what the Southerners intend. At this point, I wouldn't bet money they do. But I do know this: We can't kill those hostages, or we've already lost."

"Jewel, you're young yet."

"I'm thirty-two."

"Yes." The Terafin rose. "What good are hostages if your enemy knows, with certainty, that you will never use them?"

"They can't know—"

"They can. And they will, the moment we fail in our resolve. Those men and women who are now confined in the King's Palace—they came as both guarantee of peace and sacrifice should the situation change. Have you read Goderwin's report?"

"Yes."

"Then you know who died, and how."

Jewel, tight-lipped, said nothing.

"This is not savagery, Jewel, it is politics. Every Annagarian noble within the Tor saw those deaths; it is too close to their Festival of the Sun for things to unfold otherwise. The Annagarians respect power and its practice. If we fail in our resolve, there may well be war, and it will be entered into lightly. By the clansmen."

Jewel rose as well; the two women exchanged a brief glance. It was the younger who looked away. But as she turned for the door, she said, "I didn't start out ATerafin; I started out in the twenty-fifth holding, with no money, no luck, and my den. I love my den. I chose them. I trained them, and I protected them. But I couldn't protect them all." Hard lesson to learn, that one. "When Lander died, back then, we knew it was because of the interference of a rival den, led by a boy called Carmenta. Have I told you this?"

"I don't believe you have."

"I made sure that Carmenta died for it. Wasn't his fault, in the end; certainly wasn't the fault of the rest of his den.

"And they died horribly. Probably slowly. There were two bodies the magisterians couldn't even identify without the help of the Order's best mages."

"Jewel."

"I told myself, I didn't know. I told myself that it wasn't my hand that killed them. But I'm seer-born. I knew that a creature that was masquerading as a friend, even then, was a killer. I knew it. And I knew that if I told him that Carmenta and his gang were a threat to the undercity, they'd die."

"These situations aren't the same, Jewel. A den is not a House."

"No. A den isn't a House. As a denleader, I had the luxury of being vengeful."

Silence, utter and profound. Amarais was quiet in her anger.

Mirialyn ACormaris stood stiffly in the Hall of the Wise, listening to the rage in her father's voice. Her father, King Cormalyn, the god-born son of the Lord of Wisdom, had never once raised his voice in her living memory. He spoke now with a voice that took the years from him, and a Wisdom-born man made, at best, an uneasy compromise with youth. His golden eyes were flashing; she could see their reflection in the armor of the man he argued with. The gods were here, in strength and power.

The Queen Marieyan, silver-haired and delicate in seeming, bent her head a moment, and then lifted it, resolute. She reached out to touch her daughter's shoulder; her grip was strong. "Do not interfere," she said quietly. Beside her, standing as ill at ease as Mirialyn, stood the Queen Siodonay the Fair. Like the Princess, she was armed as for battle, and like the Princess, she was stricken into a stillness and silence that was, for her, unusual.

Mirialyn shook her head mutely. Interfere? Between these two? She could not conceive of such an action as a possibility.

King Reymalyn's face was pale, but his voice was as loud as her father's, his eyes as bright. "And where is the justice in that?"

"Where is the justice in the slaughter of innocents?"

"These are hostages, brother—or have you forgotten?" He lifted his sword—his sword, bright and gleaming, lightning with haft—in mailed fist. "Those who died were our people and our care. We have always taken steps to ensure that they would not be threatened by our actions. And how has such peaceful intent been rewarded? They were slaughtered for sport!"

"I do not deny it, but I—"

"You will do as you agreed—as we both did. Here," he said, and in his free hand he raised a signed and sealed scroll. The force of his hand should have crushed it, but such treaties were protected by the craft of the Order of Knowledge against the ravages of time or handling. "This is the treaty we signed. Read it."

"I remember it well. I wrote it."

"Then you know that the Annagarians have forfeited their rights here. A death for a death."

"Has it not occurred to you, brother, that there was a reason beyond the sport of slaughter for these deaths? Has it not become clear to you that we have, among these hostages, the one man who can lay claim to the Tor Leonne?"

"And is the Tor our desire?"

"Reymalyn—"

"No. No, I tell you. This is not a day for politics. Ask them," he said, throwing his arm wide to take in the vastness of the city that lay beneath night's cover without, "Ask them what they desire. They will tell you what they know to be *right*."

"They will tell you," Queen Siodonay said suddenly, her voice trembling, "what you desire to hear. But it will not necessarily be the answer to our predicament." As she spoke, her voice grew stronger. "No, husband, hear me. It is my right.

"This is a dangerous time for the Empire. You and King Cormalyn have been, and will be, our best defense should defense be required. But you cannot be seen thus—quarreling like angry children."

Even King Cormalyn was shocked into silence.

Queen Marieyan nodded softly.

"The Ten offered hostages. The Ten have suffered the loss. The Ten will meet—as you know they will—to discuss the fate of the Annagarians now confined in the Arannan Halls.

"You are of the gods, and your parents make their demands known now; in this matter, your blood rules you both too dearly. You are what the Empire has always needed, almost all of the time. But this atrocity, my Lords—this atrocity is a matter of men, and for men. Let The Ten decide as they must."

"Well said, Queen Siodonay." King Cormalyn bowed.

"Reymalyn?"

"They are the injured parties," he said, but it was grudging.

"Yes," she replied softly. "Trust them to make their decisions. The dead ride them harder than they ride even you."

Ser Fillipo par di'Callesta bowed very low as he entered the presence of Ser Valedan di'Leonne. He was the only clansman to do so, and Ser Valedan stared at him uneasily as he exposed the back of his neck. If Ser Fillipo par di'Callesta was aware of this singular lack of grace, he did not show it at all. He was the last of the Annagarian hostages to be escorted into the open-air courtyard; the others—those sent by Garrardi and Lorenza—had come an hour past, and had gathered in the corner farthest from both the open arches and the Swords that waited beyond.

Ser Fillipo was the most important man in the courtyard. He had six cerdan and ten serafs; he had two wives present and three children. He was tall, he fought well, and he rode a horse as if two legs were unnatural. Averda, of all the five Terreans, had taken the treaty between the Dominion and the Empire very seriously. Ser Fillipo was the brother of the ruler of Averda, a par. Serra Alina had often called him the second son of a man who was lucky beyond the whim of fortune to have one of such caliber, let alone two.

He was, in too many things, all that Valedan was not. Already, the clansmen were coming from the corners of the courtyard in which they found refuge, as if Ser Fillipo's presence could bring order, reason, and safety. Especially safety.

"Ser Valedan," Serra Alina whispered.

Valedan glanced at her, and then realized that Ser Fillipo had no intention of rising until such permission was granted. He had seen this posture many times before, during the Festival seasons when the children of the concubines could wander the Tor Leonne freely, spying on the clansmen, and joining their children in sports, in song, and in other less approved of games.

"Rise," he said, and his voice was very quiet—but it was steady.

Ser Fillipo rose. If the position was natural in seeming, it was not in truth, and he shed it quickly. "Serra Alina."

"Ser Fillipo."

"Have you had news?"

"I? But I am merely a Serra. Surely the clansmen—"

"Enough. I was considered enough of a danger that I was detained. I have not had the time, nor do we have it now. Speak."

Her smile was edged as his tone; sharp and hard. "At your command, Ser Fillipo." She bowed; the bow fell short of perfect grace. "Mirialyn ACormaris has come twice. She believes—although she will not say for certain—that The Ten meet on the morrow to decide our fate." She paused, as if to gather breath, and the simmering anger left her features, emptying them in a rush. "I was able to obtain, from another source, a written copy of the report made to The Terafin."

He held out a hand, and she reached into the folds of her sari. There was no question of etiquette, no subtle struggle, as she handed him the papers.

Valedan saw Ser Fillipo pale.

His mother began to cry.

Ser Oscari began to shout.

Serra Helena began to wail.

It was too much. This courtyard, with its fountain, its quiet, open space, its familiar stone walls and unadorned floors had oft been his retreat. He drew breath, and even the air that filled his lungs felt stale and dirty.

"ENOUGH!"

Silence descended at his word.

Serra Alina was the first to drop, and she dropped into a fully executed crouch, knees against what would, in the South, have been smooth mats, not rough stone, forehead against her knees.

Women held no legal title in the Dominion, but they held a subtle power; Serra Alina was the most notable woman present. As she, the other Serras bowed down to the floor, their unadorned hair falling like scattered strands of shadow.

Ser Valedan di'Leonne turned his gaze to the men.

Ser Fillipo par di'Callesta met the young man's gaze, held it a moment, and then raised a brow. It was a flicker of expression that held—of all things—a certain amusement. And then, he spoke a single word. "Tyr'agar."

The silence became absolute.

"Tyr'agar?" Ser Oscari, sputtering as if he'd been caught mid-drink with a joke. "Ser Fillipo, surely you jest? Why the boy's—"

The overweight, overfamiliar man gaped a moment, and then, as Fillipo turned to face him, actually reddened. "Ser Fillipo," he mumbled. And then, turning, "Tyr'agar." The five cerdan who were Fillipo's escort found the stones as well, and hugged them almost—but not quite— as closely as the women.

Ser Mauro di'Garrardi, a young man of Valedan's age, shrugged a lithe shoulder. His was the acknowledged beauty of the foreign Annagarian court, and he knew it. He did not flaunt, but he did not hide; there was nothing false, in either direction, about Mauro.

He was new to the court. A fourth son, to be sure—but cousin to the Tyr'agnate Eduardo kai di'Garrardi. His older brother, the third son, had been recalled two years ago to the Dominion. Mauro had been sent in his stead. There were rumors, of course; when a man was as comely as Mauro, there would always be rumors. To his credit, Mauro di'Garrardi paid them no heed, either to affirm or deny.

"Take the title," Ser Mauro said, bending gracefully, but slowly, at the knee. "But remember that it is just that. Tyr'agar." He had four cerdan, one of whom accompanied him at all times in the course of a normal day. There were to be no more normal days. He gestured, and they joined him.

Ser Kyro di'Lorenza was the oldest man in the group. He brought a hand to a frosted beard and then dropped it again. Looked down at the white silk that pulled slightly across the pale back of his wife, the one woman who had come with him into this foreign exile, this other court. Helena. "I do not like it," he said, speaking for the first time. "But I will abide my word, Ser Fillipo."

"What word is this?" Valedan said, speaking softly where sharpness was called for.

"Have you read Serra Alina's report, Ser Valedan?"

"No."

"Then you will not understand the covenant. But both Ser Fillipo and I have agreed to . . . abide by the decision of the foreigners. We live at their whim, instead of dying like men at our own.

"These knees," he added gruffly, motioning with a frown to his son—his adult son, Ser Gregori, who should have known better, "are not what they used to be. They haven't bent much, these past twelve years. Not much at all."

"And we don't have our swords," Ser Kyro added. "This oath, this acknowledgment—it means nothing without swords."

"No," Ser Fillipo said, turning his head to the side, that

he might see Ser Kyro. "It means more. We are under the open sky, Kyro, and the Lord watches."

"The Lord watches warriors," was the truculent reply. But the old man nodded to himself, and then, knees against the stone, he smiled grimly and raised his face to look upon a man a third his age, if that. "Tyr'agar."

CHAPTER EIGHTEEN

"Duarte."

Duarte AKalakar was just this side of being able to control the mutinous rage that had spread through the ranks of the Ospreys. The effort cost him, though; it always did. Fiara was calling for blood, and if he hadn't had use of the detention chambers, he was certain that Annagarian blood—even Annagarians gone native—would be thickening the waters of the bay. If only it were just Fiara. "What?" He looked up, and froze as he met the wide darkness of black eyes.

Kiriel.

He had two guards posted outside of his doors; he always did. Only one person got through those doors without being announced, and it certainly wasn't Kiriel.

He rose, slipping into a defensive posture as he took his place within the flat rings that had been etched—by his own power combined with that of Alexis—into the stone floor. "What," he asked carefully, "are my guards doing?"

"Guarding the door," she replied.

"And they saw fit to let you pass?"

"They didn't see me."

She was always like this, a mixture of the cunning and the blunt that never quite fit. He didn't relax, but only because he found it impossible to relax around her. "You told me that you weren't a mage."

"I'm not a mage." She swallowed. "The Kalakar said that our pasts were not at issue."

She didn't ask me, he thought, but he didn't say it. "Why did you feel it necessary to come to me unannounced?" The circle beneath his feet grew cool to his magical sight.

"Because I wasn't certain of your guards."

"Pardon?"

"I wasn't certain of your guards."

"I see." He took a deep breath, waited a moment, realized that she intended to keep him waiting, and frowned. "Continue."

"Some of the Ospreys are planning to stage a demonstration in the merchant common tonight." She met his eyes, and hers were unblinking, unnerving because they did not swerve or dip or change.

"Where did you hear this?"

"I can't tell you," she replied softly.

In everything, she was infuriating. "Kiriel, you've come here to essentially betray the confidence of the Ospreys who've planned this . . . excursion. You've come in person instead of leaving the traditional note beneath the door. You've interrupted me, by methods which you will not explain, and having done so, have given me news which I needed—and did not want—to hear. If you're trying to be ingratiating, you're failing miserably—and if you're trying to be helpful, you will give me the names of the ringleaders."

"No," Kiriel said quietly, "I won't. They bound me by my word."

"They . . . bound . . . you . . . by . . . your . . . word."

"Yes."

"Kiriel—"

"I can kill them, if you'd like."

She meant it. Even if he hadn't seen her face, he would have known it; he could hear it in her words, in the casual certainty that lay beneath the surface of her youthful voice. Exasperation turned to something else as he met her gaze.

"You don't want me to kill them."

The Ospreys were a team. A difficult team, yes; too difficult for the regulars to either train or control. They stood apart, keenly aware of the things in their temperaments that made them different. Unique. He'd found them. He'd put them together, giving to the Kings' Justice the one or two that served as example of behavior that even the Ospreys would not tolerate. He beat them into a unit that he could direct, control, manipulate.

And care for, truth be told, although it wasn't what he'd

intended so many years ago, standing in front of The Kalakar's desk with intensity written all over his face. His first real battle.

They had no family, most of these men and women. With Alexis, he had given them a home, and they looked to each other. Half of them were survivors of the Southern wars, and they knew firsthand, full well, what the Annagarians were capable of. Those scars he could not mask, could not assuage; they lay against the heart like a brand that even blood could not quench. And blood had been spilled in the attempt.

Who was it? Who was it who planned to go against his express orders into the common to slaughter the Annagarians they could find there, huddled amidst the merchant masses? Fiara was safely behind a locked door, but she was not the only one capable of such an act. Hells, she wasn't even close.

But she also wasn't the type of person who could welcome Kiriel di'Ashaf. Not because Kiriel came from the South; no one in the company believed that. Oh, her color was right for it, and her height; her face had the right lines. But she was born to the blade, and no women were trained in Annagar. No women, that is, with hands as uncallused as Kiriel's and a back so unbent by labor. No, Kiriel was the mystery woman—and Fiara disliked mystery. Because if you kept your mysteries that closely guarded, it meant you didn't trust her—and if you didn't trust her, she didn't owe you anything.

Who? Who would include this misfit among the misfits? Who would try to make her feel at home, and test her mettle so thoroughly, at the same time? Test. Test . . .

"Duarte?"

"Learn," he said, as she interrupted the abrupt turn of his thoughts, "to use ranks, Kiriel. I am Primus Duarte. You are Sentrus Kiriel."

"Yes, Primus Duarte."

She was incapable of the sarcasm that any other such tone would have conveyed. "I'm sorry. I was musing. No, I do not wish you to kill them." He paused. "Kiriel, I wish to ask you a question. I wish you to answer it truthfully."

She nodded, her eyes guarded, always guarded.

"Why did you come to me with this information?"

"Because," she replied, her brow rippling the perfect lines of her skin as she frowned, "I am to serve you."

"Yes?"

"Your orders were clear. You did not wish us to take action for the crimes of the Southerners against this House."

"And you did not agree with my decision."

She frowned again. "No."

"Why? Answer honestly," he told her. As if she would do anything else.

"Because," she said hesitantly, "it makes us look weak."

"Weak?"

"They do this to your people, and you do nothing. They will know that you do nothing, and they will not fear to do it again."

"Understood." Well understood, he'd heard the argument so many times. "Which means you agree that something should be done."

"Yes."

"Then why did you come to me?"

"Because," she said, speaking even more slowly, "I serve you."

"That's all?"

She nodded.

"Look, Kiriel, you must have hoped to gain something."

She stared at him blankly.

"You came here to tell me this. You betray the confidence of people you've given your word to. You must have hoped to gain something. My confidence? My trust?"

"They are your people, Duarte. *Yours.* They betray you." Her eyes grew oddly wide, flickering as if Duarte was watching a struggle to draw a curtain beneath their surface. In the shadows, her face looked leaner, longer; a hint of the feral made him stiffen. "You must do something, or you will appear weak. If you are weak, you will no longer rule. Do you not understand this?

"If you wish it, I will kill them."

"No," he said. "I do not wish it. Leave here, and do not speak of this to anyone else."

She nodded, and saluted, fist across chest, cool eyes shuttered. He had a momentary vision of chilling clarity;

he saw her, this one time, for what she was. And he thought that this slender, naive young woman would coolly and calmly torture a small child to death if he but requested it. Would, and could.

"And while you're out, find Alexis and tell her I want to speak with her. Now."

Cook found her.

He wasn't a cook; in fact, he was probably the worst cook in the unit. He was taller than she was, and much wider, his hair was lighter, although dark enough by Northern standards, and he wore a beard that fringed his round jaw. Sun and wind had worn lines into the sides of his face, near his eyes and mouth; he smiled, and as age caught up with him, you could see the smile linger there pleasantly.

He even smiled at her.

"Mind if I sit?"

She shrugged, moody; he shrugged, good-natured, and sat beside her on the demiwall, huffing slightly as he pulled his legs up and over the ledge. The garden, what there was of it in an estate as small as this, spread out before them in a carefully manicured sea of colors. Here and there, when the sea breeze was brisk, the whole bent and blended as if it were alive.

Which, he thought ruefully, it was. She heard his sigh, and looked up sharply.

"Just thinking," he said as he stared, "that I can even be stupid without speaking."

Sullen, she turned her gaze back to the grounds.

"Kiriel."

She said nothing, but he knew she was listening; she had ears like no one he'd ever met.

"You've been here over two weeks now."

She gave him no help at all. But he didn't mind; he'd seen this many times before.

"We've all done things we're not proud of. We've all seen things we'd forget in a minute if we could. Never works that way. We aren't the easiest to like, but you aren't either."

That caught a smile, but the smile was a grim one, turning on edge into something a bit too chilly to be friendly. Not what he'd hoped for, but it'd do. For now.

"We don't know what you want from us. Most of us wanted the regiment—and the Ospreys. Most of us were chosen by Duarte."

"Primus Duarte."

He chuckled. "We don't stand on ceremony here. But sure, if it makes you easier, Primus Duarte."

"Why do you do that?"

"Do what?"

"Laugh. What have I done to amuse you?"

"Nothing really. I laugh because I'm happy enough, it's a nice day, I have pleasant company, I'm enjoying life."

She frowned. "Do you think I'm stupid?"

"Pardon?"

"Why are you really laughing?"

"I'm really laughing," he said carefully, although he didn't move, "because none of the Ospreys would have corrected me. Duarte's a Primus, but he's a Duarte first; that's what we call him."

"But he told me he wanted to be called Primus Duarte."

"Sure. And I'd like to be called 'Your Majesty.' " He laughed again. "Kiriel, I don't understand you. I've seen every one of the Ospreys get into the drill ring and work you over with every dirty trick in the book. I know them; they haven't held anything back since you broke Corin's ribs.

"Not a single trick slips past. You've got a temper that'd usually get you knocked flat at least a couple of times, but you can't be riled to fight. Auralis hasn't managed you, and he's still up to every other Osprey in the company, Duarte included.

"Outside of the circle, though—outside of the circle it's like you don't know anything. How can you know so much about fighting—about cheating—and so little about everything else?"

"So little?" Her brows were so high they almost disappeared into her hairline. "You think *I* know so little?"

"Well, you aren't exactly the Kings' own Magi."

Her lips grew thin and pale. "I don't understand any of *you*," she said at last, and the words were almost guttural. He saw her face as she turned fully toward him; he froze. "You think that the little games you play in the circle are 'cheating'; you think them clever. They aren't. They aren't even close.

"If I were stupid enough—if I had ever been stupid enough—to fall prey to any of them, I'd be decorating the foot of a throne in the—"

She snarled, swallowing the rest of the words, the rest of the unguarded anger. Her shadow moved almost before she did. Armed, armored, hampered by boots and weighted belt, she was in the flower beds and then across the green, moving so quickly and so surely, Cook had no time to react. No time to call her back, if that's what he wanted to do. No time to be afraid.

Afraid?

Well, yes. He was afraid of her.

And why? Because she knew how to kill? They all did.

Climbing down from the demiwall, he walked away, keeping a brisk pace until the damaged flower bed was well out of sight. The Ospreys were always at the top of the gardener's trouble list, and he didn't want to compound their reputation by actually being at the scene of a crime.

But as he walked, he gave himself a strong mental shake. She was cold and distant and peculiar, but she was an Osprey—and that meant, in the end, that she needed a place to belong. At least, it did to Cook.

Fear was no open handshake, no accepting welcome.

Of course, only a stupid man would set aside his cautious behavior, his fear of her—especially after he'd sat so close to death beneath the open, afternoon sky.

Cook shook his head ruefully. He could be stupid without ever opening his mouth.

Solran Marten, the bardmaster of Senniel College, pulled a dark strand of hair from her eyes and twisted it between forefinger and thumb. At her back, the sun illuminated the colored glass which depicted The Ten, in two rows of five, as they made their way collectively to Avantari—the Palace of Kings—after the long battle with the reigning barons had finally come to its proper close. The Artisan who had crafted this towering window had captured perfectly the dignity that these Ten, in their righteous joy, displayed. They were a force, standing together, to be reckoned with; a force that the barons, with their petty bickering and their politics of assassination, could never have broken.

It was a damned good thing, Solran thought, that the Artisan had long passed into history. He would have been heartbroken otherwise.

"They aren't as bad as they have been," her companion said, modulating his voice so that it carried only to her ears.

Solran Marten was one of the few chosen bardmasters who was not bard-born; she could not reply in kind to the man who stood across the divide on the other side of the open gallery. She grimaced, the expression exaggerated enough to carry her skepticism. Lifted her hands, signing with blinding speed.

He smiled. "Yes," he said softly. "It is harder without the presence of the Kings. But the Kings have chosen not to interfere."

Solran, as head of Senniel College, knew full well why; she suspected that Kallandras did as well, but wisely did not choose to speak of it. She nodded grimly and stared down into the chamber.

Four hours had passed. Four hours, with the day getting hotter and more uncomfortable all around them.

The Terafin and The Kalakar began the morning with a motion that had shocked every other member of the Council: Do not retaliate.

Princess Mirialyn ACormaris immediately joined them— she sat in on the Council meeting with the status of adviser. She had a voice—and used it—but no vote. The Fennesar, of all The Ten the most subdued in appearance, quietly added her voice to the motion, to carry it to the table.

The Kalakar spoke with a voice most unlike her: strained, even subdued. But there was no tremor in the words, and no doubt. She held her head up with a battered pride as she finished the motion.

Where the Kalakar voted, The Berriliya could not. This was a truth almost universally acknowledged by the denizens of *Averalaan Aramarelas* to be more a rule of nature than an act of political will. Solran did not understand—and felt certain that she never would—how these two could form two sides of the triangle that had won the Southern wars for the Empire. She considered it nothing short of miraculous that they hadn't turned the armies under their command upon each other.

She was certain that, had they had them now, they would have. And it was a pity. The Berriliya was the only man on the Council who was The Kalakar's match, in more ways than one.

The Darias rose next. She was much like a younger version of The Terafin; elegant, willowy, very much a classically beautiful woman. It came as a surprise to Solran—and, judging by his momentary frown, to Kallandras—when The Darias spoke against the Annagarians in quiet but certain terms.

The Morriset declined to vote, watching the proceedings with the same quiet that marked most of his dealings. He was not a swordsman, not a soldier, and not an athlete; he had rounded with the years, developing a quiet, paternal demeanor—a demeanor which was not greatly changed by the state of emergency. She was grateful for it.

The Tamalyn also declined, although Solran thought it was more because The Tamalyn had no real idea of the significance of the events that were passing around him, than any uncertainty about the right course of action. He was a bookish man, and if not for his House Council—a bevy of mothering men and women—would no doubt have lost his rulership, or his family prestige, to the study of books and odd bits of fact and lore.

But he had a way about him that she loved. Solran, bardmaster, war-witness and sentence-speaker, hovered around him when she could, seeking to protect him—just as his council did—from the worst of the ravages of politics. Why, she couldn't say, for she was not his mother, and he was, in any event, no child, but there was something about him, curly-haired and completely honest, that held fast to the essence of childhood long after the fact of it had fled.

She shook herself ruefully. The Korisamis, long the voice of quiet and persuasive reason, stood quietly. He was unprepossessing in size or statue, but when he spoke, he was listened to. It was with regret, he said, that he found it necessary to support the motion in favor of execution of the Annagarian hostages. He did not advocate a public execution, or anything as barbarous as the Southerners had inflicted upon their own—but death, yes. Solran had long suspected that he had some bardic talent, hidden away by lack of training and years of disuse, but the bard-born among her master bards denied it, and she chose—usually—to trust their opinions, for they recognized their own. Yet his was the very voice of reason in tone and texture. Had she not counted some of the Annagarian nobles among her friends, she might have been swayed.

The Wayelyn spoke last, as he was from the least of The Ten Houses. And perhaps because his was least, the hostage the House had offered as a means of binding the Southern Dominion had been closer, personally, to The Wayelyn than any other hostage had been to their leader.

She was pained, but not surprised, to hear him call for the Annagarians' death, eye for eye. He was the only one there close to tears.

And there it was. Mirialyn with no voice made it three against five, with two abstentions. Four hours. Solran raised her ivory face, met Kallandras' eyes squarely, and exhaled. Four hours to decide the fate of over twenty people.

The Terafin rose, her face pale, her hands as steady as the scepter of office in King Cormalyn's hands. "By the will of the Council," she said, each word sharp and clear. "The message will be sent to the Dominion of Annagar." She turned to the Princess who waited, her face a white cloud. "Tell the Kings Cormalyn and Reymalyn of the decision of the Council."

"And when would you have this act carried out?"

"It would be fitting," The Berriliya said, rising, "if the hostages could be executed upon the eighth of Lattan."

Solran closed her eyes. Of course. The Festival of the Sun. He would know what it would mean to the Annagarians; it was the height of the Lord's rule, the day in which the warriors reigned. A slap—worse—in their faces. It did not surprise her at all.

When she opened her eyes to gaze across at her distant companion, she saw that the gallery was empty. Kallandras had already gone. And it was time, now, that she leave as well; the meeting was over.

Or was it?

The doors to the hall opened; the sun from the ceiling and the magnificent window shone down as if it had only been waiting for his presence. His hair was shining, ringlets of gold, for all that the years had paled them, and he walked with the sure confidence of a man in his youth. He wore workaday clothing, linen and cotton in cream white and watery blue, and his boots were the standard issue of bardic colleges throughout the Empire. Only Kallandras would have walked, so attired, into a gathering of the ten most powerful people in the realm next to the Crowns. Across his hip, Salla lay unstrummed; she was his sword, his armor, his badge.

"This is a private meeting," The Berriliya said coolly. He recognized the master bard; they all did.

"Indeed. And I would not have interrupted, Berriliya, but I have word from the hostages that will not wait."

"They are not in a position to demand that word—any word—be carried to this Council."

"They are not in a position to demand anything," was the quiet reply. "And they know it. Or at least, most of them do."

"What is this?" The Korisamis rose also. He was dwarfed by the Berriliya, but where The Berriliya was the obvious danger, The Korisamis demanded his due in more subtle fashion. "Speak plainly, Master Kallandras of Senniel. We have been here four hours, and will not look kindly upon a longer stay."

"Understood, Korisamis," the bard said, and he bowed quite low. "I will be brief.

"The Tyr'agar Markaso di'Leonne—and his clan— were assassinated almost three weeks ago."

"We're aware of this."

"No man has taken up the Sun Sword; no man has claimed the Tor and its waters. We have been told that there will be no Tyr'agar until the eighth day of Lattan. But in the eyes of the Lord of the Sun, there is a Tyr'agar—the blood-anointed ruler of the Dominion of Annagar. He has sent me to you to speak on his behalf, for he claims the right of rulership."

Mirialyn turned sharply to stare at Kallandras, but Kallandras was calm, even quiet.

"As the Tyr'agar was not responsible in any way for the deaths of the Imperial hostages, he asks that you consider the act a criminal act, and not a political one—and in defense of this argument, points out the provisions for

accidental death, death by force of nature, and death by
criminal element among the hostages of either signatory
power."

"*Accidental* death?" It was The Wayelyn.

Tread carefully, Kallandras, Solran thought.

"Your pardon, Wayelyn," the master bard said, bowing
very low. "I did not mean to imply that these deaths were
anything other than an act of brutality." His expression
was somber, his voice neutral. No bard practiced the use
of his talent in a situation of this nature.

"That's it, then." The Kalakar rose, a grim smile hardening her features. She turned to the Princess. "ACormaris," she said, as much respect as she ever showed
adorning the word, "This is not a matter for the Council of
the Ten. It is a request from the head of one state to the
heads of another."

"I beg to differ," The Berriliya said, to no one's surprise.

"You must forgive me for speaking out of turn,
Berriliya, but I must ask, how so?"

The Berriliya favored Kallandras with a grim glare.
"The boy's no Tyr."

"I must, again, disagree. The rule of the Lord's grant of
Dominion is quite clear, and if you are interested, I will
quote at length."

"I'm not interested in the babblings of moronic religious fanatics."

"But I, Berriliya, find it of some interest indeed." The
Korisamis nodded politely, but not distantly, to the master
bard. "And if it will not discomfort the other members of
this Council, I would hear what you have to say." He
glanced around the too quiet table, looking for resistance
and finding its lack in all but two faces. Neither man—
Berriliya or Wayelyn—spoke.

"Very well," Kallandras said, and he shifted Salla's
position slightly, playing the strings in a long, downward
sweep as if she were a foreign instrument and not his
beloved lute.

"We can do without the accompaniment, bard. This is
not a dramatic event."

"As you will, Berriliya." But although the strings were
still, the lute remained as he had placed it. "In the
Southern Dominion, if you are born to a clan, it owns you
unless you rule it. A slight to the clan's honor is a call to

battle that ends with the destruction of one clan or the other. When the Lord of the Sun offered the Dominion of the plains to his people, he placed them above the land by giving them the use of his most treasured beast: the horse."

"Kallandras—you try our patience."

"And you, Berriliya," The Kalakar snapped, "try mine no less."

"The men of the clans understood this gift, and they accepted it, and they rode, under the banner of the Lord, to His glory, freeing the lands from those who did not believe, and would not believe, in the light of the Sun.

"There came a time when the lands were cleansed, and the clans gathered together for the first time, and their great skills turned inward—for they were warriors, with no war. Each of the clansmen felt that it was his place to rule the others, and each boasted of his skill in battle, of his victories, of his allegiance to the ways of the Lord.

"But there was one who swayed the others, for he promised the Lord dominion over the night itself." Kallandras' fingers had found the strings once again, and played them now, gently and quietly. "The Radann spoke against this, for they understood that there is balance between light and dark, life and death—that the Lady's face is necessary, if less desirable. They were driven underground or put to death publicly.

"For decades the clan that cannot be named ruled, but they ruled falsely, bringing not light into the darkness as they had promised their people, but darkness into the light. And the Lord of the Sun saw, understood, and was not pleased. The clansmen vied now for the approbation of the Lord of the Night, thinking him fair, thinking him Bright.

"But one man followed the old ways, and such was his strength that he could not be put down by mere clansmen. The Lord of the Sun came to him in a vision, and gave into his keeping the Sun Sword. 'Take this, you who of all my people have remained true. When you wield it, those who have the spark of my fire within them will come to your call, and you will lead them to victory against the darkness.'

"Ser Valens di'Leonne lifted the sword, and it seared the darkness with its fire. 'My Lord,' he said, 'I have fought in your name since I could wield blade. I will honor you, and in your name, I will take the Dominion. But after, will we not again stand upon the same plateau?'

"And the Lord said, 'No. The clan Leonne has always proved true. The Sun Sword will be the scepter of your office. No man but the heir to Leonne will dare to lift this sword while the blood runs true. Leonne is my choice, and my choice will stand until no member of Leonne who is worthy does. Let the Sun Sword be the test and the proof that you require; let any man who dares to question my will take up the sword that will lead you to victory.'

"It passed as the Lord decreed. And when Valens di'Leonne at last found peace in the Lady's dominion, three men sought the Tor. The first of these was not of the clan Leonne. He dared to lift the sword under the Lord's sight, and he burned; his screams were the wind in the valleys, the howl upon the mountain's peak. The second man, of the clan Leonne, held the sword; it did not burn him. But the third man—the kai—lifted the Sun Sword to a blaze of perfect light. No man, no true man, could see this and not understand the Lord's will."

The music stopped abruptly, although none there could say for certain when he had started to play. "I thank you for your indulgence. There remains one member of the clan Leonne, who by blood-right and bloodline takes the title Tyr'agar and challenges any pretender to take the ancient test."

"He is no ruler," The Berriliya said, but his voice was quieter. "He is no ruler unless the test is taken."

"By Annagarian law of succession, he *is* the Tyr'agar."

"It is out of our hands," The Kalakar said again, but her expression was an odd one as she turned to face the Berriliya. "Or are you afraid? Has the Hawk lost his flight feathers?"

"No more," The Berriliya said, the same odd light in his eyes, "than the Kestrel has hers. Very well. Berriliya will abide by the decision of the Crowns."

The Korisamis was very pale. "And I pray that the Crowns tender the wise answer."

"And that answer?" Mirialyn ACormaris asked softly.

"Wisdom is not always justice, as well you know, ACormaris. I have seen war. I have seen its effects; they surround us now, and if we embark on no further conflict, we will feel the ramifications of the last Southern war for decades yet. You know, as I, how many innocents perished, and how horribly, at the hands of the Southerners. You know better than I—than any of us save The Berriliya and The Kalakar—how many of their innocents perished at the hands of our soldiers." He lifted a hand, calling for silence as The Kalakar and The Berriliya both made to speak. "Will you plunge us into this chaos again for the sake of one life? For the sake of twenty?"

She lifted her chin; her hair gleamed as if it were bronze helm, and not braid. "Yes," she said softly, "if we had no other choice, I would. Remember: Valedan di'Leonne has thrice been under threat of death—and the assassins sent were no mortal creatures." She walked to the doors, turned, and bowed. "I will carry this new word to the Crowns."

Jewel Markess ATerafin had only twice been called to the Hall of The Ten in her fifteen years of service to The Terafin. And at neither time was it for a full Council meeting, in which the Kings, the Queens, the Lord of the Compact, the bardmaster of Senniel, the representative of the Council of the Magi, and the Holy Triumvirate were also to be present. She remembered, quite clearly, the last time that she had seen most of these people assembled in one place, and she had no desire to ever be in such a position again.

Avandar had fussed—and he was not a man so inclined—to insure that her appearance at least was excruciatingly correct. That she allowed him to do so spoke volumes to anyone who knew her; she was nervous.

The Terafin sat beside her in the horse-drawn carriage, gazing out at the waters that surrounded the isle. The road to *Averalaan Aramarelas* was busy, and the carriage traffic quite slow, given the early hour of the day. Both women were tired, but wore the lack of sleep as artfully as they wore the clothing that had been chosen for them by men. To either side of the carriage were three of The Terafin's Chosen; an escort of six. The Terafin was allowed six guards and two advisers when a full meeting of the Kings' Council was called. Gabriel ATerafin was the second of the two advisers that she was allowed. The circles under his eyes were dark, long, and far too obvious. Although he normally carried himself like the ATerafin that he was, his hair had grayed in the last few days, and his face had taken on the gauntness of age. Jewel knew that he wanted the Kings to refuse the young boy's transparent attempt to save his own life, although she didn't know why. All of the Chosen did.

No one spoke the words aloud after The Terafin made her will known.

"Why take me?" Jewel had asked.

"Because," The Terafin replied, "I want you to look at Valedan di'Leonne. I want you to listen to him. I want you watch as carefully as a seer has ever watched anything in her life."

"You know that I can't just—"

"I know that answers come to you at the strangest times, without rhyme or reason. If you have an answer there. I want to know it." Her face was pale. "You mentioned war, Jewel. And I think I feel its rumble."

Duarte AKalakar rode in the procession of wagons, armed and armored although no sane man would have been either in sun as scathing as this. At his back rode Auralis, and behind Auralis, Alexis. She was in a foul mood, as was he; it was just as well that something—even someone as annoying as Auralis could be—separated them. He wasn't certain why The Kalakar had chosen Ospreys—any of them—as part of her escort; the Ospreys, sadly, were not noted for their ability to drill and present well.

What made things worse was that the mysterious Kiriel was in the carriage with The Kalakar and Verrus Korama. Verrus Vernon had been relegated to horseback. And he knew well why. . . .

"Have you ridden before?" The Kalakar had asked.

"Yes."

"Good. You will ride on the left of the carriage with Cook and Sanderson."

She'd opened her mouth to speak, and then closed it. He should have known then. But no. Preoccupied with his ongoing argument with Alexis, he ordered a horse for her. It was a big, dress warhorse—something that looked like it could carry an armored man into battle without working up a sweat.

Admit it, he thought sourly. *You chose Nightwind because the damned horse looks like it should have fangs. You knew she was uncomfortable. You wanted to drive it home. Teos, she makes you act like an overweening Sentrus.*

It wasn't Kiriel who showed fear first.

And the fear that Nightwind showed the moment she touched his flank wasn't the hesitance or even the friskiness that horses are wont to show. It was primal, and worse, it was savage. Hooves with that much weight behind them weren't meant to strike ground that hard, that fast.

Neither were slender, underweight girls in too much armor.

What was the thing that he remembered most clearly from the entire incident? She didn't kill the horse.

Just that: She hadn't killed the horse.

"Kiriel," The Kalakar said, "did you know that this would happen?"

The girl was silent, although for the first time ever, Duarte saw her sweat. What was disturbing was that the sweat was probably not from the effort of escaping the hooves, head and teeth of the stallion—she'd had longer workouts, and harder ones, in the circle. No, he felt, although he did not say it because more than just Ospreys were present, that it was due to the effort of staying her hand.

"Kiriel," The Kalakar said, "did you know that this would happen?"

The girl shook her head, sheathing her sword as she turned to face the Commander.

"Did you suspect it?"

"Yes."

"Next time that you suspect something of this nature might occur, tell us. That's an order."

"Yes, Kalakar."

"Vernon?"

"Yes, Kalakar."

Vernon rode in Kiriel's stead. Kiriel sat in his.

"Why do you want me to go to this gathering of the court?"

Korama raised a brow and glanced at the profile of the

Commander. She smiled grimly. "I was not responsible for choosing you, Kiriel. I gave Duarte the orders: Six Ospreys, no more, no less."

Kiriel nodded quietly. "But you knew that Duarte and Alexis have been arguing about the Annagarians. You knew also that the argument occurred after my visit to him."

She raised a brow, but did not reply.

"You know that he doesn't trust me."

"The Ospreys hang together."

"In more ways that one," Verrus Korama added, grimacing.

"Kiriel, if he didn't trust you, why would he choose to bring you?"

"Because he fears to have me out of his sight during this crisis." She glanced out of the window, her eyes flickering over the crowds that lined the streets as if it were Ascension. "The Ospreys are known for their lack of the diplomacy so many of you seem to value. They aren't political. They aren't well-dressed compared to the rest of the House Guards. But you asked for the Ospreys.

"Duarte feels that this is very, very important. You know him well. You know that he would choose to come himself. And if he came himself, he would choose the people he least trusts to accompany him."

"And not those that he most trusts?"

"No. Because he wants to see for himself that we do not go against his orders, and he is afraid that if we do, we will kill each other."

"I think," Korama said coolly, "that she has you there, Commander." He turned to face the young woman, his expression so neutral it felt inhuman.

"Sentrus Kiriel," The Kalakar said, "You are very observant for someone who seems to understand so little of our ways."

"I understand politics."

"Very well." She looked at Kiriel as if seeing her for the first time, and then smiled, as if what she saw there had never really been in question. "You are correct in all of your assumptions. But I am your commander. I want you present for my own reasons."

Kiriel nodded.

* * *

The Kalakar looked out the window of the carriage, watching the streets as those idle—and those dragged from their tasks by the idle—stopped to gawk at the growing procession. It was not, yet, the time for the Crowns' Challenge, so the streets, clear of the continuous run of farmers' wagons and portable stalls that the Challenge brought should have been no hardship to travel.

But there, the Ospreys' horses were already becoming skittish, hemmed in on all sides by this press of people; Vernon himself was having difficulty controlling Nightwind. She frowned. She would have words with Duarte about his choice of horse, but she would have them later.

Ah, there. She was mistaken. A flag was set up on the roadside; she recognized it as a banner of the Northern Watch. A tall, sun-bronzed giant of a man carried its pole with a good deal of pride, lifting it aloft that the horsemen might see it that much more closely. Obviously the Northern Watch had their champion for the Crowns' Challenge. She wondered who the free towns would send, and whether, this year, they politicked together or, as in some, against each other; wondered who the Annagarians might send—for although the Challenge overlapped with the Festival of the Sun, the Lord of the Sun granted his blessing to those who sought glory in warriors' endeavors in the Lord's name.

That brought her back to the problem at hand.

She wanted Kiriel present—against the advice of both Korama and Vernon—at the full Council of the Crowns because Kiriel di'Ashaf had arrived in the wake of Evayne a'Nolan, and been left to drift. Today, The Kalakar thought there might be an answer or two to her mystery. A woman—if that's what she was—like Evayne didn't do things by coincidence. Kiriel had something to do with the South. And The Kalakar wanted, against the rules she set for those who took her service, to know what it was.

Serra Alina did not fuss, although she was responsible in all ways for Ser Valedan's dress. He had no wife, and no concubines, and although he was now of an age to walk the road of the clansmen, there was no one to see him through the rituals now that his father had passed. He was a child Tyr, and those were exceedingly rare, for they did not tend to survive the rigors of their regency. Or so it was said by historians.

She prayed, silently of course, because the night was so far removed from the morning sky, that the old stories were wrong.

"Stand back, Ser Valedan. Let me look at you."

He did as she told him because there were no men to witness it. Or so she hoped. He was too Northern for the South, and if he was to save their lives, that would have to change. The frown that crossed her lips was more felt than seen, and it lingered in her memory and the memory of her image in the long looking glass. He had not walked the sword's road, and he had no serafs of his own because slavery was strictly forbidden within the Empire. But more than that, he was not comfortable with the concept of owning people; it made him uneasy. *An accident of birth,* she'd once heard him say.

"The sword hangs too low." It was Ser Kyro's sword. Kallandras had quietly come into the courtyard the evening just past, carrying it, although the weapons and armor of the hostages had been confiscated by the Imperials when word of the acts in the Tor Leonne had reached their ears. "Come here."

He came, and she tightened the belt a notch, and then a notch again. He was taller than Ser Kyro by an inch or two, but not nearly as wide around. And, if she were honest, not nearly so hawkish, so wolfish. But he was very handsome, and if judged by looks alone, the picture of an Annagarian kai in exile.

Exile. The service of a woman meant very little in the Dominion, unless you were the right woman. Serra Alina had never been so graced. The Empire was the home of her spirit, but there were shadows that the heart, no matter how long in the bright sun, did not forget.

The bells chimed, and she stepped back, turning and bowing in a single, polite motion as the representative of clan Callesta stepped into the room.

"Are you ready, Tyr'agar?" Ser Fillipo bowed low, and then rose, searching every inch of the young man standing before him as if his life depended on it. Because, of course, it did. And not his life alone, but the lives of his wife, his children. That could make a man desperate.

A different man.

"No."

"Good." Ser Fillipo nodded a dark head. "Bluster and bravado will avail us nothing; in this Northern court, they want truth and honesty, as if either could be given simply and easily, with no ties, no hint of deception. Will you speak to the Kings?"

"I have no other choice."

"Death."

The young man stared at the older man, and then nodded grimly. "Do I look the part?"

"You look the part of the clansman to perfection. It's a pity that there will be no one who can truly appreciate what this means in attendance." He knelt then, knelt low. The hostages were to remain behind; not even a cerdan was to accompany him. "Ah, here comes the Serra Marlena." His face was smooth and his tone betrayed nothing, but Valedan thought that Ser Fillipo would rather face the Crowns himself than spend another moment with his mother.

She proved herself well capable of taking Serra Alina's none-too-gentle advice, however; she greeted her son with the respect that she would have once shown his father—in fact, with the same respect, and the same fear, that she had given his father when his father rode to join the clansmen in their last charge along the Averdan borders so very long ago.

"Mother," he started to say, but Serra Alina's lips compressed into a tight line. "Serra Marlena."

"Valedan," she replied, as was her right. "I wish you strength."

He held out a hand, and she took it; her own was shaking. But she did not weep. "When will they come for you?"

"I don't know. Today, sometime." He took a deep breath and began to speak as formally as he could; the situation merited it. "Kallandras said that there will be a meeting of the important members of the Kings' Council, and not just The Ten. They will speak. They will most probably argue. They will summon me, and I will speak, and then they will have me escorted out."

"And then?"

"We will wait." He smiled gently. "If you fear for my

safety, don't. I'll be under heavier guard today than I've been in my entire life. Nothing's going to get through the Kings' Swords."

Tyr Ramiro kai di'Callesta was tired and dust-stained and back-weary with hard riding. His horses were fine and endured much, but they had been driven to the edge of their limits by a man who had always known how far to push—just. His Tyran said nothing; they were men, and younger men at that for the most part, and they served him in silence when silence was called for. He was proud of his choice, and his wife's; these were the finest Callestans that any generation had produced. Any.

And they were his half brothers, all save one.

He had watched them grow in the harem's confine. He had listened to them shriek and fight and play, too old to join them, too young to escape. In some of the Terreans, it was not uncommon practice to kill the half brothers that were born to the deceased head of the clan when one took the mantle. Half brothers, even illegitimate as they were, still had the blood, and in the case of treachery and treacherous action, they could take the clan if they were powerful enough to hold it.

Ser Karro looked up, as if discerning his brother's thoughts. Ramiro shook his head at this oldest of his Tyran, and Ser Karro returned to their brief repast. Knowledge between men shortened the use of speech.

"You don't eat," General Baredan di'Navarre said. The man moved like a cat stalking careless birds.

"Not now, no. Have you finished?"

Baredan smiled grimly. "Hard to eat, this close to the capital. You said the Northerners were friendly."

Ramiro frowned. "They were."

But the reception received on the open road these past four days had been close to murderous; he was certain that, had he been traveling alone, or with only Baredan at his side, they would both be dead in a ditch or a farmer's field. The Northerners did not believe in posting their kills.

"You understand what they're saying?"

"Well enough, General." Better, in fact, than Baredan did. "Something has happened. Some skirmish at the Mancorvan border, perhaps. People were killed."

"Perhaps," Baredan agreed. "But we had no plans for such an attack, and word takes longer to travel than that."

"Tyr Ramiro!"

Both men turned on heel, responding to the call as if they were the Lord's command on the open field of war. "Mikko?" Ramiro said, command in the name.

"A person on the road."

"A single person?"

"Yes, Tyr."

"Let him pass."

Silence. Then, cautiously, "He does not seem interested in passing us, Tyr."

"Mikko, speak plainly. I assure you, Baredan di'Navarre will not approach Serra Amara the Gentle with word of your breach of correct etiquette."

The Tyran had the grace to blush. Of the oathguards, he was youngest, and still wore his honor like a too-bright, too-shiny medal. "The person is standing in the middle of the road ten yards from our camp, watching us."

Baredan and Ramiro exchanged a single glance, and then moved forward, passing the young oathguard as if his sword, his armor and his station afforded no better protection than the weapons which they drew as one.

They found the stranger on the road, just as Mikko said, and when Ramiro saw this gray-robed, solitary figure, he forgave Mikko much. For the hood of the robes hung low under the open sky. Only those with the wasting disease wore such a guise in Annagar, where they survived the purifying fires.

He started to speak, but the stranger raised a hand, and the hand was strong and slender—not the hand of the fallen. "Hold your weapon, Tyr Ramiro kai di'Callesta." A woman. She spoke in Torra, the language of Annagar, although it was oddly accented.

"I am not in the habit of taking orders from anyone save the Tyr'agar," he replied, although he put his sword up.

"Meaning," she said, her tone wry, "that you are not in the habit of taking orders from a woman. Well spoken, especially for a Tyr so far from his Terrean in these troubled times." She lifted both her hands then, and slowly lowered her hood. Her hair was the color of the Lady's blackest night, and her eyes the color of the pale flowers that grew above the Tor Leonne's waters. He thought her very beautiful, but very cold, like a perfect death. "I carry a message."

"From whom, and to whom?"

"To you, and your traveling companion, General Baredan di'Navarre."

"Speak it, then," he said, shaking his head ever so slightly at the man who stood to his right.

"You are a half-day's ride from the capital of the Empire."

"We are aware of that."

"If you continue at your present speed, you will make it by evening."

"Indeed."

"And you will arrive too late." She looked beyond his shoulders, at the horses in the farmer's run. "There is a messenger run in the town five miles North on the road. They will not let you take the horses without a significant bribe. Pay the bribe—do not attempt to kill the keeper—and take fresh horses."

"And our own?"

She shook her head softly. "I know what they mean to you," she said softly, "and if you will, you may risk one of your own as a guard, although I would not, if I were you."

Her face grew pale, as if the sun were harsher against it. "The hostages in the Tor Leonne—the Essalieyanese Imperial hostages—were killed publicly and, by Essalieyanese standards, brutally, by the order of the powers that now rule the Tor. If you not not arrive in *Averalaan Aramarelas* before sunset tonight, you had best not arrive at all."

CHAPTER NINETEEN

The Great Hall was so crowded that The Terafin was surprised to find it cool and pleasant within until she noticed,
in the farthest reach of the upper gallery, three men
standing in the triangular form that she saw so seldom
among the Magi. It meant that they were cooperating at
some venture; some movement of air, of ice, of wind.

If this meeting were to last as long as the Council of
The Ten—and there was every indication that it would be
longer—the activity of these mages would be boon and
blessing. No doubt, she thought wryly, it would also be
expensive.

The ceremonial chairs—the ten and the six—had been
placed along the northern side of the crowded gallery,
with lesser chairs in which to position the advisers that
each of The Ten brought, and with standing room for their
personal guards. The ten and the six had been elevated,
and several of the ten were already occupied. The Princes,
and their escort, Astari all, were in the lowest of the six
thrones, an echo of their fathers in their youth. At fifteen
and sixteen, Prince Reymar and Prince Cormar were
handsome and grave; they had no youthful peccadilloes,
no youthful, mispent passions, no secrets by which they
could be embarrassed at strategic points in their later rule.
The god-born never did, at least, not those born to Reymaris and Cormaris. She smiled as she saw the glower
that had etched itself in Prince Reymar's face; his forehead was creased, and his brows drawn together in a
single red line that matched the flush of his cheeks. Prince
Cormar was more subdued in his raging. An echo, she
thought, of the conflict between the Kings.

The Kings and the Queens would arrive last; a runner—
no, two—sat beside their thrones, guarding their boredom

with carefully schooled expressions as they kept track of who had arrived, and who had not.

Two runners.

Which meant, of course, that either the Kings and Queens were not together, or more likely, the Kings themselves were divided upon the issue that was to be decided by this gathering. Not for the first time, she wondered which way it would fall. She disliked not knowing, for she was in the habit of being able to draw upon her information sources to avoid the appearance of ignorance. The Terafin was not a woman who enjoyed surprises.

Gabriel offered her an arm and she smiled at him, accepting his grace. The Terafin throne—and that was, in truth, what it was—was high, and not perhaps as easily gained as it had been a decade ago. He took the seat to her right, as was his duty; Jewel took the seat to her left. She looked down upon their heads, wondering briefly what the allure of a tall chair was. Wondering, and to her chagrin, knowing at the same time. Torvan and Alayra took positions directly behind them, although Alayra had protested her position in the honor guard. She was a weapons master now; a woman with a sharp eye and a sharper tongue—but she felt her skills too slow and too blunted by age to make her a worthy guard.

Which is why, The Terafin had said dryly, *it's called an* honor *guard. Now go to the quartermaster and requisition yourself a dress uniform if you don't fit the one you used to wear. I will not take no for an answer.*

Captain Arrendas stood beside Torvan ATerafin. These three were a part of her Chosen, and they had proved, over this last decade, that her choice was more than sound.

Enough musing. The Berriliya had entered the hall moments after The Terafin party had; he assumed his seat with a minimum of fuss and pomp. She noted that Severn ABerriliya and Garth ABerriliya were his chosen advisers. No risks there; both of these men, Severn ten years the Berriliya's junior and Garth almost twenty, were military born and bred.

The Tamalyn looked as if he'd been in the hall from the moment it was opened, which was good, because he had a tendency to be late for most Council meetings—in fact, for any of his meetings—and the Crowns did not look well upon such flagrant disregard among The Ten. Not, of course, that any of the rest of The Ten thought it flagrant disregard. Absentmindedness, yes.

But such a trait in a man who held power . . .

The Kalakar arrived, Vernon AKalakar and Korama AKalakar at her side. Where most of The Ten chose ceremonial garb, or at the very least a somber, courtly gown which would serve the throne well, The Kalakar wore a variant on a dress military uniform. She also carried a sword, and The Terafin knew it was not merely for display.

Ellora had only one other adviser—Terlin AKalakar—but it came as no surprise to The Terafin that Terlin had not been chosen as part of this group; Terlin was both young and as devoted to the Mother as she was to The Kalakar—an uneasy alliance, that. Such split loyalties were usually not tolerated within Kalakar.

Or, if she were honest, in any House.

"Terafin."

She turned, and Gabriel whispered quietly. The Exalted had arrived.

"Soon," she told him softly, lowering her head deferentially as the three made their way to the southern chairs which were theirs by right. The golden eyes of the godborn daughter of the Mother were fragments of sunlight seen through thin glass; warm, but not hot, and very lovely. They swept the gathering, and The Terafin knew, from past experience, that each and every person in the room who could see her face felt, for a moment, that she met and held their gaze with an equal measure of affection and sternness.

Likewise with the other Exalted: the son of Reymaris and the son of Cormaris, the Lords of Justice and Wisdom. They were like the Kings, almost brothers to them—which was as it should be, for they shared a parent. They appeared serene, even calm, as they took their seats and adorned themselves with the emblems of their office. But they, unlike the Kings, had the luxury of keeping their own counsel and steering their own course.

The bardmaster of Senniel College came next, and she came alone, which was unusual. The Terafin thought that Sioban would have loved this pomp and ceremony—but her successor, Solran, did not. Still, she knew how to convey the appearance of such an appreciation; she wore Senniel's colors in a sash that crossed shoulder to waist, over an elegant white shift. Her arms were empty; the harp for which she was famed had been left, as if it were a weapon or a child, at the College.

She took her place with the aid of the elderly Anduvin ANorwen, at sixty-seven years of age one of the most powerful men in the Empire. He was the Master who, in the absence of an Artisan, ruled the maker's guild; he did so with guile, cunning, and a geniune passion. His gift was metalwork in all its forms. The years had been as kind to him as one might expect of a man who was, in his own words, fond of his food and his drink.

And there, Meralonne APhaniel. Platinum-haired, slender mage, the man who by his own choice represented the often fractious Magi. Seventeen years had done very little to change him, although the signs were there in his step and the line of his shoulders.

Jewel straightened her back and sat up very correctly in her chair; The Terafin smiled softly and did the same a moment or two before the doors rolled open for the final time that day. Seeing The Terafin's expression, Jewel smiled in return.

"I didn't *see* it," she said softly, "I was paying attention to the runners."

The Kings, and their Queens, entered the great hall. The sands began to run in earnest.

Valedan expected the Kings' Swords to come for him, and he was not disappointed. As they entered the enclosure, moving in a grim silence, made shiny by unsheathed swords and gleaming helms, he bowed to the Serra Marlena, and then in turn to the Serra Alina. But he did not linger long; he feared his mother would embarrass both herself and him by crying or weeping in front of the Imperial guards.

Guards who, until these last few days, he had never feared or thought of as truly foreign. As he stepped out into the long passage that led to the footpath, he lifted his chin, knowing who he had to be, and feeling it settle upon him like a thin, weak silk.

The Kings' Swords closed ranks around him; he could feel their hostility, and while it frightened him, he knew that in their position, he would feel no less angry. He wished for finer robes, for the crown, for the very Sun Sword; they would bolster him on his long walk, where no cerdan, and no other compatriot, would be allowed to.

But he had none of these things, and when you had nothing, you did without as gracefully, gravely, and strongly as you did if you had them. Who had said that? Not his mother. He thought a moment as his steps reverberated in the silence of stone and breath and anger. Serra Tonia. Not the Tyr's wife, but the woman who coordinated the concubinage in which his mother lived, the second harem. He remembered her; her hair was pale white, gossamer and thin like a spider's web. Her skin was lined by sun and wind—the wind, his mother told him, had been so unkind to her—and her eyes were like the blue of the cloudless sky, when the Lord's face was clearest, but not harsh. She was not the Tyr'agar's concubine, but rather the concubine of his father, yet the Tyr'agar respected her, and his whim granted her power, where her husband's passing granted nothing at all.

They said, in whispers, at moon's height, that it was she who had raised and coddled Markaso di'Leonne as a small boy. Valedan somehow doubted it; he could not imagine the grim, cold man his father was as anything but Tyr.

What is a Tyr'agar? He'd asked it once, and only once, perched upon the august throne of Serra Tonia's lap.

You must never ask that question, Valedan. You must never be ignorant of so important a fact. He had nodded; he could feel the reluctant motion in the tension of his neck, as if movement had echoes. *But how can you not be ignorant if you do not ask the question?* She relented, as she often did, when there were no witnesses. *The Tyr'agar is the man chosen by the Lord of the Sun. He must be as harsh as the desert sun, for his enemies will be harsher still; he must know when to let the rains come, or the valleys will die; he must grant the Lady passage, although he is the Lord's man, when it is wise and right to do so, for there is no day without night.*

He said nothing, and she must have known what it meant, for he felt the whiffle of a sigh across the top of his head before she rested her fragile chin there a moment. *The Tyr'agar is the clansman most beloved of God.*

That he understood.

Or he thought he had.

He stumbled, because he could almost smell the sweet and delicate perfume that Serra Tonia wore that day, and every day, even though time and wind had long since carried it away. She had hugged him. Not even his mother had made him feel so safe.

And she was dead. Killed by treacherous hands just as surely as he and his compatriots would be if he failed.

If the Tyr'agar was the clansman most beloved of God, then Valedan was no Tyr. He felt small, beneath the Lord's notice, as the sound of his steps grew heavier and heavier, as if he were walking, not to an audience of Kings, but to a harsher and older Northern judgment—the embrace of the turbulent waters which surrounded the Holy Isle.

The music buoyed him.

Oh, there were no words, no song, and the notes were faint, faint tendrils of sound that should never have carried over the step of so many armed and armored men— but they did, they did.

As he came into the open light, the Kings' Swords stopped, but the music did not. He heard the Primus step forward, and heard, of all things, a familiar female voice.

"Primus Gaeton."

"ACormaris."

He could not see her; the backs of too many men blocked his gaze, and he did not wish to crane to and fro like a spectator too young to understand the importance of decorum.

"We have come to join your escort, if you will permit it."

We?

"Primus Sivari sent word, ACormaris. We would be honored. Will you take the front?"

"No," she said softly. "We will stand beside."

Mailed gloves made such a full clangor when they struck breastplate. The Swords moved to either side as one man, or one living tunnel. At their end, he saw Mirialyn ACormaris and her companion. Her companion played the lute quietly, quietly. Kallandras of Senniel.

Why, he thought, although his courage failed him and he did not dare to ask, *are you helping me? You saved my life when the demon first attacked. You saved it today, when you came with Ser Kyro's sword. If you walk beside me, everyone in the Council will know that you support me? Why?*

The bard's music answered, faintly, softly.

The moon song.

The lullaby.

He spoke Weston as if he were a native; spoke it without accent, without inflection, without blemish. He wrote it with a perfect, steady hand, and understood its nuances—or was beginning to—better than he understood the tongue he was born to.

There were fewer words for death, fewer words for battlefield, fewer words for weaponry and war.

No, that wasn't true. Old Weston had easily as many words—maybe more—but it was called Old Weston for a reason. People didn't use the words that much anymore. To most of the Essalieyanese, war was distant, a Southern blight.

Or so he had been taught.

But when the doors to the Council Halls rolled open, when he stood beneath their height, dwarfed, as even a god might have been, by their vast recessed arches, he felt the anger in the silence as if it were the call of the ancient horn, the whistle of the crescent sword descending too quickly against the wind. Had he thought the Kings' Swords angry? He forgot it. The Kings' Swords were weapons, no more, no less. Gathered here were the hands that held them.

These men and women were finely attired, and they sat in rows of softly cushioned chairs that rose steeply toward the heights, that no one might miss what took place upon the floor. They were his judge and his jury, not his peers.

And they had to be his peers, or he had already failed.

"Tyr'agar," Princess Mirialyn ACormaris said. She bowed, low, the gesture Imperial. "The Crowns and The Ten await your petition." She stepped back, and then said softly, "Stand on two feet."

Something about the words felt strange; it was a moment before he realized what. The Princess was speaking in Torra, the tongue of the Annagarians. He wanted to thank her, but knew it would have to wait; she stepped away, falling to the side as if he, and not she, were the one who was moving. The Kings' Swords did the same, as did Kallandras. He stood alone.

And on two feet.

The whispers started; he heard them as if they were the gale itself. Anger, sibilance, reflective debate. He recognized many of the men and women who sat here, waiting. To the Triumvirate, he bowed. It was not his plan, or even his intent, but as they, golden-eyed, met his gaze and held it, measuring him, he felt compelled to bend. In the Dominion, he knew that each of these three would have died before they drew a second breath. And he knew, as they watched, that they knew, and they judged.

The golden-eyed were demons' get, or so his mother oft whispered, but Valedan was no child to be scared by the tales of the harem. Eight years, almost nine, he had lived here; surely, if these were demons, then in the afterlife, hell was no punishment.

Or was it? In their stern faces, he saw no pity.

But he remembered, because he was not so very far from the time when he could listen to the tales of the valor of Leonne the Founder, that the Lord himself had said that the Northern Kings—and the Kings alone—were not of tainted blood; their eyes were the color of the sun's light and the sun's justice. And those Kings had proved true to the Lord of the Sun—they had ridden, at the behest of Leonne the Founder. They had fought, and many, many of their people had died. How, he thought, could one tell when the blood was tainted or the blood was blessed?

The Lord's words, his mother would say, and she would be stern.

"Courage, Valedan," someone said. The voice carried from the heart of the gathered crowd, but although he searched, he could not see the person who uttered those two words.

Courage.

He took a breath. Another, deeper. He was here. If he failed, he and his compatriots would die—but that sentence hung above them regardless. At worst, his actions here would change nothing. Almost too numb to think of anything but that sentence, those failures, he stepped

forward into the circle that lay against the darkwood floor
as if held there by golden, moving light.

King Cormalyn, dark-haired and golden-eyed, sat in
robes of a midnight blue such as the Lady's servants
might wear, at evening's fall, in the Tor Leonne; King
Reymalyn wore white and gold, with a cape the color of
the sea at dawn thrown back over broad shoulders. He
was fire-haired and fire-jawed, although his beard was silvered with time, and his eyes were so cold they seemed
black for all of the gold about their center. To either side,
in thrones less high but no less regal, sat the Queens
Marieyan and Siodonay; he met the eyes of the eldest
Queen, the Queen Marieyan, and almost faltered at what
he saw in them. Compassion, regret. And steel. She
looked to him to be the age that Serra Tonia had been so
many years ago. Queen Siodonay wore the ceremonial
sword of her office, and more; a glittering of chain
beneath a silken hauberk. The crown that rested upon her
brow was her face's perfect adornment. Beside each of
the Queens sat a young man. One was red-haired and
clean-shaven, the other dark-haired; they seemed to be,
both in mood and demeanor, the youthful image of the
men who ruled the Empire. Even their eyes were the same
liquid gold. The Princes Reymar and Cormar. At fifteen
and sixteen they were barely his junior, and in bearing,
they had always seemed adult by comparison. He felt that
comparison keenly now.

But he did not bow to the two Kings who sat in judgment. Silence reigned beneath their watchful eyes.

At last, King Reymalyn turned to King Cormalyn.
"You see?"

But the wisdom-born King did not meet his brother's
gaze. "Stand forward," he said, using no title, granting no
authority. "Stand forward, and speak; this is the audience
that you have requested, and it will only be granted once."

Valedan raised his eyes from the circle of light, uncertain as to when his gaze had fallen there. "I am Valedan
kai di'Leonne, the Tyr'agar of the Dominion of
Annagar."

"They cannot hear you, Valedan," a soft voice whispered in his ear. "Speak loudly, and speak without fear.
King Reymalyn is justice-born, and if you address him
well, you will be heard."

That voice again, quiet and feminine and sure. He knew, as it passed, that no one else in the room could hear it. Straightening his shoulders, he spoke again, and this time he put force behind his words. "I am Valedan kai di'Leonne. The Tor Leonne is mine by right of birth and blood; no man of honor in the Dominion may call any other Tyr'agar while I live."

The King Reymalyn, red hair bound in a plaited braid in the Northern warrior style, spoke quietly. "You are the son of a concubine."

"The Kings of Essalieyan would have taken no concubine's get as suitable hostage for the behavior of a clansman," Valedan replied. "Before the assembly of the clans, I was claimed by the Tyr Markaso kai di'Leonne. In the waters of the Tor Leonne, I was baptized. Those who did not gainsay the Tyr then cannot gainsay him now with honor."

A murmur to the left and right, the susurrus of dissapproval or surprise. Valedan met the eyes of the justice-born King as if they were the too-bright sun. And he had long been warned against staring at the Lord's exposed face.

"Well said." King Cormalyn drew Valedan's attention away from his brother's burning eyes.

Valedan did not acknowledge the praise of the King, although he felt a momentary warmth at the words that King offered. "I have come to the Kings of Essalieyan to seek justice."

"Justice." King Reymalyn, his voice a cool neutrality.

"Even so. My father has been murdered. My brothers and sisters lie in a seraf's grave, without prayer or blessing. But while I remain, clan Leonne exists, and if rumors are true, you will be the last of the assassin's blades."

"Take care," Valedan's unseen adviser said, the words sharp.

It wasn't necessary. The hall errupted in a cacophony of angry whispers, shouts, insults. In three places, he heard the sound of metal against metal—swords being drawn, men straining forward and down, as if to reach him as he stood in isolation upon the great chamber's floor.

* * *

The Kalakar nodded.

"Ellora."

"He's got spirit," she said, leaning into Korama's shoulder. "You've got to give him that."

"He's got gall," Vernon snapped.

"He has," a younger voice said softly, "nothing to lose."

The three turned to see Kiriel, staring down from the gallery as if mesmerized by the handsome young man. Only Korama smiled, and it was because he chose to believe that her attention was the same, measure for measure, as any romantic young woman's would have been when confronted with a handsome, youthful—and unmarried—monarch.

"I have committed no crime against the Empire," Valedan continued, as the Kings called for, and received, the hall's silence once again.

Jeering, wordless because he chose to ignore the suddenly foreign Weston language, replied. The King Cormalyn turned and whispered something sharp to a fair-haired boy at his side; the boy nodded grimly and disappeared. The King then turned to glance at his brother. To demand, if Valedan was any judge of gesture and expression, that Reymalyn respond.

He did.

"You have committed no crime against the Empire."

Valedan froze a moment, but the King did not give him any chance to feel false hope; he was not a cruel man.

"But you are not being judged as an individual, or a group of individuals. You are being judged as the surety that you agreed to become when you crossed the border at Averda. You are the deposit, if you will, which was to be forfeited in the event that the Dominion chose to betray the trust that we held sacred." He rose, and the runners to either side melted away as if his wrath burned. "Will you argue that you are helpless to influence the decision of those you left behind? I will agree. You are helpless. But that is not your function here. We have been made to feel a great and grievous loss. You are the instrument by which we will respond." He lifted his hand, and in it, a scroll glowed suddenly with the light of his seldom-used power. "This is the testimony of the witnesses that were allowed to pass out of the Tor Leonne after the massacre. This is how our people—each and every one—died."

The stillness of breathing left Valedan as King Reymalyn unfurled the scroll and began to read.

Ellora rose as Kalakar's House name passed the lips of the justice-born King. Rose, hand across her chest, fingers tight around the pommel of the weapon that she carried by right. Vernon stood to one side; Korama to the other. Memory hurt them, and the knowledge that there would be no other chance to make new ones. The King's voice, laden with anger and sorrow, made of the death of Madson AKalakar a loss that everyone could feel as keenly as The Kalakar and her advisers had upon first hearing word.

At once, the approval that Ellora had felt, reluctantly drawn out by the courage of a young man, was buried beneath the greater loss.

She gazed blindly across the gallery and met the dark eyes of The Terafin.

He knew how they died, of course. Serra Alina made the horrors of their executions clear. But somehow, until the King spoke their names and the manner of their individual deaths into the heights of the vaulted chambers, they had not been real. They would never, after this day, be anything else. Shaking, Valedan willed himself to stand as straight and tall as possible. He lifted his chin; his eyes held fast to dignity and shed no tears of horror, although they hovered at the edge of his open lids.

We will not escape our deaths, he thought, and knew it for truth. But he had not been sent to accept failure, and as the King's voice died into a grim, terrible silence, he cleared his throat and began to speak anew.

"These actions were carried out by the men who would rule the Tor in my stead. They asked for, and received, no blessing from me—nor would they have.

"If you kill me, they will take the Sun Sword, and the Tor, and they will hold it by the Lord's right and the Lord's test. All that they have sought to accomplish by the massacre of your people, they will have accomplished. I am the only threat they face."

It was King Cormalyn who answered, perhaps only

King Cormalyn who could. "We are aware of your claim." He paused and then smiled grimly. "Tyr'agar." The term held only a hint of respect. "And it is true that your death will accomplish nothing—for the Crowns—within the Dominion. It is for this reason, and this reason alone, that we have considered sparing your life."

The King Reymalyn's eyes were the eyes of the Sun. "It is true. For you would be a thorn in the side of those responsible for the deaths of our people. But you will stand alone if you stand after this day; your people will meet the fate that is their due.

"For we have had no word that the Tyrs of the other four Terreans have been assassinated, their clans destroyed; indeed, we hear that they flourish. Such a hand as was behind this strike is a hand that would not have been raised without the approval of the Tyrs.

"You have been abandoned. There is no clan that will follow you, and if your claim is one of blood-right, it is not the first in history to have been cast back, like shadow, by the harsh light of the Lord of the Sun." He rose. "The assembly has reached a decision, Valedan di'Leonne.

"You are the wronged party, singularly, and you are the claimant to the Tor Leonne. Should you choose it, we will grant you our amnesty. But you will accept it in isolation. The others will be executed before the sun's rise."

"I have taken the responsibility for their safety upon my House," Valedan said, his voice steady.

"That is your choice."

"Then you do not understand the rules of the Dominion, and the rules of honor. I will not flee to the skirts of your wives to plead like a coward for my life while your executioners do their work. We will share a single fate, my people and I."

"So be it," King Reymalyn said grimly. He lifted the staff of his office, and the light once again limned his hands. But the light was shed by the staff. "I pronounce judgment, in the name of Reymaris, Lord of Justice."

The doors at the far side of the hall were thrown wide, letting light and noise into the stillness of a vast audience that was hushed with the waiting of several hundreds of people.

"HOLD!"

Striding into the chamber, followed by guards who wore the dust and sweat of the open road as heavily as their armor, came two men: and one was Tyr Ramiro kai di'Callesta, and the other, General Baredan kai di'Navarre.

Tyr Ramiro kai di'Callesta was known to The Ten; he was known to the Crowns. Even dust-stained and worn from travel, his bearing was unmistakably that of a man of power. And that power had no place in this chamber, at this time.

At his back, his cerdan faced not the thrones, but the doors, and following a discreet distance behind them came the Kings' Swords in great numbers. He ignored their progress across the chamber floors; ignored the swords that they had drawn by right of liege-defense. He walked, looking neither left nor right, up nor down, until he stopped five feet away from the only other man in the chambers to stand directly upon the audience floor.

There, in the sight of the Greater Assembly of Essalieyan, he dropped to one knee and drew his sword. The Annagarians did not draw blades often from the supplicant posture; a sword was a man's weapon, after all, and a man did not live on his knees.

But he lived by his honor, and he lived to serve his liege lord.

Many of the men and women gathered in the great chamber did not understand how his action was significant, but they were runners, guards, pages, lesser priests. The Kings knew, and The Ten, and the golden-eyed, demonic Exalted: Tyr'agnate Ramiro kai di'Callesta of the Terrean of Averda, was pledging his loyalty to a boy less than half his years.

And he pledged it with no less a weapon than the Sword of Callesta, called *Bloodhame* in the North of Annagar.

Valedan's reflection was caught and trapped, lengthened and twisted by the metallic sheen of the sword's blade. He stared at himself but a moment, and then lifted a steady chin. Dark eyes met dark eyes, measuring and testing and gauging.

Tyr Ramiro raised a brow, a slight lift of muscle. Then

he nodded and lowered his head once again. But his hands were absolutely steady; they did not shake, but held firmly to what was offered.

At seventeen, untried and untested, Valedan kai di'Leonne understood that the title *Tyr'agar* had suddenly become more than a desperate charade—much more than a means to an end, even if that end was the preservation of the only people in the world that he cared for. He knew that to hesitate was to show both that newfound understanding, and his fear of what it meant.

But he hesitated as he looked once again at the blade's perfect edge. Then he straightened his shoulders, and he spoke, as loudly as he could, his young voice filling a now silent room with its determination and its gravity.

"Tyr'agnate Ramiro kai di'Callesta, why have you come?"

The older man raised his face to meet the younger man's pale visage. "I have come," he said, as strongly but more surely, "as my father before me, and his father before him, to lay the Sword of Callesta in the hands of the only man who, by blood and birth and the Lord's will, may rule the clansmen. I rule Averda by your grace, and I rule it at your whim." He paused. "The riders of Averda will stand behind your banner."

The younger man reached out slowly to touch the sword's haft, and although the older man was kneeling, it seemed for a moment that it was he who ruled. Then, Valedan kai di'Leonne lifted the sword and swung it once in a great circle above his head. Holding it, raised, he turned to face the men who sat in judgment before him.

"I *am* Tyr'*agar* Valedan kai di'Leonne. I am the last of my line, but I will not remain so. You doubted," he said to the justice-born King, "that the clans would follow the son of a concubine: I tell you that they will follow the blood of a Tyr." He turned, and only Ramiro could see that his arm—the arm that held the sword extended—was shaking slightly. "Rise, Tyr'agnate. No Tyr'agar before me has ever doubted the value of *Bloodhame*. Or the man who wields it."

Thus freed from the supplicant posture, a man who was not used to its confines rose gracefully. Rose, and then bowed, low, in the direction of The Ten, and The Six. To the Exalted, he did not offer his respects, nor did they expect it. The golden-eyed god-born did not survive for long in the harsh clime of the Southern Dominion.

"Tyr'agnate," King Cormalyn said softly. "You risked much."

"Lord of wise counsel. To remain in Averda was to risk more," Ramiro replied gravely. "Ser Fillipo is my par, and I will not deliver him to the rightful wrath of your nobility. I had no hand in, and no knowledge of, the actions taken by the men who now stand in the Tor Leonne. I will make no trek to their side; the Festival of the Sun will be held, for the second time in Callestan history, without the presence of Averda. I sent my brother, who *is* valued, to these lands as proof of my faith in your rule.

"Kill him, for the actions of men who are my enemies, and not my just ruler, and the Sword of Callesta will be raised to the North, and not to the South, for the debt of blood is a debt that not even the Tyrs can ignore. Such is," he said quietly, although the words traveled, "the will of the Lord."

"Have a care," the justice-born King said quietly. "For that sounds perilously close to a threat, and not even I would be unwise enough to utter it before *this* assembly."

"A threat? Lord of just measure, since the signing of the treaty of the Averdan valleys, I have never in word or deed threatened you, or the territory that you rule. I speak the truth, and it is the only truth that will count in the Dominion of Annagar. We are the clansmen. We have our duties, whether we will it or no."

Silence a moment, and before either King could speak, the Tyr'agnate added, with a grim, mirthless smile, "Although it pains me to do so, I will speak for Lamberto as well. Tyr Mareo di'Lamberto categorically refused to travel to the Tor Leonne for the Festival. He has allowed his Tors to travel as they see fit, but there will be repercussions for those who *have* seen fit. Whether you will it or no, war is coming. Your decision this day will decide how that war turns."

Dryly, King Cormalyn said, "We thank you for your counsel; it is, as always, enlightening. We will have a recess in the audience chamber while we discuss this turn of events. If it pleases you, wait, and you shall hear our answer."

"I am, as always, at your disposal."

Queen Marieyan, alone of the four who wore the Crowns of state, smiled very slightly, the lift of her lips both rueful and sharp. She had, on several occasions, been party to the discussions between Patris Larkasir and Tyr Ramiro di'Callesta—and their various diplomatic envoys—and she knew well that Ramiro di'Callesta waited upon no man's whim.

"Then," King Cormalyn said, rising, "we will adjourn for the hour." King Reymalyn nodded in acquiescence, but his gaze was cool and distant. The Queens, Marieyan and Siodonay the Fair, rose as well. "We will take the counsel of The Ten, if they will offer it."

The Ten rose almost as one.

Ramiro di'Callesta.

The Kalakar's gaze was caught and held by him. They had both been blooded in the valleys of Averda, and although his was not the hand that had ruled the Southern Dominion during that war, it was the hand that had been raised, again and again, in devastating Northern raids. There was a simplicity about war: He was her known enemy, and a dangerous one. She did not trust him then, nor had anyone expected it of her, but after, with pretty treaties signed and the routes opened for trade, she had trusted him less; had, in fact, waited years for a slip, some sign of his true nature, his duplicity. It galled her to see him, dust-stained and obviously just come from the road, command so much respect in this room, from this assembly.

The dead had not been so loud for a decade; she had forgotten just how bitter the sound of their voices could be.

Perhaps they crowded her; perhaps they deafened her and held her in their angry thrall a moment too long. Or perhaps time had taken its toll, and age slowed her; she was not so foolish as to think that youth's strength survived the passage of so many years, so much experience, unchanged.

Or perhaps it was because *he* looked up, from the audience chamber's grand floor, and met her eyes so precisely it was as if he knew which of the ten great chairs belonged to Kalakar; or because, although Annagar trained none of its women in the arts of war, his nod acknowledged her as his equal—as kindred spirit. And, to her chagrin, it was truth; she was both.

Or perhaps it was because the young woman that the mysterious Evayne a'Nolan had left in her keeping was not the young woman that everyone silently hoped she would be.

Whatever the reason for her distraction, she *should* have seen Kiriel in time to stop her. And she did not.

The cry that warned her, that sliced through the thoughts into which she'd fallen so cleanly she thought someone *was* dying, came from across the floor. From the Terafin group. A young voice, at that—a voice that she didn't recognize, although she kept informed about Terafin events.

"Kalakar! Your guard!" There was no question at all in Ellora's mind who that cry referred to: Kiriel.

The young House Guard stood beneath Ellora, in position, her hand hovering above the hilt of her sword as if the two—hand and weapon—were not meant to be parted. Her face, pale, was impassive; she watched the men below—Tyr Ramiro di'Callesta, General Baredan di'Navarre, and the young man carrying a sword whose full history he probably did not know—lips parted, youth absent from her young face.

When had the shadows gathered, seeping from her eyes, her lips, the tips of her fingers, leaving the mask the The Kalakar and her advisers had shied away from inspecting? One moment her face was the shuttered face of a foreigner, and the next—the next, it was a thing stripped of humanity. Of mortality.

She did not speak, but the sword was in her hand as if it had no sheath, no bonds to hold it. Ellora had not drawn breath before Kiriel gripped the rail and vaulted herself over it in a type of graceful, deadly flight. Beneath her, three rows of spectators felt her shadow passing; they had no time to glance up before she was beyond them, and into the arena itself.

"*Kiriel!*" Duarte shouted, finding the voice that had deserted his Commander. "*Kiriel, stop!*"

Men of Annagar did not often think women a threat, but there was about this one a shade and a grimness that spoke of death, and only death. To call her girl—or woman—was unthinkable. Unthought. Shadow wreathed and darkened her face, but it was no Lady's shade, no Lady's veil. This darkness, he knew at once, for he saw in it the hand of the Lord of Night, whom no Annagarian named.

Leonne.

Ramiro di'Callesta reached for his sword and froze, mid-motion, as he saw the gleaming light in Valedan's hand; Baredan di'Navarre began to draw blade. Neither man moved as quickly as she; shock held them that necessary moment.

But as she bore down upon them—*past* them—in utter silence, The Kalakar noted grimly that Ramiro di'Callesta hit the floor and rolled away from the reach of her blade, but General Baredan di'Navarre threw himself toward it—in front of the man that he had come, from the heart of the Tor Leonne, to retrieve.

Kiriel snarled; there were no other words to describe the sound that filled the vaulted chamber, unless it be *roar*. And then she leaped, up and over, landing a foot beyond Baredan's stiffening back, well clear of the reach of his weapon. The older General had time to lose all color, but not hope; he began to turn as her feet touched ground.

Not the boy, Ellora thought, with horror. *Kiriel—not the boy.*

But Kiriel could not hear what she could not even say. Turning to Duarte, Ellora shouted, "Stop her!"

"Too late!" Duarte cried, although his hands were in motion. "She's too damned fast!"

Helpless, they watched her blade rise.

He heard the roar, a single sound as vast as movements of earth in the audience chamber. He, who had come seeking the lives of his compatriots—and himself—forgot politics; no fear that came out of the machination of human treacheries could be so visceral, so immediate.

Wheeling, moving faster than he had ever moved in his life, he saw death wrapped around a slender, sharp face and a long, clean blade. Tyr Ramiro had placed *Bloodhame* in his hands as a gesture of his fealty; he held her, still, both hands wrapped tight around her grip, as if she were the Sun Sword herself. As if he were her master.

The edge beneath his feet was an edge made of, and sharpened by, fear; to one side, flight, the other defense. It would not bear his weight for long.

Decide.

His own voice.

Beyond her moving body, he thought he saw Baredan di'Navarre, his father's man, frozen in place, a statue of past times and past failure. He did not have the time to understand, although it would come, that *Bloodhame* was older than Averda—but she was not older than the war between the clans of the Lord of the Sun and the creatures of the Lord of the Night; she had been crafted for that war, and the sight of this enemy was waking her.

Valedan di'Leonne, the last surviving member of the clan that, by blood-right, ruled the Dominion of Annagar, looked up in shock as his blade struck hers. The creature's—the girl's?—charge was broken; he saw her eyes widen, although there were no whites to their depth. His grip tightened; it was all that kept the Sword of Callesta from spinning useless across the chamber floor.

"Get *down*," she said, and his knees almost buckled at the force of the single word. *"Run."*

A confidence buoyed him, then. The blade of Callesta seemed to shiver in his hands, as he brought it back. She did not move.

"Run," she said again. But there was no darkness in the word.

"I am—"

She *moved*. He barely saw her. But he felt her hands around his shirt, his collar, his cloak. He cried out; he'd time for it, and little else.

"Take him away!" She threw him.

Into the waiting arms of General Baredan di'Navarre.

The older man lurched under the sudden burden, dropping his only means of protection that he might catch Valedan safely. They both staggered as they collided, but to Valedan's great surprise, Baredan held his ground, bracing his knees and his back to do so.

Two things occurred to Valedan as he gained his bearing: The first, that he was still alive, that somehow the shadow-hollowed girl had not killed him, and the second, that General Baredan di'Navarre had not—yet—offered him the sword from the position that spoke of proferred loyalty. He steadied himself against the General's arms, and then cried out in dismay.

Bloodhame had found her mark across the older man's left cheek; he bled. He did not seem to notice the wound; it was slight enough. But he said, "When you wield a weapon, it's always a danger. It doesn't matter where you are, or with who." He looked up. "Come. We've time, but I don't know how much of it. Let us join the Tyr."

Valedan nodded, but something caught his attention; something made him stop, turn, look back.

The strange, terrifying girl stood where he had, moments before, made his stiff plea for justice to the grim-faced, dour Twin Kings, blade ready, legs planted like spikes against the floor. The cerdan who wore Callestan crests backed away from her; the Kings' Swords held their ground. Men of two nations stood, side by side, in uneasy alliance, waiting the commands of their King and their Tyr, swords drawn and shields raised against a common enemy.

The Kings said, "Hold!"

And Tyr'agnate Ramiro di'Callesta said, "Hold!" as if all men who ruled spoke with a common voice. They stood a moment, held by incomprehension.

She drew her blade back and darkness shattered the light that came from the windows and open spaces above. It also destroyed the perfectly worked floor, scattering shards of gold-inlaid marble in a wide, deadly circle. From beneath the ground, seeped in blackness that was armor and shield and weapon, a shadow rose, taking on obsidian, perfect form. He gestured, and the benches that seated the Exalted exploded in a burst of white heat and flame. There were screams that carried a moment above the crackle of wood, the shivering of timber and stone.

Cerdan cried out and stumbled, as did the Kings' Swords, although both were armored. The Tyr, standing closest to the gallery of all the men upon the audience chamber's floor, raised his arms and caught the little daggers the explosion had made in sinew and flesh, grinding his teeth to a close over the cry he might have made. He stumbled back, felt the common rail beneath his shoulders, and lowered his hands a moment to look.

"I apologize for the intrusion," the creature said, lifting his hands, "But I'm afraid that we cannot allow the Leonne pawn to be played on the field."

Darkness fell like a curtain, and with it came the ceiling. But the hands that had made this room, these chambers, were no ordinary hands; the ceiling resisted the darkness a moment, and a moment was—barely—enough. Only the center dropped, like stone into water, at the creature's command.

And in the center of the audience chamber, faces upturned in silence, stood Valedan di'Leonne and Baredan di'Navarre—the Tyr'agar and his General. The rock buried them, splintering the floor yet again with its terrible weight.

Tyr Ramiro di'Callesta pulled himself over the stone walls that separated the thrones from the floor, blooding them as the cuts and ruptures of opened skin and cloth rubbed against their surfaces. He sought the floor; the thin safety of chairs and rails and quarter-walls.

"Allasakar-Etridian," Kiriel said, standing her ground upon the broken floor as if terrain were illusion.

He spit, showing teeth that were—almost—human. "Too slow, half-breed."

Of all things to offer a creature twice her height and three times her weight, she gave laughter, and the laughter was grim and chill. "Failure." Threw an arm—not her sword arm—behind her in a wide arc. There, as dust cleared, stood Valedan kai di'Leonne and General Baredan kai di'Navarre in a grim, shocked silence beside blocks of fallen stone that had been sheared smooth in a circle—a circle that encompassed them both.

The obsidian creature snarled in rage, and hesitated a fraction of a second; his gaze went to the mages in the gallery, and to the Exalted, who rose, bloodied but unbowed, from the pyre he had made of their thrones. The desire for battle warred with the desire for survival; survival won.

Only the young woman who faced him knew how close the contest was.

"Take this back," she said, "and tell them that Kiriel sent it."

Before the mage-fires descended into the broken pit that the chamber floor had become; before the Exalted could recover and put to use those magics which were their blood heritage; before the bards could speak their words of angry command, she gestured, her arm moving so quickly it could not be seen in the shadows.

The creature cried out in fury and pain.

But his spell was cast, and the shadows took him, injured and insulted, to a safety that his enemies could not prevent him from attaining.

CHAPTER TWENTY

Ser Valedan kai di'Leonne slowly lowered the sword that he had clung to so fiercely. Lowered it, seeing beyond the circle in which he and General Baredan di'Navarre stood, as if he were waking from a nightmare—and discovering that reality was far worse. Before him, between the cracks of stone and timbers that should have been his death, he could see the black back of the person who had, somehow, saved his life. He saw her sword rise and fall, as if the motion were linked to her breath; heard that breath, loud and heavy, as she brought the blade down, as she struggled to sheath it.

And he knew, as he watched, that it *was* a struggle.

General Baredan di'Navarre stared down at the floor— at what remained of the floor beneath the huge stone blocks and joists and beams. He cursed, and the sound was so welcome—so human—it drew Valedan's almost grateful attention, breaking her spell.

"What is it? What's wrong?" As if, surrounded by the ruins of a ceiling that had stood for four centuries, fires being banked by magical means to one side, something else needed to *be* wrong.

"My sun-scorched sword!" Baredan replied. He added a few words, a few colorful words, and then a few more for good measure. Serra Alina would doubtless let him understand, by the ice of her perfectly proper stare, how grave a crime he had just committed in the presence of the Tyr'agar, were she here. She was not.

"Tyr'agar," the General said, recovering with a humor that only those who walked close to death could know. He bowed. "It appears that I must forgo the usual ceremonies in favor of practicality."

Bemused, Valedan nodded, and then he frowned slightly. But only slightly; Serra Alina had been, in most things, his teacher; he understood form well. And he understood, as he met Baredan's grim smile, that the General had lost his *sword*. He could not imagine that his own father, his own dead, distant father, would ever have smiled, grimly or no, at such a loss, regardless of circumstance.

He started to speak, but Baredan lifted a hand, as if he did not know what the young man was about to say. "You must forgive me, Tyr'agar. We are on foreign soil, and I would say—although it is less clear now—that we are not among friends. We will guard our words and our clans."

But as he stopped speaking, he looked at Valedan di'Leonne as if seeing him for the first time. His blood had dried along the edge of *Bloodhame* because the boy had refused to let go of his weapon in what was, undoubtedly, the first real combat of any sort that he'd faced.

Baredan smiled. And his smile was as sharp as the Callestan blade.

The Greater Assembly was not recalled that day. The Exalted survived the flames, but their priests did not—and the death that should have been quick was both slow and terrible for each and every one of their attendants.

The Kings called for—and received—order in the hall, and then quickly disbanded the gathering; their Swords came, and those mages who served the Crowns within the Order. The Ten chose to accept the dismissal as a request, and they left the hall with their chosen guards, on the understanding that they would reconvene on the morrow.

All, of course, except for The Kalakar.

"What-exactly-did-you-think-you-were-doing?"

Kiriel, looking very much like the girl that they could never again believe she was, met Duarte's angry words with a slightly crimson face. She said nothing.

Behind the leader of the Ospreys stood The Kalakar, with Verrus Vernon and Verrus Korama to the right and left. Beside Duarte stood Alexis, her lovely hair twisted into a knot that the most nimble-fingered of the Ospreys could not have untied. She was angry. They all were.

"Sentrus Kiriel," The Kalakar said, "I'd advise you to answer the question. We are about to be called into private session with the Crowns and the Exalted; I wish to have something to say to them. It is a matter of no little import." The Swords that lined the walls of the largest of the chambers reserved for dignitaries who waited entry to the Hall of Wise Counsel were proof enough, if it were needed, of the truth of those words. But The Kalakar was certain that Kiriel did not know the Astari were present— if the girl even knew who the Astari were. She didn't know it herself for fact, but she'd known the Kings for years, and she was a good judge of their mood. "Kiriel."

"I was saving his life," Kiriel said, each word cool and civil.

"And you didn't think to warn anyone else? Twenty-seven men and women *died* in that attack." Verrus Korama took a breath, held it, and then expelled it.

"Korama, please."

He had the grace to look embarrassed, and the presence of mind to bring his fist sharply to his chest. "Kalakar." As a military man, he had seen death before; he would, no doubt, see it again. But not here, now now, and not in this manner: The screams of the priests echoed, a building and an hour away. The fire that the creature had thrown upon them had been in some way *alive*. It hollowed them, slowly.

"Thank you. Kiriel," The Kalakar continued as if there had been no interruption. "When did you know that the danger existed?"

"When the boy walked into the room." It was not as difficult as it should have been to hear her call the heir-presumptive to the Annagarian crown a boy.

Duarte turned purple; Cook turned white.

"And it didn't occur to you to *warn* any of the rest of us?"

"Duarte." The Kalakar again, sounding less and less pleased by the interruptions, which was no easy task.

But Duarte was an Osprey. *The* Osprey.

"Primus Duarte," Kiriel said very formally, "if I had uttered any warning at all, the boy would be dead. I thought—and I apologize for the thinking—that The Kalakar wished him to live."

"And the other twenty-seven?" It was Alexis' voice, strained and heated as she met the younger woman's implacable dark eyes. Her hand hovered above her dagger's hilt.

"The other twenty-seven were not important to The
Kalakar." The dark-haired, pale girl turned to face The
Kalakar, in whose name she had just dismissed two dozen
lives. "The Kings were not in danger; their thrones—as
the thrones of the Exalted—have been magicked in a way
that I do not understand. They might have been injured,
but I do not believe that Etridian could have killed them
without risking his own existence. He chose not to try.

"Have I done wrong?"

The Kalakar met Kiriel's too-dark eyes. Then she
turned her head slightly, and found Korama's gaze upon
her. *Am I that obvious?* she thought, and was surprised at
the discomfort that she felt. But she was an honest
woman—at least with herself; she did not refute Kiriel's
claim.

It's war, she thought, and knew it for truth. Knew it,
intellectually, far later than she had on some more visceral level. Old instincts. *A lot more than twenty-seven
people are going to be dead. Some of them in worse ways.*
Although that, bless the Mother, was hard to imagine.

"No," she heard herself say. "But in the future, you're
going to have to learn some of the Kalakar signals. Not
only does your commanding officer—Primus Duarte, in
this case—have the right to know of present danger, he
has the obligation." She raised a hand to her temple and
massaged her forehead. "Kiriel, you know the Kalakar
rules, and you are a part of the House Guards. I have not
asked you the questions that you *will* be asked when we
approach the Crowns."

The young girl shrugged a slender shoulder.

"Who are you, Kiriel?"

"Kiriel di'Ashaf," the girl replied grimly, the set of her
lips white.

Ser Fillipo par di'Callesta expected many things from
this grim, cloudless day. He felt the heat on the back of
his neck and raised his head, a man's gesture of defiance
under the eyes of the Lord. He was almost done with
praying; the hours had dragged. And dragged. Serra Tara,
his dutiful wife, had come and gone in the cool air,
offering him water and sweet breads. He took some of
each, enjoying neither. It took a certain strength to face
death, to face a *man's* death, and he intended to have it.

Where was Valedan?

The Imperials were hard to understand. They did not value family, they did not cleave to blood; they did not spend their hours in the practice of war, preferring dance and letters and unfathomable art. Yet they knew how to fight. Some even understood death as well as a clansman.

His shadow, turning slowly, marked the passage of time. His hands itched; it had been many years since, in a time of danger, he had had to forgo weaponry. Were Ser Kyro di'Lorenza not at his side, he would have borne it less graciously; less gracefully. But he knew that it was his lead these men followed, with or without the presence of the boy.

And he intended to lead them into whatever glory the Lord allowed unarmed prisoners in a foreign land. His gaze crossed the fountain, and came to rest upon the stone boy, whose pathetic blindfold and spindly body told the tale of Annagarian justice.

Justice.

The only sure justice was the rule of a man of power and honor—and it lasted as long, and traveled as far, as his reach. No more. No less. The Tyr'agar had not been a particularly just or honorable man.

Where was Valedan?

Ser Fillipo was on his feet before the peal of the gong had died into stillness. Ser Kyro and Ser Mauro joined him, as did Serra Alina. Serra Marlena was with Serra Helena, and his own wife, Serra Tara. In her quiet, sweet way, she was the same anchor for the women and children that he was for the men. Alina was too understandably dangerous, and she lacked, of all traits most endearing, that lovely sentimentality which made of a woman's arms and thoughts a man's haven.

He cast a sidelong glance at the dark-haired, hawklike profile. *I would arm you,* he thought. *If such a thing were possible.* And in this Empire, it was. He smiled, and the smile was a grimmer one. *And if I thought you would follow my lead.* He wished, not for the first time, that he had been a braver man. But he was who he was, and he had not taken such a Serra to wife, and the wife that he did have, he valued. Another walk beneath the open sky; another life.

And he might be meeting it sooner than he would like.
The hangings were pushed aside, and Valedan di'Leonne
entered the courtyard.

These four hostages, Fillipo, Kyro, Mauro, and Alina,
turned hard and cold as they took in his appearance.
Where he had gone dressed finely, if not well, he returned
in disheveled, rent clothing; blood from multiple scrapes
and light cuts showed dark against his unusually fair
complexion.

To his surprise, Ser Fillipo *was* surprised. Too many
years living in the deceptive tolerance of the Essalieyanese court. He realized that, had he been in the Tor
Leonne in a similar position, he would also have felt surprise, but for a different reason; Valedan walked, he lived.
If he had been roughly handled, it was clear that he had
not—yet—been humiliated.

Ser Fillipo fell at once to his knee; his companions did
likewise, carrying the charade through to the end.

And because they knelt, heads bowed, eyes to the warm
stones beneath their feet, they did not see the men who
entered the enclosure at his back.

"Rise," Valedan said, in a completely smooth voice.

Ser Fillipo lifted his head and froze in mid-motion. And
then he smiled, although the smile was a very, very
strange one. "Try'agnate," he said, meeting the eyes of
his brother.

"Tyran," Ramiro di'Callesta replied. "Did you think I
would leave you to the Northern wolves?"

Duvari had hardly aged in sixteen years; he had softened less. It was said, among the Astari, that time itself
feared even the attempt to mark the Lord of the Compact,
and if it was said with grim humor, it was at least humor.
Devon ATerafin, who felt the years more keenly, wondered where the Kings had found such a defender, and
just what they had had to sell to gain his loyalty; he hoped
it wasn't going to be too costly in the Hall of Mandaros.

The ATerafin was not a vain man; his hair was no
longer the blue-black that had been the envy—and
desire—of many a courtier. But his back was unbent, his
shoulders straight, his arms strong. He had many years of
service left in him yet—and he acknowledged, with the

same grim humor, that the Astari were determined to have all of them.

Acknowledged, with a wry smile, that he intended to offer them. Service to the Crowns had been the focal point of his adult life, and he wasn't certain that he knew what life would be without it. Very few of the Astari retired in so undramatic a fashion.

Meralonne APhaniel stood by the side of Sigurne Mellifas. The former was tall and straight, with white hair that fell past his shoulders and down the emerald back of his cloak. He'd aged as well as Duvari, although perhaps less silently. Of all the men in this large room, he was the only one who insistently, persistently, clung to his pipe. The woman beside him did not seem to notice. Where Meralonne had aged well, she had aged into a seeming frailty of size and height. Where Meralonne was prone to fiery speech, she was prone to silence—and perhaps for that reason, when she spoke, her words were treated with gravity.

The desire, Devon knew, to protect her was strong.

And it was willfully blind. Sigurne Mellifas was no stranger to violence or darkness. Or death. The platinum medallion that hung openly around her neck on a workmanlike, solid chain bore the three faces of the moon, and quartered within the full face, the elemental symbols. Mage-born. Mage-trained.

Beside Sigurne, in quiet conversation with her, was Bardmaster Marten. She was not, to the Astari's knowledge, born to the voice, but she held the college together as effectively as her predecessor—and the woman who had chosen her—the much missed Sioban Glassen.

It will do her good, Sioban had said. *She's got the head for it—and the heart; she'll keep Senniel running in good order. She's not afraid of talent, especially not when it belongs to a young student who thinks too highly of his or her own abilities.*

In the five years since Sioban had retired—if traveling through the Empire with a harp, a lute, and a bedroll could be called retirement—Solran had lived up to her former master's choice. She was good. And she was not afraid to accept her limitations and make use of the men and women around her who did not possess them.

At her side stood Kallandras of Senniel. The Astari

knew him well, and for the most part, they trusted him. Devon did. Duvari did not. The Lord of the Compact disliked a man with an orphan boy's forgotten, mythical past; too many mysteries held danger. But he was, of all bards, the Queen Marieyan's favorite, and he had, by dint of a skill that he cared to offer no explanation for, saved her life six years past.

Mirialyn ACormaris stood by the side of her father's vacant chair, in a silence better suited to the grave. She was pale. Her hair was pulled and bound; it gleamed in the light like a brass helm. She was girded with sword, although she wore no armor, carried no shield. Her silence was telling, even frightening. She offered no counsel, as if she realized that the events had moved beyond *Avantari,* and therefore beyond her certain jurisdiction.

In front of the empty thrones stood Commander Sivari and the men who were, colloquially, called the Three-mars: Verrus Andromar, Verrus Lorimar and Verrus Kitimar. They spoke in deadly earnest, their words pitched to carry the few feet necessary to be heard by their comrades, no more. The Commander still had the bearing of Kings' Champion, although it had been many years since he'd had the time for the excess and the vanity of taking the Kings' Challenge.

The Kings' Challenge.

It was almost upon them; the summer was high, and the travelers, from the Western Kingdoms, the free towns, and, yes, the Southern Dominion, already crowded the inns, taverns, and homes that had been opened to such trade. The magisterial guards were almost beside themselves in their attempt to ensure the safety of foreign Southern men. The streets carried the anger of the Empire, and that anger, great mindless beast that it was, was turned toward all things Southern. Even the Terrean dialects so common in the hundred holdings had fallen into disuse as people afraid of the consequences of their heritage chose, wisely, to hide it. Most of the time, it worked. There had only been four deaths to date.

He was certain there would be more. Echoes of the Southern wars. Did they ever really die, or did they return, like the tide, in their time?

What will it be, Devon thought, into a room that bustled

with more power than had been gathered for such a purpose in well over a decade.

As if in answer to the unspoken question, Healer Dantallon crossed the chamber, carrying a basin full of clean, warm water, and several cool cloths. He looked up and his gaze chanced across Devon's inquisitive glance, his green eyes wide and unwavering in a pale face. Denying death, and even injury, with unshakable certainty.

He approached the Exalted with more grace than he had ever approached the people who had been taken to the healeries. Devon knew it well, having been one of them. But he did not approach with much more grace, if Devon were honest. The Exalted did not seem to notice the lack of offered courtesy, which said much for their opinion of the Kings' healer. But the Exalted of Cormaris looked— almost—exasperated as he was forced to sit and bear said healer's ministrations.

The Exalted of the Mother tended her own wounds with a bitter, bitter anger that was palpable in the room. It was a sight seldom seen; the anger of the Mother was a cold, dark thing, and it was rarely wakened. Devon had never seen it until now, perhaps because he had never been so close to her in the aftermath of tragedy.

And it was tragedy, for the Churches; in one afternoon they had lost the most highly placed members of their heirarchies with the exception of the Exalted themselves. The creature that had risen from the pit made of the audience chamber floors had targeted the Exalted—and their attendants—as if they were his natural enemy.

They were.

Devon sighed as the Kings entered the room. It was time now to begin in earnest. What was decided here today, *was* decided; there would be no backward motion.

"Tell me, Fillipo," the Tyr'agnate said. "I am here under sufferance; I am not a hostage, but even so, I am to travel among you without my Tyran." He paused. "And I am not given leave to remain. Nor is my companion." He nodded quietly at Baredan's broad back, thinking, as he did, that he had not chosen poorly. Ser Kyro di'Lorenza was speaking with the General, his large hands occasionally rising and falling as if to make a point more forcefully.

The sun was low; the lamps, such as they were, were lit. It was hot here, and the slow ebb of day allowed the heat to linger, burning what it touched. Still, these two men found a place in the shade in which they might speak a moment in privacy.

"If you are asking me," the younger man said, "to judge the value of the young Tyr'agar, I'm afraid I must disappoint."

"Oh?"

"He surprises me," Ser Fillipo replied, as if that were explanation enough. To Ramiro di'Callesta, it was. They were cut from the same cloth, these two; they understood each other well. Very little surprised them. "How do you think it will go?"

The Callestan clanleader shrugged grimly. "For now? I think the Lord will smile. I am certain that clan Callesta and clan Lamberto will not lose their kin to the Kings' chosen executioners. Nor will the boy. But beyond that? The sun is in my eyes."

"Why did you come?"

"For the boy," Ramiro replied flatly, all pretense gone. "We did not know of the events that occurred in the Tor; we left before word arrived. But we came at a hard ride when news reached us." He turned then, seeking the sky a moment before he glanced away.

Fillipo looked at his brother's profile; his brother watched the burble of fountain water at the feet of the stone child. "What do you intend, Ramiro? I will follow you," he added softly, as if it were a question of choice.

"I intended to preserve the people of Averda—and the clan that rules the Terrean." He turned his hands over and stared at the new lines that scrapes and splintered marble had drawn there. "The General Alesso di'Marente will rule the Tor by the end of the Festival, if I am not mistaken. But he will rule it," the Tyr'agnate added, with a grim smile, "without benefit of the Sun Sword and the bloodlines."

"You said, intended."

"Yes."

"Now?"

"For now it is enough to preserve the life of a par who does not know when silence serves best."

Ser Fillipo smiled; it was the first expression he had used, in his captivity, that made him look younger.

"She wasn't a demon." Jewel ATerafin massaged her forehead; her eyes throbbed, her head ached, and her throat was still raw from the force of the few words that she shouted across the floor of the Great Assembly Chamber. Across the coming chasm that she, and only one other, had *seen*. "I've seen the kin before. I know what they look like." Pausing, she lifted her face and met The Terafin's open gaze. "I've seen," she said softly, "kin who were in all ways human—and I knew what they were."

"Then what was she? You saw her as well as any of the rest of us. She certainly wasn't human."

"I don't know."

Alayra's brow was a single line, which happened seldom. Each of the times she'd witnessed the expression, Jewel had wished she were somewhere else. Today was not to be the exception. Turning, she met The Terafin's cool eyes and realized that there would be no rescue from that quarter. Or, she realized, as she took in Morretz's expression, Avandar's grim stare, and Torvan's quiet sympathy, from any quarter.

There were days when being seer-born was a blessing.

And there were days like these.

"You were surprised by her." The Terafin.

"Yes. But she wasn't a threat to you, or to me—or to anyone in that hall, I'd guess, except for the creature that rose out of the pit of the floor. I—" She closed her eyes; she couldn't help it. Her lids were almost aching with a tingle that sometimes presaged illness.

And sometimes, vision.

"You had time to shout a warning to The Kalakar." Captain Alayra. She could not see the old soldier's face, but her voice sounded mere inches away.

"Yes."

"ATerafin, *wake up!*"

Alayra made commands, not requests; over the years, Jewel had grown accustomed to this fact. Her body obeyed, where her mind could not; her eyes—no, her lids, seemed to snap up. But she could not, could *not*, see them, although the voices were clear enough. She saw what she had seen during the day. In the hall. And she understood, then.

She could hear Avandar, cursing. *Seizure. Get out of the way!* She did not answer; wouldn't have, could she. She felt his fingers, his hands, the roughness of his skin against her cheeks. Then, something rigid pressed between her lips. *It's not the seizures, you fool, it's the sight,* but her lips took the rod, willing, as if her body was, for the moment, an empty vessel that—barely—managed to hold her. *Learn how to control your power,* someone had said—but the closer she got to it, the more it controlled her. As it did now.

It was the vision.

The *same* vision that had given her the impetus to cry out across the Chamber to The Kalakar.

Kiriel was leaping from the heights, and Jewel watched her fall as if she were the edge of a blade. The ground beneath her feet shuddered as if her slight weight would sunder it. Shadow trailed from her eyes, her lips, the wildly dancing tips of her ebony hair. Her hands were gloved in darkness, and her chest; she was armed and armored and weaponed.

And behind her or beside her, armored and armed and shedding blood, not shadow, stood the young princeling: Valedan kai di'Leonne. He cried out; she did not understand the words he spoke.

No—wait— But the words would not escape the rod that Avandar had placed between her lips. She felt her eyes stop their tingling; the shadows left them, returning the normalcy of The Terafin's rooms. Spitting, and glaring at the domicis who served her, she lowered her face into her hands. *What was that?* she thought. *Vision? Sight?* Some disjointed memory of the morning?

"Jewel?"

"I . . . am well."

The Terafin nodded coolly. "And your vision?"

"I would have said—would almost have said—that I was *seeing* this morning's event."

"Jewel," The Terafin's domicis said quietly, presuming to enter a conversation into which he had not, theoretically, been invited, "there is something about this young . . . woman that speaks to you. To your sense of the future."

"Yes."

Avandar was not pleased. She knew it at once because his jaw took on that muscular, clenched look. There was, between these two men, a competition that had never died. She had asked them both about it, and neither man chose to elaborate.

"Is she a danger to us?" The Terafin again.

"Yes."

"Succinctly put," her own domicis, Avandar, said. "How?"

But to that, Jewel ATerafin had no answer.

Kiriel approached the throne room for the first time. She looked through the two-story open doors to the heights formed by an arched ceiling that had been built to catch, and hold, the sound of a King's judgment. The wisdom-born King. There were windows here that caught light just as surely as the ceiling caught sound, transforming and coloring it before it descended to ground. There were benches carved out of the stone sill of each window; they were empty now, although she had no doubt that they were often filled. It was a grand hall, and although she had seen grander in her life, the sight of it filled her with the blackness of certain familiarity. Power.

"Kiriel."

The word, a nudge of sorts from Cook, brought her back to herself. She stood two feet from the frame of the door; there were armed men to either side of the entrance. She waited for them to move, knowing the game. She had seen a foolish man expose his back to her Lord's guards once before. It had only happened once; the lesson—her lesson—had been well-learned.

"Kiriel," Cook said again, his whisper making of her name a high, quiet shriek. He meant for her to walk past these men. Was it a test? Another lesson?

But she glanced back at Cook, who, of the Ospreys, she understood least, and saw at once the shifting and the shimmering about him that spoke of no such cruelty. Oh, there was a thread of it—a hint of darkness and shadow that lay about him like a fine mesh net—but it did not pull. Not now. He smiled, but the smile was weak; she did not understand it. There was no amusement in the gesture; he was not laughing at her discomfiture. No ... she thought he smiled because he was nervous. Frustrated, she turned back to the men who barred her way; they were an easier task.

The Lord's—no, the King's, and this she must not forget, lest she give herself away—guards were lightly armored and armed. They met her gaze impassively, but they met it, taking her measure as she took theirs. These men were dangerous. She could smell it. Her hand fell to her sword's black hilt and rested there, her stance changing subtly as she shifted her weight on her legs.

"Kiriel, *please*," Cook said, for the third time. Then he did something remarkably foolish: He grabbed her arm.

Kiriel di'Ashaf announced her presence by throwing him past the two guards who waited in the open doors. They had time to react before her arm had finished its carry through; the tips of two blades were beneath her chin and chest. They were narrow blades, not swords, but they did not shake at all, not even minutely, although human hands often trembled in time of danger.

She knew at once that she had done the wrong thing, at a time when the wrong thing could be fatal. For she knew with certainty that Etridian fled the chamber because he could not survive the combined might of the humans—and the god-born—who presided within. What was certain to destroy Etridian was almost certain to destroy Kiriel.

She heard Primus Duarte's angry intake of breath; heard Alexis stop breathing, and heard Auralis chuckle grimly.

Verrus Korama AKalakar moved in the quiet of the hall at her back—she could hear his distinctive step—and whispered, "I *told* you."

The Kalakar said nothing at all.

"I see," came a voice from within the great room, "that this is going to be a most . . . unusual interview." It was King Cormalyn. "If the Lord of the Compact will be so good as to order his men to grant free passage, we will overlook this unfortunate incident. And," the King continued, the words quite chilly, "if it pleases The Kalakar, she *will* maintain order within the ranks of her House while in our presence."

"Your Majesty," The Kalakar said, in as grim a tone of

voice as Kiriel had yet heard her use. She stepped past Kiriel without deigning to look at the girl, and walked without incident between the two men who stood guard. Her advisers, Vernon and Korama, followed in perfect step behind her, although it had been a long time since either man had engaged in dress maneuvers. Duarte came to stand beside Kiriel; he was flushed. He lifted a hand, thought better of it, and dropped it again as if it were stone. "We-are-going-to-talk-about-this-later."

"Yes, Primus Duarte."

Meralonne APhaniel looked up as she entered the room. Smoke wreathed his face as the tobacco in his pipe burned to ash beneath his nose, forgotten. He said something and gestured, touching his chest, his forehead, and last, his eyes—an exaggeration of form, but one necessary to make clear to the suspicious eyes of the Astari that the spell cast was entirely personal and within the Crowns' accepted canon.

In that, he showed himself to be, well, himself. Very few were the mages, or the bards, or the god-born, who dared to practice their gifts in this chamber, before these people.

She knew at once, although this did not surprise him as his vision shifted and strengthened and he saw what she carried within. Darkness, thick, heavy, *living.* Saw her face, the slight widening—and narrowing—of her eyes. Her eyes. *Impossible.*

It was not the first time in his life he had faced the impossible, nor the first time that he had been asked to act upon it.

"Your Majesty," he said, the words clear although the shocked murmurs that rose as the thrown Kalakar House Guard did were not quiet. "This one must not be allowed to live."

That, of course, changed everything.

Duarte Samison AKalakar, known to few of the people in this room and liked by less, stepped neatly in front of Kiriel di'Ashaf, although every muscle in his body tensed with the *wrongness* of exposing his back to her. He knew that, had she not been dumped on his hands and into his unit, he would have been standing, shoulder to shoulder, with Meralonne APhaniel, a man whom he remembered well—if from the distance differing levels of power and experience imposed upon the members of the Order of Knowledge.

But she *had* been placed there. She was an Osprey, untamed, untrained, quite solitary. And he knew for the first time, in this hall with too many spectators—all of them people that Kalakar emphatically did not wish to offend—that he intended to keep her, to train her, and to send her out after prey, just as he had the rest of the Ospreys, the too-deadly, too-rebellious men and women who had become his.

"I wouldn't," he said softly, to the mage whose hair now looked like a sheen of ice, "advise it."

It was not a good day.

She should have known, when the horse tried to kill the girl, that the girl was not meant to leave Kalakar. But Ellora was stubborn in her own right, and besides, if not for the intervention of Kiriel di'Ashaf, the boy, Ser Valedan, would be dead at the hands of a creature the likeness of whose voice was buried in the heart of the woman that Ellora had been, over sixteen years ago, when the city of Averalaan lay under siege of a darkness and death that her people—to a man—were unable to stop. To even act against.

Memories dimmed with time; you could fool yourself into thinking that they had finally released all hold. But they remained, and they could catch you and tear at you at the most inconvenient of times. *Where were you,* she thought, as her gaze skirted across the features of each of the men and women who stood, staring at Duarte and Kiriel di'Ashaf in the wake of Meralonne's words. *Where were you during that Henden?*

She knew that each and every man and woman in the room could answer. Where they were when they first heard those attenuated screams. And where they had been when the last of the cries, like the flickering flame of a candle, had died into a silence that should have been blessed.

Then, the darkness had reigned.

Almost. Her hand fell to her sword a moment; the gesture was so natural she had to force it down and away.

* * *

But King Cormalyn turned a cool glance to Meralonne APhaniel. "Your advice, Member APhaniel, is noted. It would please us if, in future, you might tender that advice in a less dramatic fashion." He turned to The Kalakar. "There will be no incident, Kalakar, but there *will* be explanation." Last, he looked upon the man who wore Primus' marks. "Primus," he said distantly. "Because of the respect we bear the Commander, we will not have your marks for the audacity you have shown in this room."

Duarte looked momentarily nonplussed, and then he had the grace to flush. Very awkwardly, he sheathed his weapons, trying to remember exactly when he'd drawn them. *I warned her,* he thought. *The Ospreys are not dress guards.* Of course, he'd thought himself to be above their usual displays of inappropriate temper and awkwardness.

He lowered his hands, and then, under the royal glare, stepped out of the way, falling into the proper posture and exposing Kiriel fully to the golden-eyed regard of King Cormalyn the Wise.

"You are not," King Cormalyn said after a moment had passed in stiff silence, "of Essalieyan."

Kiriel nodded warily. She had been told how to behave in the presence of the Kings, the Exalted, the Queens, the Heirs, and The Ten, but although she remembered the words, the actions did not come to her at all. Her legs stiffened, as the silence did; she bent slightly at the knees. No one, not even Dantallon, could have mistaken that posture for bow; she was almost in a defensive crouch.

Duarte was at her side, and she could see him wince; he knew her well enough—had observed her in the Kalakar training circles—to know that she was on the edge of a fight. He didn't know her well enough to know how close she was to falling off.

Because Kiriel knew fear—knew, better, that there was only one safe way to show it. She struggled against the fabric of her life, and won, but it was close. She knelt.

"Kiriel di'Ashaf," the King said quietly, as if aware of the struggle and its result. "We wish to see what magic governs."

Duarte said something, and The Kalakar; it was clear immediately that many of the people in this too-crowded, too-large room did not understand what the King meant. But she did. And she met his golden eyes, seeing a truth in them that Ashaf would have wept to know.

Ashaf.

Almost, she pulled her sword. It was there, beneath all her resolve, the memory surfacing like a corpse too hastily thrown into deep water to properly sink. She had learned all of Ashaf's lessons, and all of Isladar's; she had taken her father's mantle. Power? She understood power. Understood its use, its allure, its imperative. And what good had it done her?

She had survived.

If that meant anything.

She felt the thrum in her throat before she heard it, but she knew that she was growling. Why did it return to her this way? Ashaf. Memory.

She could not afford to be caught by it now; not when the eyes of this King were upon her—this King, and all of the men and women who served him.

Because he knew, of course, just as she had known it of him. She was god-born. Turning her face slightly, she could see that glimmer of recognition in the eyes of the Exalted as well. Yet she knew that they were not peers; they were not kin. In this empire, they held power; they *defined* it.

Ashaf returned; Ashaf's admonition, her fear. *In this south, Na'kiri, they will kill you if they can see the color of your eyes.*

But they are the color of the sun.

No, Ashaf had said, that same sun coloring her pale hair and adding minute lines to the skin around her eyes, her lips, her cheeks. *They are not the color of the sun; what color could be so harsh and so important? They are,* Ashaf added, with a slight pursing of lips, *the mark of demons, of tainted birth. Remember,* she said, quartering herself with the moon's sign, *That the sun makes deserts.*

Tainted birth.

Kiriel could not remember how old she had been when she had first been told this; could not remember how old she had been when she had last heard it.

But she remembered sitting at the gray-covered, bent,

chubby knees of Ashaf, the smooth stone beneath her, and above it, a rug, a thing that Ashaf had made of rags and cloth and twine, with no sense of color or texture to mar it. She felt the warm touch of hands across her hair and the line of her cheek; she closed her eyes and she could smell dough, butter, sugar, sweat, and even dust—the things that made Ashaf unusual among the humans at court.

And she said, *Yes, Ashaf,* and the old woman clucked and murmured as if the thing in her lap were a child and not—

And not Kiriel.

There should have been anger. Or pain. She felt it building, like a wildling, inside of her throat. But before she could give it voice, give it vent, she felt something else. Looking down at her left hand she saw the ring that she had picked up from the earthen path that Evayne trod. It was glowing softly—so softly that she might have thought it a trick of the light, if not for the fact that it warmed her hand.

As if—

As if someone were holding it.

She tried to pull free, and it followed her, and the action, the reaction, brought back other memories.

With something approaching a sigh, she lowered her head a moment, as if in human prayer. Then she let it go.

The darkness dissolved, like tears, from her irises, trailing down the perfect, pale curve of her cheeks before evaporating, and as she lifted her face, those eyes were golden, and glowing in the room's odd light. The line of her shoulders fell slightly; it seemed to those who watched that she relaxed as the mask left her face.

Dark-haired and golden-eyed, Kiriel looked up into the face of King Cormalyn, as if his gaze were the only thing in the room.

"Who is your parent?" the King asked softly. "And does The Kalakar know that you are god-born?"

"No," Kiriel said quietly. She took a breath. "I was told to hide my birth because golden eyes are the mark of demon blood."

"You are from the South." It was not a question.

And because it was not a question, she did not need to offer a lie in return.

"And the answer to the first question?" another voice said. Both King and Kiriel turned; the slender, pale-haired mage had moved quietly, and now stood, arms at his sides, eyes a silver, unblinking gray, not twenty feet away.

"I—do not know."

"Kiriel di'Ashaf," King Cormalyn said, "it is unnecessary to hide your past, or the truth of it, here. I am Wisdom-born, and my brother, Justice-born. But we have seen the Luck-born, and the Mother-born, and in our time, we have even seen Miara's brood, although they survive only a short time before the Mother claims them. You are born of a god, but you are *not* a god, and you will not be held accountable for the actions of your parent, unless you have chosen to follow in their footsteps."

"Majesty, with all due respect, I must tell you that you are being . . . unwise."

"Oh?"

Kiriel had heard that word before, said in exactly that tone. She smiled at the familiarity of the anger in the King's tone.

"What counsel does a member of the Order offer the *son* of the Lord of Wise Counsel?"

"Just this: There are gods whose children we should not suffer."

"I have said, Member APhaniel," was the King's steely, patient reply, "that this is not the case. How will you gainsay me?"

"I will tell you, if you will hear it, whose daughter she is. And then, Majesty, you will judge for yourself."

"Very well," King Cormalyn said. "Tell me, if you deem it necessary."

"*No.* If that information is to be revealed, it will be because she chooses to divulge it."

King, mage, and god-born girl turned in the direction of a voice that was familiar to each of them for different reasons. Standing in the room's center, already surrounded by men and women who had walked, like shadows, between the standing members of this powerful, exclusive court, was a hooded figure who wore robes of midnight blue.

Lifting her hands, she pulled the cowl of those robes

away from the gaunt lines of her face. Her cheek was awash in blood, her eyes dark with exhaustion. And her hair was a peppered darkness, pulled tight and held by a knot that could not, quite, be seen.

"I know you," King Cormalyn said, the first to recover his voice. "You have aged . . . well."

"And you," was her quiet reply. She spoke as if the force of her first statement had drained what little strength remained her. "Majesty, what I have said—it is of more import than I can tell you without revealing what *cannot* be revealed. Let me say only this: This war, the coming war, and the battles that will link them—they are *defined,* for each of us, by choice, by the freedom *to* choose." She sagged, her shoulders curling inward.

"Hold her there a moment," another voice said.

"Is the entire court to feel free to interrupt an interview of this nature?" It was King Reymalyn, speaking for the first time, an edge of humor in the stiff words. He rarely showed humor, but then again, this was his brother's hall.

"Not the entire court, Majesty." A slightly built man stepped around the Kings' poorly armed guards. "But certainly the healer. Hello, Evayne."

"Hello, Dantallon."

"You know each other as well?" Meralonne asked, the words sharp.

"Oh, yes," Dantallon replied. "I first met her years ago, under the auspices of a man who recognized the early signs of my talent and thought to train and develop it." His smile was grim. "And I saw her regularly throughout my training. It seemed that we barely released her, and before we could turn around she was walking—or crawling—through our doors again."

"How is Levec?" she asked wearily.

A shadow passed over Dantallon's face.

An answering shadow crossed hers. "I see," she said quietly. "I do not have time, Dantallon." Her eyes were wide and round, her face unnaturally pale. "I cannot stay."

"Of course not," he replied, and held out his arms just quickly enough to catch her before she collapsed. He cursed then, unmindful of who might hear him. "I'm sorry, Majesty. But she must be taken to the infirmary."

He glared at the back of one of the men. "Devon," he said, between clenched teeth, "I mean *now*."

"I see," Member APhaniel said softly, as the doors closed upon the two men and their ungainly burden. "Majesty, let me withdraw my qualified advice. You are the King of Wise Counsel, and I am but a mage."

"I am not so certain that I do not wish to hear your advice," the King replied, equally thoughtful.

They both turned to look at the young woman. Her eyes were upon the door.

"You know her," Meralonne said.

Kiriel di'Ashaf nodded without turning. "She brought me here. To Kalakar." Bitterly, she added, "I owe her my life."

"You don't sound as if you think much of the debt." It was Meralonne.

"She shouldn't have interfered."

"No," he replied, as he stared at her. "But she always does. And although I do not claim to understand all of her motivation, she chose her risk when she chose you. I have been—we have all been—the beneficiary of many of her risks. Keep your counsel, Kiriel. For my part, I apologize." He paused, and then his voice grew quite cool. "But I would give much to know how your human parent and your immortal parent . . . met. And where."

Kiriel did not reply.

"Which leaves us," King Cormalyn said, "with a problem of a different nature. Kiriel di'Ashaf, you wear the colors of the Kalakar House Guard. You drew weapon, without Our permission, in the Great Chamber, and your House will be measured and fined accordingly. If we accept this as a given," he added, glancing at The Kalakar and waiting just long enough to see her quiet nod, "and we dismiss, for the moment, the question of your birth, we are left with a few facts.

"You were aware of the creature before it made its attack. You faced it, upon the chamber floor, and you recognized it. I believe that it recognized you."

Kiriel did not reply.

"You were able to stand against its attack—and you injured it before it left."

She nodded.

"Are you aware of what the creature is?"

"He is one of the kinlords," she said softly, her golden eyes narrowing. "He is the weakest."

"Why did you recognize him?"

"We've—we've fought before."

"Why did you call him Allasakar-Etridian?"

At that, she smiled, and the smile was cold. "To insult him," she said softly. "He is called Lord Etridian. To call him Allasakar-Etridian is completely correct—but it stresses his weakness and his subservience."

"I see."

Her mouth fell open; she paled.

"Does he, indeed, choose to serve the God *we* do not name?"

"Y—yes. He's kinlord. But the kin serve the King— serve their Lord. They don't have a choice. The Lord of the Hells bears the mantle."

"What did you say?" It was Sigurne who spoke. She stepped into the conversation like a frail, kindly old woman. But her eyes were clear, and her voice was strong.

Kiriel's shoulders tensed. "The mantle," she replied.

"And this mantle is?"

"It is the crown of the Lord of the Hells. It is the god-right by which He rules." She braced herself.

"And how do you know of this, Kiriel?"

Kiriel did not answer.

"And how do you know of the conventions by which these creatures are called and named?"

Meralonne turned a moment, as if to speak in her defense, but he fell silent as he met her eyes.

"Please answer her question." A new voice. A voice that Kiriel did not recognize. But she knew the man; he had stood, between the Kings, in a rigid silence, and his eyes had never left her face. Danger.

Oh, it was clear that she had said too much.

"You will answer, please."

"I—I can't."

"You're lying."

She lifted her chin, straightened her shoulders; her hand fell to the hilt of the sword that she had been allowed to keep. "Very well. I won't." She planted her legs firmly against ground. It was clear, to Kiriel, that the time to make that stand had come.

Clear to Alexis, Duarte, Auralis.

And clear to Cook. But only Cook was stupid enough to interfere—a second time—when she had already made it obvious what she thought of such interference. He did not make the mistake of touching her, and he did not make the mistake of drawing a weapon. But he moved to stand beside her, his arms crossed tight against his chest, as if he needed to hold his hands idle.

She glanced up at him—the difference in their heights would always be there—and her brow creased, as if the effort of speech was wearying. Frustrating.

"*What* do you *want*?" she demanded, breath passing between her clenched teeth as she glared at him.

"To face," he replied calmly, as if speaking to a cornered wild creature, "any danger you do. You're an *Osprey*, Kiriel. That means something in my books."

"In your books," Alexis said mockingly, as she came to join him. "You don't even read, let alone do numbers."

"Primus," The Kalakar said icily.

Duarte shrugged. "I did warn you," he said, saluting halfheartedly. "They're Ospreys for a reason, Kalakar."

"If they continue to embarrass my House with their display, they will be corpses for a reason."

"Well if *that's* the case," Auralis said, his smile a lazy accompaniment to his long drawl, "I'd hate to be excluded. Sanderson?"

Sanderson glanced at Duarte for permission. He was young, and he had been admitted into the company after the Southern wars had ended. Duarte liked him enough that he failed to give that permission.

"Kiriel," the Kalakar said. "This is not the time or the place for such a display. If the Ospreys will not stand down, they will be disciplined. But they are not under the King's eye here. You are. This *is* Essalieyan. You are in the heart of *Averalaan Aramarelas*. Not even the Kings have the right to execute by fiat those they deem dangerous. They do have the right to defend themselves. Do you understand?"

No. She wanted to shout now. Wanted to shout it as loudly as she dared; to fill the hall with the roar of a voice she knew would shock every man and woman—save perhaps the mage and the frail old woman—in the chamber. She wanted to pull her sword, and have an end to it, one way or the other.

This—this *Empire*—it was not hers. It made no *sense*. She knew human courts. She had spent time observing the Shining Court, and she knew, as only those who truly understand power could, that person for person, *this* court outranked any humans that she had seen there, save three.

Yes, humans were not of the kin, but they were cold and calculating when they chose to play their games of power against each other. They were ice and steel when they chose to watch the kin at play.

And they did not gather in such a group, for such an inquisition, without a victim. Not for long.

She had known that she was the victim when the mage had first cast his sight upon her. She had even accepted it, on some level. She was weary, but she was relieved, for here, *finally,* was something that made sense.

Evayne played her own game; Evayne played her hand. She did not understand the game itself, but to be a pawn was something that she understood, however bitterly. But even Evayne was not proof against this man, this last player. She thought him more dangerous than the mage, although she could not say why; he was darker.

At last. An enemy. A challenge. A fight.

Then *they* came, unraveling this one corner of the certainty that she had managed to weave so painstakingly around herself: Cook, who hovered about her as if he thought to protect her; Auralis, copper-haired and golden-skinned, the darkest of the Ospreys; the man she most understood—until now; Alexis, dark-haired and yet pale, oddly beautiful for her distance and her heated anger—perhaps the person she least understood.

Go away.

But she did not say the words, and if she had, they would not have listened; she felt certain of it.

Go home, she told herself, forcing her shoulders back. *You've seen these lands. There is no place for you in them. Go home. Make your place, and hold it. These lands will not survive no matter what you decide.*

Go home.

"Kiriel," the old woman said, and Kiriel looked up blindly. "How long has it been since you slept?"

"I don't need to sleep."

"Oh, my dear," the old woman said, and her eyes were full of a terrible pity. "But you do." She lifted a hand; light fell from it, dripping onto the ground like liquid water. Or liquid fire. Transfixed, Kiriel watched. She watched the light, fascinated by it.

Afraid of it.

Looking up, she saw the face of the King—King Cormalyn. And beneath his face, unquestioned, unquestionable, she saw that pale, luminous beauty that no longer existed anywhere in the Shining Court. King Reymalyn shone that brightly. The men and the woman that The Kalakar had called the Exalted were brighter still.

Isladar had taught her, years ago, to abjure the light, the light's compelling, compulsive beauty. And it had been easy, then.

What do they see in me?

She wanted to ask them, but she knew the answer: Nothing. They did not have the blood.

The light that the old woman had dropped upon the floor had crept, unwatched, to form a circle around her feet, separating her from the Ospreys. She looked up; saw that the Ospreys had not noticed the light that surrounded her, rising like a finely beaded mist—or a blood-wraith.

Yet this woman, no luminescent beauty, was not a dark one either; she was gray and light, that perfect, knowable blend of color that Kiriel had grown accustomed to, in Ashaf. That she had grown—

Say it. To love.

That was the horror of it, that she *could* say it in the silence of her thoughts, no matter how much it made her writhe.

She knew what the light would do when it touched her; she thought that the woman might even suspect it. But she saw another woman's face briefly, and she held fast, remembering.

She did not even cry out when the light burned her skin, seeking her eyes and her parted lips.

CHAPTER TWENTY-ONE

Sigurne had survived a great many things in her life, and most of them she kept in the past. She did not speak of the wars she had seen, although they were far too many; she did not speak of her life in a far away village, when magery had been a whispered curse, and its onset had almost destroyed her. She did not speak of her first master, although if pressed, she might politely say that he had passed away some time ago. In fact, Sigurne Mellifas rarely spoke at all of matters that were not issues in the here and now, although when she spoke, she could be quite decisive. And the members of the famed Order of Knowledge were certain, to their sorrow, that the grave that time dug slowly for her would be the repository of all those many years of accumulated knowledge, for she kept no diaries or journals of those early years.

Yet not a mage—or a member—of the Order itself would have ever said that she was incapable of sharing.

Sigurne knew pain when she saw it. Her brown eyes widened, clearing and darkening almost at once. "Mother's heart," she said. "What have they done to you?" She gestured, a movement of fingers and lips that ended in an abrupt stillness.

"Kiriel," she said softly. "My name is Sigurne Mellifas, and you would honor me by remembering it."

The younger woman froze; eyes that were golden by birth shone, catching the light too strongly. She looked, for that moment, like a wild, hunted creature—not a cornered one, nor a frenzied one, but like a creature at harbor who has seen that the hunter carries no weapon and cannot quite believe the lack.

"I am Kiriel di'Ashaf." She spoke quietly. "And I, too, would be honored."

"You must sleep," Sigurne said, walking toward Kiriel as if the girl was no danger—and no mystery—at all.

"Is that—is that what it was?"

"Yes. It was meant to have a—a different effect." She paused. "Have you slept since you arrived here?"

Kiriel shrugged, her dark hair dancing a moment in the light as if it had a life of its own. Or as if it sought to shake itself free from the last of the touch of her spell. "I don't need to sleep much," she said at last.

"But you do," Sigurne said, repeating the earlier words. She lifted her hands again, and reached out. Kiriel took a step back, a step away, but her movement was as slow and cautious as the older mage's.

"Who are you?" Kiriel whispered, as Sigurne drifted closer.

"Sigurne," the white-haired woman said. "And when you wake, I will be watching; none will pass the guard I set." Her hands met Kiriel's chest.

The girl froze a moment, and then her face clouded, its lines folding before they stiffened into a mask behind which she could hide. "I don't want to sleep," she said.

"I know," Sigurne replied, catching her in arms that seemed, to all who watched, too frail to bear such a burden. Awkwardly, she pulled the girl against her, while the Ospreys watched.

Who, after all, would consider Sigurne Mellifas enough of a threat that they would raise either hand or voice against her?

No one. Not even the Lord of the Compact.

"Member Mellifas," King Cormalyn said, "Will you sit with the girl?"

"I cannot carry her," was Sigurne's quiet reply. "But if you wish her to remain in *Avantari*, I believe it is best if I retire with her. She will sleep, I think, for many hours, and she will wake hungry." She gestured to Cook, and he rushed to obey the request that she did not put into words; he held out his arms and caught Kiriel.

"And that is it?" the King said softly, staring at the hushed court. "Twenty-seven men and women are dead at the hands of a creature that only she was fast enough to stop, and in the end, the answer we are to derive from her is either nothing or sleep?"

Sigurne made no reply.

"No, Majesty," The Kalakar said, her voice quite loud compared to Sigurne's. "Because the creature was not sent to kill the twenty-seven—although they are dead, unjustly, regardless—but to kill the Tyr'agar. Valedan kai di'Leonne.

"We have seen creatures of this kind before. Sixteen years ago, they almost destroyed us, and they came within an hour of shattering the city's spirit. I can still hear the screams when I close my eyes in the daylight."

"Enough," the Cormaris-born King said, flinching. "There is not a man or woman here who cannot."

"Very well. I believe you know the point I wish to make."

"Make it," the King replied.

"There is no Tyr'agar in the Dominion of Annagar. But if we do not interfere, there will be one in seven short days. The Festival of the Sun, Your Majesty. And that man is a man who has proved, at least twice now, that he is willing to use these creatures.

"We have faced this threat once before, and if it failed, it was partly because Kalliaris chose to smile." She drew breath, settling her shoulders into a more comfortable—and stiffer—position. "Only a fool or a desperate man depends on that Lady's smile. We don't even know if the man who will claim the Tor Leonne is human at all. Lord Cordufar was not."

"If a man will be declared ruler of the Tor Leonne, it will be in nine days, at Festival's close, and not seven, at its start," the King said neutrally.

The Kalakar nodded.

"And there is no guarantee that the kin who arrived here is working in the employ of the man who will be crowned. We know, certainly, that that man has much to gain from the death of our hostage—but perhaps the kin wish to consolidate power under a pawn, and that man is unaware of just how far their efforts extend. Remember, Kalakar, that Lord Cordufar was under the auspices of The Darias. I believe subsequent events proved clearly— to all of The Ten's satisfaction—that The Darias labored in ignorance of Cordufar's nature and mission."

She shrugged; it was clear that, as far as Annagar was concerned, she did not believe this to be the case. "I rode," she said neutrally, "to the Dominion's border when the father of our hostage declared war upon the Empire. It would not only not surprise me to see the clans use the Allasakari, it would surprise me if they didn't."

"Unfair," another voice said. Princess Mirialyn. "The clan Leonne would not, for weight of both history and blood, use the Allasakari. Nor, in my opinion, would the Radann. And they are not the only forces within the Dominion."

"The clan Leone is not a force at all; the Radann are puppets; they serve no true god." The Kalakar, as always when she felt her case strongly, made it bluntly.

"It seems to me," King Cormalyn said softly, "that you are advocating war."

The Kalakar lifted her chin. "No, Your Majesty. There *will* be war. We cannot prevent it. Averda and Mancorvo are already dedicated to that fight, and they are the Terreans which border us." She drew breath. "But I know the Annagarians. Valedan's a boy, and an untried one at that, but he's the bloodline. If Callesta and Lamberto will declare themselves for his clan, many of the clansmen will follow."

" 'Many.' "

She had the good grace to wince slightly. "Majesty," she said, "we believe that it is clan Marente—or possibly Ser Alesso di'Marente—that hopes to benefit from the slaughter of both the clan Leonne and the Imperial hostages. But he will do so without the benefit of the Sun Sword. And that will count against him in the war.

"If Valedan wins, we can be certain that it won't be because of *Allasakari* magic. If he rules, we know that his reign starts without the taint of that god. If we turn our backs, it is not just the Dominion that will suffer. The Empire will suffer as well. When the Allasakari ruled two centuries ago, the southern half of the Empire was raided and preyed upon by the Priests and their summoned cohort. The countryside still remembers, and while it remembers that the Twin Kings eventually rode to war to end that threat, they remember the time that it took, and the losses. Let us not repeat that history."

"And you would suggest?"

"I would suggest," she replied, as neutral in tone as the King, "that the decision to wage a war is a political one; the decision to join a war, equally political."

King Cormalyn's smile was a rare one. "We have already requested a meeting with the Averdan Try'agnate. But I believe that The Ten are not united in their views on this subject."

Ellora shook her head grimly. "They will be," she said, "after today."

"Very well. The Ten will be informed of the outcome of that meeting." His gaze narrowed. "But, Kalakar, we need the information that your young Sentrus has."

"Yes, Your Majesty," she said.

Duarte's expression was singularly stern, but he kept his silence.

"Meralonne. You've been avoiding me."

"I? Avoid Sigurne Mellifas?" Pipe smoke curled in the air beneath his chin like the tail of a ghostly cat. "If I wished to avoid you, Sigurne, I would hardly have agreed to meet you in this healerie."

"Matteos," she said dryly, "is most persuasive. It *was* Matteos who delivered the message?"

Meralonne winced.

"And it will be Dantallon," she said, "who will provide you with a bed of your own in the healerie if you don't douse the tobacco in that pipe."

"I feel, as I grow older," Meralonne replied, running a crooked finger around the pipe's black rim, "that the entirety of the Empire conspires to rob me of the few little pleasures that remain to a man in his dotage."

But she had already turned in her seat, and her eyes were upon the quiet profile of a young woman in sleep's thrall. "Allasakar," Sigurne said, her voice a whisper.

Meralonne made no reply, although his confederate spoke a name that was not spoken in the Empire.

"It is said that the Lord of the Hells cannot father a god-born child," she continued. "It *is* impossible." She reached out, and her hand hovered above the pale girl's mouth, as if catching the air that she exhaled. "And yet the evidence is here, and mounting.

"Do you think the Kings would suffer such a child to live?"

"You heard King Cormalyn. A god-born child is not held responsible for the actions of his parent."

"Yes. But you know, as well as I that he might not have

spoken so freely if it were not accepted wisdom that the Lord of the Hells *cannot* breed."

The platinum-haired mage shrugged and set about carefully emptying the bowl of his pipe. "It is accepted wisdom that the progeny will not come to term," he corrected.

"Meralonne. That woman. Evayne. Did you not once have a student by that name?"

"I always regret the fact that you spend so much of your time in silence," Meralonne replied softly. "Until you speak, Sigurne." He began to fill the bowl of his pipe. "Compared to you, my gentle lady, Dantallon is not to be feared."

She waited in companionable silence until he'd pressed the fresh leaves down and lit them with a spark and word.

"Did you understand what she said?"

"Pardon?"

"Did you understand what she meant when she referred to the mantle of the Lord?"

"Sigurne, is this another test?"

"Of your background? No, old friend. It is completely as it seems: A question. Hide behind your answer as you like; I often do."

"And today?"

"Today I will tell you that *I* understood what she meant by it. And the fact that she knows of it, and the fact that you thought to interrupt the King himself when he sought to offer this child reassurances—and that, Meralonne, I consider somewhat ill-advised—tells me more than I wanted to know."

"And you a member of the Order of Knowledge," he said, his tone gently mocking.

"And I, a member of the Magi, and the governing adviser to the magisterial guards. There are arts that have been forbidden, Meralonne, and no one has spoken against them with more force than I."

"With more force? I can think of any number. With more heart, none."

Were she a younger woman, she might have blushed. She did not, although she looked pleased at the offered compliment. Her face was lined with age and time; even her hair seemed fragile and delicate. Yet the steel was there, and Meralonne thought, as he watched her, that as long as that steel survived, she would.

"Very well," he said, and he bowed almost gallantly. "Yes, Sigurne. I know what she spoke of. I will trouble you not to repeat that confession, and I will take the trouble not to repeat yours.

"When the Lord took the throne of the Hells there were no humans—or so it is said. He could pass freely between that world and this, and until the Covenant of Man was made, he ruled two domains: a mortal domain, and an immortal one.

"Upon this world, his followers were legion, and when the Covenant was made, they were offered a choice: To stay in this world, diminished and hidden, or to accompany the Lord of their choosing.

"They chose Him, although there was little doubt that they would make such a choice—and little understanding of the choice so made. But the divide itself was not meant to be breached by those born of this world. And the kin," he added softly, "*were* born of the gods and the wildness of *this* world, whether they will it or no. He did not—and I believe does not—have the power to bring his followers, in flesh, to the Hells of his making. And his followers lack the immortal shard that humans call soul.

"He refused to agree to the terms of the Covenant, and although he was weakened greatly by the fall of his City, he was not without power. The gods spoke, and at length, because of the Mother's intervention, they joined their powers and, thread by thread, they wove the mantle of which Kiriel di'Ashaf spoke.

"Allasakar had no hand in its making," the silver-haired mage continued, staring past her, although his eyes seemed to be upon her upturned face. "And it is said that the mantle was a wondrous thing; a thing beyond compare. That the mortal eye was too impoverished to perceive its beauty.

"It matters not. The mantle was given, by the gods, to their unloved brother, that he might take his followers—who were also ill-loved—with him, instead of leaving them to trouble the human world. When he donned the mantle—if donning is the correct word—the kin became as one with him. Which had the rather fortunate effect of making the kin subservient, whether they willed it or no, to his will, like parts of a body. Although they served him in this world because he defined power, they served willingly. The mantle's creation—and use—robbed them of that patina of dignity." His smile, a sudden flash of teeth too perfect for a man his age, was cold.

"If it were merely donned," Sigurne said softly, "then it could be removed. The kin are creatures who know no quest but the search for power."

"Indeed," he replied, still distant. "They are not the only ones. But the mantle *is* donned, and it may be removed or displaced. The gods created well, Sigurne. Even if the kin could indeed overpower and destroy their Lord, no one of the kin could bear the mantle's weight without paying the ultimate price. They could not wear that mantle to gain dominion over their own. For that matter, no mortal could, either. It was made for Allasakar, and it knows its master. Or so it is said."

"Meralonne, I sometimes wonder just how deeply and how completely your knowledge runs." The words were cool. "I believe you have now said more than I knew."

"Have I? How foolish of me." He exhaled a thin stream of smoke into the air between them. "Only a god can wear the mantle, Sigurne." He smiled. "Although I'm certain that the kin would be happy to support any mortal attempt to steal such a cloak as the Lord of the Hells wears. If there is more to know, I do not know it; nor can I be certain that this knowledge is indeed fact."

She nodded almost absently. "I know how I learned of that mantle," Sigurne said quietly. "I won't ask how you did. You are of the Magi, Meralonne, and the past has scarred you.

"This one—this girl—she seems so young to me, and yet so deadly." She turned to meet Meralonne's steel-gray eyes. "I will be honest."

"Are you ever anything else?"

"Meralonne, please.

"If the Kings had ordered her death, I would have done what I had to do to aid them. And I do not think I would have been displeased.

"But I saw something in her, and that something—it underlined the truth of the words King Cormalyn spoke in his ignorance of her parent. She is not all that *he* is, or rather, he is not all that *she* is.

"These ones are always the dangerous ones," Sigurne continued, looking away again. "Because when we hope, we can be so blind and foolish."

Meralonne nodded quietly. "In youth," he said, speaking as if from a great distance, "we believe, and the death of belief forces us to disavow all belief. But that disavowal, time softens, and if we do not believe, we hope. Belief is easier to kill, somehow, and its death easier to bear."

Sigurne did not reply.

"She had no right to promise that." Alexis was pale and spoke with a soft, soft voice. Always a bad sign. Duarte was pleasantly surprised to see that her dagger remained in its sheath; it often did not when she paced in anger across the worn fragments of what had no doubt been expensive carpet. "The Ospreys—Hells, the House Guards—don't have to speak of their past when they make their oath. The past is *forgotten,* Duarte. Or don't you remember your vows?"

He knew that Alexis' temper was a reflection of the rest of the company's. He also knew that Cook had come close to unforgivable insubordination—as opposed to the customary forgivable type that the Ospreys were famous for—when Kiriel di'Ashaf had been summarily remanded into the care of the Kings' healer. He'd demanded to be left as a guard. *That* had been tricky.

But most of the Ospreys didn't understand politics. Or strategy, if it didn't involve battle.

"Duarte?"

He shook himself. "I remember my vows."

"You were conveniently silent."

"We were in the Hall of Wise Counsel. The only Osprey who hadn't already humiliated House Kalakar was Sanderson. If I'd spoken another word, the Ospreys would have a new leader."

Alexis snorted. "They barely follow the old one. The Kalakar wouldn't dare."

Duarte exhaled as if he'd been holding his breath, and in some sense, he had. This had been easier twelve years ago. He wasn't sure why. Wasn't ready to examine his own motives or reactions either.

Alexis had been demoted in rank; she was once again a

mere Sentrus—funny how most of the Ospreys were—
and didn't have farther to fall. Which was not the same as
having little to lose. The Kalakar had seen fit to discipline
the Ospreys for their disgraceful performance as honor
guards. She had not chosen to dismiss them, and the difference was lost on no one. It had been a trying day. A
long one.

And it was the will of a malignant deity—which one,
he wasn't certain, but he'd find out—that Alexis had
decided to make it longer. He folded his arms against his
chest, and tried not to think about how very lovely she
was when she was angry.

Better to think about how deadly she was instead.

"Alexis, I realize that it's irrelevant, but you don't even
like the girl, and a reliable source said that you were
trying to decide whether or not to ask my permission to
kill her."

"If I was going to wait to ask your permission," she
replied a little tartly, "I couldn't dislike her *that* much."
Her eyes narrowed until they looked like the dark edge of
small blades. "And you're right. It's irrelevant." The
smile hadn't quite vanished from the corners of her lips;
Duarte allowed himself to relax. Slightly. "You know I
don't like her much, and not just because she has no sense
of humor."

Sense of humor, Duarte thought, was not among
Alexis' many virtues either. Discretion in situations of
this nature was among his.

"None of us are very comfortable with her, and I don't
think that's likely to change much. She's just too dangerous, Duarte. Auralis can't bring her down in either of
the two ways he's used to, and he's trying. Hard." She
shrugged, but the sharp smile returned briefly to her face;
there weren't many men or women who could put Auralis
in his place—without even being aware that that's what
they were doing. "But she seems to be true to her word
when she gives it. And she's an Osprey, like it or not,
because you were too gutless to tell The Kalakar you
didn't want her, period. She's tried to fit in." Alexis
shrugged. "Doesn't matter; she's in. And we, as Kalakar
House Guards—and Ospreys—are going to be true to our
own."

"The Kalakar *is* the Commander."

"And The Kalakar will *not* force answers out of any of us." The *or else* hung unspoken in the air, as most of Alexis' genuine threats did. "Speaking of which, when can we go and collect her?"

"Alexis, I suppose it would be too much to ask you to go bother Auralis?" One glance at her glacial stare was answer enough. "The healer felt that she'd be unconscious—as opposed to asleep—for the better part of a full day. Which means that if you show up before the third, you won't be welcome."

"So what else is new?"

"Alexis."

Meralonne stood over the bed of the healerie's only other occupant. His mage-sight saw the fine mesh of light that lay against her body like a crystal lattice, and he knew better than to touch her, although he thought, if he pressed the point, he might survive unscathed. He had no desire to press that point.

She was in her prime, this woman—not the timid, angry girl-child that he had first met, and not the woman who had grown from her, replacing hostility with confidence, and a precious but naive trust in his ability. But she was, he thought, a woman who might well be the age his apprentice would be, had she lived a life like any other.

He could still hear her denial, her anger, and, yes— laced around and between the hostile words—her pain as if it were yesterday. Meralonne was not Evayne; the years, such as they were, did not soften his grudges.

What can you tell me? he thought. *Who are you, Evayne?* For though he knew who she had been, that was a long time past. Experience always scarred and twisted a man, and this woman, his equal in power, had experienced much.

As if she could hear his words, she woke at that moment; her eyes snapped open, widened as if in shock. And then she sat up, seeing him, and seeing something else besides. Before he could speak, she leaned forward unsteadily, grabbing a thin, pale hand. He was not sure if he would have allowed her to touch him, had he been aware enough to step back. But he hadn't been, and her hand was shaking and cool where it gripped his.

"Go with them," she said, her bruised lips moving

awkwardly around the words. "When they go to Averda, you *must* travel with them."

"Must?" he questioned quietly.

"Yes," she said, and she coughed, and he heard the rattle of her chest. *Fire,* he thought. Fire's air. He lifted a hand, waving it to catch someone's attention.

"The healer, Evayne," he said quietly.

"No, no healer. Meralonne—we failed."

Dantallon appeared, like sun from the folds of cloud—or in this case, the mage thought, as the healer's accusing glare fell across him like a cudgel, like cloud across a clear sky. "Evayne," he said, his voice as stern as any angry Master's. "Lie back."

"I can't," she replied, and both men heard the wildness in her voice, the exhaustion.

"What were you doing, waking her?" Dantallon's tone was icy.

"I did not wake her," was the mage's mild reply. "But if you know her, you know that she does as she does."

"Not in *my* healerie."

"Do you lay wagers, healer?"

"No."

"A pity. I—"

"Meralonne." Her hands, again, tightly curled around his own. "We failed. Don't you understand? *We failed.*"

He understood, this time, that she meant those words to include him, and they had done very little in concert since she abandoned her training after their bitter, bitter argument.

In fact, they had only done one thing as allies.

On the last day of Henden, in the year 410. The dark days that year had been darker than the Blood Barons who inspired them could have imagined.

She coughed again, but she did not release his hands.

He returned her grip, shunting the healer aside, all pretense, all deference, forgotten. "What do you mean, Evayne? What do you mean, we failed?" He shook her, as if by doing so the information would fall more cleanly out of her swollen mouth.

"I wanted to have proof before I spoke," she said. "But I couldn't be certain." Her voice held no hope at all. Her eyes held less. "And I wanted to believe that it meant something. His death. All the deaths."

"*What do you mean?*"

"The Shining City," she said. And then she did something that he had not seen her do for twenty years. She wept. "The Shining City has risen."

"Evayne—were that city to rise, we *would* know. You might remember that it resides beneath the streets of the old city."

"I've seen it," she said.

His face was the color of ash as he turned to the healer; the healer had frozen in place, unable to offer his customary indignation at Meralonne's rough handling of his patient, at Meralonne's arrogance and interference.

"Where?" he asked. "Evayne!" Then he shook her again, angry at himself for asking the wrong question. "*When?*"

"I don't know! I don't know," she said again.

"Then *how* do you know it?"

She reached into her robes, wincing in pain as she pulled out the crystal shard that she had won so many years ago. Thrusting it forward, she said, "Look yourself, look! It's there—it has to be there—"

He lifted a hand and spoke three words before the healer could stop him.

She sat upright, as if struck; she had been, although the hand was not visible.

"Tell me," he said quietly.

"I cannot tell you more," she answered, and violet steel shuttered the inside of her eyes. The glimpse of wildness was gone, and although the tears had not dried on her cheeks, he would not have believed she had cried them had he not witnessed their fall.

"Dantallon," she whispered grimly, and then she lowered her face. "Askeyia will never return." Her brow creased, her lips twisted; she closed her eyes a moment as she heard the healer's sharp voice, his broken breath.

"Evayne?" It was the only word that Dantallon spoke.

She did not answer him. Instead, she turned again to the man who had been, and never would be again, her master. "Your word, Meralonne. Your word that you will go South."

"I grant it," he replied, ignoring the nails that pressed so tightly into his hands they drew blood. "What do you believe the danger to be?"

"The kin," she said faintly. "There will be deaths in the Dominion that will make the slaughter in Averalaan seem trivial by comparison."

He met her eyes, then, silver to violet, steel to steel. *There is more,* he thought, and he knew, although knowledge and the seeking of it was his professed life, that he would have answers, and more, in the South, and that he would regret them.

Evayne rose, coughing; Dantallon lifted a hand to stop her. The hand shook. "Askeyia?"

"I'm sorry." She brushed past him, and then turned, her eyes red-rimmed. "This war will be won by heroes; it will make them; bards will sing their praises.

"But if not for the sacrifice of the faceless and the unknown, the unsung and the forgotten, we could never have come this far; the darkness would be unbreachable.

"I swear that when the time is done, and I can walk among you again—" such a hunger in the words; such a visceral desire, "I will *make* their names known."

Turning, she took a step.

And was gone.

It did not surprise Meralonne; he had half-expected it, was indeed surprised that she had remained for as long as she had, obliquely answering questions.

The obstruction that Evayne had formed was gone to air and silence, and when he looked across at the healer, he could see the younger man's ashen face; the silent stiffening of half-round mouth seemed to whiten his lips.

"Who was Askeyia?"

"She was a student," the healer replied. "I came from Levec's House when I entered the Royal Service. But I returned to it when I found those with the talent, to help ease them into the life of a healer." He paused. "She went missing."

"Missing?"

"We thought—ransom. For the first two months." The healer shook his head. "As I no longer have a patient to protect, I should be going; I have things to attend to." He did not meet Meralonne's eyes.

The mage understood and let him go, questions unasked. For the moment. He was not a man who believed in coincidence.

CHAPTER TWENTY-TWO

1st of Lattan, 427 AA
Annagar, The Tor Leonne

Tyr'agnate Eduardo kai di'Garrardi was in a fine mood when the hooves of his well-shod horse crossed the threshold of the gates to the Tor Leonne proper. The streets that wound up to the plateau had emptied of gawking merchants and common clansmen as Sword's Blood showed his leisurely paces; even the serafs knew the quality of his mount when they saw it, and they made haste not to cross his path.

Sword's Blood had cost a great deal, and many a lesser man had balked at the price, preferring, no doubt, to spend it on serafs, fields, and the collection of diminutive women that were so common in lesser harems. Not so Eduardo; he was a man whose life consisted of riding and swordplay, and he owned no less than the best. He brought no wife with him to the Tor, and at the last moment an unfortunate outburst on the part of the one sister whose common sense and elegance he was not embarrassed by meant that he came, unattended by the more graceful sex, to the Festival of the Sun.

Which was well enough. He did not intend to leave so empty-handed.

Oh, it had been three years. Three years since he had first seen the Serra Diora di'Marano. Young then, at thirteen years, she was beautiful beyond compare now—and he had been the first clansman of note to appreciate just how much that beauty would grow over time. Other women had been offered to him; the daughters of greater men. But Serra Diora had about her that perfect combination of silence, grace, and quiet wit that was so elusive.

Sword's Blood had called to him from the moment he

had laid eyes on the horse; the Serra's call was no less
strong—but the ability to satisfy the impulse not so
simple. No man in Annagar could have appreciated
Sword's Blood, and therefore no other man would pay
the price. But while no man could appreciate Diora as
he had—and would—many a man with a desire they did
not realize was lesser could afford what her father, the
Widan Sendari di'Marano, desired: influence. Power.
Connection.

She had, in the end, been claimed by the kai Leonne as
his wife. The Widan was apologetic but committed; no
one refused the request of the Tor's heir.

Eduardo had attended the ceremony of joining under
the Lady's sky. The stars had been cloud-strewn, the
shadows dark. It had been, to his satisfaction, a grim evening, although the Widan lights and spells had done their
work at alleviating the natural darkness. The waters of the
Tor had never tasted so bitter as when they were raised, in
celebratory welcome, to the kai Leonne and the woman
who bore the title of wife. His wife.

A year had passed. Serra Diora, flawless that evening,
grew more perfect—and to his abiding joy, she bore the
kai Leonne no children. There was no marring of her
form, although that form was too seldom seen.

And that had been fortunate indeed.

Had there been a child, all opportunity would be lost. A
mother did not easily surrender her kin or forget the
memory of their death.

When General Alesso di'Marente—par di'Marente—
had first approached him, he had played the game of politics and power. And Eduardo had joined him with a
decorous interest, a partial willingness. They spoke in
the silence of two men, in the privacy of a room empty
of even the most trusted of Tyran, and they did not speak
for long.

But Tyr'agnate Eduardo di'Garrardi already knew what
his price would be. He asked for the part of the Averdan
lands which bordered his own, fully expecting the General to balk. He did, but not overmuch; there was room to
negotiate, which both men desired. Three days, four; no
word. A brief and pleasant salutation was all that either
man exchanged for the better part of two weeks. He
remembered very little of the finer details that had been

arranged in the end, save this: He was granted two thirds of all that he had asked.

But as he sat, blade against the sheen of perfect silk in his lap, he stared down at the flat, wooden circle that waited his mark. The sun-circles, as they were called, were the binding marks of men of the clans; the clansmen committed little to words, but much to the sight of the Sun. He raised his blade, turning it slowly by the hilt that it might catch the Lord's light and send it skittering along the marked wooden surface. Alesso di'Marente had already made his cut in the wood's face, and waited only the crosscut that would be the final gesture of commitment.

And Eduardo hesitated. "There is one other thing that I desire, Alesso."

Alesso di'Marente was not a patient man—but he'd learned, over time, that waiting had its value. "It is not," the General said, "the accepted practice to add demands to negotiations once they have been concluded. Our swords are drawn."

"I'm aware of that," Eduardo replied. "But the lands were a political matter, and this is a personal one of lesser import."

Alesso waited, and Eduardo was amused to see the cool black of his eyes, the absolute stillness in his kneeling stance. Between them, the smooth, cut surface of the flat wooden disk lay, waiting the crossed blade strokes of the men who had made their oaths. Only when each side of the bargain had been fulfilled would the disk be destroyed—given to fire, that the Lord might bear witness that obligations had been fulfilled, and honor satisfied.

The silence stretched; Eduardo realized, with some annoyance, that Alesso had no intention of breaking it. And General Alesso di'Marente was, of the two, not the ranking man; he was General, Eduardo was Tyr'agnate. Eduardo had merely to speak, and the Tyr'agar would have this man's head—and worse—on the poles that lay evenly spaced on the roadside that led to the Tor Leonne.

But still. He had played his game, and Alesso was correct; men did not usually interrupt this final avowal with requests, however trivial. He nodded; Alesso returned that nod.

"Ser Illara kai di'Leonne's wife."

"What of her?"

"You will, no doubt, destroy the harem and the children in it."

The General did not reply; the answer was obvious.

"She has borne, and bears, no children."

A nod.

"What she did not bear for the kai of a doomed line, she will bear for me. I want her."

"She is not mine," Alesso replied evenly, "to barter away."

"Nor is Averda."

Silence.

Tyr'agnate Eduardo di'Garrardi frowned slightly; he had hoped to be able to hide his desire, or at least to cloak it more appropriately. Without speaking, he lowered his sword to his knees. His meaning, he hoped, was clear.

It surprised the General. Angered him slightly, although Alesso di'Marente was not a difficult man to anger. Nor a wise one, unless one had power and position. Eduardo had both.

And the fact that the General did not immediately capitulate told him one of the many things he desired to know: That Widan Sendari par di'Marano was one of the conspirators. Later meetings would confirm this. "I will . . . confer . . . with my confederates," the General said at last. "Although I will say this: you are not the only man to ask." He smiled.

Eduardo did not. "I warn you," he said softly, "that I am not to be toyed with."

"It was a personal request," Alesso replied softly.

"Sword's Blood," was the answer, "is my *personal* horse."

Answer enough.

Two weeks later, Alesso di'Marente returned. He agreed to the conditions set out by the Tyr'agnate, and together they placed the wooden medallions—one for the clan of Garrardi, and one for the General—on the stone block. Alesso di'Marente made the first cut on each, which was appropriate; Tyr'agnate Eduardo di'Garrardi made the crosscut, sealing their oaths, and binding them together by those oaths in the eyes of the Lord of the Sun.

The waiting had been hard. And fruitful.

*   *   *

Widan Sendari di'Marano was worried. Habit kept the worry from his face, but the lines etched around the corners of his eyes had grown deeper these past few days; the winds scoured him.

It was not over yet, and they both knew it; now was not the time to take undue risks. Yet he hesitated to correct the General who had been a friend most of his adult life. Hesitated, in fact, to expose the subject to the sun's harsh light.

Which was not the same, of course, as refusing to think about it at all. And it was dusk; the sun's light was lessening by measured degree. "Tyr'agnate Eduardo di'Garrardi arrived this afternoon."

A seraf—the Widan's and not the General's—bent briefly over his empty cup, filling it in a single fluid motion. Fiona's choices were almost without flaw, and this lovely young girl—a serving girl, to be sure, and not an ornament to a powerful man's harem, but graceful and delicate nonetheless—brought him a measure of quiet as she saw to their needs without once interrupting their discourse.

"I heard," Alesso replied, staring moodily out into the perfect green of well-watered and tended wilderness. That Eduardo had arrived late meant little; he did arrive, and his name and title were worth the price that he demanded in payment. Or it had been. *Alesso*.

The Pavilion of the Dusk exposed the sun's fall to the eyes of those who were privileged enough to sit upon its platform. Tonight, the privileged numbered two: Alesso and Sendari.

"He looks well," the older man continued. "And Sword's Blood was the only topic of cerdan interest for two hours after the stallion was stabled."

Alesso shrugged.

Sendari almost allowed himself to be put off. Almost. "Have you heard that he has entered himself as a combatant for the Lord's trial?"

"Yes." He paused, setting the evening cup aside on the panels of simple wood beneath their cushions. "Sendari."

"Not yet," Sendari replied simply.

"Perhaps."

"If we had the Sword, we could proceed with less caution. It is not ours."

"Do not be so certain."

Widan Sendari di'Marano turned a pale shade of gray in the lamplight and the moonlight of the coming night. The Lady's thoughts were upon him early, and he could not shake their darkness, or his apprehension. "They failed," he said simply, choosing two syllables that might not carry the tremor in his voice.

Alesso said nothing, but gazed out again into the woods. The crickets were already singing in a multitude of different voices. Did they carry the word of the wind? Sendari thought he felt its chill. As they sat in uncomfortable silence, Alesso di'Marente lifted his chin. "Your seraf," he told his oldest friend.

"What of her?"

"Send her away." Not a request. Not a demand. Sendari knew Alesso well enough to take the warning as the offering it was.

"Alaya." He motioned quickly; a fold of his robes brushed the edge of his evening cup, unbalancing it. Before he reacted, she did, catching it and saving its contents. The waters of the Tor were highly prized. He smiled, although the smile was empty of even a trace of his usual warmth. Taking the cup from her hands, he bid her depart. "Take the small lamp," he added. Fiona en'Marano would not be pleased if the darkness robbed her of this particular seraf.

Nor would he; she had been costly.

They sat together, in silence, a woman's unmentioned name between them. And then Sendari saw what Alesso's sharper eyes had seen first; a shadow that moved counter to the other shadows that evening produced. Alesso di'Marente stiffened, but he did not bow; nor did he arm himself. He had chosen to retreat to the pavilion without escort of any type, but he was capable enough with the sword that he wore when he chose to unsheathe it.

The shadow resolved into the heavily cloaked form of a man with a slightly awkward gait. Not a seraf; no one who had come to the Tor for *this* festival would deign to bring such an obviously damaged man, although many clans maintained those who had suffered injuries in their service otherwise. And not a seraf, Sendari thought, by the fine cut of the cloth that he did wear, although that cloth only revealed itself as the distance between the moving man and the seated ones grew smaller.

The stranger bowed, and he bowed low, pulling back the hood of his cloak.

They faced a man of deceptive height. His hair was pale in the moonlight, gold with a hint of copper highlights that might well have been reflection of their lamps—had their lamps carried an orange flame. His skin was smooth and perfect and white, his lips neither too thin nor too full. In all, when his limp was not so obvious, he was not uncomely—or he would not have been, save for his eyes.

They were utterly black.

"General Alesso di'Marente," the visitor said, bowing slightly awkwardly.

The General nodded, affecting a geniality of expression that did not reach his eyes or the tone of his voice. "Lord Isladar." He lifted the evening cup on the platform at his side, and said, "Would you care to join us?"

The demon's smile was a brief flash of acknowledgment—of both Alesso's title and the threat that was so gracefully offered it might have been mistaken for hospitality. By a foolish man, and Isladar was neither; the waters of the Tor Leonne were such that they did not suffer the touch of the kin. "I have come to offer the apologies of the Shining Court," he said. He made no move to join the two who sat upon the platform.

"Apologies?"

"We are aware that we have left your court in disarray. The internal politics of the Shining Court should never have reached this far, and I believe I have some personal responsibility in that regard."

"I see."

Of all the Allasakari-summoned creatures that he had met, this one fascinated the Widan most. For the creatures were not, once you disregarded their appearance, so different from clansmen who were confident in their own power—they did not show their weakness, they did not trust each other, and they attempted to expand their holdings.

All save this one. He apologized with diffidence, when expedient; he made no display of either his power or his ruthlessness, and he did not choose to belittle his subordinates when the occasion was appropriate. At least, Sendari amended, he had not done so while Alesso, he or any of the human members of the Shining Court were present.

Secrets were always dangerous.

"There is one other matter." Isladar bowed again—a bad sign.

"Yes?"

"At the personal request of a member of your entourage, Lord Etridian chose to venture into the heart of our enemies' territory."

Sendari frowned slightly, and glanced at Alesso; the General was now quite stiff, although the muscles of his face still held the rictus of its former geniality.

"There, he attempted to kill Ser Valedan kai di'Leonne."

"And?"

"He failed."

"I see." No movement of muscle; no falling of shoulders, no relaxing of jaw; Alesso had *expected* this.

"Perhaps. But it was a foolish risk on the part of Lord Etridian, for he chose to present himself to the assembled gathering of the Crowns, their heirs, the presiding rulers of the Three Churches, the Magi and The Ten."

"He *what*?"

A fair brow rose slightly at the tone that colored the single word. Sendari thought he saw a slight quirk of upward movement in the perfect mouth; he could not be certain that it was not a trick of the light, and he dared no magery here. The kin were sensitive to its use and prone to overreact to a spell of any nature.

"He waited beneath the floor of the Great Chamber of the Crowns. They had gathered, in assembly, to pass judgment upon the Annagarian hostages."

Alesso did not like to be reminded of failure, and the hostages had been both an expensive and bloody exercise that had borne no fruit at all. He did not understand the Northerners; it irked him. He thought they might not go to war over the deaths of their nonkin—but to let them lie, unanswered, when reprisal was obvious and accessible— *that* was a sign of weakness of spirit that he could not, did not, fathom. "And the judgment they passed?"

Isladar raised a fair brow at the tone of the voice. "King

Reymalyn chose to spare the life of Ser Valedan di'Leonne, in recognition of the fact that the crimes against the hostages were not committed by his clan."

"That was always a possibility," the Widan said softly.

"Ser Valedan," the demon continued, "refused the offer."

"He what?"

"He came, he said, as a leader—and as a leader, he refused to allow those who put their faith and trust in his ability to face an end that he would not."

"This story," the General said, his eyes narrowed, "goes no further." He did not look to the Widan, but Sendari knew an order when he heard it; he did not bridle. Because he knew that those clansmen with no understanding of the subtleties of politics would find much in this brief tale to admire in a boy thought too weak of blood to be worthy of anything more than the life of a Northern hostage.

"Wise," Isladar said. "But I stray. It appears that at least one Tyr was present in the Great Chamber."

Both men stiffened. "And he?"

"Tyr'agnate Ramiro di'Callesta."

Alesso's lips whitened at the name. "I see."

"He gave his brother to the Northerners," Sendari said softly, although it was not a defense of that most dangerous of men. "And we did not think to apprise him of the . . . situation."

"Lord Etridian attacked when the Callestan lord entered the room. Unfortunately, he failed."

"*Failed?* He is one of your much vaunted kinlords!"

"There have always been reasons why we wished the Dominion to start this war," Isladar replied coldly. "Lord Etridian's attack against the Priests of the enemy was successful. His attack against the boy was not."

"Why?"

"The internal politics of the kin of the Shining Court has a very long and very unfortunate reach." He frowned. "I am permitted to tell you that he was stopped, not by the humans, or the half-gods who play at humanity, but by a member of the Shining Court. Both players felt it was safe to expose themselves to the scrutiny of the gathered assembly." It was clear, from his icy expression, that Lord Isladar did not concur.

Nor did Sendari.

"The foreign Kings will no doubt infer that the Annagarian court consorts with demons."

"No, Alesso," Sendari lifted his evening cup and touched his lips to its rim. "They will infer that the Allasakari are at work in the Dominion. That they control it."

The two men exchanged a long glance that said much. Allasakari, demons—would it make a difference? The Essalieyanese had already been threatened once by the kin—and it had been a close thing, by all Annagarian accounts, and a darker one than the Dominion had ever faced. The Crowns had once turned a blind eye to the affairs of their Southern neighbors, and during that time, the followers of the Lord of Night had grown in strength and numbers, seeding the land with creatures that were best remembered as tales to frighten children. But after the events of sixteen years past, neither Alesso nor Sendari believed that the Crowns would turn so blind an eye again.

Of course, neither Alesso nor Sendari had believed that the Northerners would be so weak of blood and resolve that the hostages' fate would not already be sealed.

"We are not in position to go to war against the Empire," the General said coolly. "Obviously, Lord Etridian was unaware of this."

Isladar made no reply. He was not a creature to belabor the obvious. He bowed. "Until the Festival of the Sun," he said quietly.

"When," the General said softly, "will your kin be ready to place themselves at the disposal of my army as, you no doubt remember, we agreed?"

Isladar's expression was impossible to read. "After," he said, "the Festival."

"But—"

"—of the Moon."

Six months.

In the darkness, the two men sat.

"Thank you," Sendari said.

"For the seraf?"

The Widan nodded. Isladar, the night had taken, and it was of no particular comfort to wish the creature in hell, as that was its domain. What, he thought, was a fate appropriate to such a one? A question for the philosophers among the Widan. "You did not think to tell me."

Alesso shrugged. "I thought, old friend. But I intended to take the risk; I did not see a reason to argue about it." The darkness hid the General's face, but it did not hide the anger beneath the facade of civilized words. Failure. Complete failure.

Sendari swallowed the words that he wished to speak. He knew what the response would be, and the time for argument had passed. He understood why Alesso di'Marente thought it worth the risk to ask—again—for the intervention of the Lords of that Court. He could not wield the Sun Sword while Valedan lived.

And perhaps, although Sendari would never speak the thought aloud, he might never be able to wield it. For both Marente and Marano sought power by means that were forbidden the clans when Leonne cast down the Allasakari, burning in a brilliant light the last of the shadows the Lord of Night had cast upon the land.

"It is a sword," he said softly.

"Old friend," Alesso said, giving warning, "it is *the* sword. You chose the Widan's path, and while you understand much, you do not understand all. The clansmen will see the Sun Sword in the swordhaven, and not in my grasp. Their whispered doubts will be carried by the wind across the Dominion." He rose. "Men of honor will follow me because they have no one else to follow.

"But they will know that I am not the Lord's Chosen. And they will know it until the last of the Leonne heirs is dead, and the Sun Sword is finally free to seek a new—a stronger—master."

Sendari shrugged. "We were prepared for this." *I thought we were,* he added silently. "But we are not prepared for the intervention of the Northerners."

"And it may be that we can avoid such intervention." Alesso stood. "I have sent for the Captain of the Tyran. I believe that it will be clear whose overzealous orders caused the deaths of the Imperial hostages." He rose. "I will give the orders," he added. Sendari thought he caught a flash of teeth in the darkness. "And I will be glad to be rid of him."

"When?"

"We will send riders in haste." He paused. "Sendari, do

you think that we might borrow the services of the Serra
Teresa? I will send my Tyran as her personal escort."

Sendari's smile was sharp and cold. "I'm afraid," he
said, "that you will have to make that request of Adano.
He *is* the kai." The Widan lifted the waters of the Tor as if
to drink them; he froze there a moment, staring. "He will
not leave Lamberto," Sendari said. "And I do not believe
that it would be wise to send a rider to him."

"Granted." The General rose, displeased.

Sendari was also displeased. He did not rise.

Only when Alesso retreated into the shadows of the
Lady's night did Sendari accept the fact that they had not
discussed the disposition of his daughter.

Serra Teresa di'Marano sat quietly in the heat of the
midday sun, a pearl-handled fan—the gift of a Northern
poet—delicately closed in her lap. Silk the color of sunlight on water fell artfully down the gentle slope of that
lap, and as she lifted the fan, it cast a half-circle shadow.

Serra Fiona en'Marano sat beside the older woman,
self-consciously arranging—and rearranging—the fall of
delicate, dark curls. She had chosen to wear a sari of dark,
rich colors, and gold trailed the curves of her neck and the
swell of her breasts. She was younger than Serra Teresa,
and in her prime; she was, of the two, more delicate in
feature and figure, and she was aware of the fact that the
sun had not yet etched its lines in the contours of her face.

But Serra Teresa made her feel *much* younger than her
age, which was awkward. It would also be enraging—
although of course there would be no outward sign of that
particular feeling—but she could not be certain that the
Serra did not have this effect by mere presence alone,
rather than by intent.

And why, Fiona thought with displeasure, should she
feel awkward? She was, after all, Sendari's Serra, and the
Serra Teresa a mere sister who had never, in the end, been
deemed suitable by any of the clansmen who were in a
position to make the offer for her.

"Ah, look, Fiona," Serra Teresa said, drawing the
younger woman's attention.

The Pavilion of Restful Repose was situated beneath
the growth of aged trees, and at its proper time, the trees
cast full shade upon those who sought it. But the women

were granted its use during the late hour of the day, when the sun had passed the point where the trees' greenery provided complete cover. They had not petitioned for its use because of the natural shade, however much they might notice the late noon lack; the Pavilion of Restful Repose was also situated on a rise which overlooked the main road that led to the waters of the Tor Leonne—and to the men who ruled it. From this vantage, one could command a clear view of the dignitaries who came to the Festival without being too forward or vulgar in self-display.

Fiona cast a quick glance to her left, but she could not see Serra Diora, and did not know whether that young woman had also been prompted by Serra Teresa. Serra Diora played the Northern harp very gently when the breeze was strong enough to keep the notes from carrying too loudly to the ears of the men who walked—or rode—below.

The serafs filled their goblets; the breezes were cool enough this day that they need not lift and wave their heavy fans in poor mimicry of the gentle wind. But they were quiet, to a man, and graceful. Only Diora chose not to have a seraf present—although, Fiona thought, that *was* the correct choice; as a wife returned to her father's clan, she had no serafs but those that he chose to lend her.

Of course Sendari chose to be far too liberal, but Diora did not seek to take advantage of his almost embarrassing affection, and for this one thing, Fiona was grateful. She wondered if Diora knew who her husband-to-be was. With Diora it was so hard to tell. Although the women in Sendari's harem were fond of the girl—and truly treated her like the only valuable child in the ensemble, much to Fiona's annoyance—Diora herself was not very open, not even when the curtains were drawn and no men were listening or watching.

Or perhaps, Fiona thought, without too much resentment, *she is only shuttered to* me. She found herself rearranging the hair at the nape of her neck yet again and forced her hands down as the banner of the clan Lorenza came fully into view. Although many of the members of clan Lorenza chose to wear the colors and the crest of their birth, only one man was allowed the legal unfurling of banners in the Tor Leonne; Fiona knew at once that the

Tyr'agnate—what was his name? Ah, yes, Jarrani kai di'Lorenza—was present.

At the head of the procession were Tyran, four abreast. They rode, and they rode stallions that seemed built more for raiding than riding, but the horses themselves seemed, if not friendly, then at least well-controlled by their riders. They were of a color—a deep brown with black boots and mane—and Fiona suspected that these colors were not natural.

Behind the horsed Tyran walked two rows of eight men abreast; they carried swords and shields, and wore helms that gleamed in the mid-afternoon sun. They walked in step, and their colors were perfectly clean, without even the patina of dust from the road to mar their presentation. Behind *these* men came cerdan, and the cerdan bore palanquins with drawn curtains. No doubt, the Serra Maria en'Lorenza and her retinue. The Tyr'agnate's wife had died several years past, and he had never seen fit to marry again, although he was still surrounded by the comforts of his harem. No, this woman was the wife of Ser Hectore kai di'Lorenza—the man who would, in scant years, if Fiona was any judge of character—be Tyr'agnate. Hectore was a pleasant sight; a handsome man, with broad shoulders and an easy, obvious command of both men and beasts. His hair was dark, and his eyes darker; he had his father's height, but he used it to its full advantage. *That* was a man of the clans. Fiona craned forward slightly as the procession continued, searching for sight of him.

Yes. There he was, at his father's sword arm, his horse reined in so that there was half a body length between father and son. He had not changed at all since the last time she'd seen him—although distance often corrected the less capricious passages of time—and she took a half breath in spite of herself, feeling a certain envy for Serra Maria en'Lorenza. Then, aware that Teresa might certainly hear—and interpret—that sound, she glanced away to the man who theoretically held the power of the Terrean of Oerta.

The Tyr'agnate was an older man—too old, in Fiona's opinion, to be Tyr, although he indeed retained the title and its privilege, but too strong to give in to death. His hair was a pale gray with hints of the color it had once been, and although she could not see his eyes, she knew that they were green. It was one of the striking things about him.

He rode with dignity and some bearing, but his gaze wandered from side to side, almost as if he were seeking something. It was said that he was doddering and suggestible. There was, in Fiona's view, no truth to the former accusation; the latter was left open. What was not, and had never been, in doubt was the extreme pride and affection that he felt for his sons. All men knew that sons were necessary, but between father and son there was sometimes an older man's envy—and caution—of another man's youthful prowess, and a younger man's impatience with the hard-won wisdom of years, and his desire for power stripped of those limitations. Hectore had been very much the younger man of that dangerous combination, but Jarrani had never been the older.

To the Tyr'agnate's left was a younger man, with a perfect chin, a sharp eye, and hair the color of a cloudy night. He did not wear hat or helm, which was foolish, and he sat astride his great mount with a particular stiffness. But Alef di'Lorenza could do very little that deprived him of the graceful presence and beauty that he had been born to. In fact, with the exception of Ser Mauro di'Garrardi, there was no more beautiful man in the courts of the clans.

But where Mauro was carefully neutral toward his cousin, the Tyr'agnate, Alef was devoted. Hectore had the ability to bind, with loyalty, the clansmen around him. Alef proved himself to be no exception.

As she studied the lines of his face, the center of the procession stopped, horses awkwardly held back by the reins of the Tyr'agnate. Fiona froze as those green eyes looked up the slope. They skirted her shaded face, her perfect hair, and fell upon the woman who sat at her side.

"What, is that Na'tere I see?" His full, deep voice carried against the wind.

Serra Teresa laughed, and the laughter was almost song, it sounded so right. She lifted her hand, and the sweep of colored silk that was one of many forms of modesty a woman might choose caught the light as she brought it to cover her mouth and chin.

The Tyr'agnate spoke a word or two to his kai; Hectore

frowned but made no reply. Satisfied, although Fiona privately thought the son somewhat ill-mannered in his coolness, the older man shouted ahead to the Tyran; the force of his voice carried the command. They stopped at once, in a near-even line, and Fiona realized that only a very foolish man or woman could believe all that was said about this man's supposed dotage. What, she thought, did he want with Serra Teresa?

She dared a sideways glance at the Serra Teresa; the older woman's lips were turned up in a half-smile that spoke of a shared past. It was a brief smile, and Fiona was not certain that it reached her eyes. With Teresa, it was hard to tell; her face was the most expressive mask that Fiona had ever seen. And Fiona was herself no ill-trained concubine.

"Na'tere," the Tyr'agnate said, his voice still booming as his strides cut the distance between them.

She waited calmly, and then turned and whispered a word, behind the scant protection of her pretty fan, to the girl who sat to her left. Serra Diora di'Marano began to play. Fiona had thought, until the sound of the notes filled the air with a resonant clarity, that Diora had been playing all afternoon—but the sound that came from the harp now was no mere idle pleasantry, no waft of notes carried, airborne, by careless breeze. There was will behind it, and heart, and a turn of string's phrase that only a master could have executed so eloquently.

Even the Tyr'agnate seemed surprised by the quality of the wordless song that she played. He froze completely when she began to sing.

Fiona froze as well; she was certain, as she listened, that the winds themselves halted their passage a moment. *Why,* she thought, *has Sendari never commanded his daughter to sing for us? For any of his guests?* Pique—at the fact that it was Teresa, and not Fiona, under whose guidance the girl now lived—rose and asserted its dominant place, breaking the sweet quality of the younger woman's spell.

But upon the face of Tyr'agnate Jarrani kai di'Lorenza there was no such pique; nothing rose to replace the quiet hush the wake of the young Serra's song left.

He was a man, but even so, Fiona thought she caught a glimmering at the edges of his eyes. For a moment, he looked his age; his lashes, frosted white, swept down over green, bright eyes.

"The sun," the old man said, as he bowed directly to the Serra Teresa, "is in my eyes."

"And so," the Serra replied, "you will tell me that I have not aged at all; that the wind has worn no lines, the sun no common freckles, across my skin; that I am all that you remember."

Fiona was surprised; the older man, less so. His laughter started the wind again as noise returned to the hill.

"You are," Ser Jarrani said, "more than I remember. My memory holds no such vibrancy—and no such ready wit." He bowed again. "But please, if you find my request not too bold, I would be honored by an introduction to the two ladies who wait so perfectly to either side."

"You are always bold," the Serra replied, "but we would be disappointed with less, because you are first among clansmen."

He laughed again, well-pleased.

"This, Tyr'agnate, is the Serra Fiona en'Marano. She graces Widan Sendari di'Marano's harem—and his life— with her perfect companionship."

Serra Fiona blushed perfectly and bowed her head, aware as she did that her hair caught the edges of sunlight and gleamed a moment like living silk. Aware also that his interest in her was perfunctory at best, but not annoyed by it. Too great an interest would be an insult to a married woman's husband.

"And this," Serra Teresa said, turning her fan, her gaze, and the Tyr'agnate's attention, to her niece, "is the Serra Diora di'Marano."

Jarrani raised a peppered brow a moment, and then it fell as his eyes narrowed. He had never developed a courtly mask. "Di'Marano?" he asked.

"Di'Marano."

The clansman bowed to Diora, and held that bow a fraction of a second longer than politeness or rank—for she had no true rank—demanded. "It has been many a year," he told her, attempting the smile of a paternal relative, "and you were not so tall, so fair, or so strong of voice then. I did not recognize you.

"But now I understand why you—"

The Serra Teresa's perfect smile froze in place a

moment; the half-sentence hung in the air like the edge of a blade poised to strike.

He is going to refer to the dead Tyr, Fiona thought, paling completely. She averted her gaze.

"Why you are called," the Tyr'agnate continued, smoothing over awkward silence, "the Flower of the Dominion."

The Serra Diora said nothing, but lowered her head very prettily. Her fingers touched the harp's strings again.

"And I would very much be honored," the older man continued, "if, with your father's permission, I might hear the music you bring to a proper, Southern instrument. The Northern harp is pretty enough, but it does not carry the weight of our history."

"The honor," the Serra Teresa replied, very properly, "would be ours."

Ser Jarrani looked from the older woman to the younger. "Na'tere," he said at last, as Diora's wordless song opened a space for conversation, "at this moment I have two desires."

"And you will remember that you are in the company of women, with no cerdan in evidence."

Fiona felt a certain shock—or envy—at the older woman's boldness, for she was almost familiar in her term of address.

He laughed. "Could I forget, when you are among that company?" His laughter left a smile across both of their faces; genuine smiles, if momentary ones. "What was I saying before your impertinent interruption? Ah, yes, that I have two desires."

"And those?" she asked, in a most innocent tone.

"That your kai—what was his name, Adano?"

"As you know well, Tyr'agnate. He is the Tor'agar Adano kai di'Marano, and he serves the Tyr'agnate Mareo di'Lamberto."

"Yes, that does sound familiar. In fact, it sounds like the name of the man who thrice refused the offer of a Tyr for the hand of an unmarried sister." The Tyr'agnate's smile was a grim one, if genuine. It softened slightly. "I would change that, in a moment, if I could. My first desire, Na'tere, has changed very little in the last two decades. You would be a wife worthy of the title, of the clan, and of the Terrean. Even now. Especially now."

She sat very still and said nothing at all, but her face was raised to catch both sunlight and the green light of his gaze; she flinched from neither. And then, slowly, she raised the fan in her lap until it touched the tip of her nose.

"My second desire, and a more attainable one: That your niece, the Serra Diora, might grow from being the Flower of the Dominion to the Lady of the Festival."

"Ah, Ser Jarrani, you are kind, and you flatter. To be named the Lady of the Festival is the highest honor that a woman can achieve among the clansmen. I fear that there are many, many women who will be held up as worthy of that attention."

"Yes," the Tyr'agnate said. "But when she sings, there is not a clansman alive who will not desire to have that voice raised in praise of the Lord of the Sun. The Lord himself must have guided me to this hillock and this meeting. It is his will."

"It is the will," Serra Teresa replied, "of a man of power."

"Teresa."

Serra Teresa lifted her chin and turned her face slowly to meet the gaze of the one man who was allowed to enter, unannounced, into the heart of her chambers.

"Sendari."

"I do not know what game you are playing, but you *will* cease at once."

"As you command," she replied smoothly.

Giving, as usual, nothing.

Sendari was weary and angry and aware that neither of these two could directly be laid at Teresa's lap. Alesso, he had chosen to avoid for the day; they were uneasy with the unspoken, and unable to put into words the difficulties that were growing between them. Or so he felt.

To come, from the day's contemplation and study, to the side of his wife; to hear from her stilted but genuine praise of his daughter's voice—a voice which, she said, in her least pleasing tones, could have served the Widan's cause, had it been but made known—was difficult enough. To forbid Fiona to speak further of it, for his own peace, had been grating.

But to hear—after forbidding further speech—that the

Tyr'agnate Jarrani kai di'Lorenza believed that he had the right to propose that *his* daughter, his Diora, be put up on a platform with some ridiculous title, so that the whole of the clans might see and hear her—that had been far, far worse. He had slept alone that night, and had barely managed to contain his anger. He still had no desire to be confronted with the presence of his disobedient wife.

"Teresa," he said, the single word sharp enough to be a curse.

"Sendari?"

"What occurred yesterday afternoon?"

"Ser Jarrani was riding with his Tyran and his family; he happened upon us while we were making use of the Pavilion of Restful Repose."

"And that is all?"

"He heard Diora singing," she continued, and he knew that she knew what Fiona had said. "And he felt that she would be the perfect Lady of the Sun."

"And he said this to *you*, rather than to *me*?"

"The choice," was her grave reply, "is not yours alone to make, Sendari. You know as well as I that there will be a Lady of the Festival; you know, as well as I, that it is a singular honor to be so chosen—and you know, better than I, that this Festival, more than any other, the choice that is made, the Lady who is presented, will be critical. There is no Tyr," Teresa said. What she did not say loomed large between them: that the choosing of the woman, the unmarried woman, who would bear the title and the privilege of the Lady of the Sun, was—had been—the prerogative of the Tyr'agar.

"There will be no Sun Sword," the Serra continued, although the set expression of Sendari's face served as a warning. "You cannot afford to have a Festival in which there is no Lady—or worse, there is a lady who is poorly chosen, whether she be politically wise or no." She bowed her head to her knees. "Forgive my boldness, brother."

There was, of course, no contrition whatever in her voice.

"She will not be put on display again."

"She is the Flower of the Dominion. She is the woman that the Tyr himself chose as the worthy wife to the man who would have ruled the Dominion. She is alive; he is not. But think, the Flower of the Dominion is in blossom, and that is the implication that you might make clear: the kai of the Leonne clan was not man enough to hold her, to own her."

"Teresa."

"I will not continue, brother. You know the truth of the words I speak better than I, and I once again beg your forgiveness, if you find it in your heart to grant it, for my boldness."

Sendari felt cold, although the day was hot, even given the season. *I will send her home,* he thought, and then realized belatedly that home—in the Terrean of Mancorvo—was long lost. The war had already started.

"What is your game, Teresa?"

"I play no game, Sendari."

He knew the truth when he heard it; he knew that she spoke truth. And that was the trap with his lovely sister; she chose to speak as much of the truth as she could, whenever she could, and always to her own ends.

Serra Diora di'Marano sat behind the closed silk of perfectly made screens. The sun was low, the morning young; it was cool, or as cool as it would be during the daylight hours. This year, the sun's fire was hot.

The Northern harp lay, untouched, on a cushion by her lap; the samisen lay against her folded knees. Her fingers, moving in small, contained circles, touched neither. Instead, they traced a familiar path—three paths—each golden.

She spoke three names, or rather, her lips formed the syllables; she did not allow a breath to escape them.

It was hard; she realized that it would be harder still. And she pressed those circles into the flesh of her smooth, perfect palms as if they were talismans against her weakness.

She did not remember the large, friendly man who called Serra Teresa "Na'tere" with such impunity. She did not recognize anything about him but the strains of his voice, and even these were changed enough by time that they only felt familiar. Voices were always the first thing that made an impression with her; they were always the last thing that left her memory.

She liked him. She had not thought to like him.

A sound caught her attention; her hands fell at once to

her lap, and rested there gracefully, as if the lap was the only proper place for a woman's hands.

"Na'dio?"

"Ona Teresa."

"Your father has requested that you do not venture out today. He . . . fears for the sun's heat."

"Yes, Ona Teresa."

"But, Diora, please. Remember who you are, and who you will be after this Festival's passage. Dress appropriately. If you need aid, I will send Ramdan to help you."

The younger woman nodded her acquiescence without turning to look over her shoulder. She waited a moment and then nodded quietly to herself. Only Serra Teresa could move so quietly that the screens themselves barely whispered the sound of her passage.

She chose silks the color of the evening sky, with golden fires and a white border to take away the depth of darkness. These were not the colors of the open day—not a young woman's colors—but as a woman returned to her father's clan, Diora was not in a situation for which they were acceptable.

Her hair, she left long, although with the help of Ramdan she added white flowers down the left side of her face, pinning them carefully against strands of hair stiffened for just that purpose.

A woman of the clans—an unmarried woman—did not travel without cerdan. There were no cerdan at her disposal, given her father's request.

And because she was the obedient daughter and the perfectly trained wife, she waited.

Radann Fredero kai el'Sol was a tired man, and a lonely one. His hair, this past month, had lost the black sheen of shadow that spoke of youth; gray had appeared in the darkness during which the clan Leonne had been lost to the Dominion of Annagar, and it had been growing steadily paler as the season progressed. He knew that the Radann in the ranks beneath him whispered about it when his back was turned, and tried his best not to be bothered by the words they did not speak to his face.

Because the words that *were* spoken were infinitely worse.

It is not right, he thought, as he bowed his head to one knee and held it there for just as long—for longer, if truth be told, than he had ever done with the Tyr Leonne, the man whose bloodline had rid the Dominion of the taint of darkness. But right or not, he bowed; it was the way of the Lord. Alesso di'Marente had strength and power; the fact that he stood, while Fredero knelt, was proof enough of that.

"In the absence of the Leonne clan, *you* are the voice of the Lord of the Sun." Alesso made the fact sound as flimsy and inconsequential as his actions over these last two weeks had made it. For this alone, Fredero would not forgive. He rose at the almost imperceptible, and impatient, dip of the General's chin. Permission.

"I am aware of that singular honor," the Radann replied neutrally.

"Yet you have done very little to prepare yourself for the Festival."

"You are aware, General, that the Festival of the Sun requires that the hidden devotions be performed by all of the Radann."

Alesso di'Marente shrugged.

"We have lost two men to the fires, and as passage between the Terreans has been restricted for the moment, there have been no Radann to replace them." The kai clapped his hands twice, sharply, and the temple servitors came at once to do his bidding. Here, in the Tor Leonne, the serafs did not wait upon the Radann; no slave, no indentured man, was considered fit to serve these most exalted of the Lord's servants. The servitors carried weapons, and engraved upon the hilt of each sword and dagger was the symbol of the ascendant sun, although the rays were an indistinguishable halo around the golden disk itself. Their weapons were sheathed, and would remain so, unless the kai el'Sol commanded otherwise. He did not, but instead nodded as the servitors lifted a decanter.

Alesso di'Marente accepted the hospitality of the Lord, taking the water that was so carefully poured into glass cut in just such a way that the light shone brilliantly through the liquid. "I am aware," he replied, his lips still glistening, "that you have had a difficult season." His tone was perfectly neutral, and his gaze was unblinking. "But I am confident that you will rise to the occasion."

Fredero waved the armed men to one side. These servitors were loyal to the Radann kai el'Sol—or at least, that was the theory. With serafs, insuring loyalty was a much easier process. But although the servitors were clansmen of little note, they were still clansmen, and they harbored ambitions. Fredero stopped himself from running a hand through his hair. He had never felt so weary.

This year, he thought, and felt the keen edge of a cold, cold wind. He wondered if it were fancy, or if the chill were a premonition—the shadow cast by the sun's light, that spoke of things not yet seen, not yet passed. His death.

And if it came to pass? Then he would face it as a servant of the Lord, and he would die on his feet. Or a lifetime of service would mean nothing, in the end; he would be sent to the whirlwind, with the rest of the weak and the undeserving.

"Which of the many things that the Festival requires brings you to us?"

"A thing of minor consequence."

Ah. Not the Sun Sword, then. "Name it."

"As you are the representatives of the Lord for this Festival season, it falls upon you to make the choice of the woman who will be the Lord's consort for the three days."

Had he been facing any man but the General Alesso di'Marente, Fredero would have been outraged. He was outraged now, but swallowed the anger, burying it before it had a chance to reach his face. No woman, no matter how politically powerful her clan was, could be considered a matter of such urgency that *the kai el'Sol* could be pulled from his chambers with impunity before morning contemplations had been completed.

"You have candidates whom you wish us to consider for this honor."

"Indeed."

"And they are?"

"There is only one, but she is the recommended choice of the two Tyr'agnati who have come to honor the Lord's Festival—and his commandment—by coming to the Tor Leonne this year."

"I . . . see." Fredero struggled to contain his anger;

failed. He was well aware that General Alesso di'Marente knew, as fact, that the clan which had birthed him was no less a clan than Lamberto. Before he took the test and made the vow under the burning eyes of the Lord, he had been called Fredero par di'Lamberto; the fourth son of four steady sons. The younger brother of Tyr'agnate Mareo di'Lamberto, the *only* Tyr to openly rebuff the General.

He was also well aware of the fact that the General—as all the clansmen—knew full well that men of honor could serve only one master, and that master, for the Radann, was not blood but the will of the Lord. To step upon the path, to become Radann, they disavowed their birth, and the responsibilities, if not the affection, that that birth burdened them with; when they lifted sword and girded themselves again, they were *el'Sol*. Bound by word to the Lord himself—and to no other.

The implication was a slap in the face; worse. It called into question the honor of the vow taken.

The dark lashes that framed the General's eyes narrowed. The kai el'Sol said nothing. They stayed thus a moment, weighing, and then the General chose to speak. "The woman to be so honored is the Serra Diora di'Marano."

If he had hoped to shock, Fredero gratified him; his eyes widened involuntarily as the name sank roots in memory. Those roots did not have far to go.

The kai Leonne's delicate, perfect wife.

Widow, he corrected himself grimly.

"I trust that the recommendation will meet with your approval, and look forward to hearing from you before the sun reaches full height today."

CHAPTER
TWENTY-THREE

The Widan Sendari was beside himself, although the emotion that disturbed him in the isolated chambers in which he honed and sharpened his craft was not easily named. His legs ached; he had been kneeling in the posture for almost two hours, if the sands were not thickened by the odd humidity of the day. The screens were closed and guarded from without by his most trusted cerdan; he was used to the total privacy that doors provided, but if one lived within the Tor Leonne, one could not insist upon changing the architecture on a whim, be it even a Widan's.

Flames leaped up, breaking contact with the black iron of the brazier that—barely—contained them. They shone against the floor, a passing orange glow that could, if unleashed, turn hardwood into ash in mere seconds.

He was master here. The fires fought him, but there was no contest; his hold over this element was unquestioned and unquestionable.

And always, when he sat in the quiet, partly darkened rooms in which he was master of the elements, it was the things that he could not control without doubt—the things over which his study, his speciality, his authority held little sway—which came to haunt him.

Diora.

She was ice and shadow; there lay, across her perfect, perfect face no hint of the child that she had once been. Even upon the eve of her marriage to the kai Leonne, she had shown him a glimpse of that younger self, a wisp of youth's impulsiveness and double-edged innocence.

What did it mean?

Oh, he writhed, asking the question, because he was a man to whom answers—or the getting of them—had become a force of nature, an obsessive desire. And because when he thought on it—and he attempted to dismiss it as women's affairs, things beneath his notice—he turned again to Alora. Alora's brief life. Her death. Her love.

He lifted his hands; clapped twice, guttering the flames that struggled against his command.

Where are they, Teresa?

Where are what, my brother?

The rings. She wore rings, the first night.

The first night?

Damn her. Damn Alora. Let them both flee to the winds of the afterlife, and cling together, as they once had.

The night that the clan Leonne perished.

She said something, and he realized that he was close to the edge; the desire to strike her was visceral. And he could; it was his right. But to start was to start; he did not know where the end to that drama lay.

Did not know if, truly, his anger did not lie in another decade, with another woman. Did she know his daughter as well as she had known his wife? Did Diora show her more, tell her more, let her see the vulnerability that he was certain lay somewhere beneath the facade she presented him whenever they came to be together?

He had left the Serra with her serafs; he had walked the grounds of the Tor Leonne, seeing nothing but the too-sharp sparkle of sunlight from the lake's waters, a sparkle not unlike the glint of lamplight over gold, over bands of gold, and had finally retreated to his circle of contemplation, there to immerse himself in the art which had made him a man of note and power among the clansmen.

She is her mother's daughter.

And in this room, without even serafs for company, Widan Sendari di'Marano acknowledged the fact that he was both afraid for his lovely daughter, and afraid *of* her, and he could not say which of the two was worse.

Fredero kai el'Sol left his circle of contemplation a much calmer man. Rising, he gathered his robes about him, fitting them with the broad golden sash of his office. He carefully lifted his scabbard from its resting place, and girded himself. The mighty among the clansmen were attended by serafs; the mighty among the Radann knew that men relied upon their own devices and their own strength—and were so judged by God. They could, he thought, with a hint of wryness, be counted upon to dress themselves decently.

He left his chambers, and as the servitors quietly pulled the screens wide, a breeze gusted in, carrying with it the scent of the rushes and the lilies that took their life from the waters of the Tor Leonne. For a moment, he was *the kai el'Sol,* the man upon whose broad shoulders the worship of the Lord of the Sun rested.

The servitors bowed with a deep and perfect respect, and he judged that respect genuine. The Radann had survived darker days than these.

But those days, he knew, were the days before the coming of the clan Leonne. What waited now that that clan had passed? Peace was such a fragile thing.

"Kai el'Sol, the four par el'Sol await you."

"Thank you."

It was Marakas who had summoned the Radann; it was his right, as par, and it did not surprise the kai el'Sol. Marakas was most sensitive to the needs of the followers of the Church, and if the rest of the par—and the kai—felt that Marakas' attention strayed at times too close to the Lady's dominion, he was still much respected and honored among the Radann. Perhaps not as greatly feared as the rest, but that, too, was not surprising, although he was broad of shoulder and chest, and at least as tall as the kai. No, his was that rare demeanor among men of power: that of a gentle man.

But the kai el'Sol knew that when the need was great, Marakas par el'Sol could be counted upon both to wield a sword and to finish a battle. If he did not insist that lesser men live on their knees, he did not live on his. A difficult balance to maintain.

But there were other reasons that he was indulged in a way that not even the kai could be said to be indulged; other reasons why his excursions into the affairs of the common clansmen and the serafs caused most to glance in the other direction: He had a touch of the Lady's blood about him—both an unpredictable wildness and a strength. The Lady's hands. He was a healer born.

Not even the greater clansmen knew this secret.

Marakas had grayed early, a frosty patina over hair as

black as the burning rocks, although the bronze of his sun-warmed skin did not give way easily to other signs of age. He was, and insisted upon remaining, clean-shaven, although at times it had proved inconvenient. His eyes were brown, although they were neither dark enough to be mysterious nor light enough to be interesting, and if they had a haunted air about them, no one was foolish enough to wonder aloud what they'd seen.

The kai el'Sol was always pleased to see Marakas.

Or almost always pleased. He felt the smile that had come, unbidden, to his lips freeze and die there as he met the eyes of the man who was a mere three years his elder. "Marakas," he said, his tone light. "It is not the custom—"

"Kai," Marakas replied, lifting a hand and begging, with his expression, for indulgence. "I must ask you to trust me. This is a matter of urgency."

"And this," Peder par el'Sol said, "is a private meeting. You know the signs, Radann. You have given them in surety." Peder was younger than either the kai or Marakas, but he was easily a match for his elders. Smooth-tongued and soft of voice, he was good with a sword, and had never once faltered in the test of fires. He was handsome, in the way that men in their prime are; he was attractive because his arrogance permeated every aspect of his life in such a manner that it spoke of sure power.

Marakas nodded grimly. "I must ask," he said gravely, "that you trust me." He paused, glanced once at the woman—the unadorned *woman*—who sat, beneath the cloth of a poor silk sari and a too-heavy veil, and then sighed. Sliding his hands to his side, he removed the sword that he carried, and laid it to rest at the center of the circle around which the five men sat. "Before the Lord," he said, "I will renounce all claim to honor and light if I endanger the Radann by my boldness."

Peder frowned, but nodded gracefully in the kai's direction. Neither of the other two Radann—the oldest, Samadar, or the youngest, Samiel—spoke a word.

The woman did not remove her veils; she sat, with her chin bowed almost to her chest, as if aware—and how could she be otherwise—that her presence was an affront to the men who had been judged the most worthy of all those who served the Lord. Or at least it seemed so for a moment.

Her movements dashed that happy, and reasonable, illusion, although it took the kai el'Sol a moment before he realized why the lift of her hands, and their odd, supple dance through the air, seemed familiar to him. They were not the gestures of an exotic dancer; they were similar in feel and in texture to the concentration and contemplations of the Widan.

Women were not allowed to bear the Sword of Knowledge, although it had never been said that women were incapable of taking the test, and surviving it.

For they learned, it was said, when they learned the arts, in the service of the Lady.

He was almost too shocked to react; the world's strangeness, the threat and the sacrilege inherent in it, washed away the peace that the contemplations had, momentarily, given him. Had he thought the offered sword theatrical? That amusement passed. Had Marakas laid his head upon the table, divorced from neck and body, it might not have been enough to make *this* tolerable.

And yet.

And yet, he waited.

She spoke three words, her hands sliding through the air as if the air were liquid, and at that, a heavy one. And then she nodded, although she did not lift the veil from her hidden face.

Marakas inclined his head in reply, and she seemed to melt into the shadows, slight though they were, at his back. "Forgive me, kai," he said, his voice shaking slightly. "Forgive me, brothers. But I did not undertake this lightly, nor without thought."

"Marakas," Samadar said, speaking for the first time this day while he stroked a platinum beard, "we will perish of old age if you are allowed to continue your apologies to a length appropriate to the gravity of your offense."

"And I," Marakas countered, "will perish at a young age if I do not at least make an attempt. We are under the eyes of the Lord," he added.

"I believe," the oldest of the Radann replied, "we're aware of that." His voice was as dry as the desert plains.

"This . . . this visitor. I assume that she has taken pains to guard this conversation from the ears of unwanted eavesdroppers?"

"I—why, yes."

Samadar inclined a head as white as his beard in the direction of the woman who sat to one side and behind the Radann. "The Lady," he said, "has her place. It is not this one, but if the Lord hears this thing that must be said in such a protected silence, and the Lord deems it worthy, you will have done us a service."

"If the Lord hears," the woman replied, which was shocking, "and he chooses to act, you will repay the service a thousandfold before it is over."

"Be still," Radann Marakas par el'Sol said, with a very real anger. She subsided at once. "This has much to do with the death of the Leonne Clan," he then continued, breaking the uncomfortable silence left in the echo of her words, speaking to his peers as if the interruption had never taken place. Or rather, as if he wished it had not; he was not so smooth an actor.

"If you tell us that you've discovered that the General Alesso di'Marente ordered the deaths," Peder said softly, "I will lose my temper."

"I have, in fact, discovered just that," was Marakas' reply. If he noticed the sarcasm behind Peder's cool words, he did not bridle. "Although I believe we have all accepted that as fact long before today."

"Patience, Peder," Samadar said.

"Four nights after the burning waters and the butchered clan, three serafs died. They are buried in the Tor, in an unmarked and unblessed grave."

"Serafs die all the time," Peder said.

"Yes. But these men died because they served di'Marente, and they were witness to the arrival of one of the General's allies." He leaned forward, his chest touching the ground. "My brothers, the ally was one of the kin."

Marakas was not a liar; it did not occur to any of his four companions to accuse him of being one, although each man had his own reasons for wishing they could believe otherwise. As usual, after so grave a statement, it was Peder who spoke.

"How did you come by this knowledge?"

The kai took a breath as Radann Peder par el'Sol met his brother's unblinking gaze.

"There were four serafs."

"I see. And the fourth somehow managed to escape?"

"It was not immediately obvious to the four that they were to be executed for witnessing the arrival of the creature. They have served Marente for decades—or rather, had—and they have seen many things that Marente would prefer to keep hidden." Marakas frowned. "The serafs are under the Lord's dominion, but they do not serve the Lord. They have their own credo, and their own place, in this life and the next. This seraf almost did not leave, although he knew that the cerdan who would follow in the wake of the General's departure were meant to be his death.

"But he knew what the presence of the kin presaged. And in the end, he chose to end his honorable service to the General to deliver that information. It was," Marakas added, well aware that the rest of the Radann considered the time he took to speak with the serafs an indulgence of whim at best, a sign of weakness at worst, "an act of courage. The serafs believe that, in serving truly, and in enduring the test of that service, they prove their honor and their worth. To leave, not for the sake of escape, but the sake of *betrayal* may cost the man everything he has ever worked for in life. But he knows the legend of Leonne and the Lord, and he remembers the tales of the Lord of Night.

"He found, in the Tor Leonne, a woman whom he believed served the interests of the Lady."

"And she?"

"I do not know." He lifted a hand to forestall the words that were forming on Peder's lips. "It was a condition placed upon me by the woman who delivered this information, and I accepted it with honor. I will not see it broken without due cause."

"Very well, Marakas," the kai said softly. "But continue this story, and continue quickly. If I understand the working of the Lady's spell, our privacy is guaranteed at a cost, and it would not serve our cause, or the Lord's, to waste the time we've been given."

"Yes, kai el'Sol."

The kai privately wished that Marakas would dispense

with proper form altogether, but he did not correct the younger man's deferential dip of shoulders and chin. Not because he was afraid of being seen as a kai who tolerated lack of respect and slovenly behavior, but because it would have wasted time. *Later*.

"The woman in question came into contact with the Lady's servants, and this woman came, as a seraf, into the Tor Leonne. I do not know how, and again, I have chosen to remain ignorant. She demonstrated the use of her learned talent, and then told me what I have told you.

"I did not wish to believe it," he continued, his eyes growing slightly unfocused as he stared into a past that his words were slowly making real for the rest of the Radann. "But I could not dismiss such a claim—for it would explain much. I began to have the General watched."

"You . . . did . . . *what*?"

Again, Marakas flushed and bowed in the submissive posture, touching his head to the polished round upon which his sword lay. "I could not bring this to your attention, kai. Not without proof. Not now." He swallowed. "And I am not certain that the rest of the Radann—or the servitors—would share our concerns. General Alesso di'Marente is a popular man among those who follow the way of the sword; he has his friends among our number." He paled, and the kai el'Sol knew exactly what he would hear next. "I—I didn't ask the Radann for aid; I did not rely upon servitors."

Fredero raised a hand that was, surprisingly, steady. The gesture stemmed the flow of Peder's outrage. Samiel, the youngest, was remarkable in his restraint; his lips were lined white, but he said not a word.

"And two evenings ago, when the sun was almost gone from the sky and the Lady's tenure begun, one of the kin came. The General sent away the lone seraf who served him and his compatriot."

"And that compatriot?"

"The Widan Sendari par di'Marano."

"Widan," the kai said, the tone of his voice giving insult that words alone could not convey.

"The creature approached after the girl left them. It was almost entirely human in appearance, but the signs were there for those who know how to look. The ensuing conversation left little room for doubt."

"What do you mean?"

"First: That Alesso di'Marente asked for the aid of the kin—one who is called 'Lord Etridian.' "

"Kinlord," Samiel said, and he did pale.

"Don't interrupt, Samiel. Continue."

"The kinlord—if that's what it was—chose to attack the greater assembly of the Northern infidels while the Kings were in session."

Not a man at this table would shed a tear for the loss of the Northerners; in fact, Samadar's nod was a grim one that contained, for a moment, some pleasure. The enemy of an enemy was almost as good as a friend.

To a foolish man. And these five were anything but.

"The creature was not supposed to attack the Northerners. He was to assassinate a single Annagarian hostage.

"Ser Valedan kai di'Leonne."

The name hit the table as if it were an ax, and although the sound of its syllables did not even leave an echo, it marked the men who heard it. Each had become accustomed enough to hiding his scars that little of their surprise showed.

"He failed."

The kai el'Sol closed his eyes a moment. "Thank you, Marakas."

"There's more."

"How much more?"

"Only one thing. Tyr'agnate Ramiro di'Callesta was *at* the Imperial Court—and in the hall—when the attack occurred."

Fredero heard the name and nodded neutrally, thinking that, of all men, it would have to be Ramiro di'Callesta. A man who had been Lamberto's worst enemy for decades. A man who did not understand the concept of honor.

The woman collapsed before they could discuss the proper response to the news that Marakas brought. A sudden huff of air, like a weak gust of breeze, and she toppled, the closing punctuation to their debate. Fredero felt a pang, something akin to guilt; he knew the cost would be high, and hoped that she survived it.

Because they would need her services again in the days to follow.

Why, he thought, *did the enemy not hide his conversation in such a way?* There was no answer to the question, at least not until the woman regained consciousness, if she ever did. Still, the Lord had put the woman in his path, and would forgive him for keeping her hidden in the confines of the greater temple. The servitors would not, unfortunately; it meant a risk to himself. Because only those who were absolutely trusted—and there were very, very few—were allowed into the kai's personal chambers, and for that reason, he had chosen to harbor this unlikely ally there.

"Widan Sendari," the seraf said, in a rush of breath.

The Widan so named looked up from the open tome that stood, carefully propped, beneath a lamp's glow. He did not recognize the seraf, and knew by his hasty entrance and his clumsy posture that this was not one of his. Fiona was meticulous, if out of favor; she would not embarrass him by allowing a seraf with this lack of grace to serve his household. Nor would she choose to send any one of her handpicked prizes into his den while he studied; it was expressly forbidden, and he had made clear, with the execution of the first such seraf, that he would not brook her disobedience in this regard.

"I am," he told the seraf coldly, "the Widan Sendari. Why have you chosen to interrupt me?"

His voice carried his mood, and his mood was a dark one. The seraf crumpled at once into a frozen heap, head and hair—the hair was particularly fine—strewn gleaming across the kneeling mats.

"My master bid me come at once. He says it is most urgent."

"Who is your master?"

"The Widan-Designate Alberto par di'Ecclenses."

Sendari was silent for a full minute. He could sense the seraf's discomfort, but it did not amuse him; it had ceased to mean anything at all, except perhaps that Alberto was in want of a wife who could better choose the serafs in his indenture. "Tell Widan-Designate Alberto par di'Ecclenses that the Widan Sendari par di'Marano would appreciate the honor of his company in the Inner

Chamber." He turned and carefully closed the book. "Tell him that I will leave at once."

The Widan-Designate was, in Sendari's opinion, born with a strong enough talent to rise quickly in the heirarchy of the Sword of Knowledge—if he survived its testing. If he did not choose to undertake that test, he would be any Widan's worthy ally—but there were spells and histories that would never be his, by right of the Sword's test, to learn. He'd achieved the title of Widan-Designate at Sendari's behest, and with Sendari's voice behind him—which was more than many a man in his lesser position could say. But it was less than Alberto should have been able to say.

Sendari did not fully understand the younger man, because he could not see, in the younger man's study, that intensity of obsession that guided so many of the Widan. And youth was the age of such passionate risk.

Still, as Widan-Designate, Alberto was allowed the use of some of the facilities which had been set aside by the Tyrs for the Sword of Knowledge, a scabbard, a way of sheathing that double-edged weapon. He could not descend into the deeps that lay at the heart of the building itself. No man who had not faced the test of the Sword could.

But the Inner Chamber was good enough. They could speak, there.

He found Alberto, in a robe that was obviously too large, waiting in a shroud of silence that was, in itself, a commingling of awe and that terrible *meekness* that would—in Sendari's reluctant opinion—be his undoing. It was very hard not to snap at someone who seemed on the verge of cringing—but Sendari was a man who had developed enough self-control that he sat with grace and ease, putting unseen effort into making the younger man feel less ill at ease. The Lord knew that he could not be more ill at ease.

Of course, such ease as he managed to achieve would not survive the questioning.

"Widan Sendari," Alberto said, rising.

The Widan waved him back into the cushions, thinking that he had once been like this awkward man. Wondering if this man ever dreamed of being a founder, of writing his name in a bloodline for the immortality that history offered.

He put the thought aside, wondering at himself. "Alberto." He joined him, and serafs came—serafs who were, in every possible way, superior to the single seraf Alberto owned. They offered wine and sweet water and fruit; it was past the hour for the midday meal, and although neither man had taken the time to eat—for very different reasons—neither felt the desire for food.

Sendari glanced around the Inner Chamber. At any given time, the Widan who sought the company of their peers gathered here; they politicked, they ate, they debated, and they parted company. There was no bloodshed in any part of the edifice except that part which was hidden, and the Widan might, if they desired it, practice a small part of their art here.

For this reason, it was the safest of all places for two of the Widan to meet and converse.

"What have you discovered?" Sendari began, without preamble.

"Nothing," Alberto said. "I mean, it's probably nothing, Widan. But it was unusual, and you gave strict orders that I was to report the unusual."

"Report it, then, without apology. I will not fault you for obeying the orders that I have given without attempting to second-guess my desire."

"Thank you, Widan. It's the Radann," the younger man said, relaxing slightly.

It couldn't be anything else, Sendari thought, and bit the acerbic words back. Alberto had been assigned the watch—the careful, magically aided watch—of the Radann. A Widan could not constantly listen to the Radann; he could not constantly see them. Not even Cortano, the man who ruled the Sword of Knowledge, had the power for such a continuous undertaking. But he could, with the aid of a carefully placed servitor or two, be called upon at just the right time. Foci had been put into place—foci crafted by Sendari himself—that might draw and hone the listening skills of a mage of power. Alberto was assigned to take messages of import from the select servitors who spied, in Alesso's service, upon the Radann, and to invoke the power of the foci when necessary.

"The kai el'Sol called a meeting with his brethren today."

Sendari waited as patiently as he could.

"I thought it would have something to do with the request that the General made of them early this morning."

"Request?"

The word was so neutral that the younger man did not realize he could get caught by it, in it.

"The General went to the kai el'Sol this morning," Alberto said. "And had the kai el'Sol disturbed before he had finished the morning contemplations."

"I . . . see."

"The kai el'Sol was not happy. He was even less so when he discovered the trivial nature of the General's visit; he was wise enough, however, to vent his anger after the General left him." The younger man shrugged, the gesture more of a nervous twitch than an expression of nonchalance. "But he had not yet fulfilled the General's request when I left my watch and sent word to you." Alberto's voice made clear what he thought of the wisdom of that.

"I see." The Widan was quiet a moment as he considered the courses this conversation could take, and what they would reveal. Even to Alberto. He wavered, not wanting to crack the facade of perfect cooperation behind which he and Alesso often struggled, but wanting very much to *know* what he already suspected. As was often the case, the desire to know won, although the contest, which did not reach the lines of his face or the posture of his body at all, was fierce.

"I would not have had the kai el'Sol disturbed for the sake of triviality," Sendari said softly. "Although his sword has been blunted, it still girds him; I prefer to treat the kai el'Sol with caution." This was truth; and it was further truth that Alesso himself did not consider the Radann a threat—although Sendari was peripherally aware that the Shining Court did—so much as an unwieldy and uncooperative weapon, to be used until such legitimacy as the Festival of the Sun could still bring, was laid across his brow.

"There were," Sendari said, lowering his voice and changing his posture in such a way that one watching carefully might still not have understood how he suggested, by the minutiae of gesture, confederacy. "Three matters that I considered to be unworthy of the attention of the Radann. We discussed these, and the General retreated to consider my position."

"Oh," Alberto said, as if Sendari's words were heavy with meaning and significance. "The matter that he disturbed the kai el'Sol for would bring honor to your family."

"Ah," the Widan replied, lifting a hand in a call for silence. "I believe I understand. And I do not believe that it is a matter I can, with humility, discuss further." His smile was stiff, but it was there. "The kai el'Sol has not yet acceded to this request?"

"No, Widan, but I believe it inevitable. If the kai makes a stand, it will not be over something of this nature."

"I concur." The Widan paused, lifting his hand silently. A seraf came at once, as if bidden; he marveled, at times, that they could be so sensitive to the slightest movements of the men they served, even though he was aware that their lives depended on it. "Wine," he said softly, before the seraf could speak. The dark liquid—for it was the season for the deepest of the wines—was slightly chilled; the act of a Widan's power, or more likely, a Widan-Designate. Sendari breathed in the scent of the wine, and held it a moment in his lungs.

The he exhaled.

"You did not call me here to discuss the temper of the kai el'Sol."

"No, Widan."

"Good." Sendari's smile was humorless. "Tell me."

"The Council of the Five was called."

"The Hand of God?"

"Yes, Widan."

"And?"

"The Radann have either discovered, and neutralized, the foci that we had placed in the Chamber of the Five, or—or one of the Widan was with them, and cast the spell of private speech."

It was clear, from the look on Alberto's face, that he thought the latter the more likely possibility of the two, and that he found it troubling. Sendari was inclined to trust the younger man's judgment in such matters, although he asked for justification of that opinion as a matter of course. "Why do you say this?"

"Because I heard them speaking—although they may have been outside of the periphery of the chamber when they began to do so—and then I heard nothing. Absolutely nothing. No breath, no rustle of cloth, no slapping of the table, no clink of cup. Nothing."

"There was no hint of what they might have been discussing?"

"No, Widan. I pressed the power. I am—fatigued." He looked wan now; pale, as if the mission to disclose his secret had been his only source of color. "I did not press too hard."

"Could you have breached the barrier?"

Alberto frowned, and when he spoke, he spoke slowly. He was, of all things, a *modest* man, and he was uncomfortable speaking about his power. It was why so many of the Widan had passed him over—they confused weak demeanor with inability. "I—I believe so. But I did not wish to alert the Radann. Perhaps they chose to be cautious in this discussion, where they have not been in any of their other private sessions. I did not wish to fuel their suspicions by announcing my presence."

Sendari frowned and then nodded. "Very well. Did you get a sense of the power that we may be facing?"

"Not a good one, no. It is . . . easier to listen than it is to shield."

"I *am* aware of that, Alberto."

The younger man flushed. Sendari immediately regretted the words, and the irritation they conveyed. Alberto was difficult enough to put at ease. "Yes, Widan. Whoever cast that spell ceased before the Radann were finished; I caught half-sentences that stopped abruptly. Then there was noise. Movement."

"I see. The servitors?"

Alberto shook his head. "I haven't had a chance to speak with them, or to have them spoken with. I called you immediately. I thought—I thought you would want to know."

"And I do," Sendari said, smoothing all strain from the words. "You did well. I will begin my own investigation along the sharpest edge of the Sword. If the mage who cast that spell was Widan, and among the Widan here, we may be in some . . . difficulty. If he was not, well." The Widan smiled grimly. "The Widan have dealt with rogue magery before."

He set down his cup, aware that it was now empty, although he did not remember the slow savoring of a very fine wine that should accompany such an emptiness. "Alerting us to the fact before the Festival may well save us from overlooking an enemy that cannot be safely overlooked."

Every word was true; every word was meant.

He watched as a momentary color returned to Alberto di'Ecclenses' face, thinking that he and Teresa were not so different. That truth was only another mask, even if it was the best fit, the closest to skin and all that lay beneath. He saw the younger man's pride as if from a great distance; he rose with grace, nodded, and left the Inner Chamber, making his way into sunlight, heat—the world of the Tor Leonne. There were people; clansmen of note surrounded by the cerdan, Tyran or Toran who served them. There were serafs carrying water, fruits, and fans with beautiful ease. The clans—both those that ruled the Tor and those that visited it—allowed only their best to publicly display their brands upon *these* grounds. There was color; flags and banners, their sharp clap in the breeze a reminder that the Lord's dominion held the winds.

And the winds were howling; he could hear them; they grew louder with each step he took. He could not silence their voices; could not submerge, forever, his response to their mocking words.

The walk across the Tor Leonne was long and ugly; each sight was an intrusion upon the privacy that necessity demanded he make. The mood was upon his face; he saw its reflection in the hurried movements of serafs and cerdan as they averted their gaze or turned, too quickly, to the tasks that suddenly seemed to absorb the whole of their attention. Sunlight slid off the surface of gold, the darkness of rubies. He announced his presence, and his title, without speaking a word; indeed, without the desire for such an announcement.

But he could not stop, could not school his face; there

were names upon his lips, and if he spoke them at all, their syllables would reverberate across the waters of the Tor. And one of those names, spoken thus, would destroy him. How long had it been? How long, since his anger had been so clear, so complete?

Not since he had been a young man.

Not since the day *she* had died, in the arms of the sister that he could not—quite—hate, but could never forgive.

He followed the path around the building, noticing only that it was thin and long. Later, perhaps, he would appreciate the sight of the Tor Leonne at summer's height. Perhaps not. The blend of sky and tree and flower flowed past him as if they were shadows cast by the Lord's face; they had no color of their own, no smell, no texture in which the eyes might delight.

There.

Pulling his robes around him, he stopped and bowed, perfunctorily, before the closed screens that bore his mark and his name. And then, without speaking a word to the seraf—or the wife—who waited, he entered into the heart of the illusion of privacy that was his home.

Radann Peder par el'Sol waited in silence on the mats of General Alesso di'Marente's waiting platform. His knees were beneath him, his hands, palm down, upon his lap. He wore a sword; the Radann were, by the Lord's law, allowed the grace of a weapon anywhere in the Tor Leonne, and not even the Tyr'agar himself would have insulted the Lord's service, or the Lord's Chosen, by breaking that edict. This side of the Festival of the Sun, the General chose to do likewise. The servitors waited outside, in the heat of the afternoon sun. They, too, bore arms, but they bore them as guards and escorts; they were allowed into the presence of the General only if they chose to set those arms aside—or if the Radann they accompanied so ordered.

Radann Peder par el'Sol did not desire the company of servitors; no man was better aware of how easily their loyalty could be bought or broken. He left them, and they were content to remain, in the open air. Wise men avoided the counsel of the powerful when the question of power itself had become so unsettled.

The General rarely kept Peder waiting, although it was

his wont to annoy the kai el'Sol, much to Peder's private amusement. Fredero was not an easy man to like, as his arrogance was mingled with that least enjoyable of traits: self-righteousness. Although each of the Radann had taken the oaths which bound them to the Lord, birth and blood could not easily be forced into a seamless whole, and Fredero kai el'Sol proved himself, time and again, to *be* Lambertan. In all but loyalty.

If not for the interference of Samadar, Peder was almost certain that Fredero would have destroyed himself, and quite possibly the Radann, by confronting the assassins of the Leonne clan directly. Almost certain.

Never underestimate your opponents.

Years, Peder had labored within the confines of the Church, honing the skills necessary to be seen as—to *be*—a leader. He could wield a sword with an ease and skill that was almost unearthly, could ride and handle beasts better than the raiding clansmen, could speak deftly without that cloying hint of subservience that often marred the speech of diplomats. He considered himself as able a judge of character as all but Samadar.

And he, like any noble-born, loathed the evidence of mistaken judgment.

The seraf returned to the room that was serene in its simplicity, joined Peder on the mats a moment, and bowed her perfect forehead into their smooth, jade-green surface, her hair an artful cascade across downturned shoulders. Then she rose, silent, and with a gesture bid Peder follow. He did, thinking that Alesso had a perfect eye for grace and beauty—that he did not need a wife to choose these things for him.

The screens were pulled wide as he approached the largest room in the grand structure which had served the Tyr'agar's informal needs since the founding of the Tor. It was empty, or almost empty; Alesso used the Tyran, although they served him in an unofficial capacity—as volunteers, Peder thought, with a certain cynical amusement—until the Festival rites. There were cushions here, and a deep recess in the floor which, although empty, could be filled with water at an hour's notice. The support beams were decorated with the colors of the Lord, but even these seemed too small for the room.

Or the man.

He stopped at the mats, knelt in a purely perfunctory way, and then left the seraf to her duties, as he turned to his.

"General Alesso," he said.

"Radann." The General's smile was slightly sharp. "I expected word earlier."

"Indeed," Peder said, taking the edge off his shrug with the faintest of apologetic smiles. "But the Hand of the Lord was to meet today, and while the matter was raised, it was one of many to be discussed and resolved. The kai el'Sol said you spoke of the matter as a 'thing of minor consequence'; he felt that the meeting of the Five could continue to its natural conclusion before word was sent."

"And he did not choose to carry that word himself?" Before the Radann could frame a reply, Alesso smiled. "Good, I tire of the man. Come, Peder. You are fortunate to find me here; I have business which will shortly demand my attention, but for the moment, I will take the peace that is offered. Join me."

The Radann acceded gracefully to the General's request.

"A question, Alesso."

"Ask it."

"Why the Serra Diora di'Marano? It is not the first time that she has been in so public a view, and it will remind the clans of that previous occasion, under a different lord."

"Bold, Peder." But the General's tone conveyed no displeasure. He waved, and two serafs appeared from the sides of the room, walking in perfect unison to the screens—the large screens—that shielded this room from the world. "The kai el'Sol did not object to the choice?"

"He objected only to the manner of its presentation, as you must have expected." The Radann watched as sunlight haloed the room's west-facing wall, open now to catch a glimpse of the Tor Leonne's quiet surroundings.

"He is used to a power that he will never again enjoy," Alesso said, lifting a hand to catch the goblet that appeared in the hands of an older seraf.

"And will the Radann, under your rule, never be of consequence in the Dominion again?"

"The Radann," the General replied smoothly, "as we agreed, will not be under *my* rule. They will be yours; you will be kai el'Sol. Whether you lead them wisely to power or foolishly to insignificance will be your decision."

Peder said nothing; the General expected no reply. They drank the water the serafs brought in silence. Then the younger man smiled.

"Alesso," he said, "I notice that you did not answer the question."

"How refreshingly observant."

"Sarcasm is unnecessary. If you do not wish to answer the question, I will abide by the decision. However, I have a request to make."

"Make it."

"That you refrain from further debasing the authority of the kai el'Sol. After the Festival you will be free to do as we have discussed. I do not need to remind you," he added, in a tone of voice that made it clear he was about to, "that we cannot afford to have the kai el'Sol pitted against us for *this* Festival. That two of the Tyr'agnati have refused the call to the Tor Leonne is bad; that the Sun Sword itself cannot be drawn is worse. Do not add a kai that speaks against the man who will wear the crown to that list."

"It is five days from the Festival."

"It is three days to the Festival; five to Festival's Height." Peder knew that Alesso knew the difference; knew as well that to the General the only moment of consequence was the moment in which the dedication of a new Tyr could take place: Festival's Height, the day during which the Lord's grip over his earthly dominion was strongest.

"As we've discussed, a month from the Festival under these circumstances would not be enough to obtain the Lord's favor and ascertain his earthly choice. *This* kai's death is not an option if you wish the legitimacy of his— of my—office." Peder smiled coolly. "After the Festival, it no longer matters."

"I see." Alesso di'Marente emptied his cup; his jaw was slightly clenched. A bad sign.

Peder braced himself for the cool tone that conveyed the greatest anger. This once, he braced in vain.

"Tyr'agnate Jarrani kai di'Lorenza came to me yesterday or the day before. He'd heard her," the General continued, his eyes unblinking, "singing. He said he would see no other, be they even Lorenzan, take the title of Lady of the Festival.

"Tyr'agnate Eduardo di'Garrardi was present. He seemed pleased by the choice, and concurred. I do not know the girl well, although she is the favored daughter of my oldest friend. But if she can cast such a spell over the two men whose support I most need . . ." he shrugged. "It costs me little enough to honor their choice, and it pleases them both." He smiled, and the smile added a subtle menace to the lines of his expression. "Now. Tell me. The meeting."

CHAPTER
TWENTY-FOUR

There were always secrets.

Between father and son, husband and wife, brothers, sisters—there were secrets and they were kept for their own precious reasons. Hatred was a secret. Power, if it was subtle, and especially if it was wielded by a woman. Anger was a secret, although sometimes in keeping it one broke other vows. Vows. Love.

Memory.

Do you see that, Na'dio?

Yes. *Yes,* she said, gazing intently at the light that the spider web caught and reflected. Wondering at the fineness of the woven thing, the splendor of the delicate trap.

No. Closer. There.

She'd looked, following the slender fingers of her aunt's perfect hands. A small fly was caught, and as it struggled, the weave stuck and clung, and the web began to shake, a foreshadowing of the death that was to follow.

Can we save it?

Why? If the fly is freed, it will be caught and crushed by the serafs; better that its death serves some purpose.

But it's not a clean death, Diora had said.

The Serra Teresa was silent a moment, and it was the silence of a teacher who thinks a lesson is about to be learned. *No death is a clean death, Diora. But if you will, you may try.*

Dior watched the web a moment, and then left her aunt. When she returned, she bore a small, sharp dagger.

And she came late. During her search, the spider had been drawn to its victim by struggles that the web made futile, and the fly was already cocooned in something far less forgiving than the single strand that had caught it. Diora watched the spider solemnly; watched it feed.

Well?

It's too late.

Yes. But if you'd like, you may destroy them both. The fly will feel no pain, and the spider will perish for destroying something that you have decided is worthy of saving.

She'd raised her youthful hand, her shaking hand, as if the dagger's edge could crush the web and its occupants and the drama that unfolded there as they watched. And then she lowered her hand.

It is not so easy as that, Serra Teresa said. *Because the web is beautiful, and because the spider has no other life, no other means of living.*

And the lesson?

What lesson?

Serra Diora di'Marano stood at the foot of the steps that led to the Sun Sword. The sun's height had cleared the skylight, but the Sword still glittered. It would, she knew, in the darkest of nights; the only thing that guttered its fire was either of the sheaths that lay before it. At her back, the Marano Toran stood. They were two, and they wore the full dress uniform of Adano's personal guard. Serra Teresa had given them leave to follow the Serra Diora—and because they had been assigned to Serra Teresa by the clan's kai, the Toran had no choice but to obey. Yet they did not seem to mind following the commands, gently worded and implacable, of a woman.

"Serra," one of the Toran said, and she turned, folding into a deep bow as she met the gaze of Tyr'agnate Eduardo di'Garrardi. It was a chance meeting of eyes; she lowered her face and let fall the veils about her cheeks, but not before he had seen—could see—her naked face, the adornment of blush rising in either cheek.

He smiled; his face, exposed, was far easier to read than hers had been. "Serra," he said, as her Toran moved to stand between them.

"Please, Tyr'agnate," she said, again lowering her face, "forgive me. I did not realize how the sands had run."

The pleasure in his smile was unfeigned; she recognized him, and although he expected it, he was flattered at the acknowledgment. "And I," he replied, "did not realize that the clansman who kept me waiting was neither unwelcome, nor a man. You have given no offense, indeed, the opposite. Are you interested in history?"

"I am the daughter of a Widan," she said, and then she folded her hands before her and said nothing, as if the reply itself were too bold, too inappropriate.

"You are the daughter of Widan Sendari par di'Marano. I know you, Serra. I have seen you many times, each at a distance greater than I care for."

She took a step back as he took a step forward; her Toran did not follow. Instead of shifting position they changed their posture; two right hands moved, simultaneously, to the hilts of sheathed swords. The gesture made their meaning as clear as the Lord's law allowed; it was forbidden to draw swords in this chamber. This room, as her father's study in so many of his dwellings, had no screens; it had two doors, fine and old, and was made of wood and stone and magic.

Diora did not think she could live in a world where doors and walls such as these were more common than screens and light and air. They seemed so heavy, life had to be escorted in; it would never find purchase without a guardian.

"Ah," the Tyr'agnate said, "forgive me. I mean no insult to the Serra."

The Toran did not speak; it was not their place. Nor did they move.

"I heard," he said, "that you sang in the presence of the Tyr'agnate Jerrani kai di'Lorenza. I would be honored, Serra Diora, if you would consent to sing for me."

"The honor," she replied, in her perfect voice, "would be mine."

"If it pleases you, I will speak with your father."

She bowed her head again, a slow nod, a graceful, flawless movement. Then she gathered her silks about her, and the Tyr'agnate was forced to move out of her way. To let her go.

Night.

Stars, clear and clean, a slowly spreading white fan across the ebony sky. The Festival of the Sun could seem, on a night like this, the custom of a foreign country, distant and unreal. Lamps were lit across the breadth of the Tor Leonne, although their light was meager. Only during the two Festivals was the expense of oil and wood and tallow justifiable—and justified.

That light would not have been welcomed.

Alesso di'Marente stood beneath the shadows of trees. No lamplight attended him, and no seraf; he was alone, by his choice. The only man with whom to share this night was immersed in the studies of the sword-sworn.

Or, Alesso thought, *in his anger.* And that anger brought him back to the daughter: Serra Diora di'Marano.

He was not a man to throw his life into the hands of a woman, any woman, and he had viewed with a dim contempt any man who did. Even the logical and rational Sendari—Sendari had almost been destroyed by Alora en'Marano, whose life was mercifully ended, by the will of the Lord, in time for the man to become Widan, and thence, to become a force of power in the Dominion.

The Tyr'agnate Eduardo di'Garrardi's desire for Serra Diora had surprised him—and angered him greatly. He needed Garrardi's support, and to have that support depend on the disposition of one young woman, no matter how lovely or graceful, was beyond his understanding.

Had been beyond his understanding.

Better, he thought, *that she had died with her husband.* He knew it for truth. Sendari would have grieved and railed—and accepted the necessity, as he had always accepted it, as he would have accepted it that night, with power a death or two away, and the heir, his *kai*—no longer merely the eldest son of a younger brother—to the new clan in the safety of his brother's keeping.

There would be no anger now, no coolness and distance between them. There would be no hostility from the Radann, veiled ever-so-politely as it might, or might not, be. There would be no pressure from Garrardi, no interest from Lorenza.

And there would be no song, no perfect voice, the echoes of which haunted him beneath the Lady's Moon. There would be no desire, no certainty that Serra Diora di'Marano was *meant* to be the wife of the man who ruled the Dominion, and not merely a man who served it.

She is just a woman, he thought. *In the darkness, she is flesh like any other.* But in the darkness, her wordless voice denied him the peace of that truth.

He had climbed the summit, and he stood a few days journey from the plateau at its height. Yet this night felt like a Moon-night, and on such a night as this, the plans he had made for his life had changed radically; on such a night as this, the mere General had decided that the Dominion was not too great a prize for his birth and blood.

If he could fell the Tyr'agar—and no one could deny him the accolades of that success—was the possession of something as slight as a woman to be denied him?

His smile was grim.

The cost. *Old friend.*

General Alesso di'Marente faced the night, and the Lady, and she gave him no easy answer.

It was at night that he found her.

Radann Fredero kai el'Sol rarely sought the solace of the darkness, but in the darkness there was a quiet that felt almost like privacy. And besides, the woman still slept, racked with chill and fever, in his private chambers. There was no dishonor to the Lord in his actions; he knew it for truth. But it *felt* wrong, and while he was adept enough to hide that discomfort, a man could not hide from himself.

He was certain, from the moment that he crossed the threshold to his elaborate rooms, that he was being watched; how, he could not say; nor did it particularly concern him. He was a wise man. He knew that, until the longest day, his life was secure. After that, there were no guarantees, except those that a man with a sword and a will to battle might make for himself.

Lady, he thought, as the clear night air filled his chest. *I am not your servant, but I would fight and die for your right to your dominion. My Lord is Lord of the Sun, of the Light. And He knows, as You, that the Lord of the Night was enemy to us all. The Radann were misled once; they will never again follow that road.*

He seldom spoke to the Lady; he was not a man with a great patience for night thoughts. But she had sent her servant to him, with word of a treachery that he could not openly confront. To confront it openly would be the death of the Radann, before the Radann had their opportunity to act. Still, he was not a man to whom the inactivity of expedience came easily.

He listened for the sound of a breath that was not his own; listened for movements that were not the brush of leaf against leaf, grass against grass, water lapping against the Tyr's personal platform at the lake's edge. Nothing came back to him except for the sense that he was watched; would be watched.

Let them watch, he thought, with a cold smile. Turning, he strode with purpose toward the edifice that had been built for one purpose and one alone: to carry the Sun Sword. The building was small, but perfect; it was made of stone and fine, hard wood, and the Widan that had survived the battle against the minions of the Lord of the Night had cast about it the enchantments of protection and preservation. The Tyr'agar had been pleased—or so history told them—to see that the only other resting place for the Sword was worthy of it.

But in those days, when the first Leonne cleansed the lands, he had seldom set the Sword aside.

Lamps burned to either side of the heavy doors, and they did not gutter except as a precursor to the death of a careless servitor. Their light cheered him briefly, as did the thought that the General's spies—for he was certain that they belonged to no other—would report his movement. Let Alesso read it as the slap in the face that it was.

The Radann did not follow, easily, the man who could not survive the test of the Lord. And that test was simplicity defined: draw the Sword.

He had seen it kill two men in his time; one Radann par, and one Radann kai. Pride in the Lord's favor was necessary. Hubris was fatal. And Fredero kai el'Sol did not suffer from that peculiar form of hubris that said: I am equal to the Lord's Chosen clan.

There was no key; Fredero kai el'Sol reached out and pulled the doors wide, flexing his muscles as he pitted them against their heaviness. They came slowly, but all of their resistance was weight; they did not creak or groan.

There were no servitors in the Inner Chamber; none were needed. No thief had tried to steal the Sun Sword since its creation, and had they, the Sword itself would intervene. Or so the doctrines said. This accepted fact, he had never seen proved.

He offered his obeisance; as kai it was simple and short. And then he crossed the threshold, and with both peace and strength, closed the doors behind him. Let them listen now. Or let them try.

The Chamber of the Sword was also illuminated by fire, although night peered in from above. Fredero paused at the door, lifted a thin stick of sandalwood incense from the neatly kept pile, and lit it upon the fire of the closest lamp. Then he placed it carefully within the brazier and left it smoking sweetly there. It would mark his time.

"Kai el'Sol."

He froze at the voice. Not in fear, but in surprise. It was a woman's voice, here. Turning slowly, he let the lamp at his back cast a shadow; it was a long one.

Wrapped in a plain, dark cloak, a slender figure stood at the foot of the stairs. Above her, burning faintly beneath the night sky, the Sun Sword sat, waiting. She bowed, and the movement revealed the silks of the sari beneath the drab cloak; they were an emerald green, edged in gold leaf, and they shimmered like dark liquid.

Her face was shadowed by the edge of a hood; her hands were hidden in the folds of the cloak. She was not tall, but the cloth hid her dimensions. She might have been delicate, or large, young or old, bent or straight.

He saw that she carried no weapon.

It surprised him, although he could not say why.

"I am the kai el'Sol," he said sternly. "And I have chosen this hour for my contemplation."

She bowed her head, waiting.

"Do you serve the Lady?"

She made no reply, and after a moment, he realized that that was her answer. This was impertinence.

And impertinence was the least of the sins that he had discovered this day. "I perform my contemplations in isolation. But if you wish to continue to view the Sun Sword, you may do so; only tell me the hour of your departure, and I will return then."

"I cannot stay," she said, "for much longer. I will be missed." And she lifted her hands slowly. The folds of the cloak fell away from them; he saw that they were fine and thin and pale; not a seraf's hands, nor a common clanswoman.

Pulling the hood from her face, she met his eyes, unblinking.

And he could not think it bold, although it was.

"Serra Diora," he said, and he bowed. He knew her well; it was under his auspices that she had been given to Ser Illara kai di'Leonne. The kai Leonne. The dead.

"Radann kai el'Sol. It has been many weeks."

"And they have been long, Serra." He left the sandalwood burning sweetly at his back, and approached her; there were no cerdan, no Tyran, to stop him. Not even a seraf attended her. "Have you come to contemplate the Sun Sword?"

"I see it," she told him softly, raising her delicate, perfect face, "every day. I watch, and I wait. One day, it will be lifted. One day, it will be drawn."

"I await that day, Serra. And I, too, watch. But I have not seen you."

"I come," she told him, "when the sun is at its height."

"And I, when the Lady's night reigns everywhere. Everywhere but here."

They were silent.

What do you know? he thought, for seeing her, he could see the Lady's darkness beneath her eyes, and in the depths of them. He did not ask. Moments passed, and he found that he could contemplate the Sword's fire without interruption, for she did not speak, and even her breath was delicate enough that it could barely be heard.

But she herself . . .

"Kai el'Sol," she said, when he turned to her and realized that he *had* turned to her. "I have come to you, here, for help."

"And what might I do to aid you, Serra Diora?"

"It is not the wish of my father that I be granted the privilege of becoming the Lord's Consort for the Festival."

"And you wish *me* to convince him?"

"No." She lowered her gaze. "I wish you to convince the General Alesso di'Marente that I am not the appropriate choice. He is my father's oldest friend, and I believe that there is conflict between them. I do not wish to be the source of that conflict."

The kai el'Sol said nothing, but the anger of the morning returned. As if she could see it clearly, she took a step back and turned away. "Serra," he said, more abruptly than he would have liked, "it is not you that angers me." He swallowed, unwilling to unman himself;

unwilling to tell her that the choice, in the end, was his only in theory. "Most men would be proud—*are* proud—to have their daughters chosen as the Lord's Consort. Why do you think your father objects?"

She was silent a long time, and when she spoke at last, her voice was soft, although the kai el'Sol thought he heard, for a moment, a thin, thin edge there. "Because I have already been married," she replied. "Because the clansmen know who I am, and who I was, and he seeks to protect me from their curiosity." Her voice caught. "I am newly returned to Marano, and I am returned under circumstance of war; he thinks that there are those who will judge me harshly and treat me less well than—than Ser Illara once did."

It was said.

"Serra," he said, "there is not a man there who will dare to treat you poorly. As the Lady of the Festival, you will *be* the Lord's Consort. You will occupy the highest seat of the Festival's many occasions, and while you will indeed be, in all ways, in the public view, you will be above it. For those three days, you *are* the Lord's Chosen. If you speak, we will hear you—for the Lord's Consort is no mere Serra; she is the *Lady,* come to visit the realm of the Lord's dominion at his behest."

She did not speak, but brought her hands together as if in prayer. "Kai el'Sol," she said, and her voice cracked. "We both know that that is true only in theory. I will be at most a Serra, at least a woman. I will be treated as a curiosity, and if I attempt to remove myself from that curiosity, I will not even have my cerdan to call upon. There will be no modesty for me, and no power. What will they say? Will they whisper *his* name? Will they offer condolences for my loss, while they smile at what it means? Will they take it upon themselves to come close—to come far closer than any honorable clansmen would otherwise dare—while I can sit and call upon no honorable defender?" She bowed her head again, but not before he saw the crimson flush across her cheeks, the reddening around the rims of her eyes. He thought there might be tears, but she was a sword's blade; unyielding.

"I would do the honorable thing," she told him, the words stilted, "if that is your desire."

"And yours?"

"It is not mine."

"And what is your desire, Serra Diora?"

"That I be allowed to honor the memory of my dead until the Festival of the Moon. *That* is the custom. But Ser Illara kai di'Leonne—yes, I will say his name—he cannot be spoken of for fear of the political consequences. So I must behave with haste and dishonor to serve the political ambitions of men that I never vowed, before the Lord, to serve and honor. I must be pretty and delicate and happy and perfect; I must accord his passing no mourning, and no loss."

He looked at her, at the anger that was just barely contained, and he realized that she was young. It had been so easy to forget it, during her short marriage to the kai Leonne, because she had been perfectly composed, perfectly graceful, and perfectly adept at subtly easing the tension of those who surrounded her husband.

He cursed General Alesso.

Because he knew that the Serra Diora was right. At heart, he was glad that she showed herself to be, after all things, not the daughter of a traitor but the widow of a great man. But having revealed just this to him, he must disappoint her; worse, he must give her to the Festival, as a political sacrifice to Alesso di'Marente—a man who served the enemies of the Lord.

To do otherwise risked the Radann, and he could not, now that he knew the truth of the General's allies, commit such a rash act. The Dominion was his responsibility.

"Serra," he said, although he could not, quite, meet her eyes, "you have proved, more than proved, that you are indeed worthy of the choice that we have made. The Lord could find no more fitting Consort in the Tor Leonne— and I think, very few so honorable.

"You have said that you must stand without cerdan for the length of the Festival, and in this you are correct. But you will have attendants, as you choose—and they will be the handmaidens of the Lord's Consort. And you will have, if not the cerdan, the Radann." He paused, and then, before he could falter, he looked at her, met the darkness of her unblinking eyes. "I promise it, beneath the light of God. You will have the Radann, and *I* will be among them."

* * *

Moonlight. The Lady's face, turned just so, the sky a clear and perfect darkness. The Serra Teresa turned from the open air, seeing the flight of insects against the screens the serafs had drawn. A candle burned at her side, and it burned quite low. She could have called for lamps, but did not. Waiting, she touched the strings of a quiet harp.

And then she smiled.

"Na'dio," she said, in a voice that the wind carried across the Tor to the ears of her niece.

"Ona Teresa," the girl replied, as if the distance between them did not exist in the darkness.

"Is it done?"

"Yes."

"And?"

"The Radann kai el'Sol will serve me," was the cool reply, "in the place of Marano cerdan, for the Festival."

"And the other?"

Silence. Then, "I did not think it wise to ask this eve. I will return to my chambers; summon the serafs away."

"Be cautious, Na'dio. We are not the only ones who listen." The Serra Teresa rose, lifting the candle and shielding it from the huff of scant wind. Because her almost-daughter could not see her face, she let it express what she felt, where no one but the Lady stood witness. "Be careful," she said, but this time, although her speech was clear, it was unembroidered by the power of their mutual curse. "Your father was not yet decided which course of action to follow."

3rd of Lattan, 427 AA
Essalieyan, Averalaan Aramarelas

"The politics of the situation is fairly simple," Baredan di'Navarre said. "He holds the Tor Leonne, and he holds the loyalty of roughly two thirds of the army— the two thirds that are mobilized and ready to obey his command."

"The Church?"

It was difficult to be spoken to so bluntly by this particular Commander. Baredan di'Navarre had studied the customs of the Imperials for much of his adult life—the military customs, of course—and yet his knowledge did not make his reactions any easier to control. The Kalakar was not a graceful woman, nor a delicate one; she walked like a man, spoke like a man, demanded—and assumed— a man's respect. And from the scars that lined her face— pale now, at the touch of the Lord's grace—she had the right to both. She was no Imperial officer, come to the field without a sense of what she asked her people to face; she was a warrior, and she had proved it to those who needed proof: The men who served her. And the women.

He knew it. He had faced her knowledge and skill in the wars over a decade past—although she was not the anvil against which *his* sword had been forged. No, that General, defeated, now ruled in the Tor Leonne. Such were the ironies of life. The Kalakar and Alesso di'Marente had clashed in the Averdan valleys, and although she had narrowly escaped the massacre there, the victory had been granted to the Northerners. A costly victory, both to Averda and Mancorvo. Ramiro di'Callesta adapted. Mareo di'Lamberto was, well, Lambertan.

Damn it. What had she said? The Church. "The Radann serve him. They have no reason not to. But they won't like it—not if Fredero kai el'Sol proves true to his birth."

The Kalakar raised a brow. "Explain."

"He's Lambertan."

Ramiro di'Callesta grimaced. "What the General is trying so eloquently to say is that the Lambertans will often take a misguided stand, and cling blindly to it in the name of so-called honor." He raised a hand as Baredan di'Navarre opened his mouth. "Not here."

The General did not bridle.

"So he has the army and the Radann, for the time being. And he has the kin." The word brought a shadow to her face, but the shadow sharpened, rather than softened, the lines of her jaw, the slits of her eyes.

The Berriliya, a man not unlike Alesso di'Marente, leaned across the table to look at the map that had been laid out. His face was thin, and his nose pronounced, but war had been kinder to him than it had to The Kalakar. Baredan suspected it was because The Berriliya chose to govern his men in a fashion that was more traditional—in the North—than The Kalakar's "personal" style of leadership, which meant that he did not often face the naked blade. "With no disrespect," he said coolly, "Mancorvo's loss was both inevitable and a blow. Lamberto is a widely respected clan, both within and without the Terrean."

"Be that as it may," Ramiro di'Callesta said coolly, "let me merely say that the clan Marano is—was—of the Terrean of Mancorvo."

"I believe the Tor'agar Adano kai di'Marano remains in Mancorvo," was Baredan's neutral reply. "I do not know if he has disowned his par or not. Certainly, if the Widan is proven to be heavily involved in the deaths of the clan Leonne—*and* they lose the war—he will be censured."

"Let us assume, for the moment, that you did not ride to the North. You did not carry word, to either Lamberto or Callesta, and the Festival of the Sun occurred as planned. What, then, would have happened?"

Baredan looked at the map, changing the lines of his face so that he might appear to be thinking, although the time taken was purely a matter of appearance; he'd thought of little else since he'd ridden with nothing but his life and his horse—ah, Sashallon—two weeks ago. "At the festival—and please," he added to the Tyr'agnate who ranked him in both political experience and knowledge of these foreign Generals—Commanders, as they styled themselves, "correct me where you think my assumption is in error."

"As you request. But I, too, am curious to know what you think; I do not spend much of my time in the Tor Leonne. Averda is a large and prosperous Terrean."

And you spend the half year that you aren't collecting taxes raiding across the Mancorvan border. "I believe that the death of the clan Leonne was planned to occur this close to the Festival of the Sun. Most of the clansmen would already be on the road when word of the death reached them, if it reached them at all. The Tyran—" he paused to spit, for the Tyran had forever condemned themselves in the Lord's eyes for their betrayal of the man to whom they had sworn their blood-oaths. In the Lord's eyes—and in the eyes of any clansmen who understood honor. "Your pardon. The Tyran have cut off the only road that leads out of the Tor Leonne, and even serafs are given a very difficult passage. Word travels, yes, but it travels slowly.

"The Tyr'agnati were intended to assemble, as for

any Festival of the Sun. It is likely, in my mind, that Tyr'agnate Lamberto would lose his life immediately. Tyr'agnate Callesta is a more political man, and he might have been able to survive. Perhaps. The Tyr'agnati of Oerta and Sorgassa are already, I believe, among the General's supporters. It is likely that they have laid claim, for their support, to the parts of those unfriendly Terreans that border them: Oerta for Averda, and Sorgassa for Mancorvo."

"I will, of course, have to disappoint."

"Of course, Tyr'agnate.

"Regardless, once the men were in the Tor Leonne, Alesso would have the power that he needed. They would be separated from their armies, and although they could call upon the individual clansmen who owe them loyalty, even these would be outnumbered by the cerdan and Tyran that now man the Tor."

"What would the Church do?"

"In our hypothetical case, they would acclaim the new Tyr." He met the unblinking eyes of The Kalakar, unconsciously drawing himself to his full height. "It is not the way of the Dominion to follow a weak man, and the Tyr'agar proved himself to be incapable of winning a war against his Northern enemies. Worse, he gave up lands that were claimed by the Dominion—by either Callesta or Lamberto—in order to sue for this peace.

"If I were Alesso di'Marente, I would have slaughtered Callesta and sued for peace with Lamberto."

"I see," Ramiro said, the two words succinct, although the glance that he afforded the General was a genial one.

The Kalakar and The Berriliya exchanged a glance. "But they will not acclaim a new Tyr?"

"Oh, they'll do it. But they'll be split. Callesta is a clan worthy of a great hatred or a great fear. It holds the cradle of the Dominion; Averda is rich enough to feed an army, and its borders have been, because of its dalliances with Lamberto, well-defended. Its young men are raised in war, and in death; they will not blink. Kill the Callestan Tyr'agnate, and the clan would be in disarray enough that Averda's fall would not be too costly."

"You are mistaken, General."

"Oh? You are the power behind your clan, Ramiro. Your kai is not your equal, nor his par."

"As you will," Ramiro replied, although it was clear that he was ill-pleased.

"Gentleman," The Kalakar said, "Let me go back to our hypothesis. The new Tyr is acclaimed by the Radann. What of the clansmen?"

"Those that are suspect will be killed," Baredan replied, feeling the sting of being corrected by a woman. "Those that are not will be elevated. Alesso will build his support, and he will hold it."

"But he will not," Ramiro said softly, "in this hypothetical case, or in fact, wield the Sun Sword."

"No."

The two men stared at each other a moment.

"Very well." The Kalakar ran her fingers through hair that was already pulled away from the strong lines of her forehead. "In the expected unfolding of events, the assassination of the clan Leonne would have remained an internal affair. Alesso di'Marente would found a new clan, and he would rule the Dominion. Ambition often tells this tale, when the ambition is large enough."

"Yes."

"You've come North. You have asked for our intervention, and while the Kings decide, the Festival of the Sun approaches. The Tyr'agnate—two—have wisely declined the journey to the South, and with that, ruined all plans for an easy transfer of power. So. You knew the General, Baredan. What now?"

"Alesso di'Marente has the army, the Radann, the Terreans of Raverra, Oerta and Sorgassa. In theory, he holds the balance of power. But we are not a cold and logical people; we are not a people who are ruled by fear and the strength of our enemy's numbers.

"*We* have the clan Leonne, and if that clan numbers a single man, he is the only man alive who can wield the Sun Sword. And we have Averda."

"And Mancorvo?"

Uneasy silence.

"Are there other factors, other immediate factors?"

"The kin are involved, Serra," he said.

She raised a brow, and he had the grace to flush.

"To continue: I would say, although I've been wrong many times in my youth—"

"You are hardly a young man, General."

"Thank you. I would say that Alesso di'Marente will, without the benefit of the Sun Sword, raise his armies and aim them toward the Northern borders. He will make a call to war that no clansman can ignore: a chance, at last, to salve an injured pride.

"And perhaps his call will be genuine; perhaps not. But I will say this: To get to you, it is no coincidence that the armies will be placed along the borders of the two Terreans that he could not be certain of."

The Berriliya and The Kalakar exchanged glances. Baredan found them intriguing, for it was clear that they did not like each other, and it was equally clear the respect between them was profound and genuine. An honorable enemy, he thought, was the next best thing to an honorable friend.

"Thank you, gentlemen, for your time."

Ramiro di'Callesta rose. Baredan stood; he disliked these foreign chairs; they were confining and rigid and colorless. "And we thank you, Commander, Commander, for yours."

He let them go, and when the doors—and even in the so-called Annagarian quarters, doors abounded in this chilly clime—had closed, he said, "The kin are involved, General."

"Yes."

"And what do you suppose they want? What would they take in return for bestowing a kingdom upon an ambitious man?"

His soul, Baredan di'Navarre started to say, and then he snorted. What a meager prize for such a display of power. They looked, as one man, at the crossbeams above them; at the walls and the towering windows that let the light in—that made of its fall a brilliant display.

"Two hundred years ago, who did the kai Leonne turn to for aid in his crusade against the Lord of Night?"

Baredan di'Navarre was no historian; he did not need to be; the question could be answered by any child old enough to speak. *To the Northern Kings.* The golden-eyed men who alone were not considered, by the Lord, to be of demon blood.

Or so the legends went.

Himself, he was glad that he was not of enough importance yet to speak with the Kings.

* * *

Valedan kai di'Leonne sat beside the fountain that adorned the courtyard of the Arannan Halls. Although he had always liked the peace of this place, he had never liked the fountain itself; in its gaunt, still boy, replete with marble blindfold, he felt the Northern condemnation of his people. It made no difference that the sculptor had *been* Annagarian; in Annagar, such a vision would have received no attention, much less approbation. Unless it had been called *Justice* and set in the face of the Tyr'agar, in which case, it would have merited death.

Yet tonight, the waters stilled for the duration of the long, cool evening, he felt akin to not only the fountain's maker, but also the statue itself: too weak, and too blind, for such a task as he had taken on.

"Valedan."

He did not look over his shoulder, and he did not rise; there was no need to, and in fact, any such gesture would have been considered—now—a display of weakness. For the person who addressed him was Serra Alina, and Serra Alina was only a woman.

"Serra Alina," he said, seeing the moonlight touch the water as he leaned forward. "Is my mother ailing?"

"Your mother is sleeping," the Serra replied, "Do you mind if I join you?"

"No."

It wasn't true; he minded. But she seldom came to him for the sake of company alone—for company, she chose the women of the Northern Court, who were, in many ways, her equal.

"The Princess Mirialyn believes that the crisis has passed."

He heard the words as if they were spoken in a foreign tongue; they touched his ears, but only came to make sense as the seconds passed and they sank roots. He rose, leaving his resentment upon the cool stone beneath his feet. "W–when?"

"W–when what?" she said, mocking him as gently as an ungentle woman possibly could.

"When will we know it for certain?"

"Soon, I think," was Serra Alina's confident reply. "Ser Valedan, you succeeded." And she knelt, before him—*for* him—the distance between his feet and the lustrous confines of her perfectly kept hair a finger's span. "No, I should not call you that. Tyr Valedan." She rose. "I thought that you would like to know."

He wanted to thank her—and two weeks ago, he would have. But he did not know what to say, did not know what a Tyr should say. His father's face, and the dim memories of his father that childhood had not left behind, were of little help; his father had rarely shown gratitude for anything.

She turned and walked away, the moon upon her pale sari, her pale shoulders. Then she stopped, and her hair caught the scant light as she turned again. "Valedan," she said, "we are beneath the Lady's Moon; if it is not your desire to be confined by the formality of the crown you have chosen, set it aside."

I don't know how, he said, but his voice did not carry in the darkness of anything but his own doubt. "Serra Alina, what will you do?"

"I? I am the sister of Tyr'agnate Mareo di'Lamberto." As always when she spoke of her brother, her voice hardened and cooled.

"And will you remain in the Empire?"

"I do not know," she replied, her voice softening as she saw—before he did—what he would say. "The Dominion holds little for me." She waited, a shadow or a blade, giving him no words. He felt the difference between their ages as keenly as he ever had. And the difference between their ranks.

But it was Serra Alina who taught him what he needed to know about the Dominion; Serra Alina who made certain that he could read, could write, could speak with the polish of a Tyr's man. It was Serra Alina who took the time to make clear which of the laws of the Dominion were expendable, and which were not.

And it was Serra Alina, of all the Annagarians present, who had risked her life to save his. And succeeded.

She was not his mother. Nor one of his mother's co-wives. But she was, of the Annagarians here, the closest thing he had to family, whether they shared blood or no.

"I don't know how to be Tyr'agar."

"I know," she told him softly, the tenor of her voice—and nothing else about her—reminding him of Serra Tonia. "You were not raised to the rule. But you have committed yourself. Tyr'agnate Ramiro di'Callesta will follow you—or your office—and I believe that Tyr'agnate Mareo di'Lamberto can be persuaded to do so as well.

"But perhaps not. You will come with a Northern army, into territories that the Northerners savaged a little over a decade ago. He may well see you as a puppet, and the crown that you would claim as a tool, for his most hated enemies." She took a step toward him, and then stopped, affording the title more respect than he himself knew how to. "And if you would give the lie to that belief, you *must* find the Leonne blood within yourself.

"You have done it once, Valedan. It is there, if you truly wish to call upon it." Her dark hair was shadow as she nodded. "And when you call it, and you hold it, let us pray that it is stronger and truer to the Founder than your father's blood ever was."

Mareo di'Lamberto sat beside the only person in the Dominion of Annagar he trusted as much as he trusted himself, and she was silent. She did not expose her face to the light very often; her skin was fair, and unblemished by the sun's reach, although the brush of time itself could never be avoided.

"Donna," he said, and he thought, as his eyes traced the familiar lines of her face, that time had been brutal indeed in these last few weeks. Would they survive this? They had survived all else.

Even the death of their kai at the hands of the Imperials. *It was not the Lord's time,* the Tyr'agnate thought. *But he is gone, just the same.* Of course a clan of Lamberto's stature could not be left without an heir, and a new heir had been appointed after the grieving had been done in accordance with the Lord's will. But it was not a clean grief; not until those responsible lay dead, their blood a red spill beneath the open sky. He had sworn it, although his gentle wife would take no part in the swearing; the disk remained, uncrossed, in their bedroom, a thing of wood, a reminder of death.

Thus did she spare the Terrean over which he presided from a war that he could only acknowledge in his most serene moments was futile without the support of his Tyr. They swore their clan oaths together, for she was his support; wife, yes, and graceful perfection whether she wore that title for public view or in the privacy of their moments together, but more than that. Oh, she was not the frail and slender girl who had once come to him so meek and so terrified, although she hid the latter for two years before he had at last received from her the one gift that he desired: her trust. No, time had silvered the dark sheen of her hair, and thickened her body, and lined the corners of her eyes and her lips.

He saw in them the hints of the smile he loved, and knew, to be fair, that time had been no kinder to him. Or perhaps, it had been just as kind; for she did not look the part of a young girl, and she was not: she was stronger, wiser, and more just than the fear of youth allowed; she gave him the shelter that he needed, on the rare occasions that that need drove him. She trusted him, always; she looked up to him, still; he strove, in every way, to continue to live up to her expectation. She was the one person in his life he did not wish to disappoint.

Let other men tell him that he did not care enough for gold, or for the power it could buy; let them tell him that he did not pay heed to politics, and the political winds that blew through the Dominion with such force; let them call him a self-righteous fool.

She did not, and her belief was the strength that he required to stay steady in the eyes of the Lord; to live an honorable life.

One did not pray to the Lord for mercy. One prayed at night, or before dawn's light, and Mareo di'Lamberto had only ever prayed for two things, for prayer took the strength from the man, and put it in the hands of the Lord or the Lady, and he disliked to be so unmanned. Only two things.

And he watched one of them now, thinking that flesh could not contain her, that time could not degrade her; she was Donna.

Yet in spite of the fact that he adored his wife as openly as any man that he had ever known, the Tyr'agnate was a man prone to practical thoughts. It was his wife who was sensitive to the changes of moontide and time, and he moved closer to her, putting an arm around her shoulders as if by doing so he could protect her from the freedom of the Lady's darker thoughts.

She accepted the shelter of his arm for a time; the warmth was gentle between them. And then she spoke.

"War, Mareo."

"I know." He rested his chin upon the top of her head. "The Callestans have ceased their border raids. It tells us much. Word has come to me that the Tyr'agnate did not travel to the Tor Leonne."

He heard her breath; felt her surprise in the way it was drawn. To understand Donna, you had to listen for the small things, the subtle gestures.

If she heard regret in his words, she did not ask him about it; instead she said, "I would not have thought the Callestans would have valued the honor of their vows so highly."

It pleased him, and he smiled. "It has little to do with honor; the Callestans think honor and silver have the same meaning. No, it's more likely that they know they can't trust him."

She was silent for a long time; longer than was her wont, although she was not a talkative woman.

"Donna?"

"They could not trust you—not to murder the Lord to whom you swore your oath. Not to plan his death through the office of the *Tyran*."

"But?"

She pulled away from his arms, breaking the circle; reached out and very gently touched his face.

"Donna," he said, resting his chin a moment in the cup of her soft hand, "tell me."

"It may be nothing," she told him.

And her tone, of course, told the opposite tale.

"Then tell me, and be free of it. Come."

"I received a letter today."

"A letter? Not a message?"

"No. A written letter. It was—it was penned by Serra Fiona en'Marano."

"Serra Fiona? I'm not sure I recall—ah, wait—the par di'Marano's young wife. He was trapped in the capital, then?"

"Yes."

"How did this letter reach us?"

"I do not know who carried it; by the time I saw the mark at the end, the messenger had vanished."

He sat still, waiting; once she began to speak, she rarely left a tale untold. Yet she hesitated a moment before she continued. "The letter—it was harmless enough. But—"

"Might I see it?"

"I do not think that you would read the words as I read them."

"Woman's business, then."

"Yes." For a moment, a smile glimmered in her eyes, and the corners that surrounded the one feature that time did not dim crinkled. Then the night took the expression from her face so completely it might never have been there at all. "The armies will be gathered after the Festival of the Sun."

He stiffened.

"But there is a possibility that the armies need not be arrayed against us."

"And what possibility is that?"

"She tells me that the Captain of the oathguards acted in haste when he ordered the public execution of the Imperial hostages."

"His only decent act."

"—and that, for his part in both the execution and the death of the Tyr, he himself was executed, although the execution was a private matter. She . . . feels that he was not an acceptable, or an honorable, man, and that he met his just end."

"I see."

"There is no Tyr'agar, but when the Tyr is appointed, the Captain of the oathguards will be replaced."

"I see."

"She believes that there is a possibility that the General Alesso di'Marente would accept your recommendation before he makes that choice."

Silence.

Serra Donna averted her eyes, but she did not stop. "And she says that the armies that are gathering will be raised—and sent—to the North. The far North."

"Donna." He caught her chin; it trembled as he met her eyes. They were glittering brightly in the lamplight. "The Empire."

He spoke a single word then, although it was unnecessary to do so for her sake. No, he spoke it for his own,

because in speaking, a man made his will known, made
it real.

Andreas.

His kai.

His unavenged kai.

CHAPTER TWENTY-FIVE

3rd of Lattan, 427 AA
Essalieyan, Averalaan Aramarelas

The Hawk and the Kestrel stood by the seawall, the distance between them both vast and tiny. The Hawk, appropriately named for the hook of his nose and the clear piercing gray of his eyes, wore a single sword. If he carried a dagger, it was appropriately placed where eyes could not easily see it. The Kestrel, named not for any resemblance to the hunting bird most favored by the Western Essalieyanese, but rather for her ability to circle the Hawk, also wore a sword; she had chosen to leave her armor in the safety of her house. It was too hot, this summer day, for the extra padding, and in the city of Averalaan, it was also ostentatious and unnecessary.

The breeze took their words by halves, but they spoke the language of their chosen profession, and what the wind took, years of experience and knowledge filled in. It had been a languid summer night, but the humidity of the day had threatened rainfall for hours; the time was almost come.

Many a discharged soldier, and many a retired one, had seen these two before, but they seldom stood alone; there was too much anger between them, too often, over the field of battle chosen, or the rules imposed upon those soldiers, or the discipline involved—they disagreed on everything but the actual battles themselves.

One man had always stood between them in these arguments, and more often than not stood above. And he was, of course, called the Eagle.

The flight of Commanders.

The Kestrel saw him first, and her demeanor changed subtly; the Hawk, aware of her every move because he trusted them, by instinct, so little, turned as well. They waited in a companionable silence until he approached.

He was not as tall as the Hawk, nor as commanding a presence as the Kestrel, but of the Commanders, his was the eye that saw clearest, and saw farthest. Time had taken much of his hair, but if he felt self-conscious about the loss, it did not show; he was not a vain man. Not a loud one.

And yet.

"Commander Allen," the Kestrel said, offering a clipped nod that spoke both of habit and precision.

"Kalakar," he said, bowing. "Berriliya."

"Commander Allen."

They stepped apart, and he took his accustomed place between them, flanked by them and comfortable to be so. They stared at his profile, at either side of his profile; she saw a perfectly normal man whose calm smile gave nothing away. He saw the scars of an old fire, healer-doused and tended, but visible if one knew where to look.

"Well?" the Kestrel asked.

Commander Allen smiled. "You haven't gotten patient in the last decade."

"No."

"I thought ruling a great House would at least teach you that."

The Hawk snorted. "She rules her House the way she did her regiment."

The Commander lifted a hand. "It *is* her House. The regiment was the Kings'."

"You haven't answered the question."

"You noticed." He stared out at the waves upon the sea, at the clouds, gray and that deep, livid green—if green was a color that could be said to be livid, it was on days like this, with the storm gathering in its folds—and he said, "Can you see the rocks?"

It was an odd question. The Berriliya looked; The Kalakar snorted. "The only rocks I care about are the ones beneath my feet. They're stable. Allen." Pause. "Bruce."

"We haven't spoken for well over eight years, Ellora."

She shrugged.

"What have you been doing in those eight?"

"Building a House."

"Building a small personal army."

She shrugged again; it was true. "I've tended to the responsibilities that fell on my shoulders."

"And you, Devran?"

"I did not choose the House," the Berriliya said curtly, as if at an unspoken accusation. "The House chose me. I either accepted the title, or I . . . abandoned the name. The name meant, and means, much to me. But if you mean to imply that I've seen no fighting . . ."

"No," was the dry response. He waited. And then he laughed. "*I* have spent my time in the company of a very suitable woman. I have watched my grandson grow; I have sponsored my granddaughter into the House Terafin. She is not," he added, as if only then realizing that he spoke with the leaders of two of The Ten, "a military woman, and I would not have her become one.

"I have spent three months traveling in the company of Sioban Glassen, and was looking forward to doing so again." The sea's waves were almost nonexistent, but he looked down at them as if they were fascinating.

Or as if, beneath the facade of the nearly still waters, other memories were surfacing.

"Is that an answer?" The Kalakar said at length; The Berriliya was silent throughout.

"What was the question?"

"Will you come," she said quietly, "to Annagar?"

"Will I come out of retirement?"

"Yes."

"It took two years," he told her quietly, although he stared out at the sea, always at the sea, "to remember that men and women were neither weapons nor enemies. To trust them; to realize that accident and illness were more likely to take them from me than ambush or open clash."

She shrugged.

"I do not think, Ellora, that you've remembered either. Or you," he said to The Berriliya, without rancor. "But I am not of the patriciate except by military rank, should I choose to air it." He bowed his head a moment.

"Rank or no," The Berriliya said, "you know that we've elected to accompany the army."

"At the Kings' behest, and with their grave apprehension." He lifted a hand to the back of his neck; massaged the muscles there.

"Yes."

"And you know," The Kalakar said, "that our previous success was, in all ways, the success of *three* Commanders. We two are agreed on at least—and possibly only— one thing: We can't go South without you."

"Then you have asked me no question; instead, you have laid a problem at my feet." He smiled at that. "Old times."

"Allen."

"I wanted you to know what you were asking of me, but I see that neither of you are going to understand it. How unsatisfying. And how," he smiled sharply, "expected. Or it would have been, a decade ago.

"I know of the kin, Ellora. I know what happened here the last time the kin were involved—although I wasn't in the city at the time." He lifted his cloak, and in the sun's light, they saw that he was girded round with a sword, and the sword was familiar to both of them. "I have not forgotten duty. And I will not lie. If I have done other things for eight years, I have been apprentice in all of them, and master of none; they were enjoyable, but they were not what I was made for." He let the cloak fall. "But I would not lose them either. I dislike the loss of something I have struggled so hard to achieve." The seawall carried the weight of his hands for a moment; the weight of his arms and his shoulders. Then he straightened out, and as he did, he seemed taller. "Are you answered?"

"Yes," The Kalakar said, as The Berriliya nodded.

"Good. Had either The Kalakar or The Berriliya chosen to remain in Averalaan, I would not have allowed it."

"What, you don't think that the army survived our absence?"

"It survived well enough," the Commander said, "when there was no war." His smile was as sharp as the words themselves, and for the first time that day, the Kestrel and the Hawk smiled with him.

"How long do we have?"

The Hawk and the Kestrel exchanged glances.

"Intelligence is being gathered and consolidated. General Alesso di'Marente seems to have been prepared."

"And his aim?"

"We do not believe that he intends to declare war upon the Empire. He will certainly take Averda if he can; we believe he will also attempt to bring down clan Lamberto in Mancorvo."

"Internal affair," the Eagle said softly.

"Yes."

"Our angle?"

"We have," The Berriliya said neutrally, "the surviving member of the clan Leonne."

"Dangerous," the Eagle said, "but possible. When will we know for certain?"

"Either war will be declared at the height of the Festival of the Sun, or it won't; I think the Festival of the Sun, politically, will decide the course of the war for the Annagarians."

"And for us."

"Allen—"

"The levies?"

The Kalakar rolled her eyes; the man who had mourned the loss of a gentle man's life had already been buried. "We wait the Kings' orders. Speaking of which, I have an interview that I must attend."

She knew, the moment she entered the large, empty hall—or rather, the large hall that *should* have been empty—that there was going to be trouble. The Ospreys were that type of weapon; double-edged, with a grip that grew slippery when the blade had drawn too much blood.

Sentrus Auralis, cocky as ever, stood at an indolent ease, his eyes so artfully narrowed he looked as if he'd fall over if touched. Sentrus Alexis—a soldier determined to keep that rank in spite of the best intentions of her superior officers—stood with her arms crossed, her fingers tapping her upper arms. She usually stood with a dagger at hand—but not even Alexis would have been quite so bold where The Kalakar herself was concerned.

Cook stood beside the long table, arms crossed just as Alexis' were, sword girded. He did not wear armor, or a helmet, but of all the soldiers present, his presence did the least disservice to her House name. But he stood beside, and slightly behind, the young woman whose presence The Kalakar had requested.

Kiriel.

Duarte sat beside her until The Kalakar entered the hall; he rose at once to greet her, the motion a command to the Ospreys present. She knew that, until the interview was over, he would not sit again. But she wondered, idly, what he would do when she ordered him out of the hall.

Ordered them all out.

She came alone; they saw that, and she knew it served her well in their eyes. Not even Korama accompanied her, and in matters of both import and delicacy—although the combination of anything to do with the Ospreys and delicacy was almost beyond the bounds of comprehension—she never left him behind. He was not just a Verrus, but *her* Verrus; as close to domicis as The Kalakar would allow.

The Kalakar would never trust an outsider—and at that, a nonmilitary man, to see to her protection or her personal needs. She knew that many of The Ten employed the domicis, through either short- or long-term contract, and although it had been pointed out, with more or less heat depending upon who had started the age-old argument, that she certainly paid the House Guards—and especially the Verruses—in coin, she could not shake the feeling that gold or no, they were loyal to *her*.

Which didn't quite explain the Ospreys. Or why she tolerated them. In times of peace, she could barely defend them herself—but war was looming on the horizon; she could almost taste it in the winds.

The Kings would return the only right answer, and the gathering would start.

"Primus Duarte," The Kalakar said softly.

"Commander."

"You provide more of an escort for a young Sentrus than one normally sees."

His eyes flickered ever-so-slightly to his left, glancing off the steely profile of Sentrus Alexis. So.

"Kiriel," The Kalakar said, willing to bend slightly to the ill-humor of this particular company, "do you require the presence of the Ospreys for our interview?"

Kiriel's eyes turned to Duarte, but she was far less subtle than her superior officer. Ellora could see the whites of Duarte's eyes as he rolled them.

"Kalakar," he said.

"Primus. This is not the time or the place."

"There is no other," Alexis replied, and The Kalakar

took a very hard look at the single sword across her right shoulder.

"Sentrus," Duarte said, and the woman fell silent.

"Primus," The Kalakar continued, as if there had been no interruption, "this is not a torturer's session. This is an interview."

"It's more than just an 'interview,'" Auralis said, in that wonderfully attractive drawl that made him so popular among the less discriminating young of either sex. "It's an interrogation on the eve of the biggest war we've seen in twelve years." His lovely eyes were still lidded, but he'd straightened up to his full height. It made him look slightly more dangerous—and marginally more respectful.

This was the real reason why Ellora had elected to leave both of the Verruses behind. They could not tolerate obvious disrespect, and she did not wish to have to defend it when she found it distasteful enough herself.

She did not respond, but instead continued to meet the eyes of the one man she was sure of: Duarte AKalakar, fledgling mage, leader of the Ospreys.

"You know what's at stake," she said softly.

"And you," was his quiet reply. "Commander, may I speak freely?"

Ellora snorted with genuine amusement. "And I'm to stop you when I can't even keep a bunch of your sentruses in line?"

His smile was rueful, but beneath the smile of both of these leaders was steel; they knew the people who served them; they knew the promises that had been made.

Neither knew, and neither wished to know, what would happen to the service when the promises themselves were compromised. But neither wished to go to war against not only the Dominion, but some shadowy cabal that seemed to work beside it and within it, with less knowledge than they could easily have.

As if they knew what the only clean answer to their predicament was, they both turned to Kiriel. The girl, cool and pale and somehow darker than cloudy night, said nothing, and there was a quality to her silence that made Ellora realize, for the first time, that although the young Sentrus did not understand what exactly the difficulty was that she posed to the House Guards, and therefore to Kalakar, she understood, in some way, that it *was* a difficulty.

And she found it amusing.

There are times, Ellora thought, as she met, unblinking, the young woman's gaze, *when Devran's right.* Then, as if such a concession, unspoken though it was, galled her, she said, "You are required to attend the interview itself. You are not required to respond to questions that pertain to your past. While you remain a member of the House Guards, you are under my protection, and your past is not at issue."

But her voice was clipped, even cool, as she spoke, which had not been her intent. There was something about Kiriel that provoked her; something about the girl that made her, attractive and extremely competent though she was, very difficult to like.

Turning to Duarte, some of that coolness remained. "You are to leave, with the men and women under your command. Any Osprey that chooses to disobey that order—and it *is* an order, make no mistake—will find themselves debarred from House Kalakar, names stripped. Do I make myself clear?"

It was not what she had intended, but once she had set foot on that path, she could not turn back; she understood the rules of leadership.

Still, Sentrus Alexis hesitated a moment, seeking something from Primus Duarte.

Find it soon, Ellora thought, ill-amused.

The woman apparently found enough of what she sought to tender The Kalakar—the Commander—a sharp salute.

They left, and they left her alone with Kiriel di'Ashaf, a girl who had not yet served the mandatory probation required to make her Kiriel Ashaf AKalakar. *I gave her my word,* Ellora thought, as she met the girl's black eyes. Thinking of Evayne a'Nolan, and the massacre in the Averdan valleys. Thinking of what it meant, to return there now.

Thinking of demons, of darkness, of a city racked by the screams of the dying.

And Kiriel di'Ashaf's smile widened slightly, as if those screams, attenuated and distanced only slightly by years and time, were a song she could hear, could conduct.

The Kalakar rose, shuttering her face, setting the memories firmly aside. And then she opened the door to the hall.

"Gentlemen. Time is of the essence."

Before Kiriel could rise or speak, five men and two women entered the great hall. The Princess of the blood, Mirialyn ACormaris, Devon ATerafin, The Berriliya, Commander Allen, Member Meralonne APhaniel of the Order of Knowledge and the little known, but greatly respected, Jewel ATerafin.

She knew that she would be true to the word that she had given when she had accepted the service of Kiriel di'Ashaf, but her lips turned up in a slightly triumphant smile as she caught the surprise that made Kiriel seem, for just a moment, a sixteen-year-old girl.

She did not understand these people.

For a moment, fear held her; she touched her sword, pulling what shadow she could find into a tight, near impenetrable web around her body—armor that only the mage would find easy to pierce. But although her hand was on the haft of her blade, she did not draw it, and the moment passed, leaving her with a dryness in the mouth and throat. Frustration settled around her shoulders as if it were the only mantle she would ever wear again.

The mantle.

"Member APhaniel?" The Berriliya said quietly.

"It is already done," the mage replied, quick with the words, as if he did not wish to appear to be following the commands of another. Strands of platinum hair flew a moment in the absolutely still room, and then he bowed sardonically to Kiriel. "Kiriel di'Ashaf," he said softly.

"Meralonne APhaniel," she replied.

"You have a good memory, Kiriel," The Kalakar said, as she took a seat at the long table, and motioned for their visitors to do the same. They could not shed power, but they could shed the formality of it, if they so chose.

"Too good a memory." It was Member APhaniel who spoke. "I do not believe that my given name was ever used in your presence."

"You are well enough known, Member APhaniel." It

was the youngest woman in the room, save Kiriel, who spoke, tossing her dark curls out of the fringes of her lashes and binding them with a swathe of red cloth. "If she was curious, she could have asked. Devon said that the first thing you did was practically order King Cormalyn to execute her."

"True enough." Gray eyes met black ones; a platinum brow lifted. "And is that what happened?"

Kiriel shrugged coolly. "No. I did not know who you were until someone spoke your name—but I knew of you." Let him wonder. It was, after all, the truth.

"I . . . see."

"Did she do it to you, as well?" Kiriel said, the bitterness in her voice adding years to her face.

" 'She'?"

"Evayne. Did she take you from your home and bring you here?"

"From my—" He froze, and she knew at once—the *blood* knew—that he was, for a moment, afraid. It was gone before she could hold it long enough to twist; gone before she could make a weapon of it that she could use. If she could; that had never been her art, thanks to Ashaf.

Ashaf's life had cost her much.

But her death had been worse.

"No, Kiriel," the mage said gravely, "Evayne did not bring me to Averalaan; I was here long before her birth."

They don't know, she thought suddenly. *They don't know your secret. And they don't know mine. But they know I have one.*

She did not reveal what he had not revealed. Because a secret, like a concealed dagger, was only useful once, and this was not the time for it.

"How do you know of me?"

She said nothing.

"I see." He bowed slightly. Conceding? "This is The Berriliya—Commander of the second army. The Kalakar, as you know, is Commander of the third. Commander Allen," and the quietest man in the room nodded briefly, "commands the first army." He turned then to a woman whom Kiriel also recognized. "This is the Princess Mirialyn ACormaris; she represents the interests of the Crowns. This is Devon, and this is Jewel; they are both ATerafin."

"And they represent?"

"The interests of the Crown." It was the Princess who answered, drawing Kiriel's eye. Of all the people in the room, Mirialyn was hardest to look at—because once she started, Kiriel found it very, very difficult to stop. The Princess held a light like a vessel made for only that purpose; where darkness edged her it was thin and fine, a net made of life, but not a plant with deep roots. Among the kin, beauty was defined solely by power.

And yet.

And yet they saw the light as clearly—more clearly—than she. They did not hold it; could not take it; could not contain it. Given enough time, they could corrupt it and destroy it, but a light such as Mirialyn ACormaris carried would take several lifetimes to dim and tarnish. And so they disavowed it.

She is lost to us, Kiriel. Look elsewhere; look long.

No. she shook her head as a voice that she never wanted to hear again touched her memory. Speaking words that were oft spoken, deeply felt.

I will not listen to you again.

"Sentrus."

Necessary interruption was usually humiliating; this was to be no exception, although no one laughed or sneered. Kiriel felt the sting across her pale skin, the burn of blush; she looked away from the Princess and struggled to continue to do so.

Jewel ATerafin felt the shift in Kiriel di'Ashaf; she could almost *see* it in the lines of the young woman's face. For a moment—for just a moment—entranced by the Princess of the blood, the clouds had separated, and a glimpse of something completely different had shown through.

A glimpse of something familiar; something that would have attracted her when she'd been on the streets; something worth reaching out for. Something worth following.

Something that she *had* followed, and taken in, at least once. It surprised her, and Jewel ATerafin was one of the seer-born; she wasn't used to being surprised.

She was a good judge of character. It was her pride, and it was more besides; it had kept her alive for long enough to come to the notice of The Terafin. She had lived in the

twenty-fifth holding with her small den, much less worthy
of note than even the bastard child of a well off patris.
Stealing for a living *was* living, and only a fool tried to
survive *that* life in this city on her own. Jewel was, and
had been, no fool, but her lot had been slightly different
than other orphaned children: Each and every member of
the den she'd thieved with had been her personal choice.

And she had once taken in a killer.

Duster.

She hadn't thought about Duster for ten years.

Duster had been her right hand; Duster had been the
heavy. In a fight, Duster had been the muscle—if something that graceful and fast could be called muscle. She'd
been the easiest of the den to taunt into stupidity, and she
held grudges for longer than a god. They'd made jokes
about it, back then. Very quiet ones.

She'd killed three men before she became one of
Jewel's den-kin. The first one, in self-defense. The
second, in anger. The third in vengeance, although she
never would explain what had driven her to such a
revenge. It was the third death that had made of Duster a
killer.

But Duster had chosen the den. The den had chosen
Duster. And although she had killed that lone man, had
truly tested the limits of how much suffering she could
both endure and willingly, personally inflict, she had
served, in heat and cool anger, better than anyone. Had
died in that service.

"Jewel?"

"I'm sorry," she murmured. "I was—I was thinking."
Devon raised a peppered brow, and she shook her head
slightly: no threat.

Kiriel now hid behind shadows that were more than just
lack of light.

Without thinking—and Jewel, surrounded by men and
women of *this* rank, never acted without thinking—she
brushed past Devon ATerafin, past Mirialyn ACormaris,
past the three Commanders who had earned their place in
a grim and bloody history—as if they were the passersby,
and this was the open street, and this young woman was
in search of, in need of, a den.

And then, as she met dark eyes that were somehow
shining like liquid gold, she froze.

"Kiriel di'Ashaf," she said quietly. "I'm Jewel ATerafin. You can call me Jay."

Kiriel didn't answer.

Jewel didn't expect it. "You're part of the Kalakar House Guard. Pretty impressive for a newcomer. I know people who'd kill for a place here."

There was no reply.

"But you're wasted here, and we both know it."

She heard a cough at her elbow; two in fact. Ignored them both. "We are considering a declaration of war against the Dominion of Annagar; it has happened before in the history of the Empire; no doubt, it will happen again. But this declaration—it's not ours alone to make.

"This is *your* war."

Silence, one marked by the raising of eyebrows and exchanged glances between powerful men, and women, who had somehow become spectators.

"Don't tell me how to fight my battles," Kiriel said, relenting enough to show teeth.

"Jewel," Devon whispered, "what—"

"Not now." She didn't even look back at him. "I can't tell you how to fight them. I don't know enough about what they are." She shrugged again. "But I do know what I saw in the Great Chamber."

Kiriel's smile was thin and cold—but it was there. And it froze in place. "You're the one who shouted."

"Yes."

"You're fast." Respect, and Jewel knew she didn't often show it.

Jewel ATerafin didn't take respect she hadn't earned. Not from her den-kin. "No."

"Then what?"

"I'm seer-born."

Silence. Then, heavy with forced nonchalance, "What do you see for me?"

"War."

Kiriel snorted. It was odd; the single act of derision made her seem more youthful; almost her age, in fact.

"With me at your side."

"What?"

"*What?*"

What?

"*You?* You're no soldier."

"No. And neither are you. You're Kiriel. When your enemies come hunting you, they won't stop in the ranks of the foot soldiers—because you won't be there." She saw past the paling alabaster of Kiriel's skin, into the depths of eyes that were golden and cold.

Oh, the silence. Jewel wondered what in the hells she was doing, and she hoped, whatever it was, she was going to survive it.

"And where will I be, seer?"

"You'll be with the kai Leonne." Jewel *knew* the words were true the minute she said them. Just didn't know why, but it didn't concern her yet. It would, though.

"Why?"

"Because you've already saved his life once. And because, before this is out, *Allasakar-Etridian* won't seem like such a difficult foe."

Kiriel's eyes narrowed.

"Kiriel, your enemies and our enemies are the same, whether you know it or not. There will be a Sun King in the Dominion of Annagar, or there will be a puppet."

"And this so-called Sun King won't be *your* puppet?"

Jewel shrugged. "Meet him. Decide for yourself. And decide, Kiriel di'Ashaf, just how far you're willing to go to protect him."

Kiriel shrugged, but the movement was forced and edged. "His protection is not my concern. I'm part of the House Guards," she said at last. "I'm one of—one of the Black Ospreys."

Jewel was surprised. She'd heard of them, though— who hadn't? It shouldn't have been a surprise to her that that was where Kiriel was placed. But she knew that Kiriel didn't belong there—because if she had, if she'd truly found kin, she wouldn't have had that momentary look that could draw Jay Markess across both a decade and a room. "But I'm going to war beside Valedan kai di'Leonne. We need to win this war," she told Kiriel, and knew it of a sudden for absolute truth. Felt it so sharply, the fear of loss was visceral.

"You can't."

Something in the girl's tone set Jewel's teeth on edge, but she'd heard it before, a dozen times. Fear made fear a weapon—and the gods knew in the streets of the lower holdings, you needed to hone whatever weapons you could. Jewel Markess had always understood the pleasure inherent in causing fear.

She didn't bother to hide hers behind bluster; no point to it. Because she *knew* that Kiriel's taunt was also Kiriel's truth, and for an icy second the ghostly otherwhere of a battlefield strewn with corpses fogged her vision.

She understood it then. The vision. The image of Kiriel, darkness wreathed and absorbed; the sight of Valedan, bleeding, bruised—and living.

"She's right," Jewel Markess said, and her voice was the seer's voice—the distant, cool certainty that made of the speaker a vessel. "We *can't win.*"

No one spoke; the moment stretched, thinly, between each of the men and women there. Glances were joined and broken as the unsaid surfaced: That Jewel Markess ATerafin was seer-born. Then, as they watched, they realized that the seer's gaze did not waver from the face of Kiriel di'Ashaf. Her gaze held weight, and the eyes of the men and women who were in large part to decide the course of the coming battle turned to Kiriel as well.

"Kiriel," the seer said, "will you come to war with us?"

"As a member of the House Guards—" The Kalakar began, but Jewel's imperative wave cut the words off so cleanly it might as well have been a blade.

I hope, Devon thought, cringing as he saw the cloud settle into the lines of one of the ten most powerful people in the Empire, *that you know what you're doing, Jewel. Because I guarantee if you don't, you'll wish you'd never left the street.*

"You said this was my war," was the cool reply. "And if I wanted allies, I'd ask."

"You'd go to the Hells themselves in burning chains before you'd ask for anyone's help."

Kiriel smiled at that; the smile was genuine. And then it faded. "You came here to ask me questions. The Kalakar said I could answer whatever ones you asked that didn't have anything to do with my past.

"You won't ask any," she said, rising. "But let me be generous. I know what you're facing. You could field the biggest army your world has seen since Moorelas fell, and you still wouldn't win.

"They don't want you," she added softly. "At least, they don't want you yet. Stay home. Let them play in the Dominion. Maybe, by the time they're finished there, you'll have had enough time to build some sort of a defense." Her tone made it clear that if there was one, she couldn't conceive of it.

"Who?"

But she shook her head and looked away, and if there was anger in her eyes, there was a very real pain—the type of pain from which anger often springs hottest. "I am not ready," she said. "I am not ready to betray him." She spoke each word as if it were dragged from her, and Jewel felt that they had been, and by her. It was a promising start.

Duster.

"But if whoever this is deserves your loyalty, why are you here?"

"We fight our own battles." There was no warmth in the words.

"Excuse me, young lady," Commander Allen said, standing quietly by Jewel's side, although just when he'd moved, no one but Kiriel had noticed. "But the protection that you . . . enjoy . . . is at The Kalakar's behest. You are a member of her House Guards, and as long as you behave in accordance with the rules that govern the Guards, your right to protect your past will be respected.

"But the House Guards of Kalakar will go to war, if that is the Crowns' decision.

"And if you are not among the House Guards when they choose to take the field against the armies of the Dominion—and her allies—you will no longer have the right to the grace that The Kalakar has granted. I'd advise you to consider this carefully." Commander Allen's voice was so deceptively soft it was easy to miss the threat in the words—and the threat was not subtle. He bowed, curtly, to Jewel ATerafin—an apology for his interruption. He offered Kiriel nothing.

"I'm going," Jewel said, as if the Commander had not spoken. The words were a challenge. "I'm not afraid of what we'll meet on the road, and I think I see it more clearly than anyone here but you."

"I-am-not-afraid."

The Kalakar's gaze traveled the length of the connection between Jewel ATerafin and Kiriel di'Ashaf, traversing it again and again as if to find answers there. Finally she said, "Kiriel, Commander Allen speaks the truth.

"But you're an Osprey, and the Ospreys have always been trouble. Report to Primus Duarte on the morrow; he'll have your detail—and your orders. You will either follow them, or you will leave Kalakar and its protection."

Kiriel forced herself to nod, but her eyes were upon Jewel ATerafin's pale, almost ordinary face.

"You have," the seer said softly, "a decision to make."

Kiriel laughed, briefly and bitterly.

"Well, this is either very good or very bad." Duarte leaned against the wall, the seal across the scroll that bore his new orders unbroken for the moment.

"Duarte."

"Alexis," he said, mimicking her tone precisely, hoping to distract her. Then, when he realized just how futile it was, "I told you it was risky to make that stand."

"We thought the risk was worth taking. We'll live with the consequences. *Open* the damned thing."

The scroll came an inch off the desk, and then another, casting a thin shadow; neither Duarte nor Alexis had moved to touch it. "Fancy." she said coolly. "But I think we have better things to do than watch you practice a trick that couldn't kill a flea. The orders."

It was the women who were always the problem. The Kalakar. Kiriel. Alexis. Give him Cook, or Sanderson, or Auralis—well, maybe not Auralis, but Auralis wouldn't get into so much trouble if he could keep away from the women.

"Duarte, I'm waiting."

Never ever, he thought sourly, *get emotionally involved with a member of your unit. Never.* He grabbed the scroll as it lolled in the air and cracked the seal.

"What? What does it say?"

"We're to report to Verrus Andromar at *Avantari.* Tomorrow." He looked up at the sharp-faced woman he considered the most attractive person in the Empire. "In the Arannan Halls."

* * *

"Jewel."

The younger woman looked up from the scrolls that she labored over; ink stained the corner of her mouth, as it often did when she let her mind wonder. She relaxed when she saw Torvan ATerafin in the doorway, and then tensed when he drew close enough that she could see his expression.

"Does The Terafin want me?"

"Yes." He paused. "By the Shrine." He winced, and added, "I don't think she wants to wait for as long as it's going to take you to clean up. I'd avoid Avandar if at all possible, if I were you."

The woman who ruled the House and the woman who served it met in the late afternoon light. It seemed strange to Jewel ATerafin; the Shrine of Terafin was a nighttime relic; a place where ghosts and restless dreams could be either invoked or laid to rest. Shadows and darkness gave mystery; light took it away, shining too harshly across unadorned marble and bronze.

Shining just as harshly across the rather stark features of the woman whose rule over House Terafin was unquestioned. "Jewel," The Terafin said, her voice quite cool.

Jewel bowed at once, and held that bow, gathering her thoughts and her expression before she rose. Bows, she had discovered over the years, were good for that; you could use them to hide shock, anger, contempt, or fear while feigning respect. Anything that bought time acceptably was to be valued.

"I've spoken with Devon," The Terafin said.

"Oh."

"Join me." It was an order. Jewel joined her lord on the steps of the Shrine, and together, in a careful and graceful lockstep—although it had to be said that The Terafin's grace was natural, and Jewel's learned—they climbed to the altar that rested beneath the domed roof. "Now. We have peace, and we have privacy."

The breeze flew past, picking at strands of Jewel's unruly hair. Time, lessons, and a dozen different attendants had not taken the wildness out of those dark curls; she'd been told with a sniff that the color would go first.

"I did not," The Terafin said, when Jewel did not immediately speak, "grant you permission to travel with the army. You are a member of House Terafin, and you owe fealty to Terafin. You, of all people, know this." As if to make her point, she glanced around the Shrine and its confines, alluding, with that single gesture, to all of their mutual history.

"I did not," The Terafin continued, as a crimson stain spread itself across cheeks that were—or that should have been at thirty-two years of age—too old to take well to blushing, "give you leave to insult The Berriliya or The Kalakar, and while we are not perhaps the friends that we could be, our Houses owe each other the respect of rank. If anyone from Terafin is to push past them as if they don't exist, it will not be you."

"Terafin."

"The House needs you here."

Jewel bowed, the motion a bobbing of head, no more.

"And now I would appreciate it if you would tell me why the *House* needs you *there*."

There were days when she hated the sight.

"Terafin," she said quietly, "what would you give—of your House—to win this war?"

"This is not a discussion, Jewel."

And there were days when she *loathed* it. "Terafin." She swallowed, because she knew that she didn't have an answer.

"I would not give the life of my House," a third voice said, and they both turned, and neither woman was surprised. Standing before them, hands behind his back and face lined with thought, the spirit of Terafin wore a face that Jewel had never seen, and that The Terafin knew well.

Jewel had never seen the guardian of Terafin during the hours of the day before. But if she did not recognize the face that he wore, she recognized what lay beneath it: concern for Terafin, the Great House of his founding. One could not summon the spirit of Terafin; not even if one were *The* Terafin. The spirit chose his time—and his companions. And in this generation of those chosen worthy to be ATerafin, he had only two: The Terafin, and Jewel. Neither woman had ever given voice to what this meant.

Because Terafin was a big House, the most powerful of The Ten, and if The Terafin was its undisputed leader, the

House Council was not without its power. The Terafin had wisely chosen to announce no heir to the title.

"I would not give the life of my House," the guardian of Terafin said. "But I risked my House for the Kings."

"And the House became stronger for the choice," The Terafin said quietly.

"Yes," he said softly. "But we did not know that that would be the outcome. Terafin, the House is, and has been, many things; it will be many things in the future. Some of them, you envision; some you cannot.

"Many of the patriciate turned their backs upon the cause of the Kings when they came seeking support for their war against the Barons. They did it in the name of their families, of their Houses.

"Terafin did not. And if the Kings came today, Terafin *would* not."

"You do not," The Terafin said wryly, "rule Terafin. I do."

He bowed and his smile was almost rueful. Almost. "As you say, Terafin." His bow carried the respect that his tone did not. "But if I do not rule, I advise. If I might beg your indulgence?"

She laughed, and the laughter took the last of the edge out of her voice, although it was a quiet laugh, appropriate to a woman of great station.

"Jewel Markess ATerafin, go South if South calls, and do what must be done. But I will have your word, before you leave, that regardless of the state of the war, if you are summoned to Terafin, you *will* return."

"Of course!"

The guardian's smile was almost sad. "Take those who you feel are worth risking. And also take your domicis."

The hostages were freed, but in a limited fashion; they were allowed to return to their quarters, allowed to have their cerdan as escorts, allowed even to resume the style of title and dress and entertainment that had been their wont. They were not, by royal decree, allowed to leave *Averalaan Aramarelas,* and any need that required a journey beyond the confines of the Holy Isle was to be facilitated by the Kings' Swords.

Which was better than any of them, save perhaps Serra Marlena en'Leonne, had hoped for when news of the slaughter had first reached them. But they did not yet feel safe; had they, the restrictions would have already begun to chafe and annoy.

Ser Fillipo par di'Callesta was quiet as he contemplated their fortune, and their fate. He, of course, would be free to travel the moment the Kings decided to announce their decision—if, he thought grimly, they chose to *make* one—and he very much wished to do so. It had been years since he had fought by his brother's side, and his brother had proved himself, if anyone born to Callesta ever doubted it, to be worthy of the title the Wolf of Callesta.

But he also dearly wished to leave his wife and his younger son in the safety of the Imperial court. For in the Imperial court, Valedan di'Leonne had found safety against the servants of the Lord of Night—and if such a boy could find safety against such an enemy, his own family, far more important to him, and far less important to anyone else, would surely be protected.

Michaele, his oldest, was fourteen—and fourteen was not too young to blood a blade in the service of Callesta. Besides, if he elected to leave Michaele behind, he thought it would go ill; the boy was not unlike his father, and had every intention of going to war. Whether or not the Imperials declared themselves allies—and if they did, it was a very mixed blessing—Averda would see battle.

"Fillipo."

He knew the voice at once; it was a dusky voice, a sleepy one, full-throated and heavy and feminine. Andrea en'Callesta. Smiling, he turned to greet her; the smile stiffened. "What has passed?"

"Nothing yet. But Tara bid me come to find you. She is with Valedan."

He started to walk, and she touched his shoulder, catching the silk of his shirt and holding him a moment. She had always been bold, and although at times he found it annoying, he had never quite mastered the appreciation he felt for that hint of wildness—and its strength. "What?"

"Men have come. Soldiers. They bear a standard I recognize only half of."

She was sharp; she missed little, if she missed anything at all. "The half?"

"Kalakar. I believe they have come for Valedan."

He grew still at once. "Where is the Tyr'agnate?"

"I do not know. He did not leave word."

"And the General Baredan di'Navarre?"

"With the kai Leonne. He does not—he does not appear to be pleased." She paused, as if weighing the moment and necessity to speak her mind. It did not take long. "These men and women—they are old enough to have served, I think, in the wars."

Kalakar.

He cursed, a single sharp word, and pulled himself free from the grip of his wife. And then he left her, and his musings, behind, thinking that if they took the boy, and made of him some Imperial puppet, Averda had already lost.

CHAPTER TWENTY-SIX

Valedan knew Kiriel the moment he saw her, although she stood in the middle of the ranks of what appeared, for a moment of chill uncertainty, to be a small army. He did not think that he would ever forget her, and in this at least, he was right; he was to be proved wrong about many things in his life.

General Baredan swore, unmindful of the presence of the women; the women chose, with a certain pale grace, not to hear him. He understood, immediately, that it had been choice and tact on their part, and had the good sense to fall silent. But he drew his sword and held it out, at chest height, for Valedan to see. Valedan knew what he offered.

I haven't taken your oath yet, the young Tyr'agar thought. He nodded, but said, "Put it away, General. I do not believe that these soldiers have come to offer us injury."

"You don't recognize their banner," the General said softly, although he followed the orders of the man-boy that he had chosen to pledge his sword to. "I do." Valedan noticed that Baredan kept his hand upon the hilt of his sword.

The men stopped at barked orders. And then one of them stood forward, and Valedan saw, as the soldier approached, that he faced no man; this was a woman, sharp-faced and cool. But he had been trained in Essalieyan; she was not the enigma to him that she was, and would no doubt always be, to the General. Princess Mirialyn ACormaris had taught him to ride; it was the Princess, as well, who sparred with him when he reached a high enough level of skill. He knew—for his mother reminded him constantly—that in Annagar the women did not do anything so demeaning as fight or kill, at least not so brutishly; that they did not choose to smell of horse-sweat, and clomp around gracelessly in heavy boots and light armor.

But he was not in Annagar, and he wondered, briefly, if he would ever be. This woman, this Sentrus, was another soldier to him, no more, no less. Or she would have been, if not for the General's reaction. As he appraised her, she appraised him, and then she lifted her arm and performed the Imperial salute. Sloppily.

"It's good to see," the General said stonily, "that the Black Ospreys of the Kalakar House Guards can still live down to their reputation."

The soldier, thus rebuked, returned a gaze as cold as the General's tone. "The Black Ospreys of the Kalakar House Guards reporting for duty."

"WHAT?"

But Ser Valedan kai di'Leonne stood forward. "I did not realize," he said quietly, and without the coolness of his General, "that this company was so . . . large." He paused. "Do you ride?"

"Me? No—but some of us can. Sir."

"They aren't cavalry, if that's what you meant."

"Good. Are you the leader of this company?"

"No, sir. That'd be Primus Duarte."

"And he?"

She smiled, and the smile made her face look more sharp, rather than less. "Waiting your permission, Tyr'agar."

"My permission? I've already given it."

He could hear the General sputter, although the man was absolutely silent.

"Uh, well, yes, sir. But it has been brought to our attention that the customs of the Dominion are rather more complicated with regards to the presence of those who are—gifted."

Valedan frowned.

"What she's trying to say," the General explained, his voice quiet and utterly smooth, "is that he's one of the Imperial mage-born, and will therefore not approach without your express permission. Tyr'agar," he added quietly, "there are no Radann here who can perform the rites of purification."

"There were," was the young man's remote reply, "Radann in plenty in the Tor Leonne."

His meaning silenced the General.

And the Sentrus.

"Tell your Primus—that is the title?—that I have accepted the company *as* an Imperial company while we are upon Imperial soil. He may approach."

Serra Alina was proud of Valedan. She did not show it; did not so much as change posture or position. But the General was slightly off guard; it was Baredan who had shown surprise, and quite openly. Valedan appeared to be in command of the situation.

He had to be.

Take their service, but tell no one. Her advice. The only clear path she could see.

But shouldn't I ask—

That is precisely what you cannot afford to do. You are the Tyr'agar, Valedan.

But I don't know how to—

And you will learn. Ramiro di'Callesta is a dangerous man. Never tell him all that you know unless you wish to set a Callestan Tyr beside the waters of the Tor Leonne. You may trust the General—he is your man, truly.

Then I can ask him.

No.

Why?

The look of confusion and annoyance made the only surviving scion of the once great clan look younger than his years. She smiled fondly, remembering that expression.

Because, Na'Vale. He is your man, but he flutters about you like a nervous mother. Or wife. When you return to the Dominion—if you indeed return—the men of the clans will look first to Callesta and then to the General before they see you. If the General flutters and hovers and waits, if he seems to be the source of your strength and your wisdom, then it won't matter whether he's your liege, your loyal liege, or not. They will know that you are weak. And they will not follow.

Or do you wish to be a Tyr in exile?

He watched as a man detached himself from this group

of soldiers. Watched, lifting his chin slightly, as that man approached. He wore the colors of the Kalakar House Guards, that much, Valedan knew clearly from his years in Avantari. What he did not recognize—and what Baredan obviously did—was the black bird that plunged, claws extended, beneath the more familiar colors.

But he knew from the General's reaction that this crest, and this House, had not been friendly in the wars that had been the cause of his exile.

Exile? As the Primus—he knew the rank by the golden quarter-circle above the sword across the right shoulder—approached, the unspoken word echoed in the emptiness that the massacre had made of his life. He did not clearly remember the Dominion of Annagar; could not easily recall all the details of the Tor Leonne—the seat of power which, coveted, had caused the death of his distant father—even though there were some images that would never leave him. But he could recall, at will, the colors of The Ten; he knew their leaders on sight, and knew, further, many of their lesser nobles. Solran Marten and Kallandras of Sennial visited often, and if he was quiet enough, he was allowed to listen to them sing. He knew the ranking Patrises and the merchants who, holding no title, held the power of Royal Charter; he even knew, by sight, some of the Magi and the man who ruled the most important guild in the Empire: the guild of the maker-born.

Exile?

He knew the healer-born, and the men who served as healers although their skills were learned and not granted; he knew the priests, and their golden-eyed masters, and privately *knew* that the Annagrian view must be wrong, for these men and women could not be demons. He knew *Morrel's Ride* and *Moorelas' Fall*—knew, as well, the arguments that surrounded the "correct" use of this Northern hero's name—and he knew what the Six Days meant.

This was his home.

Or it had been.

The Primus saluted, and the salute was a sharp one. "Primus Duarte AKalakar reporting for duty, Tyr Leonne."

"And will you protect me from demons, Primus,"

Valedan said, as he looked at the restive rank of the men and women who followed, "or from them?"

At that, the Primus froze, and then he lifted a brow. "Permission to speak freely?"

"Granted."

"You look like a boy. You stand like one. You even sound like one."

The silence that followed the words was a thick one; no one moved.

"You can ask a question like that; you've got an edge to you beneath that youth. If you intend to go South, sharpen it." The Primus smiled. "These are the Black Ospreys. They serve Kalakar, except in time of war."

"Then?"

"They serve the Kings."

"And what do they owe to me?"

The Primus smiled again, as if he was surprised at the question. Valedan was—and he was the one who asked it.

"Inasmuch as your commands do not conflict with The Kalakar's or the Kings', we owe you service and protection."

"And who decides when those orders are in conflict?"

Silence a moment, and then the Primus smiled grimly. "Not the General," he said, acknowledging for the first time the man who stood so stiffly to Valedan's right.

"No," Valedan said, remembering Alina's words, the sharpness behind their strength. "The General serves *me*, and he will abide by my orders, once given.

"But perhaps we did not understand each other clearly. I accepted your *service*. You will tell me what that means."

"It means—"

"To you."

Ser Fillipo par di'Callesta listened from a discreet distance, watching the boy with a measured calm. He recognized the banner as quickly as the General had; perhaps more so. Bloodied but unfelled, it cast a long shadow in the memory of a man who had served in the campaign that led to the Averdan valleys. He stepped back, thinking that this was not a decision that he could have made, or could have accepted. Wondering what Baredan felt. What Ramiro would feel, upon seeing them himself.

Boy, he thought, for he had never thought of Valedan as anything else, *your blood is stronger than we thought.*

For the entire first meeting, Duarte held his breath and prayed. A lot. *I'm too old for this.*

But no one had said anything completely offensive, and after the right amount of time had passed—an eternity, more or less—the Ospreys had been dismissed to quarters, with commands to report back in the morning.

They didn't make it.

They got out of the Arannan Halls and halfway across the courtyard before the first outraged outburst; made it to the edge of the footpath before they'd stopped completely, demanding answers, reasons, explanations. From him.

At least, praise Kalliaris, they'd waited. He could be thankful for that much.

"I know it's asking a lot—"

"It's asking more than a bloody lot," Cook said grimly. He'd done something he rare did: straightened out. He was a *big* man.

"But we don't have a choice." Duarte had managed, against all odds, to get the Ospreys *to* the palace. But he'd done it not by dint of threat; he'd done it by the clear expedient of simple fact. It was a *direct* order. They could obey it, or they could be cashiered.

But having got them here, he was under no illusions: Ospreys and orders they didn't like were oil and fire.

We can fight the Dominion, he'd told The Kalakar, *but don't ask us to* serve *the Southerners. Ask any other company. Please.* Close as he'd come to begging since he'd turned fifteen. Hadn't got him anywhere.

"We've always got a choice," Auralis said, in the smooth, warm drawl that made anyone who knew him well very nervous. "We've followed orders we didn't like before."

Trust Auralis. The Ospreys could do everything short of outright mutiny under the guise of following orders. They'd done it under The Berriliya's very brief command.

"We don't do it here."

"Duarte—" Alexis began, but he cut her off.

"No. Maybe you don't realize what's at stake."

"Sure, we do," Auralis said, his voice even quieter. "We're supposed to put our lives on the line for a bunch of Annagarian nobles." He paused. "For a bunch of Annagarian nobles who serve, directly or indirectly, the interests of the Callesta clan."

Callesta.

He hated the name.

Hated the use of it, hated what it brought back. The Black Ospreys had lost two thirds of their number on a single day, and a quarter of those who had made it off the field never made it across the border again.

I told her, he thought, seeing the grim, white line of The Kalakar's lips. Knowing that she felt as he did, and that she wouldn't fight the Kings for the right to stand apart. To honor the dead, by refusing, years later, to *serve* their killers.

"It was General Alesso di'Marente who ordered the slaughter," Duarte said, his voice weak although it was wrapped around fact. "And that General will rule the Dominion if we don't intervene."

"And if we don't intervene," Cook said, his voice heated where Auralis' was smooth, "Marente and Callesta will fall in on each other. Marente served under Callesta, Duarte. We're not idiots. Not a man who served there could forget it."

"Then state your position. State it clearly. Make your choice."

"Let me make it for you," a new voice said.

They turned, as one, to look upon the still features of the man that they had been ordered to protect: Valedan di'Leonne. The son of a man whose death not a single Osprey mourned.

"I will not take your service where it is so reluctantly given. You," he said to Cook, "may continue as you like in the service of the Kalakar. I do not know how well she tolerates disobedience; it must be very well.

"You," he said, turning to Duarte, "may also continue under her service. But you will not serve *me*. Keep your old wounds, and let them bleed as you like; I have need of whole men."

"So," Alexis said slowly, "the pretty boy speaks."

He turned, as if seeing her for the first time; she smiled with teeth. But she'd forgotten momentarily that this pretty boy had been raised in Essalieyan; he didn't even blink at the sword by her side. He did flush, though; his cheeks lost their pale, even neutrality.

And then, for just a moment, he looked young.

"You've come without guards," she said casually, as she noticed Auralis sidling round his side.

"This is *Avantari*," the youth said with a shrug. "Here, I don't need them."

"This is *Avantari*," Alexis said, with the slightest of nods, "but we're the Ospreys."

Auralis laughed.

She let him.

She let it happen because it *was* something she understood; all of it. There was a point that had to be made, by either Valedan or the Ospreys. They knew it as well; they had thrown off the rules that Kiriel found so enraging and so inexplicable.

She let Duarte stand, almost openmouthed with shock and a growing horror as he realized the implications of what might occur. A shout, some strangled command, pushed its way up his throat and out of his mouth.

She let Cook stand back, let Fiara bend forward, let every member who fought under the Osprey banner take a collective breath.

She heard Alexis tell Duarte that this young slip of a pretty boy with his court-soft hands and his delusions of grandeur *needed* to be taken down a notch. Or four. Nothing deadly. Just—a lesson.

A real lesson.

And she smiled as Valedan di'Leonne leaped out of the way and landed on both feet, his hands glinting with the length of two slender, Southern daggers. He was only the second person in her time with the Ospreys who had managed to outwit—or outmove—Auralis when he was stalking his prey.

She was the first.

Valedan's back was to a wall, although he had started out in a convenient archway, and his lips were pressed and set in a thin line. Auralis, armed, stopped a moment, and then began to pace, as if circling, a large cat who had suddenly discovered that the mouse had teeth and claws of its own. She liked the ripple of shirt and muscle; it seemed fluid enough to be liquid. And it reminded her of other such confrontations, in another court, a world away.

Do I miss it?

Yes.

She thought about intervening, and took a step between Fiara and Cook, her hand on the hilt of her blade. But a circle had been drawn, invisible, across the stone, and she stood at its edge just as Duarte himself did, waiting.

It should have been an easy kill, or at least an easy wounding, if that's what Auralis had intended. It was hard to tell with Auralis; his good humor was often burned away in a flash of annoyance, and what lay beneath it was not so unfamiliar to Kiriel di'Ashaf: darkness, anger, a brooding desire to prove one's power.

But Valedan was not unprepared either.

She watched the glint of steel in his hands, and saw its reflection in his dark, Southern eyes. Saw Auralis there as well, bearing his single dagger, cutting the air in tight half circles.

He moved, copper hair flying in a single, thick tail at his back. Steel twisted, flickering like silver flame; first blood fell in a trickle from the left side of Valedan's jaw. The hush was broken by a sharp exhalation; breath was drawn again.

And then Kiriel smiled as she heard Alexis curse; for Valedan's jaw was not the only jaw so marked, and Auralis' blood trickled down the runnel of his dagger.

"Well done," Auralis said, as he felt the dagger's sting.

The boy shrugged, and in that gesture, he looked like an Osprey. "Not so," was his quiet reply. "If we were in the South, they'd be poisoned." The dagger moved, but Valedan's eyes did not leave his enemy's face.

For just a minute, Auralis froze.

Alexis snorted. "If you were in the Dominion, you would not be fighting with daggers."

"You fight," Valedan replied, "with whatever weapon is at your disposal."

Before he had finished the last word, Auralis was gone again. This time, his pride had been pricked, and if he could not be forced to foolish action by anger, he could be cruel in his attempts to salve what had been wounded.

This, too, Kiriel understood.

But Valedan knew, and Kiriel saw the light behind his

eyes flicker; she felt the tensing of his shoulders and his legs an instant before he leaped. He exposed his back to Auralis, which was risky; Auralis was in motion but not so hurried that he could not avail himself of the opportunity. He pivoted; his blade struck.

Valedan grunted, but he, too, was in motion, and instead of rolling away from Auralis, he rolled into him.

They both fell; the dagger had not been so deeply planted that Auralis could not pull it as his arms flew wide in an attempt to cushion his landing. Instinct.

Valedan kai di'Leonne, the last of his clan, rolled up, bleeding, before Auralis landed. His knee was against the older man's throat, and the points of his daggers—both daggers—hovered a hair's breadth above the Osprey's blue eyes.

That broke the circle; ended the drill.

The Ospreys moved; steel scraped against steel as they noisily drew longer blades.

And Kiriel crossed the courtyard before those blades had cleared sheaths, her own trailing a hint of shadow, her eyes far darker than lack of light could conveniently excuse. She faced the Ospreys, her back to Valedan kai di'Leonne, her meaning clear.

"Auralis chose," she told her comrades coldly. "Valedan kai di'Leonne accepted the challenge, and fought fairly." If there was criticism of Auralis in the words, no one spoke against it; they had all felt the sting of his blade, either in practice or in less friendly fights, of which there were very, very few.

"Get out of the way, Kiriel," Alexis said, the only woman to stand against the newest, and the youngest, of the Black Ospreys. She nearly spit when Duarte's hand caught and held her shoulder.

"He did choose," the Primus said coldly. "And he isn't dead, no matter how hard he tries to get that way."

"Duarte—"

"Alexis."

She fell silent as she met an expression that Kiriel had never seen upon Duarte AKalakar's face. The Primus held her eyes for just that necessary second longer before turning to look at Kiriel; to look beyond her.

"Valedan kai di'Leonne—Tyr'agar—you have something that belongs to us."

The boy, pale and sweating, did not raise his eyes. The daggers did not waver. "Yes."

"What do you require of us for his safe return?"

"Nothing," the kai di'Leonne said coldly. He leaped back, a motion that was quick and a little too fast, releasing Auralis to the Ospreys. They noted that he kept his daggers drawn and his injured back to the wall. As Auralis rose, the air crackled; light flared, turning into a burning ribbon that encircled the Osprey.

"Unnecessary, Duarte," Auralis said, running a hand across his chin.

But Kiriel could see the darkness in him; he was shrouded in shadow, in the anger and humiliation of total and unexpected defeat. He lied. She did not know if Duarte realized it.

Auralis bowed grimly to the young man. There was no friendship in the gesture, but if there was resentment, it was buried beneath an uncharacteristically subdued expression.

"Nothing?" Duarte asked.

"Nothing." He sheathed his daggers in a single motion, taking only the time necessary to wipe clean the edge of the single dagger that had drawn Auralis' blood. Later, Kiriel thought, he'd have to clean them properly, or he'd pay for the theatrical gesture.

"This isn't our best," Duarte said.

"And what is?"

Silence.

Valedan drew breath, exhaled, and drew another, sharper one. "I am not my father," he told them, his eyes leaving Duarte's face to rest, briefly, upon each of the Ospreys gathered here. "I am not Callestan. But I *am* Annagarian, and when I rule, Annagar will be mine. I came here, without guard and without adviser, because I wished to speak with you on your own terms. I trusted you because I felt secure in the honor of the Empire.

"I don't know what you suffered at the hands of the Anngarian armies. I don't care. I did not ask, or press, for your unit. *You* requested permission to serve *me,* and I accepted that service." His glance flickered off Auralis with some justified contempt. "Service such as this is better left in the hands of my enemies.

"Had you complaint with *me,* there were better ways to

raise it—more honorable ways, if you even understand the difference.

"You said," he turned, unexpectedly, to Alexis, "that I needed to be taught a lesson. Thank you."

She had the grace to blush.

"For people who claim to loathe the Annagarians, you are the closest I've seen to their match. If you think that I will plead with you; if you think that I could hold such a one hostage against your good behavior, than you do not understand Leonne, no matter how well you think you understand Annagar." He turned, then.

The wound in his back, darkening the folds of his cloth, was an accusation.

"Wait!"

It was Cook who spoke; Kiriel would remember it later, for she, too, was willing to let him pass, and to let his judgment stand. It was Cook, and Kiriel thought that had it been Duarte, Valedan kai di'Leonne would not have stopped. But he did, and he turned, and the wound disappeared.

"Yes?"

"I can't speak for the Ospreys. Hell, the Primus can't speak for the Ospreys. But swear that we won't take Callestan orders—not from them, and not from you—and I'll serve you."

The silence of the offer stretched out; Valedan's face was cold and hard.

Take it, Kiriel thought, her hand on the sword white. *You've got what you came for: they respect your personal power now.*

"So sworn," Valedan said grimly. He drew his sword, and then grimaced. "There is no circle."

"Not in Essalieyan."

"Then how will you take my oath?"

"Same as we took his," Cook said, pointing over his shoulder in Duarte's general direction. "On faith."

There was laughter, and if it was sharp, it was genuine. Another man stood forward. Sanderton. He drew his sword. "You fight pretty well," he said.

"Better with daggers than a sword," was Valedan's reply. He bowed and Sanderton sheathed the weapon.

Fiara stepped forward. "We buried two thirds of our own," she told him, "in the Averdan valleys."

"And how many of ours did you bury?"

"None; we left 'em for carrion."

"Then the winds took them; the Lord passed them over. That was then; what will you do now?"

"I'll follow the Ospreys," she told him, and she drew her sword. "Besides, I always root for the underdog, and you don't stand a chance in the South."

"Oh?"

"He stabbed you. He's still standing."

"Perhaps I didn't think I'd survive his death."

She laughed. "See what I mean?" she said, although it was to the Ospreys, and not to the Tyr, that she spoke.

Alexis nodded. "I see it. And I don't. You're right. He's too honest and he's got honorable notions—but he's still standing, and Auralis should've had him for breakfast. I think he's got a chance." She had the grace to look almost embarrassed. "I don't believe that you spared Auralis' life because you thought we'd kill you if he died. You heard her; he heard him; you knew the fight—beginning and end—was yours and yours alone." She met Valedan's eyes for the first time, and found them unwavering. "We're not all killers."

"Just mostly!"

Duarte turned sharply, but the voice fell silent before he could attach it to a face. He stepped forward, although Valedan had not yet called him.

"Service," he told the younger man, "means giving what we have, as we have it. We're not clansmen. We'll never be clansmen. And we're not cut out to be Tyran. We're not Imperial soldiers, not in the usual sense of the word, but we don't serve *under* a Commander; we serve *beside* one. The Kalakar is one of us. Looks like today you set your foot on the inside of that same circle. Two thirds of the Ospreys died in the service of Commander Ellora AKalakar—protecting her banner. If necessary, all of the Ospreys would have.

"Today—tonight," he added, as he saw the crimson of the sun, "all of the Ospreys would die to protect yours." But he grimaced. "Just try to be certain that yours and Callesta's aren't standing within thirty yards of each other, or it could get tricky."

Valedan nodded. "If you don't mind," he said, his voice

a shade quieter, "I think I'd like to see the physicians now."

Only Kiriel was not surprised when he collapsed.

Baredan di'Navarre was beside himself with rage.

What made it was worse was the quality of the anger. It was almost completely silent; it showed in the pale line around the edge of his lips and the clipped, even tone of his voice. The women would not leave, and it was not his station—although it was obvious that he would dearly have loved it to be otherwise—to order them away; it was Valedan's, and Valedan, abed in the healerie of the Queen's court, did not see fit to accommodate him.

And only partly because he wished to avoid what Baredan would, no doubt, have to say the moment the last of the women's skirts had brushed the dust clear of the doorframe. The healer's touch had not left him, and although the healer himself had claimed the touch to be a light one, it lingered every time he closed his eyes. He felt vulnerable; he felt empty.

He felt, for a moment, that he was eight years old again, and the brothers and sisters—the sisters, especially—of his life in the Tor Leonne had come and gone, offering their formal, tearful farewells. He had never been allowed to visit, and he would not see them again, although he had never accepted that fact until the moment the Imperial merchants had arrived, bearing their tales of death.

His mother had come with him, and he was glad of it—but there was so very much that he'd left behind that he'd learned over the years not to miss. It was not that he missed them now—but that sense of hollowness, of loneliness, had returned to him with a strength that memory alone could not contain.

And he did not wish to be alone with a man of the clans, for if the women were as sharp, they were not as unkind in their judgment; they were used, after all, to seeing the weakness of the men they had been chosen by, if only in the privacy of the harem. Among themselves, the men did not make their vulnerabilities known.

"I ask you again," the General said, through teeth clenched so tightly his jaw barely moved, "how you were wounded."

It wasn't a question, of course; it was a demand. "General," he said quietly. "The wound was *my* wound. It has been dealt with."

Silence. Five minutes might pass before Baredan di'Navarre began again, his temper growing more sour, rather than less, as the sands ran. Valedan thought—although he was never certain—that the Serra Alina found the General's ill humor vastly amusing.

The doors opened.

Standing between them, attended only by two Tyran, was Ramiro di'Callesta. The cushions and the hard back of a bed meant for royal injuries prevented Valedan from sinking out of sight; the expression on the Tyr's face made Baredan's seem cheery, although if pressed, Valedan could not have easily said why.

"Tyr'agar," the Callestan Tyr said, offering perfect—and quick—obeisance. His face was smooth as Northern glass when he rose. The Tyran to either side offered supplicant bows that were longer and more formal; they did not rise as he did; they did not possess his rank. Nor did he wait for the Tyr'agar's permission; having the Tyran in this room was a matter of social grace, not necessity.

"Tyr'agnate," Valedan said, nodding.

"I see that reports of your health were not exaggerated."

"Tyr'agnate," Serra Alina said, leaving her quiet place by the foot of Valedan's bed, and kneeling a moment, in deference to his rank—and his importance to Valedan di'Leonne's cause.

Ramiro di'Callesta frowned, the movement a passing ripple of lips. "Serra Alina di'Lamberto."

"I attend the Tyr'agar while he rests in this foreign hall, and unfortunately, while he rests here, I answer to the healer, Dantallon, for his rest and his recovery. If you—"

"Serra Alina," Valedan said, raising a hand. "Dantallon will not—"

"He most certainly will." They all turned then, to see the pale-haired, somewhat haggard healer as he cast a shadow in the door. "Permission was granted for the Serra—and *only* the Serra—to attend the Tyr'agar. I see that the Southerners are as disappointingly obtuse as their Northern counterparts when it comes to such rules.

"Or perhaps, gentleman, you are not familiar with the language of the court; Weston and your tongue have similar roots, but are certainly divergent languages. Let me speak more clearly, the hour being late, and your time no doubt too precious to waste on longer explanations.

"Get out."

The Tyran, still kneeling, rose as one man; their hands curved round the hilts of their swords, but they did not draw them.

"You are bold," the General said softly, "for an unarmed and unescorted man."

"He is not unescorted," a new voice said, and the Princess Royale, Mirialyn ACormaris, stepped into the light his lamp cast. "And were I you, I would not pit my blade against the blade of your Tyran, no matter how often battle has tested them." There was no bragging in her voice; there was almost no inflection.

"Valedan?" the Callestan Tyr said.

The younger man smiled amost ruefully. "He means it. If I were one of the Kings themselves, he'd have come with the Queens as escort. He's valued here. But more important, he's obeyed.

"I take no insult from it; it is the custom of the North, and if not for Northern customs, the clan Leonne would not be a clan." But he silently thanked the healer, wondering how he'd known.

And knowing.

The healer's touch still bound them together, after all.

Serra Alina sat by his side once the healer had satisfied himself of Valedan's improving condition. The Princess stopped only for long enough to formally ask if the difficulty were a difficulty that required the intervention of the Crowns; she accepted his polite refusal with much better grace than the men who had pledged to follow his rule. Of course, she accepted it with a grace and ease that implied that she already knew who had been responsible for the injury, and what the outcome of that injury was.

Valedan knew that she probably did.

I am seventeen, he thought idly, as the lamplight played against the face of his only attendant. The Serra Alina was not lovely, and he thought that she never had been; her face was too sharp, and the line of her lips too tight, for that. Her eyes were not large enough, and nowhere about her was the pleasing vulnerability, that lovely mix of modesty and grace, that made a wife so highly prized.

Yet she had about her other things that wives were highly prized for. *How old are you?* She turned, as if the words were spoken and not merely thought, and he met her eyes as if the shadows between them were a bridge that could be crossed.

It occurred to him to wonder, for the first time, how she had felt when she had been chosen and sent as a hostage to this land. She had always seemed happy here, if sharply spoken, and she treated Ser Fillipo with courtesy, although Mancorvo and Callesta were bitter enemies.

"Serra," he said.

"I'm here. Are you thirsty?"

"No." Silence. Then, "Did you—did you leave anyone behind? I mean—was there anyone you, you cared for in the Dominion?"

He thought she would laugh, and in laughter, no matter how soft, she could be unkind. But although he tensed, she offered him no cause for caution.

"I left Lamberto," she said softly. It was late. Valedan had rarely understood the importance of the night to the Annagarian court, but he knew that he was seeing its fact in the softening of her face; hearing it in the quiet folds of her voice. "But Mareo and I seldom saw eye to eye. He is a proud man, Valedan, and as just and honorable a man as the Dominion is likely to produce—but for the sake of his scruples, he would weaken our clan.

"We argued, often, about this. Let me say, beneath the Lady's Moon, that although he bears great enmity for the Empire, it is in the Empire that he would find his truest home—in this court, among these people.

"Oh, his honor impresses the clansmen, especially those who are young and have never seen battle; it impresses the serafs, for their life is an easier life beneath his rulership. But it does not impress the Tors, nor the Tyr'agnati—for they see in his scruples another weakness to be exploited.

"And Callesta has exploited that weakness. The Empire never did."

He was silent a moment. "Kyro di'Lorenza would follow your brother," he said at last, in defense of the Lambertan Tyr.

"Yes." She fell silent, and when she spoke again, it was with a hint of tartness. "Valedan, *think*. Why is Ser Kyro here, and not in the Dominion where he belongs?"

Valedan had the grace to blush.

"Yes. Because he is an honorable man—too honorable for the politics of Lorenza. For the politics of *Annagar*.

"The only man here worthy of rulership in the Dominion is Ser Fillipo di'Callesta. And perhaps young Mauro; it is not clear to me that his interest is power, but he is canny enough when he chooses to be." She turned her back to him, away from the scant light. "Callesta and Lamberto were required to surrender hostages of value to the Kings.

"Only Ramiro di'Callesta chose to take the threat seriously. Ser Fillipo was the Captain of his Tyran, and much trusted; there is affection between the two, and if Fillipo was ever asked to choose between you and his brother, Fillipo would always choose Ramiro. Do not forget it."

"You're wrong," he said.

"Wrong, am I? I know Fillipo, Valedan. I know—"

"You're wrong. Lamberto surrendered someone of value."

She did not turn; she did not speak for a moment, and he wondered if she would. But at last, she brushed her hair back and over her ear; he saw that her hand shook slightly. "You are too true to your Northern experience," she said at last. "I am a *woman*, Valedan. My role as hostage was meant to be—*was*, by the standards of the clans—an insult. What you've just said—you may say it here, in this room, to me. Never say it anywhere else. Valedan—" She turned, her face pale, no hint of pleasure at all at the compliment he'd offered coloring her cheeks. "If you are to be Tyr'agar, you will have to convince clansmen—the lowest to the very highest—that you are fit to rule.

"Say this, say only that you think that *I* was so worthy, and they will turn from you, or against you." She rose.

"Wait." He lifted his hand. "Serra Alina," he added, as she continued to walk toward the door. "That was not a request." She stopped, turned, and knelt in the full suppliant posture.

It annoyed him. "Serra Alina," he said. "You taught me

how to use the daggers that saved my life tonight. Everything I know about Annagar has been your gift.

"You've saved my life twice now—and I know that what you've taught me—and what you teach me—will save it again and again.

"You are Lambertan; you do not owe me this honor. Your brother has not declared himself for me. And if the Imperial army aids my cause, he may well refuse to join it."

"That would," she said carefully, "be Mareo."

He wished there were moonlight in the room, but the room had been chosen for its security; the windows were small and poorly lit.

"I don't want to fight this war without you."

"Valedan—"

"And I don't want to fight with you about this war."

"Valedan, don't—"

"You told me," he continued, his voice as low as hers, "that a wife could be many things—but above all, she should be trusted. That a man chooses his wife not merely for her looks, but for her wisdom and her cunning and her loyalty."

She did not speak; did not attempt to interrupt him.

"You're the wisest person I know, except for the Princess. If you would have me, I would be honored if you would accept the position of wife to the kai Leonne."

"And am I ordered to accept?" she asked, and her voice was wooden, but not—quite—cool.

"No." He felt the strength ebb from him then.

"And may I rise?"

"Yes."

Watching her, remote, the lamps lighting her poorly in the evening's dark, he felt his heart sink more surely than the sun did each day.

"I am flattered," she said, as she made her retreat to the doors. "But I do not think I can tender an answer, Valedan. Not tonight; not when the offer is so unexpected, and so large."

She was gone before he could ask her what she meant. Gone before he could think, with pride, that this was the first time that he had ever truly surprised her.

CHAPTER
TWENTY-SEVEN

She could not accept his offer, of course.

He was a boy, and she a woman so long past her prime that the thought of marriage—in the Dominion—would have been unseemly. But here, in the North, at thirty-eight, her life seemed an endless realm, a freedom, a web of possibilities.

The freedom itself, she would have thrown away in an instant, had she been even twelve years younger, for there was a challenge in what he offered, a challenge that he did not understand the depth of, and one that she felt, Lady forgive her this one vanity, she was worthy of meeting.

But she was sister to a Tyr, and if she married, she would be *the* Serra, or there would be repercussions. And Valedan kai di'Leonne was a man who was in need of a wife both young and beautiful; a woman that the clansmen would note with both admiration and silent envy. She was not a vain woman, nor one who did not know her own strengths and weaknesses. Not even in the flower of her youth had she been such a wife.

And she was Lambertan enough that she would not hurt his chances by accepting an offer that, in another time, would have pleased her greatly.

As she so often did, she found the fountain in the Arranan courtyard. In full moonlight, it was quiet wonder; the waters rippling just so at the feet of a blindfolded, spindly child—a child of stone, an accusation to the clans by the serafs who had managed to make their way across the poorly guarded borders. Or perhaps by the Voyani who chose to remain in the North, forsaking the ways of their people.

It mattered not; what mattered was that, in workmanship, it was perfect, and that it was rendered by a man who understood the South. She found comfort in that.

Her privacy did not last for long.

Moonlight casts poor shadows. But in the silence that came with the hush of night and sleep of the multitude, the footsteps of the man could be heard long before he appeared. She half hoped that he would continue on his way, but knew that the hope was a vain one, for she recognized Ser Kyro's step when she heard it. And Ser Kyro, long away from his home, found the comfort of water soothing, although the statue itself was an irritation.

He would come to the fountain; she had the choice of leaving before he arrived, or of waiting on his company.

She decided to wait.

She was not surprised to see that he came alone; Ser Kyro, honorable and inseparable from his sword and the Lord's will, was nonetheless more of a night man than many thought, or cared to think—Ser Kyro included. He paused as he saw her sitting on the fountain's marble ledge, and then, realizing that he'd been seen, continued to walk toward her.

Toward the blindfolded boy.

"I heard," he said gravely, "about the kai Leonne." He could not quite bring himself to say *Tyr'agar,* but she forgave him much; the Lord's dominion had given way to the Lady's, besides which, she found it hard herself. Valedan was a boy to her, even if he stood on the threshold of adulthood. But they had both chosen to accept him as their ruler. So much had changed, in so short a time.

"I believe," she said softly, for she spoke as softly as she could with Ser Kyro, "that the news of his injury has traveled to every Annagarian in *Avantari.* But he has chosen to keep his counsel on this."

"And you?" The older man cast a sideways glance at the Serra, and was rewarded by a glimmer of a smile.

"I, Ser Kyro, will keep his counsel as well."

"You have kept his counsel wisely, Serra Alina."

She looked up at him, and then away, thinking of how very much he reminded her of the father who had been dead these many years. Dead before the war, before the peace, before her brother had found his excuse to be rid of her at last. She had been, in many things, her father's daughter—his youngest child, his only girl. And in his approaching dotage, he'd given her much freedom.

She almost regretted it now, thinking of what she might have been had she truly known how to be the perfect wife. Thinking that she knew it, but it was not—quite—enough. "I have kept his counsel," she told Ser Kyro.

"This was his first battle. Do you think it would harm him to tell us of it?"

"Tell you what, Ser Kyro?"

"The truth," he said wryly.

"I assure you, I would never lie to a clansman."

He laughed. "And my wife would never lie; nor my daughter. My dear, all women are liars. And all men. It makes us what we are in each other's eyes. And that is why the Lord of the Sun is *the* Lord," he added, although the moon reigned in the open sky, "for he burns away all lies and all vanity to see clearly the truths which make us, and he hones those truths when we are in his service."

"And are you?"

"Am I?"

"In his service."

"Until the kai Leonne is Tyr'agar. Or dead."

She nodded as if she expected no less.

"You knew this."

"You are not Callestan," she said, with a hint of pride. "You offered him your word, and you knelt beneath the open sun. Of course I knew you would serve him."

"Yet you did not see fit to tell me more of the man I serve."

"I am not his wife, nor his daughter, nor his mother, nor his sister. I have no right to speak in his stead, where he does not seek to speak." She did not ask him what he meant; she knew.

But Ser Kyro left little unsaid. In matters of this nature, it was not his way to be silent. "Serra Alina, he was offered his life, and his clan's life, by the Imperial Kings before the servants of the Lord of Night attacked. You knew this."

"Yes."

"And he chose to refuse their offer if they would not likewise spare us."

"Yes."

"Why?"

She turned to face him then, seeing his age as if it were a great and terrible distance. *Will you survive this war,*

Ser Kyro? she thought, for she knew, at that moment, that he would ride to war unless he was strictly forbidden. Knew that his age was not so feigned that the journey would not be harsh, and knew that even if his death was certain, he would have to go, for he was known, and respected, among the lower clansmen as a man of honor. They needed that. Less than eight years had passed; when had they come to rest so heavily upon him?

"Might I keep my own counsel, Ser Kyro?"

"No. Not in this. I have sworn my service to the boy, Alina, and I will not waver from that vow. Tell me. Why did he not accept his life?"

"Because he knew that our lives depended on his, and that he was the only shield that might possibly stand between us and the wrath of the Northern Kings."

"He is young," the Serra said, cupping cool water in her hands and letting it run between her fingers. "He can face death without flinching because his enemies have already cut from him the things that he valued. He would not have been so quick to offer, if he better understood all that he had to lose by dying."

"Perhaps it is not youth," Ser Kyro said. "Perhaps it is true honor. The Leonne clan had it once or they would never have been given the Sun Sword."

"And what do you believe?"

"I believe that he is Leonne," was the older man's reply. "And I am heartened by it." His smile was a momentary warmth that transformed his features. "For I will die in this campaign, and I would rather not go to my Lord serving an unworthy man."

"What of Serra Alina di'Lamberto?"

Fillipo smiled, but the smile was slight, one his brother could easily miss in the lamplight of a night that would have been better used for sleeping than planning. "She is the preeminent Serra in the exile Court," he replied. "Sharper-tongued than any woman I've met who could still sound noble born and bred. She is no fool."

"No. That much is obvious." He frowned. "But she seems to speak for the Tyr."

"Ramiro," Fillipo said quietly, "she has spent time with the kai Leonne since he was a child of six. If he can be said to have had a teacher, it is the Serra."

"And what has she taught him? I do not need to remind you, brother," he said, in a tone of voice that gave lie to the words, "that she is Lambertan."

"Indeed. Ramiro, you have expressed some admiration for the Serra in the past."

"Yes. I have said that she would make a worthy foe." But he smiled at his brother, and it eased their tension. "And you know how I feel about worthy foes. They have their place, and it is not against me." Just as quickly as it had come, the smile dimmed. "She seldom leaves his side, whether she is given cause or no, and she is well within her rights in *this* court."

"Yes."

"You do not fear her influence."

"No. Her influence has kept the boy alive at least once."

"Twice," Ramiro said softly. "Which brings us to my second point. The Ospreys."

Fillipo shrugged. "He did not seek my advice."

"No. Nor the General's. Nor, for that matter, Ser Kyro's or Ser Mauro's."

"You believe he accepted Alina's advice."

"Yes."

"If Lamberto is said to bear enmity toward Callesta," the par said to his quiet kai, "it is nothing compared to what Mareo di'Lamberto will feel when he sees that banner flying beside Leonne's in the field of battle. If she advised him to accept their service, she is no servant of Mareo di'Lamberto's." He paused. "And for all we know, the boy made the decision himself." His eyes were dark. "Certainly the Serra Alina did not tell him to get involved in a knife fight with one of the Ospreys—and she did not urge him to protect that man by his silence. I tell you, Ramiro, the boy has surprised me, and I feel that this is not the last time that he will do so."

Ramiro was silent for a moment longer, and then he exhaled. The glint left his eyes; he seemed, for a moment, tired. "I will be glad," he told his brother quietly, "when we have crossed the Averdan border again. There are too many rules here."

Kiriel sat alone in the open sunlight.

Her head was bare, and her arms; she wore no armor.

Her sword, however, was like a limb—only an act of violence would part her from it, and the Osprey that was foolish enough to begin such an action had been winnowed from the ranks of the House Guards by actions that were not quite so foolish—but just as suicidal—many years ago.

She liked the sunlight today.

She had always found it both repelling and compelling, although she suspected the latter was a gift of Ashaf's. A gift of a valley seraf from the Dominion. Without thinking, she lifted her hand to her throat and touched the slender chain that hung there; she pulled on it, pulled it up, and let the sun touch the large, heavy crystal that hung at its end. It was not a valuable stone, and yet it pulsed with the patterns of an unfamiliar magic.

Kiriel, schooled well in the arts, found that lack of familiarity comforting—for it was a magic that she associated with Ashaf. Only with Ashaf.

Ashaf.

There was a shadow across the sun's face. She let the pendant fall into the folds of her shirt. And she waited, listening for the sounds of footsteps, passersby, anyone who sought to intrude on a moment of privacy. There was none, but still she waited.

And when her visitor came, she came in silence, and only by the slight brush of cloth against cloth did Kiriel—whose hearing was unparalleled among the kin—know that she had at last arrived.

"Evayne," she said, turning at once to see the hooded face of the blue-robed seer.

The hood lifted; the hands that rose with it were older and stronger, and Kiriel thought she saw the white lines of scars across her arms in the brief glimpse of skin that the single motion afforded. "Kiriel," the seeress said, and Kiriel saw that she was a woman of power. She was also, the younger woman thought, slightly surprised; it pleased her.

Because she *had* known that Evayne was coming, and she'd waited for her. Evayne read it in her face; triumph was not a thing that the kin guarded well.

"You were expecting me."

"Yes."

"For how long?"

She had grown used to sharp questions from weak people, and she took as little offense as she could at the words and the tone behind them. Evayne made it easy; she was not weak, no matter how she might choose to display her age and hide her power until the last possible moment. "I knew that you would come an hour ago."

The seeress cursed softly, a single word; Kiriel did not understand it.

"He grows in power," Evayne said, "if you can sense my coming; if you can know, an hour away, what *I* did not know until this courtyard appeared on the path.

"I will be brief. I came only to deliver a warning to you."

"A . . . warning?"

"Indeed. Make of it what you will," the seeress added, her face now an unbending mask.

"Who gave you the warning?"

"You learned enough on our journey here to know that I cannot answer that question," Evayne said softly, but without rancor. "The warning is this: Lord Isladar has been sent to the South."

Kiriel knew that she had lost what little color she had; knew further that her eyes showed shadow and the lines of her face, the leanness of the fight. "Thank you," she said.

"Is this bad news?"

The young girl's laugh was bitter; Ashaf had always said it was too old for her. *I'll grow into it*, she'd answered. Her jaw tightened. She wanted to be quit of these lands, for the longer she stayed in their soft facade of safety, surrounded by those that were gray and white and barely capable of being a threat to a loaf of bread, let alone each other, the more she thought of the past.

And the past was dead dead dead.

"Of course it's bad news," she said angrily.

But Evayne, having delivered it, was gone. Kiriel rose and made ready to leave, but lingered a moment in the sunlight, as if waiting for a cloud to curtain it, to draw this scene to an end.

And because she waited, there was none.

He came next, and she would have known him anywhere: Pale hair, long, white, and perfect; eyes of silver, glinting with light that the sun couldn't touch; supple arms, legs, perfect grace—in all things, beautiful.

The hair on the back of her neck rose, but she was used to this reaction by now; she bit it back; forced herself to sit at a semblance of ease. Wondering. "Member APhaniel," she said, in a polite and perfectly respectful tone of voice.

"Kiriel di'Ashaf." He bowed. She saw that he did not carry a sword. But perhaps he did not need it.

"I have come to ask a favor of you."

"A favor?"

"Yes." A white brow lifted. "You are acquainted with the concept?"

"Oh, yes," she said, although his words riled. "A favor is when I agree to do as you've requested because we have a mutual goal, and make plans to have you killed, or to kill you myself, at the moment those plans come into fruition."

He chuckled, not at all offended. "I see. Daunting, but I fear I must ask it anyway."

Nonplussed, she rose, her hand on her sword hilt. She did not trust the mage; how could she? But she did not distrust him either. And anyone that you did not distrust was dangerous, because it was through trust—or the uneasy alliances that power in a shifting clime demanded—that you opened yourself to the naked blade, the unseen attack.

"I had a visitor," he said softly.

Ah. "So did I."

They were silent a long time, or what felt like a long time; Kiriel was only comfortable with silence when it wasn't shared.

"We are not friends, she and I," the mage said; Kiriel heard the steel in his voice more clearly than she ever had. Unsheathed, she thought it would be a wonderous sound. "I do not know if you know it, but we have encountered Isladar before."

"You are here; he fled. You won."

"Yes. And I would like to see that history repeated," the mage said quietly. "But the South has always been prey to the Allasakari and their minions because of their superstitious belief that the god-born are demon-kin. They do not have effective measures at containing what

has been summoned—if they even have the desire to try."
He bowed. "We will not, I think, be friends, Kiriel
di'Ashaf. Neither you or I have that luxury—and perhaps,
if I am honest, that inclination. But we have a mutual
foe, if I understand Evayne correctly.

"Let us make the same pact that the kin make; let us
take the same risks. Let us trust one another in this field,
for this fight."

She nodded.

And then he said, "I wish the binding oath."

"No."

He shrugged. "Then I will not have it. I believe it has
been a long time since the kin have used it—if they use it
at all."

"They force the weak to it," she said with disdain. "Only
the unnamed and those a tier above it will take that oath,
and they take it to save their lives."

"Fair enough," he said coolly. "I have taken binding
oaths in my time, and I have never been forced to them.
Only forced," he added softly, "to their consequence. But
that is not a story for this day. I will travel with the
entourage of Valedan di'Leonne."

"Then why did you come to seek my permission?"

"Because the war he fights, and the war we fight, are
entwined, perhaps inseparable in this conflict—but they
are not the same war, and we two know it."

"No, Meralonne, you are wrong," a third voice said.

Kiriel's sword was out of its sheath; its shadows
drained the warmth of the sun from the balcony. But she
relaxed when she saw the young woman—the young
seer—who had come to speak with her in the Kalakar
House.

The young woman who had acknowledged that, alone,
the Northern Imperials, and the man who claimed the
waters of the Tor Leonne, could not win the war.

"Jewel," the mage said, clearly less pleased by the
intrusion than Kiriel, "this is a private matter."

"It's not a private matter," Jewel replied, as if Meralonne were merely a man, and not a man of power. "If
Valedan kai di'Leonne loses, we have lost; if he wins, we
have won reprieve." Her eyes appeared, for just that
moment, to be clear glass; a trick, no doubt, of the sun.

"The Terafin has given me permission to ride with the host. I have petitioned Valedan kai di'Leonne."

"Petition the army," Meralonne said, with an odd expression. "That's what I did."

"If it comes to that, I will. They'll take me because they'll hope I can jump through the hoops of their questions with answers they like. But I'd rather be accepted by Valedan." She paused. "And by you," she said, turning to Kiriel.

And this so-called Sun King won't be your *puppet?* She had said it to Jewel ATerafin, but did not repeat it; the words had been meant for the Commanders, and they were no longer witnesses. Kiriel shrugged briefly, but not with disdain. Because there was, in Jewel ATerafin, a kernel of light that had not been dimmed.

Oh, Kiriel knew about Jewel's background; the Ospreys delighted in telling it. But it had not tarnished her; the guilt of it, or the shame in it, were simply not there. She had done what she had to do, done it cleanly, and survived; she felt a perverse pride in the fact that she had made her living stealing out of the pockets of the rich before becoming one of those rich.

And she never pressed charges against young thieves, or so the Ospreys said.

"I remain a part of the Kalakar House Guards," Kiriel said, neutrally.

"Then you've made your decision," Jewel replied, no relief—in fact, no expression—upon her guarded face.

"Yes," Kiriel said, turning to the mage. "Please leave us, Member APhaniel."

Jewel showed her surprise at that—and it only deepened when Meralonne APhaniel tendered a respectful bow and obeyed what was, after all, barely a request. "That's not the mage I know," she muttered.

"No," Kiriel said, and she seemed surprised herself. She folded her arms across her chest and waited until his footsteps—and the echoes they left—were gone. And then she met Jewel's eyes, and hers were golden. Even though she knew it to be safe—perhaps even an asset—in the Empire to appear so, she usually remained hidden behind eyes that were dark, dark brown. "I will fight this war, your war; I will fight it by your rules as I understand them. What oaths Valedan kai di'Leonne needs, I will make, if it is necessary."

"But—" Jewel was quiet for a long moment. Kiriel could see the flicker of surprise behind her eyes; the apprehension that almost stopped her from questioning the gift that Kiriel offered. Almost. "But you said that you didn't want to fight—that we couldn't win this war."

"You said it as well," was her grim reply. "If there were an easy answer, I would give it to you—and I am not used to being questioned. Pretend that there is ease. I have seen Valedan di'Leonne. I have seen him fight, and I've seen what he chooses to do after a fight. I don't understand it; but I know that it is a weakness that is his strength. And I find it . . . compelling.

"We are not the same, you and I, and we will never be. But I see in you some of what I see in him."

"That's not all," Jewel said softly.

Kiriel raised a brow. The silence stretched between them a moment before she chose to break it. Ashaf would have recognized the hesitation; the decision implicit in that pause. "No. But I thought it would be enough."

"I'm a seer."

"I'll remember that." She shrugged and turned away. "An enemy of mine has chosen to go South. I would take any field against him that was offered to me. *Any* field. Is that what you wished to hear?" She turned as she asked the question.

Jewel grimaced. "No. But it's the truth, and it'll do." She held out a hand. Kiriel stared at it. Jewel laughed. "It's a gesture of solidarity, Kiriel."

Kiriel hesitated a moment longer, and then she took the hand, touching for the first time a person who was brighter inside than Ashaf had been. She was afraid; she had not thought to be afraid. But that light, unlike the light of Sigurne Mellifas, did not burn; it did not even flinch.

"Kiriel?"

She shook herself, angry at the awe and the awkwardness. "We don't even know if we're leaving."

"We're leaving," Jewel said, her gaze distant. "We just don't know when. And we're praying to Kallairis that it won't be until the Festival of the Moon."

Kiriel nodded, and they stood together companionably,

both women holding secrets of their own that they still sought to protect.

"You aren't used to trusting people." Jewel's voice was quiet and so matter-of-fact it seemed surprising that she bothered to say something that self-evident at all.

"And you are?"

"With my life. Every day. Well, every other day." She grinned, although Kiriel sensed the pain beneath that rueful movement of lips.

"I never trusted anyone with my life."

Jewel turned to look at the younger woman, feeling, for a moment, that she was fifteen years old, and her responsibilities extended only as far as a handful of street children she'd chosen as family. "You can, you know."

"Oh?" Kiriel replied, her voice as cold as a Northern spring. "And if I did, who'd be foolish enough to trust *me* in return?"

Jewel Markess ATerafin turned to meet eyes that were both golden warmth and icy darkness. And she laughed. "You can turn it off, you know," she said, as she saw Kiriel's brows rise. "It doesn't impress me."

Kiriel was nonplussed.

"Don't tell me. You do it naturally." She laughed again, but the laughter trailed into what would have been, from anyone else, uneasy silence. From Jewel, it was silence, plain and simple. "You're a killer," she told the younger woman.

It was Kiriel's turn to smile, but the smile faltered as Jewel ATerafin continued to speak.

"But that isn't all you are. Tell me I can trust you, and I'll trust you."

"It looks like it's going to scar," Alexis said sweetly, as she circled Auralis. He was a vain man—admittedly with good reason—and she particularly enjoyed pricking that vanity now and again. Especially in the drill circle; especially when she was the one who was on the receiving end of a temper that, three days after what was now referred to as the "incident," still hadn't worked itself out. He was off his stride. *Feeling his age,* she thought, and that made her smile as well.

Which was unfortunate, because Auralis off his stride was easily a match for Alexis distracted, and it was Alexis who ate dirt. Again. It didn't increase her affection for the young Annagarian noble who had, to the amazement of the Ospreys and the endless relief of their leader, managed to put Auralis in his place—but it did increase her respect.

Cook gave her a hand up; Auralis was already looking for his next sparring partner. Victim, she amended, as she tested her knee. "Duarte, you lazy son of a bitch—you take him!"

Duarte laughed. Yes, lazily. He was the only Osprey who could come up even against Auralis consistently, and it was *only* even. If, she amended again, you didn't count Kiriel. She was willing to fight for the girl's rights as an Osprey, but Kiriel still didn't inspire the gut reaction that was, to Alexis, what the Ospreys were all about: family, for better or worse.

"I'll wait," Duarte said. "At least another hour. Maybe two. I like to choose my battles." He smiled as he offered her a hand. "You should choose yours more carefully."

She slapped him half-playfully; he did her the grace of not dodging. "I hope he keeps this up for the rest of the week."

"Betting pool?"

She laughed. "Seven days, three hours."

"Three hours?"

Alexis shrugged. "We had to differentiate. We've all known Auralis for a *long* time." Her knee still hurt; she winced as she shifted her weight to accommodate the pain. "We're all getting older," she told him softly. "We're not the same men and women we were when we fought in the last war."

"Worried?"

"Some," she said, brooding. It surprised him; Alexis rarely condescended to worry. "Have you heard yet?"

"I'm just a lowly Primus," Duarte said. "And at that, a lowly Primus in *Avantari*. The Kalakar connections don't mean as much as they could." She didn't smile; in fact, she bent, struggling with the straps of her boots. As if, he thought, they were complicated. He started to reach for her, and stopped, remembering where they were and who she was. Alexis barely knew what the word tender meant—and never in a public place.

"I'm just too old," she said softly, without looking up.

It was probably the only way she could say it. "I thought—I thought I wanted Auralis to kill the boy. Part of me still does. Not because I think he's dangerous— even if he took Auralis down, I don't—but because he means that we have to go back to Averda." She shook her head; dark strands of hair fell, as if at unspoken command. A curtain. A shield. "When we left, it was the only thing I wanted. To go back. To raze the Terrean. To kill every man, woman, child."

"I know."

"I was younger, then. Then, I could have done it."

He willed her to lift her face; she didn't.

"But they're going to die, again, on foreign soil. Doesn't matter how good you are, or I am, or *he* is. We could be gods. Won't save them. And I can't think of more than a handful that I'd be willing to lose." She tightened the straps of her boots almost viciously. "I thought of them as comrades, back then.

"Now, I think of them as family."

"Or children," Duarte said.

"I never wanted children," she told him, elbows on her knees. "And this is why. The only person I'm not worried about is her."

"Kiriel."

She nodded.

"Maybe the Kings will decide against the boy."

She laughed bitterly. "Duarte, you used to know how to lie to me. When did you lose it?" She lifted her face then, because she was angry and anger was safe. "You were in the Great Hall. You *saw* the creature. You have to know what it means."

"I used to know how to lie to you," he told her, offering her a smile that only touched the surface of his face, "because you used to want to be lied to." They turned as Auralis finished with Fiara—barely—and drew together a moment. "Do you want to retire?"

"No."

"Then live with it, Alexis. This is a soldier's life." He was harsher than he meant to be.

Because she didn't know how to let him be anything else.

CHAPTER
TWENTY-EIGHT

5th of Lattan, 427 AA
The Tor Leonne

The silks were very fine. Although merchant travel had been much inhibited over the past two months, these bolts had been ordered by, and delivered to, no less a man than the Radann kai el'Sol. They were flawless because the penalty for flaws was so terribly high, for these silks were meant to adorn the woman chosen as the Consort of the Lord of the Sun for the duration of the Festival.

Of course, the young Serra Diora di'Marano was one of the few clanswomen who had already been gifted with a garment nearly as fine—perhaps, if he were honest, *as* fine—as the garment the servitors now labored over. He wondered if she would make the comparison. No doubt every other clansman in the realm—every clansman, he thought grimly, who had been allowed to make the trek for this year's Festival—would.

And it was for this reason, if no other, that he joined the laborers, ascertaining that the detail work was both expensive and perfect. This year, it had to be perfect, because she wore it.

It did not help his mood to know that in easing her in her role as Lord's Consort, he was aiding General Alesso di'Marente. A fool's thought, and he had no time for it; Alesso di'Marente would stand in the waters of the Tor Leonne, accept the Lord's blessing, and bear the crown which he, Fredero kai el'Sol, would place upon his brow.

Lord aid me, he thought, as he clenched his hands into shaking fists. *I will place the crown on the head of a man who is not Leonne.* He had accepted it as his duty before the name Valedan kai di'Leonne had been spoken aloud by Marakas par el'Sol; it echoed still, lingering in his ears

at every quiet moment. He strove to make certain that
there weren't many.

They'd thought him dead.

And why? Because the rest of the clan Leonne had perished with barely a whimper. In the morning after the
slaughter, their blood had already been cleaned from the
walls and the screens and the doors, and their bodies
hidden from the Lord's sight; they had raised no arms in
self-defense, left no enemies in their wake as proof of
their prowess. It was as if they had simply ceased to exist.
The will of the Lord.

But the Lord had protected Valedan.

The Imperial hostages here had been slaughtered to a
man, and their deaths had been unclean, public sport to
rival the sports of the unnamed clans who ruled by the
Lord of Night's will. Everyone knew what the outcome of
those deaths would be: the equally brutal deaths of the
Annagarian hostages.

But the Lord had protected Valedan.

The General Alesso di'Marente—the man who sought
to rule the Tor Leonne—had asked for, and received, the
aid of one of the kinlords. *Kinlord.* He had attacked the
entire assembly of the Imperial Council.

And the Lord protected Valedan.

Not even a man with the sun in his eyes could mistake
the Lord's meaning.

"Not the beads; the crystal. Use the crystal."

The servitor—a man whose entire life had been devoted to the creation of gowns such as this one, bowed a
wrinkled face. He was an old man, wiry and sun-wizened,
and although age had slowly taken the agility out of his
fingers as sure as a wound drained a body's blood, his
years of experience shored up his skill.

At too many years of age to count, Jevri was without
parallel. And it was unlike Fredero to question his choice
and his decision in so obvious a fashion. But Jevri did not
comment—and not because it wasn't his place; the Lord
knew that Jevri dared much in his quest for perfection.

As if, Fredero thought, *he knows what troubles me.*

It was more than possible. At one time, in a past that
was never distant enough, Jevri had been a seraf in the
Lambertan fold. A parting gift from his brother. The
finest of his gifts, if not the most obviously valuable.

To bring him to the temple, Fredero had been forced to give Jevri his freedom. It was a little thing; Jevri had as much freedom as any poor man did in the Dominion. Perhaps more. He had accepted both freedom and employ with silent grace; it was only when he was caught up in his craft that he became a man capable of sharp words.

And he offered not a single word today.

He sewed instead, and embroidered, pausing only to speak to the servitors who labored under his command. It was almost comforting to watch them.

And comfort of this nature could not last.

The doors burst open. As one man, the servitors stopped their work—save for Jevri, who continued with the focus of a man who knows that the job is both necessary and not yet finished, and is willing to let the rest of the world take care of itself.

"Kai el'Sol!"

He turned at once to see a young Radann, sword drawn, hair pulled back perfectly to better expose his face. His badge of office glittered brightly against the blue of his robe; he was young, and had an earnestness about him that both pleased and pained Fredero.

"Radann Nattani," he said, bowing. "Is there trouble?"

Gently rebuked, the man nodded. "Tyr'agnate Eduardo kai di'Garrardi demands an audience at once."

Fredero's face deepened in color. "Demands?"

"Uh—requests. But . . ."

"Understood." Fredero turned to his oldest servitor. "Jevri, I will leave this in your capable hands."

"Kai el'Sol," Jevri replied serenely.

The Tyr'agnate was a handsome man by any standards, although his face had a sharpness to it that discouraged trust. His temper was almost as well known as Sword's Blood; certainly as often displayed.

Fredero kai el'Sol knew a moment's bitterness; he could not refuse to deal with any man who might be a friend to the Radann in the months and years to follow. He bowed, and held that bow a fraction of a second longer than strict ritual dictated.

"Tyr'agnate."

"Kai el'Sol." The Garrardi Tyr's bow was low and respectful. It was not groveling, but it was given. He had come to expect less of the men who held the Dominion's future in their grip.

He was in no way reassured. "Come, if you have time; I have not yet taken the morning water, and if you would join me, I would be honored."

"The honor would be mine."

They repaired to the Garden of the Stone together. There, waited upon by servitors that the kai el'Sol had handpicked for loyalty, they partook of the waters of the Tor Leonne in a silence of rising sun and shrinking shadow.

"Kai el'Sol," Eduardo di'Garrardi said at last, setting his cup aside and leaning into the weathered edge of hard stone.

"Inasmuch as any garden can be, this is private," Fredero replied.

"I am not concerned with privacy at the moment. This Festival, there is very little that I fear."

Or any, Fredero thought; Eduardo was not a man driven by his fears. By his desires, yes, and those obsessions left room for little else.

"The Lord's Consort will be the Serra Diora di'Marano."

The kai el'Sol nodded.

"It has come to my attention that the General appears to have a . . . personal interest in this matter."

"I believe," the kai el'Sol said neutrally, "that the request originated with the Tyr'agnate of Sorgassa."

"I was there when he brought the request to the General. In truth, it pleased me. It pleases me less now."

There was nothing the kai el'Sol could say; he did not attempt to fill the silence.

"The Radann have been neglected since the unfortunate and unexplained assassination." Eduardo di'Garrardi sat forward. "There are matters of war that concern the General, and he, no doubt, feels that the Radann are loyal. Or that they are not to be feared."

"That may be so."

"Then, kai el'Sol, let me be blunt." Reaching into the folds of his silk robes, he drew out an unmarked wooden medallion. He set it carefully on the flat of the stone bench, between them. "With your permission?" he asked, as he touched the hilt of his sword.

"Granted."

The steel caught the sun's light and sent it scattering across the stone. Nothing but the surface of the waters of the Tor caught the sun as beautifully as the naked blade. Nothing.

"The Serra Diora di'Marano is the Consort of the Lord of the Sun, not the Lord of the Tor Leonne. If Alesso di'Marente forgets that—if he shows any sign of forgetting it—I will put the considerable wealth of Oerta behind you should you refuse to grant him the crown. Or should you, as is the law, demand that he take up the Sun Sword." The words hung in the air longer than his hands; the blade flashed down, sinking a quarter inch into wood and resting there.

"And from me?" the kai el'Sol asked, his voice deceptively soft.

"If there is treachery, it will most likely occur after the crown has graced his brow, in which case, you will call for the Sword. You will, of course, refuse to lay that crown across that brow if I deem it necessary."

"And whose brow will it adorn? Who will rule the Tor if not the architect of Leonne's demise?"

Eduardo shrugged coldly. "That," he said, "is a matter for the Lord to decide. He did well enough two hundred years ago."

Fredero kai el'Sol did not search the sky for a sign of the Lord's blessing; he knew it when it came, cloaked even as it was in the guise of Garrardi. He drew his sword and neatly crossed the cut that the Tyr'agnate had made, thinking that Garrardi was a fool, but a fool whose goodwill he required.

After all, what man would throw away such a necessary ally for the sake of a mere wife?

Affection was safe, but any deeper emotion was a trap, had always been a trap. The Serra Teresa di'Marano watched her niece as she stood in the center of a flurry of cautious, but hurried, wives and serafs. Diora was beyond understanding just how she had been caught by such a trap, if indeed she could even see the bars of the cage, but she was willing to destroy herself utterly in the memory— the *memory,* not the actuality—of such a deep and divisive love.

The Lady's hand was everywhere in a woman's heart; she could think of no woman who did not desire a home, a partner, a place which she ruled and was loved for ruling, and a place where she could go in which rules were someone else's prerogative—and problem. She had met many, many women who had not fulfilled this desire; they were not a threat.

No, the threats, as attested to by the golden rings that had been wound by strands of raven hair into invisibility, were those who had found what they sought.

Threaten things loved, and a woman might buckle in terror, fold, and give in to any demand until such a time as she might come upon the means to end the threat permanently. But destroy those things, and you destroyed the life, if not the living, of the woman who so loved. Living ghosts were always dangerous.

The time will come, she thought, as she gazed upon the icy perfection of her niece's beautiful face, *when you will want those things again; you will find the road that brings you back to a life you've forsworn.* But she would bear the scars. She would always bear the scars. If she survived.

Serra Teresa knew this from bitter experience. Knew both. Only youth's immediate passion and distant sense of mortality could keep the oaths alive when those who'd received them lay buried beneath layers of unblessed earth. Diora di'Marano was young.

And powerful for it.

"Not, I think, the diamonds," the Serra Teresa said softly, as Diora turned to face her. "They are too Northern."

Ramdan bowed immediately, but Alaya—Serra Fiona's youngest seraf, and easily the most valuable to Teresa's expert eye—spoke. "But they are perfect for her. Look at the color against her skin; they trap the Lord's light and catch the eye."

"They are," Ramdan said, "too Northern."

"But the Dominion—"

"The mines are in Mancorvo," Serra Teresa said, her perfect voice showing no hint of her extreme frustration.

It must have shown somehow; Alana en'Marano leaned over and cuffed the young seraf on the back of the head. "Don't argue with the Serra," she told the girl, in a friendly tone that was still laced with windblown sand.

"She's twice as smart as the rest of us combined—a match for Sendari on a bad day."

"Alana," Serra Teresa said softly, well-pleased but disinclined to show indulgence, "he is your husband, and more, the father of the young lady whom you are dressing. Show appropriate respect."

She could hear quite clearly the words that Alana muttered beneath her breath; no one else could, with the exception of Diora. She let them pass with the barest hint of a smile.

Because to do less than smile was to show things she did not wish to reveal.

Illia en'Marano—still the most sensuously graceful of Sendari's wives for all that she was now closer to thirty than twenty—lifted the curtain of Diora's hair thoughtfully. "I believe the Serra Teresa is right," she told Alaya, but very gently. "The pearls, or the opals, would be softer, and they would still be very fine."

Diora said nothing; she had not spoken a single word since the dress itself arrived. Mute, she had made her way to the harem's chamber, and mute, she had allowed the wives to remove her morning clothing and dress her in this stunning gift from the Radann to the woman who would honor the Lord by her presence.

The Radann had once before gifted her with a similar robe—a robe not quite as fine, and not quite as costly. Grimly, the Serra Teresa bowed her head. *You wanted this,* she thought, as she lifted an ivory fan. *Be strong enough to bear it, or we are all doomed.*

She played the Northern harp, and it was not the small instrument, but the large one, that she sat behind. The sun's rays adorned her hat and her shoulders, glinted off the fall of her robes as if they were liquid and not pale silk. Her hair was bound in a series of three combs, each a shade of green with hints of gold and a dark blue stone that must have come from the North.

Her hands were perfect and pale when they came to rest or pause, but they did not pause often. An hour, as the sun made its way toward its exit, had passed while she sang; her voice did not change or deign to notice the passage of that time.

He noticed it by the slow spread of pink across the

horizon, by the cooling of the air, by the change in the breeze. And he did not move, because if he rose to leave, there was just as good a chance that he would approach her instead. She was not attended. He had seen her arrive in her spare and simple sari almost by accident, and were it not for the harp that she carried, he would not have noticed her at all.

But the fact that she did carry it, that she chose to struggle with its weight when he had never once seen her less than perfectly graceful, caught his attention.

He had women, and if he desired, he could have many more. He would have to have a Serra after he took the Tor, for neither of his previous wives had survived to produce a living kai. *What,* he thought, as he watched her lift and struggle with a harp that she obviously did not wish to scratch or damage in any way, *possessed you to come here without a seraf?* He almost laughed, she seemed so willful, so determined.

And it was in the willful, in the awkward, in the graceless huff of breath and the strands of hair that escaped those combs, that perfect sheen, that he realized just how dangerous a trap she had become—and he had thought of little else these past few days.

For these movements were hers, they were private, they were akin to those she might make when perfection of social rule gave way to a different perfection, a different communion. She lifted a hand, brushed the strands of hair back behind her ears. Ran her tongue along her lips twice. Closed her eyes.

And then, as he stood and watched, she began to sing. The harp's accompaniment joined her, but the damage had been done, the weapon planted; he could not have moved had he needed to.

Until the moment he saw the Tyr Eduardo kai di'Garrardi approach the pavilion from the West. She saw him as well, and her hands stilled the music of the strings; silence descended, where song might have been safer. She became the Serra Diora di'Marano at once, and if her silks were a bit wrinkled, and her hair slightly windswept, it only made her more appealing.

She froze; he had come without seraf or cerdan, and she had come without seraf or cerdan. As a married woman, it would have been her death, and his, had his rank been unworthy of note. She was not a married woman, and he was not an unworthy man.

"Serra Diora," he said, bowing quite low.

"Tyr'agnate," she said, and the word was both respectful and cool. Her hands fell from harp strings to lap. She rose for long enough to extend him the courtesy his rank demanded; when she lifted her face again, her cheeks were slightly crimson.

"I would prefer," he said, as he began to walk toward the dais, "that you call me Eduardo. It is what you will call me, three days hence."

She bowed again, for in the Dominion, a Serra did not argue with a Tyr'agnate. Cerdan did, or fathers, or brothers. But she did not call him Eduardo. Instead, when she lifted her head, and saw how close he stood, she said, "I am the Consort of the Lord of the Sun; I am not unmarried for the next three days. I have been claimed. You are a man of the clans. You will not dishonor me."

He raised a dark brow, surprised and not entirely pleased—but not entirely displeased either. He walked past the harp that stood between them, and stood above her, looking down.

"My dear Diora," he said, reaching out to brush her cheeks with the barest touch of his fingers. "The women of the clan Marano have long been known to harbor willful, even wild, spirits. Yet you have always been so perfectly graceful, so entirely feminine, I do not believe that I have seen that wildness in you. Until today." He looked up at the sky, the deepening sky. "Until this eve."

She could not struggle against him; she could not cry out, although, if she wished to refuse him, she might attempt that refusal in quiet, measured tones. He knew it, and he knew that she knew it: For many a woman had been dishonored in the Dominion, and if the man so responsible was weak enough, he might pay the price of that insult if it became widely known—but a woman always suffered, if the assault were public knowledge. Better to weep in silence, to stifle cries of pain or pleas for mercy than to call for help and have it arrive too late. Serra Diora was from a family that had too much to lose, and her position was a high one; the fall would be fatal.

If he chose it, she would accept it, like it or not.

And he did not care if she liked it or not. Not now; Sword's Blood had not carried him willingly to begin with. But he carried him now although he still suffered no other man to ride him.

She saw it in his eyes; he saw her freeze; saw her lips part as if she thought to deter him with words. As if he had already made the decision instead of hovering so dangerously over its edge.

"Garrardi."

He had a moment to compose his face, but he chose not to take it, turning instead, his hand still against the velvet curve of the Serra's upturned cheek. "Marente."

"What are you doing here?"

"I might ask you the same question."

"Obviously," Alesso di'Marente said, "I am here by the whim of the Lord. It is the day before Festival's start. The Serra Diora di'Marano, at *your* request, has been chosen by the Radann as the Lord's Consort. She is not to be *touched* until the Festival is over."

"And you've become such an ardent follower of the rules the Radann lay down." The derision was clear in the tone of the Tyr'agnate's voice. "I am not a fool. Why are you here, alone, without your escort?"

"I do not have to explain my movements to you."

Eduardo di'Garrardi drew away from Diora and the pavilion, his attention focused on Alesso, and Alesso alone. "No, General, you do not. But the Serra Diora di'Marano is not yours, and she will not be yours. Or have you forgotten your word?"

"I forget nothing."

"Then say it. Tell her."

The General's face suddenly shuttered; the angry light gleaming beneath the surface of dark eyes went out. All anger left his voice, all command. But in neutrality there was a hint of the howling wind, and it was cold. "Serra Diora," he said, bowing stiffly and with great respect, "it is your father's wish that, after the Festival of the Sun, you be given to the Tyr Garrardi as wife." He turned back to the Tyr'agnate. "Will that do, Eduardo?"

"No." The ruler of the Terrean of Oerta looked down a sharp nose, his eyes as narrow as blades. "I want more. Tell me, Alesso, that you will not touch her; that you will not try; that it is *your* will that she be my wife."

"And if I say it, will you cease your insulting attempts to arrive before the ceremony does?"

"Ceremony is for those who don't have the power to avoid it. It is not an insult—it is a statement of fact. A few days here or there will not make a difference."

"They will make a difference," a new voice said. "In the eyes of the Lord."

The glare that bridged the two men snapped as they turned to face the Radann kai el'Sol and the Serra Teresa di'Marano. Servitors accompanied the kai el'Sol, and cerdan, the Serra Teresa; as well, three men that had the look of Marano serafs, they were so silent and graceful.

"Serra Diora, forgive me," the Radann kai el'Sol said, and he bowed as deeply as if she were in truth the Lord's Consort, although the morning sun would not arrive for many hours. "I detained the Serra Teresa, or you would have had a proper escort." He nodded to the servitors, and they left him immediately.

Their weapons glinted in the sun's fading light as they came to stand between the two men and the Serra.

"Diora," the Serra Teresa said, in a voice that only the two women could hear. "You are unharmed?"

"Yes," her niece replied, the voice shaky but clear. "The General was—was here unexpectedly. I'm—I'm sorry I called you—I was—"

"You were intelligent," the Serra Teresa said softly. She turned her gaze to the Tyr and the General, and her voice was like the desert night. "Tyr'agnate. General Alesso di'Marente. The Serra Diora begs your forgiveness, but she is fatigued, and it is vital that she be refreshed; she must greet the dawn's light as the Consort.

"If you will excuse us?"

Alesso di'Marente bowed at once, and he bowed very, very low. The Tyr'agnate nodded, the anger still coloring his cheeks and his gestures.

But the kai el'Sol stepped forward. "The Serra Diora will have Radann as her personal guards for the next three days. She will appear nowhere without them, either in public or in private. If you wish to speak with her, you will come to *me* and I will arrange it."

The Serra Diora raised her face, and for a moment, she looked genuinely alarmed. But she did not appear to be frightened of the Radann kai el'Sol. "Radann—"

His breath was not long enough to give her room to speak unless she forced her words between—and over—his. She was the Flower of the Dominion.

"If you, or any of the clansmen who follow either of you, lay a hand on her, or stand close enough to offer insult, I will order the Radann to kill. Do I make myself clear?"

Alesso seemed almost amused. "Perfectly, kai el'Sol. Eduardo?"

"Indeed."

"Then I believe that we will escort the Serra to her father." He turned on heel, and then stopped.

"Radann kai el'Sol," the Serra Teresa began, her voice as soft and soothing as any woman's had ever been. But he held up a hand to still her words, and she, too, was true to her training.

"You are her father's friend," he told the General. Then, as if wisdom had finally caught up with him, he stopped, his jaws clamped over lips that might otherwise have continued to move.

Teresa did not remain with Diora once they had reached the safety of Sendari's harem. The Radann did, but they remained outside of the sliding screens that were her world, their swords drawn, a sure sign of their willingness to use them.

There were things that people did not share when they desired the illusion of control, and among those was fear and its aftermath. Diora desired to be alone, and Teresa quietly acceded to the unspoken request. They knew each other well, the older woman and the younger, because they had walked many of the same roads.

In the darkness, Diora sat without benefit of lamp or torch or moon, because it was in the shadows of the Lady's night that she found the only safety she sought: privacy.

Her cheek was ice where Eduardo di'Garrardi had touched it. But the intervention of the General had not filled her with relief. It was not until the Radann Fredero kai el'Sol had arrived that she felt any certain sense of protection.

Alesso di'Marente had seemed amused by the arrival of the Radann; indeed, she would have believed that he was.

Until she heard him speak. He was good at masking what he felt; she was certain that only she and Ona Teresa heard what lay beneath the words. An anger that cold and that implacable was always wielded. She was not sure who would die for this evening's work—or when—but she was certain that someone would.

And she was afraid that it would be Radann Fredero kai el'Sol. Her plans depended on him. He could die after Festival's Height, but not a moment before, if he had to die at all.

Yes, of course. That was it.

She was afraid that the plans that she had made—plans so close to bearing fruit—were about to be uprooted by the gale and tossed against the cliffs, as the rest of her life had been, in a single, bleak night.

But she did something that she had not done since Serra Teresa arrived at the Tor. In the limited privacy of her room, she caught her hair and pulled it down, and unraveled it from the three rings that the night muted. They were cool in her hands, and weighty. She put them on. She needed to wear them again.

Because she *liked* Radann kai el'Sol.

Because she had so desperately hoped that he would not be a man that she could like.

He woke her before dawn.

The one other man who would have dared lay dead well over a month. Her father did not come here, although it was theoretically his right, and she had no serafs.

In fact, the Widan Sendari di'Marano could have refused her visitor entry. It would have been a hollow gesture; his men stood on either side of both screens—the ones that opened in, and the ones that opened into the private interior garden. The Serra was not given a room that could be reached by anyone who happened to approach the building from an exterior wall.

But she knew, when she heard the tentative knocking upon the frame of the door, and not the bells or the gong, who it was. She rose, wrapping herself quickly and carefully in the silks appropriate to greeting a man of rank, and then she said, softly, "Enter."

The Radann kai el'Sol stepped across the threshold, carrying an oil lamp that burned quite brightly.

Augmented, she thought idly. She was the daughter of a
Widan; use of magic, especially those enchantments
linked to fire, were as familiar to her as the Tor Leonne.

The Radann's bow was deep, and he held it a while.

"I am sorry to wake you, Serra," he said. She heard the
weariness in his voice and wondered if he had slept at all.
"But you must have these, and you must be prepared
before sun's first light. Today, you greet the dawn as the
Lord's Consort." As he spoke, he held out a hand; one of
the Radann who followed him stepped forward.

In the darkness of the room's shadowy light, Diora
thought there was something wrong with the man. He was
bent, too bent; age was not something that was allowed to
demean the Lord's service.

She rose, and as she did, another Radann entered the
room, pulling the hood from his face. She recognized
the Radann Samadar par el'Sol in the bright light cast
by the lamp.

Ah. That was it. The Radann who stepped forward with
the ancient, lacquered box was still somehow of the
shadows, and in them, although the light cast by the lamp
was bright indeed.

"Radann kai el'Sol. Radann par el'Sol," Diora said,
kneeling very correctly.

"Serra Diora," the par el'Sol replied gravely. "May I
approach? I mean you no harm."

She had always been wary of the Radann, and of them,
most suspicious of Samadar. He had survived far too long
not to be canny, and the wisdom that mellowed many
a man—and caused, by that mellowing, their deaths—
had not gentled Samadar at all. "Of course," she said
softly.

A fourth man entered the room behind them. He, too,
pulled back his hood. Marakas par el'Sol. A man whose
inclusion into the Hand of God she had always found
curious. He was not a dangerous man in the traditional
sense of the word, and if Samadar had survived the years
by being as hard and sharp and cold as a blade, she didn't
understand how Marakas had survived at all.

But he had. She smiled hesitantly as their eyes met.
"Par el'Sol. I am indeed honored to have three such men
attend me this festival morn."

"The honor," Marakas said gravely, "is more ours than

you know." He offered her a perfect bow. There was, in these men, more respect than she'd seen since the death of Illara kai di'Leonne. It troubled her.

The kai el'Sol had busied himself removing the emblems by which the Serra Diora's title would be known for these three days. First, a crown, a work of gold and Lord's gold and sapphires that would sit heavily upon any brow. It was elegant in line, a Southern artifact, not an ornate and ugly Northern gift. He handed the crown to Samadar, and Samadar crossed the planks of the floor in silent grace.

"Serra," he said simply. She bent her head, and he placed the crown upon it. Symbolic; she would have to remove it to have the serafs tend her hair and every contour of her face.

Next, the kai el'Sol pulled from the chest a ring; the ring, like the crown, was a work of solid gold, with highlights of the Lord's gold. Pearls were set in each of the four quarters, and they were of perfect luster: water's gift. This, Marakas par el'Sol brought.

The third thing, the final thing, was the necklace. It was pure gold, and it shone in the darkness with a light of its own. The chain seemed to be made of one piece; like a snake's body, it flexed and bent with no obvious joint. From it, in full circle, hung slender triangles—the stylized rays of the sun's light. The kai el'Sol brought this himself and lowered it gently over the crown.

The fourth Radann in the room spoke then. Serra Diora almost forgot to breathe.

"We, too, have a gift for the Lord's Consort," she said, and she pulled the hood away from her face. "A gift, and a request." She was not lovely; indeed, she was quite plain. Her hair was brown, but it had seen too much sun, too much wind. Her skin was etched with the passage of time, the howling of sand-laden wind. Her eyes were dark, and they did not blink as they met Diora's.

Serra Diora could not think of a single thing to say in reply.

The Radann had brought a woman into her rooms. A woman dressed *as* Radann. The punishment for such a crime had not been invented. Had not had to be invented.

As if she could read the thoughts that paralyzed the Flower of the Dominion, the woman smiled. And the

smile, laden with regret, very real fear, and an abiding
sorrow, was more frightening in its way than the woman's
presence.

"What gift?" the Serra Diora asked, in a perfectly modu-
lated voice.

The woman drew a knife from the sleeves of her robes.
"Just this."

The Serra held out a hand; the woman laid the sheathed
weapon across her palm. As she did, Diora glimpsed the
faint lines of scarring across the woman's wrist. "May I
draw it?"

"It is yours, Serra Diora; you may draw it or not as you
wish." She smiled. "But you've asked a wise question.
Let me answer it. Draw this weapon when you have no
other weapon that you can wield; draw it when you understand, in full, what Leonne faced. Take strength from it if
you can; it is a woman's weapon, but wielded by the right
hand, it is more than a match for a—" and she hesitated a
moment, and then, squaring her shoulders, completed the
sentence, "a man's sword."

The chill that greeted her words was to be expected.
The Serra Diora ignored it. "And the request?"

"Understand," the woman said softly, "that it *is* a
request; there is no barter between us. The gift that
we have chosen to give *is* given. It is yours; you may
do as you please with it, although I would advise you to
keep it."

"I see. The request?"

The woman touched her throat a moment, and then, her
fingers shaking slightly, she pulled a pendant from
its hiding place beneath the folds of dark fabric. The
light of the crystal that hung heavily on a chain that
wasn't even gold was so bright and clear it was hard to
look upon. Serra Diora did not squint because squinting
was an unpleasant trait that had been trained out of her
many, many years ago. But she flinched as the light
touched her face.

"Take this, Serra Diora. Take it, and when you meet your
family, give it to my oldest daughter."

"How am I to know who your oldest daughter is?"

"You will know." She took a deep breath. "I do not
think you will like her, or she you. But her name is

Margret. This is a favor," she said again, as if it were necessary.

"I do not think that I will be given leave to search for your family," the younger woman said softly.

"You won't," was the tired reply. "I only ask that you carry this and return it to my family if you do meet them. It is older than the Tor Leonne," she said, as she stared unblinking into its heart, "and it would cripple us to lose it."

"You cannot carry it back to your daughter."

"No. I will never leave this place."

The Radann kai el'Sol coughed slightly, and they both turned at once, aware suddenly that to ignore three such men, even in circumstances as unusual as these, was a display of poor judgment, if not poor manners.

But Diora studied the woman's face for a moment and then, hesitantly, she nodded.

"Wear it," the woman said.

"But I can't with—"

"You can."

For the third time that night, Diora bowed her head. She let the pendant fall into the folds of her gown and nestle between her breasts. Because she heard the truth in the woman's words, and more: She heard the knowledge of a coming death, and the struggle to accept it with grace.

What could drive such a woman to this place, to those robes, to this room? For Diora heard the desire for life in the words that were heavy with death.

The Voyani did not interfere in the politics of the clans. But she was here. She was Voyani.

And she was right. The pendant, so large and so bright, seemed to dim and fade; she could feel its weight, but she could no longer see it. For a moment she hesitated, for she had seen magery before, and she feared it with reason. But then she drew breath, lifted her chin; was she not of the clans? She had made her decision the moment she had bowed her head before this stranger, and she would accept it.

The Radann were growing less patient by the minute. "Kai el'Sol," the Serra said quietly. "Forgive me. The dawn draws near; I feel that the honor that you have granted me is almost too great to bear, and it unnerves me a little." She drew a pretty breath. "But I will not dishonor your choice, or the Lord's." She rose. "Par el'Sol," she said, bowing to Samadar.

He reached out as if to touch her chin, to draw her face up, and drag her eyes with it. She met his eyes squarely, and his hand fell away. "I almost think, little Serra, that you know more than a Serra should."

She did not answer.

"What do you know of the Widan?"

Diora flushed. "What does any woman know of the Widan?"

"Do you know," he said softly, "if any of the Widan here practice the forbidden arts?"

Her expression did not shift at all, but she froze as understanding of the words seemed to permeate. And then she said, as her eyes flickered to the impassive face of the Voyani woman, "I think it not impossible."

"The Widan Sendari?"

"I am di'Marano," she said, her voice cool and stilted.

"Understand the seriousness of the accusation," Samadar replied. "We intend no insult to you, Serra Diora, by the asking."

"Intent or not, you have offered it. If my father, the Widan Sendari di'Marano, were indeed guilty of such an offense, then I, and all of his kin, would be destroyed by the Lord's light when it finally fell." Her hands rested in her lap, stiff as ivory. "But it is said that the Lord's light falls less gently again on those who betray their fathers."

"Serra Diora," the kai el'Sol said, "we are the Radann; we speak for the Lord."

She met his eyes for an unseemly length of time, and in the end, her lids closed and her dark lashes rested against her cheeks. "No," she said, her voice almost inaudible. "My father was not a practitioner of the forbidden arts."

"And the other Widan?"

"I do not know what the other Widan do," she said, her voice sweet, her eyes dark. "The Widan are not a brotherhood."

The Radann kai el'Sol nodded, as if her words only confirmed what he feared. "The dagger that you have

been given is as old as the Leonne war," he told her
solemnly.

"It is far older than that," the woman said serenely.

Diora was mildly surprised; the Radann Samadar
par el'Sol, obviously irritated. Not even the clansmen
interrupted the Radann kai el'Sol to draw attention to his
mistakes.

But the kai el'Sol seemed somehow inured to her. "It
was given to the Voyani by the—by the Lady. The
Voyani fought their own battles against the Lord of Night.
If you—if you are approached by a servant of the Lord of
the Night, the knife will let you know."

"How?"

"I am sorry, Serra, but we—none of us—are privy to
exactly what the blade does."

She turned her dark eyes upon the Voyani woman. The
woman's smile was very sad. "I cannot help you," she
said, "any more than the Radann. But it will succor you,
Serra Diora. When we have left, give it only a taste of
your blood, no more, and it will remain with you while
you live."

"You do not wish its return?"

"I wish it," she said gravely, "to go to the person who
needs it most. It has a name, among the Voyani. *Lumina
arden.* The light that burns. You will feel its fire, Serra
Diora." She bowed to the Radann, and lifted her hood,
obscuring the feminine lines of her face. "Radann kai
el'Sol, my power is at an ebb. Soon I will no longer be
able to guard this conversation from prying ears."

The kai el'Sol nodded.

Diora looked up at his face, took a deep breath, and
said, "The Widan Cortano di'Alexes. If any man knows
the forbidden arts, it is he."

Samadar par el'Sol and Fredero kai el'Sol exchanged a
bleak glance. The Widan Cortano di'Alexes was considered, by the court of the Tor Leonne, to be the edge of the
Sword of Knowledge.

Ramdan and Alaya attended her, as did Sendari's
wives. Alana stood at a distance giving orders; they
worked in harsh lamplight because they were forced, this
one day, to work while the Lady reigned. And while the
Lady reigned, they were perhaps freer with their words

than they would otherwise have been. The next three days would demand rigid formality from each of them; they were forgiven by the Serra Teresa for their lapses in perfect grace.

Her almost-daughter suffered no such lapse; indeed, she seemed steeped in unnatural silence, as if silence itself were strength.

The gown the Radann had left her was exceedingly fine; Serra Teresa was pleased with it, and very little impressed her. The silk seemed flawless—if that were possible—and the beadwork and embroidery masterful. She had seen many, many Festivals, and had never seen a dress so fine, so perfectly suited to its wearer, as this one.

The crown was set upon the veil that hid her face; no clansman was to have sight of it before the first rays of sun danced across the waters of the Tor Leonne. The ring had been sized for her slender fingers, and the necklace shone in the uneven light.

"Na'dio," Teresa said softly.

Diora carefully turned her head. The combs that held the veil were gold and pearl, but the warmth of them framed a face that seemed cool and remote by comparison. The older Serra shook her head. "You are the Consort of the Lord of the Sun, Na'dio. Such a face will only chill him."

Her niece answered with *the* voice, taking the risk almost recklessly. "I do not owe the Lord my joy, only my obedience."

"Na'dio," she said sharply, answering in the private voice.

"Ona Teresa," she replied, answering normally.

"Can you not smile, Na'dio?"

"When I have left the harem," she told her aunt softly. At times like this, Serra Teresa could see the four-year-old girl in the face of the young woman that she'd become. "Summon the Radann. I am ready."

The Radann were ready as well.

As the Serra Diora left her chambers, she noted two things. The first: That the man who led the guards who would have responsibility of her was no less a man than the Radann Marakas par el'Sol. And the second, that her father had not come to escort her, although it was his right.

* * *

The clansmen gathered at the Lord's Pavilion; the stretch of wood and cloth and banner that surrounded the east side of the waters themselves. The Serra Diora, protected from their coarse view by the veil and the imposing formal dress of the armed Radann, did not speak; speech was not expected. The men made way for her as she passed, and if they craned to get a glimpse, she did not notice in her contemplation of her duty to the Lord.

The Radann kai el'Sol was waiting for her; he stood alone upon the platform that was raised to the Lord's worship. Beside him was a curved chair, one that did not suffer from the high backs of the Northern pretenders. There were cushions to either side, and sweet water on a table that appeared to made of solid silver.

No less a man than the Radann kai el'Sol himself offered the Serra Diora a hand as she mounted the dais.

"Strength, Serra," he said in a voice that he hoped would not carry.

She smiled, or he thought she did; the veil obscured her face and in the predawn light he could not see her expression. And then he took the seat that was meant for her, waiting in the silence until the serafs she had chosen to attend her had artfully arranged the train of her dress. It was the second dress that she had worn that had had such a train—an open sign that she was to be appreciated for the beauty of stillness and not the grace of movement.

The Radann kai el'Sol offered her water, and when she accepted, poured it himself.

But it was Ramdan who brought her her strength, the only succor that she was allowed to publicly accept for the duration of the Festival. In perfect silence, he placed her samisen in her lap.

She looked up, her eyes wide, and the Radann Fredero kai el'Sol smiled sadly and nodded.

Hands shaking, the Serra Diora gently adjusted both dress and lap. Then, as the darkness in the skies above began to fade and the last of the straggling clansmen gathered, she began to play.

She did not sing a woman's song, but rather began the lay of the Sun Sword. And her voice was so beautiful, so achingly pure, that it was impossible not to feel, for just a moment, that the hand that wielded that Sword was the only just hand in a land of weakness and cowardice.

Only after the last of the strains of this first song had died completely did anyone stop to remember that the hand that had wielded that Sword was Leonne.

The Serra Teresa had not been chosen by the Serra Diora to serve as Consort's attendant. They had agreed upon it, and Teresa bitterly regretted the agreement the moment she heard the first strains of the lay. She stood beside her brother, the Widan Sendari, and even in the poor light, she could see his face quite clearly. Many of their meetings and their arguments had occurred at dusk or dawn, the time when the will of man reigns for a moment or two.

Men of power should never love, she thought, as she stole a glance at his rigid profile. He had almost chosen not to become a man of power, for the sake of love. By the time he had chosen to forsake the memory of the dead, the living had already sunk roots in his heart. She knew her brother as well as she knew any living person, and she could not say what the cost of tearing those roots out and destroying them utterly would be.

But she saw, in his face, the certain knowledge that he would have to try. She saw bleakness, an emptiness that not even Alora's death had left there.

Or perhaps she had never been privy to what Alora's death had left Sendari.

And what was this? Pity for the man who had not, in the end, been able to save *her;* who had hesitated out of anger, out of jealousy, to use the power that was his, Widan's title or no?

You will kill my almost-daughter, she thought, as the lines of his face hardened and then smoothed into empty neutrality. *And you are beginning to know it.*

Poorly played, Diora; you have taken too bold a risk.

But she was awed in spite of herself, for the power that Diora di'Marano put into that song was a power that surpassed any the Serra Teresa had ever known. If she had started her song for political reasons, or even personal ones, by the end of the last sustained note, there was the momentary transcendence that comes with, and from, a music that reaches beyond the known and into the hidden heart.

And as that last note faded, the first rays of sun glimmered and danced across the moving waters. The Lord had come.

CHAPTER TWENTY-NINE

The Widan Cortano di'Alexes was not a friend.

It had been Cortano who, at the test of the Sword, had come closest to killing Sendari, and the spiderweb of milky white that lay across his hands was a gift of that meeting. Spells of defense were a subtle and tricky thing; offense was easy. But the Widan-Designate Sendari di'Marano had a subtle mind.

It was a dangerous game, to show superior power to a man who held power—but if a Widan did not show it, in one area or another, he did not cross the bridge; the wind consumed him, and the test of the Sword proved fatal.

He still bore scars, hidden beneath the folds of his robe; unexposed to the sun's glare, they faded slowly with the years. And they reminded him, always, that Cortano was not a man to be trusted.

If any man of power was.

"Sendari."

"Cortano." The younger man bowed, feeling his age as a lack of experience and wisdom. Feeling very much the apprentice. It was only Cortano di'Alexes who had this effect on him now; the rest, the winds had taken.

The chamber, usually full of the followers of the Sword of Knowledge, was conspicuously empty; a foolish man might have blamed that emptiness on the hour, for the Widan were known to study late into the Lady's night, and sleep long through the Lord's day.

Sendari was not a foolish man. As he rose from his bow, he examined Cortano's face. White hair framed it, and white hair fell in a spill from his chin down his chest. Only the heart of the beard itself was dark, a hint of its youthful glory. His eyes, that disturbing blue that seemed uncannily like the open sky, were unblinking. And narrowed.

"Sendari," the Sword's Edge said again. He sat on a chair, rather than the cushions that were laid about the room for the comfort of the Widan; Sendari was obliged to stand, a position which was generally reserved for inferiors.

He stood, with what grace he could muster.

"What happened this morning?"

"The Festival opened," was Sendari's neutral reply.

"Yes. I was there."

Silence.

Cortano frowned. "Sendari, your daughter sang the lay of the Sun Sword."

The Widan nodded.

"Why?"

"This may surprise you, Cortano," Sendari's reply was cool, "but my time here has not been spent attending to the needs of a single child in my harem. The girl was chosen for the Festival by Alesso, Garrardi, and Lorenza; she was approved with undue haste by the kai el'Sol. I was not consulted." He let his anger show; it was genuine enough. "I did not consider intervention either wise or necessary."

"Cleverly put," was Cortano's soft reply. He paused. "And with a single song, she has declared to the clansmen of Annagar—to those clansmen who made the trek or were allowed to make it—that it was *Leonne* who fought for justice. They will all be thinking that it was Alesso di'Marente who ended that fight. And they will be watchful now, where they might have been lulled.

"You argued for her life the night the clan Leonne perished."

"Yes."

"She is a threat to us."

"She is a girl."

The blue eyes had never been so piercing; Sendari felt as if he were standing beneath the open sky, bearing the brunt of the Lord's judgment. And who was the Lord to judge him? "If you fear her, Cortano, kill her yourself. I am not beholden to you; I do not serve you; I am not required to take your orders."

"I do not fear her, Sendari. I fear your attachment to her."

Sendari said nothing.

"Very well. If you will have it so. You will pay the price of her game if it becomes costly."

The Widan Sendari shrugged. "I was under the impression that we were to speak about matters of the Court, not matters of the Tor."

"You were correct." Cortano rose. "You are to take this word to the General: Isladar says the Lord had confirmed his initial estimate. By the Festival of the Moon the forces of the Shining Court will be at our disposal." Neither man mentioned the last war that had been called after the close of the Lady's Festival. "Regardless, Isladar does not wish the influence of the Radann to hold sway; we have given him our word that the Radann are in hand. Therefore, we will keep the Radann intact until such a time as he has tendered his troops."

Cortano was the man who had introduced the younger Alesso to the Shining Court; to the kinlords, Etridian, Assarak, Isladar; to the Allasakari, the men who became vessels for the shadows that without exception devoured them from within.

He had no wife, no heirs, no attachments; it made him a formidable opponent. No one crossed him; not even the Tyr'agar spoke against him. Cortano made it easy. He was not a man who desired power in its own right; not a man who desired a dynasty and the place such a bloodline would give him in history. He had serafs, but they did not speak; he had no concubines.

The Radann thought he was touched by the Lord of Night; they watched him like circling hawks. But although their accusations held a profound truth, they saw nothing.

Because the Widan Cortano was the first Widan in more than a hundred years who had the power of sword-flight: He could vanish from a place and appear a hundred—a thousand—miles away, with no one the wiser for it.

What does the Court offer you? It was a question that both he and Alesso had asked themselves—and each other—time and again. No easy answer came; in fact, no answer at all.

"I will carry word," Sendari said, "to the General Alesso di'Marente. Is that all?"

"No. I have carefully considered your report, and I

believe that I know what the source of the power within the Radann temple is. I will have it removed today."

Sendari's nod was cool. "You . . . breached the barrier?"

Cortano smiled. He did not answer, and the lack of answer was not lost upon the younger man.

"One more thing."

Sendari stifled his anger, muting his expression, forcing it into neutrality.

"If your daughter sings that lay again, I will be forced to kill her."

The Serra Teresa regarded her brother in the silence of the early morn. The sun had not yet reached full height, and at the Pavilion of the Dawn, the serafs and attendants struggled with cushions, with instruments, with goblets of sweet water. They made little noise in the sweet coolness of the morning breeze as it swept in across the waters of the Tor, yet their steps seemed light and easy under the glare of the Lord's notice.

Because the Serra Diora di'Marano filled the valley with the beguilement of her voice. She had sung for two hours, the songs sweetly chosen paeans to a young girl's love.

And her heart was behind them, as it had been behind the song that had broken night's light; Teresa could hear the emotion reverberate recklessly in each word, each pause, each drawn breath.

"Teresa," Sendari said, making a command of the name.

She had expected no less. Ramdan followed her, holding a flat, large cloth between her exposed face and the Lord's light. Sendari gestured him away, and after a moment, she allowed her favorite seraf to be dismissed.

"She has drawn Cortano's attention," Sendari said, without preamble.

His sister could have chosen to feign ignorance; she could have dissembled; she could have shown fear—for he knew her well enough to know that the fear was suddenly there. But she was Teresa; she did not disappoint him. "It was unavoidable."

"He will kill her yet," Sendari said quietly.

She met his eyes then, her gaze unflinching—as masculine a gaze as Alesso's when Alesso's anger was both great and quiet. The darkness of her eyes was not a cool one, although her expression did not change at all.

"You are Widan, Sendari."

Angered, he said, "And what does that mean?"

"It means," the Serra Teresa said coolly, "that you place too much value upon the word of a Widan." She turned at that moment, and they saw the Radann kai el'Sol bow, from the *kneeling* position, to the dais upon which Diora sat.

"And you place too much value upon the interference of the Radann."

"Not the Radann kai el'Sol," she replied, lifting a fan and spreading its delicate ivory leaves. "He will not survive the Festival's end unless Alesso is more of a fool than he appears."

Silence. Sendari's anger was sudden, but it was not for public consumption. "The Serra Teresa is perceptive, as always."

"Our mother's gift." She pointed with the fan, tracing a graceful arc in the air. "Ah, see? They've come to pay their respects."

Tight-lipped, Sendari di'Marano watched as his oldest friend crossed the Pavilion of the Dawn, and was unexpectedly stopped by the Radann. His sister's smile, he noted, was quite cold. "If he will not survive," she said, and he knew by the timbre of her voice that she used *the* voice, "he will make certain that for this three-day, Alesso feels his power." She turned to look at him, and their eyes met like the clash of swords.

"Widan Cortano is Widan," she told him. "As are you. What you are to each other, I have never attempted to understand. I have seen a man killed by the fire, and by the wind; both deaths at Cortano's command. I understand why you respect him. But although Cortano has the power of the Sword, Alesso has the power of the armies. Never in the history of the Dominion have the clansmen chosen to follow the Widan. The Radann, yes, although I fear this is not their season. Ah, that is a fine gesture." Sunlight glinted off the leaves of wet lilies as the General Alesso di'Marente laid them before the feet of Diora's attendant—*Illia,* Teresa thought, from the perfect grace of movement that followed as the woman carefully swept them up and offered them to Diora. "He could have offered gold or jewels, but they are to cold for such a day as this."

"Cortano is not a threat to be lightly dismissed."

"He is not a threat to be dismissed at all. And I have not dismissed him. What you cannot protect, my brother, I believe the General can." Her voice was ice; the sun did not touch it, or her, as she spoke.

For a moment, he could see the blood on her hands as clearly as if they were still wet.

Alora.

She saw understanding in his eyes; knew by his silence that he would not reply. "We both gave her our word," she said coldly. And that was accusation enough. Before it, he could say nothing at all.

While his daughter received honors and glory above all women, Sendari di'Marano retreated into the privacy of his chambers, hating the very touch of the open sky.

Thinking, and hating the thought, that he should have allowed Alesso to kill Diora when the opportunity had presented itself.

The first day passed in a blur of faces.

Diora sat beneath the gold-fringed canopy that declared her the property of the Lord. To either side were Illia and Alana, the two women she had chosen to attend her on this day; before them stood the Radann Fredero kai el'Sol and the Radann Marakas par el'Sol; to her left and right, Radann who served. She thought one of them to be in the pay of the Radann Peder par el'Sol, for his tone of voice changed when that man came to pay his respects, but it was not her position to offer advice to the Radann. Nor would it ever be; she was, after all, a woman, and women did not serve the Lord. But the Lord's servants might serve her three days longer. Just three days, and then she could rest.

Her fingers were tingling from the exertion of playing the samisen, but the instrument was both her shield and her love, and she was loath to put it aside.

And because she was so loath, she had it in her lap when the Radann came, carrying between them a limp and obviously injured woman.

Illia en'Marano gasped and lowered her face at once; Alana drew a thick breath and turned to her mistress. Her mistress was frozen, her fingers pressed tight against the strings, blessed strings, of the samisen.

"What is this?" The kai el'Sol said, stepping forward with a very real anger. "Larant—what have you done?"

The Radann Larant el'Sol met the kai el'Sol with a grim and level stare. Not, Diora thought, a friend. "This— this *woman*—was found in the temple of the Radann." He caught her chin and forced her face up.

Diora already knew who she would see. Nose broken, lips swollen, eyes darkened—the peculiarly striking but plain face of the woman who had visited her the evening before was almost gone. But her eyes, dark and bright, were the same eyes, and they met Diora's grimly. Fearfully.

Serra Diora di'Marano sat in stiff and heavy silence, her knees pressed together, her chin held as high as she dared hold it. She did not breathe.

"A—a woman? In the *temple*?"

She would never have thought that a Lambertan would be so skillful a liar. Or perhaps it was not a lie; there was an unmuted horror in the voice that he gave to the Radann, an outrage, an anger. Were they disappointed? She thought that at least one of them was.

"Radann Peder par el'Sol suggested that we make an example of her," the Radann Larant el'Sol said. "The magnitude of the crime demanded your attention. We apologize," he added, with a regret that was only insincere if one knew how to listen, "for disturbing the Consort."

Diora knew how to listen. She knew that to be the perfect Serra was to look away, as Illia en'Marano had done. She looked, but not away; instead, her eyes hugged the curve of the Radann kai el'Sol's shoulders. They were tense; even stiff. She thought for a moment that he might ruin everything, throw himself upon the fires of an angry Lord. Thought it, and was glad.

But then he spoke. "Have her displayed by the gates, where the clansmen may see her."

"Kai el'Sol. Should we—"

"No," he said. "If she survives the attention of the clansmen, and their righteous anger, for the three days, let it be a sign that the Lord knows mercy. If she does not, she is not to be given to earth; burn her and let the wind scatter her unblessed ashes."

"Kai el'Sol."

"And Larant?"

"Yes, kai?"

"If you approach the Consort's Pavilion with such ugliness one more time before the Festival is over, you will join her."

The man paled. "But I thought—"

"You will *summon me*, Radann."

He bowed, dropping his victim. "Kai el'Sol."

"Go."

The Radann went, and only when they had disappeared from sight did the kai el'Sol turn to the Lord's Consort. "I am sorry, Serra Diora," he said, and she heard the heaviness of the truth in each word.

"As am I," was the Serra Diora's reply. "But come, Radann kai el'Sol, this is the Festival of the Lord, and the judgment of the Lord has been heard." And she touched the samisen. Let the chords become single notes, let the notes carry across the waters.

Marakas par el'Sol stared at the sun-touched waters for a long time, and when at last he looked away, he did not speak at all.

They ate, and they drank, and they presided over the beginning of the Lord's Challenge. The Serra Diora, carried by Radann upon a palanquin that was fine enough for a Tyr, was called upon to view those who vied for the Lord's favor. They presented their weapons to her, and they each craned to get a glimpse of the Flower of the Dominion.

Hair as black as the Lady's night, with a mystery and a beauty that only night would ever truly reveal, she was all that they desired to see, and when she blushed, pleasingly, and looked away, she was delicacy, she was grace.

The Tyr'agnate Eduardo di'Garrardi joined these men.

He rode into the open field on the plateau, and the clansmen parted to let him through—not because they recognized his banner, although it was impossible not to know that he was the ruler of the Terrean of Oerta, but because he rode Sword's Blood. The roan stallion's eyes were dark, and the lift of his head carried it well above the lesser horses that surrounded him. As he approached,

Diora could see the scars along his coat where he had entered into combat. It was said that Eduardo di'Garrardi did very little to control Sword's Blood when Sword's Blood felt it necessary to make a challenge. It was also said that the stallion had not yet lost a fight.

"Serra Diora," the Tyr'agnate said, as he dismounted and led Sword's Blood, by bridle, to the raised palanquin.

"Tyr'agnate," she said, grateful for the Radann who stepped, weapons drawn in gentle warning, between them.

"Kai el'Sol," the Tyr said, properly addressing the guardian and not the guarded. "It is obvious that the Lord values this Consort highly to demand that you personally attend her."

The Radann shrugged. "The Lord is not the only one to prize his Consort highly—but he is the only one who has that right." The frown was evident in his voice, if not his expression. "But you, Tyr'agnate—it is unlike you to interrupt the ceremony of the Lord's Challenge."

"Interrupt? You mistake me, kai el'Sol," he said, looking past Fredero to the woman who sat upon the shoulders of the Radann. "I intend to win it."

He drew his sword, and in the light of the clear sky, the blade flashed white.

"Alesso."

The General turned, and when he saw who called him, his expression cooled. "Sendari."

They stood a moment, watching each other like wary beasts of prey. It was the General who at last broke the silence. "We have not spoken for the past few days.'"

"We have both been busy." Sendari bowed. "But I have come with word."

"Ah. You play the messenger." Before the Widan could respond, he added, "And as usual, it suits you ill. Come, old friend. Take the water with me." Serafs came at once, dressed in the white, gold, and blue that were the Lord's colors. They set a silver pitcher upon the flat, low table, and then bowed their heads to the ground. They were dismissed, leaving the General and the Widan to sit in quiet isolation, measuring each other.

"We do not make good enemies," Alesso said at last.

"No," the Widan replied. He lifted the pitcher and

poured, knowing that if he waited for Alesso, he would wait long. It was not that the task was beneath his dignity—the waters were, after all, from the lake of the Tor itself—it was merely a detail, in an afternoon that was full of too many details, each requiring his attention. They would be parched with speech—or the effort of stilted silence—before he thought to lift glass.

Sendari understood the failing well; had he not, many times, left food untouched while he embarked upon the study of the Sword?

He was silent as he sat in the presence of his oldest friend—a man who, by his recent actions, had become more of a stranger than the sister he almost hated. "Alesso, Diora has been promised to Garrardi." It was said.

A man did not like to discuss the disposition of his daughter with his friend; there was a wrongness to it, a feeling of things forbidden by men who followed the ways of the Lord. And neither he nor Alesso were such men, except as it suited them. But still.

"Yes," Alesso said, the single word curt.

Sendari felt the chill of anger settle about his shoulders; he lifted his chin and met Alesso's brittle stare. And then, of all things, the General Alesso di'Marente laughed. It was a bark of a laugh, sharp and harsh, and the bitterness in it reminded Sendari of youthful anger.

But all anger was youthful, in its way.

"I cannot lie to you, Sendari, except by omission."

"You endanger us, Alesso."

"Yes." He laughed again. "And if I were so enamored of safety, I would have remained the faithful vassal to the end of my days, toiling for a fat and mediocre Tyr." He raised a hand. "I could tell you that I am insulted that you think I would endanger our alliances and our plans for the sake of a woman—any woman. I could accuse you of valuing your daughter so highly that you think any man couldn't help but do the same. I could fence with words, Sendari, and it would solve *nothing*. Let us leave them behind. Between us, there should be truth."

"There is the matter of Diora."

"Yes," Alesso said. "And it would have been cleanest had she died with her husband." The accusation was in the words, but it was not a harsh one.

"She almost did."

"I know. You have helped me in all things, Sendari. And you know what I desire. You know also that we need Eduardo kai di'Garrardi, and you might as well know that we've already clashed once over the girl."

"I might as well," the older man said, and his smile was forced out of him by the General's will, not his own.

"Help me, then. She was made the Lady of the Lord for the Festival, and it did not displease me."

"You did not seek to consult me."

"No more than I would have consulted the Tyr about the timing of his assassination. You would have refused."

That was Alesso. Against his will, Sendari felt himself relax. "You have already killed two wives," he said coldly.

"Childbirth killed one," was Alesso's soft reply. About the other, he did not speak.

Sendari had never asked. He was silent a long time, thinking about Teresa's words, and Cortano's threat. "Alesso," he said at last, "she will not make a good wife."

"She was good enough for the kai Leonne."

"Yes. But there is something about her that has become disquieting. If you would take my advice—"

"I won't."

"—you would search elsewhere. Did you hear what she sang at dawn?"

Alesso frowned. "It is always sung at the Festival," he said at last, with a feigned nonchalance.

"Yes. And at every other Festival, the Sun Sword is drawn. They remember it now."

"They would have remembered it anyway. You saved her life," the General Alesso di'Marente told his oldest friend. "Did you save her for a man who is willing to offer her dishonor before she has been lawfully given?"

Sendari was silent for a long moment; his face was carefully expressionless.

And Alesso di'Marente laughed. "She didn't tell you," he said softly.

"I have not spoke with Diora since—"

"Not Diora, old man. Teresa. She came to the rescue at the side of the Radann kai el'Sol."

"Very well. Enough, Alesso! We do not make good

enemies. Let us cease this bickering." He paused, and then added, "And how exactly did you come to be aware of such an infraction against my family's honor, when I was not? I doubt very much that either the kai el'Sol or the Serra Teresa would come, with such news, to you."

"I wish, by the Lord's grace, that I could for once succeed in an attempt to omit the slightest of facts in a discussion with you. I was aware, of course, because I was there." The laughter left his face. "I would never dishonor you."

"I know." He drained his cup, and smiled. "And now that we've put this difference aside, there is another. What," he said sweetly, "of the last assassination attempt against the boy?"

"Sendari!"

Light and heat. Light and heat.

The sway of the fans her attendants held did little to quench the summer's hand; it was midday.

The Serra Diora di'Marano, Consort to the Lord of Day, sat beneath a canopy that was both fine and simple. Much of its workmanship was on the exterior: the dyes in the cloth that formed the tented dome, the engraving on the wooden beams that held it, the inlay of gold and pale wood and silver upon the steps that led to where she sat.

"They will rest," the kai el'Sol told her softly, as he stood stoically beyond the reach of the heavy fans.

She gazed at the ranks of the men who had passed the first of the tests—a series of interlaced armed combats that had quickly separated the wheat from the chaff. Those that were injured were tended by personal physicians or serafs; those that were too injured were carried from the field by cerdan. She recognized the banners of many of the men here, and knew that they were vying for the title of the Lord's Champion. And the favor of the Lord's Consort. The Lord's Champion and the Lord's Consort were the highest ranks given to one who was not Tyr or Radann kai el'Sol at the Festival of the Sun.

This afternoon, after the proper respect had been paid to the sun's most dangerous hour, there would be the basic tests of horsemanship, both handling and racing. Racing was always interesting, because the fastest horses were often the lightest, and they did not take well to mounted combat. The final stretch of the Lord's Challenge always began between mounted men. So the clansmen had to choose their horses carefully, by their paces, but also by their abilities in the arts of war. The Widan Sendari di'Marano was one of few men who had had little love of, or little interest in, horses; his daughter had been properly trained to show little interest in them as well, although by the grace of her aunt, she knew more than her father professed to—and less than he actually did, which was the case for many things.

She thought that Sword's Blood would be too heavy a horse for the races, and she was proved wrong, although in the proving of it, two clansmen withdrew their animals from the field because they had dared come too close to the mount that had made Eduardo di'Garrardi famous among the clans. It would cost Garrardi.

Although this seat was the favored seat in which to view the games, she was not the only woman who sat so; nor the only noble who watched. To either side, at the edge of the plateau, the clansmen and their wives—carefully protected from exposure to either the Lord's face or the clansmen's gaze—took their places, watching those who bore their name. Exchanging money, although it was frowned upon.

She had watched these games with Ser Illara kai di'Leonne. Attended by his wives—her wives, the women of her choosing; he had no children who were old enough to be trusted to view the full ordeal in its entirety with the appropriate demeanor, but in a few years, they would have joined them.

"Serra Diora?"

She shook her head and smiled gently at the Radann kai el'Sol, wondering if he would mistake her distance for delicacy and heat-fatigue. Hoping.

In the silence, the wind carried a scream up the slope.

The only assassins she could trust were never summoned during the Festival of the Lord. They served the Lady, and during this threeday, the Lady's dominion was at its weakest. Out of respect for the Lord and the customs of the Lord, the assassins did not choose to accept a name—or so the popular wisdom went.

The Serra Diora di'Marano had been taught only a little about summoning the servants of the Lady; she had been tutored in other skills of a more personal nature: the arts of poison, the ability to administer cures to those poisons that were swiftly diagnosed, the deft handling of a small blade in close quarters. To summon the Lady's servants took a different type of knowledge—one that she had little of.

And the Serra Teresa had refused to aid her.

"We do not summon the Lady's servants during the Festival of the Lord," she said. Diora knew finality of tone when she heard it, no matter how gracefully it was given.

As if she read in the silence all that remained unspoken, the Serra Teresa said, "We do not have the resources it would require at our disposal this Festival." She had taken care to use the voice to hide the words, offering the words as if they could somehow cushion the blow.

As if she knew what a blow they would be.

Moonlight was at its height. It was not a bright light, not a full one, but it was more than enough to see by. The Serra Diora di'Marano listened for the movement of Radann at her doors; listened for the quiet huff of seraf's breath. Both came to her, neither as real as the piteous cries that memory would not let fade.

Squaring her shoulders, she closed her eyes. She did not rise; the serafs had been trained from birth to hear the slightest of her movements and attend them at once, and as their lives often depended upon such hearing and such instinctive reaction, they were more difficult to escape than guards. Than men. She focused her thoughts and opened her lips, hardening them with the strength of her determination so that they would not tremble.

"Sleep. Hear nothing. Wake in the morn."

You cannot order a man to do a thing that is against his nature—not for long. You can hold him with the force of your voice if you intend to kill him, but if you intend to avoid notice, if you desire secrecy or privacy without threat of discovery, find a thing in that man's nature and exploit it. Work with his intent and his desires, not against.

She listened for a moment longer and then nodded. Turning her face, she rose quickly.

The seraf, Alaya, was younger than she, but in size they were almost identical. For this reason, Diora had chosen her, and for no other; she was Fiona's girl, after all, and if she was foolish and sweet, it was to Fiona that she would report when her tenure here was done.

Without another word, she donned the seraf's simple robes, and with the paints of the day, she drew upon her wrist the brand by which Alaya was known. Her hands shook; this was not her skill, but it was night, and in the darkness, it would serve.

She did not wish to kill the Radann, but to order them to ignore her was difficult and not certain to succeed. Success, of course, meant safety—but failure meant that a member of the Radann would know that she had the voice, and that she was willing to use it against the servants of the Lord.

Against one man, she would have tried. The Radann kai el'Sol had left no less than four. She was happy with the four, however; they were well-behaved, and not one of them would have considered it appropriate to their station to harass a young seraf in the dead of a quiet night, even though her Serra would never discover the misdeed in time to attempt to protect her.

Gathering the folds of her robes, she walked to the corner of the room and picked up a delicate, porcelain pitcher—a gift from a Northern noble, dead this past month. Then she drew the hood above her face, and made her way to the doors, pausing only long enough to retrieve a small object from beneath the hard mats.

She knelt, as she had seen Alaya kneel a hundred times, slid the screen doors open a crack, bowed to the Radann, and rose. Their lamps made her shadow seem long as she crossed the threshold, holding the pitcher in perfectly steady hands because she knew, of course, that the Serra Diora valued it. She knelt on the other side of the doors, bowed again, and slid them shut.

The Radann glanced down at her, but serafs came and went, and besides, the pitcher in her hands made clear that she was to travel to the waters of the Tor Leonne, at the behest of her Serra. The kai el'Sol's permission to gather those waters, strictly and quietly granted, had been given at the gathering of the Radann who were to serve in the unusual position of guards to the Lord's Consort for the Festival.

They were meant, these Radann, to keep clansmen from entering, not to keep serafs from leaving. They did not shift position to acknowledge this seraf's presence, although she knew that they were well aware of it.

She passed two other serafs in the halls before she found her passage to the outside; the cerdan who served her father and her aunt nodded quietly as she left. Not a single one of them paid close attention to her face.

Even so, she did not breathe easily until the stars, and not broad wooden beams, were above her head. She walked quickly to the lake, and there, the Tyran that served the General Alesso di'Marente did stop her, but they were perfunctory in their inspection—for Diora had, every night for the last four, sent Alaya to the lake to retrieve the waters. This night was no different.

Her hands did not shake as they touched the waters, although the waters were surprisingly cool. She filled the pitcher carefully and then, in her kneeling position, bowed respectfully to the Tyran. They were clansmen of note, if not merit; they would expect respect.

Carefully balancing the full pitcher, she lingered a moment to catch the soothing lap of waves against the shore, desiring a moment of peace, no matter how brief. Then she left the waters of the Tor Leonne behind, carrying only this small portion with her.

She did not return to the harem.

Instead, she found the long and carefully tended road that led to the gates of the Tor Leonne; the gates through which any lawful visitor must pass. In the shadows, they were still very fine, and she paused a moment as she saw the lights that glowed brightly by them.

Did she falter?

A moment, no more. If the Tyran were at their duties, she was safe; if they were not, she would make no approach.

The night was very dark.

She heard his voice before she saw him, because she knew how to listen better than she knew how to do almost anything except breathe. And sing.

The Voyani's voice she would have heard in any case,

and the listening magnified it, made of it a piercing, horrible scream instead of the whimper she knew it to be. A plea for mercy. A denial of knowledge.

"You know this is not necessary," he said, his voice a blend of neutrality and distaste. "Only tell us what we wish to know, and we will leave you in peace."

We.

She froze; she knew how to stand in a silence that was almost absolute.

"Who sent you?"

"Cortano, with all due respect, I believe that I am better able to handle this interrogation."

"Lord Isladar, with all due respect, I believe that you are not within your jurisdiction."

They were of a kind; they spoke with the same precision, the same distance, the same surety of power. She measured the silence after this short exchange by the labored breathing of their victim. Her knees bent; she knelt, slowly, the folds of her robe crinkling beneath the breaths, heavy and hoarse, of the Voyani woman.

"You were with the Radann." Not a question. "Who sent you?"

Serra Diora di'Marano knew how to wait.

Folding her knees, bowing her perfect, ivory face, she began her vigil, praying to the Lady's Moon for strength and guidance and an end to this—and all—torments.

"Well, Peder?"

"I don't know. I did as you instructed, and discovered her presence—but I do not know how she was used, or at whose instructions." She heard his shrug. "I assure you," he said blandly, "that she was not present during the meetings of the Radann; Fredero is weak, but is not a fool."

A lie.

She tensed and then relaxed, fighting her reactions. She had never trusted Radann Peder par el'Sol, and she did not trust him now—but he lied to his allies, and he lied about the Radann kai el'Sol, and in that, he found some small favor.

They did not hear it.

"Well?"

"The wanderers caused us trouble once before," the

man called Lord Isladar said softly. "They were a great people once, and they had cities that make the Tor Leonne seem paltry and dim by comparison. We thought them scattered, but the Annagarian winds seem to carry the dust and debris for a very long time. Cortano, may I?"

Silence.

No, Diora thought, willing the answer.

But she knew by the time it took him to answer, what the reply would be. "Yes." There was warning in the word.

"Thank you."

She heard him step forward, and then she heard the woman *scream,* and every cry that she had ever heard—save only one—lost strength and meaning; from this point on, pain would be defined by a lone Voyani woman, one who was almost a stranger.

One that she had come this distance to kill. Quickly. Cleanly.

She could never have said why afterward, for it was her habit when in danger to sit perfectly, rigidly still. But this once she lifted her hands—both of them, and clutched a pendant that sat, unseen by even her own eyes, around her neck. It bit into the flesh of her palms as her fingers locked around it.

Light flared in her eyes, blinding her with its flash. But it was a light more *felt* than seen, and although it terrified her, it was not because she feared the exposure it would bring. She moved; felt something beneath her feet—although she knew her feet were folded under her legs—and moved forward.

Into the clearing.

There were three men there; she could see their backs as she approached. One wore the robes of the Radann's office, one the silks of an evening's disturbed leisure. And one wore black, a color darker than the night or her hair or the nightmares that had plagued her since the death of the clan Leonne. She wondered what hand had fashioned the cloth, and then wondered if it were cloth at all.

She did not wonder long; they did not see her. And she was drawn forward by a compulsion that she could not explain, and would never have ignored. The light bit her palms. Standing before the three men, she cast no shadow at all; they could not see her. And she could not look back

to see their faces, for she found what she had come
seeking, and it held her gaze and all of her attention.

In the savaged ruins of the woman's face, Diora could
still recognize the rictus of humiliation and agony. Blood
was there as punctuation, and bone where flesh had been
casually gouged away. She did not think that a body could
suffer so much and still cling to life.

Or be forced to it.

The Voyani woman lifted her face with effort; the
collar that clung to her neck far too tightly came with it,
clinking and rattling. She raised hands—a single hand—
and it, too, trailed chains.

Margret, she said, although her lips did not appear to
move, *this is your mother's death. Understand what it is
that you face.* As if pushed, Diora turned—and when she
saw the visage of Lord Isladar of the kin, she froze anew.
For the darkness of his robes was nothing compared to the
darkness that was his eyes. Beneath a face that was
strangely, savagely beautiful was a chill that the wind's
loudest voice could barely touch.

She had never seen a creature that was outside of the
Lord's dominion before. Having seen him this once, she
would not forget. And she would try, at least once, before
this war was over.

*This is our damnation and our salvation. I have come
to the end that the Oracle's road decreed. And the bearer
of this gem has paid the price to bring it back to the
Voyani. Do not let our past be forgotten; do not let your
past rob us all of a future.*

This is your mother's death, she said again, and Diora
turned. *Blessed death. Peaceful death.*

Avenge it.

She reached out, the chains grew taut with the whole of
the force she could muster. The three men watched in
unseeing silence as the Serra Diora di'Marano lifted one
hand, one free hand, and reached out, touching the fingertips of the Voyani woman with her own fingers, as if, for
a moment, they stood on either side of a piece of glass.

Aye, you are the Lady's dagger, the woman said, *Grant
me the Lady's death.*

Diora reached into the fold of her robes with her hand,
with the one free hand, and pulled out the dagger that she
had slid so carefully from beneath her bed. She had meant

to blood it. She had meant to end both threat and torment. But as she looked at her hand, she saw that it was translucent, a ghostly image of a hand.

I did not break. They know nothing.

"What is this?" Lord Isladar said, stepping suddenly forward. "Cortano—are we watched?"

"No. There are none within the boundary save us."

The creature bent forward, and caught the woman's chin in his hands.

Diora raised the dagger, and it, too, seemed translucent, but shone with a pale light. She hesitated a moment, for the creature was now in her path, but the woman faced her, unblinking.

"There *is* someone. We are at risk—

Lady's daughter, please—hurry. He is kinlord; if he is prepared, he will hold my spirit for the Three Days, and this will be nothing in comparison. Please. Strike.

"There is an older magic here. They have it. Hold, Cortano. I need a moment or she will escape us."

"Escape?"

"There are many avenues of escape," Lord Isladar said coolly. "Death among them. But I almost have her now."

Diora drove the dagger into the Voyani woman's open left eye. It slid through the flesh as if it had no substance; the ghost of a knife, and not the knife itself.

But the kinlord cried out for the first time in anger. His hands tightened. She could see the struggle beneath the woman's torn flesh; a struggle that eyes alone were not meant to see. And she could see that death was somehow losing. Without thought, she drew the dagger again, but this time, brought it about in an arc that drew blood from the creature's hand. Real blood.

His grip faltered for a second, for less than a second, but it was enough. He was left with empty flesh, a shell, devoid of the ability to offer either answers or pleasure.

Diora took a step back and froze; the clearing was gone. She sat, her hands clenched around the pendant that pulsed like a heart of light in her palms; to either side was a bush in full bloom in the darkness. *Roses,* she thought, *or another exotic bloom.* She did not dare open her palms; did not dare to release the crystal or let it fall back into the folds of her robes. Rising clumsily, she began to run with her hands clasped in front of her—for she knew that he would come for her.

The last thing she had seen had been his eyes, and their gazes, for an instant, had met.

CHAPTER THIRTY

The Radann Marakas par el'Sol was waiting for her, although she did not realize this until they collided.

The Serra Diora had not been the cause of a collision such as this since she was a child of four or five; she was stunned a moment, and before she could continue to run, he caught her wrists. Her hands were pressed into the pendant; the strength of his grip did not break the strength of hers.

She wondered if anything could; the pendant seemed a part of her flesh; she could not tell whether the pulse she felt was hers or the crystal's. It didn't matter. The presence of a man without the Lord of Night's eyes was a blessing and a comfort, even though he was a man of power.

"Radann par el'Sol." Her soft voice was completely natural.

"Serra Diora di'Marano," he replied. "It is late, and it is not seemly that a woman of the clans should be seen, alone, with a Radann of the Lord. You will forgive me, but I have taken the liberty of assuring your privacy, and I believe it is best that we retire immediately."

That way.

The words came on the crest of a warm summer wind.

"As you say," she replied, but she could not stop herself from glancing over her shoulder. Moonlight silvered shadowed trees; the Tor Leonne seemed to be sleeping within the Lady's night.

He pulled her along, and after a moment, noticed how her hands were clasped. Marakas was not known for his attention to detail, either among the Radann, or among clansmen who were powerful enough to have to be wary of them. "Follow," he told her softly, releasing one wrist. "Speed is of the essence."

He did not tell her where she was going, and she did not care to argue; she could hear what he could not: the movement of the kinlord; the words of the Widan; the curses, quiet but heartfelt, of the Radann Peder par el'Sol. And although the listening was exhausting, she could not stop.

So she listened, sparing only enough of her attention that she might walk in the Radann's wake while clutching the pendant's warm crystal in the folds of her palms. And because of this, she did not recognize where their retreat took them until she lifted her face to the wide doors that guarded the sanctuary of the Sun Sword.

The Radann Marakas par el'Sol opened them and led her in.

There were servitors within: four, each armored and armed as if for combat and not the duty of guarding a highly placed official. They were watchful, but they took a moment to pay the Lord's Consort her due; they bowed, very low, and held that bow a fraction of a second longer than etiquette demanded. Respect. Why?

"We were not followed," the Radann told his servitors.

"My apologies, Radann par el'Sol, but I believe that we may well have been followed," Diora said softly.

"I saw nothing," the Radann par el'Sol replied, but he watched her face intently and took no insult from her contradiction.

"You knew," she said, her wide, dark eyes narrowing into slender crescents.

"Yes. I had you followed."

"But I—"

"I had your seraf followed each of the last four nights. Tonight, I followed personally." He paused, and then added, "No man who looked at your face could mistake you for even a fleeting moment for Serra Fiona's child."

"But why—"

"Because, Serra Diora, I did not trust you."

She was stunned, and she was not used to being stunned. It was summer, but the air was as chill as the sharp sea winds in the rainy seasons on the Northern coast.

"Who follows us?"

Silence.

He stepped forward and caught her by the arms. She thought he would shake her, but he did not; he closed his eyes instead and she felt—she felt a warmth in the palms of his hands. "Serra," he said gently, "please. You must answer the question."

"Radann par el'Sol," one of the servitors said, "I believe that it is not necessary to question the Lord's Lady."

They both looked, the Lord's Consort and the Lord's Radann. Glowing fiercely bright beneath the window that gazed out at the Lady's night was the Sun Sword. And the light that flared was a clarion call, a call to battle—if there were a hand that could wield it.

Leonne legend told of a light that harsh, and it shone for one thing alone.

"Tell me," Marakas said, his voice gentle but insistent.

She had, for the moment, no fear of him. Later she would marvel at herself; later she would deride her lack of control, the weakness that such immediate trust—that any trust, here, in this place, showed. "The Widan Cortano, the Radann Peder par el'Sol, and—and a servant of the Lord of Night."

She had not thought his face capable of anger, but it was, and the anger was cold and implacable. "Why were you there?"

She looked at her hands. Tried to open them.

"Serra Diora?"

"I was there," she told him softly, although she did not meet his eyes, "to kill the Voyani woman." She added, as if in defense of the action, "She had information which could harm us all."

He nodded. "I would have done no less, but she had been under guard for the day." He paused. "And I would not see her suffer the three days. Clansmen are cruel, where they are given the lawful right to be so."

"She died," Diora told him softly, "without revealing anything."

"How?"

She lifted her cupped, stiff hands, and he took them, and with care pried them loose. Blood ran then, from the cuts in her hands that matched, exactly, the facets of the large gem. The crystal itself bore no sign of the stain; it was clear and bright as the Sun Sword itself.

"This killed her?"

She did not reply.

"May I?" he asked her, as he looked at the crystal.

She stepped back, and he bowed.

"As you wish," he told her softly. "But I believe that this is one of the Voyani artifacts. Families are defined, among the Voyani, by the old magics that they keep. Do you know who she was?"

Diora shook her head; wild strands of dark hair clung to her face. She felt exposed, dressed as she was, with no finery and no paints behind which to hide.

"She was Evallen of the Arkosa Voyani; the matriarch of the family."

It was expedient to feign ignorance; it was also honest. Diora knew very little about the wanderers. They did not affect the politics of the realm, and it was in the politics of the Dominion that the Serra Diora di'Marano was steeped.

"Evallen served the Lady," he continued. "And she has passed that burden to you, and you have accepted it, whether you know it or not." He turned to face the Sun Sword. "There is one Leonne left alive," he said quietly. "And until he is either united with the Sword, or dead, this Sword will not be raised in war against our enemies." And then he smiled, and the smile was sharp. "But I wander, as always. The pendant that you carry exacts a blood price, and you have paid it, aware or no. You will be weakened for the next week, and the Festival is only one day old." He unfurled her fingers, and they battled him with a will of their own while she watched. "We will be safe here; if they have followed, they will not follow into the swordhaven. The Sun Sword protects us from that much.

"They will know that these magics were used if they are following. But they will be looking, I think, for these." He touched the wounds upon her hands. "And these are deep enough, and clear enough, that you would not be able to hide them."

"He saw me," she said. "The creature. He *saw* me."

"When?"

"When I killed her."

"He was *there* and you escaped?"

"I wasn't—physically—there."

"What do you mean?"

"I—forgive me, Radann par el'Sol. I babble like a

child. I was not physically present. I approached upwind of the gates, and I heard their voices. I could not kill the woman in the presence of witnesses, for I would be acting against the orders of the kai el'Sol himself. But as I sat in hiding, awaiting the right moment, I heard two voices I recognized, and a third I did not. I don't know why, but I picked up the crystal, and held it between my palms.

"And it took me to them—but not in the flesh. I looked, in my own sight, a spirit, a ghost. They were—questioning the Voyani. She could see me; they could not. She asked me to kill her before he had a chance to bind her, for she feared what he would do in the Three Days that he could hold her spirit. I—did as she asked. But as I did, he turned to face me, and he saw *me*."

Marakas smiled with a weary relief. "What he saw, Serra Diora, was your spirit. And the Dominion's women have housed the spirits of Tyrs in the frail flesh of lambs. The only way they will know you is by your wounded hands, although they will not know exactly what they seek until they see it."

She raised a brow, motioning with that minute gesture to the four who stood guard and bore witness to the words that had passed between them.

He was not a subtle man. "These men are my personal servitors. I trust them absolutely."

"Then you are—you are not a man who has many wives." She smiled; the smile was shaky, but genuine.

His face darkened, although he returned her smile bitterly. "I had one," he told her. "And I only ever wanted one." She wanted to know how he, not of the Widan, knew so much about the Voyani arts. But Marakas' background had always been hidden; he claimed no great clan, and no Terrean, and no matter how her sources had searched, she had never unearthed his secrets.

And now, she knew suddenly, he was going to give them to her. And she wasn't certain if she wanted to know.

He closed his eyes and then took her hands. The movement was so sure that it took her a moment to realize that it was subtly wrong. The hands that now held hers were warm, and they grew warmer, although she knew that they would not become uncomfortably hot; they reminded her, in some ways, of the pendant; they offered protection, comfort.

Comfort.

She knew, then, that she could trust him. Knew that he was of the clans, but of a clan so minor there was little difference between it and a family of serafs. Knew that he had loved his wife, and knew that he felt her loss as keenly as any bereaved husband, although the loss was not a new one. She knew that he valued the serafs, that the servitors that he had said he could trust *were* trustworthy, that he served the Lord's cause because he valued the Dominion, but that he did not value the Radann over-much, and that he saw, always, a profound role for the Lady and the Lady's night. That he valued things lost, and valued them profoundly.

His anger was not hers; it was not so cold and so absolute; it allowed for grief. But Faida, Ruatha, and Deirdre were a loss that not even he could begin to feel. How could she—

She cried out then, and pulled her hands away.

"Healer," she whispered, her face pale with both loss of blood and shock.

"Yes."

"You didn't—you didn't warn me."

His eyes were lidded; his expression was suddenly neutral. "No."

"Because you didn't trust me."

"Yes."

"And you thought to—to read this from me, while you healed these?" She raised her hands in anger and before he could reply, she struck him. He caught her hand before she could strike again; it would have been hard to say which of the two was more surprised by her action— the Radann or the Serra herself. The silence between them stretched out in the darkness until one of the Radann's servitors coughed.

"It was wrong," Marakas said. By that open admission to an inferior, he once again set himself apart from the clansmen. "But these are not times in which the right and the wrong done to one man or one woman may rule us. I apologize."

"And are you satisfied?"

"No, Serra, I am not. But I will heal the hands, and you will be forewarned enough to keep your thoughts upon what you will; the injury does not require a deeper communion."

The Serra Teresa di'Marano sat alone in the garden beneath the face of the open moon. In her lap the Northern harp's strings resonated with the dance of her fingers, and her voice rose and fell in an Imperial lament for a wildness and time long past. At least, that was what the bard who gave her the song had said; she sang in a tongue that was both foreign and old. She understood the Imperial court tongue, but was less well-versed in its variants.

And she believed the bard, and sang with that belief. Wondering, as she did, whether or not two people who had the voice could lie to each other at all.

She was surprised to see Diora step from between two barely opened screens into the lambent moonlight. Her almost-daughter's hair was drawn back in combs and pearls, and she was dressed for the day and not the night, yet she seemed a shadow, a thing not meant for sunlight.

"Ona Teresa," Diora said softly.

"Na'dio," her aunt replied, stilling the music of the strings with the gentlest touch of a hand. "Join me, if you like, but remember that you must greet the dawn with the Radann."

Diora nodded. She made a place for herself on the cushions that lay upon stone smoothed by the passage of water, wind, and time. And then she drew her legs up, sitting with her chin upon her knees, the very picture of a child.

"What," Serra Teresa said, resuming the play of finger across taut string but giving her attention to other matters, "has happened?"

"Ona Teresa," her almost-daughter said, and Teresa knew, then, that one never wondered an idle question beneath the full face of the Lady's Moon. "Did you know that my father was in league with the servants of the Lord of Night?"

They both spoke in the voice, with the voice; they bound their words as tightly as they dared. Teresa thought, if the light were sharper, that she would see the signs of it in Diora's face—and they were signs that the Consort to the Lord could not afford to expose to the clansmen. The Flower of the Dominion was expected to be exactly that: perfect when in bloom.

"Did you not?"

"No."

Of course she hadn't known; Teresa herself had not known it until the night that a lone seraf had come to her, in darkness, praying that all of the rumors that surrounded the unmarried Marano sister were true.

"Why didn't you tell me?"

"Because the voice is no guarantee, Diora, that we will not be discovered. To know what I knew—and what you now profess to know—is death."

Her Na'dio turned to face her then, and she played something brighter, something softer, than the Northern dirge. Because her daughter's eyes held more than simple knowing; they held understanding. Vision.

"It is worse than death, I think," Diora said at last.

"Tell me. Tell me, if you will."

"I went to kill the Voyani woman."

Teresa nodded, unsurprised. Although Diora was ice and shadow to the clansmen and women who watched her with envy or desire, her aunt could not help but hear the horror and pity that had colored the words that she spoke when the Voyani woman had been led away, words whose meaning had nothing at all to do with pity. In that, at least, she was well-trained. But Teresa had more than half-expected, after Diora's attempt to find an assassin, that the young Serra would attempt to kill the woman herself.

And she knew that, no matter what her almost-daughter might say, pity and mercy were no small part of her motivation. Weakness.

"I had to kill her," Diora continued, hearing the unspoken, unvoiced criticism. "Because she knew too much. About the Radann kai el'Sol—"

"Diora, I told you, he is already doomed—"

"And me."

Serra Teresa froze. "You met her."

"Yes."

"You did not inform me."

"No. It appears, Ona Teresa, that we have both been playing our own games. How very like my father we both are."

"Like his General, perhaps," the older woman said. "Here. Play the harp a while, Diora, if you wish to continue speaking. My hands tire."

Her niece played the Northern harp as if she'd been born to the North, and for one weary moment, Teresa wished it had been so. "When did you meet Evallen?"

"You knew her."

"Oh, yes," her aunt said, keeping everything she felt out of her voice; schooling it, so that Diora might know for certain that she was offering privacy and asking for it at the same time.

"Am I anything but another pawn to you?"

"Yes," Teresa said, holding her heart's words back. "Diora—when?"

"Festival eve."

"And did she—give you anything?"

Surprise. Anger. Resignation. Even a hint of admiration. "Yes."

"Will you tell me what it was?"

"No."

"Ah. Then let me hope that she has not laid the responsibility of the Family upon you, for if she has, you will be forced to bear it, or you will pay the price."

"What price? What price could possibly be more costly than the price I have already paid?"

If Teresa offered privacy, Diora offered none; although her expression did not change, her voice did.

Teresa bowed her head, feeling the sting of another woman's tears, the endless ache of another's loss. Diora's voice was very, very powerful. "Nothing," she said at last. "I forget myself, and you, in the warning. Diora—"

"You called her here."

Teresa did not answer.

"And she perished for it."

"Evallen's path was decided long before it crossed yours, Na'dio," Teresa said coolly. "She is dead now. We are not. You killed her?"

"Yes. But not—but not immediately. The Sword's Edge was there. The Radann Peder par el'Sol. And one other. Ona Teresa, he was not just a servant of the Lord of Night. He was a vessel. One of his *kin*."

"And does it change your course, Na'dio? Does it change the plans that we have crafted?"

The silence of music played without heart, a curtain behind which the actors prepare for the play, uncertain of whether or not there will be an audience, but certain that an unfavorable audience is death.

"I don't know. I don't know what your plans were, or are—and I think you understand now that you don't know all of mine.

"But if the Lord of Night was the hand behind the Sword and the General, then I will take him into account, and there will be a reckoning." She lifted her youthful face, and the moonlight whitened it, hiding any imperfection, robbing it of any expression that was not grim and cold. "I swear it, by the Lady. I swear it by Faida, by Ruatha, by Deirdre."

"Diora—"

"Help me, Ona Teresa. This has grown beyond me, and I *cannot* allow that. I have sworn."

And what of my oaths, Teresa thought, as she carefully caught her almost-daughter's icy hands and stilled the singing of the harp for the evening. *What of my oaths to protect you, to watch over you, to keep you safe? What of my oaths to my own ghosts, my own dead?*

But she nodded, not trusting herself to speak with a voice that Diora would accept as truthful.

Alesso di'Marente stood shoulder to shoulder with Sendari di'Marano as they faced the Widan Cortano di'Alexes—*the* Sword's Edge—and his two companions, the kinlord, Isladar, and another emissary from the Shining Court, one whose human seeming was superficial enough that no one, on second glance, could mistake him for anything other than what he was: kin to the Lord of Night. Cortano had dispensed with the pretense of procedure and summoned them, from their sleep, to his personal chambers.

Alesso was furious.

Sendari knew it by the stillness and the silence in which he cloaked himself. He carried two swords; Sendari thought that these were not his only weapons, although they were the only visible ones. Beneath his robes, he wore the gift of Baredan di'Navarre—an old friend, a new enemy, and a man with a canny sense of what was valuable and useful.

"Widan Cortano," the General said, his eyes slightly narrowed in the poor light. "You summoned me, and I have chosen to answer that summons. I am pleased that Sendari had the forethought to warn me of the possible presence of the kin; the carelessness of the Shining Court in sending their emissaries has already cost me four of my most valued serafs. It is not yet dawn, but it will be; my presence will be required. Shortly."

The Widan Cortano looked neither concerned nor angered by Alesso di'Marente's words; the General's tone was neutral, and if the words were—almost—confrontational, they were not offensive enough to force the sword-sworn hand, unless the Widan already desired to move. "General," he said, inclining a majestically white head, "it was not at my insistence that you were summoned, but at the forceful request of our allies."

"I see." The General turned on his heel, pivoting neatly to face Lord Isladar. His anger was no better concealed. "What did you feel so important that it could not wait until our agreed upon meeting?"

The kinlord gave a low bow.

It unsettled Sendari, and readied him. Of the kin, this Lord was the quietest. He did not possess the overweening arrogance that made the kinlords so insulting; nor did he insist upon displaying his power as if it were plumage, and he a peacock in season. He was quiet in most things, and offered his counsel seldom, but when he did, the Lord of Night listened. Or so it was said. Sendari had not yet met the Lord of Night, and he had no intention of ever doing so. Let the rest of the Court please itself.

"General Alesso," Isladar said smoothly, "please, allow me to introduce Kovakar. He is a lieutenant in the army of Lord Assarak."

"Lord Assarak has no dealing with the Tor."

"Indeed, General Alesso, that was my response. But it appears that Lord Assarak is impatient."

"Lord Assarak is impatient," Kovakar hissed, "because of *your* folly, *Lord* Isladar. How much longer will we be forced to defer to *these*?" He raised his head, and lifted his shoulders; the robes that he wore bore the sudden shift in growth for no more than five seconds. "The only threat to us in the South are the Wandering clans. You know what they were before they abandoned their cities. Cortano, you yourself assured us—"

"I said that they were not a political force," the Widan said, in a deceptively mild tone.

"We will no longer tolerate these games of human politics," Kovakar replied, raising hands that were now long, clawed ebony. "Lord Assarak has dealt with humans before, and he has decided that it is time to deal with them again.

"You, *General,*" he spit to the side as the word left his lips, "are to finish the Radann. They were in league with the Wanderer that *Lord* Isladar lost—you will bring them to me. Now.

"If you do not," he added, "remember that there are thousands of clansmen who desire the Tor Leonne; we require only one of them to achieve our goals."

"And those goals, Kovakar?"

Kovakar seemed momentarily nonplussed at the tone of the General's voice. He glanced to the side, but Lord Isladar was studiously examining the screen opposite them.

"To defeat the Empire, of course."

"And you intend to do this on your own when you cannot even field a small unit of the kin to join a greater army of clansmen at the agreed upon time? You will remember that it was the delay of the Shining Court, and not the delay of the Tor and its human politics, that has crippled the war?"

Kovakar's smile was hideous and triumphant as he again glanced at Lord Isladar. "Lord Isladar did not have control of his little pet, and she escaped, destroying two thirds of the kin that had been assembled to serve you."

"Pet? What is this, Isladar?" Cortano said softly, touching the black center of his beard as he often did when the hunt for answers was upon him. "Did you lose little Kiriel?"

Lord Isladar shrugged, as neutral in expression as Alesso. "She is what she is, Cortano. The *Kialli* are not born; they have always been. But children grow, and before they reach their full strength and accept their duty and their destiny, they test the limits of authority placed upon them. They break ties that they do not understand,

and only when they have retreated to stand on their own, to *know* their own power, do they return.

"But she *will* return; I have seen it. And she will rule."

Cortano smiled and shook his head. "A worthy endeavor, or so I have always thought. You are the study of a lifetime, Isladar. It is my honor to preside over the Sword's Edge while you attempt your long return."

"*Attempt?*" Kovakar spoke, the two syllables the strike of lightning and the thunder that follows. He turned to the kinlord, Isladar, with open surprise. "You *allow* this? You allow these to question you?"

"I am not so fearful of my own status that I must see it slavishly worshiped at every possible moment, Kovakar," the kinlord responded. "It bores me. And besides, I've noted your tendency to defer, with what might pass for grace among the *Kialli,* to the mortal members of the Shining Court."

"Not so," Cortano said softly. "I do not believe that Kovakar has graced the upper chamber."

"The upper chamber is attended by footservants and Generals who have been placed under our Lord's geas," Kovakar replied, unriled. "And the Lord Assarak has decided that this will change. Starting now."

He was agile when he moved. He was deadly, and of the kin, he was powerful enough to take no master's name as part of his known identity. He was Lieutenant to Assarak, a step away from the Fist of God, and he intended to show these humans who they dealt with.

His victim's eyes were barely rounding in the way shocked mortal's eyes often did as he covered the distance between them, moving slowly for a *Kialli* of his stature.

Isladar was not a threat; in matters of the Court, he involved himself only when his pet was threatened, and even then, seldom. The mage, Cortano, was dangerous— but he was ambitious, and he desired things that the merely human court could never offer him.

But the human General's mage was disposable. Lord Assarak had made that quite clear. *The Lady Sariyal says that these two are not merely allies, but "friends." A weakness, Kovakar. Use it.*

He caught the mage-born human by the throat, closing his hand in just such a way as to allow breath through. He would also, in time, allow a scream or two to reach the ears of the man who needed to learn this lesson: The *Kialli* served no human interest for long; they were masters.

Kovakar did not intend to be quick or clean. The Lord kept a very tight rein upon subjects who had not seen the flats of this world since the Sundering and the Choice, and the sweet songs of the fields of Hell no longer slaked a thirst that had been ordained by that Choice. He had desired this return, but found—as his kin did—that the world was a much changed place. The glory had gone out of it, and the grandeur; there were mortals, and more mortals, and their pigs and cows and sheep. Here, wilderness meant the absence of human "civilization"; the trees were short and silent, the grasses tame, the forests devoid of the shadows and the light that had always been the bane of the *Kialli*.

Oh, there were souls, little flickering shards of immortality trapped in flesh that aged so quickly one could almost smell it decay, but they were the only compelling thing that remained in the Sundered Realm.

We will change that, he thought.

At his back, he heard the hiss of steel, slowly drawn, a lingering lovely sound that sent the mildest of shivers along his ear ridges. He turned, holding the mage whose hands now burned ineffectually at an ebony claw, and smiled, showing teeth. "General," he said, making of the word an insult. "You are almost beneath notice, but not quite. I would not turn my back upon the steel you wield if I were not guaranteed an alternate form of protection. But come. You have shown an interest in the fate of this mage-born mortal. I assure you that I will not disappoint that interest.

"Remember who *we* are."

"I have never forgotten it," the General Alesso di'Marente said calmly. He turned to the Widan Cortano di'Alexes. "Cortano."

"General."

"If you feel that the demon is correct, then you will find another clansman to replace me." He turned to the kin-lord. "Isladar, if you interfere, you will be forced to dirty your hands with the blood of the Dominion."

"Indeed." The kinlord's expression was completely neutral, but his lips turned up at the corners in what was almost—but not quite—a human smile.

The Sword's Edge narrowed, becoming sharper and brighter and infinitely more dangerous as it glittered in the eyes of the man who held the title. "Alesso—"

The General smiled.

"You are not as young a man as you were."

"No. Neither of us are." His smile broadened. "But it *is* the Festival of the Sun, old man." He drew his second sword as Sendari's body stiffened in the shock of Kovakar's care.

And then he lifted his hand and very carefully touched the sash that he wore across his chest; felt its warmth beneath his palm as he spoke three words. A gift from Baredan di'Navarre, whose name, for the first time in this longest of months, he did not curse.

He had one chance, and it was a short one; he was no fool. He had seen the demon move, and knew that in speed he was overmastered. But in cunning, the kin underestimated their allies when they were certain of their power. Their certainty of power was matched only by that power itself; in raw terms, a mortal did not challenge the kin in man-to-man combat and win.

Not unless he had come prepared, if hastily.

With a contempt akin to a demon's, Alesso di'Marente drove the points of both swords into the creature's exposed spine, cutting to either side as he dragged them out. Light lanced from his blades in visible sparks as steel effortlessly crossed the barrier demonic magic had made.

Kovakar snarled in rage and pain; Sendari fell. Alesso did not pause to see whether or not the Widan had made the fall intact; he leaped back, landing nimbly, his swords—edge out—crossed before him.

Kovakar turned, his hands extended; in the light, the hard sheen of his dark palms cast a reflection against the walls and screens. Alesso had not expected the wounds to kill him, for he had seen enough of the *Kialli* to know that such hope was futile. But the demon was slowed; the near-severing of his spine had damaged him greatly to bring him almost to his knees. A demon fighting on his knees was not a threat to be taken lightly—but it was one that *could* be taken.

"Alesso!" He barely heard his name—it was too quiet, and the syllables were choked almost beyond recognition. But he heard it, and he smiled. And it had been a long time since he had had this freedom, had walked this line, had lifted his sword in a combat that demanded no less than his best.

He came this close to death. And this close to death, there was no need for a pretty expression, a neutral guise; this close to death there was no room for fear—there was reaction, action, the swing of blades, the dance of death.

Alesso had never succumbed to the call of the dance; it required a trust in a partner's intent—and skill—that he had never felt. As close as he got was this: not a dance, but a contest, with death the only arbiter, and the only reward.

He felt the demon's claws cut the flesh from his arm, tearing through layers of cloth and chain as if they were quill-paper. But he almost didn't feel the pain because his body responded before it had registered, twisting and striking as the demon discovered that the only power it had over him was physical.

He heard the demon's breath; felt his own; the room became two men—two combatants—on a wide stretch of planked floor, wielding their chosen weapons. The creature feinted, but the feint was clumsy; he returned in kind, striking flesh that resisted as if it were armor.

Blood fell in a ring beneath his feet as the sword came back; he parried, left-handed, struck with his right, saw the sizzle of shadow as the vessel of the Lord of Night was ruptured.

And he smiled.

Sendari moved away from the fighting, hand around his throat as if to protect it from a grip that still burned. He rose at the edge of the mats, on the left hand side of the kinlord, Isladar, a foot and a half from the support of the nearest wall. The kinlord looked down, stepped aside, and watched him rise—which was proper etiquette; he did not comment on the weakness of the Widan. Instead, he said, "Your General has hidden much from the sight of the kin."

"The kin," Sendari replied, "have hidden much from

themselves. Alesso was chosen by Cortano for good reason. He is a man that the clansmen will follow."

"Indeed," Cortano added softly, although he was obscured by the kinlord's height, "he is. And I will say, Sendari, that he has lost little of his form over the last decade."

"It is the Festival season."

"And it irked him, to be a politician during the Lord's trial by combat."

"We could not afford to enter a challenge that we couldn't be certain of winning." Sendari winced and turned aside as his oldest friend took another glancing blow from the ebony claws of the kin. He lifted his hands, opened his mouth, and then dropped them, waiting. At times like this—and he had witnessed very, very few—Alesso was an elemental force, a thing, like the fires over which Sendari had at so much cost gained mastery, to be contained, to be feared, and to be respected.

Not to be protected.

Isladar raised a dark brow. "You would let him fight alone?"

"I would," Sendari said, and then added, "reluctantly. He has a way of being . . . unthankful . . . for intervention."

"Yes," Cortano said. "Youthful pride."

"He is not so young as that."

Sendari's throat hurt too much to allow him to laugh. "Proof," he said to Cortano, although the white-haired Widan was still obscured by the kinlord's frame, "that power and knowledge are not one and the same."

"You don't know if he's going to win."

Not a question. Sendari glanced at the demon, and then at the man upon whom their plans depended. "No," he said. "Does that please you, kinlord?"

"Not much," was Isladar's neutral answer. "You do not suffer with fear or guilt as you say it; you are both Widan, and you are both curiously unruffled by this turn of events. In fact, if I read what I see correctly, Cortano is actually pleased."

"Satisfied," the Edge of the Sword said curtly.

Sendari did not reply. He disliked this reminder of the demon's ability to read the lines written upon a man's soul, possibly because of what it implied. Lips narrowing into a thin line, he gave the fight his full attention. Or the semblance of it.

"Widan Sendari."

"Kinlord."

"Why do you not interfere? You have struggled for decades to reach these three days—and the Festival Height will be your reward."

"The Festival's Height," Cortano replied, "will be our declaration, no more; the fruits of success still hang from a fiercely guarded tree."

"Cortano, please."

"Very well, but you will not understand his answer."

At that, Sendari allowed himself to glance at the kinlord—and he was gratified for the first time in the length of a trying day, for the kinlord looked angry, even insulted, by Cortano's words. To a Widan, they would have been a spur to greater knowledge—or a slap in the face.

"We both see things that we have not seen before," the younger Widan said. "This is Alesso's test in the eyes of the Lord."

"You do not believe the Sun Lord even exists."

"Isladar," Cortano's voice was cold with warning.

"Very well, Widan—but I hardly think, with a demon on the mats, an eavesdropper is likely to pay attention to a statement that is widely believed if never publicly spoken."

Sendari said, "I do not believe, although that is beside the point. Alesso believes it, in his fashion. And he has chosen this as a test. He will win, and we will continue, or he will die, and we will continue."

"He chose this battle to save your life."

"Are you saying that to elicit guilt or to show your ignorance?"

Isladar laughed. The sound was deep and cold and beautiful. "Widan, you are wise. Very well. I am *Kialli*. Yet I will say this: You were some part of what motivated him."

"It was not a matter of my life—it was a matter of his dominion."

"And if I ended the battle now, he would never know whether or not he passed the test that he set for himself."

"Isladar," Cortano's voice.

The kinlord lifted a hand and pointed. Magical fire streamed from him like a solid bridge made of twisted ebony and burning ember. It struck Kovakar in the chest and bore him down to the mats that were already a cindered ruin.

"I apologize, General, but I am afraid that this particular creature is not without his import to our cause. I must ask that you forgo the pleasure of his death." Before Alesso could even react, the fire-laced shadow sprang out like a cage around the demon, harboring him.

The General turned slowly. "Release him, kinlord."

Isladar raised a brow. "I am afraid, General, that I do not have that option."

Black-eyed, bloodied, and unbowed, Alesso di'Marente looked kin to the kin as he turned slightly to face the Sword's Edge. "Cortano," he said softly, a single, cold word.

"Do not," the kinlord said, "interfere."

No breath was drawn in the room as this second of contests shifted ground and place.

The Widan who controlled the Sword of Knowledge paused a moment and then stepped at last into the range of Sendari's vision. In front of the kinlord. "Isladar." He appeared almost apologetic. "I must ask this, as a favor."

"And if I choose not to grant it?"

Cortano's expression did not shift; no muscle moved.

"I see," the kinlord said, "that we do not understand each other at all. You are not Allasakari."

At this, the Sword's Edge stiffened. "I have offered you no insult, old *friend*."

"But you offered no warning either."

"Your curiosity has been satisfied, Isladar. You have the answer to the question that Kovakar was sent to pose. You now know how much humiliation we are willing to suffer—and how much we fear to engage you." His smile was thin. "If you wish, you will have the answer to the question that you are about to pose. And I give you my word that you will not appreciate it." He paused. "There are those who will throw the whole of a struggle for the sake of pride. I am such a man. As is the General. Sendari, oddly enough, is not.

"Are you, *Kialli* kinlord?"

Isladar's smile was out of place, for his eyes were chill and narrow. "No," he replied, "as you well know."

"Then dissolve your protections, Isladar. You require our aid; there will be no three like us in the whole of the Dominion in this generation, and were there, you would not have the time to search; Etridian's ill-planned intervention has seen to that.

"The Empire is moving. Your ancient enemies have taken to roads that are older than our memory. You need the Dominion's weight against the Empire to be assured the swift victory you desire.

"You are kinlord, and you are not without your power—but your power and mine have never been matched and tested." He did not speak or move, but the light trapped him in its orange cocoon, glittering with sparks of white and blue that lit the length of his pale beard.

"If we do not have a swift victory, we will have one nonetheless."

"And you are so certain?"

"You have seen the Lord of the Shining City."

"Yes." Cortano's voice wavered for just a second, and then his expression hardened. "And I have heard the Northern Lays—past *and* present."

Isladar gestured; the shadow-spun fire that kept the General and the kin apart was banked in that instant.

"It is never wise," he said softly, "to point out the weakness of your enemy and then let him live."

"Is wisdom weakness?" Cortano shrugged, unruffled.

But Sendari saw that the shields he wore intensified as both the kinlord and the Sword's Edge turned once again to a battle that was still not decided.

Both Alesso and the creature had taken the moment's respite to catch their breath and horde their energy. They met like small giants; he was surprised that the wide, slender planks under the gored and bloodied mats did not collapse beneath their weight. Watching, he forgot to breathe as claw struck flesh, and sword struck claw, and as the blood flew, as it thickened and mottled Alesso's skin, Sendari thought, if not for the weapon, he would not have been able to distinguish between the two.

He was wrong; Alesso's sword style was a signature that no man in the Dominion had come close to forging.

In the end, in an almost florid series of strokes, Alesso di'Marente severed Kovakar's head from his spine and sent it rolling down the mats.

He was no fool; he did not pause to relish the moment. When the kin were dead, they left no corpse, no corporeal remnant. But each of the three witnesses marked the end of the battle in that beheading.

Bleeding and victorious, Alesso di'Marente carefully wiped his sword's blade. The only blood on it was his, but blood was corrosive regardless. He had no illusions; he was injured, and the loss of blood unsteadied him. The armor was beyond repair—or at least beyond the repair of the moment, and the sun's rays were glittering across the face of the waters of the Tor.

He bowed to the lake and the Lord, and then rose, touching his chest. The sash was almost ruined, but he could feel its warmth, ebbing as the minutes passed, beneath his sticky palm. What the Wanderers had crafted, they had crafted well; he would pay much to know where Baredan had found the sash, and what it had cost. The Voyani parted from their history for no mere coin.

Turning, he started to sheathe his swords, but the Lord's glory was still upon him. In a silence that was warm and not icy, he crossed the mats to where Isladar stood, waiting.

Without a word of warning, he brought the short sword up and across in a short, swift arc. Isladar's hand was already out, palm up, to catch the blade; he moved far too quickly to dodge. But dodging was not Alesso's intent.

He smiled as he heard the kinlord's grunt and saw the spill of nightshadow down the sword's edge. "A warning," he told the kinlord, for he knew that the kinlord had not expected to feel the edge of the sword at all.

Isladar smiled grimly and twisted his hand. A rain of light glanced off the ceiling as the blade shattered.

They stared at each other for a long moment, and then the General bowed. "Give Lord Assarak my thanks. It has been a long time. I would offer them myself, but I must retire and prepare for the Festival of the Sun." He paused for just long enough to catch Cortano's eye. "Widan."

"General. Most impressive."

The Widan Sendari par di'Marano remained conspicuously silent until he received the unspoken order to retreat. But he was grateful—to whom, he did not care to say—that the sword that had been shattered was not the blade by which Alesso had made his name. Of the two weapons in his possession, Alesso had chosen to strike with the short sword. A practical man.

CHAPTER THIRTY-ONE

Light, pink and hazy, spread across the sky's lowest edge, the curtain of day dropping—or the curtain of night burning slowly away. The Serra Diora di'Marano sat upon the dais that faced the lake, her hands cupped around a ceremonial goblet; it was cool, a balm to new skin. The lines of night were hidden beneath white masque powder, and the posture of graceful attention was one that was almost more natural to her than breathing, but she knew that Alana, oldest of her father's wives, saw immediately that something was wrong.

Although it was dawn, she thanked the Lady that the men who ruled were not as dangerously perceptive as the women who served them. Holding the goblet, she waited until enough of the sun had crested the horizon. Then, raising it in a flash of silver and precious stone, she spoke the Lord's blessing. The Radann kai el'Sol could not see the expression on her face, for he stood beside her, lifting the goblet's twin.

Below, at the very edge of the lake, the men who had survived the first test of the Lord lifted their swords in a silence that was almost eerie. Long shards of light were cast groundward as they held their salute. Only when the Radann kai el'Sol lowered his goblet did they lower their weapons and bow.

"We will meet within the hour upon the plateau. Let all clansmen who seek to continue the Lord's test meet us there."

They bowed, not to the Radann, but to the Lord's Consort. And none there held a bow so graceful—or so deep—as the Tyr'agnate Eduardo kai di'Garrardi.

"Well, Teresa, the world is full of foolish men indeed if the only ones who attend you are cerdan and seraf."

The cerdan looked up at the approaching visitor, and straightened themselves out to their full height and full bearing. Burnished medallions hung at their chests, and their swords gleamed like their too-bright youth in the early part of the day. The Serra liked youth, not for its obvious physical beauty—although it had that—but for its painful idealism, its charming naïveté. She rarely had the chance to indulge in her choice of cerdan, but at this particular Festival Sendari must be well attended, and his wife, even more so; the senior cerdan were spoken for.

And the junior cerdan were proud to bear up under the attention of a Tyr.

Serra Teresa did not need to look up from the fringe of her fan to know who spoke; she had a gift for voices, and once she'd heard one, she was unlikely to forget it. And this man had more, beside the timbre of a deep voice, to recommend him: height, bearing, a gift of charm and a faded ability to fight and to ride with the best of the clansmen. He was not known for the quality of his mercy, but his foibles, when he chose to exercise them, ran toward affection and loyalty.

"Tyr'agnate," she said properly, bowing her head in a perfect show of respect.

" 'Tyr'agnate is it?" Jarrani kai di'Lorenza laughed. "It's an odd Festival. I don't think I've ever seen you so . . . alone."

"Alone?" At this, she did look up.

"Well, for one you're usually surrounded by Northerners." He coughed. "If you'll forgive my lack of tact."

"I shall choose," she said sweetly, "not to notice it."

"That's the problem with women. You've no idea whether or not you've actually behaved well; they don't say a damned thing."

"I am sure," she replied, as sweet in tone as the waters of the Tor, "that if you truly wished such honesty, you would find yourself a wife."

He laughed at that, and ruefully. "Marano," he said, to the young cerdan who seemed to be in charge, "I assure you that I intend your Serra no disrespect; my own Tyran will vouch for my behavior."

They were not so shiny a group as the cerdan the Serra had been granted, but they were older and cannier. They were also, she thought, a trifle bored, but had the training not to show it.

"Ramdan," she said to her personal seraf. It was, of course, unnecessary; she could see his shadow shrink as he knelt to retrieve goblets and the appropriate decanter. "I apologize, Tyr'agnate; had I known that I would have the honor of your company, I would have attempted to secure a more appropriate pavilion to receive it."

"The only such pavilions are far from the fighting." He stood a moment, shading his eyes from the rays of the early morning's sun. "It's been a bloody morn."

"Yes," she said quietly, all archness gone from her voice. "I don't know why."

"Well," the Tyr'agnate said, drawing the word out into several syllables worth as he bent his knees and made a show of settling into the cushions that the seraf provided, "as I have no wife for you to offend—and none to turn to for guidance—might I ask you your opinion on a matter or two?"

"You may, of course, always ask. And if I am able, I will answer. But you are a Tyr'agnate—"

"And you are a woman who does not need to dissemble. If I wanted a child, I'd have searched for a child."

Her lifted fan hid the smile of momentary pleasure that spread across her lips, but it did not conceal her eyes. "You have Hectore," she said.

"Yes, well. Perhaps another today. On this one he's like a blade that's too sharp; he'd cut silk as soon as flesh, and probably with as much vigor. He's in a foul mood."

"Ah. A flaw in a man his age," Serra Teresa said serenely, "to take a loss so poorly."

"Was it that obvious?"

"Eduardo di'Garrardi is not exactly a graceful winner."

"No." Jarrani frowned. "But speaking of Eduardo, has the wind taken his sense and dashed it against the cliffs?"

She raised both brows in exaggerated—but quite real—surprise.

He laughed, pleased with himself, and she saw the child in him—that youth, so bright and shiny, which was so often completely extinguished in men half his age.

"I am not your wife," she said, a little tartly, "and I will remind you of that fact. Your Tyran are listening, and they will expect you to show a proper respect for your peers."

"They'll expect no such thing," he told her. "First, we're too boring for them; they've half an eye and half a brain on the testing. Second, if your brothers weren't such tiresome and clingy fools I would gladly remedy the first complaint in a moment."

She composed her face into perfect neutrality.

"Teresa, don't. You know how I feel about this."

"Adano *is* the kai of Marano."

"Yes, well." He took the water that Ramdan offered without glancing up. "But about Garrardi."

"If you are asking me why he exposes himself to the danger of the Lord's test, I cannot answer. He is of an age—and a rank—where such testing isn't necessary, and is in all probability not advisable. Short of winning, he will only damage his reputation among the clansmen."

"He's fighting like a demon."

"Jarrani."

"I'm not to profane either?"

"Not a bit." She sipped the waters and then turned her face toward the plateau as if seeking a cooling breeze. "I would have said he was being completely foolish—but I would also have ventured to advise you against allowing Hectore to enter the competition."

"Well, yes." She waited; she was one of the most famous Serras in the Dominion, and she could outwait the Lord and the Lady when she so chose. Eventually, he laughed.

"It was the kai's idea, but I didn't discourage it. We're short a Tyr or two—had he placed well, it would have drawn the attention of clansmen who are now seeking new masters. Neither of us expected Garrardi to seek the title.

"And you haven't answered my question."

"Very well, Tyr'agnate, but I answer the question to incur no favor and would appreciate the asking and the answering to remain a private act.

"Eduardo di'Garrardi has taken to the plateau in an attempt to prove himself worthy of the Flower of the Dominion."

He did not laugh, and he should have; he did not deride

the younger man's wisdom. Instead he caught her hand. It was a risky action. "Teresa," he said, all affection and all joviality gone, as if they were masks too heavy, for this instant, not to fall. "This alliance—it is not to my liking."

She did not flinch or blush or pale. Jarrani was a man of power, but he was, in his fashion, a man of honor; the threat that he offered he did not offer to her, but through her, and this was wise.

"It is not," she said, extricating her fingers with care not to draw attention to the gesture, "to her liking either, and I believe he knows it." The fan's ivory spindles fell open in her lap as she smoothed them into the perfect crescent. "This is not a matter of alliance, Jarrani." Her voice was as cold as his, but infinitely more musical. "To Garrardi, Diora is a creature like Sword's Blood; she is not attached to Marano—or Marente—excepting only that he requires her father's permission before he makes his claim known. I am not my brother's wife, and I am not taken into all of his counsel, so I am, of course, guessing.

"And as I am guessing, Tyr'agnate—"

"Jarrani."

"—Tyr'agnate, I will say that I think neither my brother nor the man he serves is fond of the choice made, and you may be surprised by the Festival's end." Her fan rose, and delicate though it was, it was a wall.

"And the price for this advice?"

She did not answer.

"Teresa, I did not mean to offend."

"I know. And you did not offend, Tyr'agnate. Rather, you offered a reminder. No more."

He stared at her face, and the fan that punctuated it, in a silence of words considered and words rejected. Then he rose. "I would still pay almost any price for the privilege, Serra Teresa."

Her smile was soft and bitter, but he did not see it; he had already returned to his Tyran.

She was quiet as she watched his retreat. Thinking that he was a dangerous man, because he spoke the truth when he spoke, and because his affections and his loyalties were a part of that truth. And they were rare enough that it was easy—even for a woman of her experience—to forget that they were only a part.

* * *

Eduardo di'Garrardi killed two men before the sun's height brought the testing to a temporary end. They were not the first men he had killed, nor the first killed in combat, but even Diora was surprised at the ease with which they were dismissed. Here, with clansmen as witness, there were honors to be paid, forms to observe. The Tyr'agnate made a great show of neither; he was conspicuous in his arrogance. The men that he faced were enemies, not rivals; when vanquished, they lay like any enemy beneath the sun's hot face: devoid of life or purpose.

Each time he won a combat—whether it ended in death or no—he turned not to the Lord but to the Lord's Consort; each time he so turned, she tilted her head farther into the folds of the fan that had been the Serra Teresa's gift.

The Radann kai el'Sol was furious, but hid it as well as any born Lambertan might. When he sought her gaze at all, she smiled, but her smile was both tentative and easily missed. It was also rarely offered.

The General Alesso di'Marente chose to grace them with his presence just before the morning's testing was called to an end, and he had the privilege of watching Eduardo di'Garrardi's last battle. He said nothing as he watched the rise and fall of sword, but it was a graceless combat, so close to sun's height.

"Kai el'Sol."

"General. We missed your presence at the opening ceremony."

If there was criticism in the tone—and there was—the General chose to ignore it. He stood, hands clasped loosely behind his back, and watched the battle intently, eyes narrowed against the flash of sun off blade, the consequence of a sky bereft of cloud and storm.

The Lord renders one *judgment.*

"This is the last?"

"It is."

"And the result?"

"Five men, General. Five men will advance."

The General frowned. "Not six."

"The Tyr'agnate's second contest with the man who would have otherwise held the sixth place ended in his death."

"I see. And the Tyr'agnate?"

"The judgment is not mine to make."

"Kai el'Sol," was the almost amused reply, "is he among the six?"

"Yes."

"Impressive."

Grudging even this agreement, the kai el'Sol was silent for a moment. The moment ended as Eduardo di'Garrardi's opponent drove his blade point first into the sheath of the plateau itself: surrender. It was a near thing, but this closely watched, Eduardo had no choice; he held his hand. The man's kin came to him, quickly, as if that moment of control were a passing cloud in a brisk wind. They gathered and they retreated, giving the defeated combatant the opportunity to display both dignity and strength—such as it was—by walking off the field. But they did not sheathe the weapons they had drawn, and no witness could think it coincidence that the honor guard they formed was heaviest at the rear.

Alesso laughed. "I see that Garrardi has indeed distinguished himself."

The day waned slowly; the Lord's face was harsh and complete in its dominion of the sky. Food had been brought to the Serra, and water, but she touched neither. Alaya's seraf hands held a fan that caught air and used it; the hint of cool breeze wafted across downturned cheek, an echo of the rainy season.

Brave girl, to try to mime the winds.

Fire could be contained, but air, never. Hold out your hands, and it passed through your fingers more quickly than water. It lifted the veil of sand, casting it into unwary eyes, and at the peak of the storm, that sand buried those who had not managed to find shelter from the wind's full fury.

The Tor Leonne was far enough from the desert winds that it was not troubled by them, yet close enough that the wind's whisper still held menace and warning.

She heard its whisper.

And contained within it, words.

"Diora."

"Ona Teresa."

"Have you spoken with the kai el'Sol?"

She raised the lashes of her perfect eyes and gazed a

moment upon the broad back of the man who had kept his word. He protected her from the curiosity of the clansmen, and from those who might—just might—seek a chance to gloat at the fate of the Serra who had, a year past, been the most envied young woman in the Dominion. She thought he might leave an honor guard during those times that Festival duties demanded his attention, but not even Marakas par el'Sol had been allowed to stand alone with the Radann the kai el'Sol had chosen; what she endured, he endured, and for the same length of time.

Once, she might have thought him brave and honorable.

Then, as she grew wiser and more learned, a fool.

And now?

"No."

"The time is now, Diora. If you do not do this thing, you will—"

"I know what I must do."

And now she would consider him a doomed man. She hoarded her voice and her voice's strength. Because tonight she intended to speak in private with the Radann kai el'Sol. To offer him not the soothing tones of the Flower of the Dominion, but the command—the implacable command—of the oathsworn wife.

Silence then. Ona Teresa's blessed and cursed voice became wind, hot and languid in its silence. But the silence was a lull, a trick of timing.

"You need the Sun Sword."

I know.

And the man who dared to bring the Sun Sword into the open at the height of this particular Festival was a doomed man, for the General could not overlook the insult and the implication of the weapon's presence.

He is dead, no matter what happens. This way, his death serves a purpose.

She tried, as Alaya bent just a little too close and caught the edge of her chin with the soft, thick leaves of the fan, to believe it. And because she was born of Sendari di'Marano and his long dead wife, because she was trained and taught by the Serra Teresa di'Marano, she could.

But another truth came to her as she sat, waiting for sunfall, counting the truths she did know: that men of power should never be trusted. The obvious reasons had been given her: that they were not trustworthy, that they valued nothing above their survival and their supremacy, that they made, of those Serras foolish enough to dally, pawns—or serafs.

She had found one more: that they *could* be trustworthy. That they could value honor and prize something greater and deeper than their power over the realm they had chosen for their dominion. And that they, not the Serra, might become the pawn that was sacrificed in the hunt for a larger piece.

She had not thought to like the Radann kai el'Sol, but she did, and it was a terrible thing.

Later, she would remember that the Festival of the Sun was marked not by light, but the shadows the sun cast; those shadows fell long, and when the season passed, they remained, scars against the hidden heart, evidence of a wound that had only just missed its mark. Only just failed to grant its peace.

But she thought that those shadows were night, and she thought that night, even as brief a night as the Lord granted at his Festival, was the Lady's dominion. So much of the world slept, and the parts of it that woke— serafs and cerdan, crickets and night blossoms—were, as she was, a part of the invisible world, the world in which power was measured in little things because it could never be measured in greatness.

She could not say that she had never wondered what it would have been like to be born a man, a clansman's son. But at thirteen she had lost the illusion that that would grant freedom, for she had seen many men trapped by bonds as strong as hers, into different services, whether they wielded sword and rode stallion or swept the open courtyards after the clansmen and their Serras had passed.

Freedom.

She turned the word around in the silence of closed lips; it was a Northern word. It had no roots in the Tyrian tongue, although it had been adopted in some fashion, and used. The closest analogy that the Tyrian tongue could offer to the Weston language was *Tyr'agar*. First ruler.

What, in the end, was freedom?

Serra Diora took a deep breath and then, very quietly,

she touched the door of the swordhaven and pushed it. It was ajar, and it swung toward the interior on a newly oiled hinge. Within there were lamps, light, and a window into the nightworld by which the Sword might be seen if the Lady chose to look.

"Radann kai el'Sol?"

"Serra Diora." The Radann kai el'Sol stood at the foot of the stairs. To his left and his right were two men; they wore hoods, but by their sunbursts, she knew them to be par el'Sol. "Close the door behind you, make the offering, and join us."

She bowed in respect and accepted his command as if obedience was reflex. It was. Incense touched her fingers, leaving a hint of fragrance that fire would make less cloying. Then, rising, she made her way to the steps.

The Radann kai el'Sol bowed, which surprised her. "Tomorrow," he said softly, "is the Festival's Height."

"Yes." She met his eyes squarely, because she knew, at that moment, that he expected no less. She had no seraf and no cerdan; he had no attendants but these two. There were none to witness either her boldness or his deference. "Forgive me, Radann kai el'Sol." *Speak truth where truth will do.* "Forgive me, but I did not choose this site because I desired privacy."

He waited, grave, a stillness about him that was more substantial, suddenly, than the robes or the rank that made them so desirable.

To his right, Radann Samadar par el'Sol lowered his hood. To his left, Radann Peder par el'Sol.

The hood fell away from the latter's face as the night lost its aura of safety; she remembered, meeting his eyes, that safety was illusion, that only the desire for safety was real. That lesson, she'd learned the night the clan Leonne perished, but it was a lesson that she forgot, time and again; a lesson that, like real pain, and not the memory of pain, could only truly be felt when one walked its terrain again. The desire for safety was that strong.

And the desire for love, and neither could ever be guaranteed.

The dagger was in her hand; she had taken it with the ease and immediacy that she had once—and never would again—grasped her father's hand.

"Serra Diora," the kai el'Sol said, his voice low and gentle.

She did not shift in either gaze or stance, and they did not approach her, for the use of daggers was an art in which the women of the clans often excelled. "Kai el'Sol. I am . . . surprised at your choice of companion."

The Radann Peder par el'Sol grimaced. "Of course. You *are* the Widan's daughter, and the Widan serves the General."

"Of course." Her lips were set in a thin line. "This man," she told the kai el'Sol, "intends to preside over the Radann after your death." She looked for some sign of surprise in the kai's features; there was none. Instead, and far worse, was the hint of a bitter resignation, a turning of the corner of lips, a momentary drop of shoulder and brow.

"Yes, Serra, I know. You are . . . observant. And I should have expected no less; you were wife to the kai Leonne." He turned away from her—and from his companions, neither of whom spoke, and made his way to the steps that lay before the Sun Sword. "Join me, Serra."

She had to walk between the Radann to reach him, but she did not hesitate. Nor did she sheathe her dagger.

The steps, wide and flat, she mounted with ease, pulling up the hem of her sari with a twist of her left hand. He waited for her, and as she joined him, he knelt before the weapon crafted by the Lord. She thought he was praying, and perhaps he was, for very little else could bring a Radann to his knees.

But he said, "Serra Diora, is this the favor that you have come to ask?"

And she looked at the gleaming flat of the blade beneath the torches that marked and honored it with an echo of the Lord's light. "Yes." She hesitated for a moment longer and then sheathed the dagger in the folds of her sari. "Kai el'Sol—the Radann—"

"Serves the interests of the General. Yes, I know."

"But you—"

"He told me, Serra."

She was silent as she absorbed this. "He spied for you?"

"No. He intended to take the Radann."

Silence. Then she raised her face, slowly, to the night sky. "The Lord of Night."

"Yes. Peder is a man of great ambition, but he *is* Radann. To offer his support for my death and the title of kai," the kai el'Sol shrugged. "But to offer his support for a return of the Lord of Night?" He bowed his head. "I am not the man for this game, Serra Diora. I am the Lord's servant, but the game that is played here is a game for men who understand treachery better than I."

She turned then, and saw that the face of the Radann Peder par el'Sol was turned up, toward the Sword, or the kai. Or both.

"And if I were the man for this game, I think it would matter little," the kai continued. "But I will serve the Lord, and the Lord's work, as I can." He rose. "The Sun Sword is always displayed at Festival's Height. It has always been drawn and wielded by the Tyr'agar. I would be honored to bring it, as has been my duty for my tenure as the kai el'Sol, to the celebration of Festival's Height."

She knew what it would cost, and she had thought to use her gift to influence a man of pride and honor to do exactly as he pledged to do. But she had thought to use him while he remained ignorant, and she was ashamed of the thought, and for it, for she saw clearly that he knew what the cost of his action would be.

As if he could read what could not be upon her face, he smiled. "A General knows when to surrender some of the men in his command to his enemy's slaughter, that the war effort elsewhere might continue.

"But I will ask a boon, daughter of our enemy."

She waited in silence.

"Do not judge the Radann Peder par el'Sol too harshly, for he *will* be kai el'Sol." He offered her an arm, as if the steps were steep, and she took it. "The only loyalty required of the Radann is loyalty to the Lord. If he were to be judged by the Lord tomorrow, at the height of the Lord's power, he would not be judged unworthy." He took a step and then stopped. "But I must say in honesty that he does not know about the . . . gift the Voyani woman left you. He knows of the woman."

"He had her killed."

"He had no choice. You will understand that, one day, or you will never understand it. Her power was detected.

It was detected by the Sword's Edge. Peder could expose her, and maintain his role, or he could attempt to save her and doom us all.

"We are fighting a war, Serra. We are all, singly, expendable. All.

"The Tor Leonne will not be open to travel until Alesso wears the crown and holds the Tor. Until open travel is possible, we can send no word, gather no information, inform no others. The Tor will be the General's; we cannot prevent it. But I swear before the Lord's Sword that it will never belong to the General's allies."

As he spoke, she turned and the light along the blade flashed starkly and sharply in the poor light.

"Alesso di'Marente would never serve the Lord of Night." It was pulled from her grudgingly, as if it pained her to say anything about the man at all.

"No? Perhaps not willingly. But he overestimates himself, or underestimates his allies. If Peder believed that the General could withstand the forces of the Lord of Night, he would never have come to me. Peder par el'Sol is no loyal friend—but he is no fool."

"Kai el'Sol, with your permission, I would like a moment alone."

His arm fell away from hers, as if it had become too heavy; he bowed, and waited for her to make her descent. She ascended instead, and stood, as he had stood, before the gleaming crescent sword. And then she knelt, as he knelt, and pressed her head against the stone.

But her prayer, spoken, was silent; her gift and her curse protected the words from the ears of any save the Lord himself.

If the Lord listened.

He heard her sing from a distance enforced on all sides by the Radann, and although the song had ended and the sweet stillness of the Tor had passed, he remained to greet the fall of night in the same position that he had held when she departed. The healers had done their work—at cost, and not to him alone—but the skin was new and pulled when he moved quickly; his clothing, heavy enough to protect him from the full heat of the sun, chafed.

The demon was gone, but others remained, less easy to destroy and far less gratifying.

"Alesso."

"Sendari." He did not look away from the pavilion.

"The Tyr'agnate of Oerta has been looking for you."

"Let him look."

Sendari chuckled dryly. "It is early for that game, Alesso. We have already agreed. Until the Festival's end we cannot afford this antagonism."

"Whether we can afford it or no, old friend, we will pay. I have done as you required, and I have mollified Garrardi in a fashion. But he was not soothed by Calevro's death."

"Calevro was the Captain of the oathguards. He broke his oath for personal gain. If Garrardi thought that we could afford the stain of his allegiance, he is a greater fool than I would have thought."

"Which," Alesso replied, lifting and swinging his arm as if the morning's exercise was not yet done, "says much."

"Indeed."

"Sendari, might I not—"

"No."

The frown flashed across the General's face and passed in an instant, yet it could not be easily forgotten. A harbinger of the storm to come.

"It is not my choice," Sendari said, matching his friend's momentary anger. "And we will not argue about this again, I swear it by the Lord's grace. The Radann guard her at all times. If she is awake, the kai el'Sol attends her personally. If she is asleep, she is attended by his personally appointed servitors. Not even I am allowed into her presence."

"And you accept this? She *is* your daughter."

Sendari said nothing, but turned instead to gaze up at the face of the moon in the clear, clear sky. It was a long moment before he answered, but although the shallows of night hid the twist of his lips and the quickly changing contours of his jaw, Alesso knew him well enough to wait.

"Yes," he said at last, and softly. "She is my daughter." His shoulders fell.

"I will not dishonor her," the General said, almost awkward.

Sendari shrugged. "Alesso, leave it be. You are right; I cannot think clearly where she is concerned. She is—she is much like her mother before her."

The General's silence was less complex, but longer. At last he said, "What will Isladar do?"

"Nothing. He will take word back to Assarak. In fact, I believe he will enjoy that, although I cannot say for certain. They are not allies."

"The kin cannot form alliances."

Sendari laughed. "And what are we, Alesso?"

"Pawns." The General's smile was a gleam. "But we need them."

"For now, yes. And later?"

"Later, Sendari, we will form a different alliance, with another enemy. Why do you think they want this war, the Shining Court? Because they have already faced the Empire once."

Sendari lifted a hand, calling for quiet in a silence made of magic and intensity. "Yes. Do not underestimate the Northerners. And do not underestimate the Lord of Night."

"Sendari—"

"We do not know what occurred in Averalaan; not well. We know of the three weeks, and we know of the shadow that rose from the heart of the old city. But the shadow's grip was a poor one; the sea winds blew it away in the dawn of their First Day.

"This time, Alesso, the shadow's grip is not so poor or so uncertain."

"And how do you know so much, Sendari, when you speak so little?"

"I see it," the Widan said, his eyes taking on the half-vacant look of a man staring into the ephemera of his past, "in Cortano's face. I hear it in Isladar's word. I know it by the fact that the kinlords and their servants are growing both in strength and in number. If you know how to look, you can distinguish between even the imps."

"We plan to make use of the kin."

"And they, of us. But the game is growing dangerous if Assarak feels he can make a point of rulership," he paused to touch the bruises across his throat, "with impunity."

They had chosen their course; there was no turning aside. Nor would Sendari have requested it. But although it was the Festival of the Sun, they thought of the Lord of Night, wondering when his reach had grown so long.

The night was cool, and the breeze was silent beside the waters of the Tor Leonne.

The Radann kai el'Sol found dressing almost painful—but not nearly so much as the servitor Jevri did. For Jevri was almost an Artisan, and the Radann kai el'Sol was not the demure and graceful clanswoman for whom his designs had been intended. He was a man, with a man's impatience for purity of detail, and had he been any other man, Jevri would have given up in quiet disgust two hours past. Had he been any other man, the servitor would have given up in noisy disgust one hour past. And this servitor had been raised seraf and trained in a powerful clan's house.

But they had been together a long time, these two. Jevri held the needle between his lips as he paused to inspect the detail of his work in the poor light. Of course it would be poor light; the Radann kai el'Sol was expected to greet the dawn. And the most annoying thing about such a meeting was that he would greet the dawn in the same fine but serviceable robes that he had greeted Jevri wearing.

The needle pricked the old man's lip, drawing both blood and a curse.

He had been given to Fredero on a whim, a request made, gently and firmly, by the kai el'Sol's mother of her husband, the Tyr'agnate of Mancorvo, a mere week before he left the fold of clan Lamberto forever, choosing the halls of the Lord's Service over the halls of his blood kin. The Tyr'agnate had not been happy with his choice—but then, what man would see his family forsaken, even if the cause be as noble a cause as the Lord's service?—but he had granted his wife's wish.

Fredero was ever the stoic, and Jevri, the dutiful seraf. But both men could not help but think the change in station inappropriate, for Jevri was not the seraf to serve the harsh and spare Radann.

Oh, he worked.

When Fredero came to tell him that he was to be given his freedom, Jevri acquiesced, as ordered. When he in turn offered his service to the Radann as servitor, Fredero accepted without question. Such had been the Serra Carlatta's will, and Fredero had rarely argued with his mother's wisdom.

Beadwork caught the lamplight; trailed down the edge of a knife and a needle; softened the sheen of crushed silk. Darkness brought a subtle beauty to the light.

And the clansmen were not known for either their subtlety or their appreciation of subtlety. At least, the clansmen of honor were not. Among these, Lamberto was first.

How had it started? Fredero had learned to fight. He was not a small man, and not a fool for all that he chose to wear honor's righteous face. He understood cunning and deceit; he merely chose not to practice either. Jevri saw in this man, daily, a man worthy of a seraf's service. Even the best of the serafs.

But it was not in combat in the service of the Lord that the kai el'Sol was to distinguish himself, for the Radann were all well-versed in the arts of war, and to compare a kill—and the Imperial war provided many—in a roomful of warriors was no way to set oneself apart from the rest of the Radann.

He took care to adjust the inner straps of the headdress that the Radann kai el'Sol would wear. He took less care when offering the Radann kai el'Sol directions on how best to stand—with straight shoulders, for one—while it was being fitted.

This finery was reserved for the height of the moment: the declaration of the winner of the Lord's test. Rumors and money were exchanged with equal facility as the servitors and the cerdan played their favorites from among the five who were to meet for the final time in the sun's heat. Jevri's coin had never been added to that game, although this one year he had been sorely tempted to place his bet upon the Tyr'agnate; the man fought like one sun-maddened.

And if Jevri was almost willing to be parted from his coin, it meant he would earn little for it; he was not a man given to games of chance.

No, it was certainty that he valued. He let the hem of the robe fall away and ran a hand across his weary eyes.

"We're not finished yet," he told the kai el'Sol.

"Jevri—"

"No. It *must* be perfect today."

Their eyes met; they both glanced away like shy children, not turned blades. Oh, they knew how to argue, at times like this, when no one was there to witness such impropriety. But not today.

Jevri knelt at the hem of the kai el'Sol and found his needle. The beadwork had already been glued into place, but he had had to be certain that the fall was perfect before he fastened with thread and needle these little repositories of sunlight.

He understood the importance of light at the Festival of the Sun.

For a long time—many years—he had tried to understand the puzzle of the Serra Carlatta's choice, for he knew, with some piqued pride, that he had been among the most favored of her serafs; certainly, the one most envied her by other Serras. In the meantime, he had cooked, swept, cleaned, and mended as the Radann Fredero el'Sol required, puzzling, always puzzling.

Until the morning that he saw his first Festival at his Ser's side. Others had eyes for the clansmen, for the combat, for the Serras, the wine, the food, and the Sun Sword. He had eyes for only one thing: the raiment that the Lord's Consort wore. It was splendid in its fashion, a work that was almost—almost—art.

And seeing it, he knew that he could better it, given only time and the proper materials. He had never made a dress so fine, although he was well capable of it, for such a dress was beyond ostentatious; only here, only upon this platform, in this company, could a Serra—the choice of the particular Serra did not concern him—truly shine, wife to the Lord for the Festival's stay.

Oh, it was selfish, and he knew it.

And he wondered, as his heart raced, if the Serra Carlatta understood what she had given him to. Because it was the Radann who decided what dress and what style was appropriate for the Lord's Consort.

It was important; it was so important that he had had to strain and work to prevent himself from blurting it like a common market seraf to his clansmen. But he did wait. And after the Festival's end, he asked for the only favor that he had ever asked. Asked with humility, as befit his station. Asked with grace. Asked with a plea that, try as he might, he could not keep out of his voice.

"Jevri, I am not a rich man. To do as you ask—to get you the material you require—would beggar me. And for what? A woman's *dress*?"

He had not said no.

Jevri had one weapon left him; he used it now. "Fredero, please."

Silence—a long, almost uncomfortable one. Two men, separated by birth and experience, and bound together by birth and experience, waited to see who would break it.

It was, of course, the Radann Fredero el'Sol. "This must be important. I've known you all my life, and you've never once called me by my adult name."

"I will never ask you for anything else again."

"Don't say that."

But he hadn't. Asked for anything, and certainly not anything as important.

He made his dress, scrimping and saving where he could without injuring the whole—this perfect, singular garment, this creation for the Lord's glory. And just under one year later, fingers near bleeding and eyes reddened by sleep's lack, he presented the garment to the Radann Fredero el'Sol, who in turn presented it to the Lord's Consort.

And the Lord's Consort wore the dress in marvel, in wonder, and in perfect glory, when she was presented to the clansmen. And to the first among clansmen: the Tyr'agar Markaso kai di'Leonne.

The Radann had never seen such an expression cross the Tyr'agar's face. But the Serra who had been chosen Consort was his eldest daughter, and she looked—she looked a thing beyond man, the very Consort made flesh for the Lord's Festival. He had—he, a clansman—reached out to touch the fabric of her skirt, where no other man would have dared, to sully it by giving it the *feel* of reality. But the wonder remained, and the smile that crept up the left corner of his mouth—for that was where his smile always started—was both reward for Jevri, and reward for his master.

Jevri made every dress for every Festival from that day on. And with each Festival, he outdid himself in the name of, and service of, the Radann Fredero el'Sol. The Radann Fredero par el'Sol. And the Radann Fredero *kai* el'Sol.

"Jevri?"

But he had never, before this day, given more than a cursory nod to the garments of the Radann.

"Jevri?"

He swore softly, swore to the seraf's god, swore at the seraf's god. His fingers *were* bleeding in the uneven light.

"Jevri, get help."

"No."

"Why? You've had help before." Fredero craned his neck to the side and down, attempting to catch a glimpse of his shadowed servant. "It doesn't have to be perfect. It just has to be finished."

Jevri started to argue and then looked at the flickering lamp; the oil was low. Had he truly been so long at so little? He stared down at his hands, shadows welled in the curves time had worn there revealing more than they concealed: He was not a young man, nor even one in the midst of life.

Age settled around his shoulders with a grip that could not be shaken. Nor would be.

"Yes," he told the kai el'Sol, urging his hands on but watching the progress of bent fingers as if they belonged to someone else.

"Good. I'll—"

"It has to be finished. By me."

"Jevri—"

Jevri had never been good with words, although he knew how to listen to nuance. He knew that among the women and the wives there were things that could be asked, and things that must never be questioned. As a seraf in service to the Serra Carlatta, he had had less chance to observe the way the men spoke, but he knew, nonetheless, that there were things that could never be said, fears that had no natural expression.

Not to a man of the clans.

Not to Fredero par di'Lamberto.

"Fredero. Please."

Silence, always this pause, this uneasiness. Anger would have been a welcome visitor, but between them there was none; not this eve. Nor was there fear, although fear sheltered in different places behind each man's words. There was resignation, a search for, and abandoning of, a dozen different phrases.

"What will you do?" The kai el'Sol said awkwardly.

"I? I will not serve the Radann par el'Sol, no matter what mantle he wears."

"Jevri—"

"I am not a seraf," the older man replied serenely. "And the choice will, this time, be fully my own."

"I see." Silence. "But have you—"

"Kai el'Sol, I will not speak of it. I will not think of it until it is time. You can worry if you like," he added tartly.

"Why thank you."

There was much that was familiar in the passage of time; the slow change in the tinge of the sky's hue; the lowering of the oil that somehow held the Lord's fire in the darkness of night, although it was liquid; the lengthening of shadows and the flickering of vision that accompanied sleep's lack.

But although he had often labored well into the Lady's hours, Jevri el'Sol, born kep'Lamberto, found no comfort in the task, for it was the first, and it was the last, and he knew that when the rays of Sun touched the farthest walls, the robes would not be all that he had hoped for.

He prayed to the Lady for strength and time.

But it was the Lord who answered, pushing the curtain of night away as was his right on this, the longest day of the year.

CHAPTER THIRTY-TWO

Eduardo kai di'Garrardi stood on the plateau. His cerdan had left and the man who would meet him in combat had not yet entered the field; he stood alone. The sun was high; the shadow he cast was shorter and squatter than he.

Sword's Blood had been retired from the field, and not unharmed, but the gashes across flank and foreleg were not deep, and in the gaining of those scars he had more than proved his worth to the clansmen who watched the penultimate battle. Let them talk in their scornful way about the small village that had been the stallion's price; he knew, from this day on, that they would remember the stallion's name when the village was scattered by raiders or worse.

And they would remember his rider.

What Tyr had entered the field of the Lord's Chosen while they held their title? What Tyr had dared to take the political risk, choosing instead to send their par—or, if brave, their kai—to the fight by which a true clansman made himself known?

He had been cautioned against it, but quietly, although he was not a man known for accepting the caution of the timid. But there was more to be won than a combat or two. More than the regard of the nameless clans who gathered in the heat of the high sun on this one day that combat, no matter how terrible the Lord's heat, could not be halted.

He turned his face into the breeze and saw the Flower of the Dominion as she blossomed beneath the blue of the open sky, and he offered her a bow and a wordless promise.

Fredero kai el'Sol was nowhere in sight; she would have seen him, no matter where he stood, for the Serra

Diora di'Marano knew how to look. If a fan's folds could protect her from the Lord's gaze, might it not protect her from the gaze of the merely mortal?

She wore gold as if gold were light, as if light were a thing of weight and solidity. Gold hung in strands that were old when her clan was founded, crossing and touching and twining in a heavy spill down pale silk. Gold bound her wrists, catching light and making of it a liquid thing, a warmth that was unmarred by Northern stones; gold sent the light scattering at every movement of every finger.

And upon her finger, like a binding, nestled among the heirlooms in the keeping of the Lord's Radann, three rings, three plain and unadorned rings, as new in their manufacture as the borrowed rings of the Lord's Consort were ancient.

The kai el'Sol had paused a moment when he offered her the rings of the High Festival, for her hands were already adorned. But he had no arguments to offer, and she no defense; it was as if the evening past had robbed them of the ability to speak in any way that was both meaningful and elegant. All that remained was the awkward hesitation of a man and a woman who do not know each other well enough to speak freely, but who know each other too well to be served by the musical syllables of social veneer.

She wondered, idly, if the Serra Teresa had noticed. Wondered, less idly, why it was that the Radann who stood guard were Samadar par el'Sol and Peder par el'Sol. Marakas was, like his kai, nowhere in evidence.

Perhaps, just perhaps, the strangest of the Radann intended to somehow save the life of the kai el'Sol. He was a healer born; it was his gift and curse. Just as the voice was hers. Perhaps, hidden, he thought to wait out the wrath of the General and catch the former Lambertan clansman by the thread of his life.

It was, she thought, very like Marakas.

He did not tend to the fallen on the Lord's field.

Upon that field, no healers were allowed.

The clansmen wanted a death.

Their desire was contained by the muted silence of their breaths and the slight rise of their shoulders, but it found voice in hands that strayed to—and remained

upon—the hilts of sheathed swords. Shoulder to shoulder,
men sat in their clans' groupings, their banners a wall or a
circle around the plateau. If wine or song or the charms of
the serafs the clansmen made available had kept the men
away for the first two days of the Challenge, none missed
the third—for on the third day matters of honor called
them, or matters of money, or both. On this day, the title
was decided.

The birds in the sky above, circling with black wings
spread the height of a man from wingtip to wingtip,
caught the wind and made of it a stable platform; they
floated, leisurely in their observance of the men below.

And perhaps, just perhaps, one could see such birds and
find them beautiful; one could see their flight and their
fall without expecting a death must presage it. Perhaps
one could see the clansmen watching and find them handsome and honor-bound; could see in the slight flare of
nostrils, in the narrowing of eyes and the intensity of
attention, no hint of blood-scent, no desire for the spoils
of the kill.

Diora could not remember a day when she did not
know what vultures did, and the knowledge robbed their
flight of beauty in her eyes, although if she studied them
carefully, and took care to ignore the revulsion that carrion eaters brought by their very nature, she could see
both power and grace in their lazy flight.

In the men, she saw death, but although she could
remember no innocence when it came to the flight of vultures, she could remember a time—one so removed it
came back to her unexpectedly and awkwardly, very
much the reminder of all the things she was not—when
she had seen things bright and shiny and expected that
there was mercy beneath the patina of power that wielded
sword and armor.

That wielded fire and the knowledge of fire.

She turned slightly, scanning the crowd that had gathered across the ring of the plateau, looking for the Radann
kai el'Sol.

She saw instead a Widan and his General, and her eyes
stayed a moment, surrounded as she was by the tension of
a coming kill. In all her hours of prayer, knees bent, eyes
upon the face of the moon in the rippling waters of the
Tor Leonne, no answer came to her for the one question

she asked, time and again—the one thing that she could not explain: Why had she been allowed to live? She was not a selfless woman, but had she a choice of lives to preserve, there was one—one single life—that she would have placed above her own. No choice was offered, and she, ringbound, oathbound, sheltering grief and rage behind her perfectly schooled face, was left without choice. But the *why* haunted her almost as strongly as the ghosts.

Her father was Widan. And if not for the General Alesso di'Marente, he would not have been a *powerful* man. What had he been, before the ascent of the man he called friend? Widan? No; less than that. Widan-Designate—a man born to power, with no will to use it. Who had given him the will, and when? When had he ceased to be—to be what her memory told her he *was*? When had he become just another dangerous man, another enemy in a pool of enemies too wide and too deep for the simple Leonne Tyr?

The corner of her lips did not dimple or turn downward; her face was her best mask and she wore it for the world to see.

He was not a stupid man. He knew that, having chosen this course, he could not choose another, not now; there could be no turning back. No backward glance.

Yet she thought she saw his eyes upon her before she lifted her fan with delicate grace and turned away, finding it easier to watch the combat for which the clansmen were assembled.

Finding it easier to watch a strange man's death at such a distance that the blood was just a trick of the light, a blur of color that might have easily been the workmanship of a weaver. The sun was at its height; the day was, of the long days in this year, the hottest, the brightest. The living man stopped a moment, lifting a weapon that caught the sun in such a flash it might have been pure light.

From the ground, an answering flash, but weaker; the fallen man was not yet dead, or had not yet accepted the fact. But his defense—such as it was—was meager, weak on a day when weakness itself was the worst of sins. Death was the winner's, to grant or to deny.

She knew that Eduardo di'Garrardi stood as the Lord's Chosen because of the relish with which the death was delivered to the clansmen who waited.

It was not the outcome that Alesso di'Marente desired. He turned to the Widan at this side and saw a frown that was, line for line, his own. It made him chuckle. "Not what we wanted, old friend."

"I fai· to see what you find amusing, Alesso. We need Garrardi as an ally—but a *Tyr'agnate* who has passed the Lord's test is a threat."

"Yes."

"You do not wear the crown yet. There are those who will try to acclaim the Tyr'agnate in your place."

"They will fail."

"Perhaps. If I had thought he would win, I would have—"

"Entered yourself? Or entered me?"

"You," was the ill-humored reply. "I saw you this morning, Alesso. Nothing Garrardi offered on the field could match it."

Sendari par di'Marano spoke with such inflectionless certainty that he might have been speaking of the weather, or of the harvest the season in his lands might bring. There was no intent to flatter; it was not his way. And because of it, Alesso was flattered.

"It is done," he told his oldest friend. "And we will abide by it. Decide what must be done to collar him if he chooses to rise above his station."

Sendari turned as the Radann made their way to where Eduardo kai di'Garrardi stood. Their formal robes wafted in the day's first strong breeze; it was as if the Lord himself chose to draw breath only at that moment. "There is a problem," he said, in as carefully neutral a tone as he used when speaking with the Sword's Edge.

It was the tone that Alesso least liked. "And that?"

"He has gained power today by gaining stature in the eyes of the clans. If I know Eduardo di'Garrardi, it is now that he will attempt to claim the prize that he was offered for our alliance." Before Alesso could speak, Sendari raised a hand. "It is clever, Alesso, give him that. He will come from the field anointed with the blood of weaker men, and he will approach the Lord's Consort as Champion, *as is his right.* Deny him, and he will take his stand against you before the close of the ceremony."

"Before," Alesso said coolly, "my rulership is confirmed by the Radann. I understand, old friend."

"Alesso," Sendari said, understanding well what lay beneath the words, "she is just a woman."

"*You* say that to *me*?"

The anger was back in the Widan's eyes; a cold flash that settled into stillness and distance.

"Do not offer me anger, Sendari. What will you say? That I cannot compare love for the daughter with love for the mother?" He caught the Widan's clenched fist. "Or will you say instead that what you had was love, and what I have is desire, that I am incapable of love?"

"Clansmen," the Widan said coolly, "do not speak of love." But the anger left his face as he retrieved his hand. "As you well know, it's a woman's word, and a woman's binding."

"Strong bonds, for all that."

"In the end, you won."

"Because in the end, she died." The sun was too hot, the day's glare too bright. "Very well, old friend," he said, his face grim and taut with the effort of this particular speech. "I will accept the Lord's judgment."

A Serra in the Dominion was no stranger to violence, but the violence was rarely that of open combat. Another man's blood, spread like an accident of color or a celebration of death, was almost like a man's sex; best left for men to boast about or of.

The Serra Diora was not to be so favored. This Festival was a man's festival, and this test, a man's test. That she sat in the position of honor was due to a man's choice; that she was finely adorned, perfectly outfitted, and completely visible, a man's decree. She could no more turn away from the Lord's Champion than she might have from her own husband when eyes that were not friendly watched; in public circumstance, the watcher decreed all by his presence. No matter that the privacy of the harem protected a different form of communication, allowed for greater liberty; safety was illusion, after all.

Where was the Radann kai el'Sol?

"Lady," the Tyr'agnate said, as he approached the Radann who stood, a slender human wall, before her. They had no choice but to turn to the side, and they faced each other like well-trained cerdan in the absolute silence.

"Tyr'agnate," she replied, acknowledging the respect—and the evident desire—in the single spoken word with a nod of the head.

He chose his ascent, stepping with care upon the man-made stairs that one had to climb in order to approach anything that the Lord claimed. His trail was dark, and as he drew near, Diora could see that not all of the blood was his enemy's. She hid her smile beneath the perfect fold of her lips.

But when he held out his hand, she very carefully closed her fan and laid it in his palm. She was rewarded with his smile, and it was both dark and lovely. The plateau spoke with the hushed approbation of the clansmen.

She rose, delicate and graceful, carrying the weight of the Lord's gold; the Lord's Champion offered her the hand that did not clutch her token. But she would not take it, for it was sticky now with drying blood and sweat. He grimaced as he looked at his empty hand, seeing it for the first time as a Tyr of the court and not a combatant.

"Your pardon," he said softly, so softly that it might not have reached her ears at all. But he came to stand beside her, and as he did, the hushed murmurs that walled the plateau became shouts. Light glinted off swords raised in salute; wind gave to the flight of flags the sound of applause.

The General Alesso di'Marente chose to greet them at this moment, climbing, as Eduardo had done before him, the steps of the dais unhindered.

The shouts grew and then dimmed as the significance of his approach became clear.

Some of the clansmen gathered here had crossed the threshold of the Tor Leonne proper for the first time; they were in the strength of their youth, and they had been summoned by Tyrs or Tors who understood the need for numbers at this Festival. But most had come, yearly, with their entourage. They had seen many combatants emerge victorious, and they had seen many Consorts rise to greet them.

But they had never seen, until this day, a clansman who

did not carry the Leonne blood in his veins join them upon the Lord's dais. Very, very few of the clansmen below did not recognize Alesso di'Marente, and even those who did not, understood what he attempted to claim by his presence.

Eduardo di'Garrardi's smile was smooth as steel. "General."

"Tyr'agnate. A most impressive display."

The Tyr's lazy smile was genuine; he was pleased. But flattery was not the reward that he had fought to receive. Nor was the Lord's favor. "Is that the Widan I see below?"

Alesso made no game of his response. "It is."

"I would speak with him. Now."

"As you wish. You are the Lord's Champion, Tyr'agnate."

"Yes."

"You will be content with the title and the . . . Serra."

Silence; Eduardo was heady from his victory, and the cries from the plateau were close enough that memory and action could not easily be separated. He did not reply.

The Widan Sendari par di'Marano walked stiffly and silently up the steps to the platform's height. There he joined the Marente General, making it clear to any and all where his loyalty lay. Eduardo could not mistake what the action meant; the Marano clan was known for their cunning and their caution, but when they chose to ally themselves, they had examined all avenues, and all foreseeable possibilities; they were steady; they saw far. A wise man gained much forsaking old allies at the right moment, and Sendari was a wise man—but Eduardo did not see the moment at hand that would sway the Widan.

Did he want to rule? He gazed at the gathered clans, and then at the General, stiff-lipped and cool under the sun's height. "A General," he said softly, "never knows the glory of the fight."

He was rewarded with the first smile that Alesso di'Marente had offered him, which is to say, he was not rewarded at all. "Do not play this game, Eduardo. Or play it," the General continued, his hand upon the hilt of his sword, "to its end."

"And you challenge me?"

"I neither challenge," the General said, "nor refuse one, if it is offered."

Eduardo di'Garrardi met the unblinking gaze of the man who should have ruled Marente. Alesso was the older of the two, and although the Tyr'agnate had the advantage of size, he had not passed the Lord's test unscathed. Still, his hand touched the hilt of his sword, and he smiled crookedly. The Garrardi sword had history; the Marente sword, none.

As if aware of the unspoken words, the General said, "Ah yes. *Ventera* is a blade with much history, some of it honorable. *Terra Feure* is a blade that will *make* history."

"Tyr'agnate. General." The Widan Sendari par di'Marano spoke quietly—and in a tone that was generally reserved for the young. "If you will play this game, may I respectfully suggest that you choose a different time for it?"

"Sendari—"

"Or you may, if you desire, play it *now*. But the clansmen wait, and they grow impatient. We are already walking on treacherous ground, and our allies are not those who would gracefully ignore weakness in our own court." Although he seemed to pause for breath, the pause was illusory, for both the kai Garrardi and the par Marente had words to say, but it was the Widan who spoke. "Your loss would hurt us," he said to Eduardo, "and yours. None here would benefit by it.

"The war cannot be called today—although it should be. We have no choice but to wait until the passing of the Festival Moon—and the Shining Court wishes that practice to end *here;* to disappoint them poses a risk that you should both understand. In between, we must hold power against any Tyr or Tor who thinks to take it, and the Dominion, from the men who are best fit to rule it. We may gather and build our armies; we may build those structures that will support a long campaign against the Imperials, should it become one.

"Tyr'agnate, for my part I am willing to honor our bargain, and before the assembled clans, I will declare the Serra Diora di'Marano the keep of the kai Garrardi, in the Lord's name. More than that is beyond me; as you well know the rites cannot be performed on the Lord's Day.

even suggest it, and the Radann will show you how little
armed they are.

"Either you will accept this in good faith, or you will
not. We—both of us—do not have the luxury of a
leisurely decision."

The Tyr'agnate met the eyes of the Widan before
glancing briefly at the shuttered gaze of the General. Then
he turned to the Serra who stood, in perfect silence, at his
side, and for her, he reserved the brunt of his attention.

"Done," he said at last, and softly. "But you will
declare this thing before the Radann offer the General the
Lord's crown."

"Of course," Sendari replied. He offered his daughter
his hand, and she took it without hesitation.

And as she did, he saw them: the three rings. The oath
rings. He froze, and then met her eyes, and he saw in the
darkness there a fire akin to Alesso's fire, a steel as sharp,
or sharper. He could not hold her gaze for long, although
her gaze held answers, and he was Widan.

He had spoken truth: There was little time. His grip was
harsher than he intended, but it was always thus: the
things that one feared or valued—or both—were always
clutched tightly, in caution or care.

She was his perfect daughter; she was Teresa's perfect
niece. She neither noticed the ferocity of his grip, nor
cared. The Flower of the Dominion—the Serra that each
and every clansman gathered knew had once belonged to
the kai Leonne—stood as tall as her diminutive height
allowed. That she might be seen.

And that she might, being seen, be known as a worthy
Consort to the Lord of the Sun. A hush followed as the
father raised the daughter's gold-laden hand; a hush that
held expectancy, a desire for the *rightness* of the moment.

"I call the Lord to witness," Sendari said, his voice surprisingly strong. "That this, the Serra Diora, is of Marano,
and she is blood of my blood, and she is wholly mine by
birth, and no other clan has lawful claim to her.

"And I call the Lord to witness that this, the Lord's
Chosen Champion, the Tyr'agnate Eduardo kai di'Garrardi,
has proved himself worthy, in the eyes of the clans of
Annagar, and of the Lord of the Sun, of the keep of the
Serra who has been the Lord's Consort.

"Therefore I, Sendari par di'Marano, grant the keep of

my daughter, Diora di'Marano, to Eduardo kai di'Garrardi, such keep to be consummated upon the appropriate rites and observances, and further grant that all children borne to that union are of the Garrardi clan by birth and blood, and that Marano shall exert no claim to such offspring."

It was, Alesso thought, a statement worthy of Sendari; no simple sentence when addressing a crowd where a complicated one would do.

"Who will bear witness?"

The clansmen across the plateau roared with a single breath.

"Then let it be witnessed, and let no man of honor revoke what has been in honor offered to witnesses such as these!"

The cheering was very like the roar of the wind across the open plains.

The Tyr'agnate bowed, and then, unsheathing his sword—the Garrardi sword, with its subtle curve and its obvious weight—he turned to the General Alesso di'Marente and plunged the point of the weapon into the wooden planks. There was an audible crack, and many a swordsmith flinched at the noise, although they were probably the only men there to worry about the stress upon the sword, and not the stress upon the Dominion— for by his action, the Tyr'agnate Eduardo di'Garrardi proclaimed the General his rightful liege lord.

The General stood his ground a moment, that the clansmen who were less quick of wit might have a chance to understand what had occurred. Then he gripped the haft of the sword and levered it out of the wooden platform. He strained; it was not an easy motion.

Only Sendari was close enough to see the way his eyes narrowed, and even if Eduardo had seen the slight contraction of lids he might not have understood how close he came to receiving the sword back, edge first. But Alesso's temper had long since, like all else in his life, come under his dominion; he was graceful as he returned the weapon to this, the first and now the most famous of his servants.

There were murmurs; there would be dissent. They expected no less. But the murmurs were weaker than the breeze on the plateau, and the chants of the Radann—for they had begun their interminable song, although at what exact moment he did not remember. He was pleased to find they were to prove useful for something this Festival.

They approached, three of the four par el'Sol who served the kai; the kai el'Sol was not present. Nor was he expected to be now, although he should have been witness to the resolution of the Lord's test; his place was by the waters of the Tor Leonne. The par el'Sol were granted the right and privilege of crowning the Lord's Champion—but only the kai el'Sol could give the power of rulership over the Lord's Dominion to a clansman.

"General," the Radann Peder par el'Sol said, bowing with genuine respect. "The time has come."

"Par el'Sol. Lead, in the Lord's name, and in the Lord's name, I will follow."

At the head of the procession the Radann par el'Sol walked; they wore robes of pure white, with gold borders and gold collars, each embroidered in the form of the sun ascendant with eight rays, all of perfect fire. They seemed a brotherhood of dignity and silence, although their swords had a history as long as the Garrardi sword, and names as venerable. Alesso di'Marente had never seen them drawn, but he knew their names; what clansmen did not? Five swords had been crafted for the Radann by the Lord, and if they were not as fine as the Sun Sword, they were more jealously guarded, for the Sun Sword alone had its methods of destroying the hand of one not meant to wield it.

Samadar el'Sol wore *Mordagar,* Samiel el'Sol, *Arral* and Peder el'Sol, *Saval.* Marakas el'Sol bore *Verragar,* the least of the five, and the Radann kai el'Sol, *Balagar,* the greatest. It was said that when these five swords were joined, no enemy of the Lord could stand against them—and it was said that when they fought alongside the Sun Sword, the Sun Sword granted them a measure of its power.

Myth and legend—folklore which had never been, would never be, proved. And what was proof to any but one Widan-trained? Something cold and hard, a weapon. And a weapon's only place in the heart was to still it.

He joined the Radann in their long, slow walk, feeling, as he followed them, the weight of the Dominion's history. This was the triumphal march, and in truth he was triumphant, but he felt out of step with the Lord's will, and it disturbed him greatly. Markaso kai di'Leonne had been, and would have continued to be, a weak Tyr; a man with more control over his harem and his serafs than he could ever exert over either his Tyrs or his enemies. He had called one war in his life, and failed to win it, losing both precious land and face in the process. No doubt he would have been forced to call another, and that, too, he would have lost.

Alesso did not intend to lose any game he played, be it war or no. But he did not have the authority of time and tradition. He did not have the blood.

What of it? He squared his shoulders, and felt the new skin pull across the breadth of his chest. Beneath armor, beneath silk, beneath things visible. It was enough. He brought his hand to the hilt of *Terra Feure,* and he followed the slowly growing shadows of the Radann.

The path that wound in and around the Tor Leonne took on an edge of clarity that it had never had. His shadow was sharp as he walked the winding footpath, seeing each upturned leaf, each blossoming flower, each plant that, uprooted from its desert clime, still sought to deny the sun's heat by closing its armored petals, before he realized what the flowers were: Nightblossom. Odd, to see the Lady's flowers in the citadel of the Lord, on this Festival day. He frowned, thinking that serafs would have to be found and dispatched, if serafs were indeed the ones who had chosen so poorly. If Serras, then he would tread more carefully.

The waters of the Tor Leonne opened up as the procession reached the peak of the path. The path itself had widened, and stonework, tended and kept free of the creeping plants that alone seemed to require no work, had been laid. No natural wonder here, no hidden dell or quiet recess. This was the seat of power, and in the Dominion, power did not hide.

But the face it wore was not painted and pretty; it was not overly ornate. To the east of the lake was the dwelling which the Tyr'agar claimed as his own; it was recessed into hill and surrounded by trees, but it stood, thick-beamed and pale, as the most important edifice by the lake. The roof's wind chimes caught the breeze and made of it something delicate and soothing as they danced above the treetops. Elegance and simplicity were the rules of the Tor Leonne, and they were followed nowhere so closely as here. Gold? The light of the sun was brighter. What need of color, of banner, of flag? No man could mistake this building—or the man who dwelled within it—for anything other than it was. The home of the Tyr'agar towered above all else.

But it was not to the Tor Leonne that the procession went, although it slowed in its passage in silent respect. The edifice was, officially, empty of all but its ghosts. And ghosts held no sway beneath the height of the sun.

There was the platform by which the waters could be viewed in the dawn's light; the platform by which the moon could best be seen as its face rippled in pleasant reflection; the platform by which the waters, under the open sun, could be seen beneath the cover of trees that just—barely—obeyed the edicts of height.

The procession came to none of these, but instead followed the path to the rocky shore of the lake itself. There were stones here that were smooth as glass, but harder, and stones that were larger across than a prone horse. But there were smaller stones and beneath them sand, and the lake lapped their edges in the silence of the day.

Standing, his feet a sword's edge from the water, was a lone man. And he wore sunlight as if it were raiment, and as he turned to greet them the lake caught his reflection. Above his brow, light glittered, and behind his head; his hair was the dark brown-black of the Annagarian clans, except where light touched and streaked it. Across his chest, burning like fire, the sun ascendant; across his wrists, for as he lifted his hands, the sleeve of his robe fell away, the white tracery of fire, of the fire's test.

The Radann par el'Sol—all of them—fell to their knees at once, their movements neither graceful nor practiced. Alesso understood this because his own knees bent in reflex, as if someone had placed firm hands on either shoulder and pushed him forcefully down.

To the feet of the Radann kai el'Sol. He rose as the kai el'Sol nodded, and he approached this man, this sudden stranger.

The General was not a man who liked surprise.

From behind came the Lord's Chosen Champion, the bloodied and unbowed Eduardo di'Garrardi. At his side, taking care not to bloody the intricate, perfect dress she wore, was the Lord's Consort, the Flower of the Dominion. The Radann par el'Sol receded, for they remained on their knees as these three, the man who would be ruler and the two Chosen of the Lord, stepped forward.

In his raised hands, the kai el'Sol carried the simple crown with which the Leonne Tyrs had been proclaimed since the founding. The Northern crowns were ornate, and they were golden, and they were covered in etching and gem work and runes. This crown, this emblem was different: It was of one piece, and it was not fashioned of gold. It was made of steel, and in shape it looked exactly like a sword might had the blade been blunted and turned in on itself, in a circlet.

This was the only crown that Leonne the Founder would wear, and it had been protected from the ravages of time by the arts of Voyani long dead. It should have looked ridiculous, and perhaps to foreign eyes it did. But the clansmen were a better breed.

"General Alesso di'Marente," the Radann kai el'Sol said, his voice carrying far in the hushed silence of lapping water and stillness. "The Lord's law *is* law. The rulership of the Tor Leonne has passed, kai to kai, by the bloodline that the Lord decreed.

"But where there is no living member of the line, the Radann must deliberate and decide. The Hand of the Lord holds the Sword, and it seeks no man too weak to bear the crown in these times. There is," he said, his eyes dark and unblinking, "a darker time ahead than any of us have yet seen."

Alesso's eyes narrowed as he met the Radann's flat gaze, hearing beneath the words all of the accusations that the kai el'Sol had never dared—and would never dare—to make.

Or so he had thought. Yet this man, this man was the very Radann, the wielder of *Balagar,* and until this moment, beneath the open sky, with the end of his long struggle balanced between two hands, he had forgotten it.

It was not his way to make such a mistake.

"The Lord's will," Alesso said softly, so softly that the words carried only to the Radann and the two who stood beside him.

"The Radann have made their decision. Step forward, Alesso par di'Marente. Step forward and receive this, the crown of Leonne. Receive it in glory, and understand the weight that it places upon you."

Alesso was not a short man, but in such ceremony— and only in this one—he was not required to kneel to receive the benediction of the Radann.

Fredero kai el'Sol bent, and with so much care the gesture seemed oddly gentle, he lowered the crown into the waters of the Tor Leonne. His lids closed over dark eyes; his brow creased. He whispered the words of the water, and then he rose.

"Step forward, General."

Alesso di'Marente took a breath and then stepped into the waters of the lake. They were cool, but not cold, as they ringed his ankles with ripples that traveled into the stillness at the heart of the water.

Water.

The kai el'Sol had to reach, but Alesso did not bow his head to accommodate the Radann; instead, he sought the sun as drops of water trickled down steel to touch his brow, his cheeks, his eyes.

This was his moment.

"Tyr'agar," the kai el'Sol said. He turned, then, and before Alesso could reply, he cried out, "The Radann have chosen General Alesso par di'Marente as their Tyr. To him, the Tyr'agnate will pledge their allegiance—and from him, receive their commands.

"From this day forward, let there be the clan Alesso, and let this man, Alesso the Founder, be known as Tyr'agar until his death. Thus, the will of the Radann!"

There was silence, and then, beneath it, a murmur.

The Tyr'agar, Alesso the Founder, turned; the sun was at his back and above his head. Clansmen, one by one, drew sword as they met his gaze; the quiet of the lake was disturbed, again and again, by the sound of metal against metal; the unsheathed sword.

The first of these clansmen was also the most powerful: Tyr'agnate Jarrani kai di'Lorenza. He stepped forward, leaving the semicircle that had made a ragged wall across the flat stones and the sparse shore. His sword was *Bane,* dressed in ceremonial scabbard until the moment of the crowning.

"Tyr'agar," the Tyr'agnate said, and pushed the sword, point down, into a space between the rocks. It was a gentle movement, one unlikely to damage either sword or pride, as different from the gesture of the Lord's Chosen Champion as the Lady from the Lord.

"Tyr'agnate," the Tyr'agar replied.

Jarrani rose and smiled. "The long road is not so harsh a road now."

Alesso's grin was fierce. "No. Your Tors?"

"They come," Jarrani said. "All but four."

The four, he would deal with later. The Tyr'agnate stood at the water's edge while the Tor'agars and Tor'agnati who owed him loyalty and service made their trek to the water's edge. To the only man not of the Lord's Radann who had the right, by law, to stand within the waters themselves. Twenty-six.

The Oertan clansmen came next; there were twenty-eight. Of the Mancorvan clansmen, he had a handful, but among those, the clan Marrani, Tor'agar, and so of import. And of Averda, he had more, but they were so close to seraf in rank they served him only by what their presence said to the others. That even the common and the lowly were less afraid of their Tors than they were of the new Tyr'agar.

As the last of the clansmen retrieved his sword and returned to the rocks, Alesso di'Marente smiled. His shadow had grown long with the passage of time, for this ceremony was no small and trivial affair; each clansman had to meet his eyes, and see in them the power that Markaso kai di'Leonne—the last of the Leonne Tyrs—had never truly possessed.

Still, if it was triumph, it was also grueling; he wore light armor, as befit a warring clansman, and it trapped the warmth of the sun too well. The heat was lessened by the touch of the water.

And then it was taken away completely as the Radann kai el'Sol spoke again.

"The Radann," the kai el'Sol said, "have chosen." He bent, placed both hands into the waters of the Tor Leonne, and when he raised them he carried a scabbard, one rich and fine and unmistakable.

Alesso cursed him without need for words; he had

waited until the ceremony's end, so that he might be certain that each and every clansman—or woman—of significance had gathered to bear witness.

The gasp of the gathered crowd was followed by the silence of held breath, of inability to draw breath. "But the Lord has not.

"Tyr'agar, will you not take up the Sun Sword, as the Lord of the Sun has decreed all Tyrs *must* do? Will you not let the Lord speak?"

The lilies floated upon the surface of the waters behind the shining back of the Radann kai el'Sol, theirs the only motion in the stillness. Light, pale in color, they rested always above the water, never in it, yet the two could not be separated.

Diora ceased to breathe. The lightness that came with breath's lack made her feel like a lily upon the surface of the world. The kai el'Sol had told her that he would present the Sun Sword, and she knew voices well enough to hear the truth in his words. But in her mind's eye, in the privacy of thought, she had seen the Sword brought to the lake by servitors, as it was always brought; she had seen the Sword presented, almost as afterthought, a reminder to the clansmen of the one thing that the General lacked: the blood.

Subtlety was the way of a Serra, by necessity; it was not the way of a Lambertan. Not this man. She felt fear, and tried to wrap it around herself like a shawl; tried to grip and cling to it as if it were the skirts of her mother, and she a child.

Because she stood this close to the only action that she had conceived of for every waking hour of every day since the slaughter, and she could not afford to lose all fear, because without fear, there was no caution.

And without caution . . .

Her hands caught the light as they trembled, and she stared at the things that bound her: three simple rings.

Silence stretched, unbroken until the Radann Peder par el'Sol stood forward. "Kai el'Sol," he said softly, "you overstep yourself. The Lord's truest test of rulership has always been the warrior's path, and it is clear to all assembled here that *this* Tyr'agar rules because of his strength, where the last fell because of his weakness.

"Or do you claim that the Lord's true choice was a man who died without fight or cost in a *single evening's* slaughter? The Radann were chosen *by* the Lord. Our choice is the only choice. There is no other."

But the kai el'Sol was implacable in the face of Peder's words; he met the silent death in Alesso's eyes without flinching.

"The Sun Sword," the Tyr'agnate Jarrani kai di'Lorenza said, entering a fray that could not be resolved with weapon skill, his voice loud enough to carry but somehow calm enough that he did not appear to be shouting, "is myth. It is a part of the Leonne legend, as is the crown. You'll note," he said, with a wryness that held no warmth, "the crown rests upon the General's head in far more fitting a fashion than it ever sat upon Markaso di'Leonne's."

"The Tyr'agar has chosen to play the games of the Radann; he has followed the rules that you have set. He has paid his respect to the will of the Lord—and more—by leading armies rather than cowering behind the safety of stone walls in 'worship.'

"He is not beholden to you, kai el'Sol. Both the Tyr'agar and the kai el'Sol wear the sun ascendant, in full blossom. In the Lord's eyes, you are equals; you will not order him to perform to your will."

"It is not *my* will," the kai el'Sol said, untouched by the open edge of the Tyr'agnate's words. "It is the Lord's will. And I note, Tyr'agnate, that the crowning, which is also part of the 'Leonne legend,' was of the utmost import to the Tyr'agar. The legend is a body, and it *is* alive; you cannot cleave off the arm or the leg and say that it is the same as the whole because it is flesh."

"Have I been struck down, kai el'Sol?" the newly crowned Tyr'agar asked. "Have the winds come to bear me away? I am not a child. The clansmen gathered here are not children. We are not to be frightened by the partisan politics of a fool."

"And that is your answer?"

"It is."

"The Sword is a sword; it is significant because it is a symbol of office," Jarrani kai di'Lorenza said coldly.

There was a murmur in the crowd, a mixture of approbation and disapproval, of encouragement and fear. For there were men who were of the same mind as the Lorenzan Tyr'agnate. History for such men seemed to be a thing of the past, always of the past; only things witnessed were real.

Fredero, born of Lamberto, turned to face the clansmen of Annagar for the last time. Thinking, oddly, that it would have been nice to see Mareo one more time. That it might have been nice if Jevri kep'Lamberto—Jevri el'Sol—had been of high enough rank that he might join the clansmen and be present for this last of performances; this singular bow. Or that it might have been nice to have the opportunity to apologize—yet again—for his shortness in the early hours of morning; the robes that had been wrung, bead by bead, out of the hands of the reluctant servant, had been far more than Fredero thought he could ask in so short a time.

What might it have been like, a life like Mareo's, with a wife at his side, and a kai?

And then he remembered the kai's loss, and he was still.

It is time, he told himself, but his hands shook. He was ready, but he was not ready, and he balanced upon this edge for a moment longer.

Until he met the eyes of the Serra Diora di'Marano. The Serra Diora en'Leonne. The Lord's Consort. In finery she was second only to Fredero, both of them clothed by the genius of Jevri. In strength, in determination, he thought her second to none. Almost, he bowed.

And she surprised him. Surprised them all.

Because she *did* bow, lowering her fan to expose her face to the kai el'Sol.

Serra Diora di'Marano had from Fredero kai el'Sol all that she required, but she was speechless. Voiceless. Such a gift as he had given her he had given freely; not even her father had ever offered so much. And her father had never been a man of the kai el'Sol's political stature.

She did not tell herself that Fredero kai el'Sol gave her this pretty act of treachery because he knew his days were numbered. It wasn't true. She could see that clearly. His convictions alone had brought him to the Radann, and his convictions held him now; they were such that she thought, had he made a different choice, he might have met the same end. No Lambertan man could escape what he was, after all.

The Lambertans had always been loyal.

Oh, she heard the murmurs. She listened to the steel beneath the very thin veneer of the Tyr'agnate's words, and she found its power persuasive. But no matter how he—or the Tyr'agar—might try to gloss over the truth, it had been made clear: that he did not dare to take the Sun Sword.

It would do him some damage.

And the words that she had practiced, in secret prayer, in fantasy, and in tearless anger, would do the rest. It would not be his death though he deserved it. But it was the damage that she, a widowed Serra, could do, and she had worked this long month for no other goal. Yet before she could speak, the kai el'Sol turned from her, to the restless crowd.

"I have served the Lord, and serve him still, in the only way I can.

"These men tell you that they will not see the Sword raised because they do not wish to play *my* games. I play no game. If there is a man among you who feels that my tenure as kai el'Sol has been unworthy of the Lord—unworthy of the *clans*—let him speak now."

The silence was unbroken, although Alesso's face was as white as the sun's full glare.

"The Lord has his laws, and they were broken once before. And in that break, the darkness found purchase in lands where the Sun's might reigns. There are reasons for the laws that he has made, *and the Lord makes no exception.*

"The Tyr'agar of the Dominion, by the laws of the Lord, *is* the man who can wield the Sun Sword. Not a man worthy of the title Lord's Champion; not a man worthy of the title General; not a man whose prowess in battle is unmatched or unmatchable. It is not power, not service, and not loyalty that defines this law. Do you allow your serafs to decide to serve or disobey at their own whim, and through the merits of their own wisdom?

"We *are* the Lord's servants. We obey the Lord's will. He makes no exception.

"I offer this as proof." And to her horror, Fredero kai el'Sol gripped the Sun Sword firmly by the hilt.

And drew it.

She stepped forward, the motion involuntary, and Eduardo di'Garrardi gripped her arms, drawing her back. She could not struggle without losing all dignity, all power; she stilled at once, and the Tyr'agnate was forced to release her.

The Radann par el'Sol—all of them—watched in tight-lipped fascination. And she realized, as she looked at their set faces, that not a single one of them was surprised.

Nor were they surprised when the Radann kai el'Sol began to burn. But by the reflected fire in the eyes of Marakas par el'Sol, she knew that he alone grieved.

The fire was not one that came from without; she saw it first in his eyes, and second between his lips as he opened his mouth to draw breath, or to scream, or both. She wanted a good death for him, for he had had the strength to choose this death, but there was only the reality of fire, and she knew—as all the clansmen did—that the fire burned from the heart out. That all that would be left of this, a man of honor, was ashes that the winds would scatter forever.

Thus, the Lord's law.

It seemed to go on forever, this burning, this terrible fire. She thought that it would, for if the fire first consumed the heart, it was a burning that must, by its nature, be without end, for his heart seemed vast and boundless.

But the legends must lie, for the fire blossomed from his chest, devouring flesh, emptying his body of what little life might remain within it. Shining raiment became a garment of flame, and then a thing of ash, a thing without shape. The waters boiled a moment, steaming with the heat of the unnatural flame.

With no hands to support it, the Sun Sword fell, unsheathed, into the waters of the Tor Leonne.

Lady, Lady be merciful. Keep him from the winds, who takes this step in your service. Lady show mercy. Lady, please.

She almost forgot the words that she had come this far to speak, so intent was the prayer. But she was a Serra, and she was Diora, and she was the Flower of the Dominion, grieving for her dead in the only way she knew how.

Before the last of the flames had consumed even the crystal with which the kai el'Sol's robes had been beaded, she walked into the waters of the Tor Leonne. Eduardo di'Garrardi could not stop her, nor the Tyr'agar, nor the man who had been her father; they were transfixed.

To stand in the lake itself was a crime, but she stood, for the Festival's Height had not yet passed and on this day she was still the Consort of the Lord of the Sun.

Hands shaking, she knelt—or so it first appeared. But she had not stepped into the waters to kneel; she merely bent to retrieve.

The flat of the Sun Sword rested in her palms as she brought it out of the water's cradle. "I am Serra Diora di'Marano, the Lord's Consort," she said, pitching her voice so it carried the width and length of the Tor Leonne, stretching her abilities so that she might clearly be heard by not only clansmen, but serafs and Serras and those who tended the grounds. "And I say to you, clansmen all, that I was promised, in the eyes of the Lord, to the man who would be Tyr. Where the kai el'Sol has given his life, I give less, for he was a man of honor, and I am a simple Serra. But in honor of the laws of the Lord, and in honor of the memory of Ser Illara *kai* di'Leonne, I say to you that I will never survive to marry a lesser man—a man who cannot wield *this* Sword."

She turned to Alesso and Eduardo and Jarrani, wielding the Sword although she never once touched its hilt.

Eduardo's anger was instantaneous, but quenched—slightly—by the pallor of Sendari's suddenly aged face. "A Serra does not choose her husband," he said, his voice a growl. "You have developed too fine a notion of yourself, little Serra, if you feel that you may dictate to *us*."

"And you," she said coolly, "have developed too little esteem if you feel that you cannot meet the challenge of a simple Serra."

"Enough, Garrardi. You demean yourself," Jarrani said, beneath his breath. His eyes, as he met the unblinking gaze of the diminutive Serra who held the Sun Sword, were dark and clear. "You will revoke that vow. Now." He would have taken a step forward, but it would have carried him into the lake itself.

"No, Tyr'agnate, I will not."

"Sendari."

The Widan shook his head, almost wordless. "Na'dio . . ."

"Force is only one form of strength," she said evenly. "There are others."

Alesso was like the Sword itself: Steel. But he stepped where Jarrani could not, for he wore the crown, and the waters were not forbidden him.

She turned then, for the shadows the sun cast once again started to lengthen. "Clansmen of Annagar, I appeal to you, for yours is the power, and mine the supplication. If you will it, I will remain di'Marano until one of these three men can in honor and truth draw this sword from its scabbard. **You know that any woman of honor cannot dishonor her husband's memory by taking a lesser man in his stead. Lend me your support. Tell the Tyrs that you have heard the Lord's Consort, and you find her words fair.**"

Kneeling, she plunged her hands into the water, that their shaking might not be seen. But when she rose again, she drew from the Lake of the Tor Leonne the Sun Sword's scabbard. With perfect grace, although both sword and scabbard seemed unwieldy in her delicate hands, she joined these two. But she did not rise.

The clansmen did. Their voices carried her words, filling the hollows of the gently sloped hills, removing, temporarily, all the silence behind which a man might hide.

The Flower of the Dominion for the Tyr of the Dominion.

She faced Alesso without so much as a smile.

And then she turned once again to the clansmen, but not before she met her father's gaze, and held it, and saw in it his knowledge of a truth that he had never seen before: that she was Alora's daughter.

And that she bore Teresa's blood.

CHAPTER
THIRTY-THREE

Moonlight. Stars. Pale reflection on water that would not be still. He saw all of these things with new eyes. Saw all of these things without seeing.

He had won, and he had lost, and it was the loss that was the freshest wound. At his side, as silent as the reflection across the waters, but darker and humbler, the only man not of his kin that he counted friend: Sendari di'Marano, Widan. Father.

The sun's height was as far away as it could be; the darkness carried all of the sky with its weight and its freedom. "Cortano?"

"Beside himself with rage."

"She *is* your daughter," Alesso said. "And if anyone's kin could outsmart the Sword's Edge, it would be yours." He said it with affection, but there was no answering smile, no chuckle, no wry grin. Just darkness and silence.

There was much to be angry about, certainly. They had all been bested by a woman. They had seen to their enemies within the court; they had taken precautions and caused all of the right deaths. Only Cortano had seen a glimmer of danger in the song of a willful girl, and he had seen it late; she was already the Lord's Consort, and guaranteed of His protection by the kai el'Sol.

The kai el'Sol.

Garrardi made it clear—before retreating to the pavilion which served as his home when he chose to grace the Tor Leonne with his presence—that political concerns were not his concerns; he would have Sendari abide by his given word. Cortano and Jarrani argued against him, in a terse, short way; they knew, as Alesso and Sendari did, that by her actions this Festival, Diora di'Marano— Diora en'Leonne—had given herself a role as vital to the

Anngarian Tyr'agar as either the crown which graced the Tyr'agar's brow or the Sword which he dared not wield.

Throughout the argument, Sendari had been uncharacteristically silent; he was silent now; the water lapping against small rocks made more noise than he.

"Tell me," Alesso said.

The Widan stared at the waters a long time before answering; long enough that Alesso thought he would not. But when he spoke, he said, "She will never be yours, Alesso."

There was no possessive anger, no heat, in the words, no parental protectiveness. He spoke as Widan, cool and distant. Alesso grimaced. "Am I that obvious?"

"Is it obvious that you think you can make this work in your favor? Is it obvious that, as you intend to wield the Sun Sword at the end of this war, you are not nearly as angry as you should be?" Sendari snorted. His exasperation was as close as he had yet come to humor since the close of the Festival.

"I see."

"Alesso," the Widan said, the exasperation leaving his face and taking the momentary warmth with it, "I know my daughter now. She will never be yours. What she wants, and why she wants it—I cannot fathom. But she works against us. And it is not in furtherance of her goals; I believe her goal *is* to oppose us."

"And what would you have us do?"

Sendari was silent. At last he said, "We have been so long at the work of the Lord that I have forgotten the moonlight."

"Sendari—"

The Widan turned to his friend in the darkness, and Alesso took a step back as he saw, in the moon's light, the lines of Sendari's face.

"Go," he said, "and seek the Lady's solace. I will be waiting, and I will still be Tyr'agar."

"And is it enough?"

"To be Tyr?" Alesso shrugged and turned back to the lake that was now his most prized possession. "I don't know, old friend," he said softly. "I don't know."

The shrine was not neglected, but neither was it well tended; the serafs had been instructed to stay their hand until the Festival—and the attention—of the Lord had passed. Tucked away in a corner made of trees and tall rocks, the small monument of weathered stone stood at the northernmost part of the lake; here, the Tyr'agar and his family came to pay the Lady her due.

Sendari found the steps, built into earth and greenery, that led to the shrine, but not without difficulty; the lamp he carried was a pale orange glow, and his eyes—his eyes could not easily discern what was path and what decoration that led nowhere.

He felt betrayed by Diora.

And he felt as if he were her betrayer.

Both of these, he thought dispassionately, were true. Oh, not by the law of the Dominion; in the Dominion's law, she was guilty, and there was no mitigating circumstance that allowed a daughter to act not only against her father's wishes, but against her father himself. But the Dominion's law was not the law of the heart, not the law of the Lady, and it was to the Lady's shrine that he now repaired.

Sendari, give me your word that you will be as you are, for it is the man that you are that I love. Tell me that you will not seek the Widan's title, the Widan's art.

I promise. Alora. What word I have, I give you.

There were no words that could be said that could cut a man as deeply as his own. They were his words; he had walked away from them, thinking that he could just disentangle himself from the past, that he could leave it behind. But the words were a weave, and their mesh was of a thin, fine mettle; they pulled and cut.

Na'dio . . .

Father, will you always love me?

Always.

What did it mean? What was *always*? Was it significant that it was only the child that had asked the question, and only to the child that he had given the word? He set the lamp on a stair a moment and ran his hand over his eyes; he was getting old, to see so poorly. To see so much so poorly. Had he left her, or had she left him? For he was not the father of her youth, nor she the daughter of his memory.

Why? Why, Na'dio?

He picked up the lamp and continued the slow climb.

But when he reached the shrine, and stood beneath the peaked roof that protected the altars, he saw that he was not to be alone beneath the Lady's Moon.

The Serra Teresa di'Marano stood in the shadows cast by another lamp, almost as if waiting. For him. He wanted to withdraw, but he froze a moment, or perhaps drew breath too sharply; she turned.

"Sendari."

He gestured, sharply, the mage-light crackling from his hands as he struggled for focus. She did not flinch; her expression, the epitome of neutrality, allowed for no display of fear or worry. Or perhaps she knew him too well. A silence descended around them that would not be broken by any listener, casual or otherwise, who did not possess the art, and the craft, of the Widan.

"Teresa."

It was always tangled, this meeting of kin. He felt that he had never liked his sister, that he had, in fact, hated her. But she *was* his sister, and blood of his blood, and he could not easily walk away from her. Just as he could never have killed Adano. It was a weakness.

A terrible weakness.

"Sendari," she said again. "I did not expect to see you here again."

Did he hear too much in her words?

"This is not a game, Teresa."

"Oh, but it is. Because it is war, and men of power play at war as if it were a game that requires everything they can give it."

"And women?"

"There are no women of power in the Dominion," she said softly. As if it were fact. As if she believed it.

He wanted to strike her. Instead, he set the lamp upon the altar, illuminating the carvings across its face. These were contemplation carvings, circles and spheres and patterned mandalas whose whole purpose was to give concentration in the place of anxiety. Or anger. Or fear.

"How long?" he said, staring at the surface of the rock. It was more giving than the face of his sister. "How long have you known?"

Her silence was too long; he glanced up quickly, furtively, and saw that she was paler, if no less composed. But she did not lie to him.

"Since the Festival of the Moon, Sendari. The Festival in which you chose to forsake your vows to Alora en'Marano." She, too, looked down. "I would have told you, brother."

"And you did not?"

"No." She started to speak, and then fell silent; he saw a glimmer of anger, and something that might have been guilt. They did not expose themselves to each other. Or rather, she did not expose herself to him. He knew that her gift told her what lay beneath his words—all the anger, the fear, the lies, if he chose to attempt them.

"Why, Teresa? Why did she do this? She must have known what it would cost."

Her eyes widened as he spoke, and then her face softened slightly, losing the quality of edge that made her seem so like a fine weapon. "You could ask her," she told him quietly. "I believe that she would answer, if you ever chose to ask."

Silence. Then, "I chose to ask you."

"And if I answer, as I see fit, you will answer a question I pose of you?"

"Perhaps."

"What would you have done, had a man you trusted been responsible for the death of Alora?"

He started to answer, and then he stopped. Thinking that, in all these years, his daughter had become a woman, unfathomable, and lost to him. That she had walked the path from a daughter who was much loved, to a wife, with a wife's friends and loves and loyalties. Loves that he was not privy to, that he would never—quite—understand.

What would he have done?

Anything.

"And how," the Serra Teresa continued, her gaze now intent, "would that man stop you from exacting vengeance?"

There was only one way, and they both knew it. She picked up her lamp and swung its shadows in the darkness of the Lady's night. Then she crossed the small space between them—the necessary space, the terrible distance—and she placed a palm on his shoulder. "Sendari, what will you do with her?"

"Is that your question?"

"Yes. And it is the only question I have, tonight,

tomorrow night, and in the nights to follow. It is the only question I will have until it is answered and I—and we—move on, following one path or another."

He raised a palm, as if to ward her, and said, "What other choice do I have?"

And because it was as much of an answer as he could give, and her gift would make this clear, he waited in silence until she left. Because until she left, taking with her the question that he had not been able to ask of himself, he could not breathe.

The Serra Diora di'Marano was weeping.

You must not move.

The hardest thing she had ever done was to sit in the harem's Inner Chamber and listen. To the voices that she recognized, distorted by screams of pain and fear, ended by death. Knowing that she could use the voice, that she could force these men to stop for long enough that they might somehow, some way, escape.

Aie, she *knew* that she could not have done it. But her heart did not know it. And it never would. She had sat, while their blood splashed her lap, and she had lifted no hand, spoken no word. *She had done nothing.*

The rings that bound her fingers bound her heart; she swore to the Lady that she would never again remove them.

She had hoped, somehow, that the act of striking at the men who had been responsible for the deaths of her sister-wives—and her child, her son, no matter that Deirdre had borne him—would give her peace.

But there was no peace.

Because the last word that had been spoken to her had been a single word: her name.

And she could hear it now, rebounding in the emptiness of the room that was, for the moment, her prison.

Diora!

Ruatha's voice. Ruatha's shocked and terrified voice. Ruatha's angry, betrayed voice. Of the wives, only Ruatha had seen her, sitting, the power of her voice completely silent while the treacherous Tyran killed them all.

Killed—

her son.

She could not breathe, except to weep. Her arms, she

wrapped around her body, as if the ghost of Na'dani could be caught and held, just held, just one more time.

Diora!

And could she offer explanation? She told them all, in the private voice, that she loved them—that she would not let them be forgotten or unmourned. But she knew that Na'dani did not understand the words—and that Ruatha, her Ruatha, of the wives the one that she had loved most fiercely, had gone to her death bitter and betrayed.

If she could, she would go, now, and claw through the earth with her hands, digging up grass and worms and flesh until she found them where they lay in their bed of earth. And she thought, oh, she thought, that she might join them at last.

The Serra Diora was weeping.

Because she was the Flower of the Dominion, and her work was not yet done, and she did not know how she could continue it without them; they had been her strength. What remained of their memory, the months had leached from her, until all she could remember was their deaths, and her part in them.

Evayne, she thought, as her voice quieted, as she struggled to ride it and tame it, *you were wrong. I have righted nothing.*

Ruatha, please, forgive me. If you watch from the heart of the whirlwind, forgive. I have struck the first of the blows I will strike, and I strike it in your name.

She had not lifted a hand.

Please forgive me.

She had not raised her voice.

Please.

She had not used *the* voice.

Ruatha . . .

The night was endless; she had swallowed it, and it was devouring her. She knew that in the morning, when the sun rose, she would carry this night within her; the only people who could have gentled it with the coming of dawn lay dead.

And the worst of it was this: She was the Serra Diora *en'Leonne.* In the morning, she would wake, and she would plan. Because she had declared war, and now she must fight it. Nothing else was left her. Nothing at all.

* * *

The Tyr'agar was crowned, and the crowning both lifted, and lowered, his shadow. The blockade of the Tor ended with the Festival; the merchants who had been corralled within its walls were granted passage to their Terreans, be they North or South. Death had come, dramatic and terrible, and death had gone, and in its wake, a new leader had risen: the Tyr'agar Alesso di'Alesso; the founder of a new line.

The clansmen left the Tor with their entourages, large and small, like a human river moving down the plateau. And among that mass, no one noticed or remarked on a single unremarkable man.

He dressed like a clansman, albeit in garb that was a bit too broad for his shoulders, and he carried with him two swords, one girded and one strapped to his back. He had only a small pack with the possessions that he valued, and they were few indeed, and on his sleeve he bore the emblem of the sun with indistinct rays on a field of blue.

He was tired.

Four days had passed since the crowning glory of the Festival's Height; four days since the Radann kai el'Sol had chosen both his death and his weapon.

This man was not a man with rank or station that allowed him to witness the event, and he had no desire to do so.

But someone had to. Someone had to bear witness, bear it with honor, and carry it home.

So he had done something that he knew the Radann kai el'Sol would never have approved of: He had stolen a set of Radann's robes from the temple, and he had come to the water's edge, as the rest of the clansmen had come, both to witness the crowning of a Tyr—and its aftermath.

After this, he had done the second of three things that he knew the Radann kai el'Sol would not approve of. He had taken the liberty—and it was a liberty punishable by death, although death was fast approaching regardless—of filling three skins with the waters of the Tor Leonne. Because the waters contained all that remained of his master—the waters and the wind.

He had then returned to the temple, put away his needles, his shears, his crystals and pearls—those things which, as a master with little funding, he would have found difficult to replace. He took soldi as well, gold

coins and silver, although he privately thought Fredero
would forgive him that trespass.

What he would not forgive, what he would *never* forgive, was the third of the three things.

Jevri el'Sol, born Jevri kep'Lamberto, had taken the
sword, *Balagar,* from its place of honor. If it objected, it
did not make its voice known—not even when Jevri had,
cautiously but with quiet determination, unsheathed the
blade, wielding it. It was not the Lord's way, and he
understood this, but he had never served the Lord; he had
served Fredero. And while he understood that Fredero
forgave the Radann Peder par el'Sol his treachery and his
betrayal for the greater good of the Dominion, Jevri was
under no obligation to do any such thing.

This sword had belonged to his master; the master of
his adult years, and the master of his choosing. He had
been blessed and privileged, and he would honor that
privilege before he sought another master.

If he ever did. He was not a young man.

The sun was hot during the day; the nights, cold. Not
until he was well quit of the Terrean of Raverra did he
sleep without the terrible ache in the bones of his fingers,
his feet. But the roads were safe for an old man such as
he, bearing the crest that he did. He stayed with men who
accepted coin for hospitality, and he walked, cane in
hand, watching the merchant caravans as they fought for
space on roads that would soon see rain.

He expected pursuit. There was none.

When, he thought, would Peder par el'Sol—he could
not bring himself to even *think* of the name kai el'Sol as
any man's but Fredero's—notice the loss of the sword?

It was in the Lord's hands.

And the Lord did not choose, this time, to hinder. The
days passed; he walked through them all, keeping a
steady, a stately pace. The three skins, he did not touch,
nor the sword, but he ate traveling rations, honeyed wheat
and nuts and dried fruits. There were rivers and brooks as
he proceeded North, into the plains that produced the
finest horses in the Dominion.

Jevri el'Sol crossed the Mancorvan border.

To reach the city of Amar was less easy than he
expected it would be; at every point along the road that a
man could be stopped, he was stopped; if it were not for

the symbol of the Lord across his shoulder, he thought his detention might have been rougher and lasted longer.

Hard times, but he was calm; he expected no less.

Lamberto was not a friend of the new Tyr'agar. How could it be, when the man ruled by treachery, by darkness?

Politics, Jevri thought. And he continued to walk. Because this was his gift to Fredero kai el'Sol, the youngest of the Lambertan Tyr's brother's—youngest and most loved.

Days passed. He thought the sun etched lines more deeply into his hands, his arms; he could not see his face, and was not particularly sorry for the lack. But he missed Fredero, perhaps because he carried so many responsibilities with him.

Perhaps because they were friends.

But Jevri el'Sol was patience personified in everything but his craft, and his craft was behind him; his past before. He walked from the heart of the Tor Leonne to the heart of the city of Amar, the home of the clan Lamberto, and although the road and the wind and the weather slowed him down, nothing stopped him.

The gates were not as he remembered them, and he felt a twinge at that, a stab of surprise. There were Tyran here, bristling like angry boars.

This was, however, Amar, and the Tyran here served the Lord with honor. They did not—a single one of them—recognize him, although he thought he recognized a few of their faces; it was hard to tell, the years changed men so.

"I have come," he told the oathguard who barred his way, "to speak with Tyr Mareo kai di'Lamberto."

"The Tyr is a busy man," the Tyran replied.

"Yes. And he is a man who serves the Lord. He will hear what I have to say."

But these men, they were determined, and in the end, Jevri had become curt. "I am tired, I am road weary, and I have come from the side of the Radann kai el'Sol to speak with Mareo. I *will not* be put off by young, self-important men. Do I make myself clear?"

"You most certainly do," a familiar voice said.

And the Tyran parted at once, as if they were a tunnel

and not a wall. At the end, flanked by them, stood the Tyr'agnate who ruled Mancorvo.

"Jevri," he said, with a broad smile, "welcome to our home."

But Jevri did not return the smile. "Tyr'agnate," he said, although he had called him a good many things when they had lived under the roof of Serra Carlatta's harem together, and none of them had been that. "I have come from the Tor Leonne to deliver to you the tale of the last day of the Radann kai el'Sol."

Mareo's face grayed at once, turned grim and dark. He waved the Tyran away, and said, simply, "Follow." As if he spoke to a seraf, a familiar seraf.

And Jevri, born kep'Lamberto, obeyed.

In the privacy of the harem—the same harem in which he had watched Fredero grow up—he told the Tyr his story. He was quiet as he spoke, as was his wont, and Mareo did little to interrupt.

"I will do my penance," Jevri told him, "for the theft of the robe, but I have served the Lord faithfully these many years, and it is in the service of the Lord that I have come."

But Mareo said, "It was in the service of Fredero that you came, and you came to Lamberto. You know that my brother forswore his family, to my father's dismay, and joined the Radann."

"Rather well," Jevri replied, almost dryly. "But he thought of you often, and he would have wanted word of his fate to travel.

"He drew the Sun Sword, Tyr'agnate, that all clansmen of honor might see for themselves the Lord's wrath, and make the honorable choice."

"And you wished me to understand what my brother felt the only choice to be."

"Yes. And more." He knelt and unstrapped the sword at his back. "This is *Balagar*."

Mareo paled. "You *stole* the sword of the Radann kai el'Sol?"

Jevri nodded grimly.

"But why?"

"Because when the armies ride, they will ride through Mancorvo. And it was the kai el'Sol's fervent belief that the demons who once served the Lord of Night will ride at their head. This sword was a sword that could stand against those creatures; it was a lesser sword than the Sun Sword, but it *is* a sword of right, one meant to be raised in defense of the Lord of the Sun.

"Had he lived, he would have wielded it, taking the war to the kinlords and their master. But he did not live. And I have taken the sword," Jevri said softly, "to the only other man I consider worthy of bearing it, Lord forgive my presumption.

"You need it, Tyr'agnate."

The Tyr'agnate was silent a long time. At last, he said, "Do you know what they offered me?"

Jevri felt a cold, sharp sting, as if something had passed through his heart. He said nothing.

"The choice of the Captain of the Tyr'agar's Tyran. And a war with the Northern Empire and its demon kings."

They stared at each other, these two men, and it was Mareo di'Lamberto who looked away. He had aged.

"What news you have brought us, Jevri. What terrible news. And the rites?"

"We could not say them without risking the wrath of the new Tyr'agar. But here," Jevri said, removing the first of the skins. "This is water from the lake of the Tor; his ashes were taken by water and wind.

"With these, we can offer the Lady's blessing."

And then, weary, Jevri el'Sol closed his eyes and leaned back into the cushions that Mareo di'Lamberto had provided for the oldest of his family's serafs. He made no pretense of freedom, did Jevri, although by Lord's law, it was his.

"Thank you, old friend," Mareo told the sleeping man as he rose, and very quietly ran a hand along his eyes. "Thank you for bringing my brother home."

Jevri, sleeping, did not answer.

"I'll speak to you again in the morning, after we have performed the Lady's rites for our fallen."

Again no reply.

But Mareo di'Lamberto knew that Jevri el'Sol, that Jevri kep'Lamberto, was awake because, from beneath the lids of wrinkled eyes that had seen far too much, came a thin trail of tears.

He set *Balagar* beside the old man, and said, softly, "You guarded this all the way home, Jevri kep'Lamberto. Guard it for one more night."

And Jevri lifted an aged, wrinkled hand and placed it gently upon the scabbard of Fredero kai el'Sol's sword. For the heart and the soul of a man *was* his sword, and he would guard this sword with his life.

But he would much rather have guarded the man who had wielded it, and in the silence of an empty harem, he heard that man's young voice.

And he thought that it would be fitting and merciful if it was the last voice he heard.

But he was faithful, was Jevri kep'Lamberto, and when he woke, and knew that no death would take him yet, he prepared to pay his respects.

And to continue living for as long as the Lady decreed.

IRENE RADFORD

☑ THE GLASS DRAGON   UE2634—$5.99

Within a realm which has always been protected by its magicians, and in a kingdom whose ruler's own life is intricately linked with that of the dragons, the disappearance of these magical beasts could well see the land fall to invaders.

☑ THE PERFECT PRINCESS   UE2678—$5.50

Without the dragons and their magic to back his claim to the throne, Prince Darville—only recently freed from an enchantment that had kept him imprisoned in the form of a wolf—might soon see his realm lost to these enemies.

☑ THE LONELIEST MAGICIAN   UE2709—$5.99

The kingdom of Coronnan and its new liege, Darville, are once again threatened by Lord Krej and a magical coven determined to seize the Dragon Crown. And even as Senior Magician Baylor struggles to protect the king and kingdom from these enemies capable of wielding powerful, long-forbidden magics, the young apprentice Yaakke undertakes a dangerous dragon-led quest to find and save the dragon Shayla, to learn the truth about his own identity and powers.
